JAMES M.CAIN

FOUR COMPLETE NOVELS

JAMES M.CAIN

FOUR COMPLETE NOVELS

The Postman Always Rings Twice

Mildred Pierce

Double Indemnity

Serenade

AVENEL BOOKS·NEW YORK

This omnibus edition was previously published as four separate volumes
under the titles:
The Postman Always Rings Twice copyright MCMXXXIV, © renewed MCMLXII by James M. Cain
Mildred Pierce copyright MCMXLI, © renewed MCMLXIX by James M. Cain
Double Indemnity copyright MCMXXXVI, © renewed MCMLXIV by James M. Cain
Serenade copyright MCMXXXVII, © renewed MCMLXIV by James M. Cain

This 1982 edition is published by Avenel Books, distributed by Crown
Publishers, Inc., by arrangement with Alfred A. Knopf, Inc.

Manufactured in the United States of America

h g f e d c b a

Library of Congress Cataloging in Publication Data

Cain, James M. (James Mallahan), 1892–1977.
  Four complete novels.

  Contents: The postman always rings twice—Mildred
Pierce—Double indemnity—Serenade.
  I. Title.
PS3505.A3113A6 1982   813'.52   81-19079
ISBN: 0-517-36249X   AACR2

CONTENTS

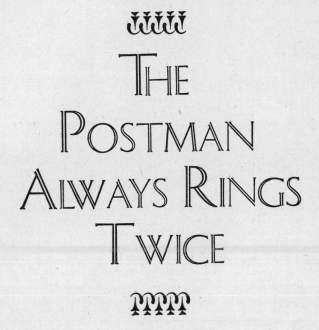

THE
POSTMAN
ALWAYS RINGS
TWICE

TO
VINCENT LAWRENCE

Chapter 1

THEY THREW ME OFF the hay truck about noon. I had swung on the night before, down at the border, and as soon as I got up there under the canvas, I went to sleep. I needed plenty of that, after three weeks in Tia Juana, and I was still getting it when they pulled off to one side to let the engine cool. Then they saw a foot sticking out and threw me off. I tried some comical stuff, but all I got was a dead pan, so that gag was out. They gave me a cigarette, though, and I hiked down the road to find something to eat.

That was when I hit this Twin Oaks Tavern. It was nothing but a roadside sandwich joint, like a million others in California. There was a lunchroom part, and over that the house part, where they lived, and off to one side a filling station, and out back a half dozen shacks that they called an auto court. I blew in there in a hurry and began looking down the road. When the Greek showed, I asked if a guy had been by in a Cadillac. He was to pick me up here, I said, and we were to have lunch. Not today, said the Greek. He laid a place at one of the tables and asked me what I was going to have. I said orange juice, corn flakes, fried eggs and bacon, enchilada, flapjacks, and coffee. Pretty soon he came out with the orange juice and the corn flakes.

"Hold on, now. One thing I got to tell you. If this guy don't show up, you'll have to trust me for it. This was to be on him, and I'm kind of short myself."

"Hokay, fill'm up."

I saw he was on, and quit talking about the guy in the Cadillac. Pretty soon I saw he wanted something.

"What you do, what kind of work, hey?"

"Oh, one thing and another, one thing and another. Why?"

"How old you?"

"Twenty-four."

"Young fellow, hey. I could use young fellow right now. In my business."

"Nice place you got here."

"Air. Is a nice. No fog, like in a Los Angeles. No fog at all. Nice, a clear, all a time nice a clear."

"Must be swell at night. I can smell it now."

"Sleep fine. You understand automobile? Fix'm up?"

"Sure. I'm a born mechanic."

He gave me some more about the air, and how healthy he's been since he bought this place, and how he can't figure it out, why his help won't stay with him. I can figure it out, but I stay with the grub.

"Hey? You think you like it here?"

By that time I had put down the rest of the coffee, and lit the cigar he gave me. "I tell you how it is. I got a couple of other propositions, that's my trouble. But I'll think about it. I sure will do that all right."

Then I saw her. She had been out back, in the kitchen, but she came in to gather up my dishes. Except for the shape, she really wasn't any raving beauty, but she had a sulky look to her, and her lips stuck out in a way that made me want to mash them in for her.

"Meet my wife."

She didn't look at me. I nodded at the Greek, gave my cigar a kind of wave, and that was all. She went out with the dishes, and so far as he and I were concerned, she hadn't even been there. I left, then, but in five minutes I was back, to leave a message for the guy in the Cadillac. It took me a half hour to get sold on the job, but at the end of it I was in the filling station, fixing flats.

"What's your name, hey?"

"Frank Chambers."

"Nick Papadakis, mine."

We shook hands, and he went. In a minute I heard him singing. He had a swell voice. From the filling station I could just get a good view of the kitchen.

Chapter 2

ABOUT THREE O'CLOCK a guy came along that was all burned up because somebody had pasted a sticker on his wind wing. I had to go in the kitchen to steam it off for him.

"Enchiladas? Well, you people sure know how to make them."

"What do you mean, you people?"

"Why, you and Mr. Papadakis. You and Nick. That one I had for lunch, it was a peach."

"Oh."

"You got a cloth? That I can hold on to this thing with?"

"That's not what you meant."

"Sure it is."

"You think I'm Mex."

"Nothing like it."

"Yes, you do. You're not the first one. Well, get this. I'm just as white as you are, see? I may have dark hair and look a little that way, but I'm just as white as you are. You want to get along good around here, you won't forget that."

"Why, you don't look Mex."

"I'm telling you. I'm just as white as you are."

"No, you don't look even a little bit Mex. Those Mexican women, they all got big hips and bum legs and breasts up under their chin and yellow skin and hair that looks like it had bacon fat on it. You don't look like that. You're small, and got nice white skin, and your hair is soft and curly, even if it is black. Only thing you've got that's

Mex is your teeth. They all got white teeth, you've got to hand that to them."

"My name was Smith before I was married. That don't sound much like a Mex, does it?"

"Not much."

"What's more, I don't even come from around here. I come from Iowa."

"Smith, hey. What's your first name?"

"Cora. You can call me that, if you want to."

I knew for certain, then, what I had just taken a chance on when I went in there. It wasn't those enchiladas that she had to cook, and it wasn't having black hair. It was being married to that Greek that made her feel she wasn't white, and she was even afraid I would begin calling her Mrs. Papadakis.

"Cora. Sure. And how about calling me Frank?"

She came over and began helping me with the wind wing. She was so close I could smell her. I shot it right close to her ear, almost in a whisper. "How come you married this Greek, anyway?"

She jumped like I had cut her with a whip. "Is that any of your business?"

"Yeah. Plenty."

"Here's your wind wing."

"Thanks."

I went out. I had what I wanted. I had socked one in under her guard, and socked it in deep, so it hurt. From now on, it would be business between her and me. She might not say yes, but she wouldn't stall me. She knew what I meant, and she knew I had her number.

That night at supper, the Greek got sore at her for not giving me more fried potatoes. He wanted me to like it there, and not walk out on him like the others had.

"Give a man something to eat."

"They're right on the stove. Can't he help himself?"

"It's all right. I'm not ready yet."

He kept at it. If he had had any brains, he would have known there was something back of it, because she wasn't one to let a guy help himself, I'll say that for her. But he was dumb, and kept crabbing. It was just the kitchen table, he at one end, she at the other, and me in the middle. I didn't look at her. But I could see her dress.

It was one of these white nurse uniforms, like they all wear, whether they work in a dentist's office or a bakeshop. It had been clean in the morning, but it was a little bit rumpled now, and mussy. I could smell her.

"Well for heaven's sake."

She got up to get the potatoes. Her dress fell open for a second, so I could see her leg. When she gave me the potatoes. I couldn't eat.

"Well there now. After all that, and now he doesn't want them."

"Hokay. But he have'm, *if* he want'm."

"I'm not hungry. I ate a big lunch."

He acted like he had won a great victory, and now he would forgive her, like the big guy he was. "She is a all right. She is my little white bird. She is my little white dove."

He winked and went upstairs. She and I sat there, and didn't say a word. When he came down he had a big bottle and a guitar. He poured some out of the bottle, but it was sweet Greek wine, and made me sick to my stomach. He started to sing. He had a tenor voice, not one of these little tenors like you hear on the radio, but a big tenor, and on the high notes he would put in a sob like on a Caruso record. But I couldn't listen to him now. I was feeling worse by the minute.

He saw my face and took me outside. "Out in a air, you feel better."

" 'S all right. I'll be all right."

"Sit down. Keep quiet."

"Go ahead in. I just ate too much lunch. I'll be all right."

He went in, and I let everything come up. It was like hell the lunch, or the potatoes, or the wine. I wanted that woman so bad I couldn't even keep anything on my stomach.

Next morning the sign was blown down. About the middle of the night it had started to blow, and by morning it was a windstorm that took the sign with it.

"It's awful. Look at that."

"Was a very big wind. I could no sleep. No sleep all night."

"Big wind all right. But look at the sign."

"Is busted."

I kept tinkering with the sign, and he would come out and watch me. "How did you get this sign anyway?"

"Was here when I buy the place. Why?"

"It's lousy all right. I wonder you do any business at all."

I went to gas up a car, and left him to think that over. When I got back he was still blinking at it, where it was leaning against the front of the lunchroom. Three of the lights were busted. I plugged in the wire, and half the others didn't light.

"Put in new lights, hang'm up, will be all right."

"You're the boss."

"What's a matter with it?"

"Well, it's out of date. Nobody has bulb signs any more. They got neon signs. They show up better, and they don't burn as much juice. Then, what does it say? Twin Oaks, that's all. The Tavern part, it's not in lights. Well, Twin Oaks don't make me hungry. It don't make me want to stop and get something to eat. It's costing you money, that sign is, only you don't know it."

"Fix'm up, will be hokay."

"Why don't you get a new sign?"

"I'm busy."

But pretty soon he was back, with a piece of paper. He had drew a new sign for himself, and colored it up with red, white, and blue crayon. It said Twin Oaks Tavern, and Eat, and Bar-B-Q, and Sanitary Rest Rooms, and N. Papadakis, Prop.

"Swell. That'll knock them for a loop."

I fixed up the words, so they were spelled right, and he put some more curlicues on the letters.

"Nick, why do we hang up the old sign at all? Why don't you go to the city today and get this new sign made? It's a beauty, believe me it is. And it's important. A place is no better than its sign, is it?"

"I do it. By golly, I go."

Los Angeles wasn't but twenty miles away, but he shined himself up like he was going to Paris, and right after lunch, he went. Soon as he was gone, I locked the front door. I picked up a plate that a guy had left, and went on back in the kitchen with it. She was there.

"Here's a plate that was out there."

"Oh, thanks."

I set it down. The fork was rattling like a tambourine.

"I was going to go, but I started some things cooking and I thought I better not."

"I got plenty to do myself."

"You feeling better?"

"I'm all right."

"Sometimes just some little thing will do it. Like a change of water, something like that."

"Probably too much lunch."

"What's that?"

Somebody was out front, rattling the door. "Sounds like somebody trying to get in."

"Is the door locked, Frank?"

"I must have locked it."

She looked at me, and got pale. She went to the swinging door, and peeped through. Then she went into the lunchroom, but in a minute she was back.

"They went away."

"I don't know why I locked it."

"I forgot to unlock it."

She started for the lunchroom again, but I stopped her. "Let's— leave it locked."

"Nobody can get in if it's locked. I got some cooking to do. I'll wash up this plate."

I took her in my arms and mashed my mouth up against hers . . . "Bite me! Bite me!"

I bit her. I sunk my teeth into her lips so deep I could feel the blood spurt into my mouth. It was running down her neck when I carried her upstairs.

Chapter 3

FOR TWO DAYS after that I was dead, but the Greek was sore at me, so I got by all right. He was sore at me because I hadn't fixed the swing door that led from the lunchroom into the kitchen. She told him it swung back and hit her in the mouth. She had to tell him something. Her mouth was all swelled up where I had bit it. So he said it was my fault, that I hadn't fixed it. I stretched the spring, so it was weaker, and that fixed it.

But the real reason he was sore at me was over the sign. He had fallen for it so hard he was afraid I would say it was my idea, 'stead of his. It was such a hell of a sign they couldn't get it done for him that afternoon. It took them three days, and when it was ready I went in and got it and hung it up. It had on it all that he had drew on the paper, and a couple of other things besides. It had a Greek flag and an American flag, and hands shaking hands, and Satisfaction Guaranteed. It was all in red, white, and blue neon letters, and I waited until dark to turn on the juice. When I snapped the switch, it lit up like a Christmas tree.

"Well, I've seen many a sign in my time, but never one like that. I got to hand it to you, Nick."

"By golly. By golly."

We shook hands. We were friends again.

Next day I was alone with her for a minute, and swung my fist up against her leg so hard it nearly knocked her over.

"How do you get that way?" She was snarling like a cougar. I liked her like that.

"How are you, Cora?"

"Lousy."

From then on, I began to smell her again.

One day the Greek heard there was a guy up the road undercutting him on gas. He jumped in the car to go see about it. I was in my room when he drove off, and I turned around to dive down in the kitchen. But she was already there, standing in the door.

I went over and looked at her mouth. It was the first chance I had had to see how it was. The swelling was all gone, but you could still see the tooth marks, little blue creases on both lips. I touched them with my fingers. They were soft and damp. I kissed them, but not hard. They were little soft kisses. I had never thought about them before. She stayed until the Greek came back, about an hour. We didn't do anything. We just lay on the bed. She kept rumpling my hair, and looking up at the ceiling, like she was thinking.

"You like blueberry pie?"

"I don't know. Yeah. I guess so."

"I'll make you some."

"Look out, Frank. You'll break a spring leaf."

"To hell with the spring leaf."

We were crashing into a little eucalyptus grove beside the road. The Greek had sent us down to the market to take back some T-bone steaks he said were lousy, and on the way back it had got dark. I slammed the car in there, and it bucked and bounced, but when I was in among the trees I stopped. Her arms were around me before I even cut the lights. We did plenty. After a while we just sat there. "I can't go on like this, Frank."

"Me neither."

"I can't stand it. And I've got to get drunk with you, Frank. You know what I mean? Drunk."

"I know."

"And I hate that Greek."

"Why did you marry him? You never did tell me that."

"I haven't told you anything."

"We haven't wasted any time on talk."

"I was working in a hash house. You spend two years in a Los

Angeles hash house and you'll take the first guy that's got a gold watch."

"When did you leave Iowa?"

"Three years ago. I won a beauty contest. I won a high school beauty contest, in Des Moines. That's where I lived. The prize was a trip to Hollywood. I got off the Chief with fifteen guys taking my picture, and two weeks later I was in the hash house."

"Didn't you go back?"

"I wouldn't give them the satisfaction."

"Did you get in movies?"

"They gave me a test. It was all right in the face. But they talk, now. The pictures, I mean. And when I began to talk, up there on the screen, they knew me for what I was, and so did I. A cheap Des Moines trollop that had as much chance in pictures as a monkey has. Not as much. A monkey, anyway, can make you laugh. All I did was make you sick."

"And then?"

"Then two years of guys pinching your leg and leaving nickel tips and asking how about a little party tonight. I went on some of them partios, Frank."

"And then?"

"You know what I mean about them parties?"

"I know."

"Then he came along. I took him, and so help me, I meant to stick by him. But I can't stand it any more. God, do I look like a little white bird?"

"To me, you look more like a hell cat."

"You know, don't you. That's one thing about you. I don't have to fool you all the time. And you're clean. You're not greasy. Frank, do you have any idea what that means? You're not greasy."

"I can kind of imagine."

"I don't think so. No man can know what that means to a woman. To have to be around somebody that's greasy and makes you sick at the stomach when he touches you. I'm not really such a hell cat, Frank. I just can't stand it any more."

"What you trying to do? Kid me?"

"Oh, all right. I'm a hell cat, then. But I don't think I would be so bad. With somebody that wasn't greasy."

"Cora, how about you and me going away?"

"I've thought about it. I've thought about it a lot."

"We'll ditch this Greek and blow. Just blow."

"Where to?"

"Anywhere. What do we care?"

"Anywhere. Anywhere. You know where that is?"

"All over. Anywhere we choose."

"No it's not. It's the hash house."

"I'm not talking about the hash house. I'm talking about the road. It's fun, Cora. And nobody knows it better than I do. I know every twist and turn it's got. And I know how to work it, too. Isn't that what we want? Just to be a pair of tramps, like we really are?"

"You were a fine tramp. You didn't even have socks."

"You liked me."

"I loved you. I would love you without even a shirt. I would love you specially without a shirt, so I could feel how nice and hard your shoulders are."

"Socking railroad detectives developed the muscles."

"And you're hard all over. Big and tall and hard. And your hair is light. You're not a little soft greasy guy with black kinky hair that he puts bay rum on every night."

"That must be a nice smell."

"But it won't do, Frank. That road, it don't lead anywhere but to the hash house. The hash house for me, and some job like it for you. A lousy parking lot job, where you wear a smock. I'd cry if I saw you in a smock, Frank."

"Well?"

She sat there a long time, twisting my hand in both of hers. "Frank, do you love me?"

"Yes."

"Do you love me so much that not anything matters?"

"Yes."

"There's one way."

"Did you say you weren't really a hell cat?"

"I said it, and I mean it. I'm not what you think I am, Frank. I want to work and be something, that's all. But you can't do it without love. Do you want that, Frank? Anyway, a woman can't. Well, I've made one mistake. And I've got to be a hell cat, just once, to fix it. But I'm not really a hell cat, Frank."

"They hang you for that."

"Not if you do it right. You're smart, Frank. I never fooled you for a minute. You'll think of a way. Plenty of them have. Don't worry. I'm not the first woman that had to turn hell cat to get out of a mess."

"He never did anything to me. He's all right."

"The hell he's all right. He stinks, I tell you. He's greasy and he stinks. And do you think I'm going to let you wear a smock, with Service Auto Parks printed on the back, Thank-U Call Again, while he has four suits and a dozen silk shirts? Isn't that business half mine? Don't I cook? Don't I cook good? Don't you do your part?"

"You talk like it was all right."

"Who's going to know if it's all right or not, but you and me?"

"You and me."

"That's it, Frank. That's all that matters, isn't it? Not you and me and the road, or anything else but you and me."

"You must be a hell cat, though. You couldn't make me feel like this if you weren't."

"That's what we're going to do. Kiss me, Frank. On the mouth."

I kissed her. Her eyes were shining up at me like two blue stars. It was like being in church.

Chapter 4

"GOT ANY HOT WATER?"

"What's the matter with the bathroom?"

"Nick's in there."

"Oh. I'll give you some out of the kettle. He likes the whole heater full for his bath."

We played it just like we would tell it. It was about ten o'clock at night, and we had closed up, and the Greek was in the bathroom, putting on his Saturday-night wash. I was to take the water up to my room, get ready to shave, and then remember I had left the car out. I was to go outside, and stand by to give her one on the horn if somebody came. She was to wait till she heard him in the tub, go in for a towel, and clip him from behind with a blackjack I had made for her out of a sugar bag with ball bearings wadded down in the end. At first, I was to do it, but we figured he wouldn't pay any attention to her if she went in there, where if I said I was after my razor, he might get out of the tub or something and help me look. Then she was to hold him under until he drowned. Then she was to leave the water running a little bit, and step out the window to the porch roof, and come down the stepladder I had put there, to the ground. She was to hand me the blackjack, and to go back to the kitchen. I was to put the ball bearings back in the box, throw the bag away, put the car in, and go up to my room and start to shave. She would wait till the water began dripping down in the kitchen, and call me. We would break the door down, find him, and call the doctor. In the end, we figured it would look like he had slipped in the tub, knocked himself out, and then drowned. I got the idea from a piece in the paper where a guy had said that most accidents happen right in people's own bathtubs.

"Be careful of it. It's hot."

"Thanks."

It was in a saucepan, and I took it up in my room and set it on the bureau, and laid my shaving stuff out. I went down and out to the car, and took a seat in it so I could see the road and the bathroom window, both. The Greek was singing. It came to me I better take note what the song was. It was "Mother Machree." He sang it once, and then sang it over again. I looked in the kitchen. She was still there.

A truck and a trailer swung around the bend. I fingered the horn. Sometimes those truckmen stopped for something to eat, and they were the kind that would beat on the door till you opened up. But they went on. A couple more cars went by. They didn't stop. I looked in the kitchen again, and she wasn't there. A light went on in the bedroom.

Then, all of a sudden, I saw something move, back by the porch. I almost hit the horn, but then I saw it was a cat. It was just a gray cat, but it shook me up. A cat was the last thing I wanted to see then. I couldn't see it for a minute, and then there it was again, smelling around the stepladder. I didn't want to blow the horn, because it wasn't anything but a cat, but I didn't want it around that stepladder. I got out of the car, went back there, and shooed it away.

I got halfway back to the car, when it came back, and started up the ladder. I shooed it away again, and ran it clear back to the shacks. I started back to the car, and then stood there for a little bit, looking to see if it was coming back. A state cop came around the bend. He saw me standing there, cut his motor, and came wheeling in, before I could move. When he stopped he was between me and the car. I couldn't blow the horn.

"Taking it easy?"

"Just came out to put the car away."

"That your car?"

"Belongs to this guy I work for."

"O.K. Just checking up."

He looked around, and then he saw something. "I'll be damned. Look at that."

"Look at what?"

"Goddam cat, going up that stepladder."

"Ha."

"I love a cat. They're always up to something."

He pulled on his gloves, took a look at the night, kicked his pedal a couple of times, and went. Soon as he was out of sight I dove for the horn. I was too late. There was a flash of fire from the porch, and every light in the place went out. Inside, Cora was screaming with an awful sound in her voice. "Frank! Frank! Something has happened!"

I ran in the kitchen, but it was black dark in there and I didn't have any matches in my pocket, and I had to feel my way. We met on the stairs, she going down, me going up. She screamed again.

"Keep quiet, for God's sake keep quiet! Did you do it?"

"Yes, but the lights went out, and I haven't held him under yet!"

"We got to bring him to! There was a state cop out there, and he saw that stepladder!"

"Phone for the doctor!"

"You phone, and I'll get him out of there!"

She went down, and I kept on up. I went in the bathroom, and over to the tub. He was laying there in the water, but his head wasn't under. I tried to lift him. I had a hell of a time. He was slippery with soap, and I had to stand in the water before I could raise him at all. All the time I could hear her down there, talking to the operator. They didn't give her a doctor. They gave her the police.

I got him up, and laid him over the edge of the tub, and then got out myself, and dragged him in the bedroom and laid him on the bed. She came up, then, and we found matches, and got a candle lit. Then we went to work on him. I packed his head in wet towels, while she rubbed his wrists and feet.

"They're sending an ambulance."

"All right. Did he see you do it?"

"I don't know."

"Were you behind him?"

"I think so. But then the lights went out, and I don't know what happened. What did you do to the lights?"

"Nothing. The fuse popped."

"Frank. He'd better not come to."

"He's got to come to. If he dies, we're sunk. I tell you, that cop saw the stepladder. If he dies, then they'll know. If he dies, they've got us."

"But suppose he saw me? What's he going to say when he comes to?"

"Maybe he didn't. We just got to sell him a story, that's all. You were in here, and the lights popped, and you heard him slip and fall, and he didn't answer when you spoke to him. Then you called me, that's all. No matter what he says, you got to stick to it. If he saw anything, it was just his imagination, that's all."

"Why don't they hurry with that ambulance?"

"It'll be here."

Soon as the ambulance came, they put him on a stretcher and shoved him in. She rode with him. I followed along in the car. Halfway to Glendale, a state cop picked us up and rode on ahead. They went seventy miles an hour, and I couldn't keep up. They were lifting him out when I got to the hospital, and the state cop was bossing the job. When he saw me he gave a start and stared at me. It was the same cop.

They took him in, put him on a table, and wheeled him in an operating room. Cora and myself sat out in the hall. Pretty soon a nurse came and sat down with us. Then the cop came, and he had a sergeant with him. They kept looking at me. Cora was telling the nurse how it happened. "I was in there, in the bathroom I mean, getting a towel, and then the lights went out just like somebody had shot a gun off. Oh my, they made a terrible noise. I heard him fall. He had been standing up, getting ready to turn on the shower. I spoke to him, and he didn't say anything, and it was all dark, and I couldn't see anything, and I didn't know what had happened. I mean I thought he had been electrocuted or something. So then Frank heard me screaming, and he came, and got him out, and then I called up for the ambulance, and I don't know what I would have done if they hadn't come quick like they did."

"They always hurry on a late call."

"I'm so afraid he's hurt bad."

"I don't think so. They're taking X rays in there now. They can always tell from X rays. But I don't think he's hurt bad."

"Oh my, I hope not."

The cops never said a word. They just sat there and looked at us.

They wheeled him out, and his head was covered with bandages. They put him on an elevator, and Cora, and me, and the nurse, and the cops all got on, and they took him up and put him in a room. We all went in there. There weren't enough chairs, and while they were putting him to bed the nurse went and got some extra ones. We all sat down. Somebody said something, and the nurse made them keep quiet. A doctor came in and took a look, and went out. We sat there a hell of a while. Then the nurse went over and looked at him.

"I think he's coming to now."

Cora looked at me, and I looked away quick. The cops leaned forward, to hear what he said. He opened his eyes.

"You feel better now?"

He didn't say anything, and neither did anybody else. It was so still I could hear my heart pounding in my ears. "Don't you know your wife? Here she is. Aren't you ashamed of yourself, falling in the bathtub like a little boy, just because the lights went out. Your wife is mad at you. Aren't you going to speak to her?"

He strained to say something, but couldn't say it. The nurse went over and fanned him. Cora took hold of his hand and patted it. He lay back for a few minutes, with his eyes closed, and then his mouth began to move again and he looked at the nurse.

"Was a all go dark."

When the nurse said he had to be quiet, I took Cora down, and put her in the car. We no sooner started out than the cop was back there, following us on his motorcycle.

"He suspicions us, Frank."

"It's the same one. He knew there was something wrong, soon as he saw me standing there, keeping watch. He still thinks so."

"What are we going to do?"

"I don't know. It all depends on that stepladder, whether he tumbles what it's there for. What did you do with that slung shot?"

"I still got it here, in the pocket of my dress."

"God Almighty, if they had arrested you back there, and searched you, we'd have been sunk."

I gave her my knife, made her cut the string off the bag, and take the bearings out. Then I made her climb back, raise the back seat, and put the bag under it. It would look like a rag, like anybody keeps with the tools.

"You stay back there, now, and keep an eye on that cop. I'm going to snap these bearings into the bushes one at a time, and you've got to watch if he notices anything."

She watched, and I drove with my left hand, and leaned my right hand on the wheel. I let one go. I shot it like a marble, out the window and across the road.

"Did he turn his head?"

"No."

I let the rest go, one every couple of minutes. He never noticed it.

We got out of the place, and it was still dark. I hadn't had time to find the fuses, let alone put a new one in. When I pulled in, the cop went past, and was there ahead of me. "I'm taking a look at that fuse box, buddy."

"Sure. I'm taking a look myself."

We all three went back there, and he snapped on a flashlight. Right away, he gave a funny grunt and stooped down. There was the cat, laying on its back with all four feet in the air.

"Ain't that a shame? Killed her deader than hell."

He shot the flashlight up under the porch roof, and along the stepladder. "That's it, all right. Remember? We were looking at her. She stepped off the ladder on to your fuse box, and it killed her deader than hell."

"That's it all right. You were hardly gone when it happened. Went off like a pistol shot. I hadn't even had time to move the car."

"They caught me down the road."

"You were hardly out of sight."

"Stepped right off the ladder on to the fuse box. Well, that's the way it goes. Them poor dumb things, they can't get it through their head about electricity, can they? No sir, it's too much for them."

"Tough, all right."

"That's what it is, it's tough. Killed her deader than hell. Pretty cat, too. Remember, how she looked when she was creeping up that ladder? I never seen a cuter cat than she was."

"And pretty color."

"And killed her deader than hell. Well, I'll be going along. I guess that straightens us out. Had to check up, you know."

"That's right."

"So long. So long, Miss."

"So long."

Chapter 5

W E DIDN'T DO ANYTHING about the cat, the fuse box, or anything else. We crept into bed, and she cracked up. She cried, and then got a chill so she was trembling all over, and it was a couple of hours before I could get her quiet. She lay in my arms awhile, then, and we began to talk.

"Never again, Frank."

"That's right. Never again."

"We must have been crazy. Just plain crazy."

"Just our dumb luck that pulled us through."

"It was my fault."

"Mine too."

"No, it was my fault. I was the one that thought it up. You didn't want to. Next time I'll listen to you, Frank. You're smart. You're not dumb like I am."

"Except there won't be any next time."

"That's right. Never again."

"Even if we had gone through with it they would have guessed it. They *always* guess it. They guess it anyway, just from habit. Because look how quick that cop knew something was wrong. That's what makes my blood run cold. Soon as he saw me standing there he knew it. If he could tumble to it all that easy, how much chance would we have had if the Greek had died?"

"I guess I'm not really a hell cat, Frank."

"I'm telling you."

"If I was, I wouldn't have got scared so easy. I was so scared, Frank."

"I was scared plenty myself."

"You know what I wanted when the lights went out? Just you, Frank. I wasn't any hell cat at all, then. I was just a little girl, afraid of the dark."

"I was there, wasn't I?"

"I loved you for it. If it hadn't been for you, I don't know what would have happened to us."

"Pretty good, wasn't it? About how he slipped?"

"And he believed it."

"Give me half a chance, I got it on the cops, every time. You got to have something to tell, that's it. You got to fill in all those places, and yet have it as near the truth as you can get it. I know them. I've tangled with them plenty."

"You fixed it. You're always going to fix it for me, aren't you, Frank?"

"You're the only one ever meant anything to me."

"I guess I really don't want to be a hell cat."

"You're my baby."

"That's it, just your dumb baby. All right, Frank. I'll listen to you, from now on. You be the brains, and I'll work. I can work, Frank. And I work good. We'll get along."

"Sure we will."

"Now shall we go to sleep?"

"You think you can sleep all right?"

"It's the first time we ever slept together, Frank."

"You like it?"

"It's grand, just grand."

"Kiss me goodnight."

"It's so sweet to be able to kiss you goodnight."

Next morning, the telephone waked us up. She answered it, and when she came up her eyes were shining. "Frank, guess what?"

"What?"

"His skull is fractured."

"Bad?"

"No, but they're keeping him there. They want him there for a week, maybe. We can sleep together again tonight."

"Come here."

"Not now. We've got to get up. We've got to open the place up."

"Come here, before I sock you."

"You nut."

It was a happy week, all right. In the afternoon, she would drive in to the hospital, but the rest of the time we were together. We gave him a break, too. We kept the place open all the time, and went after the business, and got it. Of course it helped that day when a hundred Sunday school kids showed up in three buses, and wanted a bunch of stuff to take out in the woods with them, but even without that we would have made plenty. The cash register didn't know anything to tell on us, believe me it didn't.

Then one day, 'stead of her going in alone, we both went in, and after she came out of the hospital, we cut for the beach. They gave her a yellow suit and a red cap, and when she came out I didn't know her at first. She looked like a little girl. It was the first time I ever really saw how young she was. We played in the sand, and then we went way out and let the swells rock us. I like my head to the waves, she liked her feet. We lay there, face to face, and held hands under water. I looked up at the sky. It was all you could see. I thought about God.

"Frank."

"Yes?"

"He's coming home tomorrow. You know what that means?"

"I know."

"I got to sleep with him, 'stead of you."

"You would, except that when he gets here we're going to be gone."

"I was hoping you'd say that."

"Just you and me and the road, Cora."

"Just you and me and the road."

"Just a couple of tramps."

"Just a couple of gypsies, but we'll be together."

"That's it. We'll be together."

Next morning, we packed up. Anyway, she packed. I had bought a suit, and I put that on, and it seemed to be about all. She put her things in a hatbox. When she got done with it, she handed it to me. "Put that in the car, will you?"

"The car?"

"Aren't we taking the car?"

"Not unless you want to spend the first night in jail, we're not. Stealing a man's wife, that's nothing, but stealing his car, that's larceny."

"Oh."

We started out. It was two miles to the bus stop, and we had to hike it. Every time a car went by, we would stand there with our hand stuck out, like a cigar store Indian, but none of them stopped. A man alone can get a ride, and a woman alone, if she's fool enough to take it, but a man and a woman together don't have much luck. After about twenty had gone by, she stopped. We had gone about a quarter of a mile.

"Frank, I can't."

"What's the matter?"

"This is it."

"This is what?"

"The road."

"You're crazy. You're tired, that's all. Look. You wait here, and I'll get somebody down the road to drive us in to the city. That's what we ought to done anyhow. Then we'll be all right."

"No, it's not that. I'm not tired. I can't, that's all. At all."

"Don't you want to be with me, Cora?"

"You know I do."

"We can't go back, you know. We can't start up again, like it was before. You know that. You've got to come."

"I told you I wasn't really a bum, Frank. I don't feel like no gypsy. I don't feel like nothing, only ashamed, that I'm out here asking for a ride."

"I told you. We're getting a car in to the city."

"And then what?"

"Then we're there. Then we get going."

"No we don't. We spend one night in a hotel, and then we start looking for a job. And living in a dump."

"Isn't that a dump? What you just left?"

"It's different."

"Cora, you going to let it get your goat?"

"It's got it, Frank. I can't go on. Goodbye."

"Will you listen to me a minute?"

"Goodbye, Frank. I'm going back."

She kept tugging at the hatbox. I tried to hold on to it, anyway to carry it back for her, but she got it. She started back with it. She had looked nice when she started out, with a little blue suit and blue hat, but now she looked all battered, and her shoes were dusty, and she couldn't even walk right, from crying. All of a sudden, I found out I was crying too.

Chapter 6

I CAUGHT A RIDE TO San Bernardino. It's a railroad town, and I was going to hop a freight east. But I didn't do it. I ran into a guy in a poolroom, and began playing him one ball in the side. He was the greatest job in the way of a sucker that God ever turned out, because he had a friend that could really play. The only trouble with him was he couldn't play good enough. I hung around with the pair of them a couple of weeks, and took $250 off them, all they had, and then I had to beat it out of town quick.

I caught a truck for Mexicali, and then I got to thinking about my $250, and how with that much money we could go to the beach and sell hot dogs or something until we got a stake to take a crack at something bigger. So I dropped off, and caught a ride back to Glendale. I began hanging around the market where they bought their stuff, hoping I would bump into her. I even called her up a couple of times, but the Greek answered and I had to make out it was a wrong number.

In between walking around the market, I hung around a poolroom, about a block down the street. One day a guy was practicing shots alone on one of the tables. You could tell he was new at it from the way he held his cue. I began practicing shots on the next table. I figured if $250 was enough for a hot dog stand, $350 would leave us sitting pretty.

"How you say to a little one ball in the side?"

"I never played that game much."

"Nothing to it. Just the one ball in the side pocket."

"Anyhow, you look too good for me."

"Me? I'm just a punk."

"Oh well. If it's just a friendly game."

We started to play, and I let him take three or four, just to feel good. I kept shaking my head, like I couldn't understand it.

"Too good for you, hey. Well, that's a joke. But I swear, I'm really better than this. I can't seem to get going. How you say we put $1 on it, just to make it lively?"

"Oh well. I can't lose much at a dollar."

We made it $1 a game, and I let him take four or five, maybe more. I shot like I was pretty nervous, and in between shots I would wipe off the palm of my hand with a handkerchief, like I must be sweating.

"Well, it looks like I'm not doing so good. How about making it $5, so I can get my money back, and then we'll go have a drink?"

"Oh well. It's just a friendly game, and I don't want your money. Sure. We'll make it $5, and then we'll quit."

I let him take four or five more, and from the way I was acting, you would have thought I had heart failure and a couple more things besides. I was plenty blue around the gills.

"Look. I got sense enough to know when I'm out of my class all right, but let's make it $25, so I can break even, and then we'll go have that drink."

"That's pretty high for me."

"What the hell? You're playing on my money, aren't you?"

"Oh well. All right. Make it $25."

Then was when I really started to shoot. I made shots that Hoppe couldn't make. I banked them in from three cushions, I made billiard shots, I had my english working so the ball just floated around the table, I even called a jump shot and made it. He never made a shot that Blind Tom the Sightless Piano Player couldn't have made. He miscued, he got himself all tangled up on position, he scratched, he put the one ball in the wrong pocket, he never even called a bank shot. And when I walked out of there, he had my $250 and a $3 watch that I had bought to keep track of when Cora might be driving in to the market. Oh, I was good all right. The only trouble was I wasn't quite good enough.

"Hey, Frank!"

It was the Greek, running across the street at me before I had really got out the door.

"Well Frank, you old son a gun, where you been, put her there, why you run away from me just a time I hurt my head I need you most?"

We shook hands. He still had a bandage around his head and a funny look in his eyes, but he was all dressed up in a new suit, and had a black hat cocked over on the side of his head, and a purple necktie, and brown shoes, and his gold watch chain looped across his vest, and a big cigar in his hand.

"Well Nick! How you feeling, boy?"

"Me, I feel fine, couldn't feel better if was right out a the can, but why you run out on me? I sore as hell at you, you old son a gun."

"Well, you know me, Nick. I stay put awhile, and then I got to ramble."

"You pick one hell of a time to ramble. What you do, hey? Come on, you don't do nothing, you old son a gun, I know you, come on over while I buy'm steaks I tell you all about it."

"You alone?"

"Don't talk so dumb, who the hell you think keep a place open now you run out on me, hey? Sure I'm alone. Me a Cora never get to go out together now, one go, other have to stay."

"Well then, let's walk over."

It took him an hour to buy the steaks, he was so busy telling me how his skull was fractured, how the docs never saw a fracture like it, what a hell of a time he's had with his help, how he's had two guys since I left and he fired one the day after he hired him, and the other one skipped after three days and took the inside of the cash register with him, and how he'd give anything to have me back.

"Frank, I tell you what. We go to Santa Barbara tomorrow, me a Cora. Hell boy, we got to step out a little, hey? We go see a fiesta there, and you come with us. You like that, Frank? You come with us, we talk about you come back a work for me. You like a fiesta a Santa Barbara?"

"Well, I hear it's good."

"Is a girls, is a music, is a dance in streets, is swell. Come on, Frank, what you say?"

"Well, I don't know."

"Cora be sore as hell at me if I see you and no bring you out.

Maybe she treat you snotty, but she think you fine fellow, Frank. Come on, we all three go. We have a hell of a time."

"O.K. If she's willing, it's a go."

There were eight or ten people in the lunchroom when we got there, and she was back in the kitchen, washing dishes as fast as she could, to get enough plates to serve them.

"Hey. Hey Cora, look. Look who I bring."

"Well for heaven's sake. Where did he come from?"

"I see'm today a Glendale. He go to Santa Barbara with us."

"Hello, Cora. How you been?"

"You're quite a stranger around here."

She wiped her hands quick, and shook hands, but her hand was soapy. She went out front with an order, and me and the Greek sat down. He generally helped her with the orders, but he was all hot to show me something, and he let her do it all alone. It was a big scrapbook, and in the front of it he had pasted his naturalization certificate, and then his wedding certificate, and then his license to do business in Los Angeles County, and then a picture of himself in the Greek Army, and then a picture of him and Cora the day they got married, and then all the clippings about his accident. Those clippings in the regular papers, if you ask me, were more about the cat than they were about him, but anyway they had his name in them, and how he had been brought to the Glendale Hospital, and was expected to recover. The one in the Los Angeles Greek paper, though, was more about him than about the cat, and had a picture of him in it, in the dress suit he had when he was a waiter, and the story of his life. Then came the X rays. There were about a half dozen of them, because they took a new picture every day to see how he was getting along. How he had them fixed up was to paste two pages together, along the edges, and then cut out a square place in the middle, where the X ray was slipped in so you could hold it up to the light and look through it. After the X rays came the receipted hospital bills, the receipted doctors' bills, and the receipted nurses' bills. That rap on the conk cost him $322, believe it or not.

"Is a nice, hey?"

"Swell. It's all there, right on the line."

"Of course, is a not done yet. I fix'm up red, a white, a blue, fix'm up fine. Look."

He showed me where he had put the fancy stuff on a couple of the pages. He had inked in the curlicues, and then colored it with red, white, and blue. Over the naturalization certificate, he had a couple of American flags, and a eagle, and over the Greek Army picture he had crossed Greek flags, and another eagle, and over his wedding certificate he had a couple of turtle doves on a twig. He hadn't figured out yet what to put over the other stuff, but I said over the clippings he could put a cat with red, white, and blue fire coming out of its tail, and he thought that was pretty good. He didn't get it, though, when I said he could have a buzzard over the Los Angeles County license, holding a couple of auctioneer's flags that said Sale Today, and it didn't look like it would really be worth while to try to explain it to him. But I got it, at last, why he was all dressed up, and not carrying out the chow like he used to, and acted so important. This Greek had had a fracture of the skull, and a thing like that don't happen to a dumb cluck like him every day. He was like a wop that opens a drug store. Soon as he gets that thing that says Pharmacist, with a red seal on it, a wop puts on a gray suit, with black edges on the vest, and is so important he can't even take time to mix the pills, and wouldn't even touch a chocolate ice-cream soda. This Greek was all dressed up for the same reason. A big thing had happened in his life.

It was pretty near suppertime when I got her alone. He went up to wash, and the two of us were left in the kitchen.

"You been thinking about me, Cora?"

"Sure. I wouldn't forget you all that quick."

"I thought about you a lot. How are you?"

"Me? I'm all right."

"I called you up a couple of times, but he answered and I was afraid to talk to him. I made some money."

"Well, gee, I'm glad you're getting along good."

"I made it, but then I lost it. I thought we could use it to get started with, but then I lost it."

"I declare, I don't know where the money goes."

"You sure you think about me, Cora?"

"Sure I do."

"You don't act like it."

"Seems to me I'm acting all right."

"Have you got a kiss for me?"

"We'll be having supper pretty soon. You better get ready, if you've got any washing to do."

That's the way it went. That's the way it went all evening. The Greek got out some of his sweet wine, and sang a bunch of songs, and we sat around, and so far as she was concerned, I might just as well have been just a guy that used to work there, only she couldn't quite remember his name. It was the worst flop of a homecoming you ever saw in your life.

When it came time to go to bed, I let them go up, and then I went outside to try and figure out whether to stay there and see if I couldn't get going with her again, or blow and try to forget her. I walked quite a way off, and I don't know how long it was, or how far away I was, but after a while I could hear a row going on in the place. I went back, and when I got close I could hear some of what they were saying. She was yelling like hell and saying I had to leave. He was mumbling something, probably that he wanted me to stay and go back to work. He was trying to shut her up, but I could tell she was yelling so I would hear it. If I had been in my room, where she thought I was, I could have heard it plain enough, and even where I was I could hear plenty.

Then all of a sudden it stopped. I slipped in the kitchen, and stood there listening. But I couldn't hear anything, because I was all shook up, and all I could get was the sound of my own heart, going bump-bump, bump-bump, bump-bump, like that. I thought that was a funny way for my heart to sound, and then all of a sudden I knew there was two hearts in that kitchen, and that was why it sounded so funny.

I snapped on the light.

She was standing there, in a red kimono, as pale as milk, staring at me, with a long thin knife in her hand. I reached out and took it away from her. When she spoke, it was in a whisper that sounded like a snake licking its tongue in and out.

"Why did you have to come back?"

"I had to, that's all."

"No you didn't. I could have gone through with it. I was getting so I could forget you. And now you have to come back. Goddam you, you have to come back!"

"Go through with what?"

"What he's making that scrapbook for. *It's to show to his children!* And now he wants one. He wants one right away."

"Well, why didn't you come with me?"

"Come with you for what? To sleep in boxcars? Why would I come with you? Tell me that."

I couldn't say anything. I thought about my $250, but what good was it telling her that I had some money yesterday, but today I lost it playing one ball in the side?

"You're no good. I know that. You're just no good. Then why don't you go away and let me alone instead of coming back here again? Why don't you leave me be?"

"Listen. Stall him on this kid stuff just a little while. Stall him, and we'll see if we can't figure something out. I'm not much good, but I love you, Cora. I swear it."

"You swear it, and what do you do? He's taking me to Santa Barbara, so I'll say I'll have the child, and you—you're going right along with us. You're going to stay at the same hotel with us! You're going right along in the car. You're—"

She stopped, and we stood there looking at each other. The three of us in the car, we knew what that meant. Little by little we were nearer, until we were touching.

"Oh, my God, Frank, isn't there any other way out for us than that?"

"Well. You were going to stick a knife in him just now."

"No. That was for me, Frank. Not him."

"Cora, it's in the cards. We've tried every other way out."

"I can't have no greasy Greek child, Frank. I can't, that's all. The only one I can have a child by is you. I wish you were some good. You're smart, but you're no good."

"I'm no good, but I love you."

"Yes, and I love you."

"Stall him. Just this one night."

"All right, Frank. Just this one night."

Chapter 7

"There's a long, long trail a-winding
Into the land of my dreams,
Where the nightingale is singing
And the white moon beams.

"There's a long, long night of waiting
Until my dreams all come true,
Till the day when I'll be going down
That long, long trail with you."

FEELING GOOD, ain't they?"

"Too good to suit me."

"So you don't let them get hold of that wheel, Miss. They'll be all right."

"I hope so. I've got no business out with a pair of drunks, I know that. But what could I do? I told them I wouldn't go with them, but then they started to go off by themselves."

"They'd break their necks."

"That's it. So I drove myself. It was all I knew to do."

"It keeps you guessing, sometimes, to know what to do. One sixty for the gas. Is the oil O.K.?"

"I think so."

"Thanks, Miss. Goodnight."

She got in, and took the wheel again, and me and the Greek kept on singing, and we went on. It was all part of the play. I had to be drunk, because that other time had cured me of this idea we could pull a perfect murder. This was going to be such a lousy murder it wouldn't even be a murder. It was going to be just a regular road accident, with guys drunk, and booze in the car, and all the rest of it. Of course, when I started to put it down, the Greek had to have some too, so he was just like I wanted him. We stopped for gas so there would be a witness that she was sober, and didn't want to be with us anyhow, because she was driving, and it wouldn't do for her to be drunk. Before that, we had had a piece of luck. Just before we closed up, about nine o'clock, a guy stopped by for something to eat, and stood there in the road and watched us when we shoved off. He saw the whole show. He saw me try to start, and stall a couple of times. He heard the argument between me and Cora, about how I was too drunk to drive. He saw her get out, and heard her say she wasn't going. He saw me try to drive off, just me and the Greek. He saw her when she made us get out, and switched the seats, so I was behind, and the Greek up front, and then he saw her take the wheel and do the driving herself. His name was Jeff Parker and he raised rabbits at Encino. Cora got his card when she said she might try rabbits in the lunchroom, to see how they'd go. We knew right where to find him, whenever we'd need him.

Me and the Greek sang "Mother Machree," and "Smile, Smile, Smile," and "Down by the Old Mill Stream," and pretty soon we came to this sign that said "To Malibu Beach." She turned off there. By rights, she ought to have kept on like she was going. There's two main roads that lead up the coast. One, about ten miles inland, was the one we were on. The other, right alongside the ocean, was off to our left. At Ventura they meet, and follow the sea right on up to Santa Barbara, San Francisco, and wherever you're going. But the idea was, she had never seen Malibu Beach, where the movie stars live, and she wanted to cut over on this road to the ocean, so she could drop down a couple of miles and look at it, and then turn around and keep right on up to Santa Barbara. The real idea was that this connection is about the worst piece of road in Los Angeles County, and an accident there wouldn't surprise anybody, not even a cop. It's dark, and has no traffic on it hardly, and no houses or anything, and suited us for what we had to do.

The Greek never noticed anything for a while. We passed a little summer colony that they call Malibu Lake up in the hills, and there was a dance going on at the clubhouse, with couples out on the lake in canoes. I yelled at them. So did the Greek. "Give a one f' me." It didn't make much difference, but it was one more mark on our trail, if somebody took the trouble to find it.

We started up the first long upgrade, into the mountains. There were three miles of it. I had told her how to run it. Most of the time she was in second. That was partly because there were sharp curves every fifty feet, and the car would lose speed so quick going around them that she would have to shift up to second to keep going. But it was partly because the motor had to heat. Everything had to check up. We had to have plenty to tell.

And then, when he looked out and saw how dark it was, and what a hell of a looking country those mountains were, with no light, or house, or filling station, or anything else in sight, the Greek came to life and started an argument.

"Hold on, hold on. Turn around. By golly, we off the road."

"No we're not. I know where I am. It takes us to Malibu Beach. Don't you remember? I told you I wanted to see it."

"You go slow."

"I'm going slow."

"You go plenty slow. Maybe all get killed."

We got to the top and started into the downgrade. She cut the motor. They heat fast for a few minutes, when the fan stops. Down at the bottom she started the motor again. I looked at the temp gauge. It was 200. She started into the next upgrade and the temp gauge kept climbing.

"Yes sir, yes sir."

It was our signal. It was one of those dumb things a guy can say any time, and nobody will pay any attention to it. She pulled off to one side. Under us was a drop so deep you couldn't see the bottom of it. It must have been 500 feet.

"I think I'll let it cool off a bit."

"By golly, you bet. Frank, look a that. Look what it says."

"Whassit say?"

"Two hundred a five. Would be boiling in minute."

"Letta boil."

I picked up the wrench. I had it between my feet. But just then, away up the grade, I saw the lights of a car. I had to stall. I had to stall for a minute, until that car went by.

"C'me on, Nick. Sing's a song."

He looked out on those badlands, but he didn't seem to feel like singing. Then he opened the door and got out. We could hear him back there, sick. That was where he was when the car went by. I looked at the number to burn it in my brain. Then I burst out laughing. She looked back at me.

" 'S all right. Give them something to remember. Both guys alive when they went by."

"Did you get the number?"

"2R–58–01."

"2R–58–01. 2R–58–01. All right. I've got it too."

"O.K."

He came around from behind, and looked like he felt better. "You hear that?"

"Hear what?"

"When you laugh. Is a echo. Is a fine echo."

He tossed off a high note. It wasn't any song, just a high note, like on a Caruso record. He cut it off quick and listened. Sure enough, here it came back, clear as anything, and stopped, just like he had.

"Is a sound like me?"

"Jus' like you, kid. Jussa same ol' toot."

"By golly. Is swell."

He stood there for five minutes, tossing off high notes and listening to them come back. It was the first time he ever heard what his voice sounded like. He was as pleased as a gorilla that seen his face in the mirror. She kept looking at me. We had to get busy. I began to act sore. "Wot th' hell? You think we got noth'n t' do but lis'n at you yod'l at y'self all night? C'me on, get in. Le's get going."

"It's getting late, Nick."

"Hokay, hokay."

He got in, but shoved his face out to the window and let go one. I braced my feet, and while he still had his chin on the window sill I brought down the wrench. His head cracked, and I felt it crush. He crumpled up and curled on the seat like a cat on a sofa. It seemed a year before he was still. Then Cora, she gave a funny kind of gulp that ended in a moan. Because here came the echo of his voice. It took the high note, like he did, and swelled, and stopped, and waited.

Chapter 8

WE DIDN'T SAY ANYTHING. She knew what to do. She climbed back, and I climbed front. I looked at the wrench under the dash light. It had a few drops of blood on it. I uncorked a bottle of wine, and poured it on there till the blood was gone. I poured so the wine went over him. Then I wiped the wrench on a dry part of his clothes, and passed it back to her. She put it under the seat. I poured more wine over where I had wiped the wrench, cracked the bottle against the door, and laid it on top of him. Then I started the car. The wine bottle gave a gurgle, where a little of it was running out the crack.

I went a little way, and then shifted up to second. I couldn't tip it down that 500-foot drop, where we were. We had to get down to it afterward, and besides, if it plunged that far, how would we be alive? I drove slow, in second, up to a place where the ravine came to a point, and it was only a 50-foot drop. When I got there, I drove over to the edge, put my foot on the brake, and fed with the hand throttle. As soon as the right front wheel went off, I stepped hard on the brake. It stalled. That was how I wanted it. The car had to be in gear, with the ignition on, but that dead motor would hold it for the rest of what we had to do.

We got out. We stepped on the road, not the shoulder, so there wouldn't be footprints. She handed me a rock, and a piece of 2 x 4 I had back there. I put the rock under the rear axle. It fitted, because I had picked one that would fit. I slipped the 2 x 4 over the rock and under the axle. I heaved down on it. The car tipped, but it hung

there. I heaved again. It tipped a little more. I began to sweat. Here
we were, with a dead man in the car, and suppose we couldn't tip it
over?

I heaved again, but this time she was beside me. We both heaved.
We heaved again. And then all of a sudden, there we were, sprawled
down on the road, and the car was rolling over and over, down the
gully, and banging so loud you could hear it a mile.

It stopped. The lights were still on, but it wasn't on fire. That was
the big danger. With that ignition on, if the car burned up, why
weren't we burned too? I snatched up the rock, and gave it a heave
down the ravine. I picked up the 2 x 4, ran up the road with it a way,
and slung it down, right in the roadway. It didn't bother me any. All
over the road, wherever you go, are pieces of wood that have
dropped off trucks, and they get all splintered up from cars running
over them, and this was one of them. I had left it out all day, and it
had tire marks on it, and the edges were all chewed up.

I ran back, picked her up, and slid down the ravine with her. Why
I did that was on account of the tracks. My tracks, they didn't worry
me any. I figured there would be plenty of men piling down there
pretty soon, but those sharp heels of hers, they had to be pointed in
the right direction, if anybody took the trouble to look.

I set her down. The car was hanging there, on two wheels, about
halfway down the ravine. He was still in there, but now he was down
on the floor. The wine bottle was wedged between him and the seat,
and while we were looking it gave a gurgle. The top was all broken
in, and both fenders were bent. I tried the doors. That was important, because I had to get in there, and be cut up with glass, while
she went up on the road to get help. They opened all right.

I began to fool with her blouse, to bust the buttons, so she would
look banged up. She was looking at me, and her eyes didn't look
blue, they looked black. I could feel her breath coming fast. Then it
stopped, and she leaned real close to me.

"Rip me! Rip me!"

I ripped her. I shoved my hand in her blouse and jerked. She was
wide open, from her throat to her belly.

"You got that climbing out. You caught it in the door handle."

My voice sounded queer, like it was coming out of a tin phonograph.

"And this you don't know how you got."

I hauled off and hit her in the eye as hard as I could. She went down. She was right down there at my feet, her eyes shining, her breasts trembling, drawn up in tight points, and pointing right up at me. She was down there, and the breath was roaring in the back of my throat like I was some kind of a animal, and my tongue was all swelled up in my mouth, and blood pounding in it.

"Yes! Yes, Frank, yes!"

Next thing I knew, I was down there with her, and we were staring in each other's eyes, and locked in each other's arms, and straining to get closer. Hell could have opened for me then, and it wouldn't have made any difference. I had to have her, if I hung for it.

I had her.

Chapter 9

WE LAY THERE A few minutes, then, like we were doped. It was so still that all you could hear was this gurgle from the inside of the car.

"What now, Frank?"

"Tough road ahead, Cora. You've got to be good, from now on. You sure you can go through it?"

"After that, I can go through anything."

"They'll come at you, those cops. They'll try to break you down. You ready for them?"

"I think so."

"Maybe they'll pin something on you. I don't think they can, with those witnesses we got. But maybe they do it. Maybe they pin it on you for manslaughter, and you spend a year in jail. Maybe it's as bad as that. You think you can take it on the chin?"

"So you're waiting for me when I come out."

"I'll be there."

"Then I can do it."

"Don't pay any attention to me. I'm a drunk. They got tests that'll show that. I'll say stuff that's cock-eyed. That's to cross them up, so when I'm sober and tell it my way, they'll believe it."

"I'll remember."

"And you're pretty sore at me. For being drunk. For being the cause of it all."

"Yes. I know."

"Then we're set."

"Frank."

"Yes?"

"There's just one thing. We've got to be in love. If we love each other, then nothing matters."

"Well, do we?"

"I'll be the first one to say it. I love you, Frank."

"I love you, Cora."

"Kiss me."

I kissed her, and held her close, and then I saw a flicker of light on the hill across the ravine.

"Up on the road, now. You're going through with it."

"I'm going through with it."

"Just ask for help. You don't know he's dead yet."

"I know."

"You fell down, after you climbed out. That's how you got the sand on your clothes."

"Yes. Goodbye."

"Goodbye."

She started up to the road, and I dived for the car. But all of a sudden, I found I didn't have my hat. I had to be in the car, and my hat had to be with me. I began clawing around for it. The car was coming closer and closer. It was only two or three bends away, and I didn't have my hat yet, and I didn't have a mark on me. I gave up, and started for the car. Then I fell down. I had hooked my foot in it. I grabbed it, and jumped in. My weight no sooner went on the floor than it sank and I felt the car turning over on me. That was the last I knew for a while.

Next, I was on the ground, and there was a lot of yelling and talking going on around me. My left arm was shooting pain so bad I would yell every time I felt it, and so was my back. Inside my head was a bellow that would get big and go away again. When it did that the ground would fall away, and this stuff I had drunk would come up. I was there and I wasn't there, but I had sense enough to roll around and kick. There was sand on my clothes too, and there had to be a reason.

Next there was a screech in my ears, and I was in an ambulance. A state cop was at my feet, and a doctor was working on my arm. I went out again as soon as I saw it. It was running blood, and between the wrist and the elbow it was bent like a snapped twig. It was broke. When I came out of it again the doctor was still working on it, and I thought about my back. I wiggled my foot and looked at it to see if I was paralyzed. It moved.

The screech kept bringing me out of it, and I looked around, and saw the Greek. He was on the other bunk.

"Yay Nick."

Nobody said anything. I looked around some more, but I couldn't see anything of Cora.

After a while they stopped, and lifted out the Greek. I waited for them to lift me out, but they didn't. I knew he was really dead, then, and there wouldn't be any cock-eyed stuff this time, selling him a story about a cat. If they had taken us both out, it would be a hospital. But when they just took him out, it was a mortuary.

We went on, then, and when they stopped they lifted me out. They carried me in, and set the stretcher on a wheel table, and rolled me in a white room. Then they got ready to set my arm. They wheeled up a machine to give me gas for that, but then they had an argument. There was another doctor there by that time that said he was the jail physician, and the hospital doctors got pretty sore. I knew what it was about. It was those tests for being drunk. If they gave me the gas first, that would ball up the breath test, the most important one. The jail doctor won out, and made me blow through a glass pipe into some stuff that looked like water but turned yellow when I blew in it. Then he took some blood, and some other samples that he poured in bottles through a funnel. Then they gave me the gas.

When I began to come out of it I was in a room, in bed, and my head was all covered with bandages, and so was my arm, with a sling besides, and my back was all strapped up with adhesive tape so I could hardly move. A state cop was there, reading the morning paper. My head ached like hell, and so did my back, and my arm had shooting pains in it. After a while a nurse came in and gave me a pill, and I went to sleep.

·   ·   ·

When I woke up it was about noon, and they gave me something to eat. Then two more cops came in, and they put me on a stretcher again, and took me down and put me in another ambulance.

"Where we going?"

"Inquest."

"Inquest. That's what they have when somebody's dead, ain't it."

"That's right."

"I was afraid they'd got it."

"Only one."

"Which?"

"The man."

"Oh. Was the woman bad hurt?"

"Not bad."

"Looks pretty bad for me, don't it?"

"Watch out there, buddy. It's O.K. with us if you want to talk, but anything you say may fall back in your lap when you get to court."

"That's right. Thanks."

When we stopped it was in front of a undertaker shop in Hollywood, and they carried me in. Cora was there, pretty battered up. She had on a blouse that the police matron had lent her, and it puffed out around her belly like it was stuffed with hay. Her suit and her shoes were dusty, and her eye was all swelled up where I had hit it. She had the police matron with her. The coroner was back of a table, with some kind of a secretary guy beside him. Off to one side were a half dozen guys that acted pretty sore, with cops standing guard over them. They were the jury. There was a bunch of other people, with cops pushing them around to the place where they ought to stand. The undertaker was tiptoeing around, and every now and then he would shove a chair under somebody. He brought a couple for Cora and the matron. Off to one side, on a table, was something under a sheet.

Soon as they had me parked the way they wanted me, on a table, the coroner rapped with his pencil and they started. First thing, was a legal identification. She began to cry when they lifted the sheet off, and I didn't like it much myself. After she looked, and I looked, and the jury looked, they dropped the sheet again.

"Do you know this man?"

"He was my husband."

"His name?"

"Nick Papadakis."

Next came the witnesses. The sergeant told how he got the call and went up there with two officers after he phoned for an ambulance, and how he sent Cora in by a car he took charge of, and me and the Greek in by ambulance, and how the Greek died on the way in, and was dropped off at the mortuary. Next, a hick by the name of Wright told how he was coming around the bend, and heard a woman scream, and heard a crash, and saw the car going over and over, the lights still on, down the gully. He saw Cora in the road, waving at him for help, and went down to the car with her and tried to get me and the Greek out. He couldn't do it, because the car was on top of us, so he sent his brother, that was in the car with him, for help. After a while more people came, and the cops, and when the cops took charge they got the car off us and put us in the ambulance. Then Wright's brother told about the same thing, only he went back for the cops.

Then the jail doctor told how I was drunk, and how examination of the stomach showed the Greek was drunk, but Cora wasn't drunk. Then he told which cracked bone it was that the Greek died of. Then the coroner turned to me and asked me if I wanted to testify.

"Yes sir, I guess so."

"I warn you that any statement you make may be used against you, and that you are under no compulsion to testify unless you so wish."

"I got nothing to hold back."

"All right, then. What do you know about this?"

"All I know is that first I was going along. Then I felt the car sink under me, and something hit me, and that's all I can remember until I come to in the hospital."

"*You* were going along?"

"Yes sir."

"You mean you were driving the car?"

"Yes sir, I was driving it."

That was just a cock-eyed story I was going to take back later on, when we got in a place where it really meant something, which this inquest didn't. I figured if I told a bum story first, and then turned around and told another story, it would sound like the second story was really true, where if I had a pat story right from the beginning, it would sound like what it was, pat. I was doing this one different from the first time. I meant to look bad, right from the start. But if I wasn't driving the car, it didn't make any difference how bad I looked, they couldn't do anything to me. What I was afraid of was that perfect murder stuff that we cracked up on last time. Just one little thing, and we were sunk. But here, if I looked bad, there could be quite a few things and still I wouldn't look much worse. The worse I looked on account of being drunk, the less the whole thing would look like a murder.

The cops looked at each other, and the coroner studied me like he thought I was crazy. They had already heard it all, how I was pulled out from under the back seat.

"You're sure of that? That you were driving?"

"Absolutely sure."

"You had been drinking?"

"You heard the results of the tests that were given you?"

"I don't know nothing about the tests. All I know is I didn't have no drink."

He turned to Cora. She said she would tell what she could.

"Who was driving this car?"

"I was."

"Where was this man?"

"On the back seat."

"Had he been drinking?"

She kind of looked away, and swallowed, and cried a little bit. "Do I have to answer that?"

"You don't have to answer any question unless you so wish."

"I don't want to answer."

"Very well, then. Tell in your own words what happened."

"I was driving along. There was a long upgrade, and the car got hot. My husband said I had better stop to let it cool off."

"How hot?"

"Over 200."

"Go on."

"So after we started the downgrade, I cut the motor, and when we got to the bottom it was still hot, and before we started up again we stopped. We were there maybe ten minutes. Then I started up again. And I don't know what happened. I went into high, and didn't get enough power, and I went into second, right quick, and the men were talking, or maybe it was on account of making the quick shift, but anyhow, I felt one side of the car go down. I yelled to them to jump, but it was too late. I felt the car going over and over, and next thing I knew I was trying to get out, and then I was out, and then I was up on the road."

The coroner turned to me again. "What are you trying to do, shield this woman?"

"I don't notice her shielding me any."

The jury went out, and then came in and gave a verdict that the said Nick Papadakis came to his death as the result of an automobile accident on the Malibu Lake Road, caused in whole or in part by criminal conduct on the part of me and Cora, and recommended that we be held for the action of the grand jury.

There was another cop with me that night, in the hospital, and next morning he told me that Mr. Sackett was coming over to see me, and I better get ready. I could hardly move yet, but I had the hospital barber shave me up and make me look as good as he could. I knew who Sackett was. He was the District Attorney. About half past ten he showed up, and the cop went out, and there was nobody there but him and me. He was a big guy with a bald head and a breezy manner.

"Well, well, well. How do you feel?"

"I feel O.K., judge. Kind of shook me up a little, but I'll be all right."

"As the fellow said when he fell out of the airplane, it was a swell ride but we lit kind of hard."

"That's it."

"Now Chambers, you don't have to talk to me if you don't want to, but I've come over here, partly to see what you look like, and partly because it's been my experience that a frank talk saves a lot of breath afterwards, and sometimes paves the way to the disposition of a whole case with a proper plea, and anyway, as the fellow says, after it's over we understand each other."

"Why sure, judge. What was it you wanted to know?"

I made it sound pretty shifty, and he sat there looking me over. "Suppose we start at the beginning."

"About this trip?"

"That's it. I want to hear all about it."

He got up and began to walk around. The door was right by my bed, and I jerked it open. The cop was halfway down the hall, chinning a nurse. Sackett burst out laughing. "No, no dictaphones in this. They don't use them anyway, except in movies."

I let a sheepish grin come over my face. I had him like I wanted him. I had pulled a dumb trick on him, and he had got the better of me. "O.K., judge. I guess it was pretty silly, at that. All right, I'll begin at the beginning and tell it all. I'm in dutch all right, but I guess lying about it won't do any good."

"That's the right attitude, Chambers."

I told him how I walked out on the Greek, and how I bumped into him on the street one day, and he wanted me back, and then asked me to go on this Santa Barbara trip with them to talk it over. I told about how we put down the wine, and how we started out, with me at the wheel. He stopped me then.

"So you *were* driving the car?"

"Judge, suppose *you* tell *me* that."

"What do you mean, Chambers?"

"I mean I heard what she said, at the inquest. I heard what those cops said. I know where they found me. So I know who was driving, all right. She was. But if I tell it like I remember it, I got to say I was driving it. I didn't tell that coroner any lie, judge. *It still seems to me I was driving it.*"

"You lied about being drunk."

"That's right. I was all full of booze, and ether, and dope that they give you, and I lied all right. But I'm all right now, and I got sense enough to know the truth is all that can get me out of this, if anything can. Sure, I was drunk. I was stinko. And all I could think of was, I mustn't let them know I was drunk, because I was driving the car, and if they find out I was drunk, I'm sunk."

"Is that what you'd tell a jury?"

"I'd have to, judge. But what I can't understand is how she came to be driving it. I started out with it. I know that. I can even remember a guy standing there laughing at me. Then how come she was driving when it went over?"

"You drove it about two feet."

"You mean two miles."

"I mean two feet. Then she took the wheel away from you."

"Gee, I *must* have been stewed."

"Well, it's one of those things that a jury might believe. It's just got that cock-eyed look to it that generally goes with the truth. Yes, they might believe it."

He sat there looking at his nails, and I had a hard time to keep the grin from creeping over my face. I was glad when he started asking me more questions, so I could get my mind on something else, besides how easy I had fooled him.

"When did you go to work for Papadakis, Chambers?"

"Last winter."

"How long did you stay with him?"

"Till a month ago. Maybe six weeks."

"You worked for him six months, then?"

"About that."

"What did you do before that?"

"Oh, knocked around?"

"Hitchhiked? Rode freights? Bummed your meals wherever you could?"

"Yes sir."

He unstrapped a briefcase, put a pile of papers on the table, and began looking through them. "Ever been in Frisco?"

"Born there."

"Kansas City? New York? New Orleans? Chicago?"

"I've seen them all."

"Ever been in jail?"

"I have, judge. You knock around, you get in trouble with the cops now and then. Yes sir, I've been in jail."

"Ever been in jail in Tucson?"

"Yes sir. I think it was ten days I got there. It was for trespassing on railroad property."

"Salt Lake City? San Diego? Wichita?"

"Yes sir. All those places."

"Oakland?"

"I got three months there, judge. I got in a fight with a railroad detective."

"You beat him up pretty bad, didn't you?"

"Well, as the fellow says, he was beat up pretty bad, but you ought to seen the other one. I was beat up pretty bad myself."

"Los Angeles?"

"Once. But that was only three days."

"Chambers, how did you come to go to work for Papadakis, anyhow?"

"Just a kind of an accident. I was broke, and he needed somebody.

I blew in there to get something to eat, and he offered me a job, and I took it."

"Chambers, does that strike you as funny?"

"I don't know how you mean, judge."

"That after knocking around all these years, and never doing any work, or even trying to do any, so far as I can see, you suddenly settled down, and went to work, and held a job steady?"

"I didn't like it much, I'll own up to that."

"But you stuck."

"Nick, he was one of the nicest guys I ever knew. After I got a stake, I tried to tell him I was through, but I just didn't have the heart, much trouble as he had had with his help. Then when he had the accident, and wasn't there, I blew. I just blew, that's all. I guess I ought to treated him better, but I got rambling feet, judge. When they say go, I got to go with them. I just took a quiet way out."

"And then, the day after you came back, he got killed."

"You kind of make me feel bad now, judge. Because maybe I tell the jury different, but I'm telling you now I feel that was a hell of a lot my fault. If I hadn't been there, and begun promoting him for something to drink that afternoon, maybe he'd be here now. Understand, maybe that didn't have anything to do with it at all. I don't know. I was stinko, and I don't know what happened. Just the same, if she hadn't had two drunks in the car, maybe she could have drove better, couldn't she? Anyway, that's how I feel about it."

I looked at him, to see how he was taking it. He wasn't even looking at me. All of a sudden he jumped up and came over to the bed and took me by the shoulder. "Out with it, Chambers. Why did you stick with Papadakis for six months?"

"Judge, I don't get you."

"Yes you do. I've seen her, Chambers, and I can guess why you did it. She was in my office yesterday, and she had a black eye, and was pretty well banged up, but even with that she looked pretty good. For something like that, plenty of guys have said goodbye to the road, rambling feet or not."

"Anyhow they rambled. No, judge, you're wrong."

"They didn't ramble long. It's too good, Chambers. Here's an automobile accident that yesterday was a dead open-and-shut case of manslaughter, and today it's just evaporated into nothing at all. Every place I touch it, up pops a witness to tell me something, and when I fit all they have to say together, I haven't got any case. Come on, Chambers. You and that woman murdered this Greek, and the sooner you own up to it the better it'll be for you."

There wasn't any grin creeping over my face then, I'm here to tell you. I could feel my lips getting numb, and I tried to speak, but nothing would come out of my mouth.

"Well, why don't you say something?"

"You're coming at me. You're coming at me for something pretty bad. I don't know anything to say, judge."

"You were gabby enough a few minutes ago, when you were handing me that stuff about the truth being all that would get you out of this. Why can't you talk now?"

"You got me all mixed up."

"All right, we'll take it one thing at a time, so you won't be mixed up. In the first place, you've been sleeping with that woman, haven't you?"

"Nothing like it."

"How about the week Papadakis was in the hospital? Where did you sleep then?"

"In my own room."

"And she slept in hers? Come on, I've seen her, I tell you. I'd have been in there if I had to kick the door down and hang for rape. So would you. So *were* you."

"I never even thought of it."

"How about all those trips you took with her to Hasselman's Market in Glendale? What did you do with her on the way back?"

"Nick told me to go on those trips himself."

"I didn't ask you who told you to go. I asked you what you did."

I was so groggy I had to do something about it quick. All I could think of was to get sore. "All right, suppose we did. We didn't, but you say we did, and we'll let it go at that. Well, if it was all that easy, what would we be knocking him off for? Holy smoke, judge, I hear tell of guys that would commit murder for what you say I was getting, when they weren't getting it, but I never hear tell of a guy that would commit murder for it when he already had it."

"No? Well I'll tell you what you were knocking him off for. A piece of property out there, for one thing, that Papadakis paid $14,000 for, cash on the nail. And for that other little Christmas present you and she thought you would get on the boat with, and see what the wild waves looked like. *That little $10,000 accident policy that Papadakis carried on his life.*"

I could still see his face, but all around it was getting black and I was trying to keep myself from keeling over in bed. Next thing, he was holding a glass of water to my mouth. "Have a drink. You'll feel better."

I drank some of it. I had to.

"Chambers, I think this is the last murder you'll have a hand in for some time, but if you ever try another, for God's sake leave insurance companies out of it. They'll spend five times as much as Los Angeles County will let me put into a case. They've got detectives five times as good as any I'll be able to hire. They know their stuff from A to izzard, and they're right on your tail now. It means money to them. That's where you and she made your big mistake."

"Judge, I hope Christ may kill me, I never heard of an insurance policy until just this minute."

"You turned white as a sheet."

"Wouldn't you?"

"Well, how about getting me on your side, right from the start? How about a full confession, a quick plea of guilty, and I'll do what I can for you with the court? Ask for clemency for you both."

"Nothing doing."

"How about all that stuff you were telling me just now? About the truth, and how you'd have to come clean with the jury, and all that? You think you can get away with lies now? You think I'm going to stand for that?"

"I don't know what you're going to stand for. To hell with that. You stand for your side of it and I'll stand for mine. I didn't do it, and that's all I stand for. You got that?"

"The hell you say. Getting tough with me, hey? All right, now you get it. You're going to find out what that jury's really going to hear. First, you were sleeping with her, weren't you? Then Papadakis had a little accident, and you and she had a swell time. In bed together at night, down to the beach by day, holding hands and looking at each other in between. Then you both had a swell idea. Now that he's had an accident, make him take out an accident policy, and then knock him off. So you blew, to give her a chance to put it over. She worked at it, and pretty soon she had him. He took out a policy, a real good policy, that covered accidents, and health, and all the rest of it, and cost $46.72. Then you were ready. Two days after that, Frank Chambers accidentally on purpose ran into Nick Papadakis on the street, and Nick tries to get him to go back to work for him. And what do you know about that, he and his wife had it already fixed up they were going to Santa Barbara, had the hotel reservations and everything, so of course there was nothing to it but Frank Chambers had to come with them, just for old times' sake. And you went. You got the Greek a little bit drunk, and did the same for yourself. You stuck a couple of wine bottles in the car, just to get the cops good and sore. Then you had to take that Malibu Lake Road, so she could see Malibu Beach. Wasn't that an idea, now. Eleven o'clock at night, and she was going to drive down there to look at a bunch of houses with waves in front of them. But you didn't get there. You stopped. And while you were stopped, you crowned the Greek with one of the wine bottles. A beautiful thing to crown a man with, Chambers, and nobody knew it better than you, because that was what you crowned that railroad dick with, over in Oakland. You crowned him, and then she started the car. And while she was climbing out on the running board, you leaned over from behind, and held the wheel, and fed with the hand throttle. It didn't need much gas, because it was in second gear. And after she got on the running board, she took the wheel and fed with the hand throttle, and it was your turn to climb out. But you were just a little drunk, weren't you? You were too slow, and she was a little too quick to shoot the car over the edge. So she jumped and you were caught. You think a jury won't believe that, do you? It'll believe it, because I'll prove every word of it, from the beach trip to the hand throttle, and when I do, there won't be any clemency for you, boy. It'll be the rope, with you hanging on the end of it, and when they cut you down they'll bury you out there with all the others that were too goddam dumb to make a deal when they had the chance to keep their neck from being broke."

"Nothing like that happened. Not that I know of."

"What are you trying to tell me? That *she* did it?"

"I'm not trying to tell you that anybody did it. Leave me alone! Nothing like that happened."

"How do you know? I thought you were stinko."

"It didn't happen that I know of."

"Then you mean she did it?"

"I don't mean no such a goddam thing. I mean what I say and that's all I mean."

"Listen, Chambers. There were three people in the car, you, and she, and the Greek. Well, it's a cinch the Greek didn't do it. If you didn't do it, that leaves her, doesn't it?"

"Who the hell says anybody did it?"

"I do. Now we're getting somewhere, Chambers. Because maybe you didn't do it. You say you're telling the truth, and maybe you are. But if you are telling the truth, and didn't have any interest in this woman except as the wife of a friend, then you've got to do something about it, haven't you? You've got to sign a complaint against her."

"What do you mean complaint?"

"If she killed the Greek, she tried to kill you too, didn't she? You can't let her get away with that. Somebody might think it was pretty funny if you did. Sure, you'd be a sucker to let her get away with it. She knocks off her husband for the insurance, and she tries to knock off you too. You've got to do something about that, haven't you?"

"I might, if she did it. But I don't know she did it."

"If I prove it to you, you'll have to sign the complaint, won't you?"

"Sure. *If* you can prove it."

"All right, I'll prove it. When you stopped, you got out of the car, didn't you?"

"No."

"What? I thought you were so stinko you didn't remember anything. That's the second time you've remembered something now. I'm surprised at you."

"Not that I know of."

"But you did. Listen to this man's statement: 'I didn't notice much about the car, except that a woman was at the wheel and one man was inside laughing when we went by, and another man was out back, sick.' So you were out back a few minutes, sick. That was when she crowned Papadakis with the bottle. And when you got back you never noticed anything, because you were stinko, and Papadakis had passed out anyhow, and there was hardly anything to notice. You sat back and passed out, and that was when she slid up into second, kept her hand on the hand throttle, fed with that, and as soon as she had slid out on the running board, shot the car over."

"That don't prove it."

"Yes it does. The witness Wright says that the car was rolling over and over, down the gully, when he came around the bend, *but the woman was up on the road, waving to him for help!*"

"Maybe she jumped."

"If she jumped, it's funny she took her handbag with her, isn't it? Chambers, can a woman drive with a handbag in her hand? When she jumps, has she got time to pick it up? Chambers, it can't be done. It's impossible to jump from a sedan car that's turning over into a gully. She wasn't in the car when it went over! That proves it, doesn't it?"

"I don't know."

"What do you mean you don't know? Are you going to sign that complaint or not?"

"No."

"Listen, Chambers, it was no accident that car went over a second too soon. It was you or her, and she didn't mean it would be you."

"Let me alone. I don't know what you're talking about."

"Boy, it's still you or her. If you didn't have anything to do with this, you better sign this thing. Because if you don't, then I'll know. And so will the jury. And so will the judge. And so will the guy that springs the trap."

He looked at me a minute, then went out, and came back with another guy. The guy sat down and made out a form with a fountain pen. Sackett brought it over to me. "Right here, Chambers."

I signed. There was so much sweat on my hand the guy had to blot it off the paper.

Chapter 10

AFTER HE WENT, the cop came back and mumbled something about blackjack. We played a few rounds, but I couldn't get my mind on it. I made out it got on my nerves to deal with one hand, and quit.

"He kind of got to you, hey?"

"Little bit."

"He's tough, he is. He gets to them all. He looks like a preacher, all full of love for the human race, but he's got a heart like a stone."

"Stone is right."

"Only one guy in this town has got it on him."

"Yeah?"

"Guy named Katz. You've heard of him."

"Sure, I heard of him."

"Friend of mine."

"It's the kind of a friend to have."

"Say. You ain't supposed to have no lawyer yet. You ain't been arraigned, and you can't send for nobody. They can hold you forty-eight hours incommunicado, they call it. But if he shows up here, I got to let him see you, you get it? He might show up here, if I happened to be talking to him."

"You mean you get a cut."

"I mean he's a friend of mine. Well, if he didn't give me no cut, he wouldn't be no friend, would he? He's a great guy. He's the only one in this town can throw the headlock on Sackett.

"You're on, kid. And the sooner the better."

"I'll be back."

He went out for a little while, and when he came back he gave me a wink. And pretty soon, sure enough, there came a knock on the door, and in came Katz. He was a little guy, about forty years old, with a leathery face and a black moustache, and the first thing he did when he came in was take out a bag of Bull Durham smoking tobacco and a pack of brown papers and roll himself a cigarette. When he lit it, it burned halfway up one side, and that was the last he did about it. It just hung there, out the side of his mouth, and if it was lit or out, or whether he was asleep or awake, I never found out. He just sat there, with his eyes half shut and one leg hung over the arm of the chair, and his hat on the back of his head, and that was all. You might think that was a poor sight to see, for a guy in my spot, but it wasn't. He might be asleep, but even asleep he looked like he knew more than most guys awake, and a kind of a lump came up in my throat. It was like the sweet chariot had swung low and was going to pick me up.

The cop watched him roll the cigarette like it was Cadona doing the triple somersault, and he hated to go, but he had to. After he was out, Katz motioned to me to get going. I told him about how we had an accident, and how Sackett was trying to say we murdered the Greek for the insurance, and how he made me sign that complaint paper that said she had tried to murder me too. He listened, and after I had run down he sat there awhile without saying anything. Then he got up.

"He's got you in a spot all right."

"I ought not to signed it. I don't believe she did any such a goddam thing. But he had me going. And now I don't know where the hell I'm at."

"Well, anyhow, you ought not to have signed it."

"Mr. Katz, will you do one thing for me? Will you see her, and tell her—"

"I'll see her. And I'll tell her what's good for her to know. For the rest of it, I'm handling this, and that means I'm handling it. You got that?"

"Yes sir, I've got it."

"I'll be with you at the arraignment. Or anyhow, somebody that I pick will be with you. As Sackett has made a complainant out of you, I may not be able to appear for you both, but I'll be handling it. And once more, that means that whatever I do, I'm handling it."

"Whatever you do, Mr. Katz."

"I'll be seeing you."

That night they put me on a stretcher again, and took me over to court for the arraignment. It was a magistrate's court, not a regular court. There wasn't any jury box, or witness stand, or any of that stuff. The magistrate sat on a platform, with some cops beside him, and in front of him was a long desk that ran clear across the room, and whoever had something to say hooked his chin over the desk and said it. There was a big crowd there, and photographers were snapping flashlights at me when they carried me in, and you could tell from the buzz that something big was going on. I couldn't see much, from down there on the stretcher, but I got a flash at Cora, sitting on the front bench with Katz, and Sackett, off to one side talking to some guys with briefcases, and some of the cops and witnesses that had been at the inquest. They set me down in front of the desk, on a couple of tables they had shoved together, and they hadn't much more than got the blankets spread over me right than they wound up a case about a Chinese woman, and a cop began rapping for quiet. While he was doing that, a young guy leaned down over me, and said his name was White, and Katz had asked him to represent me. I nodded my head, but he kept whispering that Mr. Katz had sent him, and the cop got sore and began banging hard.

"Cora Papadakis."

She stood up, and Katz took her up to the desk. She almost touched me as she went by, and it seemed funny to smell her, the same smell that had always set me wild, in the middle of all this stuff. She looked a little better than she had yesterday. She had on another blouse, that fitted her right, and her suit had been cleaned and pressed, and her shoes had been polished, and her eye was black, but not swelled. All the other people went up with her, and after they had spread out in a line, the cop told them to raise their right hand, and began to mumble about the truth, the whole truth, and nothing but the truth. He stopped in the middle of it to look down and see if I had my right hand raised. I didn't. I shoved it up, and he mumbled all over again. We all mumbled back.

The magistrate took off his glasses, and told Cora she was charged with the murder of Nick Papadakis, and with assault against Frank Chambers, with intent to kill, that she could make a statement if she wanted to, but any statement she made could be used against her, that she had the right to be represented by counsel, that she had eight days to plead, and the court would hear her plea at any time during that period. It was a long spiel, and you could hear them coughing before he got done.

Then Sackett started up, and told what he was going to prove. It was about the same as he had told me that morning, only he made it sound solemn as hell. When he got through, he began putting on his witnesses. First there was the ambulance doctor, that told when the Greek had died, and where. Then came the jail doctor, that had made the autopsy, and then came the coroner's secretary, that identified the minutes of the inquest, and left them with the magistrate, and then came a couple of more guys, but I forget what they said. When they got done, all that the whole bunch had proved was that the Greek was dead, and as I knew that anyway, I didn't pay much attention. Katz never asked any of them anything. Every time the magistrate would look at him, he would wave his hand and the guy would step aside.

After they had the Greek dead enough to suit them, Sackett really straightened out, and put some stuff in that meant something. He called a guy that said he represented the Pacific States Accident Assurance Corporation of America, and he told how the Greek had taken out a policy just five days before. He told what it covered, how the Greek would get $25 a week for 52 weeks if he got sick, and the same if he got hurt in an accident so he couldn't work, and how he would get $5,000 if he lost one limb, and $10,000 if he lost two limbs, and how his widow would get $10,000 if he was killed in an accident, and $20,000 if the accident was on a railroad train. When he got that far it began to sound like a sales talk and the magistrate held up his hand.

"I've got all the insurance I need."

Everybody laughed at the magistrate's gag. Even I laughed. You'd be surprised how funny it sounded.

Sackett asked a few more questions, and then the magistrate turned to Katz. Katz thought a minute, and when he talked to the guy, he did it slow, like he wanted to make sure he had every word straight.

"You are an interested party to this proceeding?"

"In a sense I am, Mr. Katz."

"You wish to escape payment of this indemnity, on the ground that a crime has been committed, is that correct?"

"That is correct."

"You really believe that a crime has been committed, that this woman killed her husband to obtain this indemnity, and either tried to kill this man, or else deliberately placed him in jeopardy that might cause his death, all as part of a plan to obtain this indemnity?"

The guy kind of smiled, and thought a minute, like he would return the compliment and get every word straight too. "Answering that question, Mr. Katz, I would say I've handled thousands of such cases, cases of fraud that go over my desk every day, and I think I have an unusual experience in that kind of investigation. I may say that I have never seen a clearer case in all my years' work for this and other companies. I don't only believe a crime has been committed, Mr. Katz. I practically know it."

"That is all. Your Honor, I plead her guilty on both charges."

If he had dropped a bomb in that courtroom, he couldn't have stirred it up quicker. Reporters rushed out, and photographers rushed up to the desk to get pictures. They kept bumping into each other, and the magistrate got sore and began banging for order. Sackett looked like he had been shot, and all over the place there was a roar like somebody had all of a sudden shoved a seashell up against your ear. I kept trying to see Cora's face. But all I could get of it was the corner of her mouth. It kept twitching, like somebody was jabbing a needle into it about once every second.

Next thing I knew, the guys on the stretcher picked me up, and followed the young guy, White, out of the courtroom. Then they went with me on the double across a couple of halls into a room with three or four cops in it. White said something about Katz, and the cops cleared out. They set me down on the desk, and then the guys on the stretcher went out. White walked around a little, and then the door opened and a matron came in with Cora. Then White and the matron went out, and the door closed, and we were alone. I tried to think of something to say, and couldn't. She walked around, and didn't look at me. Her mouth was still twitching. I kept swallowing, and after a while I thought of something.

"We've been flimflammed, Cora."

She didn't say anything. She just kept walking around.

"That guy Katz, he's nothing but a cop's stool. A cop sent him to me. I thought he was on the up-and-up. But we've been flim-flammed."

"Oh no, we ain't been flimflammed."

"We been flimflammed. I ought to have known, when the cop tried to sell him to me. But I didn't. I thought he was on the level."

"I've been flimflammed, but you haven't."

"Yes I have. He fooled me too."

"I see it all now. I see why I had to drive the car. I see it, that other time, why it was me that had to do it, not you. Oh yes. I fell for you because you were smart. And now I find out you're smart. Ain't that funny? You fall for a guy because he's smart and then you find out he's smart."

"What are you trying to tell me, Cora?"

"Flim-flammed! I'll say I was. You and that lawyer. You fixed it up all right. You fixed it up so I tried to kill you too. That was so it would look like you couldn't have had anything to do with it. Then you have me plead guilty in court. So you're not in it at all. All right. I guess I'm pretty dumb. But I'm not that dumb. Listen, Mr. Frank Chambers. When I get through, just see how smart you are. There's just such a thing as being too smart."

I tried to talk to her, but it wasn't any use. When she had got so that even her lips were white, under the lipstick, the door opened and Katz came in. I tried to jump for him, off the stretcher. I couldn't move. They had me strapped so I couldn't move.

"Get out of here, you goddam stool. *You* were handling it. I'll say you were. But now I know you for what you are. Do you hear that? Get out of here!"

"Why, what's the matter, Chambers?"

You would have thought he was a Sunday school teacher, talking to some kid that was crying for his chewing gum that had been taken away. "Why, what's the matter? I *am* handling it. I told you that."

"That's right. Only God help you if I ever get you so I got my hands on you."

He looked at her, like it was something he just couldn't understand, and maybe she could help him out. She came over to him.

"This man here, this man and you, you ganged up on me so I would get it and he would go free. Well, he was in this as much as I was, and he's not going to get away with it. I'm going to tell it. I'm going to tell it all, and I'm going to tell it right now."

He looked at her, and shook his head, and it was the phoniest look I ever saw on a man's face. "Now my dear, I wouldn't do that. If you'll just let me handle this—"

"You handled it. Now I'll handle it."

He got up, shrugged his shoulders, and went out. He was hardly gone before a guy with big feet and a red neck came in with a little portable typewriter, set it on a chair with a couple of books under it, hitched up to it, and looked at her.

"Mr. Katz said you wanted to make a statement?"

He had a little squeaky voice, and a kind of a grin when he talked.

"That's right. A statement."

She began to speak jerky, two or three words at a time, and as fast as she said it, he rattled it off on the typewriter. She told it all. She went back to the beginning, and told how she met me, how we first began going together, how we tried to knock off the Greek once, but missed. A couple of times, a cop put his head in at the door, but the guy at the typewriter held up his hand.

"Just a few minutes, sarge."

"O.K."

When she got to the end, she said she didn't know anything about the insurance, we hadn't done it for that at all, but just to get rid of him.

"That's all."

He gathered his sheets together, and she signed them. "Will you just initial these pages?" She initialed them. He got out a notary stamp, and made her hold up her right hand, and put the stamp on, and signed it. Then he put the papers in his pocket, closed his typewriter, and went out.

She went to the door and called the matron. "I'm ready now." The matron came in and took her out. The guys on the stretcher came in and carried me out. They went on the double, but on the way they got jammed in with the crowd that was watching her, where she was standing in front of the elevators with the matron, waiting to go up to the jail. It's on the top floor of the Hall of Justice. They pushed on through, and my blanket got pulled so it was trailing on the floor. She picked it up and tucked it around me, then turned away quick.

Chapter 11

THEY TOOK ME BACK to the hospital, but instead of the state cop watching me, it was this guy that had taken the confession. He lay down on the other bed. I tried to sleep, and after a while I did. I dreamed she was looking at me, and I was trying to say something to her, but couldn't. Then she would go down, and I would wake up, and that crack would be in my ears, that awful crack that the Greek's head made when I hit it. Then I would sleep again, and dream I was falling. And I would wake up again, holding on to my neck, and that same crack would be in my ears. One time when I woke up I was yelling. He leaned up on his elbow.

"Yay."

"Yay."

"What's the matter?"

"Nothing's the matter. Just had a dream."

"O.K."

He never left me for a minute. In the morning, he made them bring him a basin of water, and took out a razor from his pocket, and shaved. Then he washed himself. They brought in breakfast, and he ate his at the table. We didn't say anything.

They brought me a paper, then, and there it was, with a big picture of Cora on the front page, and a smaller picture of me on the stretcher underneath it. It called her the bottle killer. It told how she had pleaded guilty at the arraignment, and would come up for sentence today. On one of the inside pages, it had a story that it was believed the case would set a record for speed in its disposition, and another story about a preacher that said if all cases were railroaded through that quick, it would do more to prevent crime than passing a hundred laws. I looked all through the paper for something about the confession. It wasn't in there.

About twelve o'clock a young doctor came in and went to work on my back with alcohol, sopping off some of the adhesive tape. He was supposed to sop it off, but most of the time he just peeled it, and it hurt like hell. After he got part of it off, I found I could move. He left the rest on, and a nurse brought me my clothes. I put them on. The guys on the stretcher came in and helped me to the elevator and out of the hospital. There was a car waiting there, with a chauffeur. The guy that had spent the night with me put me in, and we drove about two blocks. Then he took me out, and we went in an office building, and up to an office. And there was Katz with his hand stuck out and a grin all over his face.

"It's all over."

"Swell. When do they hang her?"

"They don't hang her. She's out, free. Free as a bird. She'll be over in a little while, soon as they fix up some things in court. Come in. I'll tell you about it."

He took me in a private office and closed the door. Soon as he rolled a cigarette, and half burned it up, and got it pasted on his mouth, he started to talk. I hardly knew him. It didn't seem that a man that had looked so sleepy the day before could be as excited as he was.

"Chambers, this is the greatest case I ever had in my life. I'm in it, and out of it, in less than twenty-four hours, and yet I tell you I never had anything like it. Well, the Dempsey-Firpo fight lasted less than two rounds, didn't it? It's not how long it lasts. It's what you do while you're in there.

"This wasn't really a fight, though. It was a four-handed card game, where every player has been dealt a perfect hand. Beat that, if you can. You think it takes a card player to play a bum hand, don't you. To hell with that. I get those bum hands every day. Give me one like this, where they've all got cards, *where they've all got cards that'll win if they play them right*, and then watch me. Oh, Chambers, you did me a favor all right when you called me in on this. I'll never get another one like it."

"You haven't said anything yet."

"I'll say it, don't worry about that. But you won't get it, you won't know how the hand was played, until I get the cards straightened out for you. Now first. There were you and the woman. You each held a perfect hand. Because that was a perfect murder, Chambers. Maybe you don't even know how good it was. All that stuff Sackett tried to scare you with, about her not being in the car when it went over, and having her handbag with her, and all that, that didn't amount to a goddam thing. A car can teeter before it goes over, can't it? And a woman can grab her handbag before she jumps, can't she? That don't prove any crime. That just proves she's a woman."

"How'd you find out about that stuff?"

"I got it from Sackett. I had dinner with him last night, and he was crowing over me. He was pitying me, the sap. Sackett and I are enemies. We're the friendliest enemies that ever were. He'd sell his soul to the devil to put something over on me, and I'd do the same for him. We even put up a bet on it. We bet $100. He was giving me the razz, because he had a perfect case, where he could just play the cards and let the hangman do his stuff."

That was swell, two guys betting $100 on what the hangman would do to me and Cora, but I wanted to get it straight, just the same.

"If we had a perfect hand, where did his hand come in?"

"I'm getting to that. You had a perfect hand, but Sackett knows that no man and no woman that ever lived could play that hand, not if the prosecutor plays his hand right. He knows that all he's got to do is get one of you working against the other, and it's in the bag. That's the first thing. Next thing, he doesn't even have to work the case up. He's got an insurance company to do that for him, so he doesn't have to lift a finger. That's what Sackett loved about it. All he had to do was play the cards, and the pot would fall right in his lap. So what does he do? He takes this stuff the insurance company dug up for him, and scares the hell out of you with it, and gets you to sign a complaint against her. He takes the best card you've got, which is how bad you were hurt yourself, and makes you trump your own ace with it. If you were hurt that bad, it had to be an accident, and yet Sackett uses that to make you sign a complaint against her. And you sign it, because you're afraid if you don't sign it he'll know goddam well you did it."

"I turned yellow, that's all."

"Yellow is a color you figure on in murder, and nobody figures on it better than Sackett. All right. He's got you where he wants you. He's going to make you testify against her, and he knows that once you do that, no power on earth can keep her from ratting on you. So that's where he's sitting when he has dinner with me. He razzes me. He pities me. He bets me $100. And all the time I'm sitting there with a hand that I know I can beat him with, if I only play the cards right. All right, Chambers. You're looking in my hand. What do you see in it?"

"Not much."

"Well, what?"

"Nothing, to tell you the truth."

"Neither did Sackett. But now watch. After I left you yesterday, I went to see her, and got an authorization from her to open Papadakis's safe deposit box. And I found what I expected. There were some other policies in that box, and I went to see the agent that wrote them, and this is what I found out:

"That accident policy didn't have anything to do with that accident that Papadakis had a few weeks ago. The agent had turned up on his calendar that Papadakis's automobile insurance had pretty near run out, and he went out there to see him. She wasn't there. They fixed it up pretty quick for the automobile insurance, fire, theft, collision, public liability, the regular line. Then the agent showed Papadakis where he was covered on everything but injury to himself, and asked him how about a personal accident policy. Papadakis got interested right away. Maybe that other accident was the reason for that, but if it was the agent didn't know anything about it. He signed up for the whole works, and gave the agent his check, and next day the policies were mailed out to him. You understand, an agent works for a lot of companies, and not all these policies were written by the same company. That's No. 1 point that Sackett forgot. But the main thing to remember is that Papadakis didn't only have the new insurance. He had the old policies too, *and they still had a week to run.*

"All right, now, get this set-up. The Pacific States Accident is on a $10,000 personal accident policy. The Guaranty of California is on a $10,000 new public liability bond, and the Rocky Mountain Fidelity is on an old $10,000 public liability bond. So that's my first card. He had an insurance company working for him up to $10,000. I had two insurance companies working for me up to $20,000, whenever I wanted to call them in. Do you get it?"

"No, I don't."

"Look. Sackett stole your big card off you, didn't he? Well, I stole the same card off him. You were hurt, weren't you? You were hurt bad. Well, if Sackett convicts her of murder, and you bring suit against her for injuries sustained as a result of that murder, then a jury will give you whatever you ask for. And those two bonding companies are liable for every cent of their policies to satisfy that judgment."

"Now I get it."

"Pretty, Chambers, pretty. I found that card in my mitt, but you didn't find it, and Sackett didn't find it, and the Pacific States Accident didn't find it, because they were so busy playing Sackett's game for him, and so sure his game would win, that they didn't even think of it."

He walked around the room a few times, falling for himself every time he passed a little mirror that was in the corner, and then he went on.

"All right, there it was, but the next thing was how to play it. I had to play it quick, because Sackett had already played his, and that confession was due any minute. It might even come at the arraignment, as soon as she heard you testify against her. I had to move fast. So what did I do? I waited till the Pacific State Accident man had testified, and then got him on record that he really believed a crime had been committed. That was just in case I had a false arrest action against him later on. And then, wham, I pleaded her guilty. That ended the arraignment, and for that night, blocked off Sackett. Then I rushed her in a counsel room, claimed a half hour before she was locked up for the night, and sent you in there with her. Five minutes with you was all she needed. When I got in there she was ready to spill it. Then I sent Kennedy in."

"The dick that was with me last night?"

"He used to be a dick, but he's not a dick any more. He's my gumshoe man now. She thought she was talking to a dick, but she was really talking to a dummy. But it did the work. After she got it off her chest, she kept quiet till today, and that was long enough. The next thing was you. What you would do was blow. There was no charge against you, so you weren't under arrest any more, even if you thought you were. Soon as you tumbled to that, I knew no tape, or sore back, or hospital orderly, or anything else would hold you, so after he got done with her I sent Kennedy over to keep an eye on you. The next thing was a little midnight conference between the Pacific States Accident, the Guaranty of California, and the Rocky Mountain Fidelity. And when I laid it in front of them, they did business awful quick."

"What do you mean, they did business?"

"First, I read them the law. I read them the guest clause, Section 141 3/4, California Vehicle Act. That says if a guest in an automobile gets hurt, he has no right of recovery, *provided*, that if his injury resulted from intoxication or willful misconduct on the part of the driver, then he can recover. You see, you were a guest, and I had pleaded her guilty to murder and assault. Plenty of willful misconduct there, wasn't there? And they couldn't be sure, you know. Maybe she did do it alone. So those two companies on the liability policies, the ones that had their chin hanging out for a wallop from you, they chipped in $5,000 apiece to pay the Pacific States Accident policy, and the Pacific States Accident agreed to pay up and shut up, and the whole thing didn't take over a half hour."

He stopped and grinned at himself some more.

"What then?"

"I'm still thinking about it. I can still see Sackett's face just now when that Pacific States Accident fellow went on the stand today and said his investigation had convinced him that no crime had been committed, and his company was paying the accident claim in full. Chambers, do you know what that feels like? To feint a guy open and then let him have it, right on the chin? There's no feeling like it in the world."

"I still don't get it. What was this guy testifying again for?"

"She was up for sentence. And after a plea of guilty, a court usually wants to hear some testimony to find out what the case is really about. To determine the sentence. And Sackett had started in howling for blood. He wanted the death penalty. Oh, he's a blood-thirsty lad, Sackett is. That's why it stimulates me to work against him. He really believes hanging them does some good. You're playing for stakes when you're playing against Sackett. So he put his insurance man on the stand again. But instead of it being *his* son of a bitch, after that little midnight session it was *my* son of a bitch, only Sackett didn't know it. He roared plenty when he found it out. But it was too late. If an insurance company didn't believe she was guilty, a jury would never believe it, would it? There wasn't a chance in the world of convicting her after that. And that was when I burned Sackett. I got up and made a speech to the court. I took my time about it. I told how my client had protested her innocence from the beginning. I told how I didn't believe it. I told how I knew there existed what I regarded as overwhelming evidence against her, enough to convict her in any court, and that I believed I was acting in her best interest when I decided to plead her guilty and throw her on the mercy of the court. But. Chambers, do you know how I rolled that *but* under my tongue? But, in the light of the testimony just given, there was no course open to me but to withdraw the pleas of guilty and allow the cases to proceed. Sackett couldn't do a thing, because I was still within the limit of eight days for a plea. He knew he was sunk. He consented to a plea for manslaughter, the court examined the other witnesses itself, gave her six months, suspended sentence, and practically apologized even for that. We quashed the assault charge. That was the key to the whole thing, and we almost forgot it."

There came a rap on the door. Kennedy brought Cora in, put some papers down in front of Katz, and left. "There you are, Chambers. Just sign that, will you? It's a waiver of damages for any injuries sustained by you. It's what they get out of it for being so nice."

I signed.

"You want me to take you home, Cora?"

"I guess so."

"One minute, one minute, you two. Not so fast. There's one other little thing. That ten thousand dollars you get for knocking off the Greek."

She looked at me and I looked at her. He sat there looking at the check. "You see, it wouldn't be a perfect hand if there hadn't been some money in it for Katz. I forgot to tell you about that. Well. Oh, well. I won't be a hog. I generally take it all, but on this, I'll just make it half. Mrs. Papadakis, you make out your check for $5,000, and I'll make this over to you and go over to the bank and fix up the deposits. Here. Here's a blank check."

She sat down, and picked up the pen, and started to write, and then stopped, like she couldn't quite figure out what it was all about. All of a sudden, he went over and picked up the blank check and tore it up.

"What the hell. Once in a lifetime, isn't it? Here. You keep it all. I don't care about the ten grand. I've got ten grand. This is what I want!"

He opened his pocketbook, took out a slip, and showed it to us. It was Sackett's check for $100. "You think I'm going to cash that? I am like hell. I'm going to frame it. It goes up there, right over my desk."

Chapter 12

W E WENT OUT OF THERE, and got a cab because I was
so crippled up, and first we went to the bank, and put the
check in, and then we went to a flower shop, and got two big
bunches of flowers, and then we went to the funeral of the Greek. It
seemed funny he was only dead two days, and they were just burying
him. The funeral was at a little Greek church, and a big crowd of
people was there, some of them Greeks I had seen out to the place
now and then. They gave her a dead pan when we came in, and put
her in a seat about three rows from the front. I could see them
looking at us, and I wondered what I would do if they tried to pull
some rough stuff later. They were his friends, not ours. But pretty
soon I saw an afternoon paper being passed around, that had big
headlines in it that she was innocent, and an usher took a look at it,
and came running over and moved us up on the front bench. The
guy that did the preaching started out with some dirty cracks about
how the Greek died, but a guy went up and whispered to him, and
pointed at the paper that had got up near the front by that time,
and he turned around and said it all over again, without any dirty
cracks, and put in about the sorrowing widow and friends, and they
all nodded their head it was O.K. When we went out in the church-
yard, where the grave was, a couple of them took her by the arm,
and helped her out, and a couple more helped me. I got to blubbering while they were letting him down. Singing those hymns will do
it to you every time, and specially when it's about a guy you like as
well as I liked the Greek. At the end they sang some song I had

heard him sing a hundred times, and that finished me. It was all I could do to lay our flowers out the way they were supposed to go.

The taxi driver found a guy that would rent us a Ford for $15 a week, and we took it, and started out. She drove. When we got out of the city we passed a house that was being built, and all the way out we talked about how not many of them have gone up lately, but the whole section is going to be built up as soon as things get better. When we got out to the place she let me out, put the car away, and then we went inside. It was all just like we left it, even to the glasses in the sink that we had drunk the wine out of, and the Greek's guitar, that hadn't been put away yet because he was so drunk. She put the guitar in the case, and washed the glasses, and then went upstairs. After a minute I went up after her.

She was in their bedroom, sitting by the window, looking out at the road.
"Well?"
She didn't say anything. I started to leave.
"I didn't ask you to leave."
I sat down again. It was a long while before she snapped out of it.
"You turned on me, Frank."
"No I didn't. He had me, Cora. I had to sign his paper. If I didn't, then he would tumble to everything. I didn't turn on you. I just went along with him, till I could find out where I was at."
"You turned on me. I could see it in your eye."
"All right, Cora, I did. I just turned yellow, that's all. I didn't want to do it. I tried not to do it. But he beat me down. I cracked up, that's all."
"I know."
"I went through hell about it."
"And I turned on you, Frank."
"They made you do it. You didn't want to. They set a trap for you."
"I wanted to do it. I hated you then."
"That's all right. It was for something I didn't really do. You know how it was, now."
"No. I hated you for something you really did."
"I never hated you, Cora. I hated myself."

"I don't hate you now. I hate that Sackett. And Katz. Why couldn't they leave us alone? Why couldn't they let us fight it out together? I wouldn't have minded that. I wouldn't have minded it even if it meant—you know. We would have had our love. And that's all we ever had. But the very first time they started their meanness, you turned on me."

"And you turned on me, don't forget that."

"That's the awful part. I turned on you. We both turned on each other."

"Well, that makes it even, don't it?"

"It makes it even, but look at us now. We were up on a mountain. We were up so high, Frank. We had it all, out there, that night. I didn't know I could feel anything like that. And we kissed and sealed it so it would be there forever, no matter what happened. We had more than any two people in the world. And then we fell down. First you, and then me. Yes, it makes it even. We're down here together. But we're not up high any more. Our beautiful mountain is gone."

"Well what the hell? We're together, ain't we?"

"I guess so. But I thought an awful lot, Frank. Last night. About you and me, and the movies, and why I flopped, and the hashhouse, and the road, and why you like it. We're just two punks, Frank. God kissed us on the brow that night. He gave us all that two people can ever have. And we just weren't the kind that could have it. We had all that love, and we just cracked up under it. It's a big airplane engine, that takes you through the sky, right up to the top of the mountain. But when you put it in a Ford, it just shakes it to pieces. That's what we are, Frank, a couple of Fords. God is up there laughing at us."

"The hell he is. Well we're laughing at him too, aren't we? He put up a red stop sign for us, and we went past it. And then what? Did we get shoved off the deep end? We did like hell. We got away clean, and got $10,000 for doing the job. So God kissed us on the brow, did he? Then the devil went to bed with us, and believe you me, kid, he sleeps pretty good."

"Don't talk that way, Frank."

"Did we get that ten grand, or didn't we?"

"I don't want to think about the ten grand. It's a lot, but it couldn't buy our mountain."

"Mountain, hell, we got the mountain and ten thousand smackers to pile on top of that yet. If you want to go up high, take a look around from that pile."

"You nut. I wish you could see yourself, yelling with that bandage on your head."

"You forgot something. We got something to celebrate. We ain't never had that drunk yet."

"I wasn't talking about that kind of a drunk."

"A drunk's a drunk. Where's that liquor I had before I left?"

I went to my room and got that liquor. It was a quart of bourbon, three quarters full. I went down, got some Coca-Cola glasses, and ice cubes, and White Rock, and came back upstairs. She had taken her hat off and let her hair down. I fixed two drinks. They had some White Rock in them, and a couple of pieces of ice, but the rest was out of the bottle.

"Have a drink. You'll feel better. That's what Sackett said when he put the spot on me, the louse."

"My, but that's strong."

"You bet it is. Here, you got too many clothes on."

I pushed her over to the bed. She held on to her glass, and some of it spilled. "The hell with it. Plenty more where that came from."

I began slipping off her blouse. "Rip me, Frank. Rip me like you did that night."

I ripped all her clothes off. She twisted and turned, slow, so they would slip out from under her. Then she closed her eyes and lay back on the pillow. Her hair was falling over her shoulders in snaky curls. Her eye was all black, and her breasts weren't drawn up and pointing up at me, but soft, and spread out in two big pink splotches. She looked like the great-grandmother of every whore in the world. The devil got his money's worth that night.

Chapter 13

W E KEPT THAT UP for six months. We kept it up, and it was always the same way. We'd have a fight, and I'd reach for the bottle. What we had the fights about was going away. We couldn't leave the state until the suspended sentence was up, but after that I meant we should blow. I didn't tell her, but I wanted her a long way from Sackett. I was afraid if she got sore at me for something, she'd go off her nut and spill it like she had that other time, after the arraignment. I didn't trust her for a minute. At first, she was all hot for going too, specially when I got talking about Hawaii and the South Seas, but then the money began to roll in. When we opened up, about a week after the funeral, people flocked out there to see what she looked like, and then they came back because they had a good time. And she got all excited about here was our chance to make some more money.

"Frank, all these roadside joints around here are lousy. They're run by people that used to have a farm back in Kansas or somewhere, and got as much idea how to entertain people as a pig has. I believe if somebody came along that knew the business like I do, and tried to make it nice for them, they'd come and bring all their friends."

"To hell with them. We're selling out anyhow."

"We could sell easier if we were making money."

"We're making money."

"I mean good money. Listen, Frank. I've got an idea people would be glad of the chance to sit out under the trees. Think of that. All this nice weather in California, and what do they do with it? Bring people inside of a joint that's set up ready-made by the Acme Lunch Room Fixture Company, and stinks so it makes you sick to your stomach, and feed them awful stuff that's the same from Fresno down to the border, and never give them any chance to feel good at all."

"Look. We're selling out, aren't we? Then the less we got to sell the quicker we get rid of it. Sure, they'd like to sit under the trees. Anybody but a California Bar-B-Q slinger would know that. But if we put them under the trees we've got to get tables, and wire up a lot of lights out there, and all that stuff, and maybe the next guy don't want it that way at all."

"We've got to stay six months. Whether we like it or not."

"Then we use that six months finding a buyer."

"I want to try it."

"All right, then try it. But I'm telling you."

"I could use some of our inside tables."

"I said try it, didn't I? Come on. We'll have a drink."

What we had the big blow-off over was the beer license, and then I tumbled to what she was really up to. She put the tables out under the trees, on a little platform she had built, with a striped awning over them and lanterns at night, and it went pretty good. She was right about it. Those people really enjoyed a chance to sit out under the trees for a half hour, and listen to a little radio music, before they got in their cars and went on. And then beer came back. She saw a chance to leave it just like it was, put beer in, and call it a beer garden.

"I don't want any beer garden, I tell you. All I want is a guy that'll buy the whole works and pay cash."

"But it seems a shame."

"Not to me it don't."

"But look, Frank. The license is only twelve dollars for six months. My goodness, we can afford twelve dollars, can't we?"

"We get the license and then we're in the beer business. We're in the gasoline business already, and the hot dog business, and now we got to go in the beer business. The hell with it. I want to get out of it, not get in deeper."

"Everybody's got one."

"And welcome, so far as I'm concerned."

"People wanting to come, and the place all fixed up under the trees, and now I have to tell them we don't have beer because we haven't any license."

"Why do you have to tell them anything?"

"All we've got to do is put in coils and then we can have draught beer. It's better than bottled beer, and there's more money in it. I saw some lovely glasses in Los Angeles the other day. Nice tall ones. The kind people like to drink beer out of."

"So we got to get coils and glasses now, have we? I tell you I don't *want* any beer garden."

"Frank, don't you ever want to *be* something?"

"Listen, get this. I want to get away from this place. I want to go somewhere else, where every time I look around I don't see the ghost of a goddam Greek jumping out at me, and hear his echo in my dreams, and jump every time the radio comes out with a guitar. I've got to go away, do you hear me? I've got to get out of here, or I go nuts."

"You're lying to me."

"Oh no, I'm not lying. I never meant anything more in my life."

"You don't see the ghost of any Greek, that's not it. Somebody else might see it, but not Mr. Frank Chambers. No, you want to go away just because you're a bum, that's all. That's what you were when you came here, and that's what you are now. When we go away, and our money's all gone, then what?"

"What do I care? We go away, don't we?"

"That's it, you don't care. We could stay here—"

"I knew it. That's what you really mean. That's what you've meant all along. That we stay here."

"And why not? We've got it good. Why wouldn't we stay here? Listen, Frank. You've been trying to make a bum out of me ever since you've known me, but you're not going to do it. I told you, I'm not a bum. I want to *be* something. We stay here. We're not going away. We take out the beer license. We amount to something."

It was late at night, and we were upstairs, half undressed. She was walking around like she had that time after the arraignment, and talking in the same funny jerks.

"Sure we stay. We do whatever you say, Cora. Here, have a drink."

"I don't want a drink."

"Sure you want a drink. We got to laugh some more about getting the money, haven't we?"

"We already laughed about it."

"But we're going to make more money, aren't wc? On the beer garden? We got to put down a couple on that, just for luck."

"You nut. All right. Just for luck."

That's the way it went, two or three times a week. And the tip-off was that every time I would come out of a hangover, I would be having those dreams. I would be falling, and that crack would be in my ears.

Right after the sentence ran out, she got the telegram her mother was sick. She got some clothes in a hurry, and I put her on the train, and going back to the parking lot I felt funny, like I was made of gas and would float off somewhere. I felt free. For a week, anyway, I wouldn't have to wrangle, or fight off dreams, or nurse a woman back to a good humor with a bottle of liquor.

On the parking lot a girl was trying to start her car. It wouldn't do anything. She stepped on everything and it was just plain dead.

"What's the matter? Won't it go?"

"They left the ignition on when they parked it, and now the battery's run out."

"Then it's up to them. They've got to charge it for you."

"Yes, but I've got to get home."

"I'll take you home."

"You're awfully friendly."

"I'm the friendliest guy in the world."

"You don't even know where I live."

"I don't care."

"It's pretty far. It's in the country."

"The further the better. Wherever it is, it's right on my way."

"You make it hard for a nice girl to say no."

"Well then, if it's so hard, don't say it."

She was a light-haired girl, maybe a little older than I was, and not bad on looks. But what got me was how friendly she was, and how she wasn't any more afraid of what I might do to her than if I was a kid or something. She knew her way around all right, you could see that. And what finished it was when I found out she didn't know who I was. We told our names on the way out, and to her mine didn't mean a thing. Boy oh boy what a relief that was. One person in the world that wasn't asking me to sit down to the table a minute, and then telling me to give them the low-down on that case where they said the Greek was murdered. I looked at her, and I felt the same way I had walking away from the train, like I was made of gas, and would float out from behind the wheel.

"So your name is Madge Allen, hey?"

"Well, it's really Kramer, but I took my own name again after my husband died."

"Well listen Madge Allen, or Kramer, or whatever you want to call it, I've got a little proposition to make you."

"Yes?"

"What do you say we turn this thing around, point her south, and you and me take a little trip for about a week?"

"Oh, I couldn't do that."

"Why not?"

"Oh, I just couldn't, that's all."

"You like me?"

"Sure I like you."

"Well, I like you. What's stopping us?"

She started to say something, didn't say it, and then laughed. "I own up. I'd like to, all right. And if it's something I'm supposed not to do, why that don't mean a thing to me. But I can't. It's on account of the cats."

"Cats?"

"We've got a lot of cats. And I'm the one that takes care of them. That's why I had to get home."

"Well, they got pet farms, haven't they? We'll call one up, and tell them to come over and get them."

That struck her funny. "I'd like to see a pet farm's face when it saw them. They're not that kind."

"Cats are cats, ain't they?"

"Not exactly. Some are big and some are little. Mine are big. I don't think a pet farm would do very well with that lion we've got. Or the tigers. Or the puma. Or the three jaguars. They're the worst. A jaguar is an awful cat."

"Holy smoke. What do you do with those things?"

"Oh, work them in movies. Sell the cubs. People have private zoos. Keep them around. They draw trade."

"They wouldn't draw my trade."

"We've got a restaurant. People look at them."

"Restaurant, hey. That's what I've got. Whole goddam country lives selling hot dogs to each other."

"Well, anyway, I couldn't walk out on my cats. They've got to eat."

"The hell we can't. We'll call up Goebel and tell him to come get them. He'll board the whole bunch while we're gone for a hundred bucks."

"Is it worth a hundred bucks to you to take a trip with me?"

"It's worth exactly a hundred bucks."

"Oh my. I can't say no to that. I guess you better call up Goebel."

I dropped her off at her place, found a pay station, called up Goebel, went back home, and closed up. Then I went back after her. It was about dark. Goebel had sent a truck over, and I met it coming back, full of stripes and spots. I parked about a hundred yards down the road, and in a minute she showed up with a little grip, and I helped her in, and we started off.

"You like it?"

"I love it."

We went down to Caliente, and next day we kept on down the line to Ensenada, a little Mexican town about seventy miles down the coast. We went to a little hotel there, and spent three or four days. It was pretty nice. Ensenada is all Mex, and you feel like you left the U.S.A. a million miles away. Our room had a little balcony in front of it, and in the afternoon we would just lay out there, look at the sea, and let the time go by.

"Cats, hey. What do you do, train them?"

"Not the stuff we've got. They're no good. All but the tigers are outlaws. But I do train them."

"You like it?"

"Not much, the real big ones. But I like pumas. I'm going to get an act together with them some time. But I'll need a lot of them. Jungle pumas. Not these outlaws you see in the zoos."

"What's an outlaw?"

"He'd kill you."

"Wouldn't they all?"

"They might, but an outlaw does anyhow. If it was people, he would be a crazy person. It comes from being bred in captivity.

These cats you see, they look like cats, but they're really cat lunatics."

"How can you tell it's a jungle cat?"

"I catch him in a jungle."

"You mean you catch them *alive?*"

"Sure. They're no good to me dead."

"Holy smoke. How do you do that?"

"Well, first I get on a boat and go down to Nicaragua. All the really fine pumas come from Nicaragua. These California and Mexican things are just scrubs compared to them. Then I hire me some Indian boys and go up in the mountains. Then I catch my pumas. Then I bring them back. But this time, I stay down there with them awhile, to train them. Goat meat is cheaper there than horse meat is here."

"You sound like you're all ready to start."

"I am."

She squirted a little wine in her mouth, and gave me a long look. They give it to you in a bottle with a long thin spout on it, and you squirt it in your mouth with the spout. That's to cool it. She did that two or three times, and every time she did it she would look at me.

"I am if you are."

"What the hell? You think I'm going with you to catch them goddam things?"

"Frank, I brought quite a lot of money with me. Let's let Goebel keep those bughouse cats for their board, sell your car for whatever we can get, and hunt cats."

"You're on."

"You mean you will?"

"When do we start?"

"There's a freight boat out of here tomorrow and it puts in at Balboa. We'll wire Goebel from there. And we can leave your car with the hotel here. They'll sell it and send us whatever they get. That's one thing about a Mexican. He's slow, but he's honest."

"O.K."

"Gee I'm glad."

"Me too. I'm so sick of hot dogs and beer and apple pie with cheese on the side I could heave it all in the river."

"You'll love it, Frank. We'll get a place up in the mountains, where it's cool, and then, after I get my act ready, we can go all over the world with it. Go as we please, do as we please, and have plenty of money to spend. Have you got a little bit of gypsy in you?"

"Gypsy? I had rings in my ears when I was born."

I didn't sleep so good that night. When it was beginning to get light, I opened my eyes, wide awake. It came to me, then, that Nicaragua wouldn't be quite far enough.

Chapter 14

WHEN SHE GOT OFF the train she had on a black dress, that made her look tall, and a black hat, and black shoes and stockings, and didn't act like herself while the guy was loading the trunk in the car. We started out, and neither one of us had much to say for a few miles.

"Why didn't you let me know she died?"

"I didn't want to bother you with it. Anyhow, I had a lot to do."

"I feel plenty bad now, Cora."

"Why?"

"I took a trip while you were away. I went up to Frisco."

"Why do you feel bad about that?"

"I don't know. You back there in Iowa, your mother dying and all, and me up in Frisco having a good time."

"I don't know why you should feel bad. I'm glad you went. If I'd have thought about it, I'd have told you to before I left."

"We lost some business. I closed down."

"It's all right. We'll get it back."

"I felt kind of restless, after you left."

"Well my goodness, I don't mind."

"I guess you had a bad time of it, hey?"

"It wasn't very pleasant. But anyhow, it's over."

"I'll shoot a drink in you when we get home. I got some nice stuff out there I brought back to you."

"I don't want any."

"It'll pick you up."

"I'm not drinking any more."

"No?"

"I'll tell you about it. It's a long story."

"You sound like plenty happened out there."

"No, nothing happened. Only the funeral. But I've got a lot to tell you. I think we're going to have a better time of it from now on."

"Well for God's sake. What is it?"

"Not now. Did you see your family?"

"What for?"

"Well anyway, did you have a good time?"

"Fair. Good as I could have alone."

"I bet it was a swell time. But I'm glad you said it."

When we got out there, a car was parked in front, and a guy was sitting in it. He got a silly kind of grin on his face and climbed out. It was Kennedy, the guy in Katz's office.

"You remember me?"

"Sure I remember you. Come on in."

We took him inside, and she gave me a pull into the kitchen.

"This is bad, Frank."

"What do you mean, bad?"

"I don't know, but I can feel it."

"Better let me talk to him."

I went back with him, and she brought us some beer, and left us, and pretty soon I got down to cases.

"You still with Katz?"

"No, I left him. We had a little argument and I walked out."

"What are you doing now?"

"Not a thing. Fact of the matter, that's what I came out to see you about. I was out a couple of times before, but there was nobody home. This time, though, I heard you were back, so I stuck around."

"Anything I can do, just say the word."

"I was wondering if you could let me have a little money."

"Anything you want. Of course, I don't keep much around, but if fifty or sixty dollars will help, I'll be glad to let you have it."

"I was hoping you could make it more."

He still had this grin on his face, and I figured it was time to quit the feinting and jabbing, and find out what he meant.

"Come on, Kennedy. What is it?"

"I tell you how it is. I left Katz. And that paper, the one I wrote up for Mrs. Papadakis, was still in the files, see? And on account of being a friend of yours and all that, I knew you wouldn't want nothing like that laying around. So I took it. I thought maybe you would like to get it back."

"You mean that hop dream she called a confession?"

"That's it. Of course, I know there wasn't anything to it, but I thought you might like to get it back."

"How much do you want for it?"

"Well, how much would you pay?"

"Oh, I don't know. As you say, there's nothing to it, but I might give a hundred for it. Sure. I'd pay that."

"I was thinking it was worth more."

"Yeah?"

"I figured on twenty five grand."

"Are you crazy?"

"No, I ain't crazy. You got ten grand from Katz. The place has been making money, I figure about five grand. Then on the property, you could get ten grand from the bank. Papadakis gave fourteen for it, so it looks like you could get ten. Well, that makes twenty five."

"You would strip me clean, just for that?"

"It's worth it."

I didn't move, but I must have had a flicker in my eye, because he jerked an automatic out of his pocket and leveled it at me. "Don't start anything, Chambers. In the first place, I haven't got it with me. In the second place, if you start anything I let you have it."

"I'm not starting anything."

"Well, see you don't."

He kept the gun pointed at me, and I kept looking at him. "I guess you got me."

"I don't guess it. I know it."

"But you're figuring too high."

"Keep talking, Chambers."

"We got ten from Katz, that's right. And we've still got it. We made five off the place, but we spent a grand in the last couple weeks. She took a trip to bury her mother, and I took one. That's why we been closed up."

"Go on, keep talking."

"And we can't get ten on the property. With things like they are now, we couldn't even get five. Maybe we could get four."

"Keep talking."

"All right, ten, four, and four. That makes eighteen."

He grinned down the gun barrel a while, and then he got up. "All right. Eighteen. I'll phone you tomorrow, to see if you've got it. If you've got it, I'll tell you what to do. If you haven't got it, that thing goes to Sackett."

"It's tough, but you got me."

"Tomorrow at twelve, then, I phone you. That'll give you time to go to the bank and get back."

"O.K."

He backed to the door and still held the gun on me. It was late afternoon, just beginning to get dark. While he was backing away, I leaned up against the wall, like I was pretty down in the mouth. When he was half out the door I cut the juice in the sign, and it blazed down in his eyes. He wheeled, and I let him have it. He went down and I was on him. I twisted the gun out of his hand, threw it in the lunchroom, and socked him again. Then I dragged him inside and kicked the door shut. She was standing there. She had been at the door, listening, all the time.

"Get the gun."

She picked it up and stood there. I pulled him to his feet, threw him over one of the tables, and bent him back. Then I beat him up. When he passed out, I got a glass of water and poured it on him. Soon as he came to, I beat him up again. When his face looked like raw beef, and he was blubbering like a kid in the last quarter of a football game, I quit.

"Snap out of it, Kennedy. You're talking to your friends over the telephone."

"I got no friends, Chambers. I swear, I'm the only one that knows about—"

I let him have it, and we did it all over again. He kept saying he didn't have any friends, so I threw an arm lock on him and shoved up on it. "All right, Kennedy. If you've got no friends, then I break it."

He stood it longer than I thought he could. He stood it till I was straining on his arm with all I had, wondering if I really could break it. My left arm was still weak where it had been broke. If you ever tried to break the second joint of a tough turkey, maybe you know how hard it is to break a guy's arm with a hammerlock. But all of a sudden he said he would call. I let him loose and told him what he was to say. Then I put him at the kitchen phone, and pulled the lunchroom extension through the swing door, so I could watch him and hear what he said and they said. She came back there with us, with the gun.

"If I give you the sign, he gets it."

She leaned back and an awful smile flickered around the corner of her mouth. I think that smile scared Kennedy worse than anything I had done.

"He gets it."

He called, and a guy answered. "Is that you, Willie?"

"Pat?"

"This is me. Listen. It's all fixed. How soon can you get out here with it?"

"Tomorrow, like we said."

"Can't you make it tonight?"

"How can I get in a safe deposit box when the bank is closed?"

"All right, then do like I tell you. Get it, first thing in the morning, and come out here with it. I'm out to his place."

"His *place*?"

"Listen, get this, Willie. He knows we got him, see? But he's afraid if she finds out he's got to pay all that dough, she won't let him, you get it? If he leaves, she knows something is up, and maybe she takes a notion to go with him. So we do it all here. I'm just a guy that's spending the night in their auto camp, and she don't know nothing. Tomorrow, you're just a friend of mine, and we fix it all up."

"How does he get the money if he don't leave?"

"That's all fixed up."

"And what in the hell are you spending the night there for?"

"I got a reason for that, Willie. Because maybe it's a stall, what he says about her, and maybe it's not, see? But if I'm here, neither one of them can skip, you get it?"

"Can he hear you, what you're saying?"

He looked at me, and I nodded my head yes. "He's right here with me, in the phone booth. I want him to hear me, you get it, Willie? I want him to know we mean business."

"It's a funny way to do, Pat."

"Listen, Willie. You don't know, and I don't know, and none of us don't know if he's on the level with it or not. But maybe he is, and I'm giving him a chance. What the hell, if a guy's willing to pay, we got to go along with him, haven't we? That's it. You do like I tell you. You get it out here soon as you can in the morning. Soon as you can, you get it? Because I don't want her to get to wondering what the hell I'm doing hanging around here all day."

"O.K."

He hung up. I walked over and gave him a sock. "That's just so you talk right when he calls back. You got it, Kennedy?"

"I got it."

I waited a few minutes, and pretty soon here came the call back. I answered, and when Kennedy picked up the phone he gave Willie some more of the same. He said he was alone that time. Willie didn't like it much, but he had to take it. Then I took him back to the No. 1 shack. She came with us, and I took the gun. Soon as I had Kennedy inside, I stepped out the door with her and gave her a kiss.

"That's for being able to step on it when the pinch comes. Now get this. I'm not leaving him for a minute. I'm staying out here the whole night. There'll be other calls, and we'll bring him in to talk. I think you better open the place up. The beer garden. Don't bring anybody inside. That's so if his friends do some spying, you're right on deck and it's business as usual."

"All right. And Frank."

"Yes?"

"Next time I try to act smart, will you hang one on my jaw?"

"What do you mean?"

"We ought to have gone away. Now I know it."

"Like hell we ought. Not till we get this."

She gave me a kiss, then. "I guess I like you pretty well, Frank."

"We'll get it. Don't worry."

"I'm not."

I stayed out there with him all night. I didn't give him any food, and I didn't give him any sleep. Three or four times he had to talk to Willie, and once Willie wanted to talk to me. Near as I could tell, we got away with it. In between, I would beat him up. It was hard work, but I meant he should want that paper to get there, bad. While he was wiping the blood off his face, on a towel, you could hear the radio going, out in the beer garden, and the people laughing and talking.

About ten o'clock the next morning she came out there. "They're here, I think. There are three of them."

"Bring them back."

She picked up the gun, stuck it in her belt so you couldn't see it from in front, and went. In a minute, I heard something fall. It was one of his gorillas. She was marching them in front of her, making them walk backwards with their hands up, and one of them fell when his heel hit the concrete walk. I opened the door. "This way, gents."

They came in, still holding their hands up, and she came in after them and handed me the gun. "They all had guns, but I took them off them in the lunchroom."

"Better get them. Maybe they got friends."

She went, and in a minute came back with the guns. She took out the clips, and laid them on the bed, beside me. Then she went through their pockets. Pretty soon she had it. And the funny part was that in another envelope were photostats of it, six positives and one negative. They had meant to keep on blackmailing us, and then hadn't had any more sense than to have the photostats on them when they showed up. I took them all, with the original, outside, crumpled them up on the ground, and touched a match to them. When they were burned I stamped the ashes into the dirt and went back.

"All right, boys. I'll show you out. We'll keep the artillery here."

After I had marched them out to their cars, and they left, and I went back inside, she wasn't there. I went out back, and she wasn't there. I went upstairs. She was in our room. "Well, we did it, didn't we? That's the last of it, photostats and all. It's been worrying me, too."

She didn't say anything, and her eyes looked funny. "What's the matter, Cora?"

"So that's the last of it, is it? Photostats and all. It isn't the last of me, though. I've got a million photostats of it, just as good as they were. Jimmy Durante. I've got a million of them. Am I mortified?"

She burst out laughing, and flopped down on the bed.

"All right. If you're sucker enough to put your neck in the noose, just to get me, you've got a million of them. You sure have. A million of them."

"Oh no, that's the beautiful part. I don't have to put my neck in the noose at all. Didn't Mr. Katz tell you? Once they just made it manslaughter, they can't do any more to me. It's in the Constitution or something. Oh no, Mr. Frank Chambers. It don't cost me a thing to make you dance on air. And that's what you're going to do. Dance, dance, dance."

"What ails you, anyhow?"

"Don't you know? Your friend was out last night. She didn't know about me, and she spent the night here."

"What friend?"

"The one you went to Mexico with. She told me all about it. We're good friends now. She thought we better be good friends. After she found out who I was she thought I might kill her."

"I haven't been to Mexico for a year."

"Oh yes you have."

She went out, and I heard her go in my room. When she came back she had a kitten with her, but a kitten that was bigger than a cat. It was gray, with spots on it. She put it on the table in front of me and it began to meow. "The puma had little ones while you were gone, and she brought you one to remember her by."

She leaned back against the wall and began to laugh again, a wild, crazy laugh. "And the cat came back! It stepped on the fuse box and got killed, but here it is back! Ha, ha, ha, ha, ha, ha! Ain't that funny, how unlucky cats are for you?"

Chapter 15

SHE CRACKED UP, then, and cried, and after she got quiet
she went downstairs. I was down there, right after her. She
was tearing the top flaps off a big carton.

"Just making a nest for our little pet, dearie."

"Nice of you."

"What did you think I was doing?"

"I didn't."

"Don't worry. When the time comes to call up Mr. Sackett, I'll
let you know. Just take it easy. You'll need all your strength."

She lined it with excelsior, and on top of that put some woolen
cloths. She took it upstairs and put the puma in it. It meowed a
while and then went to sleep. I went downstairs to fix myself a Coke.
I hadn't any more than squirted the ammonia in it than she was at
the door.

"Just taking something to keep my strength up, dearie."

"Nice of you."

"What did you think I was doing?"

"I didn't."

"Don't worry. When I get ready to skip I'll let you know. Just
take it easy. You may need all your strength."

She gave me a funny look and went upstairs. It kept up all day,
me following her around for fear she'd call up Sackett, her following
me around for fear I'd skip. We never opened the place up at all. In
between the tiptoeing around, we would sit upstairs in the room.

We didn't look at each other. We looked at the puma. It would meow and she would go down to get it some milk. I would go with her. After it lapped up the milk it would go to sleep. It was too young to play much. Most of the time it meowed or slept.

That night we lay side by side, not saying a word. I must have slept, because I had those dreams. Then, all of a sudden, I woke up, and before I was even really awake I was running downstairs. What had waked me was the sound of that telephone dial. She was at the extension in the lunchroom, all dressed, with her hat on, and a packed hat box on the floor beside her. I grabbed the receiver and slammed it on the hook. I took her by the shoulders, jerked her through the swing door, and shoved her upstairs. "Get up there! Get up there, or I'll—"

"Or you'll what?"

The telephone rang, and I answered it.

"Here's your party, go ahead."

"Yellow Cab."

"Oh. Oh. I called you, Yellow Cab, but I've changed my mind. I won't need you."

"O.K."

When I got upstairs she was taking off her clothes. When we got back in bed we lay there a long time again without saying a word. Then she started up.

"Or you'll what?"

"What's it to you? Sock you in the jaw, maybe. Maybe something else."

"Something else, wasn't it?"

"What are you getting at now?"

"Frank, I know what you've been doing. You've been lying there, trying to think of a way to kill me."

"I've been asleep."

"Don't lie to me, Frank. Because I'm not going to lie to you, and I've got something to say to you."

I thought that over a long time. Because that was just what I had been doing. Lying there beside her, just straining to think of a way I could killed her.

"All right, then. I was."

"I knew it."

"Were you any better? Weren't you going to hand me over to Sackett? Wasn't that the same thing?"

"Yes."

"Then we're even. Even again. Right back where we started."

"Not quite."

"Oh yes we are." I cracked up a little, then, myself, and put my head on her shoulder. "That's just where we are. We can kid ourself all we want to, and laugh about the money, and whoop about what a swell guy the devil is to be in bed with, but that's just where we are. I was going off with that woman, Cora. We were going to Nicaragua to catch cats. And why I didn't go away, I knew I had to come back. We're chained to each other, Cora. We thought we were on top of a mountain. That wasn't it. It's on top of us, and that's where it's been ever since that night."

"Is that the only reason you came back?"

"No. It's you and me. There's nobody else. I love you, Cora. But love, when you get fear in it, it's not love any more. It's hate."

"So you hate me?"

"I don't know. But we're telling the truth, for once in our life. That's part of it. You got to know it. And what I was lying here thinking, that's the reason. Now you know it."

"I told you I had something to tell you, Frank."

"Oh."

"I'm going to have a baby."

"*What?*"

"I suspicioned it before I went away, and right after my mother died I was sure."

"The hell you say. The hell you say. Come here. Give me a kiss."

"No. Please. I've got to tell you about it."

"Haven't you told it?"

"Not what I mean. Now listen to me, Frank. All that time I was out there, waiting for the funeral to be over, I thought about it. What it would mean to us. Because we took a life, didn't we? And now we're going to give one back."

"That's right."

"It was all mixed up, what I thought. But now, after what happened with that woman, it's not mixed up any more. I couldn't call up Sackett, Frank. I couldn't call him up, because I couldn't have this baby, and then have it find out I let its father hang for murder."

"You were going to see Sackett."

"No I wasn't. I was going away."

"Was that the only reason you weren't going to see Sackett?"

She took a long time before she answered that. "No. I love you, Frank. I think you know that. But maybe, if it hadn't been for this, I would have gone to see him. Just *because* I love you."

"She didn't mean anything to me, Cora. I told you why I did it. I was running away."

"I know that. I knew it all along. I knew why you wanted to take me away, and what I said about you being a bum, I didn't believe that. I believed it, but it wasn't why you wanted to go. You being a bum, I love you for it. And I hated her for the way she turned on you just for not telling her about something that wasn't any of her business. And yet, I wanted to ruin you for it."

"Well?"

"I'm trying to say it, Frank. This is what I'm trying to say. I wanted to ruin you, and yet I couldn't go to see Sackett. It wasn't because you kept watching me. I could have run out of the house and got to him. It was because, like I told you. Well then, I'm rid of the devil, Frank. I know I'll never call up Sackett, because I had my chance, and I had my reason, and I didn't do it. So the devil has left me. But has he left you?"

"If he's left you, then what more have I got to do with him?"

"We wouldn't be sure. We couldn't ever be sure unless you had your chance. The same chance I had."

"I tell you, he's gone."

"While you were thinking about a way to kill me, Frank, I was thinking the same thing. Of a way you could kill me. You can kill me swimming. We'll go way out, the way we did last time, and if you don't want me to come back, you don't have to let me. Nobody'll ever know. It'll be just one of those things that happen at the beach. Tomorrow morning we'll go."

"Tomorrow morning, what we do is get married."

"We can get married if you want, but before we come back we go swimming."

"To hell with swimming. Come on with that kiss."

"Tomorrow night, if I come back, there'll be kisses. Lovely ones, Frank. Not drunken kisses. Kisses with dreams in them. Kisses that come from life, not death."

"It's a date."

.   .   .

We got married at the City Hall, and then we went to the beach. She looked so pretty I just wanted to play in the sand with her, but she had this little smile on her face, and after a while she got up and went down to the surf.

"I'm going out."

She went ahead, and I swam after her. She kept on going, and went a lot further out than she had before. Then she stopped, and I caught up with her. She swung up beside me, and took hold of my hand, and we looked at each other. She knew, then, that the devil was gone, that I loved her.

"Did I ever tell you why I like my feet to the swells?"

"No."

"It's so they'll lift them."

A big one raised us up, and she put her hand to her breasts, to show how it lifted them. "I love it. Are they big, Frank?"

"I'll tell you tonight."

"They feel big. I didn't tell you about that. It's not only knowing you're going to make another life. It's what it does to you. My breasts feel so big, and I want you to kiss them. Pretty soon my belly is going to get big, and I'll love that, and want everybody to see it. It's life. I can feel it in me. It's a new life for us both, Frank."

We started back, and on the way in I swam down. I went down nine feet. I could tell it was nine feet by the pressure. Most of these pools are nine feet, and it was that deep. I whipped my legs together and shot down further. It drove in on my ears so I thought they would pop. But I didn't have to come up. The pressure on your lungs drives the oxygen in your blood, so for a few seconds you don't think about breath. I looked at the green water. And with my ears ringing and that weight on my back and chest, it seemed to me that all the devilment, and meanness, and shiftlessness, and no-account stuff in my life had been pressed out and washed off, and I was all ready to start out with her again clean, and do like she said, have a new life.

When I came up she was coughing. "Just one of those sick spells, like you have."

"Are you all right?"

"I think so. It comes over you, and then it goes."

"Did you swallow any water?"

"No."

We went a little way, then she stopped. "Frank, I feel funny inside."

"Here, hold on to me."

"Oh, Frank. Maybe I strained myself, just then. Trying to keep my head up. So I wouldn't gulp down the salt water."

"Take it easy."

"Wouldn't that be awful? I've heard of women that had a miscarriage. From straining theirself."

"Take it easy. Lie right out in the water. Don't try to swim. I'll tow you in."

"Hadn't you better call a guard?"

"Christ no. That egg will want to pump your legs up and down. Just lay there now. I'll get you in quicker than he can."

She lay there, and I towed her by the shoulder strap of her bathing suit. I began to give out. I could have towed her a mile, but I kept thinking I had to get her to a hospital, and I hurried. When you hurry in the water you're sunk. I got bottom, though, after a while, and then I took her in my arms and rushed her through the surf. "Don't move. Let me do it."

"I won't."

I ran with her up to the place where our sweaters were, and set her down. I got the car key out of mine, then wrapped both of them around her and carried her up to the car. It was up beside the road, and I had to climb the high bank the road was on, above the beach. My legs were so tired I could hardly lift one after the other, but I didn't drop her. I put her in the car, started up, and began burning the road.

We had gone in swimming a couple of miles above Santa Monica, and there was a hospital down there. I overtook a big truck. It had a sign on the back, Sound Your Horn, the Road Is Yours. I banged on the horn, and it kept right down the middle. I couldn't pass on the left, because a whole line of cars was coming toward me. I pulled out to the right and stepped on it. She screamed. I never saw the culvert wall. There was a crash, and everything went black.

When I came out of it I was wedged down beside the wheel, with my back to the front of the car, but I began to moan from the awfulness of what I heard. It was like rain on a tin roof, but that wasn't it. It was her blood, pouring down on the hood, where she went through the windshield. Horns were blowing, and people were jumping out of cars and running to her. I got her up, and tried to stop the blood, and in between I was talking to her, and crying, and kissing her. Those kisses never reached her. She was dead.

Chapter 16

THEY GOT ME FOR IT. Katz took it all this time, the
$10,000 he had got for us, and the money we had made, and
a deed for the place. He did his best for me, but he was licked from
the start. Sackett said I was a mad dog, that had to be put out of the
way before life would be safe. He had it all figured out. We murdered the Greek to get the money, and then I married her, and
murdered her so I could have it all myself. When she found out
about the Mexican trip, that hurried it up a little, that was all. He
had the autopsy report, that showed she was going to have a baby,
and he said that was part of it. He put Madge on the stand, and she
told about the Mexican trip. She didn't want to, but she had to. He
even had the puma in court. It had grown, but it hadn't been taken
care of right, so it was mangy and sick looking, and yowled, and tried
to bite him. It was an awful-looking thing, and it didn't do me any
good, believe me. But what really sunk me was the note she wrote
before she called up the cab, and put in the cash register so I would
get it in the morning, and then forgot about. I never saw it, because
we didn't open the place before we went swimming, and I never
even looked in the cash register. It was the sweetest note in the
world, but it had in it about us killing the Greek, and that did the
work. They argued about it three days, and Katz fought them with
every law book in Los Angeles County, but the judge let it in, and
that let in all about us murdering the Greek. Sackett said that fixed
me up with a motive. That and just being a mad dog. Katz never
even let me take the stand. What could I say? That I didn't do it,

because we had just fixed it up, all the trouble we had had over killing the Greek? That would have been swell. The jury was out five minutes. The judge said he would give me exactly the same consideration he would show any other mad dog.

So I'm in the death house, now, writing the last of this, so Father McConnell can look it over and show me the places where maybe it ought to be fixed up a little, for punctuation and all that. If I get a stay, he's to hold on to it and wait for what happens. If I get a commutation, then he's to burn it, and they'll never know whether there really was any murder or not, from anything I tell them. But if they get me, he's to take it and see if he can find somebody to print it. There won't be any stay, and there won't be any commutation, I know that. I never kidded myself. But in this place, you hope anyhow, just because you can't help it. I never confessed anything, that's one thing. I heard a guy say they never hang you without you confess. I don't know. Unless Father McConnell crosses me, they'll never know anything from me. Maybe I'll get a stay.

I'm getting up tight now, and I've been thinking about Cora. Do you think she knows I didn't do it? After what we said in the water, you would think she would know it. But that's the awful part, when you monkey with murder. Maybe it went through her head, when the car hit, that I did it anyhow. That's why I hope I've got another life after this one. Father McConnell says I have, and I want to see her. I want her to know that it was all so, what we said to each other, and that I didn't do it. What did she have that makes me feel that way about her? I don't know. She wanted something, and she tried to get it. She tried all the wrong ways, but she tried. I don't know what made her feel that way about me, because she knew me. She called it on me plenty of times, that I wasn't any good. I never really wanted anything, but her. But that's a lot. I guess it's not often that a woman even has that.

There's a guy in No. 7 that murdered his brother, and says he didn't really do it, his subconscious did it. I asked him what that meant, and he says you got two selves, one that you know about and the other that you don't know about, because it's subconscious. It shook me up. Did I really do it, and not know it? God Almighty, I can't believe that! I didn't do it! I loved her so, then, I tell you, that I would have died for her! To hell with the subconscious. I don't believe it. It's just a lot of hooey, that this guy thought up so he could fool the judge. You know what you're doing, and you do it. I didn't do it, I know that. That's what I'm going to tell her, if I ever see her again.

I'm up awful tight, now. I think they give you dope in the grub, so you don't think about it. I try not to think. Whenever I can make it, I'm out there with Cora, with the sky above us, and the water around us, talking about how happy we're going to be, and how it's going to last forever. I guess I'm over the big river, when I'm there with her. That's when it seems real, about another life, not with all this stuff how Father McConnell has got it figured out. When I'm with her I believe it. When I start to figure, it all goes blooey.

No stay.

Here they come. Father McConnell says prayers help. If you've got this far, send up one for me, and Cora, and make it that we're together, wherever it is.

MILDRED PIERCE

THE LOCALE of this book is California, and the Californian will find much in it that is familiar to him; the characters, however, are imaginary, as are the situations, and in one instance, a whole neighborhood; they do not represent, and are not intended to represent, actual persons, events, or places.

Chapter 1

I N T H E S P R I N G of 1931, on a lawn in Glendale, California, a man was bracing trees. It was a tedious job, for he had first to prune dead twigs, then wrap canvas buffers around weak branches, then wind rope slings over the buffers and tie them to the trunks, to hold the weight of the avocados that would ripen in the fall. Yet, although it was a hot afternoon, he took his time about it, and was conscientiously thorough, and whistled. He was a smallish man, in his middle thirties, but in spite of the stains on his trousers, he wore them with an air. His name was Herbert Pierce. When he had finished with the trees, he raked the twigs and dead branches into a pile, carried them back to the garage, and dropped them in a kindling box. Then he got out a mower and mowed the lawn. It was a lawn like thousands of others in southern California: a patch of grass in which grew avocado, lemon, and mimosa trees, with circles of spaded earth around them. The house, too, was like others of its kind: a Spanish bungalow, with white walls and red-tile roof. Now, Spanish houses are a little outmoded, but at the time they were considered high-toned, and this one was as good as the next, and perhaps a little bit better.

The mowing over, he got out a coil of hose, screwed it to a spigot, and proceeded to water. He was painstaking about this too, shooting the water all over the trees, down on the spaded circles of earth, over the tiled walk, and finally on the grass. When the whole place was damp and smelled like rain, he turned off the water, pulled the hose through his hand to drain it, coiled it, and put it in the garage. Then he went around front and examined his trees, to make sure the water hadn't drawn the slings too tight. Then he went into the house.

The living room he stepped into corresponded to the lawn he left. It was indeed the standard living room sent out by department stores as suitable for a Spanish bungalow, and consisted of a crimson velvet coat of arms, displayed against the wall; crimson velvet drapes, hung on iron spears; a crimson rug, with figured border; a settee in front of the fireplace, flanked by two chairs, all of these having straight backs and beaded seats; a long oak table holding a lamp with stained-glass shade; two floor lamps of iron, to match the overhead spears, and having crimson silk shades; one table, in a corner, in the Grand Rapids style, and one radio, on this table, in the bakelite style. On the tinted walls in addition to the coat of arms, were three paintings: one of a butte at sunset, with cow skeletons in the foreground; one of a cowboy, herding cattle through snow, and one of a covered-wagon train, plodding through an alkali flat. On the long table was one book, called *Cyclopedia of Useful Knowledge*, stamped in gilt and placed on an interesting diagonal. One might object that this living room achieved the remarkable feat of being cold and at the same time stuffy, and that it would be quite oppressive to live in. But the man was vaguely proud of it, especially the pictures, which he had convinced himself were "pretty good." As for living in it, it had never once occurred to him.

Today, he gave it neither a glance nor a thought. He hurried through, whistling, and went back to a bedroom, which was filled with a seven-piece suite in bright green, and showed feminine touches. He dropped off his work clothes, hung them in a closet, and stepped naked into the bathroom, where he turned on water for a bath. Here again was reflected the civilization in which he lived, but with a sharp difference. For whereas it was, and still is, a civilization somewhat naïve as to lawns, living rooms, pictures, and other things of an aesthetic nature, it is genius itself, and has forgotten more than all other civilizations ever knew, in the realm of practicality. The bathroom that he now whistled in was a utile jewel: it was in green tile and white tile; it was as clean as an operating room; everything was in its proper place, and everything worked. Twenty seconds after the man tweaked the spigots, he stepped into a bath of exactly the temperature he wanted, washed himself clean, tweaked the drain, stepped out, dried himself on a clean towel, and stepped into the bedroom again, without once missing a bar of the tune he was whistling, or thinking there was anything remarkable about it.

After combing his hair, he dressed. Slacks hadn't made their appearance then, but gray flannels had: he put on a fresh pair, with polo shirt and blue lounge coat. Then he strolled back to the kitchen, a counterpart of the bathroom, where his wife was icing a cake. She was a small woman, considerably younger than himself; but as there was a smear of chocolate on her face, and she wore a loose green smock, it was hard to tell what she looked like, except for a pair of rather voluptuous legs that showed between smock and shoes. She was studying a design, in a book of such designs, that showed a bird holding a scroll in its beak, and now attempted a reproduction of it, with a pencil, on a piece of tablet paper. He watched for a few moments, glanced at the cake, said it looked swell. This was perhaps an understatement, for it was a gigantic affair, eighteen inches across the middle and four layers high, covered with a sheen like satin. But after his comment he yawned, said: "Well— don't see there's much else I can do around here. Guess I'll take a walk down the street."

"You going to be home for supper?"

"I'll try to make it, but if I'm not home by six don't wait for me. I may be tied up."

"I want to know."

"I told you, if I'm not home by six—"

"That doesn't do me any good at all. I'm making this cake for Mrs. Whitley, and she's going to pay me three dollars for it. Now if you're going to be home I'll spend part of that money on lamb chops for your supper. If you're not, I'll buy something the children will like better."

"Then count me out."

"That's all I want to know."

There was a grim note in the scene that was obviously out of key with his humor. He stood around uncertainly, then made a bid for appreciation. "I fixed up those trees. Tied them up good, so the limbs won't bend down when the avocados get big, the way they did last year. Cut the grass. Looks pretty nice out there."

"You going to water the grass?"

"I *did* water it."

He said this with quiet complacency, for he had set a little trap for her, and she had fallen into it. But the silence that followed had a slightly ominous feel to it, as though he himself might have fallen into a trap that he wasn't aware of. Uneasily he added: "Gave it a good wetting down."

"Pretty early for watering the grass, isn't it?"

"Oh, one time's as good as another."

"Most people, when they water the grass, wait till later in the day, when the sun's not so hot, and it'll do some good, and not be a waste of good water that somebody else has to pay for."

"Who, for instance?"

"I don't see anybody working around here but me."

"You see any work I *can* do that I *don't* do?"

"So you get done early."

"Come on, Mildred, what are you getting at?"

"She's waiting for you, so go on."

"Who's waiting for me?"

"I think you know."

"If you're talking about Maggie Biederhof, I haven't seen her for a week, and she never did mean a thing to me except somebody to play rummy with when I had nothing else to do."

"That's practically all the time, if you ask me."

"I wasn't asking you."

"What do you do with her? Play rummy with her awhile, and then unbutton that red dress she's always wearing without any bras-sière under it, and flop her on the bed? And then have yourself a nice sleep, and then get up and see if there's some cold chicken in her icebox, and then play rummy some more, and then flop her on the bed again? Gee, that must be swell. I can't imagine anything nicer than that."

His tightening face muscles showed his temper was rising, and he opened his mouth to say something. Then he thought better of it. Then presently he said: "Oh all right, all right," in what was intended to be a lofty, resigned way, and started out of the kitchen.

"Wouldn't you like to bring her something?"

"Bring her—? What do you mean?"

"Well, there was some batter left over, and I made up some little cakes I was saving for the children. But fat as she is, she must like sweets, and—here, I'll wrap them up for her."

"How'd you like to go to hell?"

She laid aside the bird sketch and faced him. She started to talk. She had little to say about love, fidelity, or morals. She talked about money, and his failure to find work; and when she mentioned the lady of his choice, it was not as a siren who had stolen his love, but as the cause of the shiftlessness that had lately come over him. He broke in frequently, making excuses for himself, and repeating that there *was* no work, and insisting bitterly that if Mrs. Biederhof had come into his life, a guy was entitled to some peace, instead of a constant nagging over things that lay beyond his control. They spoke quickly, as though they were saying things that scalded their mouths, and had to be cooled with spit. Indeed, the whole scene had an ancient, almost classical ugliness to it, for they uttered the same recriminations that have been uttered since the beginning of marriage, and added little of originality to them, and nothing of beauty. Presently they stopped, and he started out of the kitchen again, but she stopped him. "Where are you going?"

"Would I be telling you?"

"Are you going to Maggie Biederhof's?"

"Suppose I am?"

"Then you might as well pack right now, and leave for good, because if you go out of that door I'm not going to let you come back. If I have to take this cleaver to you, you're not coming back in this house."

She lifted the cleaver out of a drawer, held it up, put it back, while he watched contemptuously. "Keep on, Mildred, keep right on. If you don't watch out, I may call you one of these days. I wouldn't ask much to take a powder on you right now."

"You're not calling me. I'm calling you. You go to her this afternoon, and that's the last you've seen of this house."

"I go where I goddam please to go."

"Then pack up, Bert."

His face went white, and their eyes met for a long stare. "O.K., then. I will."

"You better do it now. The sooner the better."

"O.K. . . . O.K."

He stalked out of the kitchen. She filled a paper cornucopia with icing, snipped the end off with a pair of scissors, and started to ice the bird on the cake.

By then he was in the bedroom, pitching traveling bags from the closet to the middle of the floor. He was pretty noisy about it, perhaps hoping she would hear him and come in there, begging him to change his mind. If so, he was disappointed, and there was nothing

for him to do but pack. His first care was for an outfit of evening
regalia, consisting of shirts, collars, studs, ties, and shoes, as well as
the black suit he called his "tuxedo." All these he wrapped tenderly
in tissue paper and placed in the bottom of the biggest bag. He had,
in truth, seen better days. In his teens he had been a stunt rider for
the movies, and was still vain of his horsemanship. Then an uncle
had died and left him a ranch on the outskirts of Glendale. Glendale
is now an endless suburb, bearing the same relation to Los Angeles
as Queens bears to New York. But at that time it was a village, and a
pretty scrubby village at that, with a freight yard at one end, open
country at the other, and a car track down the middle.

So he bought a ten-gallon hat, took possession of the ranch, and
tried to operate it, but without much success. His oranges didn't
grade, and when he tried grapes, the vines had just started when
Prohibition came along and he dug them out, in favor of walnuts.
But he had just selected his trees when the grape market zoomed on
the bootleg demand, and this depressed him so much that for a time
his land lay idle, while he tried to get his bearings in a dizzily
spinning world. But one day he was visited by three men who made
him a proposition. He didn't know it, but southern California, and
particularly Glendale, was on the verge of the real-estate boom of
the 1920's, such a boom as has rarely been seen on this earth.

So, almost overnight, with his three hundred acres that were located in the exact spot where people wanted to build, he became a
subdivider, a community builder, a man of vision, a big shot. He and
the three gentlemen formed a company, called Pierce Homes, Inc.,
with himself as president. He named a street after himself, and on
Pierce Drive, after he married Mildred, built this very home that he
now occupied, or would occupy for the next twenty minutes. Although at that time he was making a great deal of money, he declined to build a pretentious place. He told the architect: "Pierce
Homes are for folks, and what's good enough for folks is good
enough for me." Yet it was a little better, in some ways, than what is
usually good enough for folks. It had three bathrooms, one for each
bedroom, and certain features of the construction were almost luxu-
rious. It was a mockery now, and the place had been mortgaged and
remortgaged, and the money from the mortgages long since spent.
But once it had been something, and he liked to thump the walls,
and comment on how solidly they were built.

Instead of putting his money in a bank, he had invested it in A. T.

& T., and for some years had enjoyed daily vindication of his judgment, for the stock soared majestically, until he had a $350,000 "equity" in it, meaning there was that much difference between the price of the stock and the margin on which he carried it. But then came Black Thursday of 1929, and his plunge to ruin was so rapid he could hardly see Pierce Homes disappear on his way down. In September he had been rich, and Mildred picked out the mink coat she would buy when the weather grew cooler. In November, with the weather not a bit cooler, he had had to sell the spare car to pay current bills. All this he took cheerfully, for many of his friends were in the same plight, and he could joke about it, and even boast about it. What he couldn't face was the stultification of his sagacity. He had become so used to crediting himself with vast acumen that he could not bring himself to admit that his success was all luck, due to the location of his land rather than to his own personal qualities. So he still thought in terms of the vast deeds he would do when things got a little better. As for seeking a job, he couldn't bring himself to do it, and in spite of all he told Mildred, he hadn't made the slightest effort in this direction. So, by steady deterioration, he had reached his present status with Mrs. Biederhof. She was a lady of uncertain years, with a small income from hovels she rented to Mexicans. Thus she was in relative affluence when others were in want, and had time on her hands. She listened to the tales of his grandeur, past and future, fed him, played cards with him, and smiled coyly when he unbuttoned her dress. He lived in a world of dreams, lolling by the river, watching the clouds go by.

He kept looking at the door as though he expected Mildred to appear, but it remained closed. When little Ray came home from school, and scampered back for her cake, he stepped over and locked it. In a moment she was out there, rattling the knob, but he kept still. He heard Mildred call something to her, and she went out front, where other children were waiting for her. The child's name was really Moire, and she had been named by the principles of astrology, supplemented by numerology, as had the other child, Veda. But the practitioner had neglected to include pronunciation on her neatly typewritten slip, and Bert and Mildred didn't know that it was one of the Gaelic variants of Mary, and pronounced Moyra. They took it for a French name of the more exclusive kind, and pronounced it Mwaray, and quickly shortened it to Ray.

His last bag strapped up, he unlocked the door and walked dramatically to the kitchen. Mildred was still at work on the cake, which by now was a thing of overwhelming beauty, with the bird sitting on a leafy green twig, holding the scroll, "Happy Birthday to Bob," perkily in its beak, while a circle of rosebuds, spaced neatly around the rim, set up a sort of silent twittering. She didn't look up. He moistened his lips, asked: "Is Veda home?"

"Not yet she isn't."

"I laid low when Ray came to the door just now. I didn't see any reason for her to know about it. I don't see any reason for either of them to know about it. I don't want you to tell them I said good-bye or anything. You can just say—"

"I'll take care of it."

"O.K., then. I'll leave it to you."

He hesitated. Then: "Well, good-bye, Mildred."

With jerky steps, she walked over to the wall, stood leaning on it, her face hidden, then beat on it once or twice, helplessly, with her fists. "Go on, Bert. There's nothing to say. Just—go on."

When she turned around he was gone, and then the tears came, and she stood away from the cake, to keep them from falling on it. But when she heard the car back out of the garage, she gave a low, frightened exclamation, and ran to the window. They used it so seldom now, except on Sundays if they had a little money to buy gas, that she had completely forgotten about it. And so, as she saw this man slip out of her life, the only clear thought in her head was that now she had no way to deliver the cake.

She had got the last rosebud in place, and was removing stray flecks of icing with a cotton swab wound on a toothpick, when there was a rap on the screen door, and Mrs. Gessler, who lived next door, came in. She was a thin, dark woman of forty or so, with lines on her face that might have come from care, and might have come from liquor. Her husband was in the trucking business, but they were more prosperous than most truckers were at that time. There was a general impression that Gessler trucks often dropped down to Point Loma, where certain low, fast boats put into the cove.

Seeing the cake, Mrs. Gessler gave an exclamation, and came over to look. It was indeed worth the stare which her beady eyes gave it. All its decorations were now in place, but in spite of their somewhat conventional design, it had an aroma, a texture, a totality that proclaimed high distinction. It carried on its face the guarantee that every crumb would meet the inexorable confectioners' test: It must melt on the tongue.

In an awed way, Mrs. Gessler murmured: "I don't see how you do it, Mildred. It's beautiful, just beautiful."

"If you have to do it, you can do it."

"But it's *beautiful!*"

Only after a long final look did Mrs. Gessler get to what she came for. She had a small plate in her hand, with another plate clamped over it, and now lifted the top one. "I thought maybe you could use it. I fricasseed it for supper, but Ike's had a call to Long Beach, and I'm going with him, and I was afraid it might spoil."

Mildred got a plate, slid the chicken on it, and put it in the ice-box. Then she washed Mrs. Gessler's plates, dried them, and handed them back. "I can use practically anything, Lucy. Thanks."

"Well, I've got to run along."

"Have a nice time."

"Tell Bert I said hello."

". . . I will."

Mrs. Gessler stopped. "What's the matter?"

"Nothing."

"Come on, baby. Something's wrong. What is it?"

"Bert's gone."

"You mean—for good?"

"Just now. He left."

"Walked out on you, just like that?"

"He got a little help, maybe. It had to come."

"Well what do you know about that? And that floppy-looking frump he left you for. How can he even look at her?"

"She's what he wants."

"But she doesn't even *wash!*"

"Oh, what's the use of talking? If she likes him, all right then, she's got him. Bert's all right. And it wasn't his fault. It was just—everything. And I did pester him. I nagged him, he said, and he ought to know. But I can't take things lying down, I don't care if we've got a Depression or not. If she can, then they ought to get along fine, because that's exactly the way he's built. But I've got my own ideas, and I can't change them even for him."

"What are you going to do?"

"What am I doing now?"

A grim silence fell on both women. Then Mrs. Gessler shook her head. "Well, you've joined the biggest army on earth. You're the great American institution that never gets mentioned on Fourth of July—a grass widow with two small children to support. The dirty bastards."

"Oh, Bert's all right."

"He's all right, but he's a dirty bastard and they're all dirty bastards."

"We're not so perfect."

"We wouldn't pull what they pull."

The front door slammed and Mildred held up a warning finger. Mrs. Gessler nodded and asked if there was anything she could do, today. Mildred wanted desperately to say she could give her a lift with the cake, but there had been one or two impatient taps on an automobile horn from across the yard, and she didn't have the nerve. "Not right now."

"I'll be seeing you."

"Thanks again for the chicken."

The child who now entered the kitchen didn't scamper in, as little Ray had a short time before. She stepped in primly, sniffed contemptuously at the scent left by Mrs. Gessler, and put her schoolbooks on the table before she kissed her mother. Though she was only eleven she was something to look at twice. In the jaunty way she wore her clothes, as well as the handsome look around the upper part of her face, she resembled her father more than her mother: it was commonly said that "Veda's a Pierce." But around her mouth the resemblance vanished, for Bert's mouth had a slanting weakness that hers didn't have. Her hair, which was a coppery red, and her eyes, which were light blue like her mother's, were all the more vivid by contrast with the scramble of freckles and sunburn which formed her complexion. But the most arresting thing about her was her walk. Possibly because of her high, arching chest, possibly because of the slim hips and legs below it, she moved with an erect, arrogant haughtiness that seemed comic in one so young.

She took the cake her mother gave her, a chocolate muffin with a white V iced upon it, counted the remaining ones, and calmly gave an account of her piano practice. Through all the horrors of the last year and a half, Mildred had managed fifty cents a week for the lessons, since she had a deep, almost religious conviction that Veda was "talented," and although she didn't exactly know at what, piano seemed indicated, as a sound, useful preliminary to almost anything. Veda was a satisfactory pupil, for she practiced faithfully and showed lively interest. Her piano, picked out when Mildred picked out her coat, never actually arrived, so she practiced at her Grandfather Pierce's, where there was an ancient upright, and on this account always arrived home from school somewhat later than Ray.

She told of her progress with the Chopin *Grand Valse Brillante*, repeating the title of the piece a number of times, somewhat to Mildred's amusement, for she employed the full French pronunciation, and obviously enjoyed the elegant effect. She spoke in the clear, affected voice that one associates with stage children, and indeed everything she said had the effect of having been learned by heart, and recited in the manner prescribed by some stiff book of etiquette. The waltz disposed of, she walked over to have a look at the cake. "Who's it for, Mother?"

"Bob Whitley."

"Oh, the paper boy."

Young Whitley's sideline, which was soliciting subscriptions after school hours, Veda regarded as a gross social error, and Mildred smiled. "He'll be a paper boy without a birthday cake if I don't find some way to get it over there. Eat your cake now, and then run over to Grandfather's and see if he minds taking me up to Mrs. Whitley's in his car."

"Can't we use our car?"

"Your father's out with it, and—he may be late. Run along now. Take Ray with you, and Grandfather'll ride you both back."

Veda stalked unhurriedly out, and Mildred heard her call Ray in from the street. But in a minute or two she was back. She closed the door carefully and spoke with even more than her usual precision. "Mother, where's Father?"

"He—had to go somewhere."

"Why did he take his clothes?"

When Mildred promised Bert to "take care of it," she had pictured a vague scene, which would end up with "Mother'll tell you more about it some day." But she had forgotten Veda's passion for her father's clothes, the proud inspection of his tuxedo, his riding breeches, his shiny boots and shoes, which was a daily ritual that not even a trip to her grandfather's was going to interfere with. And she had also forgotten that it was impossible to fool Veda. She began examining some imaginary imperfection on the cake. "He's gone away."

"Where?"

"I don't know."

"Is he coming back?"

"No."

She felt wretched, wished Veda would come over to her, so she could take her in her arms and tell her about it in some way that didn't seem so shame-faced. But Veda's eyes were cold, and she didn't move. Mildred doted on her, for her looks, her promise of talent, and her snobbery, which hinted at things superior to her own commonplace nature. But Veda doted on her father, for his grand manner and fine ways, and if he disdained gainful work, she was proud of him for it. In the endless bickerings that had marked the last few months, she had invariably been on his side, and often withered her mother with lofty remarks. Now she said: "I see, Mother. I just wanted to know."

Presently Ray came in, a chubby, tow-haired little thing, four years younger than Veda, and the picture of Mildred. She began dancing around, pretending she was going to poke her finger into the cake, but Mildred stopped her, and told her what she had just told Veda. She began to cry, and Mildred gathered her into her arms, and talked to her as she had wanted to talk in the first place. She said Father thought the world of them both, that he hadn't said good-bye because he didn't want to make them feel badly, that it wasn't his fault, but the fault of a lot of things she couldn't tell about now, but would explain later on some time. All this she said to Ray, but she was really talking to Veda, who was still standing there, gravely listening. After a few minutes Veda evidently felt some obligation to be friendly, for she interrupted to say: "If you mean Mrs. Biederhof, Mother, I quite agree. I think she's distinctly middle-class."

Mildred was able to laugh at this, and she seized the chance to gather Veda to her, and kiss her. Then she sent both children off to their grandfather's. She was glad that she herself hadn't said a word about Mrs. Biederhof, and resolved that the name should never pass her lips in their presence.

Mr. Pierce arrived with the car and an invitation to supper, and after a moment's reflection, Mildred accepted. The Pierces had to be told, and if she told them now, after having supper with them, it would show there were no hard feelings, and that she wanted to continue relations as before. But after the cake had been delivered, and she had sat around with them a few minutes, she detected something in the air. Whether Bert had already stopped by, or the children had made some slip, she didn't know, but things weren't as usual. Accordingly, as soon as supper was over and the children had gone out to play, she got grimly at it. Mr. Pierce and Mom, both originally from Connecticut, lived in a smaller, though just as folksy Pierce Home, on a pension he received as a former railroadman. But they were comfortable enough, and usually took their twilight ease in a small patio back of the house. It was here that Mildred broke the news.

A silence fell on them, a glum silence that lasted a long time. Mom was in the swing. She began touching the ground with her foot and it began rocking, and as it rocked it squeaked. Then she began to talk, in a bitter, jerky way, looking neither at Mildred nor at Mr. Pierce. "It's that Biederhof woman. It's her fault, from beginning to end. It's been her fault, ever since Bert started going with her. That woman's a huzzy. I've known it ever since I first laid eyes on her. The idea, carrying on like that with a married man. And her own husband not dead a year yet. And the filthy way she keeps house. And going around like she does with her breasts wobbling every which way, so any man's got to look at her, whether he wants to or not. What did she have to pick on my boy for? Wasn't there enough men, without she had to . . ."

Mildred closed her eyes and listened, and Mr. Pierce sucked his pipe, and put in melancholy remarks of his own. It was all about Mrs. Biederhof, and in a way this was a relief. But then a sense of vague apprehension stirred within her. This evening, she knew, was important, for what was said now would be written indelibly on the record. For the children's sake, if no other, it was vital that she give no word of false testimony, or omit words essential to a fair report, or in any way leave a suspicion of untruthfulness. Also, she felt a growing annoyance at the facile way in which everything was being blamed on a woman who really had very little to do with it. She let Mom run down, and after a long silence, said: It's not Mrs. Biederhof."

"Who is it, then?"

"It's a whole lot of things, and if they hadn't happened, Bert wouldn't any more have looked at her than he would have looked at an Eskimo woman. It's—what happened to Bert's business. And the awful time we had getting along. And the way Bert got fed up. And—"

"You mean to tell me this is *Bert's* fault?"

Mildred waited a minute, for fear the rasp in Mom's voice would find an answering rasp in her own. Then she said: "I don't say it was *anybody's* fault, unless it was the Depression's fault, and certainly Bert couldn't help that." She stopped, then doggedly plowed on with what she dreaded, and yet felt had to be said: "But I might as well tell you, Bert wasn't the only one that got fed up. *I* got fed up too. He didn't start this thing today. *I* did."

"You mean—*you put Bert out?*"

The rasp in Mom's voice was so pronounced now, her refusal to admit basic realities so infuriating, that Mildred didn't trust herself to speak at all. It was only after Mr. Pierce had interposed, and a cooling five minutes had passed, that she said: "It had to come."

"It certainly did have to come if you went and put that poor boy out. I never heard of such a thing in my life. Where's he at now?"

"I don't know."

"And it's not even your *house.*"

"It'll be the bank's house pretty soon if I don't find a way to raise the interest money."

When Mom replied to that, Mr. Pierce quickly shushed her down, and Mildred smiled sourly to herself that the barest mention of interest money meant a rapid change of subject. Mr. Pierce returned to Mrs. Biederhof, and Mildred thought it diplomatic to chime in: "I'm not defending her for a minute. And I'm not blaming Bert. All I'm trying to say is that what had to come had to come, and if it came today, and I was the one that brought it on, it was better than having it come later, when there would have been still more hard feelings about it."

Mom said nothing, but the swing continued to squeak. Mr. Pierce said the Depression had certainly hit a lot of people hard. Mildred waited a minute or two, so her departure wouldn't seem quite so pointed, then said she had to be getting the children home. Mr. Pierce saw her to the door, but didn't offer a ride. Falteringly, he said: "You need anything right now, Mildred?"

"Not yet a while, thanks."

"I sure am sorry."

"What had to come had to come."

"Goodnight, Mildred."

Shooing the children along, Mildred felt a hot resentment against the pair she had just left, not only for their complete failure to get the point, but also for their stingy ignoring of the plight she was in, and the possibility that their grandchildren, for all they knew, might not have anything to eat. As she turned into Pierce Drive the night chill settled down, and she felt cold, and swallowed quickly to get rid of a forlorn feeling in her throat.

After putting the children to bed she went to the living room, pulled a chair to the window, and sat there in the dark looking out at the familiar scene, trying to shake off the melancholy that was creeping over her. Then she went to the bedroom and turned on the light. It was the first time she had slept here since Bert started his attentions to Mrs. Biederhof; for several months now, she had been sleeping in the children's room, where she had moved one of the twin beds. She tiptoed in there, got her pajamas, came back, took off her dress. Then she sat down in front of the dressing table and started combing her hair. Then she stopped and began looking at herself, grimly, reflectively.

She was a shade under medium height, and her small size, mousy blond hair, and watery blue eyes made her look considerably younger than she actually was, which was twenty-eight. About her face there was no distinction whatever. She was what is described as "nice-looking," rather than pretty; her own appraisal she sometimes gave in the phrase, "pass in a crowd." But this didn't quite do her justice. Into her eyes, if she were provoked, or made fun of, or puzzled, there came a squint that was anything but alluring, that betrayed a rather appalling literal-mindedness, or matter-of-factness, or whatever it might be called, but that hinted, nevertheless, at something more than complete vacuity inside. It was the squint, Bert confessed afterward, that first caught his fancy, and convinced him there was "something to her." They met just after her father died, when she was in her third year at high school. After the garage business had been sold and the insurance collected, her mother had toyed with the idea of buying a Pierce Home, using her small capital as a down payment, and taking in roomers to pay the rest. So Bert came around, and Mildred was excited by him, mainly on account of his dashing ways.

But when the day of the grand tour of Pierce Homes arrived, Mrs. Ridgely was unable to go, and Bert took Mildred. They drove in his sports roadster, and the wind was in her hair, and she felt a-tingle and grown-up. As a grand climax they stopped at the Pierce Model Home, which was really the main office of Pierce Homes, Inc., but was built like a home, to stimulate the imaginations of customers. The secretaries had gone by then, but Mildred inspected everything, from the great "living room" in front to the cozy "bedrooms" at the rear, lingering longer in these than was perhaps exactly advisable. Bert was very solemn on he way home, as befitted one who had just seduced a minor, but gallantly suggested a re-inspection next day. A month later they were married, she quitting school two days before the ceremony, and Veda arriving slightly sooner than the law allowed. Bert persuaded Mrs. Ridgely to give up the idea of a Pierce Home for boardinghouse purposes, possibly fearing deficits, and she went to live with Mildred's sister, whose husband had a ship chandler's business in San Diego. The small capital, at Bert's suggestion, was invested in A. T. & T.

And Mildred's figure got her attention in any crowd and all crowds. She had a soft, childish neck that perked her head up at a pretty angle; her shoulders drooped, but gracefully; her brassière ballooned a little, with an extremely seductive burden. Her hips were small, like Veda's, and suggested a girl, rather than a woman who had borne two children. Her legs were really beautiful, and she was quite vain of them. Only one thing about them bothered her, but it bothered her constantly, and it had bothered her ever since she could remember. In the mirror they were flawlessly slim and straight, but as she looked down on them direct, something about their contours made them seem bowed. So she had taught herself to bend one knee when she stood, and to take short steps when she moved, bending the rear knee quickly, so that the deformity, if it actually existed, couldn't be noticed. This gave her a mincing, feminine walk, like the ponies in a Broadway chorus; she didn't know it, but her bottom switched in a wholly provocative way.

Or possibly she did know it.

The hair finished, she got up, put her hands on her hips, and surveyed herself in the mirror. For a moment the squint appeared in her eyes, as though she knew this was no ordinary night in her life, and that she must take stock, see what she had to offer against what lay ahead. Leaning close, she bared her teeth, which were large and white, and looked for cavities. She found none. She stood back again, cocked her head to one side, struck an attitude. Almost at once she amended it by bending one knee. Then she sighed, took off the rest of her clothes, slipped into her pajamas. As she turned off the light, from force of long habit she looked over to the Gesslers', to see if they were still up. Then she remembered they were away. Then she remembered what Mrs. Gessler had said: ". . . the great American institution that never gets mentioned on Fourth of July, a grass widow with two small children to support"—and snickered sourly as she got into bed. Then she caught her breath as Bert's smell enveloped her.

In a moment the door opened, and little Ray trotted in, weeping. Mildred held up the covers, folded the little thing in, snuggled her against her stomach, whispered and crooned to her until the weeping stopped. Then, after staring at the ceiling for a time, she fell asleep.

Chapter 2

For a day or two after Bert left, Mildred lived in a sort of fool's paradise, meaning she got two orders for cakes and three orders for pies. They kept her bustlingly busy, and she kept thinking what she would say to Bert, when he dropped around to see the children: "Oh, we're getting along all right—no need for you to worry. I've got all the work I can do, and more. Just goes to show that when a person's willing to work there still seems to be work to be done." Also, she conned over a slightly different version, for Mr. Pierce and Mom: "Me? I'm doing fine. I've got more orders now than I can fill—but thank you for your kind offers, just the same." Mr. Pierce's faint-hearted inquiries still rankled with her, and it pleased her that she could give the pair of them a good waspish sting, and then sit back and watch their faces. She was a little given to rehearsing things in her mind, and having imaginary triumphs over people who had upset her in one way and another.

But soon she began to get frightened. Several days went by, and there were no orders. Then there came a letter from her mother, mainly about the A. T. & T., which she had bought outright and still held, and which had fallen to some absurd figure. She was quite explicit about blaming this all on Bert, and seemed to feel there was something he could do about it, and should do. And such part of the letter as wasn't about the A. T. & T. was about Mr. Engel's ship chandler business. At the moment it seemed that the only cash customers were bootleggers, but they all used light boats, and Mr. Engel was stocked with heavy gear, for steamers. So Mildred was directed to drive down to Wilmington and see if any of the chandlers there would take this stuff off his hands, in exchange for the lighter articles used by speedboats. Mildred broke into a hysterical laugh as she read this, for the idea of going around, trying to get rid of a truckload of anchors, struck her as indescribably comic. And in the same mail was a brief communication from the gas company, headed "Third Notice," and informing her that unless her bill was paid in five days service would be discontinued.

Of the three dollars she got from Mrs. Whitley, and the nine she got from the other orders, she still had a few dollars left. So she walked down to the gas company office and paid the bill, carefully saving the receipt. Then she counted her money and stopped by a market, where she bought a chicken, a quarter pound of hot dogs, some vegetables, and a quart of milk. The chicken, first baked, then creamed, then made into three neat croquettes, would provision her over the weekend. The hot dogs were a luxury. She disapproved of them, on principle, but the children loved them, and she always tried to have some around, for bites between meals. The milk was a sacred duty. No matter how gritty things got, Mildred always managed to have money for Veda's piano lessons, and for all the milk the children could drink.

This was a Saturday morning, and when she got home she found Mr. Pierce there. He had come to invite the children over for the weekend, "—no use coming back here with them. I'll bring them direct to school Monday morning, and they can come home from there." By this Mildred knew there was dirty work afoot, probably a trip to the beach, where the Pierces had friends, and where Bert would appear, quite by coincidence. She resented it, and resented still more that Mr. Pierce had delayed his coming until she had spent the money for the chicken. But the prospect of having the children fed free for two whole days was so tempting that she acted quite agreeably about it, said of course they could go, and packed a little bag for them. But unexpectedly, as she ran back in the house after waving them good-bye, she began to cry, and went in the living room to resume a vigil that was rapidly becoming a habit. Everybody in the block seemed to be going somewhere, spinning importantly down the street, with blankets, paddles, and even boats lashed to the tops of their cars, and leaving blank silence behind. After watching six or seven such departures Mildred went to the bedroom and lay down, clenching and unclenching her fists.

Around five o'clock the bell rang. She had an uneasy feeling it might be Bert, with some message about the children. But when she went to the door it was Wally Burgan, one of the three gentlemen who had made the original proposition to Bert which led to Pierce Homes, Inc. He was a stocky, sandy-haired man of about forty, and now worked for the receivers that had been appointed for the corporation. This was another source of irritation between Mildred and Bert, for she thought he should have had the job, and that if he had bestirred himself a little, he *could* have had it. But Wally had got it, and he was out there now, without a hat, greeting her with a casual wave of the cigarette that seemed to accompany everything he did. "Hello, Mildred. Is Bert around?"

"Not right now he isn't."

"You don't know where he went?"

"No, I don't."

Wally stood thinking a minute, then turned to go. "All right, I'll see him Monday. Something came up, little trouble over a title, I thought maybe he could help us out. Ask him if he can drop over, will you?"

Mildred let him get clear down the walk before she stopped him. She hated to wash the dirty linen in front of any more people than she could help, but if straightening out a title would mean a day's work for Bert, or a few dollars in some legal capacity, she had to see that he got the chance. "Ah—come in, Wally."

Wally looked a little surprised, then came back and stepped into the living room. Mildred closed the door. "If it's important, Wally, you'd better look Bert up yourself. He—he's not living here any more."

"*What?*"

"He went away."

"Where?"

"I don't know exactly. He didn't tell me. But I'm sure old Mr. Pierce would know, and if they've gone away, why—I think Maggie Biederhof might know, at least how to reach him."

Wally looked at Mildred for a time, then said: "Well—when did all this happen?"

"Oh—a few days ago."

"You mean you've busted up?"

"Something like that."

"For good?"

"As far as I know."

"Well, if you don't know I don't know who does know."

"Yes, it's for good."

"You living here all alone?"

"No, I have the children. They're away with their grandparents for the weekend, but they're staying with me, not with Bert."

"Well say, this is a hell of a note."

Wally lit another cigarette and resumed looking at her. His eyes dropped to her legs. They were bare, as she was saving stockings, and she pulled her skirt over them self-consciously. He looked several other places, to make it appear that his glance had been accidental, then said: "Well, what do you do with yourself?"

"Oh, I manage to keep busy."

"You don't look busy."

"Saturday. Taking a day off."

"I wouldn't ask much to take it off with you. Say, I never did mind being around you."

"You certainly kept it to yourself."

"Me, I'm conscientious."

They both laughed, and Mildred felt a little tingle, as well as some perplexity that this man, who had never taken the slightest interest in her before, should begin making advances the moment he found out she had no husband any more. He talked along, his voice sounding a little unnatural, about the swell time they could have, she replying flirtatiously, aware that there was something shady about the whole thing, yet a bit giddy at her unaccustomed liberty. Presently he sighed, said he was tied up for tonight, "But look."

"Yes?"

"What you doing tomorrow night?"

"Why, nothing that I know of."

"Well then—?"

She dropped her eyes, pleated her dress demurely over her knee, glanced at him. "I don't know why not."

He got up and she got up. "Then it's a date. That's what we'll do. We'll step out."

"If I haven't forgotten how."

"Oh, you'll know how. When? Half past six, maybe?"

"That suits me fine."

"Make it seven."

"Seven o'clock I'll be ready."

Around noon next day, while Mildred was breakfasting off the hot dogs, Mrs. Gessler came over to invite her to a party that night. Mildred, pouring her a cup of coffee, said she'd love to come, but as she had a date, she wasn't sure she could make it. "A date? Gee, you're working fast."

"You've got to do something."

"Do I know him?"

"Wally Burgan."

"Wally—well, bring him!"

"I'll see what his plans are."

"I didn't know he was interested in you."

"Neither did I . . . Lucy, I don't think he was. I don't think he'd ever looked at me. But the second he heard Bert was gone, well it was almost funny the effect it had on him. You could see him get excited. Will you kindly tell me why?"

"I ought to have told you about that. The morals they give you credit for, you'd be surprised. To him, you were a red-hot mamma the second he found out about you."

"About *what?*"

"Grass widow! From now on, you're fast."

"Are you serious?"

"I am. And they are."

Mildred, feeling no faster than she had ever felt, pondered this riddle for some little time, while Mrs. Gessler sipped her coffee and seemed to be pondering something else. Presently she asked: "Is Wally married?"

"Why—not that I know of. No, of course he's not. He was always gagging about how lucky the married ones were on income-tax day. Why?"

"I wouldn't bring him over, if I were you."

"Well, as you like."

"Oh, it's not that—he's welcome, so far as that goes. But—you know. These are business friends of Ike's, with their lady friends, all-right guys, trying to make a living same as anybody else, but a little rough, and a little noisy. Maybe they spend too much time on the sea, playing around in their speedboats. And the girls are the squealing type. None of them are what you ought to be identified with, specially when you've got a single young man on your hands, that's already a little suspicious of your morals, and—"

"Do you think I'm taking Wally seriously?"

"You ought to be, if you're not. Well if not, why not? He's a fine, upstanding, decent young man, that looks a little like a pot-bellied rat, but he's single and he's working, and that's enough."

"I don't think he'd be shocked at your party."

"I haven't finished yet. It's not a question of whether he'd be shocked at my party, it's a question of whether you're making proper use of your time. What *are* his plans, so far as you know them?"

"Well, he's coming here and—"

"When?"

"Seven."

"That's mistake No. 1. Baby, I wouldn't let that cluck buy your dinner. I'd sit him right down and give him one of those Mildred Pierce specials—"

"What? Me work when he's willing to—"

"As an investment, baby, an investment in time, effort, and raw materials. Now shut up and let me talk. Whatever outlay it involves is on me, because I've become inspired and when inspired I never count little things like costs. It's going to be a perfectly terrible night." She waved a hand at the weather, which had turned gray, cold, and overcast, as it usually does at the peak of a California spring. "It won't be no fit night out for man or beast. And what's more, you've already got dinner half fixed, and you're not going to have things spoil just because he's got some foolish notion he wants to take you out."

"Just the same, that was the idea."

"Not so fast, baby—let us pause and examine that idea. Why would he want to take you out? Why do they ever want to take us out? As a compliment to us, say they. To show us a good time, to prove the high regard they have for us. They're a pack of goddam liars. In addition to being dirty bastards, and very dumb clucks, they are also goddam liars. There's practically nothing can be said in favor of them, except they're the only ones we've got. They take us out for one reason, and one reason only: so *they* can get a drink. Secondarily, so *we* can get a drink, and succumb to their fell designs after we get home, but mainly so *they* can have a drink. And, baby, right there is where I come in."

She ducked out the screen door, ran across the yards, and presently was back with a basket, in which were quite a few bottles. She set them out on the kitchen table, then resumed her talk. "This stuff, the gin and the Scotch, is right off the boat, and better than he's tasted in years. All the gin needs is a little orange juice, and it'll make a swell cocktail; be sure to cut it down plenty with ice. Now this other, the wine, is straight California, but he doesn't know it, and it's O.K. booze, so lean on it. That's the trick, baby. Handle the wine right and the high-priced stuff will last and last and last. Fill him up on it—much as he wants, and more. It's thirty cents a quart, half a cent for the pretty French label, and the more he drinks of that, the less he'll want of Scotch. Here's three reds and three whites, just because I love you, and want you to get straightened out. With fish, chicken and turkey, give him white, and with red meat, give him red. What are you having tonight?"

"Who says I'm having anything?"

"Now listen, have we got to go all over that? Baby, baby, you go out with him, and he buys you a dinner, and you get a little tight, and you come home, and something happens, and then what?"

"Don't worry. Nothing'll happen."

"Oh something'll happen. If not tonight, then some other night. Because if it don't happen, he'll lose interest, and quit coming around, and you wouldn't like that. And *when* it happens, it's Sin. It's Sin, because you're a grass widow, and fast. And he's all paid up, because he bought your dinner, and that makes it square."

"He must have a wonderful character, my Wally."

"He's got the same character they've all got, no better and no worse. *But*—if you bought *his* dinner, and cooked it for him the way only you can cook, and you just happened to look cute in that little apron, and something just happened to happen, then it's Nature. Old Mother Nature, baby, and we all know she's no bum. Because that grass widow, she went back to the kitchen, where all women belong, and that makes it all right. And Wally, he's not paid up, even a little bit. He even forgot to ask the price of the chips. He'll find out. And another thing, this way is quick, and the last I heard of you, you were up against it, and couldn't afford to waste much time. You play it right, and inside of a week your financial situation will be greatly eased, and inside of a month you'll have him begging for the chance to buy that divorce. The other way, making the grand tour of all the speako's he knows, it could go on for five years, and even then you couldn't be sure."

"You think I want to be kept?"

"Yes."

For a while after that, Mildred didn't think of Wally, at any rate to know she was thinking of him. After Mrs. Gessler left, she went to her room and wrote a few letters, particularly one to her mother, explaining the new phase her life had entered, and going into some detail as to why, at the moment, she wouldn't be able to sell the anchors. Then she mended some of the children's clothes. But around four o'clock, when it started to rain, she put the sewing basket away, went to the kitchen, and checked her supplies, from the three or four oranges in reserve for the children's breakfast to the vegetables she had bought yesterday in the market. The chicken she gave a good smelling, to make sure it was still fresh. The quart of milk she took out of the icebox with care, so as not to joggle it, and, using a tiny ladle intended for salt, removed the thick cream at the top and put it into a glass pitcher. Then she opened a can of huckleberries and made a pie. While that was baking she stuffed the chicken.

Around six she laid a fire, feeling a little guilty that most of the wood consisted of the dead limbs Bert had sawed off the avocado trees the afternoon he left. She didn't build it in the living room. She built it in the "den," which was on the other side of the chimney from the living room and had a small fireplace of its own. It was really one of the three bedrooms, and had its own bathroom, but Bert had fixed it up with a sofa, comfortable chairs, and photographs of the banquets he had spoken at, and it was here that they did their entertaining. The fire ready to light, she went to the bedroom and dressed. She put on a print dress, the best she had. She examined a great many stockings, found two that showed no signs of runs, put them on. Her shoes, by careful sparing, were in fair shape, and she put on simple black ones. Then, after surveying herself in the mirror, admiring her legs, and remembering to bend the right knee, she threw a coat around her and went to the den. Around ten minutes to seven she put the coat away and turned on one button of heat. Then she pulled down the shades and turned on several lamps.

Around ten after seven, Wally rang the bell, apologetic for being late, anxious to get started. For one long moment Mildred was tempted: by the chance to save her food, by the chance to eat without having to cook, most of all by the chance to go somewhere, or to sit under soft lights, perhaps even to hear an orchestra, and dance. But her mouth seemed to step out in front of her, and take charge in a somewhat gabby way. "Well my goodness, I never even dreamed you'd want to go out on a night like this."

"Isn't that what we said?"

"But it's so awful out. Why can't I fix you something, and maybe we could go out some other night?"

"Hey, hey, I'm taking *you* out."

"All right, but at least let's wait a few minutes, in case this rain'll let up a little. I just hate to go out when it's coming down like this."

She led him to the den, lit the fire, took his coat, and disappeared with it. When she came back she was shaking an orange blossom in a pitcher, and balancing a tray on which were two glasses.

"Well say! *Say!*"

"Thought it might help pass the time."

"You bet it will."

He took his glass, waited for her to take hers, said "Mud in your eye," and sipped. Mildred was startled at how good it was. As for Wally, he was downright reverent at how good it was. "What do you know about that? Real gin! I haven't tasted it since—God knows when. All they give you in these speaks is smoke, and a guy's taking his life in his hands, all the time. Say, where did *you* tend bar?"

"Oh, just picked it up."

"Not from Bert."

"I didn't say where."

"Bert's hooch was God-awful. He was one of these home-laboratory guys, and the more stuff he put in it to kill the taste, the worse it tasted. But his—say, Bert must be crazy if he walked out on *you*."

He looked at her admiringly and she refilled his glass. "Thanks, Mildred. I couldn't say no if I tried. Hey, what about yours?"

Mildred, not much of a drinker under any circumstances, had decided that tonight might be an excellent time to exercise a certain womanly restraint. She laughed, shook her head. "Oh—one's all I take."

"Don't you like it?"

"I like it all right, but I'm really not used to it."

"You've got to get educated."

"I can see that right now. But we can attend to that part a little bit at a time. Tonight, the rest of it's yours."

He laughed excitedly, strolled over to the window, stood looking out at the rain. "You know, I'm thinking about something. . . . Maybe you were right about not going out. That look's wetter than a Chinaman's wash. Did you really mean it, what you said about knocking something together that we could eat?"

"Of course I meant it."

"Putting you to one hell of a lot of trouble, though."

"Don't be silly, it's no trouble at all. And I bet you get a better meal here than you would outside. That's another thing you might have noticed, all the time you've been coming here. I don't know how much of a bartender I am, but I'm an awfully good cook."

"Quit kidding me. That was the hired girl."

"That was me. Want to watch?"

"I sure do."

She really was a marvelous cook, and he watched delightedly while she popped the chicken into the oven, scraped four potatoes, shelled a little dish of peas. They went back to the den until it should be time to put the vegetables on to boil, and he had another cocktail. By now she was wearing a little blue apron, and he oafishly admitted that he "sure would like to give those apron strings a pull."

"You'd better not."

"Why?"

"I might tie it on you, and put you to work."

"O.K. by me."

"Would you like to eat here? By the fire?"

"I'd love it."

She got a bridge table out of the closet and set it up in front of the fireplace. Then she got out silver, glassware, and napkins, and arranged them for two. He followed her around like a puppy, his cocktail glass in his hand. "Hey, this looks like a real dinner."

"I told you. Maybe you weren't listening."

"From now on, I'm nothing but ears."

The dinner was a little more of a success than she bargained for. For soup, she served some chicken jelly she had had left over from the middle of the week, and it struck him as very high-toned. When she had taken away the cups, she came in with the wine, which by a curious coincidence had been in the icebox since Mrs. Gessler left, and poured it, leaving the bottle on the table. Then she came in with the chicken, the potatoes, and peas, all deftly arranged on one platter. He was enthusiastic about everything, but when she came in with the pie, he grew positively lyrical. He told how his mother made such pies, back in Carlisle, Pa. He told about the Indian School, and Mt. Pleasant, the quarterback.

But the food, much as it delighted him, seemed almost incidental. He insisted that she sit beside him, on the sofa, and wear the apron. When she came in with the coffee, she found he had turned out the lights, so they drank it by firelight alone. When they finished it he put his arm around her. Presently, deciding she ought to be sociable, she dropped her head on his shoulder, but when he touched her hair with his fingers she got up. "I've got to take these things out."

"I'll put the table away for you."

"Then all right, and when you get done with that, if you want the bath, it's right beyond you, and that's the door over there. As for the cook, as soon as she gets the dishes out of sight, she's going to put on a warmer dress."

What with the rain, and the general clammy feel of the night, the little print dress was becoming more and more uncomfortable, despite its pleasing appearance. She went to the bedroom, slipped out of it, and hung it up in the closet. But when she reached for her dark blue woolen dress, she heard something and turned around. He was standing in the door, a foolish grin on his face. "Thought you might need a little help."

"I don't need help, and I didn't ask you in here."

She spoke sharply, for her resentment at this invasion of her privacy was quick and real. But as she spoke, her elbow touched the closet door, and it swung open, revealing her. He caught his breath and whispered "Jesus." Then he seemed bewildered, and stood looking at her and yet not looking at her.

Badly annoyed, she took the woolen dress off its hanger and slipped it over her head. Before she could close the snaps, however, she felt his arms around her, heard him mumbling penitently in her ear. "I'm sorry, Mildred. I'm sorry as hell. But it didn't break like I figured it would. I swear to God, I came in here for nothing but to pull those apron strings. It was just a gag, that's all. Hell, you know I wouldn't pull any cheap tricks like that on you, don't you?" And as though to prove his contempt for all cheap tricks, he reached over and turned out the light.

Well, was she angry at him or not? In spite of the way in which she had followed all instructions, and the way he had justified all predictions, she still didn't know what she wanted to do about Wally. But as she twisted her head to keep her mouth from meeting his, it flitted through her mind that if she didn't have to open the Scotch, she might be able to get six dollars for it somewhere.

Along about midnight, Wally lit a cigarette. Feeling warm, Mildred kicked the covers off and let the cold damp air prickle her quite lovely nakedness. She raised one leg, looked at it judiciously, decided once and for all it was not bowed, and that she was going to stop worrying about it. Then she wiggled her toes. It was a distinctly frivolous operation, but there was nothing frivolous about Wally as he set an ashtray near him, and pulled the covers over his more or less lovely nakedness. He was silently, almost ostentatiously glum as he lay there and smoked, so much so that Mildred said: "Penny."

"I'm thinking about Bert."

Without hearing any more about it, she knew what this meant: Wally had had his fun, and now he was getting ready to get out from under. She waited a moment or two, as she often did when angered, but in spite of her effort to sound casual, her voice had a vibrant sound to it. "And what about Bert?"

"Oh—you know."

"If Bert left me, and he's out of my life, why do you have to do all this thinking about him, when nobody else is?"

"We're good friends. Goddam good friends."

"But not so goddam good that you wouldn't block him off from a job he was entitled to have, and then go around playing all the politics you knew how, to get it for yourself."

"Mildred, cussing's no good, coming from you."

"And double-crossing's no good, coming from anybody."

"I don't like that."

"I don't care whether you like it or not."

"They needed a lawyer."

"After you talked to them they did. Oh yes, at least a dozen people came to Bert, and warned him what you were doing, and begged him to go down and put his claim in, and he wouldn't do it, because he didn't think it was proper. And then he found out what was proper. And what a pal you were."

"Mildred, I give you my word—"

"And what's that worth?"

She jumped out of bed and began marching around the dark room, bitterly reviewing the history of Pierce Homes, Inc., the incidents of the crash, and the procedure of the receivers. He started a slow, solemn denial. "Why don't you tell the truth? You've had all you wanted of me, haven't you? A drink, a dinner, and other things I'd prefer not to mention. And now you want to duck, and you start talking about Bert. Funny you didn't think about Bert when you came in here, wanting to pull those apron strings. You remember them, don't you?"

"I didn't hear you saying no."

"No, I was the sap."

She drew breath to say he was just like the rest of them, and then add Mrs. Gessler's phrase, "the dirty bastards," but somehow the words didn't come. There was some core of honesty within her that couldn't quite accept Mrs. Gessler's interpretations of life, however they might amuse her at the moment. She didn't really believe they were dirty bastards, and she had set a trap for Wally. If he was wriggling out of it the best way he could, there was no sense in blaming him for things that were rapidly becoming too much for her, but that he certainly had nothing to do with. She sat down beside him. "I'm sorry, Wally."

"Hell, that's all right."

"I've been a little upset lately."

"Who wouldn't be?"

Next morning, Mildred was glumly washing the dinner dishes when Mrs. Gessler dropped over, to give an account of the party. She rather pointedly didn't refer to Wally until she was leaving, and then, as though she had just thought of it, asked how he was. Mildred said he was all right, and listened while Mrs. Gessler added a few more details about the party, and then said abruptly: "Lucy."

"Yes?"

"I'm on the town."

"Well—you don't mean he actually left the money on the bureau, do you?"

"All but."

Mrs. Gessler sat on the corner of the table, looking at Mildred. There didn't seem to be much to say. It had all seemed so pat, so simple, and amusing yesterday, but neither of them had allowed for prophecies that merely half came true, or for dirty bastards that were goddam liars, but not quite such clucks as they should have been. A wave of helpless rage set over Mildred. She picked up the empty wine bottle, heaved it into the pantry, laughed wildly as it smashed into a hundred pieces.

Chapter 3

ROM THEN ON, Mildred knew she had to get a job. There came another little flurry of orders for cakes and pies, and she filled them, but all the time she was thinking, in a sick, frightened kind of way, or trying to think, of something she could do, some work she could get, so she could have an income, and not be put out of the house on the first of July, when the interest would be due on the mortgages Bert had put on the house. She studied the help-wanted advertisements, but there were hardly any. Each day there would be notices for cooks, maids, and chauffeurs, but she skipped quickly by them. The big advertisements, headed "Opportunity," "Salesmen Wanted," and "Men, Women, Attention"—these she passed over entirely. They savored too much of Bert's methods in getting rid of Pierce Homes. But occasionally something looked promising. One advertisement called for: "Woman, young, pleasing appearance and manners, for special work." She answered, and was excited a day or two later when she got a note, signed by a man, asking her to call at an address in the Los Feliz section of Holly-wood. She put on the print dress, made her face up nicely, and went over there.

The man received her in sweat shirt and flannels, and said he was a writer. As to what he wrote, he was quite vague, though he said his researches were extensive, and called him to many different parts of the world, where, of course, she would be expected to travel with him. He was equally vague about her duties: it appeared she would help him "collect material," "file documents," and "verify citations"; also take charge of his house, get some order into it, and check his bills, on which he feared he was being cheated. When he sat down near her, and announced he felt sure she was the person he was looking for, she became suspicious. She hadn't said a word that indicated any qualifications for the job, if indeed a job existed, and she came to the conclusion that what he wanted wasn't a research assistant, but a sweetie. She left, feeling sullen over her wasted afternoon and wasted bus fare. It was her first experience with the sexological advertiser, though she was to find out he was fairly common. Usually he was some phony calling himself a writer, an agent, or a talent scout, who had found out that for a dollar and a half's worth of newspaper space he could have a day-long procession of girls at his door, all desperate for work, all willing to do almost anything to get it.

She answered more ads, got repeated requests to call, and did call, until her shoes began to show the strain, and she had to take them constantly to the shoemaker's, for heel-straightening and polishing. She began to feel a bitter resentment against Bert, for taking the car when she needed it so badly. Nothing came of the ad-answering. She would be too late, or not qualified, or disqualified, on account of the children, or unsuitable in one way and another. She made the rounds of the department stores, and became dismally familiar with the crowd of silent people in the hallway outside the personnel offices, and the tense, desperate jockeying for position when the doors opened at ten o'clock. At only one store was she permitted to fill out a card. This was at Corasi Bros., a big place in downtown Los Angeles that specialized in household furnishings. She was first through the door here, and quickly sat down at one of the little glass-topped tables reserved for interviews. But the head of the department, addressed by everybody as Mrs. Boole, kept passing her by, and she grew furious at this injustice. Mrs. Boole was rather good-looking, and seemed to know most of the applicants by name. Mildred was so resentful that they should be dealt with ahead of her that she suddenly gathered up her gloves and started to flounce out, without being interviewed at all. But Mrs. Boole held up a finger, smiled, and came over. "Don't go. I'm sorry to keep you waiting, but most of these people are old friends, and it seems a pity not to let them know at once, so they can call at the other stores, and perhaps have a little luck. That's why I always talk to new applicants last, when I really have a little time."

Mildred sat down again, ashamed of her petulant dash for the door. When Mrs. Boole finally came over, she began to talk, and instead of answering questions in a tight-lipped, defensive way, as she had at other places, opened up a little. She alluded briefly to the break-up of her marriage, stressed her familiarity with all things having to do with kitchens, and said she was sure she could be useful in that department, as saleswoman, demonstrator, or both. Mrs. Boole measured her narrowly at that, then led her into an account of what she had been doing about getting a job. Mildred held nothing back, and after Mrs. Boole cackled gaily at the story of Harry Engel and his anchors, she felt warm tears swimming into her eyes, for she felt if she didn't have a job, at least she had a friend. It was then that Mrs. Boole had her fill out the card. "There's nothing open right now, but I'll remember what you said about the kitchenware, and if anything comes up, at least I'll know where to get hold of you."

Mildred left in such a pleasant glow that she forgot to be disappointed, and she was halfway down the hall before she realized her name was being called. Mrs. Boole was standing in the hallway, the card still in her hand, and came toward her nervously. She took Mildred's hand, held it a moment or two while she looked down at the street, many stories below. Then: "Mrs. Pierce, there's something I've got to tell you."

"Yes?"

"There aren't any jobs."

"Well, I knew things were slack, but—"

"Listen to me, Mrs. Pierce. I wouldn't say this to many of them, but you seem different from most of the applicants that come in here. I don't want you to go home thinking there's any hope. There isn't. In this store, we've taken on just two people in the last three months—one to take the place of a gentleman who was killed in an automobile accident, the other to take the place of a lady who had to retire on account of ill health. We see everybody that comes in, partly because we think we ought to, partly because we don't want to close up the department altogether. There just aren't any jobs, here or in the other stores either. I know I'm making you feel bad, but I don't want you to be—kidded."

Mildred patted her arm, and laughed. "Well my goodness, it's not your fault. And I know exactly what you mean. You don't want me to be wearing out shoes, for nothing."

"That's it. The shoes."

"But if you *do* have something—"

"Oh, if I have anything, don't worry. I'll be only too glad to let you know—by paid telegram. And, if you're down this way again, will you drop in on me? We could have lunch."

"I'll be only too glad to."

Mrs. Boole kissed her, and Mildred left, feeling footsore, hungry, and strangely happy. When she got home there was a notice hanging on the door, asking her to call for a paid telegram.

"Mrs. Pierce, it was like something in a movie. You had hardly stepped into the elevator, honestly. In fact I had you paged downstairs, hoping you hadn't left the store."

They sat down, in Mrs. Boole's private office this time, Mrs. Boole behind her big desk, Mildred in the chair beside it. Mrs. Boole went on: "I was watching you step into the down car, I was admiring your figure if you have to know why I was watching you, when this call came from the restaurant."

"You mean the store restaurant?"

"Yes, the tea room on the roof. Of course, the store doesn't have anything to do with that. It's sublet, but the manager likes to take people from our lists, just the same. He feels it makes a better tie-up, and then of course we do quite a lot of sifting ourselves, before we place a name on file, and it puts him in touch with a better class of girls."

"And what is the job?"

Mildred's mind was leaping wildly from cashier to hostess to dietician: she didn't quite know what a dietician was, but felt she could fill the bill. Mrs. Boole answered at once: "Oh, nothing very exciting. One of his waitresses got married, and he wants somebody to take her place. Just a job—but those girls do very well for a four-hour day; they're only busy at lunch, of course—and it would give you plenty of time with your own children, and home—and at least it's a job."

The idea of putting on a uniform, carrying a tray, and making her living from tips made Mildred positively ill. Her lips wanted to flutter, and she ran her tongue around inside them to keep them under control. "Why, thanks ever so much, Mrs. Boole. I realize, of course, that it's quite a nice opening—but I doubt if I'm really fitted for it."

Mrs. Boole suddenly got red, and began to talk as though she didn't quite know what she was saying. "Well, I'm sorry, Mrs. Pierce, if I got you down here about something that—perhaps you don't feel you could accept. But I somehow got the idea that you wanted work—"

"I do, Mrs. Boole, but—"

"But it's perfectly all right, my dear—"

Mrs. Boole was standing now, and Mildred was edging toward the door, her face feeling hot. Then she was in the elevator again, and when she got out on the street she hated herself, and felt that Mrs. Boole must hate her, and despise her, and regard her as a fool.

Shortly after this, she registered with an employment agency. To decide which agency, she consulted the phone book, and decided on Alice Brooks Turner, mainly on account of the crisp succinctness of her advertisement:

ACCOUNTANTS

CASHIERS

SALESMEN

SALESWOMEN

OFFICE MANAGERS

Alice Brooks Turner
Skilled Personnel Only

Miss Turner, who had a small suite in one of the downtown office buildings, turned out to be a trim little person, not much older than Mildred, and a little on the hard-boiled side. She smoked her cigarette in a long holder, with which she waved Mildred to a small desk, and without looking up, told her to fill out a card. Mildred, remembering to write neatly, furnished what seemed to her an absurd amount of information about herself, from her age, weight, height, and nationality, to her religion, education, and exact marital status. Most of these questions struck her as irrelevant, and some of them as impertinent. However, she answered them. When she came to the question: What type of work desired?—she hesitated. What type of work did she desire? Any work that would pay her something, but obviously she couldn't say that. She wrote: Receptionist. As in the case of Dietician, she wasn't quite sure what it meant, but it had caught her ear these last few weeks, and at least it had an authoritative sound to it.

Then she came to the great yawning spaces in which she was to fill in the names and addresses of her former employers. Regretfully she wrote: Not previously employed. Then she signed the card, walked over, and handed it in. Miss Turner waved her to a chair, studied the card, shook her head, and pitched it on the desk. "You haven't got a chance."

"Why not?"

"Do you know what a receptionist is?"

"I'm not sure, but—"

"A receptionist is a lazy dame that can't do anything on earth, and wants to sit out front where everybody can watch her do it. She's the one in the black silk dress, cut low in the neck and high in the legs, just inside the gate, in front of that little one-position switchboard, that she gets a right number out of now and then, mostly then. You know, the one that tells you to have a seat, Mr. Doakes will see you in just a few minutes. Then she goes on showing her legs and polishing her nails. If she sleeps with Doakes she gets twenty bucks a week, if not she gets twelve. In other words, nothing personal about it and I don't want to hurt your feelings, but by the looks of this card I'd say that was you."

"It's quite all right. I sleep fine."

If this bravado had any effect on Miss Turner, there was no sign of it. She nodded, and said: "I'm sure you sleep fine. Don't we all? But I'm not running a house of call, and it just happens that at the moment receptionists are out. That was then. In those good old days. When even a hockshop had to have this receptionist thing out there in front to show it had class. But then they found out she wasn't strictly necessary. They began sleeping with their wives, and I guess it worked all right. Anyway, the birth rate went up. So I guess you're out of luck."

"Receptionist isn't the only thing I can do."

"Yes, it is."

"You don't give me much chance to tell you."

"If there was something else you could do, you'd have put it down in great big letters, right on this card. When you say receptionist, that's all I want to know. There's no more after that, and no use your wasting my time, and me wasting yours. I'll file your card, but I told you once and I'm telling you again, you haven't got a chance."

The interview, obviously, was ended, but Mildred forced herself to make a little speech, a sales talk. As she talked she warmed up to it, explaining that she was married before she was seventeen, and that while other women were learning professions, she had been making a home, raising two children, "not generally regarded as a disgraceful career." Now that her marriage had broken up, she wanted to know if it was fair that she be penalized for what she had done, and denied the right to earn her living like anybody else. Furthermore, she said, she hadn't been asleep all that time, even if she had been married. She had taught herself to be a good housekeeper and a fine cook, was in fact earning such little income as she had by peddling her cookery around the neighborhood. If she could do that, she could do other things. She kept repeating: "What I do, I do well."

Miss Turner pulled out a lot of drawers, set them in a row on her desk. They were filled with cards of different colors. Looking intently at Mildred, she said: "I told you you're not qualified. O.K., you can take a look here and see what I mean. These three drawers are employers, people that call me when they want somebody. And they call me, too. They call me because I'm on the level with them and save them the trouble of talking to nitwits like you. You see those pink ones? That means 'No Jews.' See the blues? 'No Gentiles' —not many of them, but a few. That's got nothing to do with you, but it gives you an idea. People are sold over this desk just like cattle in the Chicago yards, and for exactly the same reason: they've got the points the buyer wants. All right, now take a look at something that does concern you. See those greens? That means 'No Married Women.' "

"Why, may I ask?"

"Because right in the middle of rush hour you wonderful little homemakers have a habit of getting a call that Willie's got the croup, and out you run, and maybe you come back next day, and maybe you come back next week."

"Somebody has to look after Willie."

"These people, these employers on the greens, they're not much interested in Willie. And another habit you wonderful homemakers have got is running up a lot of bills you thought friend husband would pay, and then when he wouldn't you had to get a job. And then the first pay check you draw, there's eighteen attachments on it—and life's too short."

"Do you call that fair?"

"I call them green. I go by the cards."

"I don't owe a cent."

"Not one?"

Mildred thought guiltily of the interest that would be due July 1, and Miss Turner, seeing the flicker in her eye, said: "I thought so. . . . Now take a look at these other drawers. They're all applicants. These are stenographers—a dime a dozen, but at least they can do *something*. These are qualified secretaries—a dime a dozen too, but they rate a different file. These are stenographers with scientific experience, nurses, laboratory assistants, chemists, all able to take charge of a clinic, or run an office for three or four doctors, or do hospital work. Why would I recommend you ahead of any of them? Some of those girls are Ph.D.'s and Sc.D.'s from U.C.L.A. and other places. Here's a whole file of stenographers that are expert bookkeepers. Any one of them could take charge of all the office work for a small firm, and still have time for a little sleeping. Here are sales people, men and women, every one of them with an A-1 reference—they can really move goods. They're all laid off, there's no goods moving, but I don't see how I could put you ahead of them. And here's the preferred list. Look at it, a whole drawerful, men and women, every one of them a real executive, or auditor, or manager of some business, and when I recommend one, I know somebody is getting something for his money. They're all home, sitting by their phones, hoping I'll call. I won't call. I've got nothing to tell them. What I'm trying to get through your head is: You haven't got a chance. Those people, it hurts me, it makes me lie awake nights, that I've got nothing for them. They deserve something, and there's not a thing I can do. But there's not a chance I'd slip you ahead of any one of them. You're not qualified. There's not a thing on earth you can do, and I hate people that can't do anything."

"How do I qualify?"

Mildred's lips were fluttering again, the way they had in Mrs. Boole's office. Miss Turner looked quickly away, then said: "Can I make a suggestion?"

"You certainly can."

"I wouldn't call you a raving beauty, but you've got an A-1 shape and you say you cook fine and sleep fine. Why don't you forget about a job, hook yourself a man, and get married again?"

"I tried that."

"Didn't work?"

"I don't seem to be able to kid you much. It was the first thing I thought of, and just for a little while I seemed to be doing all right. But then, I guess two little children disqualified me, even there. That wasn't what he said, but—"

"Hey, hey, you're breaking my heart."

"I didn't know you had a heart."

"Neither did I."

The cold logic of Miss Turner's harangue reached Mildred's bowels, where the tramping, waiting, and hoping of the last few weeks hadn't. She went home, collapsed, and wept for an hour. But next day she doggedly registered at three more agencies. She took to doing desperate things, like turning suddenly into business places, as she was passing them on the street, and asking for an opening. One day she entered an office building and, beginning at the top floor, called on every firm, in only two places getting past the gate. All the time the thought of July 1 haunted her, and she got weaker, paler, and tackier-looking. The print dress was pressed so many times that she searched the seams anxiously every time she put the iron on it. She lived on oatmeal and bread, reserving for the children such eggs, chicken, and milk as she could buy.

One morning, to her surprise, there came a card from Miss Turner, asking her to call. She dressed in about four minutes, caught the nine o'clock bus, and was in the familiar little office by nine thirty. Miss Turner waved her to a seat. "Something's come up, so I dropped you that card."

"What is it?"

"Housekeeper."

". . . Oh."

"It's not what you think, so don't employ that tone of voice. I mean, there's no sleeping in it, so far as I know. And it means nothing to me. I don't handle domestic help, so I won't collect a dime. But I was over in Beverly the other night, and got talking with a lady that's going to marry a director, and he doesn't know it yet, but his house is due for a big shake-up. So she wants a housekeeper. So, on account of all that fine domestic efficiency you were telling me about, I told her about you, and I think it's yours if you want it. Children O.K. You'll have your own quarters and I think you can nick her for one fifty if you get tough, but you'd better ask for two hundred and come down. That's over and above all your uniforms, food, laundry, heat, light, and quarters, and quite a lot more than most of my talented stable are making."

"I hardly know what to say."

"Make up your mind. I've got to let her know."

"Why did you think of me, for this?"

"Didn't I tell you? You broke my goddam heart."

"Yes but—it's the second time lately I've had an offer of this kind. Not long ago a lady offered me a job as—a waitress."

"And you turned it *down?*"

"I had to."

"Why?"

"I can't go home and face my children if they know I've been working all day at taking tips, and wearing a uniform, and mopping up crumbs."

"But you can face them with nothing for them to eat?"

"I'd rather not talk about that."

"Listen, this is just one woman's opinion, and it may be all wrong. I've got my own little business, and it's all shot, and I'm just about holding my own if I eat in the tea rooms instead of the Biltmore. But if that goes, and I have to choose between my belly and my pride, I'm telling right now, I'm picking my belly every time. I mean, if I had to wear a uniform, I'd do it."

"I'll go over there, as a courtesy to you."

For the first time, Miss Turner departed from her hard-boiled manner, and showed some sign of annoyance. "What have I got to do with it? Either you want this place or you don't. If you don't, just say so and all I've got to do is call up and tell her, and that lets me out. But if you do want it, for God's sake get over there and act like you mean it."

"I'll go, as a courtesy to you."

Miss Turner got out a card and savagely wrote a note on it, her eyes snapping as she handed it over to Mildred. "All right, you wanted to know why that lady offered you a job as waitress, and why I recommended you for this. It's because you've let half your life slip by without learning anything but sleeping, cooking, and setting the table, and that's all you're good for. So get over there. It's what you've got to do, so you may as well start doing it."

Shaken, Mildred got on the Sunset bus, but the address was unfamiliar to her, and she had to ask the conductor where to get off. At Coldwater Canon Drive, where he set her down, there was no sign of the street. and she started wandering around an unfamiliar neighborhood, trying to get her bearings. The houses were big and forbidding, with driveways in front of them and clipped grass all around, and she couldn't find the courage to approach one. Of pedestrians there were none, and she plodded around for the better part of an hour, peering at each street sign, losing all sense of direction in the winding streets. She got into a hysteria of rage at Bert, for taking the car, since if she had that, she would not only be saved walking, but could slip into a filling station and inquire in a self-respecting way, having the attendant produce maps. But here there were no filling stations, nobody she could ask, nothing but miles of deserted pavments, shaded by frowning trees. Finally a laundry truck pulled up, and she got the driver to straighten her out. She found the house, a big mansion with a low hedge around it, went up to the door and rang. A white-coated house man appeared. When she asked for Mrs. Forrester he bowed and stepped aside for her to enter. Then he noticed she had no car, and froze. "Housekeeper?"

"Yes, I was sent by—"

"Back way."

His eyes glistening with suddenly secreted venom, he closed the door, and she savagely trudged around to the back. Here he admitted her, and told her to wait. She was in a sort of service foyer, and in the kitchen, which was only a few steps away, she could see a cook and a waitress eyeing her. He returned, led her through dark, cool halls to a library, and left her. She sat down, glad to rest her aching feet. In a few minutes Mrs. Forrester came in. She was a tall woman in flowing negligee, who wafted graciousness all around her, putting the world at its ease. Mildred got up, handed over Miss Turner's note, and sat down while Mrs. Forrester read it. Evidently it was flattering, for it evoked one or two nods and clucks. Then Mrs. Forrester smilingly looked up. "It's customary, Mildred, for the servant to sit on the *Mistress's* invitation, not on her own *initiative*."

Mildred was so startled at hearing herself addressed by her first name that it was a second or two before the sense of this made its way to her mind. Then she shot up as though her legs were made of springs, her face hot, her mouth dry. "Oh. I beg your pardon."

"It's perfectly all right, but on little things, especially with an inexperienced woman, I find it well to begin at the beginning. Do sit down. We've many things to talk about, and it'll make me quite uncomfortable to have you standing there."

"This is all right."

"Mildred, I *invited* you to sit *down*."

Her throat throbbing, tears of rage swimming into her eyes, Mildred sat down, while Mrs. Forrester spoke grandly of her plans for reorganizing the house. Apparently it was her intended husband's house, though what she was doing in it, in negligee, a full month before the wedding, she didn't bother to explain. Mildred, it appeared, would have her own quarters, above the garage. She herself had two children by a former marriage, and of course no fraternization between children could be permitted, though there need be no trouble about that, as Mildred would have her own entrance on the lane, and "all such questions can be worked out." Mildred listened, or tried to, but suddenly a vision leaped in front of her eyes. She saw Veda, haughty, snobbish Veda, being told that she had to come in the back way, and that she couldn't fraternize with Forrester offspring. Then Mildred knew that if she took this place she would lose Veda. Veda would go to her father, her grandfather, the police, or a park bench, but not even whips could make her stay with Mildred, in the Forrester garage. A surge of pride in the cold child swept over her, and she stood up. "I don't think I'm quite the person you want here, Mrs. Forrester."

"The *Mistress* terminates the *interview*, Mildred."

"Mrs. Pierce, if you don't mind. And I'm terminating it."

It was Mrs. Forrester's turn to shoot up as though her legs were made of springs, but if she contemplated further instruction in the relation of the servant to the Mistress, she thought better of it. She found herself looking into Mildred's squint, and it flickered somewhat ominously. Pressing a button, she announced coldly: "I'll have Harris show you out."

"I'll find my way, thank you."

Picking up her handbag, Mildred left the library, but instead of turning toward the kitchen, she marched straight for the front door, closing it calmly behind her. She floated to the bus stop on air, rode into Hollywood without seeing what she was passing. But when she found she had got off too soon, and had to walk two blocks for the Glendale connection, she wilted and moved on trembling legs. At Hollywood Boulevard, the bench was full, and she had to stand. Then everything began spinning around, and the sunshine seemed unnaturally bright. She knew she had to sit down, or topple over, right there on the sidewalk. Two or three doors away was a restaurant, and she lurched into it. It was crowded with people eating lunch, but she found a small table against the wall, and sat down.

After picking up the menu, and dropping it quickly so the girl wouldn't notice her trembling hands, she asked for a ham sandwich, with lettuce, a glass of milk, and a glass of water, but she was an interminable time getting served. The girl puttered about, complained of the service that was demanded of her, and the little that she got for it, and Mildred had a vague suspicion that she was being accused of stealing a tip. She was too near collapse for argument, however, and beyond repeating that she wanted the water right away, said nothing. Presently her order arrived, and she sat apathetically munching it down. The water cleared her head, and the food revived her, but there was still a quivering in her bowels that didn't seem to have anything to do with the walking, fretting, and quarreling she had done all morning. She felt gloomy indeed, and when she heard a resounding *slap*, a few inches from her ear, she barely turned her head. The girl who had served her was facing another girl, and even as Mildred looked, proceeded to deal out a second loud slap. "I caught you, you dirty little crook! I caught you red-handed, right in the act!"

"Girls! *Girls!*"

"I caught her! She's been doing it right along, stealing tips off my tables! She stole ten cents off eighteen, before that lady sat down, and now she stole fifteen out of a forty-cent tip right here—*and I seen her do it!*"

In a moment the place was like a beehive, with other girls shouting their accusations, the hostess trying to restore order, and the manager flying out of the kitchen. He was a rotund little Greek, with flashing black eyes, and he summarily fired both girls and apologized profusely to the customers. When the two of them sullenly paraded out, in their street clothes, a few minutes later, Mildred was so lost in her reflections that she didn't even give her girl a nod. It was not until the hostess appeared in an apron, and began serving orders, that she woke up to the fact that she was face to face with one of the major decisions of her life. They needed help, that was plain, and needed it now. She stared at the water glass, twisted her mouth into a final, irrevocable decision. She would not do this kind of work, if she starved first. She put a dime on the table. She got up. She went to the cashier's desk, and paid her check. Then, as though walking to the electric chair, she turned around, headed for the kitchen.

Chapter 4

THE NEXT TWO HOURS, to Mildred, were a waking nightmare. She didn't get the job quite as easily as she had supposed she would. The proprietor, whose name was apparently
Makadoulis, but whom everybody addressed as Mr. Chris, was willing enough, especially as the hostess kept shrilling in his ear:
"You've got to put somebody on! It's a mess out there! It's a mess!"
But when the girls saw Mildred, and divined what she was there for,
they gathered around, and passionately vetoed her application, unless Anna was taken back. Anna, she gathered, was the girl who had
waited on her, and the aggressor in the fight, but as all of them
apparently had been victims of the thefts, they seemed to regard her
as their representative in a sense, and didn't propose to have her
made a goat. They argued their case in quite noisy fashion, letting
the counters pile up with orders while they screamed, and making
appropriate gestures. One of these gestures wiped a plate into space,
with a club sandwich on it. Mildred caught it as it fell. The sandwich was wholly wrecked, but she put it together again, with deft
fingers, and restored it to its place on the counter. The Chef, a gigantic man addressed as Archie, watched her exhibition of juggling
with impassive stolidity, but when the reconstructed sandwich was
back on the counter he gave her a curt nod. Then he began banging
on the steam table with the palm of his hand. This restored quiet as
nothing else had been able to do. Mr. Chris turned to the girls.
"Hokay, hokay."

The question of Anna being thus settled, the hostess hustled Mildred back to the lockers, where she unlocked a door and held out a menu. "Take off your dress and while I'm finding a uniform to fit, study this menu, so you can be some use. What size do you wear?"

"Ten."

"You worked in a restaurant before?"

"No."

"Study it, specially prices."

Mildred took off her dress, hung it in the locker, and stared at the menu. There were fifty-five- and sixty-five-cent lunches on it, as well as appetizers, steaks, chops, desserts, and fountain drinks, most of these bearing fancy names that were unintelligible to her. In spite of her best concentration most of it was a jumble. In a minute or two the hostess was back with her uniform, a pale blue affair, with white collar, cuffs, and pockets. She slipped into it. "And here's your apron. You furnish your uniform; it comes off your first check, three ninety-five; you get it at cost, and you keep it laundered. And if you don't suit us, we charge you twenty-five cents' rent on the uniform; that comes out of your check too, but you don't have the whole uniform to pay for unless we really take you on. The pay is twenty-five cents an hour, and you keep your own tips."

"And what's your name, Miss?"

"Ida. What's yours?"

"Mildred."

They started for the dining room, but going through the kitchen Ida kept talking into her ear. "I'm giving you a light station, see? Three, four, five, and six, all them little booths against the wall. That's so you don't get no fours. Singles and twos are easier. All them that's just come in, you take them, and them that's already started on their lunches, I'll take care of them myself. That's so you don't get mixed up on them other girls' books."

They reached the dining room, and Ida pointed out the station. Three of the tables were occupied by people who had given their orders before the fight started, the fourth by a pair of women who had just come in. All were getting annoyed at the delay in service. But still Mildred wasn't permitted to start. Ida led her to the cashier, a fish-faced blonde who began savagely telling Ida of the complaints she had received, and of the five people who had already walked out. Ida cut her off, had her issue Mildred a new book. "You've got to account for every check, see? In here you mark your number, you're No. 9. Here you mark the number of the table, here the number of customers on the check. Down here, put down everything they order, and the first thing you got to learn: don't make no mistake on a check. It's all booked against you, and if you make a mistake, it's deducted, *and you got to pay for it.*"

With this ominous warning in her ears, Mildred at last approached the two women who were waiting to have their orders taken, handed them their menus, and inquired what they were going to have. They replied they weren't sure they were going to have anything, and wanted to know what kind of place this was anyway, to let people sit around without even asking them if they minded waiting. Mildred, almost in hysteria by now with what she had been through that day, felt a hot impulse to take them down a few notches, as she had taken Mrs. Forrester. However, she managed a smile, said there had been a little trouble, and that if they could just be patient a minute or two, she would see they were served at once. Then, taking a quick lunge at the only thing she remembered about the menu, she added: "The roast chicken is awfully good today."

Slightly mollified, they chose chicken on the sixty-five-cent lunch, but one of them said loudly: "See there's no gravy on mine in any way, shape, or form. I hate brown gravy."

"Yes, Miss. I'll remember."

Mildred started for the kitchen, barely missing a girl who appeared at the *out* door. Swerving in time, she dived through the *in* door and called to Archie: "Two roast chicken. One without gravy."

But the ubiquitous Ida was at her elbow, calling frantically to Archie: "Hold one gravy, hold it!" Then she yanked Mildred aside, and half screamed at her: "You got to call it right! You can't work nowhere without you're in good with the Chef, and you got to call it right for him. Get this: If there's any trimmings they don't want, you don't call it *without* 'em, you call it *hold* 'em!"

"Yes, Miss."

"You got to be in good with the Chef!"

Dimly Mildred began to understand why that great paw, banging on the steam table, had restored order when Mr. Chris had been mobbed like a Junebug in a flock of angry hens. She had observed that the waitresses dipped their own soup, so she now got bowls and filled them with the cream of tomato that her customers had ordered. But there was no surcease from Ida. "Pick up your starters! Pick up your starters!" At Mildred's blank look, Ida grabbed two plates of salad from the sandwich counter, whipped two pats of butter onto two small plates, and motioned Mildred to get the four plates in there, quick. "Have they got water?"

"Not yet."

"For crying out loud."

Ida made a dive for the lift spigot, drew two glasses of water, slid them expertly so they fetched up beside the four plates. Then she pitched two napkins up against the water glasses. "Get in there with them—if they haven't walked out on you."

Mildred blinked helplessly at this formidable array. "Well—can I have a tray?"

In despair, Ida picked up plates, glasses, and napkins, so they were spread across her fingers like playing cards, and balanced halfway up her arm. "Get the soup, and come on." She was gone before Mildred could recover from the speed of her legerdemain. The soup Mildred picked up gingerly, kicking the *out* door open as she saw the others doing. Taking care not to spill any of it, she eventually reached the table. Ida was smoothing the two women down, and from their glances Mildred knew it had been fully explained to them that she was a new girl, and that allowances had to be made for her. At once they began amusing themselves by calling her January and Slewfoot. Lest she show resentment, she started for the kitchen, but it seemed impossible to get away from Ida. "Pick up something! Don't never make a trip, in or out, without something in your hand. You'll trot all day and you'll never get done! Get them dirty dishes over there, on No. 3. Pick up something!"

The afternoon dragged on. Mildred felt stupid, heavy, slow, and clumsy. Try as she would to "pick up something," dirty dishes piled on her tables, and unserved orders in the kitchen, until she thought she would go insane from the confusion. Her trouble, she discovered, was that she hadn't the skill to carry more than two dishes at a time. Trays were prohibited here, Ida informed her, because the aisles were so narrow they would lead to crashes, and this meant that everything had to be carried by hand. But the trick of balancing half a dozen dishes at a time was beyond her. She tried it once, but her hand crumpled under the weight, and a hot fudge sundae almost went on the floor. The climax came around three o'clock. The place was empty by then and the fish-faced cashier came back to inform her she had lost a check. The subsequent figuring showed that the check was for fifty-five cents, which meant that her whole hourly wage was lost. She wanted to throw everything in the place at the cashier's head, but didn't. She said she was sorry, gathered up the last of her dirty dishes, and went back with them.

In the kitchen, Mr. Chris and Ida were in a huddle, evidently talking about her. From their expressions as they started toward her, she sensed that the verdict was unfavorable, and she waited miserably for them to get it over with, so she could get away from Ida, and the Filipino dish washers, and the smell, and the noise, and drearily wonder what she was going to do next. But as they passed Archie, he looked up and made a gesture such as an umpire makes in calling a man safe at the plate. They looked surprised, but that seemed to settle it. Mr. Chris said "hokay, hokay," and went into the dining room, Ida came over to Mildred. "Well personally, Mildred, I don't think you're suited to the work at all, and Mr. Chris, he wasn't a bit impressed either, but the Chef thinks you'll do, so against our better judgment we're going to give you a trial."

Mildred remembered the reconstructed club sandwich and the little nod she had received from Archie, realized that it was indeed important to be in good with the Chef. But by now her dislike of Ida was intense, and she made no effort to keep the acid out of her voice as she said: "Well please thank Archie for me and tell him I hope I won't disappoint him." She spoke loud enough for Archie to hear, and was rewarded with a loud, ursine cackle.

Ida went on: "Your hours are from eleven in the morning, ten thirty if you want breakfast, to three in the afternoon, and if you want lunch then, you can have it. We don't do a big dinner business here, so we only keep three girls on at night, but they take turns. You're on call twice a week from five to nine, same wages as in the daytime. Sundays we're closed. You'll need white shoes. Ask for nurses' regulation at any of the stores, two ninety-five. Well what's the matter, Mildred, don't you want the job?"

"I'm a little tired, that's all."

"I don't wonder, the way you trot."

When she got home, the children had just arrived from school. She gave them milk and cookies and shooed them out to play. Then she changed her dress and put slippers on her aching feet. She was about to lie down, when she heard a yoo-hoo, and Mrs. Gessler joined her, in a somewhat dark humor. Ike, it appeared, hadn't come home last night. He had phoned around nine, telling her of a hurry call that would prevent his arrival until next morning. It was all in his line of work, he had appeared at ten as he said he would, and yet . . . The extent to which Mrs. Gessler trusted Ike, or anybody, was evidently very slight.

Mildred presently asked: "Lucy, can you lend me three dollars?"

"More if you want it."

"No, thanks. I've taken a job, and need some things."

"Right away?"

"In the morning."

Mrs. Gessler went out, and Mildred went back to the kitchen to make her some tea. When she came back she sat down gratefully to the smoking cup, and flipped Mildred a bill. "I didn't have three, but here's five."

"Thanks. I'll pay it back."

"What kind of a job?"

"Oh—just a job."

"I'm sorry . . . But if it's that kind of a job, I hope you picked a five-dollar house. You're too young for the two-dollar trade, and personally I wouldn't like sailors."

"I'm a waitress. In a hash house."

"It rhymes up the same way."

"Just about."

"That's funny, though. It was none of my business, but all the time you were answering those ads, and trying to get hired on as a saleswoman, or whatever it was—I kept wondering to myself why you didn't try something like this."

"Why, Lucy?"

"Suppose you did get a job as a saleswoman? What would you get for it? No matter how they figure it up, when you're selling goods you get paid on commission, because it stands to reason if you weren't making commission they wouldn't pay you. But who's buying any goods? You'd have just stood around some store, all day long, waiting for the chance to make a living, and not making it. People *eat*, though, even now. You'll have something coming in. And then, I don't know. It may sound funny but at selling, I'd say you just weren't the type. At *this*, though—"

All that Mrs. Boole had said, all that Miss Turner had said, all that her bowels had told her, after that trip to Beverly Hills, came sweeping over Mildred, and suddenly she dived for the bathroom. The milk, the sandwich, the tea, all came up, while moaning sobs racked her. Then Mrs. Gessler was beside her, holding her head, wiping her mouth, giving her water, leading her gently to bed. Here she collapsed in a paroxysm of hysteria, sobbing, shaking, writhing. Mrs. Gessler took her clothes off, massaged her back, patted her, told her to let it come, not to try to hold back. She relaxed, and cried until tears gushed down her face, and let Mrs. Gessler wipe them away as they came. After a long time she was quiet, but it was a glum, hopeless quiet. Then: "I can't do it, Lucy! I—just—can't—do —it."

"Baby! Do what?"

"Wear a uniform. And take their tips. And face those awful people. They called me names. And one of them grabbed my leg. Ooh—I can feel it yet. He put his hand clear up to—"

"What do they pay you?"

"Twenty-five cents an hour."

"And tips extra?"

"Yes."

"Baby, you're nuts. Those tips will bring in a couple of dollars a day, and you'll be making—why, at least twenty dollars a week, more money than you've seen since Pierce Homes blew up. You've got to do it, for your own sake. Nobody pays any attention to that uniform stuff any more. I bet you look cute in one. And besides, people have to do what they can do—"

"Lucy, stop! I'll go mad! I'll—"

At Mrs. Gessler's look, Mildred pulled herself together, at least tried to make intelligible her violent outburst. "That's what they've been telling me, the employment people, everybody, that all I'm good for is putting on a uniform and waiting on other people, and—"

"And maybe they're right, just at the present moment. Because maybe what they're trying to tell you is exactly what I'm trying to tell you. You're in a spot. It's all right to be proud, and I love you for it. But you're starving to death, baby. Don't you suppose my heart's been heavy for you? Don't you know I'd have sent roast beef in here, or ham, or whatever I had, every night, except that I knew you'd hate me for it? You've just got to take this job—"

"I know it. I can't, and yet I've got to."

"Then if you've got to you've got to, so quit bawling."

"Promise me one thing, Lucy."

"Anything."

"Don't tell anybody."

"I wouldn't even tell Ike."

"I don't care about Ike, or any of these people, what they think. It's on account of the children, and I don't want anybody at all to know it, for fear somebody'll say something to them. They mustn't know it—and specially not Veda."

"That Veda, if you ask me, has some funny ideas."

"I respect her ideas."

"I don't."

"You don't understand her. She has something in her that I thought I had, and now I find I haven't. Pride, or whatever it is. Nothing on earth could make Veda do what I'm going to do."

"That pride, I wouldn't give a snap of my finger for it. You're quite right about her. Veda wouldn't do it herself, but she's perfectly willing to let you do it and eat the cake."

"I want her to have it. Cake—not just bread."

During the six weeks Mildred had been looking for work, she had seen quite a little of Wally. He had dropped around one night, after the children had gone to bed, and was quite apologetic about what he had said, and penitently asserted he had made a sap of himself. She said there were no hard feelings, and brought him into the den, though she didn't bother to light a fire or serve a drink. But when he sat down beside her and put his arm around her, she got up and made one of her little speeches. She said she would be glad to see him any time, she wanted him as a friend. However, it must be distinctly understood that what was past was past, not to be brought up again under any circumstances. If he wanted to see her on that basis, she would try to make him welcome, and she really wanted him to come. He said gee that was swell of her, and if she really meant it, it was okey-doke by him.

Thereafter he dropped by rather often, arriving usually around nine, for she didn't want the children to know quite how much she was seeing him. Once, when they were spending a weekend at the Pierces', he came on Saturday evening and "took her out." She expressed a preference for a quiet place, for she was afraid the print dress wouldn't pass muster anywhere else, so they took a drive and ate in a roadside inn near Ventura. But one night, when her affairs were beginning to get desperate, he happened to sit beside her on the sofa again, and she didn't move. When he put his arm around her, in a casual, friendly kind of way, she didn't resist, and when he pulled her head on his shoulder she let it stay there. They sat a long time without speaking. So, with the door tightly locked, the shades pulled down, and the keyhole stuffed up, they resumed their romance, there in the den. Romance, perhaps, wasn't quite the word, for of that emotion she felt not the slightest flicker. Whatever it was, it afforded two hours of relief, of forgetfulness.

This evening, she found herself hoping that Wally might come, so she wouldn't have to think about the uniform she would have to buy in the morning, or the sentence she would begin serving. But when the bell rang she was a little surprised, for it was only a few minutes after seven. She went to the door, and instead of Wally standing there, it was Bert. "Oh. Why—hello, stranger."

"Mildred, how are you?"

"Can't complain. How's yourself?"

"O.K. Just thought I'd drop around for a little visit, and maybe pick up a couple of things I left in the desk, while I'm about it."

"Well come in."

But suddenly there were such whoops from the back of the house that any further discussion of his business had to be postponed indefinitely. Both children came running, and were swept into his arms, and solemnly measured, to determine how much they had grown since he saw them. His verdict was "at least two inches, maybe three." As Mildred suspected he had seen them both the previous weekend, this seemed a rapid rate of growth indeed, but if this was supposed to be a secret, she didn't care to unmask it, and so acquiesced in three inches, and it became official. She brought them all back to the den, and Bert took a seat on the sofa, and both children snuggled up beside him. Mildred told him the main news about them: how they had got good report cards from school, how Veda was doing splendidly with her piano practice, how Ray had a new tooth. It was forthwith exhibited, and as it was a molar, required a deal of cheek-stretching before it came clearly into view. But Bert admired it profusely, and found a penny to contribute, in commemoration thereof.

Both children showed him their new possessions: dolls, brought by Mrs. Gessler from San Pedro a few days before; the gold crowns they were to wear at the pageant that would mark the closing of school in two weeks; some balls, translucent dice, and perfume bottles they had obtained in trades with other children. Then Bert asked Mildred about various acquaintances, and she answered in friendly fashion. But as this took the spotlight off the children, they quickly became bored. After a spell of ball-bouncing, which Mildred stopped, and a spell of recitations from the school pageant, which wound up in a quarrel over textual accuracy, Ray began a stubborn campaign to show Daddy the new sand bucket her grandfather had given her. As the bucket was in the garage, and Mildred didn't feel like going out there, Ray began to pout. Then Veda, with an air of saving a difficult situation, said: "Aren't you terribly thirsty, Father? Mother, would you like me to open the Scotch?"

Mildred was as furious as she ever permitted herself to get at Veda. It was the same old Scotch, and she had been saving it against that dreadful day when she might have to sell it, to buy bread. That Veda even knew it existed, much less how to open it, she had no idea. And if it were opened, that meant that Bert would sit there, and sit there, and sit there, until every drop of it was gone, and there went her Scotch, and there went her evening.

At Veda's remark, Ray forgot about the sand bucket, and began to shriek: "Yes, Daddy, we're going to have a drink, we're going to get drunk!" When Bert said, "I might be able to stand a drink, if coaxed," Mildred knew the Scotch was doomed. She went to the bedroom, got it out of the closet, went to the kitchen, and opened it. She turned out ice cubes, set glasses on a tray, found the lone seltzer siphon that had been there since winter. When she was nearly done, Veda appeared. "Can I help you, Mother?"

"Who asked you to go snooping around my closet to find out whether there was any liquor there or not?"

"I didn't know there was any secret about it."

"And hereafter, I'll do the inviting."

"But, Mother, it's Father."

"Don't stand there and look me in the eye and pretend you don't know what I'm talking about. You know you had no business saying what you did, and you knew it at the time, I could tell by the cheeky look on your face."

"Very well, Mother. It shall be as you say."

"And stop that silly way of talking."

"But I remind you, just the same, that there was none of this kind of stinginess when Father was doing the inviting. Things have indeed changed here, and not for the better, alas. One might think peasants had taken over the house."

"Do you know what a peasant is?"

"A peasant is a—very ill-bred person."

"Sometimes, Veda, I wonder if you have good sense."

Veda stalked out, and Mildred grimly arranged the tray, wondering why Veda could put her so easily on the defensive, and hurt her so.

Having a drink was a gay ritual in the household, one that had started when Bert made his bathtub gin, and that proceeded on its prescribed course tonight. First he poured two stiff drinks for the children, cluck-clucking loudly at what rummies they were getting to be, and observing that he didn't know what the younger generation was coming to anyway. Then he poured two light drinks for himself and Mildred, containing perhaps two drops of liquor apiece. Then he put in ice and fizz water, set the drinks on the tray and offered them around. But by a fascinating switcheroo, which Mildred never quite understood, he always contrived to give the children the light drinks, himself and Mildred the others. So adroit was this sleight-of-hand, that the children, in spite of their sharpest watching and concentrating, never got the drinks that were supposedly prepared for them. In the day when all the drinks were exactly the same color, there was always a delightful doubt about it: Bert said the children *had* got their drinks, and as there was at least a whiff of juniper in all the glasses, they usually decided to agree. Tonight, although the switcheroo went off as smoothly as ever, the color of the Scotch betrayed him. But on his plea of fatigue, and the need of a stimulant, they agreed to accept the light drinks, so he set one of the stiff ones for Mildred, and took the other himself.

It was a ritual, but after the preliminaries were out of the way, it was enjoyed by each child differently. To Veda, it was an opportunity to stick out her little finger, to quaff elegantly, to play Constance Bennett. She regarded it as an occasion for high-toned conversation, and plied her father with lofty questions about "conditions." He replied seriously, and at some length, for he regarded such inquiries as signs of high mentality on Veda's part. He said that while things had been mighty bad for some time, he now saw definite signs of improvement, and believed "we're due to turn the corner pretty soon."

But to Ray, it was a chance to "get drunk," as she called it, and this she did with the utmost enthusiasm. As soon as she got half of her fizz water down, she jumped up and began spinning around in the middle of the floor, laughing at the top of her lungs. Mildred caught her glass when this started, and held it for her, and she spun around until she was dizzy and fell down, in a paroxysm of delight. Something always caught in Mildred's throat when this wild dance began. She felt, in some vague way, that she ought to stop it, but the child was so delightful that she never could make herself do it. So now she watched, with the tears starting out of her eyes, for the moment forgetting the Scotch. But Veda, no longer the center of the stage, said: "Personally, I think it's a disgusting exhibition."

Ray now went into the next phase of the ritual. This was a sing-song recitation her father had taught her, and went as follows:

> *I went to the animals' fair,*
> *The birds and the beasts were there,*
> *The old baboon*
> *By the light of the moon*
> *Was combing his auburn hair;*
> *The monkey he got drunk,*
> *And fell on the elephant's trunk,*
> *The elephant sneezed*
> *And fell on his knees—*
> *And what became of the monkety-monk?*

However, as Ray recited it, there were certain changes. "Beasts" was a little beyond her, so the line became "the birds and the bees." "Auburn" was a little difficult too, so the old baboon acquired a coat of "old brown hair." The "monkety-monk" was such a tempting mouthful that he became the "monkety-monkety-monkety-monkety-monk," a truly fabulous beast. While she was reciting, her father contrived to slip off his belt and stuff the buckle down the back of his neck, so that suddenly, when he pulled the free end over his head and began trumpeting on all fours, he was a sufficiently plausible elephant for any animals' fair. Ray began circling around, coming nearer and nearer with her recitation. When she was almost on him, and had tweaked his trunk two or three times, he gave a series of mighty sneezes, so that they completely prostrated him. When he opened his eyes Ray was nowhere to be seen. He now went into a perfect dither of anxiety over what had happened to her, put his head in the fireplace and called loudly up the chimney: "Monkety, monkety, monk."

"Have you looked in the closet?"

"Mildred, I bet that's just where she is."

He opened the closet, put his head in, and called: "Hey." Mildred suggested the hallway, and he looked out there. Indeed, he looked everywhere, becoming more alarmed every minute. Presently, in a dreadful tone, he said: "Mildred, you don't suppose that monk was completely *atomized*, do you?"

"I've heard of things like that happening."

"That would be terrible."

Veda picked up her glass, stuck out her little finger, took a fastidious sip. "Well, Father, I don't really see why you should get so upset about it. It seems to me anybody could see she's right behind the sofa."

"For that, you can go to bed."

Mildred's eyes blazed as she spoke, and Veda got up very quickly. But Bert paid no attention. He draped the belt over his head again, got down on his hands and knees, said "woof-woof," and charged around the sofa with the cut-out open. He grabbed the ecstatically squealing Ray in his arms, said it was time they both went to bed, and how would they like Daddy to tuck them in? As he raised the child high in the air, Mildred had to turn her head, for it seemed to her that she loved Bert more than she could love any man, so that her heart was a great stifling pain.

But when he came back from the tucking in, put the belt on his trousers again, and poured himself another drink, she was thinking sullenly about the car. It didn't occur to her that he was the half-dozenth person she had been furious at that day, and that all of them, in one way or another, were but the faces worn by her own desperate situation. She was a little too literal-minded for such analysis: to her it was a simple matter of justice. She was working, he wasn't. He wasn't entitled to something that would make things so much easier for her, and that he could get along well enough without. He asked her again how she had been, and she said just fine, but all the time her choler was gaining pressure, and she knew that before long it would have to come out.

The bell rang, and she answered. But when Wally gave her a friendly pat on the bottom she quickly whispered: "Bert's here." His face froze for a moment, but then he picked up his cue with surprising convincingness. In a voice that would be heard all over the house, he bellowed: "Why, Mildred! Say, I haven't seen you in a coon's age! Gee you're looking great! Say, is Bert in?"

"He's right in here."

"I'll only be a minute, but I got to see him."

If Wally elected to believe Bert still lived here, Bert evidently preferred to follow suit. He shook hands with a fine show of hospitality, offered a drink as though the liquor was his own, and asked how was every little thing quite as though nothing had happened. Wally said he had been trying to see him for a couple of months now, over something that had come up, and so help him God, this was the first chance he had had. Bert said don't tell him, he simply didn't know what made the time fly. Wally said it was those three houses in Block 14, and what he wanted to know was, had any verbal promise been made at the time of the sale that the corporation would put a retaining wall in the rear? Bert said absolutely not, and launched into details as to how the lots were sold. Wally said it had all sounded pretty funny to him, but he wanted to make sure.

Mildred half listened, no longer in any humor for Wally, her mind on the car, and thinking only how she would begin. But then a perfectly hellish idea entered her mind, and she no sooner thought of it than she acted on it. "My but it's hot in here! Aren't you boys uncomfortable in those coats? Don't you want to take them off?"

"I think she said something, hey, Bert?"

"I'll say she did."

"Don't get up. I'll take them."

They took off their coats, and she draped them over her arm, and stepped into the closet to put them on hangers. When she had them nicely hung up, she slipped her fingers into Bert's change pocket, and there, as she knew it would be, was the key to the car. She took it out, slipped it into her shoe. When she came out of the closet she picked up her drink, which she had barely touched. "I think *I'll* get tight."

"'Atta girl!"

"Lemme freshen it for you."

Bert put fresh ice in her glass, and a little more liquor, and a squirt of seltzer, and she took two or three quick swallows. She tinkled her ice, told the story of Harry Engel and the anchors, which amused the two gentlemen greatly. When she finished, she felt the key tickling her instep, and let out the first ripple of real laughter that had come out of her in months. She had a charming laugh, a little like Ray's, and it startled the two men, too, so for a time they laughed with her, as though there had never been a Depression, a break-up of the marriage, or a sour feeling over who got the job with the receiver.

But Wally, evidently a little nervous, and more than a little uncertain about his status, decided presently that he had to leave. Bert took him ceremoniously to the door, but he discovered that he had forgotten his coat, and this gave him a chance to dash back for a quick word with Mildred. "Hey, is he back? I mean, is he living here?"

"Just saying hello."

"Then I'll be seeing you."

"I certainly hope so."

When Bert came back he resumed his seat, took a meditative sip out of his glass, and said: "Looked like he hadn't heard anything. About us, I mean. I figured there was no need to tell him."

"You did exactly right."

"What he don't know won't hurt him."

"Certainly not."

The bottle was getting low now, but he poured himself another drink, and got around to what he had come for. "Before I go, Mildred, remind me to get a couple things out the desk. Nothing important, but might as well take them along."

"Can I find them for you?"

"My insurance policy."

His voice was a little ugly, as though he expected an argument. The policy was for $1,000, paid-up value $256, and he had never taken out more because he didn't believe in insurance as an investment, preferring A. T. & T. There had been wrangles about it, Mildred insisting that if anything happened to him "it's the one thing between the children and the poor house." Yet she knew it was the next item for sacrifice, and obviously he was bracing himself for opposition. But she blandly got it for him, and he said "Thanks, Mildred." Then, apparently relieved at the easy way he got it, he said: "Well, goddammit, how you been, anyway?"

"Just fine."

"Let's have another drink."

They had the last two in the bottle, and then he said he had to go.

Mildred got him his coat, and took him to the door, and submitted to a teary kiss, and he went. Quickly she turned out the lights, went to the bedroom, and waited. Sure enough, in a few minutes the bell rang. She opened, and he was standing there, looking a little foolish. "Sorry to bother you Mildred, but my car key must have fallen out of my pocket. You mind my looking?"

"Why, not at all."

He went back to the den, snapped on the light, and looked all over the floor where he had been playing with Ray. She watched him with pleased, slightly boozy interest. Presently she said: "Well come to think of it, perhaps *I* took that key."

"*You* took it?"

"Yes."

"Well gimme it. I got to go home. I . . ."

She stood smiling as the dreadful truth dawned on him, and his face sagged numbly. Then she stepped quickly aside as he pawed at her. "I'm not going to give it to you, and there's no use in your trying to take it from me, because I've got it in a place where I don't think you'll find it. From now on, that car's mine. I'm working, and I need it, and you're not, and you don't need it. And if you think I'm going to pound around on my feet, and ride buses, and lose all that time, and be a sap, while you lay up with another woman and don't even use the car, you're mistaken, that's all."

"You say you're working?"

"Yes, I am."

"Then O.K. Why didn't you say so sooner?"

"Would you like me to ride you back?"

" 'Preciate that very much."

"You staying with Maggie?"

"Prefer not to say where I'm staying. I'm staying where I'm staying. But if you drop me by Maggie's, it's all right. Got to see her for a minute, so you can drop me there—if it's convenient for you."

"Anywhere's convenient for me."

They went out together, and got in the car. Fishing the key out of her shoe they started off, and rode silently to Mrs. Biederhof's, where she said she was awfully glad he dropped around, and wanted him to feel welcome any time, not only for the children's sake but for her sake. He solemnly thanked her, said he had enjoyed the evening, and opened the door to get him. Then he grabbed for the key. However, she had foreseen exactly that contingency, and palmed the key as soon as she turned on the ignition. She laughed, quite gaily malicious. "Didn't work, did it?"

"Guess it didn't."

"Goodnight, Bert. And I have a couple of old brassières at the house, tell her. They're clean and fresh and she can have them any time she drops around."

"Listen, goddammit, you got the car. Now kindly shut up."

"Anything you say."

She pulled away and drove home. When she got there the light was still on, and everything was as she had left it. Glancing at the gas, she saw there were two gallons in the tank, and kept on straight ahead. At Colorado Avenue she turned. It was the first through boulevard she had been on, and the traffic signals were off, with yellow blinkers showing. She gave the car the gun, excitedly watching the needle swing past 30, 40, and 50. At 60, on a slight upgrade, she detected the gravelly sound of ping, made a mental note to have the carbon removed. Then she eased off a little on the gas, breathed a long, tremulous sigh. The car was pumping something into her veins, something of pride, of arrogance, of regained self-respect, that no talk, no liquor, no love, could possibly give. Once more she felt like herself, and began thinking about the job with cool detachment, instead of shame. Its problems, from balancing the dishes to picking up starters, flitted through her mind one after another, and she almost laughed that a few hours ago they had seemed formidable.

When she put the car in the garage, she inspected the tires with a flashlight, to see how they looked. She was pleased to find that there was considerable rubber left, so that new ones wouldn't be needed at once. Then she ran humming into the house, turned out the light, and undressed, in the dark. Then she went to the children's room, put her arms around Veda, and kissed her. As Veda stirred sleepily, she said: "Something very nice happened tonight, and you were the cause of it all, and I take everything back that I said. Now go to sleep and don't think about it any more."

"I'm so glad, Mother."

"Goodnight."

"Goodnight."

Chapter 5

WITHIN A FEW DAYS, Mildred's financial troubles had eased a little, for she quickly became the best waitress in the place, not only at giving service, but at bagging tips. The trick of balancing dishes she learned by practicing after the children had gone to bed. She used tin plates, weighting them with stones from the garden, and got so that she could spread three on the fingers of her left hand, lay two more on her arm, remember not to stick her tongue out, and go sailing around the kitchen table without dropping any.

Tips, she knew instinctively, were a matter of regular customers who left dimes instead of nickels. She cultivated men, as all the girls did, as they were better tippers than women. She thought up little schemes to find out their names, remembered all their little likes, dislikes, and crotchets, and saw that Archie gave them exactly what they wanted. She had a talent for quiet flirtation, but found that this didn't pay. Serving a man food, apparently, was in itself an ancient intimacy; going beyond it made him uncomfortable, and sounded a trivial note in what was essentially a solemn relationship. Simple friendliness, coupled with exact attention to his wants, seemed to please him most, and on that basis she had frequent invitations to take a ride, have dinner, or see a show. At first she didn't quite know what to do about them, but soon invented a refusal that wasn't a rebuff. She would say she wanted him to "keep on liking her," that he "might feel differently if he saw her when she wasn't in uniform." This had the effect of arousing a good lively fear that perhaps she wasn't so hot in her street clothes, and at the same time of leaving enough pity for the poor working girl to keep him coming back, so she could serve his lunch. Having her leg felt, it turned out, was practically a daily hazard, and this she found best not to notice. Even a leg feeler, if properly handled, could be nursed into a regular who left good tips, no doubt to prove he really had a heart of gold.

She held aloof from the restaurant itself, and the people connected with it. This wasn't entirely due to her ideas of social superiority. In her own mind, she was highly critical of the kitchen, and was afraid to get drawn into talk, for fear she would say what she thought, and lose her job. So she confined her observations to Mrs. Gessler, and every night gave a savage account of the way things were done. Her special grievance was the pies. They were bought from the Handy Baking Company, and Mrs. Gessler often laughed loudly at Mildred's description of their uninviting appearance, their sticky, tasteless filling, and their hard, indigestible crusts. But in the restaurant she held her peace, until one day she heard Ida bawling out Mr. Chris. "I'm that ashamed to put it on the table! I'm that ashamed to ask a customer to eat it! It's just awful, the pie you put out here, and expect people to pay for it." Mr. Chris, who took all bawlings-out with a martyred shrug, merely said: "Maybe a pie is lousy, but what you expect, times like these now? If he no eat, see me, I hokay a new check." Mildred opened her mouth to take Ida's side, and hotly proclaim that a new check wouldn't make the pie taste any better. But at that moment it flashed through her mind that perhaps the real remedy was to get the pie contract herself. With the chance to make these precious dollars, her whole attitude changed. She knew she had to capture Ida, and not only Ida, but everybody else in the place.

That afternoon she was rather more helpful to the other girls than strict ethics demanded, and later, at lunch, sat down with them and got sociable. Meanwhile, she reflected what she was going to do about Ida. She was working that evening, and after the place closed, noticed Ida hurrying out with a glance at the clock, as though she might be catching a bus. Holding the door open, she asked: "Which way do you go, Ida? Maybe I could give you a lift."

"*You* got a car?"

"Anyway, it goes."

"Me, I live on Vermont. Up near Franklin."

"Why it's right on my way. I live in Glendale."

The iciness was gone by the time they climbed in the car. As they parted, Mildred asked Ida if she'd like her to stop by and pick her up, on the way over in the morning. From then on Ida had a ride, and Mildred had a better station, and more importantly, she had Ida's ear, with no possible interruptions, for a considerable time every day. They became bosom friends, and somehow the talk always got around to pies. Ida was bitter indeed at the product Mr. Chris offered his customers, and Mildred listened sympathetically. And then one night she innocently inquired: "What does he pay for those pies, Ida?"

"If he pays two bits, he's being swindled."

"Yes, but *how* much."

"I don't know . . . Why?"

"I make pies. And if he pays anything at all, I'd meet the price and make him some that people would really want to eat. I'd make him some that would be a feature."

"Could you do it, honest?"

"I sell them all the time."

"Then I'll find out what he pays."

From then on, pies became a feverish conspiracy between Mildred and Ida, and one Sunday Mildred drove over to Ida's with a fine, wet, beautifully made huckleberry pie. Ida was married, to a former plasterer not working at the moment, and Mildred suspected that a pie might help with the Sunday-night supper. Next day, during the luncheon rush, while Mr. Chris had stepped over to the bank to get more change, Ida stopped Mildred in the aisle, and said in a hoarse stage whisper: "He pays a straight thirty-five cents for them and takes three dozen a week."

"Thanks."

That night, Ida was full of the information she had filched from the file, and on Mildred's calculation that she could furnish pies at thirty-five cents, she became masterful. "You leave it to me, Mildred. Just leave it to me. You won't have to say one word. I've been knowing it all along I had to have a showdown about them pies, and now it's coming. Just leave it all to me."

The showdown, next morning, was a little noisier than Mildred had expected. Mr. Chris said he had dealt with the Handy Baking Company for years, and wasn't going to change, and Ida said he'd been losing customers for years too, and didn't have sense enough to know it. And besides, Ida went on, here's a girl that makes grand pies, and what was the matter, didn't he *want* customers? Mr. Chris said not to bother him, he was busy. Ida said look at the variety she's got, cherry, huckleberry, strawberry—

"No chilly, no hooklabilly, no strawbilly!" Mr. Chris fairly shouted his emphasis. "All a pieces fall down in a juice, waste half a pie, no good! Appliss, poomkin, limmon—no other kind, won't have'm."

At this Ida went into the dining room, beckoning Mildred after her. When they were alone she whispered excitedly: "You heard what he said? Apple, pumpkin, lemon—no other kind. That means he wants to switch, but he's too bullheaded to say so. Now listen, Mildred. Tomorrow you bring three pies, one apple, one pumpkin, one lemon. Just three, no more. And I'll see that they're served. They're samples, but you've got to remember one thing: It's got to be *his* idea."

Ida put her head through the door and beckoned, and Anna came out. Anna, the girl with the sock, had been reinstated some time before. Ida pulled her into the huddle. "Listen, Anna, you heard what I said to him in there?"

"Ida, them pies are a disgrace, and—"

"O.K., then you do just like I say, and we'll get Mildred's pies in here, 'stead of them cow pies we got now. Anna, they're just wonderful. But you know how he is, so tomorrow, when I put out the samples Mildred's going to bring, you put the bee on him and say that's what he's been up to all along. Then he thought it up, and we break through his bullheadedness."

"Just leave it to Little Orphan Annie."

"And put it on thick."

"I'll take that Greek like Grant took Richmond. Don't worry, Mildred. We'll sell your pies for you."

Mildred had a warm, wet-eyed feeling toward them both, and decided that Anna rated a free pie now and then, too. That afternoon she made the samples, and next morning Ida took charge of them herself, hurrying back to the kitchen with them like a spy carrying bombs. Changing into her uniform, Mildred was as nervous as an actress on opening night, and when she went into the kitchen there was expectancy in the air. Mr. Chris was at his desk, in the corner, and presently got up and went over to the *out* door. Here he posted, with a thumbtack, a piece of cardboard on which was written, in his Mediterranean handwriting, the special order for the day:

Sell
Ham & S Potato

All gathered around and looked at it. Ida went over to the desk, picked up the blue pencil, came back to the door and added:

& Pie

One by one, the girls filed in the dining room.

Lunch had barely started when Mildred managed to sell two pieces of pie. Mr. Rand, one of her regular customers, came in early with another man, and when she handed him the menu to pick out his dessert, she asked innocently: "Would you care for a piece of pie, Mr. Rand? The lemon is very good today."

Mr. Rand looked at his companion. "That just shows how much principle she's got. The pie stinks, she knows it stinks, and yet she says the lemon is very good today. Lay off the pie—unless you're really tired of this life, and prefer to be dead."

"We have a new line of pie today, Mr. Rand."

"Well—is it any *good*?"

"You try a piece. I think you'll like it."

The other man chose chocolate ice cream, and Mildred hurried to the kitchen to get the orders. As she came back with both desserts and the coffee, her heart gave a leap as she heard a customer say: "That pie looks good." When she set it in front of Mr. Rand the other man didn't even let her put the ice cream down. "Say, I want some of that! Can I switch?"

"Why certainly!"

"Principle? She's got principle plus. Say, that meringue looks two inches thick."

By noon, the lemon pie was a few smears of filling in an empty plate, and by one o'clock, all three pies were gone. By three, Ida had opened up on Mr. Chris, with everybody standing around, to watch the result. She said just look how them pies went. She said the lemon was gone before she could even turn around, and one customer wanted a second cut, and she didn't have it to give him. She said it was just terrible what the people said, when Mildred's pies ran out and she had to serve the bakery pies. To all of this, Mr. Chris made no reply whatever, merely hunching over his desk, and acting as though he was deaf. Ida plowed on, louder and louder. She said there was one lady, in a party of four, that wanted to know where they got such wonderful pies, and when she pointed out Mildred, she was that amazed. Mr. Chris twisted uneasily, and said not to bother him, he was busy, and—

"So that's what you was up to!"

He jumped up, and found Anna's finger not six inches from his nose, leveled at him as though it were a six-shooter. Giving him no time to recover, she went on: "So that's why you been asking all them questions about Mildred! That's why you been foxing around! And who told you she made pies, I'd like to know? Well can you beat that. Every time you take your eye off him he's up to something!"

To this not unflattering harangue Mr. Chris at first returned a blank stare. Then he burst into loud laughter, and pointed a derisive finger at Ida, as though it was a great joke on her. Ida professed to be highly indignant, that he should "let her go on like that" when he knew about Mildred's pies all the time, and had already made up his mind to take them. The more she talked the louder he laughed, and then, after he had wiped his streaming eyes, the bargain was struck. There was a little difficulty about price, he trying to beat Mildred down to thirty cents, but she held out for thirty-five, and presently he agreed. That night Mildred stood treat to Ida and Anna in a speako Wally had taken her to, and helped Anna pick up a man at a nearby table. Still with her first half dozen pies to make, she drove home very late, full of a gulpy love for the whole human race.

On the strength of her new contract, she had a phone put in, and began to drum up more trade with the neighborhood customers, on the theory that a few extra pies were no more trouble, but that the extra money would be so much velvet. For pies one at a time, she had charged, and still charged, eighty-five cents each. Shortly, as a result of the neighborhood trade, there dropped into her lap another restaurant contract. Mr. Harbaugh, husband of one of her customers, spoke of her pies one night at the Drop Inn, a cafeteria on Brand Boulevard, not far from Pierce Drive, and they called her up and agreed to take two dozen a week. So within a month of the time she went to work as a waitress, she was working harder than she knew she could work, and still hold out until Sunday, when she could sleep. Taking care of the children was out of the question, so she engaged a girl named Letty, who cooked the children's lunch and dinner, and helped with the washing, stirring, and drudgery that went with the pies. She bought two extra uniforms, so she could launder all three at once, over the weekend. This chore, however, she did in the bathroom, behind locked doors. She made no secret of the pies; she couldn't, very well. But she had no intention that either the children or Letty should know about the job.

And yet, tired as she was most of the time, there was a new look in her eye, even a change in her vocabulary. Talking with Mrs. Gessler, she spoke of "my pies," "my customers," "my marketing"; the first personal pronouns predominated. Unquestionably she was becoming a little important, in her own eyes, at least, a little conceited, a little smug. Well, why not? Two months before, she barely had pennies to buy bread. Now she was making eight dollars a week from her Tip-Top pay, about fifteen dollars on tips, more than ten dollars clear profit on pies. She was a going concern. She bought a little sports suit, got a permanent.

Only one thing bothered her. It was now late in June, and on July 1 seventy-five dollars was due on the mortgages. Her affluence was recent, and she had saved less than fifty dollars toward what she needed, but she was determined not to worry. One night, driving with Wally, she said abruptly: "Wally, I want fifty dollars out of you."

"You mean—now?"

"Yes, now. But it's to be a loan, and I'll pay you back. I'm making money now, and I can let you have it in a month, easy. But the interest is due on those mortgages Bert took out, and I'm not going to be foreclosed out of my home for a measly fifty bucks. I want you to get it to me tomorrow."

"O.K. I think I got it."

"Tomorrow."

"Hell, I'll write you a check tonight."

One day not long after that, she came home to find Letty in one of her uniforms. She hadn't bought uniforms for Letty yet. She had her put an apron on, over the wash dresses she came to work in, and said the uniform question would be postponed until it was certain she was satisfactory. Now, seeing Letty in restaurant regalia, she felt her face prickle, but left the kitchen for fear of what she might say. But Letty caught the look and followed. "I told her you wouldn't like it, Mrs. Pierce. I told her right off, but she hollered and carried on so I put it on, just to keep her quiet."

"*Who* hollered and carried on?"

"Miss Veda, ma'm."

"*Miss* Veda."

"She makes me call her that."

"And she told you to put that uniform on?"

"Yes'm."

"Very well. It's quite all right, if that's how it happened, but you can take it off now. And hereafter, remember I'm giving orders around here, not Miss Veda."

"Yes'm."

Mildred made her pies, and nothing more was said about it that afternoon, or at dinner, Veda taking no notice of Letty's change of costume. But after dinner, when Letty had gone home, Mildred summoned both children to the den, and talking mainly to Veda, announced they were going into the question of the uniform. "Certainly, Mother. It's quite becoming to her, don't you think?"

"Never mind whether it's becoming or not. The first thing I want to know is this: Those uniforms were on the top shelf of my closet, under a pile of sheets. Now how did you happen to find them there?"

"Mother, I needed a handkerchief, and went to see if any of mine had been put with your things by mistake."

"In the closet?"

"I had looked everywhere else, and—"

"All your handkerchiefs were in your own top drawer, and they still are, and you weren't looking for any handkerchief at all. Once more you were snooping into my things to see what you could find, weren't you?"

"Mother, how can you insinuate such—"

"*Weren't* you?"

"I was not, and I resent the question."

Veda looked Mildred in the eye with haughty, offended dignity. Mildred waited a moment, and then went on: "And how did you happen to give one of those uniforms to Letty?"

"I merely assumed, Mother, that you had forgotten to tell her to wear them. Evidently they had been bought for her. If she was going to take my things to the pool, I naturally wanted her decently dressed."

"To the pool? What things?"

"My swimming things, Mother."

Little Ray laughed loudly, and Mildred stared bewildered. School being over, she had left a book of bus tickets, so the children could go down and swim in the plunge at Griffith Park. But that Letty was included in the excursion she had no idea. It quickly developed, however, that Veda's notion of a swim in the pool was for herself and Ray to go parading to the bus stop, with Letty following two paces behind, all dressed up in uniform, apron, and cap, and carrying the swimming bags. She even produced the cap, which Mildred identified as the collar of one of her own dresses. It had been neatly sewed, so as to make a plausible white corona, embroidered around the edges.

"I never heard of such goings-on in my life."

"Well, Mother, it seems to me wholly proper."

"Does Letty go in swimming?"

"Certainly not."

"What does she do?"

"She sits by the pool and waits, as she should."

"For *Miss* Veda, I suppose?"

"She knows her place, I hope."

"Well hereafter, there'll be no more Miss Veda. And if she goes with you to the pool, she goes in her own clothes, and she has a swim. If she hasn't a suit, I'll get her one."

"Mother, it shall be as you say."

Little Ray, who had been listening to all this with vast delight, now rolled on the floor, screaming with laughter, and kicking her heels in the air. "She can't swim! She can't swim, and she'll get drownded! And Red will have to pull her out! He's the life guard, *and he's stuck on her!*"

At this, Mildred began to understand Letty's strange conduct, and had to laugh in spite of herself. Veda thereupon elected to regard the inquest as closed. "Really, Mother, it seems to me you made a great fuss over nothing. If you bought the uniforms for her, and certainly I can't imagine who else you could have bought them for— then why shouldn't she wear them?"

But Veda had slightly overdone it. In a flash, from the special innocence with which she couldn't imagine who *else* the uniforms could have been bought for, Mildred divined that she knew the truth, and that meant the whole thing had to be dealt with fundamentally. For Veda's purpose, in giving Letty the uniform, might be nothing more sinister than a desire to make a peafowl's progress to the pool, but it might be considerably more devious. So Mildred didn't act at once. She sat looking at Veda, the squint hardening in her eye; then she scooped up Ray in her arms, and announced it was time to go to bed. Undressing her, she played with her as she always did, blowing into the buttonholes of the little sleeping suit, rolling her into bed with a loud whoosh and a final blow down the back of her neck. But all the time she was thinking of Veda, who never took part in these frivolities. Out of the corner of her eye, she could see her, camped in front of the dressing table for a period of primping, whose main object seemed to be the spreading of as many combs, brushes, and bottles in front of her as the table would hold. She was none too agreeable about it when Mildred finished with Ray, and ordered her to the den for more talk. She got up angrily and threw down a brush. "Yee gods—what now?"

When they got to the den, Mildred closed the door, sat down in the armchair, and stood Veda in front of her. "Why did you give Letty that uniform?"

"For heaven's sake, Mother, haven't I told you once? How often do I have to tell you? I won't have you questioning me this way. Goodnight—I'm going to bed."

Mildred caught her arm, pulled her back. "You knew, when you gave it to Letty, that that was my uniform, didn't you?"

"*Your* uniform?"

Veda's simulation of surprise was so cool, so calculated, so insolent, that Mildred waited longer than she usually did, when angered. Then she went on: "I've taken a job as a waitress in a restaurant in Hollywood."

"As a—*what?*"

"As a waitress, as you very well know."

"Yee gods! Yee—"

Mildred clipped her on the cheek, but she gave a short laugh, and brazenly finished: "—gods and little fishes!"

At this, Mildred clipped her a terrific wallop on the other cheek, that toppled her to the floor. As she lay there, Mildred began to talk. "So you and your sister can eat, and have a place to sleep, and a few clothes on your backs. I've taken the only kind of a job I could get, and if you think I'm going to listen to a lot of silly nonsense from you about it, you're mistaken. And if you think your nonsense is going to make me give up the job, you're mistaken about that, too. How you found out what I was doing I don't know—"

"From the uniform, stupid. You think I'm dumb?"

Mildred clipped her again, and went on: "You may not realize it, but everything you have costs money, from the maid that you ordered to go traipsing with you to the pool, to your food, and everything else that you have. And as I don't see anybody else doing anything about it—"

Veda had got up now, her eyes hard, and cut in: "Aren't the pies bad enough? Did you have to degrade us by—"

Mildred caught her by both arms, threw her over one knee, whipped the kimono up with one motion, the pants down with another, and brought her bare hand down on Veda's bottom with all the force her fury could give her. Veda screamed and bit her leg. Mildred pulled loose, then beat the rapidly reddening bottom until she was exhausted, and Veda screamed as though demons were inside of her. Then Mildred let Veda slide to the floor, and sat there panting and fighting the nausea that was swelling in her stomach.

Presently Veda got up, staggered to the sofa, and flung herself down in tragic despair. Then she gave a soft laugh, and whispered, in sorrow rather than anger: "A waitress."

Mildred now began to cry. She rarely struck Veda, telling Mrs. Gessler that "the child didn't need it," and that she "didn't believe in beating children for every little thing." But this wasn't the real reason. The few times she had tried beating, she had got exactly nowhere. She couldn't break Veda, no matter how much she beat her. Veda got victory out of these struggles, she a trembling, ignoble defeat. It always came back to the same thing. She was afraid of Veda, of her snobbery, her contempt, her unbreakable spirit. And she was afraid of something that seemed always lurking under Veda's bland, phony toniness: a cold, cruel, coarse desire to torture her mother, to humiliate her, above everything else, to hurt her. Mildred yearned for warm affection from this child, such as Bert apparently commanded. But all she ever got was a stagy, affected counterfeit. This half loaf she had to accept, trying not to see it for what it really was.

She wept, then sat with a dismal feeling creeping over her, for she was as far from settling the main point as she had ever been. Veda had to be made to accept this job she had taken, else her days would be dull misery, and in the end she would have to give it up. But how? Presently, not conscious of having hatched any idea, she began to talk. "You never give me credit for any finer feelings, do you?"

"Oh Mother, please—let's not talk about it any more. It's all right. You're working in a—in Hollywood, and I'll try not to think about it."

"As a matter of fact, I felt exactly about it as you do, and I certainly would never have taken this job if it hadn't been that I—" Mildred swallowed, made a wild lunge at something, anything, and went on: "—that I had decided to open a place of my own, and I had to learn the business. I had to know all about it and—"

At least Veda did sit up at this, and show some faint sign of interest. "What kind of a place, Mother? You mean a—"

"Restaurant, of course."

Veda blinked, and for a dreadful moment Mildred felt that this didn't quite meet Veda's social requirements either. Desperately she went on: "There's money in a restaurant, if it's run right, and—"

"You mean we'll be *rich?*"

"Many people have got rich that way."

That did it. Even though a restaurant might not be quite the toniest thing that Veda could imagine, riches spoke to the profoundest part of her nature. She ran over, put her arms around her mother, kissed her, nuzzled her neck, insisted on being punished for the horrible way she had acted. When Mildred had given her a faltering pat on the bottom, she climbed into the chair, and babbled happily to Mildred about the limousine they would have, and the grand piano, on which she could practice her music.

Mildred gladly promised all these things, but later, when Veda was in bed and she herself was undressing, she wondered how long she could keep up the pretense, and whether she could get another job before her bluff was called. And then a hot, electric idea flashed through her mind. Why not have her own restaurant? She looked in the mirror, and saw a calculating, confident woman's face squinting back at her. *Well, why not?* Her breath began to come just a little bit fast as she canvassed her qualifications. She could cook, she had such a gift for it as few ever have. She was learning the business; in fact, so far as pies went, she was in business already. She was young, healthy, stronger than she looked. She had two children, all she wanted, all she could be expected to bring into the world, so there need be no more of that. She was implacably determined to get ahead, somehow. She put on her pajamas, turned out the light, but kept walking around the room, in the dark. In spite of herself, the limousine, the chauffeur, and the grand piano began to gleam before her eyes, but as real this time, not imaginary. She started for bed, then hurried to the children's room. "Veda?"

"Yes, Mother. I'm awake."

She went over, knelt down, put her arms around the child, hugged her passionately. "You were right, darling, and I was wrong. No matter what I say, no matter what anybody says, never give up that pride, that way you have of looking at things. I wish I had it, and—never give it up!"

"I can't help it, Mother. It's how I feel."

"Something else happened tonight."

"Tell me."

"Nothing to tell. Only now I feel it, now I *know* it, that from now on things are going to get better for us. So we'll have what we want. Maybe we won't be rich, but—we'll have something. And it'll all be on account of you. Every good thing that happens is on account of you, if Mother only had sense enough to know it."

"Oh Mother, I love you. Truly I do."

"Say it again . . . Say it—just once—more."

Chapter 6

A GAIN MILDRED'S attitude toward the restaurant changed, from critical disapproval to eager curiosity. Mr. Chris, while his cuisine might not excite her, had been in business many years, and it dawned on her now that his system was the ancient system that any restaurant must use, if it is to run at all. She began to study it hard, noting the bookkeeping, the marketing, the method of using up leftovers, particularly the tricks used by Archie, who did many things that annoyed her but never used two motions where one would suffice, never wondered if a dish was done but always knew, and at that moment picked it up. Some of his principles she adopted at once in making her pies, for she was addicted to a deal of peeping into the oven, and giving them one more minute, just to make sure. Now she put them in by the clock and took them out by the clock, and saved herself much fretting, and made better pies.

All the time her confidence was growing, her ideas clarifying as to the kind of place she meant to have. But one thing vexed her constantly. Where was she going to get the money? In the afternoons, if she had an hour, she drove to the restaurant supply houses on Main Street, in Los Angeles, and priced, calculated, and added up. As well as she could tell, she would need a thousand dollars' worth of equipment before she could start, even in a small way. A range, icebox, steam table, and sink were going to cost at least half that, and furniture, dishes, silver, and linen would account for the rest. To save this money, at her present income, was going to take a long time, and there was always the risk that she would lose her job, or that some shift in the pie situation would wipe her out completely, and leave her exactly where she was in the spring. She had to get started, but on whose money she didn't know. She thought about Wally, and even about Mrs. Gessler, but she doubted if they were good for such a sum, and some instinct told her not to ask them.

For a short time she flirted with the idea of getting it from Mr. Otis, a retired butcher turned federal meat inspector, who was a regular customer, and always left her a quarter. She worked on his romantic nature to the point where he suggested meeting her outside, and then realized she should have her notes and memoranda in some kind of order if she was to impress him enough to make a deal. So one night, when Wally had reached the stage of yawns and a cigarette, she turned on the light and sat down at the desk. "Wally, want to help me with something?"

"Not particularly."

"I have to have it soon. Tomorrow, maybe."

"What is it?"

"I don't know what you'd call it. An estimate of costs, something like that. For a man that may back me in business. But I want it all written down, with the right words for what I mean, so it looks businesslike."

Wally, snapping his cigarette ashes into the fireplace, turned around and blinked. "What kind of business?"

"Just a restaurant."

"Hey, wait a minute, *wait* a minute."

He squashed his cigarette and came over to her. Then he pulled up a chair and sat down. "Start all over again. And at the beginning. Not in the middle."

Haltingly, feeling suddenly self-conscious about it, she told him her plan: a small restaurant, where she would do the cooking herself, and sell nothing but chicken. "They have steak places. And fish places. And I thought—well, down where I work practically every other order is for chicken, so it looks to me as though I ought to have plenty of customers. And then I wouldn't have to fool with all those à la carte prices, or bookkeeping, or menus, or leftovers, or anything like that. Everybody gets a chicken-and-waffle dinner, or chicken and vegetables, if they want, but all at the same price. And then I'll have pies to take out, and keep on getting all the wholesale pie business that I can, and—well, it looks like one would help the other. I mean, the pies would help the restaurant and the restaurant would help the pies."

"And who is this guy?"

"Just an old fogy that eats lunch with me every day. But I think he's got money. And if I could show him it was a good investment, he might let me have what I need."

Wally took several turns around the room, looking at her as he went. She was so accustomed to think of him as a fat blob that she occasionally forgot what a cold little eye he really had. Presently he asked: "You really think you can put that across?"

"Well—don't you?"

"I'm asking *you*."

"It seems as though it ought to pay. I've worked it all out in my mind and I'm pretty *sure* I've thought of everything. I can certainly cook. And I've studied the business down there, every little thing I could think of. I mean, the system. And how to save money. That's the main thing, Wally, about this idea of mine. What costs in a restaurant is waste, and the extras, like printing, for the menus, and the people you have to have, for every little feature you put in. But this way, there wouldn't *be* any waste. All the leftovers would go into gravy and soup, and there wouldn't be any printing, or extras of any kind. I certainly think I can put it across."

"Then if you can, I might be able to put you in on a deal. One that would start you off with a bang. A deal that would leave you sitting so pretty you wouldn't even *need* a backer."

"Wally! If you don't look out, I'll cry."

"You do the crying later and listen to what I'm going to say to you. You know that model home we had? That dream house that Bert built, so we could take the prospects in there and show them what their place was going to look like if they spent twice as much dough as any of them had?"

"Yes, of course." She had special, rather romantic reasons for remembering the model home.

"O.K. They got to get rid of it."

"Who?"

"The receivers. For Pierce Homes, Inc. The outfit that pays me to be their attorney, and messenger boy, and thief, and anything else they can think of. They've got to get rid of it, and if you'll take it over and put this chicken place in it, it's yours. And believe me, Mildred, if that's not a natural for a restaurant, I never saw one. Why, that place even smells like chicken. Right there under the trees, with the old colonial architecture that Bert spent all that dough on—is that a place to gnaw wishbone! Dump a little gravel on one side—free parking for everybody that comes in. That big reception room—perfect for the restaurant part. The model Pierce bedroom—there's your pantry. The streamlined Pierce office—there's your kitchen. Every stick in the place complies with the fire law and the health law, even to the toilets, and there's two of them, not just one. If you really mean this, I can get it for you for four thousand bucks, house, lot, and every improvement that's on it."

"Wally, now I *am* going to cry."

"Was I asking if you had four thousand bucks? I know what you've got and what you haven't got, and I'm telling you, if you want it, it's yours."

He leaned down close, looked melodramatically around, as though to make sure nobody could hear. Then, in a low voice: "They've got to establish losses."

"Who?"

"The receivers! On their federal income tax, the return due next March, for the year 1931, they've got to show losses. If they don't, they're sunk. That's why it's yours, for four thousand bucks."

"Wally, I'd still have to have money!"

"Who says you would? That's the beauty of it. Once you take title to a piece of property around this town, that's all they want to know —you can get all the credit you want, more than you can use. You think those supply houses aren't feeling this Depression too? They can't give the stuff away, and all they ask is: Do you own property, or not? They'll deliver anything you want, and connect it up for you, too. You need a little cash, two, three hundred dollars, maybe, I can take care of that. All you've got to do is take over that property and get going, quick."

For the first time in her life, Mildred felt the quick, hot excitement of a conspiratorial deal. She comprehended the credit aspect of it, once Wally explained it, and she didn't need to be told how perfect the place was for her purposes. In her mind's eye she could already see the neon sign, a neat blue one, without red or green in it:

MILDRED PIERCE
Chicken   Waffles   Pies
Free Parking

But it all seemed too good to be true, and when she asked eager questions about it, Wally explained: "There's no catch to it. They're in one hell of a hole. On those other properties, even if they did get rid of one, the federal rulings leave them worse off than they were before. I mean, when *we* didn't build the houses, even if we had to recapture when the buyer defaulted, there's no way we can show losses. But on this, there's the twenty-five hundred the corporation paid Bert for the lot, that not even a government auditor can question. And there's the eleven thousand five hundred that Bert spent on the house, and the corporation's money, not his. Fourteen grand all together, and if we let you have it for four, there's a loss of ten thousand dollars that just about takes care of every little thing for 1931, and then some."

"But why *me?*"

"Why not? Who else wants it? Nobody can live in that dump, you know. All Bert was building was a real estate office, but for some reason nobody seems to want a real estate office right now. It's got to be somebody that can use it for something else, and that means you."

"I know, but before I get too excited about it, you'd better make sure. Because if they're just giving it away, it looks as though there'd be somebody, on the inside—"

"Oh—I see what you mean. As a matter of fact, a couple of them did have that bright idea. I put my foot down. They were original incorporators, and I've dealt with the government enough to know that if some fast stuff like that was pulled, we'd all land in jail. On a thing like this, it's got to be bona fide, and that's where *you* come in. If the government agent don't like it, he can go up and see your place, and eat the chicken, and satisfy himself you're using it for the purposes you said you were going to use it for. And then he can take a look at our files and see that we took the best offer we could get. It'll be on the up-and-up. You're no insider. You're no original incorporator. You're—"

He broke off, sat down, and began cursing, first softly, then with rising vehemence. Sensing something wrong, she asked: "What is it, Wally?"

"Bert."

"What's he got to do with it?"

"Original incorporator."

"Well?"

"He's an original incorporator, and you're married to him, and there goes your restaurant, and the prettiest deal I've had a chance to put across since Pierce Homes folded."

It was ten minutes before Mildred could get through her head the ramifications of community property, and the fact that Bert, by merely being married to her, would be co-owner of the restaurant, and therefore subject to a ruling. Then she argued about it, indignantly and passionately, but she could see by Wally's face that the point was serious. He left presently, saying he would talk to his colleagues and look up the law, and she went to bed frantic lest this, her first big chance, would be lost on a legal technicality. She had a recurrence of her bitter fury against Bert, and the way he seemed to thwart her at every turn. Next night Wally was back, looking more cheerful. "Well, it's O.K., but you'll have to get a divorce."

"Is that the only way?"

"Well? Bert left you, didn't he?"

"I wish there was some other way."

"Why?"

"Because I don't know how Bert's going to act about it. You never can count on Bert. If it was just his heart, that would be all right. But he's got some twist in his head, and you never know what he's going to do. He might make trouble."

"*How?*"

"He'd think of some way."

"There's no way. If he'll let you get a divorce on the ground of cruelty, do it nice and quiet, all well and good. If he gets tough, you spring that Biederhof woman on him, and he's got to give way, because on infidelity he can't block it. You don't ask him. You tell him."

"It takes a year, doesn't it?"

"You getting cold feet?"

"No, but if it's no use, why do it?"

"It takes a year before your decree becomes final. But as soon as it's entered, that ends the community property, and that's all you've got to worry about."

"Well—I'll see him."

"Cut out that 'well' stuff. Look, Mildred, you might as well get this thing cleaned up. Because even if it wasn't for this federal thing, you'd hardly dare go into business, still married to Bert. You don't know where he gets his money. For all you can tell, you'd no sooner hang out a sign than you'd have more judgments and attachments and garnishees slapped on you than you could count. You'd be broke before you started. But, soon as you shake Bert, you're all right."

"I said I'd see him."

"If it's money that's worrying you, forget it. In court, I'll represent you myself, and the rest of it's nothing. But get going. The deal's hot, and you haven't got one day to lose."

Next Sunday, when the children were invited to dinner by the Pierces, Mildred knew Bert was coming over. She had sent word to him that she wanted to see him, and this obviously was an arrangement that would insure his finding her alone. She started her pies early, in the hope she would be done before he got there, but she was up to her elbows in dough when he walked in the kitchen door. He asked how she had been, and she said just fine, and she asked how he had been, and he said he couldn't complain. Then he sat down quite sociably and watched her work. It was some time before she could bring herself to broach the subject, and when she did broach it, she did so after considerable beating around the bush. She told about the model home, and the legal points involved, and quoted Wally in places that became difficult. Then, gulping a little, she said: "So, it looks as though we've got to get a divorce, Bert."

He received this statement with a very grave face, and waited a long time before he spoke. Then he said: "That's something I'll have to think about."

"Have you any *particular* objections?"

". . . I've got plenty of objections. For one thing, I belong to a church that's got some pretty strict rules on this matter."

"Oh."

She couldn't keep the acid out of her voice as she spoke. That he should bring up his perfunctory connection with the Episcopal church struck her as pretty farfetched, particularly as her understanding was that what his church objected to wasn't divorce itself, but remarriage of divorced persons. But before she could make the point, he went on: "And I'd have to know more about this deal of Wally Burgan's. A whole lot more."

"What have you got to do with that?"

"You're my wife, aren't you?"

She turned away quickly, thrust her hands into the dough, tried to remember that arguing with Bert was like arguing with a child. Presently she heard him saying: "I probably know ten times as much about federal taxes as Wally Burgan does, and all I can say is it sounds to me like a lot of hooey. It comes down to a straight question of collusion: Is there any, or isn't there? In all cases involving collusion, the burden of proof is on the government, and in this case there can't be any proof, because I can testify, any time they call me, that there wasn't any."

"Bert, don't you see that it isn't a question of proving anything to a court, one way or another? It's whether they *let* me have the property or they don't. And if I don't get a divorce, they won't."

"No reason for them to act that way at all."

"And what am I going to tell Wally?"

"Just refer him to me."

Bert patted his thighs, stood up, and seemed to regard the discussion as closed. She worked furiously at the dough, tried to keep quiet, then wheeled on him. "Bert, I want a divorce."

"Mildred, I heard all you said."

"What's more, I'm going to get one."

"Not unless I say the word."

"How about Maggie Biederhof?"

"*And how about Wally Burgan?*"

In his palmiest days as a picture extra, Bert never did such a take'm as he did at that moment, with the dough doing service as a pie. It caught him square in the face, hung there a moment, then parted to reveal tragic, injured dignity. But by the time it had cascaded in big blobs to the floor, dignity had given way to hot anger, and he began to talk. He said he had friends, he knew what was going on. He said she ought to know by now she couldn't pull the wool over his eyes. Then he had to go to the sink to wash his face, and while he clawed the dough away, she talked. She taunted him with not making a living for his family, with standing in her way every time she tried to make the living. He tried to get back to the subject of Wally, and she shrilled him down. He said O.K., but just let her try to bring Maggie Biederhof into it, and see what happened to her. He'd fix it so she'd never get a divorce, not in this state she wouldn't. As she screamed once more that she would have a divorce, she didn't care what he did, he said they'd see about that, and left.

Mrs. Gessler listened, sipped her tea, shook her head. "It's the funniest thing, baby. Here you lived with Bert—how long was it?—

ten or twelve years, and still you don't understand him, do you?"

"He's got that contrary streak in him."

"No he hasn't. Once you understand Bert, he's not contrary at all. Bert's like Veda. Unless he can do things in a grand way, he's not living, that's all."

"What's grand about the way he acted?"

"Look at it, for once, the way he looks at it. He doesn't care about the church, or the law, or Wally. He just put all that in to sound big. What's griping him is that he can't do anything for the kids. If he has to stand up in court and admit he can't pay one cent for them, he'd rather die."

"Is he doing anything for them now?"

"Oh, but now is just a trifling detail, a temporary condition that he doesn't count. When he puts over a deal—"

"That'll be never."

"Will you just let me talk for a while? It's his fear of being a flat tire, I'm telling you, at one of those big dramatic moments of any man's life, that's making him dog it. But he can't hold out very long. For one thing, there's the Biederhof. She won't like it when she finds out you asked for a divorce and he wouldn't give it to you. She's going to wonder if he really loves her—though how anybody could love her is beyond me. And all the time, he's got it staring him in the face that the harder he makes it for you the harder he's making it for the kids. And Bert, he loves those kids, too. Baby, Bert's on the end of the plank, and there's nowhere for him to jump but off."

"Yes, but *when?*"

"When he gets the pie."

"What pie?"

"The pie you're going to send him. It's going to be a very special pie. It doesn't appeal to his stomach, except incidentally. It appeals to his higher nature, and in Bert, that means his vanity. It's a pie you've been fooling around with, and you want his opinion on its commercial possibilities."

"I don't really mind making Bert a pie."

"Then get at it."

So Mildred made him a pie, a deep-dish creation, filled with crab-apples cunningly candied with sugar so as to bring out the tart of the apples as well as the crystal sweetness of the sugar. It was about as commercial as a hand-whittled clothespin, but she wrote a little note, asking his opinion, and a little P.S., saying she had put his

initials on it to see if she could still do monograms. She sent it by
Letty, and sure enough, around the middle of the week, there came
another invitation to the children, for Sunday dinner. That time she
took care to have her pies out of the way early, and to make a cold
lunch. It was Letty's Sunday on, and Mildred had her serve the
lunch in the den, preceding it with a cocktail. These attentions Bert
accepted gravely, and discussed the pie at length, saying he thought
it would be a knockout. There was a great field, he said, in ready
pastries, since people no longer kept the servants they used to, and
were often stumped for a company dessert. All this was what Mildred had been thinking for some time, but that didn't occur to her
particularly, and she was genuinely happy to hear such hopeful opinion. Then Bert said it all over again, and then a pause fell between
them. Then he said: "Well Mildred, I told you I'd think that little
matter over, and I have."

"Well?"

"Of course any way you look at it, it's unpleasant."

"It certainly is for me."

"It's just one of those things that two people hate to think about.
But we really got nothing to do with it."

"I don't know what you mean, Bert."

"I mean, whether it's unpleasant for us, that's not it. It's what's
best for those kids that counts, and that's what we got to think
about. And talk about."

"Did I ever have any other reason? It's for them that I want to
take advantage of this opportunity. If I can make a go of it, I can
give them what I want them to have, and what you ought to want
them to have, too."

"I want to do my share."

"Nobody's asking you to do anything. I know that when you're
able, you'll be only too glad to do anything you can. But now—did I
say one word about it? Did I?"

"Mildred, there's one thing I can do, and if you're set on this, I
want to do it. I can see that you have a place to sleep, and that the
kids have, and that nobody can take it away from you. I want to give
you the house."

Mildred, caught wholly by surprise, wanted to laugh and wanted
to cry. The house had long ceased to be a possession, so far as she
was concerned. It was a place that she lived in, and that crushed her
beneath interest, taxes, and upkeep. That Bert, with a straight face,

should offer it to her at this time struck her as merely grotesque. And yet she remembered what Mrs. Gessler had said, and knew she was in the presence of a man and his pride. She got up suddenly, went over, and put her arms around him. "You don't have to do that."

"Mildred, I want to."

"If you want to, there's only one thing I can do, and that is, take it. But you don't have to. I want you to know that."

"All right, but you've got to take it."

"I'm sorry I said what I did about Mrs. Biederhof."

"I've been hating myself for what I said about Wally. Christ, I know there'd never be anything between you and that fat slob. But—"

"We keep saying things."

"That's it. That we don't mean."

"That we couldn't mean, Bert. Don't you think I hate this just as much as you do? But it's got to be. For their sake."

"Yeah, for their sake."

They talked low and close for a long time, and then got to laughing over the way he looked when she hit him with the dough. Then they got to laughing over the charges she would have to bring, and the cruelties he had been guilty of. "I guess you'll have to hit me, Bert. They all say the defendant hit her, and caused her great mental and physical anguish."

"You talk like Veda. She's always wanting to be hit."

"I'm glad there's a little of me in her."

He doubled his fist, brushed her chin with it. Then they both burst into shaking, uncontrollable sobs.

"The gams, the gams! Your face ain't news!"

It was a moment before Mildred quite knew what was meant, but then she gave her skirt a little hitch, and wasn't exactly displeased when a photographer whistled.

Mrs. Gessler, having no gams to speak of, stood behind her, and the bulbs went off. Next thing she knew, she was in court, raising her hand, swearing to tell the truth, the whole truth, and nothing but the truth, so help her God, and giving her name, address, and occupation, which she described as "housewife." Then she was answering questions put to her by a Wally she had never seen before, a solemn, sympathetic, red-haired man who gently urged her to tell an elderly judge the story of Bert's unendurable cruelties: his silences, during which he wouldn't speak to her for days on end; his absences from home, his striking her, "in an argument over money." Then she was sitting beside Wally, and Mrs. Gessler was up there, corroborating everything she said, with just the right shade of repressed indignation. When Mrs. Gessler got to the blow, and Wally asked her sternly if she had actually seen it, she closed her eyes and whispered, "I did."

Then Mildred and Mrs. Gessler were out in the corridor where Wally presently joined them. "O.K. Decree's entered."

"My—so soon?"

"That's how it goes when you got a properly prepared case. No trouble about a divorce if it's handled right. The law says cruelty, and that's what you got to prove, but that's all you got to prove. That sock in the jaw was worth two hours of argument."

He drove them home, and Mildred made drinks, and Bert came in, to sign papers. She was glad, somehow, that since the real estate deal started, Wally had been curiously silent about romance. It permitted her to sit beside Bert without any sense of deceit, and really feel friendly toward him. The first chance she got, she whispered in his ear: "I told them the property settlement had been reached out of court. The reporters, I mean. Was that all right?"

"Perfectly."

That this elegant announcement should come out in the papers, she knew, meant a great deal to him. She patted his hand, and he patted back. Wally left, and then Bert, after a wistful look at his glass, decided he had to go too. But something caught in Mildred's throat as he went down the walk, his hat at what was intended to be a jaunty angle, his shoulders thrown bravely back. Mrs. Gessler looked at her sharply. "Now what is it?"

"I don't know. I feel as though I'd picked his bones. First his kids, and then his car, and now the house, and—everything he's got."

"Will you kindly tell me what good the house would do *him?* On the first call for interest he'd lose it, wouldn't he?"

"But he *looked* so pitiful."

"Baby, they all do. That's what gets us."

Chapter 7

IT WAS A HOT morning in October, her last at the restaurant. The previous two weeks had been a mad scramble in which it had seemed she would never find time for all she had to do. There had been visits to Los Angeles Street, to order the equipment her precious credit entitled her to; calls on restaurant proprietors, to get her pie orders to the point where they would really help on expenses; endless scurrying to the model home, where painters were transforming it; hard, secret figuring about money; work and worry that sent her to bed at night almost too exhausted to sleep. But now that was over. The equipment was in, particularly a gigantic range that made her heart thump when she looked at it; the painters were done, almost; three new pie contracts were safely past the sample stage. The load of debt she would have to carry, the interest, taxes, and installments involved, frightened her, and at the same time excited her. If she could ever struggle through the first year or two, she told herself, then she would "have something." So she sat with the girls at breakfast, listening to Ida instruct Shirley, who was to take her place, with a queer, light feeling, as though she were made of gas, and would float away.

Ida talked with her customary earnestness. "Now when you got to make a customer wait, you can't just leave him sit there, like you done with that old party yesterday. You got to take an interest in him, make him feel you're watching out for him. Like you could ask him if he wouldn't like a bowl of soup or something, while he's waiting."

"At leas' ask him don't he want to feel your leg."

Ida took no notice of Anna's interruption, but went grimly on. When a customer came in and sat down at Anna's station, Mildred motioned Anna back to her coffee. "Sit down. I'll take care of him."

She paid little attention to the customer, except to wonder whether his bald spot was brown by nature, or from sunburn. It was a tiny bald spot, with black hair all around it, but it was a bald spot just the same. While he fingered the menu, she decided for sunburn. Then she noticed he was heavily sunburned all over, but even this didn't account for a slightly Latin look about him. He was quite tall, and rather lanky, and a bit boyish looking in his battered flannels. But his eyes were brown, and the little clipped moustache was decidedly continental. All these things, though, she noted without interest until he put down the menu and glanced at her. "What in the hell am I looking at that for? Why does anybody ever look at a menu for breakfast? You know exactly what you're going to have, and yet you keep looking at it."

"To find out the prices, of course."

She had no intention of making a gag, but his eyes were friendly, and it slipped out on her. He snapped his fingers as though this were the answer to something that had worried him all his life, and said: "*That's* it." Then they both laughed, and he got down to business. "O.K.—you ready?"

"Shoot."

"Orange juice, oatmeal, bacon and eggs, fried on one side and not too much, dry toast, and large coffee. You got it?"

She recited it back to him, with his own intonations, and they laughed again. "And if you could step on it slightly, show just a little speed—why, I might get to Arrowhead in time for a little swimming before the sun goes down."

"Gee, I wish *I* could go to Arrowhead."

"Come on."

"You better look out. I might say yes."

When she came back with his orange juice, he grinned and said: "Well? I meant it."

"I told you to look out. Maybe I did too."

"You know what would be a highly original thing for you to do?"

"What's that?"

"Say yes, right away—like that."

A wild, excited feeling swept over her. It suddenly occurred to her that for the moment she was free as a bird. Her pies were all made and delivered, the children were with the Pierces at the beach, the painters would be done by noon, there was nothing to detain her at all. It was as though for just a little while she was unlisted in God's big index, and as she turned away from him she could feel the wind in her hair. She went to the kitchen, and beckoned to Ida. "Ida, I think the real trouble with that girl is me. I think I make her nervous. And she's got to start some time. Why don't I just quietly get out?"

Ida looked over toward Mr. Chris, who was doing his morning accounts. "Well *he'd* just love to save a buck."

"Of course he would."

"All right, Mildred, you run along, and I wish you all kinds of luck with your little restaurant, and I'll be out the very first chance I get, and—oh, your check!"

"I'll pick it up next week."

"That's right, when you come with the pies."

Mildred got the bacon and eggs, went out with them. His eyes met hers before she was through the kitchen door, and she couldn't repress a little smile as she approached. As she set down the plate she asked: "Well, what are you grinning about?"

"And what are *you* grinning about?"

"Oh—might as well be original once in a while."

"Damn it, I *like* you."

The rest of it was quick, breathless, and eager. He wanted to get started, she insisted she had to take her car home. He wanted to tail her there, she said she had an errand to do after she got there. The errand was to see that the model home was locked after the painters got out, but she didn't go into that. They made the rendezvous at the Colorado Pharmacy, at twelve fifteen. Then Anna approached, to take over and collect her tip. Mildred hurried to her locker, changed, said her hasty good-byes, and scooted.

She didn't, however, go home at once. She raced over to the Broadway Hollywood and bought swimming things, thanking her luck that she had money enough with her to pay for them. Then she raced to her car and started home. It was fourteen minutes to twelve, by the dash clock, when she whirled up the drive. She put the car away, closed the garage, and ran into the house with her bundles, glancing from habit toward the Gesslers', but the shades were all down, they apparently having gone away for the weekend. Inside, she pulled her own shades down, locked all doors, checked icebox, range, water heater, and spigots. Then she whipped off her dress, changed into the little sports suit and floppy hat. She ripped open the new beach bag, stuffed her purchases into it. From her dressing table she took a comb, dropped that in. From the bathroom she got a clean towel and cake of soap, dropped them in. Then she closed the bag, got out a light coat, and dived out the door. Then, trying it to make sure it was locked, she started down the drive, but at a pace in comic contrast with the haste of a moment before. For the benefit of all who might be looking, she proceeded at demure leisure, merely a lady out for a Saturday swim, the beach bag dangling innocently from her hand, the coat thrown carelessly over one arm.

But when she got out of the block her pace quickened. She was almost running when she reached the model home. It was properly locked, and a glance through the windows told her the painters had gone. She tiptoed around it, her eyes shooting into every precious part. Then, satisfied that everything was in order, she started for the drugstore. She had gone only a block or two when she heard a horn, so close it made her jump. He was within a few feet of her, at the wheel of a big blue Cord. "I honked you before, but I couldn't make you stop."

"Anyway, we're both on time."

"Get in. Say, you look great."

Going through Pasadena they decided it was time to tell names, and when he heard hers, he asked if she was related to Pierce Homes. When she said she was "married to them for a while," he professed to be delighted, saying they were the worst homes ever built, as all the roofs leaked. She said that was nothing to how the treasury leaked, and they both laughed gaily. His name, Beragon, he had to spell for her before she got it straight, and as he put the accent on the last syllable she asked: "Is it French?"

"Spanish, or supposed to be. My great-*great*-grandfather was one of the original settlers—you know, the gay caballeros that gypped the Indians out of their land, the king out of his taxes, and then sold out to the Americans when Polk started annexing. But if you ask me, the old coot was really a wop. I can't prove it, but I think the name was originally Bergoni. However, if he Spanished it up, it's all right with me. Wop or spig, I wouldn't trust either one as far as a snail can hop, so it doesn't make much difference, one way or the other."

"And what's your first name?"

"Montgomery, believe it or not. But Monty's not so bad."

"Then, if I ever get to know you well enough to call you by your first name, I'll call you that."

"Is that a promise, Mrs. Pierce?"

"It is, Mr. Beragon."

She was pleased at all these particulars about himself, for they told her he was giving her his real name, and not a phony invented for a somewhat irregular occasion. She settled back, lost a slightly uneasy feeling she had had, of being just a pick-up.

From Glendale to Lake Arrowhead, for any law-abiding citizen, is a trip of two hours and a half. But Mr. Beragon didn't pay much attention to the law. The blue car climbed into the seventies and stayed there, and when they pulled up at the gate of the settlement it was only a little after two. They didn't enter it, however. They took the little road to the right, and in a moment were stealing through great mountain pines that ladened the air with their smell. Presently they nosed down a rough dirt track, twisted through bushes that whacked the windshield, and pulled up with a jerk behind a little shingled shack. Mr. Beragon set his brake, started to get out, and then said, as though he had just thought of it: "Or would you prefer a bathhouse, around on the other side? I keep this shack here, but—"

"I think this is fine."

He took her bag, and they went clumping around a boardwalk to the front. He unlocked the door, and they stepped into the hottest, stuffiest room that Mildred had ever been in.

"Wooh!"

He strode around, throwing up windows, going out back and opening doors, letting air circulate in a place that evidently hadn't been opened for a month. While he was doing this she looked around. It was the living room of a rough mountain shack, with a rough board floor through whose chinks she could see the red earth beneath. Two or three Mexican rugs were scattered around, and the furniture was oak, with leather seats. However, there was a stone fireplace, and a horsy, masculine look to everything, so she half liked it. He reappeared presently, and said: "Well, are you hungry? We can get lunch at the tavern, or would you rather swim first?"

"Hungry? You just *had* breakfast!"

"Then we'll swim."

He picked up her bag and led the way to a small back room whose only furnishings were a cotton rug, a chair, and an iron bed, made up neatly with blankets. "If you can manage here, I'll use the front room, and—see you in a few minutes."

"I won't be long."

Both of them spoke with elaborate casualness, but she was no sooner alone than she pitched the bag on the bed and zipped it open even more quickly than she had zipped it shut. She was terrified he would reappear before she had finished dressing. Yet the possible consequences, as such, weren't what frightened her. The heat, and now the piny breeze that was blowing in, filled her with a heavy, languorous, South Seas feeling that wanted to dawdle, to play, to get caught half dressed, without any shame whatever. But as he left her, she had caught a whiff of her hair, and it reeked of Archie's bacon grease. It often did, she knew, especially when she was a day or so late at the beauty shop, but as to whether Wally noticed this, or liked it, or didn't like it, she cared no more than she cared whether he dropped by or didn't drop by. But that this man should notice it was a possibility that made her squirm. She had an obsession to get overboard, to get washed, before he came near her.

She slipped feverishly out of her clothes, put them on a chair, slipped on the suit. This was before the day of sarongs, and it was a simple maroon affair that made her look small, soft, and absurdly childish. She put on the rubber slippers, picked up the soap. Near her was a door that seemed to lead to some sort of small corridor. She opened it and peeped. Out back was a lattice, and beyond that the walk that circled the house. She pattered out and around, then ran straight down to the little jetty, with its small float. Clutching the soap in her hand, she dived off. The water was so cold she flinched, but she swam down until she was within a few inches of the stones she could see on bottom. Now safely out of sight, she ground the soap into her hair, swimming down with her free hand, holding her breath until her heart began to pound.

When she came up he was standing there, on the float, so she let the soap flutter to the bottom. "You were certainly in one hell of a hurry."

"I was hot."

"You forgot your cap."

"I—? I must be a sight."

"You look like a drowned rat."

"If you could only see what *you* look like!"

At this pert remark he dived in, and there ensued an immemorial chase, with the immemorial squeals, kicks, and splashes. She retreated out of his reach, he followed with slow, lazy strokes; sometimes they stopped and floated, then resumed, as he thought of some new stratagem to catch her. After a while she tired, and began circling to get back to the float. Then he was in front of her, having swum under water to cut her off. Then she was caught, and the next thing she knew was being carried bodily into the shack. As she felt its warmth again, the dopey South Seas feeling returned. She felt limp and helpless, and barely had strength to kick the beach bag off the bed.

It was dark when they got up, and they drove over to the tavern for dinner. When they got back it was cold, and they decided to build a fire, of pine knots. But then they decided they hadn't had enough to eat, and got in the car, and drove down to San Bernardino, for a steak, which she offered to broil. When they got back it was late, but they gathered pine knots by the car lights, and carried them in, and started them going. When they were glowing red she laid the steak on them, to burn it, and then held it with the tongs while it cooked. Then he got plates, and they cut hungrily into it, chewing it down like a pair of wolves. Then he helped her wash up. Then he asked solemnly if she was ready to go home, and she solemnly replied that she was. Then he carried her into the bedroom, and they shivered at the unexpected cold, and in five minutes were exclaiming at how good the blankets felt.

After a while they got to talking, and she learned that he was thirty-three years old, that he had attended the University of California at Los Angeles, that he lived in Pasadena, that his family lived there too, or at any rate his mother and sister, who seemed to be all the family he had. When she asked him what he did, he said: "Oh I don't know. Fruit I guess. Oranges, grapefruit, something like that."

"You mean you work for the Exchange?"

"I should say not. That damned California Fruit Growers' Exchange is taking the bread right out of my mouth. I hate *Sunkist*, and *Sunmaid*, and every other kind of a label with that wholesome-looking girl on it."

"You mean you're an independent?"

"Damn it, what difference does it make what I am? Yes, I guess I'm an independent. I have a company. Fruit export. I don't *have* it. I own part of it. Land too, part of an estate I came into. Every quarter they send me a check, and it's been getting smaller since this Sunkist thing cut it, too. I don't *do* anything, if that's what you mean."

"You mean you just—loaf?"

"You can call it that, I suppose."

"Aren't you ever going to do something?"

"Why should I?"

He seemed quite nettled, and she stopped talking about it, but she found it disturbing. She had a complex on the subject of loafing, and hated it, but she detected there was something about this man's loafing that was different from Bert's loafing. Bert at least had plans, grandiose dreams that he *thought* would come true. But this loafing wasn't a weakness, it was a way of life, and it had the same effect on her that Veda's nonsense had: her mind rejected it, and yet her heart, somehow, was impressed by it; it made her feel small, mean, and vulgar. The offhand dismissal of the subject put her on the defensive too. Most of the men she knew were quite gabby about their work, and took the mandate of accomplishment seriously. Their talk might be tiresome, but it was what she accepted and believed in. This bland assumption that the whole subject was a bore, not worth discussing, was beyond her ken. However, her uneasiness vanished with a little ear-twiddling. At daybreak she felt cold, and pushed her bottom against him. When he took her in his arms she wriggled into his belly quite possessively, and dropped off to sleep with a sigh of deep content.

Next day they ate and swam and snoozed, and when Mildred opened her eyes after one of these naps, she could hardly believe it was late afternoon and time to go home. But still they dawdled, he arguing they should stay another day, and make a weekend of it. The Monday pies, however, were on her mind, and she knew she had to get at them. It was six o'clock when they drove over to the tavern for an early dinner, and seven before they got started. But the big blue Cord went down even faster than it had come up, and it was barely nine as they approached Glendale. He asked where she lived, and she told him, but then she got to thinking. "Want to see something, Monty?"

"What is it?"

"I'll show you."

He kept following Colorado Boulevard, and then at her direction he turned, and presently stopped. "You wait here. I won't be a minute."

She got out her key and ran to the door, her feet crunching on the gravel that had been dumped for the free parking. Inside, she groped her way to the switchbox, and threw on the neon sign. Then she ran out to observe its effect. He was already under it, peering, blinking. It was, indeed, a handsome work of art, made exactly as she had pictured it, except that it had a blazing red arrow through its middle. Monty looked first at the sign, then at Mildred. "Well what the hell? Is this yours?"

"Don't you see whose name is on it?"

"Wait a minute. The last I heard, you were slinging hash in that—"

"But not any more. Yesterday was my last day. I quit early to run off with you. From now on, I'm a businesswoman."

"Why didn't you tell me?"

"I didn't get any chance, that I noticed."

At this tribute to his prowess as a lover, he grinned, and she pulled him inside, to see the rest of it. She switched on the lights and took him through, lifting the painters' cloths to show him the new maple tables, pointing out the smart linoleum floor covering, explaining it was required by the Department of Health. She took him to the kitchen, opened up the heat range. He kept asking questions, and she poured out the whole story, excitedly flattered that a professional loafer could be interested. Yet it was an amended version. There was little in it of Wally, or Bert, or any of the circumstances that had actually figured in it, a great deal about her ambitions, her determination "to be something before I die." Presently he asked when she was going to open. "Thursday. The cook's night out. I mean everybody's cook."

"Next Thursday?"

"At six o'clock."

"Am I invited?"

"Of course you are."

She switched off the lights, and for a moment they were standing there in the dark, with the smell of paint all about them. Then she caught him in her arms. "Kiss me, Monty. I guess I've fallen for you."

"Why didn't you tell me about all this?"

"I don't know. I was going to, but I was afraid you might just think it was funny."

"I'll be here Thursday. With bells."

"Please. It won't be the same without you."

He took her home, handed her to the door, made sure she had her key. As she was waving goodbye to the disappearing Cord she heard her name called. Automatically she looked toward the Gesslers', but their house was still dark. Then she saw a woman coming across lawns, and saw it was Mrs. Floyd, who lived two doors away.

"Mrs. Pierce?"

There was a sharp note in the voice, and Mildred had a quick prescience that something was wrong. Then, in a tone of virtuous indignation that the whole street could hear, Mrs. Floyd cut loose. "Where in the world have you been? They've been a-trying to reach you ever since last night, and—*where have you been?*"

Mildred choked back an impulse to tell her it was none of her business where she had been, managed to inquire civilly: "What did they want with me, Mrs. Floyd?"

"It's your daughter."

"My—"

"Your daughter Ray. She's got the flu, and they've taken her to a hospital, and—"

"Which hospital?"

"I don't know which hospital, but—"

Mildred dashed into the house and back to the den, snapping on lights as she went. As she picked up the phone a horrible feeling came over her that God had had her number, after all.

Chapter 8

As MOM MADE HER dozenth remark about Mildred's disappearance over the weekend, Mildred's temper flared. It had been, indeed, a trying hour. She had rung a dozen numbers without finding out anything, while Mrs. Floyd sat there and kept up a running harangue about mothers who run off with some man and leave other people to take care of their children. As a last resort she had rung Mrs. Biederhof, and while that lady told her which hospital Ray had been taken to, and one or two other things, her syrupy good wishes hadn't exactly put Mildred in a good humor. Now, after a dash to Los Angeles and a quick look at Ray, she was sitting with Bert, Veda, Mom, and Mr. Pierce at one end of the hospital corridor, waiting for the doctor, listening to Bert rehearse exactly what had happened: Ray had been dull Friday night, and then yesterday at the beach, when she seemed to be running a temperature, they had called Dr. Gale, and he had advised taking her to a hospital. Mom interrupted Bert and corrected: The doctor hadn't done no such a thing. He had ordered her home and they had taken her home. But when they got there with her the house was all locked up and they rang him again. It was *then* that he ordered her to a hospital, because there was no other place to take her. Mildred wanted to ask what was the matter with the Pierces' house, but made herself swallow it back.

Bert took up the story again: There was nothing serious the matter, just a case of grippe, not flu, as Mildred had been told. "That strip of adhesive on her lip don't mean a thing. They opened a little pimple she had, that's all." Mom took the floor again, making more insinuations, until Mildred said: "I don't know that it's any of your business where I was, or anybody else's."

Mom turned white, and sat bolt upright, but Mr. Pierce spoke quickly, and she sank back, her lips compressed. Then Mildred, after trying to keep quiet, went on: "I was at Lake Arrowhead, if you have to know. When some friends invited me up to their cottage by the lake, I didn't see why I was the one person on earth that had to stay home. Of course I should have. That I readily admit. But I didn't know at the time that I had a set of in-laws that couldn't even find place for a sick child that had been left in their care. I'll certainly know better next time."

"I think Mother's perfectly right."

Up to now, Veda had been coldly neutral, but when she heard about the swank cottage by the lake, she knew exactly where she stood. Bert looked unhappy, and said nothing. Mr. Pierce had a solemn rebuke: "Mildred, everybody did the best they knew, and I don't see any need for personal remarks."

"Who started these personal remarks?"

Nobody had an answer for this, and for a time there was silence. Mildred had little appetite for the wrangle, for deep down in her heart she had a premonition that Ray was really sick. After an interminable time Dr. Gale arrived. He was a tall, stooped man who had been the family doctor ever since Veda was born. He took Mildred into the sickroom, looked at Ray, listened to the night nurse's whisper. Then he spoke reassuringly: "We get a lot of these cases, especially at this time of year. They shoot up a temperature, start running at the nose, refuse everything you give them to eat, and you'd think they were blowing up something really bad. Then next day they're out running around. Though I don't mind telling you I'm glad we've got her here instead of home. Even in a case of grippe you can't be too careful."

"I'm glad you opened that pimple. I meant to, day before yesterday—and then I forgot it."

"Well I'm glad you didn't open it. Those things, the rule is to let them strictly alone, especially on the upper lip. I didn't open it. I put that little strip over it to keep her fingers off it, that's all."

Mildred took Veda home, improvising a tale about the people who had stopped by Saturday and invited her up to the lake. She named no names, but made them quite rich and high-toned. She was undressed, with the light out, before she remembered her pies. It was three o'clock before she got to bed, and she was exhausted.

All next day she had an unreasoning, hysterical sense of being deprived of something her whole nature craved: the right to sit with her child, to be near it when it needed her. And yet the best she could manage was a few minutes in the morning, an hour after supper. She had got to the hospital early, and wasn't at all reassured by the nurse's cheery talk. And her heart had contracted when she saw Ray, all her bubbling animation gone, her face flushed, her breathing labored. But she couldn't stay. She had to go, to deliver pies, to pay off painters, to check on announcements, to contract for chickens, to make more pies. It was dinnertime before she got another respite, and then she couldn't eat. She fidgeted while Letty served Veda, then loaded Veda in the car, and took her in for another vigil. Home again, she put Veda to bed, but when she went to bed herself, she couldn't sleep.

She called the hospital at eight the next morning, and after getting a favorable report, stayed on the phone, crowding her business into the next two hours. Around ten, she loaded her pies into the car, made the rounds of delivery, and arrived at the hospital about eleven. She was surprised to find Dr. Gale already there, whispering in the corridor with a big hairy man in an undershirt, with tattoo marks on his arm. He called Mildred aside. "Now I don't want you to get alarmed. But her temperature's gone up. It's a hundred and four now, and I don't like it. I don't like it, and I don't like that thing on her lip."

"You mean it could be infected?"

"I don't know, and there's no way to tell. I've taken a smear from the pimple, another from the mucus that's coming from her nose, and a couple of CC's of blood. They're on their way to the laboratory now. They'll ring me as soon as they possibly can. But Mildred, here's the point. If we've got trouble there, she can't wait for any lab report. She's got to have a transfusion, right away. Now I've got this man here, he's a professional donor, but it's his means of livelihood, and he won't go in the room till he gets his twenty-five dollars. It's entirely up to you, but—"

Without a thought of what twenty-five dollars would do to her little reserve, Mildred was writing the check before he finished talking. The man demanded an indorsement. Dr. Gale signed, and Mil·

dred, her hands sweating with fear, went into the sickroom. She had that same terrible feeling in her bowels that she had had that day on the boulevard. The child's eyes were dull, her face hot, her whimpering a constant accompaniment to her rapid breathing. There was a new strip on her lip, a bigger one, covering a pack of gauze stained with the livid red of mercurochrome. A nurse looked up, but didn't stop spooning ice into the fluttering little mouth. "This happened after I talked to you, Mrs. Pierce. She had a nice night, temperature constant, and we thought she'd be all right in a few hours. Then just like that it went up."

Ray began to fret, and the nurse began talking to her, saying it was her mother, and didn't she know her mother? Mildred spoke to her. "It's Mamma, darling."

"Mamma!"

Ray's voice was a wail, and Mildred wanted to gather her into her arms, but she merely took one of the little hands and patted it. Then Dr. Gale came in, and other doctors, in white smocks, and nurses, and the donor, his sleeves rolled high this time, showing a veritable gallery of tattoo marks. He sat down and Mildred stood like a woman of stone while a nurse swabbed his arm. Then she went out in the corridor and started walking up and down, quietly, slowly. Somehow, by a supreme effort of will, she made time pass. Then two nurses came out of the room, then one of the doctors, then the donor, and some orderlies. She went in. The same nurse, the one who had spoken to her before, was at the head of the bed, busy with thermometer and watch. Dr. Gale was bent over, peering intently at Ray. "Her temperature's down, doctor."

"Good."

"A hundred and one."

"That's just great. How's the pulse?"

"Down too. To ninety-six."

"That's wonderful. Mildred, I've probably put you to a lot of expense over nothing. Just the same—"

They walked out to the corridor, came to an angle, went on. He resumed talking in a casual way: "I hated to do it, Mildred, just hated to slap that outlay on you—though I'll see that every charge is as reasonable as they can make it. But if I had it to do over again, I'd tell you just what I told you before. You see, here's what we're up against. Any infection above the mouth drains into the lateral sinus, and that means the brain. Now with that little pip on her lip there

was no way to tell. Every symptom she had spelled grippe, but just
the same, all of those symptoms *could* have been caused by strep,
and if we had waited until we were sure, it would have been too late.
The way she's reacting to that transfusion shows it was all a false
alarm—but I'm telling you, if it had been that other, and we hadn't
moved fast, I'd never have forgiven myself, and neither would you."

"It's all right."

"These things happen, they can't be helped."

Somewhere on the floor a buzzer sounded, then sounded again,
sharply, insistently. It seemed to Mildred that Dr. Gale turned
rather quickly, that their saunter was no longer a saunter. As they
approached the room an orderly hurried past them, carrying hot-
water bottles. He entered the room. When they went in, the nurse
was jamming them under the covers, which were thick with the
extra blankets she had already piled on. "She's having a chill, doctor."

"Orderly, get Dr. Collins."

"Yes sir."

From the ice that was forming around her heart, Mildred knew it
was no false alarm this time. She sat down, watched Ray's face turn
white, then blue; when the little teeth began to chatter she looked
away. An orderly came in with more bottles, which the nurse pushed
under the covers without looking up. He was followed by Dr. Collins, a short, heavy man who bent over Ray and studied her as
though she were an insect. "It's the pimple, Dr. Gale."

"I can't believe it. She reacted to that transfusion—"

"I know it."

Dr. Collins turned to an orderly and snapped orders in a curt,
clipped voice: for oxygen, adrenalin, ice. The orderly went. Both
doctors studied Ray in silence, the chattering of her teeth the only
sound in the room. After a long time the nurse looked up. "Her
pulse is faster, Dr. Collins."

"What is it?"

"A hundred and four."

"Take off the hot water bottles."

As the nurse pulled out the hot water bottles and dropped them
to the floor the room began to fill. Other nurses appeared, wheeling
an oxygen apparatus and a white table full of vials and syringes.
They stood around, as though waiting. Ray's teeth stopped chatter-

ing and her face lost the blue look. Then red spots appeared on her cheeks, and the nurse felt her forehead. "Her temperature's rising, Dr. Collins."

"Take off the blankets."

Two nurses stripped off the blankets and a third stepped forward with icebags, which she packed around Ray's head. For a long time they were all motionless, and there was no sound except Ray's labored breathing, and the first nurse's report on the pulse: "A hundred and twelve. . . . A hundred and twenty-four. . . . A hundred and thirty-two. . . ."

Presently Ray was panting like a little dog, and her whimpering had a pitiful note in it that made Mildred want to cry out against the injustice that one so small, so helpless, should have to bear such agony. But she sat perfectly still, not distracting by so much as a movement the attention of those on whom Ray's chance depended. The child's struggle went on and on, and then suddenly Mildred tightened. The breathing stopped for a second, then resumed in three or four short, harrowing gasps, then stopped altogether. Dr. Collins motioned quickly, and two nurses stepped forward. They had scarcely begun their rapid lifting and lowering of Ray's arms before Dr. Gale had the mask of the oxygen apparatus over her face, and Mildred caught the thunderstorm smell of the gas. Dr. Collins filed the neck of a vial, snapped it off. Quickly filling a syringe, he lifted the covers and jabbed it into Ray's rump. The first nurse had Ray's wrist, and Mildred saw her catch Dr. Collins's eye and glumly shake her head. The artificial respiration went steadily on. After a minute or two, Dr. Collins refilled his syringe, again jabbed it into Ray's rump. Another minute went by, and Mildred saw glances exchanged between nurses. As Dr. Collins refilled his syringe, she stood up. She knew the truth, and she also knew that one more jab into the lifeless little bottom would be more than she could stand. She lifted the mask of the oxygen apparatus, bent down, kissed Ray on the mouth, and pulled the sheet over her face.

She was sitting in the alcove again, but here it was Dr. Gale who broke down, not she. The cruel suddenness of it had left her numb, as though she had no capacity to feel, but as he approached, his stoop was a tottering slump. He dropped down beside her, took off his glasses, massaged his face to keep it from jerking. "I knew it. I knew it when I saw that orderly, running with the bottles. From then on there was no hope. But—we do everything we can. We can't give up."

Mildred stared straight ahead of her, and he went on: "I loved her like she was mine. And there's only one thing I can say. I did everything I could. If anything could have saved her, that transfusion would—and she had it. And you too, Mildred. We both did everything that could have been done."

They sat for a few minutes, both swallowing, both locking their teeth behind twitching lips. Then, in a different tone, he asked: "You got any choice on an undertaker, Mildred?"

"I don't know any undertaker."

"I generally recommend Mr. Murock, out there in Glendale, just a few blocks from you. He's reasonable, and won't run up charges on you, and he'll attend to everything the way most people want it done."

"If you recommend him, then it's all right."

"I'll call him."

"Is there a phone around?"

"I'll find you one."

He took her to a little office on the same floor, and she sat down and dialed Mrs. Biederhof. She asked for Bert, but he was out, and she said: "Mrs. Biederhof, this is Mildred Pierce. Will you tell Bert that Ray died a few minutes ago? At the hospital. I wanted him to know, right away."

There was a long, bellowing silence, and then: "Mrs. Pierce, I'll tell him. I'll tell him just as soon as I can find him, but I want to tell you that I'm sorry from the bottom of my heart. Now is there anything I can do?"

"No, thank you."

"Can I take Veda for a little while?"

"No, thanks ever so much."

"I'll tell him."

"Thank you, Mrs. Biederhof."

She drove home mechanically, but after a few blocks she began to dread the stop signals, for sitting there, waiting for the light to change, she would have time to think, and then her throat would clutch and the street begin to blur. When she got home, Bert came out to meet her, and took her into the den, where Letty was trying to quiet Veda. Letty went back to the kitchen, and Veda broke into loud sobs. Over and over, she kept saying: "I owed her a nickel! Oh, Mother, I cheated her out of it, and I meant to pay it back, but—*I owed her a nickel!*"

Soothingly, Mildred explained that if she really meant to pay it back, this was the main thing, and presently Veda was quiet. Then she began to fidget. Mildred kissed her and said: "Would you like to go over to your grandfather's, darling? You could practice your piano lessons, or play, or whatever you want to do."

"Oh Mother, do you think it would be right?"

"Ray wouldn't mind."

Veda trotted out of the house, and Bert looked a little shocked. "She's a child, Bert. They don't feel things the way we feel them. It's better that she not be here while—arrangements are being made."

Bert nodded, wandered about the room. A match in the fireplace caught his attention, and he stooped to pick it up. So doing, he bumped his head. If he had been hit with an axe he couldn't have collapsed more completely. Instinctively, Mildred knew why: poking into the fireplace had brought it all back, the game he used to play with Ray, all the gay nonsense between the elephant and the monk. Mildred led him to the sofa, took him in her arms. Then together, in the darkened room, they mourned their child. When he could speak, he babbled of Ray's sweet, perfect character. He said if ever a kid deserved to be in heaven she did, and that's where she was all right. *Goddam* it, that's where she was. Mildred knew this was a solace from a pain too great for him to bear: that he was taking refuge in the belief she wasn't really dead. Too realistic, too literal-minded, to be stirred much by the idea of heaven, she nevertheless craved relief from this aching void inside of her, and little heat lightnings began to shoot through it. They had an implication that terrified her, and she fought them off.

The phone rang. Bert answered, and sternly said there had been a death in the family, and that Mrs. Pierce couldn't possibly talk business today. Mildred barely heard him. The restaurant seemed remote, unreal, part of a world that no longer concerned her.

Around three thirty, Mr. Murock arrived. He was a roly-poly little man, and after seven seconds of purring condolences, he got down to brass tacks. Everything in connection with the body had been taken care of. In addition, notices had been placed in the afternoon papers, though the morning notices would have to wait until Mildred decided when she wanted the funeral, so perhaps that should be the first thing to consider. Mildred tried to get her mind on this, but couldn't. She was grateful to Bert when he patted her hand and said he would attend to all that. "Fact of the matter, Pop wants to stand the expense, anyhow. He and Mom, they both wanted to come over when I came, but I told them to wait a little while."

"I'm glad you came alone."

"But Pop, he wants to stand the expense."

"Then you attend to it."

So Bert talked to Mr. Murock, apparently knowing instinctively what she wanted. He set the time of the funeral at noon the next day. "No use stringing it out," a point to which Mr. Murock instantly agreed. The grave could be dug in the Pierce family plot in Forest Lawn Cemetery, which had been acquired on the death of the uncle who left Bert the ranch. Services were to be conducted at the house, by the Rev. Dr. Aldous, whom Mr. Murock said he knew very well, and would call at once. Dr. Aldous was Bert's rector, and for a miserable moment Mildred felt ashamed that she could claim no rector as her own. As a child she had gone to the Methodist Sunday school, but then her mother had begun to shop around, and finally wound up with the astrologers who had named Veda and Ray. Astrologers, she reflected unhappily, didn't quite seem to fill the bill at this particular time.

On the choice of a casket, Bert haggled bravely, bringing all his business judgment to bear, and presently settled on a white enameled one, with silver handles and satin lining, which would be furnished complete for $200, with two limousines and the usual bearers. Mr. Murock got up. The body, he said, would be delivered at five, and they took him to the door, on which two assistants had already fastened a white crepe. Mr. Murock paused a moment to inspect the wire frames they were erecting in the living room, for flowers. Then he started. "Oh—I almost forgot. The burial clothes."

Mildred and Bert went back to the children's room. They decided on the white dress Ray had worn at the school pageant, and with the little pants, socks, and shoes, they packed it in one of the children's little valises. It was the gilt crown and fairy wand that broke Bert up again, and Mildred once more had to pat him back to normal. "She's in heaven, she's *got* to be."

"Of course she is, Bert."

"I know goddam well she's not anywhere else."

A minute or two after Mr. Murock left, Mrs. Gessler came over and joined them in the den. She slipped in without a greeting, sat down beside Mildred, and began patting her hand with the infinite tact that seemed to be the main characteristic of her outwardly bawdy nature. It was a minute or two before she spoke. Then: "You want a drink, Bert?"

"Not right now, Lucy."

"It's right there, and I'm right here."

"Thanks, I'd rather not."

Then to Mildred: "Baby, Mamma's listening."

"There's a couple of things, Lucy."

Mildred took her to the bedroom, wrote a number on a piece of paper. "Will you call my mother for me, and tell her? Say I'm all right, and the funeral is tomorrow at twelve, and—be nice to her."

"I'll do it on my phone. Anything else?"

"I have no black dress."

"I'll get one for you. Size twelve?"

"Ten."

"Veil?"

"Do you think I should?"

"I wouldn't."

"Then no veil. And no hat. I have one that's all right. And no shoes. I have them too. But—gloves. Size six. And I think I ought to have a mourning handkerchief."

"I'll have everything. And—"

"What is it, Lucy?"

"They be dropping in now. People, I mean. And—I'll probably pull something. I just thought I'd tell you, so you'll know I had a reason."

So a little while later, Mrs. Gessler was back, and certainly pulled something. By then, quite a few people were there: Mrs. Floyd, Mrs. Harbaugh, Mrs. Whitley, Wally, and to Mildred's surprise Mr. Otis, the federal meat inspector, who had seen the notice in one of the afternoon papers. Letty's contribution was tea and sandwiches, which she had just begun to pass when Mrs. Gessler came in, hatted, gloved, and carrying a gigantic set of lilies. With a wave of the hand she dismissed the florist's driver, and finding the card, read: "Mr.

and Mrs. Otto Hildegarde—oh, aren't they beautiful, just *beautiful!*" Then, to everybody in the room: "You know, the couple Mildred visited over the weekend, up at the lake. Lovely people. I'm just crazy about them."

Then Mildred knew that there had indeed been talk, serious talk. But she also knew, from the look that went around, that now it was squelched, once and for all. She felt a throb of gratitude to Mrs. Gessler, for dealing with something she would have been helpless to deal with herself. Bert took the lilies outside, where he spread them on the lawn. Then, coupling up the hose, he attached the revolving nozzle, so they were gently refreshed by the edge of the whirling spray. Other flowers came, and he set them out too, until there was a canopy of blossoms on the grass, all glistening with tiny drops. There was a basket of gladioluses from the Drop Inn, which touched Mildred, but the one that made her swallow hardest was a mat of white gardenias, to which was attached a bluebird card, reading:

Ida	Anna	Chris Makadoulis
Ernestine	Laura	Sam
Ethel	Maybelle	Archie
Florence	Shirley	$\times$ (Fuji)

As she was fingering this a hush fell over the room, and she turned to see Mr. Murock's assistants carrying Ray in the door. Under Bert's direction, they set up trusses near the window, arranged the casket, and stepped back to permit the guests to pass by. Mildred couldn't look. But then Mrs. Gessler caught her arm, and she was looking in spite of herself. In the setting sun, a rainbow was shimmering over the spray, framing Ray's head. This broke Bert up again, and most of the guests tiptoed silently out. But it left Mildred unstirred. There was something unreal about Ray's appearance. The hot flush of the last few minutes was gone, also the animation of life, also the deadly pimple. All that remained was a waxy pallor that suggested nothing but heaven, which Bert was now babbling about for the fourth or fifth time.

Letty served the rest of the sandwiches for supper, and Bert and Mildred ate tremulously, silently, hardly tasting what was put in front of them. Then Mr. Pierce and Mom arrived, with Veda, and after viewing Ray, came back to the den. Then Dr. Aldous arrived, a tall, gray, kindly man who sat near Mildred, and didn't put her on the defensive at all for not being a member of his church. Then Mom and Dr. Aldous were in an argument, or rather Mom was, with Dr. Aldous having little to say, and Mr. Pierce, correcting Mom on a number of points of ritual. The trouble was that Mom, who had been originally a Methodist, only joining the Episcopal church after marrying Mr. Pierce, was somewhat confused as to the service that was to be used tomorrow. As Mr. Pierce told her, she had the burial service, the communion service, the psalms, and perhaps even the wedding service, so thoroughly mixed up that it was rather difficult to disentangle them. Mom said she didn't care, she wanted the Twenty-third Psalm, it was only right they should have it when the child was dead, and also there was no use telling her there would be no praying for the child's soul. What were they doing there, anyway? Mr. Pierce sharply reminded her that the burial service had nothing to do with a soul. The whole point was that the soul had already gone, and the burial was nothing but the commitment of a body. As Bert listened unhappily, Mr. Pierce kept calling on Dr. Aldous, as a sort of referee. That gentleman, listening with bowed head, presently said: "As the child wasn't baptized, certain changes will have to be made in the service anyway. Small omissions, but I'm required to make them. Now, in that case, there's no reason why the Twenty-third Psalm, and the little passage in the Communion Service that Mrs. Pierce evidently has in mind, and whatever else we want, can't be included. At the end of the service, special prayers can be, and often are, offered, and I'll be very glad to include these passages—that is, if the mother feels the need of them too."

He looked at Mildred, who nodded. At first, she had resented Mom's taking charge in this high-handed way, and felt mean remarks rising within her. Just in time, she had remembered that the Pierces were paying for everything, and kept her reflections to herself. Now she went to the children's room and packed Veda's things, so the Pierces could have her back in the morning, properly dressed. When she came out with the little suitcase, the Pierces decided it was time to go. Dr. Aldous, however, stayed a few minutes longer. Taking Mildred's hand, he said: "I've often thought the burial service could be a little more intimate, a little more satisfying to the emotions than it is. It's quite true, as Mr. Pierce said, that it is the commitment of a body, not the consecration of a soul. Just the same, most people find it hard to make the distinction, and—to them, what they see isn't a body. It's a person, no longer alive, but still the same person, loved and terribly mourned . . . Well, I hope I can arrange a little service that will be satisfactory to the old lady, and the mother, and father, and—everybody."

After Dr. Aldous left, Bert and Mildred were able to talk a little more naturally. She still had to make the inexorable pies, and as he kept her company in the kitchen, and even helped her where he could, he gave details of what had happened at the beach, and she reciprocated with a final version of what happened at the lake, making it correspond with Mrs. Gessler's version, though not feeling any particular desire to deceive. She merely wanted to be friendly. Bert nodded when she got to the part about Mrs. Floyd. "One hell of an end to a nice vacation."

"I didn't care what she thought. But about Ray, I could feel it, even before I got to the hospital. I knew it, even then."

When the pies were made, they sat with Ray for a time, then went back to the den. She said: "You don't have to worry about me, Bert. If Mrs. Biederhof is waiting up for you, why don't you run along?"

"She's not waiting up."

"You sure?"

"Yeah, I'm sure."

". . . She was awfully nice."

"Mildred, can I tell you something? About what really happened Saturday?"

"Certainly."

"Mom, she was just scared, that was all. Mom was never any good in a spot like that. And me, maybe I take after her, because I was scared too. That's why, when Doc Gale began talking hospital I fell for it so quick. But Maggie, she wasn't scared. We had to stop there, on our way to the hospital, because I was still in my beach shorts, and I had to put on some pants. And Maggie, she raised hell about taking Ray to the hospital. She wanted to bring her right in, then and there. That's what I wanted too. It seemed a hell of a note; a poor little kid, and nobody even had a place for her. But—I didn't know how you'd feel about it."

"If that's what happened, it does her credit."

"She's a goddam good friend."

"If that's what she did, I want you to thank her for me, and tell her I would have been only too glad. It was better that she *was* brought to the hospital, but if she had been put in Mrs. Biederhof's care, I wouldn't have had any objection at all. And I know she'd have been properly taken care of, *well* taken care of."

"She's as broken up as if it was her own child."

"I want you to tell her."

"And will she be glad to hear it."

Bert got wood, and made a fire, and lit it. The next Mildred knew, it was daylight, and one arm was asleep, and her head was on Bert's shoulder. He was staring into the embers of the fire. "Bert! I must have been asleep."

"You slept three or four hours."

"Did you sleep?"

"I'm all right."

They went in with Ray for a few minutes, and then Bert went out to look at the flowers. The spray was still whirling, and he reported they were "as fresh as when they were cut." She got a dustcloth and began moving about the house, cleaning, dusting, putting things in order. Presently she got breakfast, and they ate it in the kitchen. Then he took his departure, to dress.

Around ten, Mrs. Gessler came over, with the black dress, and took the pies, for delivery. Then the Pierces arrived, with Bert, in a dark suit, and Veda, in white. Then Letty arrived, in a Sunday dress of garnet silk. Before her clean apron could be issued, Mildred saw the Engels drive up with her mother, and sent her out to let them in. When Mildred heard them in the den, she sent Veda to say she would be there in a minute. Then she tried on the dress, noted with relief that it was a fair fit. Quickly she got into the rest of her costume. Carrying the black gloves, she went to the den.

Her mother, a small, worried-looking woman, got up and kissed her, as did her sister Blanche. Blanche was several years older than Mildred, and had a housewifey look, with some touch about her of the ineffectuality that seemed to be the main characteristic of the mother. Neither of them had the least trace of the resolute squint that was the most noticeable thing about Mildred's face, nor did they share her voluptuous figure. Harry Engel, the unfortunate possessor of the anchor inventory, got up and shook hands, awkwardly and self-consciously. He was a big, raw-boned man, with a heavy coat of sunburn and a hint of the sea in his large blue eyes. Then Mildred saw William, a boy of twelve, in what was evidently his first long-pants suit. She shook hands with him, then remembered she should kiss him, which she did to his acute embarrassment. He sat down, and resumed his unwinking stare at Veda. To Veda, the Engels were the scum of the earth, and William was even scummier than his parents, if that was possible. Under his stare she became haughtily indifferent, crossing one bored leg over the other, and fingering the tiny cross which hung from a gold chain around her neck. Mildred sat down, and Mr. Pierce resumed his account of the catastrophe, giving a fair version this time, with full faith and credence to Mildred's visit to the Hildegardes, at Lake Arrowhead. Mildred closed her eyes and hoped he would make it long and complete, so she wouldn't have to talk herself. Bert tiptoed over and took the receiver off the hook, so there would be no jangling phone bell.

But when Letty, now aproned, came in to ask if anybody wanted coffee, the Engels stiffened, and Mildred knew something had gone wrong. As soon as the girl had gone, it developed that when she had let them in, they had all shaken hands, taking her for "a friend." Mildred tried to shrug it off, but Blanche was quite bitter about it, obviously feeling that Letty had compromised her social position in front of the Pierces. Mildred began getting annoyed, but it was Veda who put an end to the discussion. With an airy wave of her hand, she said: "Well personally, I don't see why *you* should object to shaking hands with *Letty*. She's really a *very* nice *girl*."

While all of Veda's delicately shaded accents were soaking in, the sound of the hose stopped. When Mildred went to look, Mr. Murock was carrying flowers in the front door, to place them on the wire racks, and his assistants were carrying in chairs.

I am the resurrection and the life, saith the Lord; he that believeth in me, though he were dead, yet shall he live; and whosoever liveth and believeth in me, shall never die.

It wasn't the words, it was the voice, that crumpled Mildred as though something had struck her. Sitting there in the bedroom with Bert and Veda, the door open so they could hear, she had expected something different, something warm, something soothing, particularly after Dr. Aldous's remarks of last night. And then this flat, faraway whine, with a dreadful note of cold finality in it, began intoning the service. Not naturally religious, she bowed her head as if from some ancient instinct, began shuddering from the oppression that closed over her. Then Veda said something. Somewhere she had dug up a prayer book, and it was a moment before Mildred realized she was reading responses: *"For they shall see God. . . . Henceforth, world without end. . . . And let our cry come unto thee. . . ."* To the critical ear, Veda's enunciation might have seemed a bit too loud, a shade too clear, as though intended for the company in the living room, rather than God. But to Mildred, it was the purest of childish trebles, and once more the heat lightnings began to flicker within her, and once more she fought them down. After a long time, when she thought she would scream if she didn't get some relief from her woe, the far-away voice stopped, and Mr. Murock appeared at the door. She wondered if she could walk to the curb. But Bert took her arm and Veda her hand, and she went slowly through the living room. Quite a few people were there, half-remembered faces from her youth, grotesquely marked by time.

Jesus saith to his disciples, Ye now therefore have sorrow.
It was the same cold, faraway voice, and looking across the open grave, with the casket over it, Mildred saw it indeed came from Dr. Aldous, though he looked old and frail in his white robes. In a moment, however, he dropped his voice, adopted a softer, more sympathetic tone, and as she caught the familiar words, "The Lord is my shepherd; I shall not want." Mildred knew that the moment had come for the special prayers made necessary by Mom's stipulations, and for intimate solace. They murmured on, and her lips began to twitch as she realized they were mainly for her benefit, to ease her pain. They only made her feel worse. Then, after an interminable time, she heard: *"O God, whose mercies cannot be numbered; Accept our prayers on behalf of the soul of Moire, thy servant departed, and grant her an entrance into the land of light and joy, in the fellowship of the saints; through Jesus Christ our Lord. Amen."*
And as the child sank down, on Mr. Murock's patent pulleys, Mildred realized, with bitter shame, that now for the first time, in death, it heard itself correctly addressed, that it had lived its brief life without even knowing its name.

The worst came that evening, when she was left alone, with nobody to console, nobody to be brave in front of, nobody to face but herself. The Pierces left in the afternoon, taking Bert with them, and the Engels shortly after, taking her mother, so as to reach San Diego before dark. Then, after an early supper, she had Letty take Veda to a moving picture show. Then she found herself in a house from which all flowers, all chairs, all wire racks had been removed, which was exactly as it had been before. Desolation swept over her. She tramped around, then changed into her smock and began making pies. Around eleven she drove to the theatre, took Letty home, and held tight to Veda's hand on the way back to the house. Veda had a glass of milk, and talked gaily about the picture. It was called *The Yellow Ticket*, and Mildred winced at the circumstantial account of how Miss Elissa Landi had pulled out the gun and shot Mr. Lionel Barrymore in the stomach. When Veda went to bed, Mildred helped her undress, and couldn't bring herself to leave. Then: "Would you like to sleep with me tonight, darling?"

"But Mother, of *course!*"

Mildred was pretending to herself that she was doing Veda a kindness, but Veda wasn't one to let such a spot go to somebody else. She immediately began to *give* comfort, in large, clearly articulated, perfectly grammatical gobs. "Why you poor, dear Mother! You *lamb*. Think of all she's been through today, and the beautiful way she's looked after everybody, without giving one thought to herself! Why of *course* I'll sleep with you, Mother! You poor darling!"

To Mildred it was fragrant, soothing oil in a gaping wound. They went to her bedroom, and she undressed, and got into bed, and took Veda into her arms. For a few minutes she breathed tremulous, teary sighs. But when Veda nestled her head down, and blew into her pajamas, the way she used to blow into Ray's, the heat lightnings flickered once, then drove into her sorrow with a blinding flash. There came torrential, shaking sobs, as at last she gave way to this thing she had been fighting off: a guilty, leaping joy that it had been the other child who was taken from her, and not Veda.

Chapter 9

ONLY AN ACT of high consecration could atone for this, and some time during the night Mildred knew what it would be, and so knowing, found peace. She may have found a little more than peace. There was something unnatural, a little unhealthy, about the way she inhaled Veda's smell as she dedicated the rest of her life to this child who had been spared, as she resolved that the restaurant must open today, as advertised, and that it must not fail. She was up at daybreak carrying out this resolution, setting out pie plates, flour, utensils, cans of supplies, all sorts of things, for removal to the model home. There was a great deal of stuff, and she packed it carefully into the car, but it required several trips. On the last one, she found her staff waiting for her: a waitress named Arline and a Filipino, to do double service as dish washer and vegetable peeler, named Pancho. Both had been engaged the previous week, on the recommendation of Ida. Arline, a small, half pretty girl of twenty-five, hadn't looked very promising, but Ida had recommended her highly. Pancho, it seemed, was addicted to flashy clothes, and had thus incurred the enmity of Archie, but once he was in his kitchen regimentals he was absolutely all right.

Mildred noted Pancho's cream-colored suit, but wasted no time on it. She handed out uniforms and put them both to work. They were to give the place a thorough cleaning, and as soon as the front room was done, they were to hang the percale drapes that lay in a pile on the floor. She showed how the fixtures worked, and on Pancho's assurance that he was a virtuoso with the screwdriver, she drove back to the house, picked up her pies, and made the rounds of delivery.

When she got back she caught her breath at what she saw. Pancho had indeed made a fine job of the drapes: the fixtures were all up and he was hanging the last of them. Arline had put the tables around, so that what had been a dreary pile of wood, metal, and cloth in one corner was now a restaurant, warm, clean, and inviting. Mildred still had many things to do, but when the laundry service delivered her napkins and doilies, she couldn't resist setting a table to see how it looked. To her, it was beautiful. The red-and-white check of the linen combined pleasantly with the maple, and with Arline's brick-red uniform, just as she had hoped it would. For a few minutes she lingered, drinking in the picture with her eyes. Then, after pointing out what was to be done in the kitchen, she got in the car again, to resume her errands.

At the bank, she drew $30, filling out the stub quickly, and trying not to think of the 7 she had to write, under "Balance Forward." She asked for $10 in change, against the requirements of the evening, dropped the rolls of coin into her handbag, and went on. At the ranch where her chickens were on order, she found twenty-six waiting for her, instead of the stipulated twenty. Mr. Gurney, the rancher, was quite voluble about it, saying them birds was in such prime condition he hated to see anybody else get them. Just the same, she was annoyed. He did raise fine chickens, honestly corn-fed, not milk-fed, and fine chickens she had to have. And yet she couldn't have him overselling her like this. After fingering them for a time, she rejected two because they weren't properly picked and took the rest, paying $8, the price being three for a dollar. Loading them into the car, she went to the U-Bet market, for vegetables, eggs, bacon, butter, and groceries. She spent $11, almost having to dig into her reserve of coin.

Back at the restaurant, she inspected the kitchen, found it fairly satisfactory. Arline had mopped the floor and Pancho had washed the new dishes without breaking any. Letty arrived, and Mildred had her make lunch for Arline and Pancho, then settled down to what she really liked, which was cooking. She got out the chickens, went over them carefully for pinfeathers, found Mr. Gurney's picking a great deal better than most market picking. Then she took a small cleaver and sectioned them up. She was going to serve half a fried chicken, with vegetables or waffle, for 85¢, but she hated the half chicken that was served in most places. It came on the table in one loathsome piece, and she wondered how people could possibly eat it. She was going to do it differently. First, she cut off the necks, then cut the chickens in half. Then she took off the wings and the legs. The legs she separated into second joints and drumsticks, and then she trimmed the breasts so there was only a sliver of breastbone backing them, without any wishbone or rib. Then, remembering Archie's system for such things, she packed breasts, drumsticks, second joints, and wings into four different dishes, and placed them in the icebox so she could pick up a portion with one motion. The necks and bones she pitched into a pot, for soup. The giblets she cut up and put in a pan, for gravy. She started her other soup, the cream of tomato, and put Pancho to preparing vegetables.

Around four, Wally came in, to inspect the alterations, and report. His main activity, since she had seen him, had been to send out the announcements, and for this he had drafted his secretary. She had utilized all the old Pierce Home lists so that every person who had bought a home, or had even thought of buying a home, had been covered. Mildred listened, pleased that all this had been so well attended to, but he kept hanging around, and she wished he would go, so she could work. Then she noticed him looking at the showcase. This was the most expensive piece of furniture she had, and the only one that had been made to order. The base and back were of maple, but the sides, top, and shelves were of glass. It was to display the pies she hoped to sell to the "take-out" trade, and presently, looking rather self-conscious, Wally asked: "Well, how did you like that little surprise I fixed up for you?"

"—? What surprise?"

"Didn't you see it?"

"I haven't seen anything."

"Hey—you go back to the kitchen, then, and wait, and believe me pretty soon you're going to see something."

Mystified, she went to the kitchen, and still more mystified, saw Wally appear there in a moment or two, find her pies, and carry two into the restaurant, then two more, then two more. Then she could see him arranging the pies in the showcase. Then she could see him fumbling with something against the wall. Then suddenly the show-case lighted up, and she gave a little cry, and went running out. Wally beamed. "Well, how do you like it?"

"Why Wally, it's *beautiful!*"

"Something I did for you while—well, the last few days. I slipped in here at night and worked on it." He proudly pointed out the tiny reflectors that screwed into the maple, almost invisibly, to shoot the light downward, on the pies; the bulbs, no bigger than her finger; the wiring, cunningly tacked to the back in such manner as to leave the panels free to slide. "You know how much that little job cost?"

"I haven't any idea."

"Well, let's see now, the reflectors, they were seven cents apiece, six of them, that's forty-two cents. The lights, a nickel apiece—say, they're Christmas tree bulbs, can you beat that? Thirty cents for them, that's seventy-two cents. The wire, ten cents. The sockets, screws, and plug, maybe a dollar. Say altogether, a couple of bucks. How's that?"

"I just can't believe it."

"Took me maybe an hour. But it ought to sell pies."

"And get a free dinner."

"Oh, never mind that."

"A free dinner, and second helpings."

But the clock was ticking inexorably on, and she hurried back to work as soon as he left, though in a pleasant glow now, feeling that everybody was trying to help her. The vegetables, started before Wally came, were now ready, and they took them up. She put them in their pots and turned the hot water into the steam table. She made waffle batter, laid beside it the dipper that held exactly one waffle. She made pie crust, for biscuits. Her ice cream arrived: choco-late, strawberry, and vanilla. She had Pancho set all three freezers on a bench, where they could be easily reached, and showed Arline how to dip it up, reminding her she would be responsible for desserts as well as starters. She made salad, started the coffee.

At five thirty she went to the ladies' room to change for the eve-ning. She had given considerable thought to what she would wear. She had decided on white, but not the sleazy white of the nurse uniforms then becoming so common. She went to Bullocks, and bought sharkskin dresses, of a shade just off white, white with a tint of cream in it, and had little Dutch caps made to go with them. Always vain of her legs, she had the dresses shortened a little. Now, she hurriedly got into one, put on her Tip-Top shoes, stuck on the little cap. As she hurried out carrying the apron she would wear in the kitchen, and slip off when she came out to greet the customers, she looked like the cook in a musical comedy.

However, she didn't go into a number. She assembled Pancho, Letty, and Arline for final instructions, paying most attention to Arline. "I'm not expecting many people, because it's my first night and I haven't had a chance yet to build up my trade. But if you should be rushed, *remember*: Get their orders. I've got to know whether they're having vegetables or waffle before I can start, so don't keep me waiting."

"Call them both?"

"Call the waffle only."

"Call biscuits?"

"I'll keep biscuits out all the time, and you pick them up yourself. Pick up your own bread and your own biscuits, but put them in separate baskets and don't forget that biscuits call for a napkin, to keep them hot. Three biscuits to a person, more if they want them, but don't be stingy with them and don't take time to count. Pick them up quick, and pick up enough."

Arline surveyed the place with a practiced eye, counting tables. There were eight tables for two, around the wall, and two tables for four, in the middle. Mildred saw the look, and went on: "You'll be able to take care of them, *if* you get their orders. There's plenty of room here, you're using a tray, and that'll help. Any time you need her, I'll send Letty out to bus up your tables for you, and—"

"Can't she do that right from the start? So we get used to working together, and don't commence bumping and stepping all over each other's feet?"

"Then all right."

Letty nodded, with a self-conscious grin. She was already in the brick-red uniform, which was quite becoming to her, and obviously wanted to be part of the show. Mildred went back to the kitchen, lit the oven, and started the waffle irons to heat. She was using a gas waffle, instead of the usual electric waffle, "because that's the old-fashioned kind of round waffle that people really like." She went to the switch box, put on the lights. The last switch worked the outside sign, and when it was on, she went out to look. There it was, as

beautiful as ever, casting a bluish light over the trees. She drew a
deep breath and came inside. At last she was open, at last she had
her own business.

There ensued a long wait. She sat nervously at one of the tables
for two, while Arline, Letty, and Pancho stood in a corner whispering. Then they started to giggle, and a horrible pain shot through
Mildred. It was the first time it had occurred to her that she could
open a restaurant, and then have nobody show up. She lurched suddenly to her feet and went to the kitchen. She kept touching the
waffle irons, to see if they were hot. Outside, a car door slammed.
She looked up. A car was there, and four people were entering the
restaurant.

She had a moment of complacency as she reached for the chicken:
now she would reap her reward for all her observing, thinking, and
planning. She had had the free parking located in the rear, so she
could see exactly how many customers she had, even before they
came in; she had simplified her menu, so she could start the chicken
without waiting for the waitress to report; she had placed her icebox,
range, materials, and utensils so she could work with the minimum
of effort. Feeling as though she were starting a well-tuned machine,
she took out four each of breasts, second joints, drumsticks, and
wings, rolled them in the flour box beside the range, gave them a
squirt from the olive oil bottle that stood beside the flour. She
shoved them in the oven, for the brief baking that preceded frying
in butter. Not yet closing the oven door, she shoved a pan of biscuits
in, beside them. Arline appeared. "Four at No. 9, soup right and
left, two and two, one waf."

She reminded Arline she was not to call soup, but dip it up herself, then went out to greet her first guests. They were strangers to
her, a man, woman, and two children, but she made them a pretty
little speech, saying they were her first guests, and she hoped they
liked her place and would keep on being her guests. Arline came in
with the starters, the soup, crackers, butter, napkins, water, and
salad. Salad, for some reason, is served first in California. Mildred's
eye checked the tray, finding it in order. Two more people came in.
She vaguely remembered them as Pierce Homes buyers of six or
seven years ago, but her waitress training came at once to her aid.
Their names were on her tongue before she fairly saw their faces:

"Why how do you do, Mrs. Sawyer, and Mr. Sawyer! I'm so glad you were able to come!"

They seemed pleased, and she seated them at a table in the corner. As soon as Arline came over to get their orders, she went back to the kitchen, to start more chicken.

The first order went out smoothly, with Letty bussing the dirty dishes to Pancho, who went to work at once. But then Arline appeared, looking worried. "Two at No. 3, but one of them's a kid that won't have soup. Says she wants tomato juice with a piece of lemon and some celery salt—I told her we don't serve it, but she says she's got to have it and what do I do now?"

It was no trouble to guess who that was.

She found Bert with Veda, at one of the tables for two. Bert was in a light suit, conscientiously groomed and brushed, but with a black band on one arm. Veda was in a school dress that hadn't been worn yet, and Mildred's floppy hat. Both of them looked up with a smile, Veda exclaiming how pretty Mildred's dress was, Bert nodding approvingly at the restaurant. "By God, this looks like something. You got yourself a piece of property this time, Mildred. This place is real."

He stamped his foot. "And it's built. I saw to that. I bet there was no trouble with the Department of Health when they inspected *this* floor."

"They passed it without even looking."

"How about those toilets?"

"They passed them too. Of course, we had to cut a door through, so both of them opened into the old secretary's office. We made that into a kind of lounge. It's against the law for a toilet to open into the kitchen, you know. But that, and the painting, and the gravel, and the swing doors, were about all we had to do. It cost money though. Whew!"

"I bet it did."

"Would you like to look around?"

"I'd love it."

She took them both through, and felt proud when Bert admired everything profusely, not quite so proud when Veda said: "Well Mother, I think you've done very well, considering everything." Then she heard a car door slam, and turned to greet her new customer. It was Wally, and he was quite excited. "Say, you're going to have a mob. You heard me, a mob. That's the thing to remember with direct-mail advertising. It's not what you send. It's where you send it. I got that stuff of yours right to the people that know you, and they're coming. I bumped into six different people that told me they'd be here—and that's just six I happened to bump into. I said a mob."

Wally pulled over a chair and sat down with Bert and Veda. Bert asked him sharply if he had attended to the transfer of beneficiary on the fire insurance. Wally said he figured he'd wait till the place burned down. Bert said O.K., he was just asking.

When Mildred looked up, Ida was standing in the door. She went over and kissed her, and listened while she volubly explained that her husband had wanted to come, but got a call on a job, and simply had to look into it. Mildred took her to the table that now had only one chair, the other having been borrowed by Wally. Ida looked around, taking things in. "Mildred, it's just grand. And the space you got. You can get two more fours in easy, just by shifting those twos a little bit. And you can use trays, big as you want. You got no idea how that'll help. It'll save you at least one girl. At least."

It was high time for Mildred to get back to the kitchen, but she lingered, patting Ida's hand, basking in her approval.

The well-oiled machine was in high now, humming smoothly, pulling its load. So far, Mildred had found a few seconds for each new arrival, and particularly for each new departure, to give a little reminder of the homemade pies she had for sale, and wouldn't they like to take home one? But now she was working a bit feverishly, frying chickens, turning waffles. When she heard a car door slam she didn't have a chance to look out and count customers. Then she heard another door slam. Then Arline appeared. "Two fours just come in, Mrs. Pierce. I got room for one but what do I do with the other? I can shove two twos together, but not till I get Miss Ida moved out—"

"No no! Let her alone."

"But what'll I do?"

"Seat four, ask the others to wait."

In spite of herself, her voice was shrill. She went out, asked the second party of four if they minded waiting. She said she was a little rushed now, but it would only be for a few minutes. One of the men nodded, but she hurried away, ashamed that she hadn't foreseen this, and provided extra chairs. When she got to the kitchen, Arline was jabbering at Pancho, then turned furiously to Mildred: "He's washing plates, and the soup bowls are all out, and if he don't let me have them I can't serve my starters! *Soup bowls, stupid, soup bowls!*"

Arline screamed this at Pancho, but as Mildred shushed her down, Letty came in, heavy-footed and clumsy at unaccustomed work, and dumped more soup bowls on the pile, which went down with a crash, three breaking. Mildred made a futile dive to save them, and heard another car door slam. And suddenly she knew that her machine was stalled, that her kitchen was swamped, that she had completely lost track of her orders, that not even a starter was moving. For one dreadful moment she saw her opening turning into a fiasco, everything she had hoped for slipping away from her in one nightmare of an evening. Then beside her was Ida, whipping off her hat, tucking it with her handbag beside the tin box that held the cash, slipping into an apron. "O.K., Mildred, it's them dishes that's causing it all. Now *she* ain't no good out there, none whatever, so let *her* wipe while *he* washes, and that'll help."

As Mildred nodded at Letty and handed her a towel, Ida's quick eye spotted dessert dishes, and she set them out on a tray. Then, to Arline: "Call your soup."

"I want a right and left for two, three and one, chicken and tomato for four, and they been waiting for—"

Ida didn't wait to hear how long they had been waiting. She dipped soup into the dessert dishes, dealt out spoons with one hand and crackers with the other, and hurried out with the tray, leaving butter, salad, and water to Arline. In a minute she was back. "O.K., Mildred, I got your family to take a walk outside. They was all through eating anyway. Then I put two at my table, and that took care of four. Then soon as I get the check for that first party of four, that'll take care of four more, and—"

The twanging voice, the voice that Mildred had hated, twanged on, and Mildred responded to it with a tingle that started in her heart and spread out through the rest of her. Her nerve came back, her hands recovered their skill, as things began moving again. She was pouring a waffle when Mrs. Gessler appeared at the door, and came tiptoeing over to her. "Anything I can do, baby?"

"I don't think so, Lucy. Thanks just the—"

"Oh yes there is."

Ida seized Mrs. Gessler by the arm as she usually seized the members of her command. "You can take off that hat and get out there and sell pies. Don't bother them while they're eating but stay near the showcase and when they get through see what you can do."

"I'll be doing my best."

"Containers in the drawer under the case, they're out flat and you'll have to fold them, then tie them up and put the carrying handles on. If you have any trouble, just call for me or ask Mildred."

"What's the price, Mildred?"

"Eighty-five cents. Everything's eighty-five cents."

Mrs. Gessler laid her hat beside Ida's and went out. Soon Mildred saw her come back, lay a dollar bill in the tin box, take change, and go out. In a short time she saw many bills in the box, as Ida repeatedly came in, made change, and sent Arline out with it, so she would get her tip. When she had a lull, she slipped off her apron and went out. Nobody was standing now, but every seat was filled, and she felt as she had felt yesterday, at the funeral, when she walked through the living room and saw all those half-remembered faces. These were people she hadn't seen in years, people reached by Wally's clever system of mailing. She spoke to them, asked if everything was all right, received their congratulations, and from a few, words of sympathy about Ray.

It was well after eight when she heard another car door slam. Bert, Wally, and Veda had adjourned their meeting, on Ida's invitation, to the running board of Wally's car, and for some time she had heard them talking out there, while she worked. But now, as a foot crunched on the gravel, the conversation stopped, and then Veda burst in the back door. "Mother! Guess who just came in!"

"Who was it, darling?"

"Monty Beragon!"

Mildred's heart skipped a beat, and she looked at Veda sharply. But Veda's shining eyes didn't suggest knowledge of scandal, so cautiously she asked: "And who is Monty Beragon?"

"Oh, Mother, don't you *know?*"

"I guess not."

"He plays polo for Midwick, and he lives in Pasadena, and he's rich, and good-looking, and all the girls just *wait* for his picture to come out in the paper. He's—*keen!*"

It was the first she had known that Monty was anybody in particular, but she was too busy to be excited much. Veda began dancing up and down, and Bert came in, followed by Wally, who looked as though he had just beheld God. "Sa-a-a-a-y! If that guy's here, Mildred, you're in! Why there's not a restaurant in L.A. that wouldn't pay him to eat there. Isn't that so, Bert?"

"He's very well-known."

"Known? Hell, he's a shot."

Arline came in, from the dining room. "One waf."

Veda went to the *out* door, peeped, and disappeared into the dining room. Wally began speculating as to how Monty knew about the opening. He wasn't on any list, and it seemed unlikely he had seen the Glendale papers. Bert, with some irritation, said that Mildred's reputation as a cook had spread far and wide, and that seemed sufficient reason, at least to him, without doing any fancy sleuthing about it. Wally said by God he had a notion to find out, when all of a sudden he was standing there with open mouth, and Mildred felt herself being turned slowly around. Monty was there, looking down at her gravely, intently. "Why didn't you tell me about the little girl?"

"I don't know. I—couldn't call anybody."

"I didn't hear about it until her sister told me, just now."

"She seems to be quite an admirer of yours."

"She's the most delightful little thing I've met in a long time, but never mind about her. I'd like you to know that if I'd had any idea about it, you'd have heard from me."

As though to corroborate this declaration, a box of flowers appeared suddenly under Mildred's nose, together with a slip the messenger was offering her to sign. She opened the box, found herself staring at two gigantic orchids. But Monty took the card and tore it up. "I doubt if you're in the humor for gags."

She put the flowers in the icebox, and introduced Bert and Wally. She was relieved when Ida came over, demanding that the kitchen be cleared. Monty gave her a little pat and went to the dining room. Bert and Wally went outside, eyeing her a little queerly.

By nine o'clock there were only two customers left, and as they were eating the last of the chickens, Mildred went to the switchboard and cut off the sign. Then she counted her cash. She had hoped for thirty people, and had ordered five extra chickens to be safe. Now, having been high-pressured into taking four more than that, she had barely had enough. Truly, as Wally had promised, there had been a mob, and she found she had taken in $46, or $10 more than her wildest hopes. She folded all the bills together, so she could feel their fat thickness. Then, having little to do until Arline, Pancho, and Letty finished up, she slipped off her apron, pinned on her orchids, and went into the dining room.

Ida was still waiting on the last customers, but Bert, Wally, Monty, Veda, and Mrs. Gessler were sitting sociably at one of the tables for four. Bert and Monty were discussing polo ponies, a subject that Bert seemed impressively familiar with. Veda had curled herself into the crook of his arm and was drinking in the heavenly words about the only world that could mean anything to her. Mildred pulled up a chair and sat down beside Mrs. Gessler, who at once began making queer noises. Staring into each face, she repeated "H'm? H'm?" in an insistent way, evoking only puzzled stares. It was Monty who got it. His face lit up and he bellowed "Yes!"

Then everybody bellowed yes, and Mrs. Gessler went out to her car. When she came back she had Scotch and White Rock. Mildred had Arline bring glasses, ice, and an opener, and Mrs. Gessler began her ancient rites. Bert took charge of Veda's drink, but Mildred forbade the usual switcheroo. She knew it would remind him of Ray, and she didn't want that. Veda received her drink, with its two drops of Scotch, without any tricks, and Bert suddenly got to his feet. Raising his glass to Mildred, he said: "To the best little woman that any guy was crazy enough to let get away from him."

"You ought to know, you cluck."

Mrs. Gessler was quite positive about it, and everybody laughed, and raised a glass to Mildred. She didn't know whether to raise her glass or not, but finally did. Then Ida, having disposed of the customers, was standing beside her, taking in the conviviality with a twisted grin that seemed strange and pathetic on her extremely plain face. Mildred jumped up, quickly made her a drink, and said: "Now *I'm* going to propose a toast." Raising her glass, she intoned: "To the best little woman that nobody was *ever* crazy enough to let get away from them.' Wally said: " 'Ray!" Everybody said " 'Ray!" Ida was flustered, and first giggled, then looked as though she was going to cry, and paid no attention when Mildred introduced her around. Then she plopped down in a chair and began: "Well Mildred I wish you could have heard the comment. You got no idea how they went for that chicken. And how amazed they was at them waffles. Why, they said, they never got such waffles since they was little, and they had no idea anybody knew how to make them any more. It's a hit, Mildred. It's going to do just grand." Mildred sipped her drink, feeling trembly and self-conscious and unbearably happy.

She could have sat there forever, but she had Veda to think of, and Ida to think of too, for after such help, she had to give her a lift home. So she reminded Bert that Veda had to go to school, stuffed the precious cash into her handbag, and prepared to lock up. She shook hands with them all, looking away quickly when she came to Monty, and finally got them outside. On the lawn, the party gathered around Mrs. Gessler's car, and Mildred suspected the Scotch was being finished somewhat informally, but she didn't wait to make sure. Calling to Bert not to keep Veda up late, she loaded Ida into her car, and went roaring down the boulevard.

When she got home she was surprised to find the blue Cord outside. Inside, the house was dark, but she could see a flicker of light from the den, and there she found Monty and Veda, in the dark except for the fire they had lit for themselves, and evidently getting on famously. To Mildred, Monty explained: "We had a date."

"Oh, you did."

"Yes, we made a date that I was to take her home, so I did. Of course we had to take Pop home first—"

"Or at least, to the B—"

But before Veda could finish her languid qualification, she and Monty burst into howls of laughter, and when she could get her breath she gasped: "Oh Mother! We saw the Biederhof! Through the window! And—*they flopped!*"

Mildred felt she ought to be shocked, but the next thing she knew she had joined in, and then the three of them laughed until their stomachs ached and tears ran down their faces, as though Mrs. Biederhof and her untrammeled bosom were the funniest things in the world. It was a long time before Mildred could bring herself to send Veda to bed. She wanted to keep her there, to warm herself in this sunny, carefree friendliness that had never been there before. When the time finally came, she took Veda in herself, and helped her undress, and put her in bed, and held her tight for a moment, still ecstatic at the miracle that had come to pass. Then Veda whispered: "Oh Mother, isn't he just *wonderful!*"

"He's terribly nice."

"How did you meet him?"

Mildred mumbled something about Monty's having come into the Hollywood restaurant once or twice, then asked: "And how did *you* meet him?"

"Oh Mother, I didn't! I mean, I didn't say anything to him. *He* spoke to *me*. He said I looked so much like you he knew who I was. Did you tell him about me?"

"Yes, of course."

"Then he asked for Ray, and when I told him about her, he turned perfectly pale, and jumped up, and—"

"Yes, I know."

"And Mother, those orchids!"

"You want them?"

"Mother! Mother!"

"All right, you can wear them to school."

From the sofa came a voice, a little thick, a little unsteady: "I've been looking at that damned costume all night, and with great difficulty restrained myself from biting it. Now, get it off."

"Oh, I'm not much in the humor for—"

"Get it off."

So the costume came off, and she submitted to what, on the whole, seemed a reasonably appropriate finale to the evening. Yet she was too excited really to have her mind on Monty. When she went to bed she was tired, happy, and weepy, and Bert, Wally, Mrs. Gessler, Ida, Monty, the sign, the restaurant, and the $46 were all swimming about in a moonlit pool of tears. But the face that shimmered above it, more beautiful than all the rest, was Veda's.

Chapter 10

O NE MORNING, some months after this, she was driving down from Arrowhead with Monty. He was part of her life now, though on the whole not quite so satisfactory a part as it had seemed, in that first week or two, that he might be. For one thing, she had discovered that a large part of his appeal for her was physical, and this she found disturbing. So far, her sex experiences had been limited, and of a routine, tepid sort, even in the early days with Bert. This hot, wanton excitement that Monty aroused in her seemed somehow shameful; also, she was afraid it might really take possession of her, and interfere with her work, which was becoming her life. For in spite of mishaps, blunders, and catastrophes that sometimes reduced her to bitter tears, the little restaurant continued to prosper. Whether she had any real business ability it would be hard to say, but her common sense, plus an industry that never seemed to flag, did well enough. She early saw that the wholesale pie business was the key to everything else, and doggedly kept at the job of building it up, until it was paying all expenses, even above the wages of Hans, the baker that she hired. The restaurant intake had been left as clear profit, or what would become profit as soon as her debts, somewhat appalling still, were paid. That Monty might throw her out of step with this precious career was a possibility that distinctly frightened her.

And for another thing, she felt increasingly the sense of inferiority that he had aroused in her, that first night at the lake. Somehow, by his easy flippancy, he made her accomplishments seem small, of no consequence. The restaurant, which to her was a sort of Holy Grail, attained by fabulous effort and sacrifice, to him was the Pie Wagon, a term quickly taken up by Veda, who blandly shortened it to The Wagon. And even though he sometimes brought his friends there, and introduced them, and asked her to sit down, she noticed they were always men. She never met any of his women friends, and never met his family. Once, unexpectedly, he had pointed the car at Pasadena, and said he wanted her to see his home. She was nervous at the idea of meeting his mother, but when they got there it turned out that both mother and sister were away, with the servants off for the night. At once she hated the big stuffy mansion, hated the feeling she had been smuggled in the back door, almost hated him. There was no sex that night, and he professed to be puzzled, as well as hurt, by her conduct. She had a growing suspicion that to him she was a servant girl, an amusing servant girl, one with pretty legs and a flattering response in bed, but a servant girl just the same.

Yet she never declined his invitations, never put on the brake that her instinct was demanding, never raised the hatchet that she knew one day would have to fall. For there was always this delicious thing that he had brought into her life, this intimacy with Veda that had come when he came, that would go, she was afraid, when he went. Monty seemed devoted to Veda. He took her everywhere, to polo, to horse shows, to his mother's, granting her all the social equality that he withheld from Mildred, so that the child lived in a horsy, stream-lined heaven. Mildred lived in a heaven too, a heaven of more modest design, one slightly spoiled by wounded pride, but one that held the music of harps. She laved herself in Veda's sticky affection, and bought, without complaining, the somewhat expensive gear that heaven required: riding, swimming, golf, and tennis outfits; overnight kits, monogrammed. If Mildred knew nobody in Pasadena, she had the consolation that Veda knew everybody, and had her picture on the society pages so often that she became quite blasé about it. And so long as this went on, Mildred knew she would put up with Monty, with his irritating point of view, his amused condescension, his omissions that cut her so badly—and not only put up with him, but cling to him.

This particular morning, however, she was in a pleasant humor. She had slept well, after a romantic night; it was early fall again, with the mountain trees turning yellow, and she was pontificating amiably about Mr. Roosevelt. She pontificated a great deal now, particularly about politics. She hadn't been in business very long before she became furiously aware of taxes, and this led quite naturally to politics and Mr. Roosevelt. She was going to vote for him, she said, because he was going to put an end to all this Hoover extravagance and balance the budget. Why the very idea, she said, of all those worthless people demanding help, and this Hoover even considering doing anything for them. There was nothing the matter with them except they were too lazy to work, and you couldn't tell her that anybody couldn't get along, even if there was a Depression, if they only had a little gump. In this, Monty may have detected a smug note, an allusion to what *she* had done with a little gump. At any rate, he listened with half an ear, and then asked abruptly: "Can I tell you something?"

"If it's pro-Hoover I don't want to hear it."

"It's about Veda."

"What's she up to now?"

"Music. . . . Well what the hell, it's not up to me to give you any advice. All I know is how the kid feels."

"She takes lessons."

"She takes lessons from some cheap little ivory thumper over in Glendale, and she has a squawk. She doesn't think she's getting anywhere. Well—it's none of my affair."

"Go on."

"I think she's got something."

"I always said she had talent."

"Saying she has talent and doing the right thing about it are two different things. If you don't mind my saying so, I think you know more about pies than you do about music. I think she ought to be put under somebody that can really take charge of her."

"Who, for instance?"

"Well, there's a fellow in Pasadena that could do wonders with her. You may have heard of him—Charlie Hannen, quite well-known, up to a few years ago, in the concert field. Then his lungs cracked up and he came out here. Doesn't do much now. Organist, choir master, whatever you call it, at our church, leads a quiet life, but takes a few pupils. I'm sure I can get him interested in her. If he takes her on, she'll be getting somewhere."

"When did *you* learn so much about music?"

"I don't know a thing about it. But my mother does. She's been a patroness of the Philharmonic for years and she knows all about it. She says the kid's really got it."

"Of course I never met your mother."

This slightly waspish remark Monty let pass without answering, and it was some minutes before he went on. "And another thing that makes *me* think she's got it is the way she works at it. All right, all I know is horses, but when I see a guy on top of one, out there in the morning when there's nobody else around, popping away with a mallet to improve his backhand, I think to myself, maybe one day he'll be a polo player."

"Isn't *that* something to be."

"It's the same way with her. So far as I know, she never misses a day on that dry-goods box at her grandfather's, and even when she comes over to Mother's she does her two hours of exercises every morning, before she'll even talk about tennis, or riding, or whatever Mother has in mind for her. She *works*, and you don't even have to be a musician to figure that out."

In spite of her almost religious conviction that Veda had talent, Mildred wasn't much impressed: she knew Veda too well to read the evidence quite as Monty read it. Veda's earnest practicing at Mrs. Beragon's might mean a consuming passion for music, and it might mean a consuming passion for letting the whole household know she was around. And Mr. Hannen might have been a celebrated pianist once, but the fact that he was now organist at one of Pasadena's swank churches cast a certain familiar color over his nomination as teacher. All in all, Mildred was sure she detected one of Veda's fine schemes. And in addition to that, she resented what was evidently becoming a small conspiracy to tell her what she should do about her child, and the implication that what she was already doing, by Pasadena standards, wasn't anything like good enough.

So for some time she said nothing about this subject to Veda. But it kept gnawing on her mind, setting up the fear that perhaps she was denying the child something she really ought to have. And then one night Veda broke into a violent denunciation of Miss Whittaker, the lady to whom Mildred had been paying 50¢ a week to give Veda lessons; but something about the tirade didn't have the usual phony sound to it. Troubled, Mildred asked suddenly if Mr. Hannen, of Pasadena, would be better. This produced such excited dancing around that she knew she was in for it. So she called up, made an engagement, and on the appointed afternoon rushed through her work so she could dash home and take Veda over there.

For the occasion, she laid out some of Veda's new finery: a brown silk dress, brown hat, alligator-skin shoes, and silk stockings. But when Veda got home from school, and saw the pile on the bed, she threw up her hands in horror. "Mother! I can't be dressed *up!* Ooh! It would be so *provincial!*" Mildred knew the voice of society when she heard it, so she sighed, put the things away, and watched while Veda tossed out her own idea of suitable garb: maroon sweater, plaid skirt, polo coat, leather beret, woolen socks, and flat-heeled shoes. But she looked away when Veda started to dress. A year and a half had indeed made some changes in Veda's appearance. She was still no more than medium height, but her haughty carriage made her seem taller. The hips were as slim as ever, but had taken on some touch of voluptuousness. The legs were Mildred's, to the last grace-ful contour. But the most noticeable change was what Monty bru-tally called the Dairy: two round, swelling protuberances that had appeared almost overnight on the high, arching chest. They would have been large, even for a woman: for a child of thirteen they were positively startling. Mildred had a mystical feeling about them: they made her think tremulously of Love, Motherhood, and similar milky concepts. When Monty had denounced them as indecent, and told Veda for Christ's sake to get a hammock to sling them in, Mildred had been shocked, and pink-faced, and furious. But Veda had laughed gaily, and got brassières in a completely matter-of-fact way. It would have been hard to imagine her pink-faced about anything. What with the chest, the Dairy, and the slightly swaying hips, she moved like some proud, pedigreed pigeon.

Mr. Hannen lived just off the Pasadena traffic circle, in a house that looked usual enough from the outside, but which, inside, turned out to be one gigantic studio, with all the first floor and most of the second given over to it. It startled Mildred, not only by its size, but by its incredible bareness. There was nothing in it but a big piano, long shelves of music, a wooden wall seat across one end, and a bronze bust, in one corner, labeled BAUER. Mr. Hannen himself was a squat man of about forty, with bandy legs, thick chest, and big hands, though a slight stoop, as well as streaky white hair hinted at the illness that Monty had mentioned. He was quite friendly, and chatted with Mildred until she was off guard, and grew gabby. When she mentioned the restaurant, Veda tossed her head impatiently, but Mr. Hannen said "Ah!" in a flattering way, remembered he had heard of it, copied down the address, and promised to come in. Then, rather casually, he got around to Veda, had a look at the music she had brought, and said they might as well get the horrible part over. Veda looked a little set back on her heels, but he waved her to the piano and told her to play something—anything, so it was short. Veda marched grandly over, sat down on the bench, twisted her hands in a professional way, and meditated. Mr. Hannen sat down on the wall seat, near Mildred, and meditated. Then Veda launched into a piece known to Mildred as Rachmaninoff Prelude.

It was the first time, in recent months, that Mildred had heard Veda play, and she was delighted with the effect. The musical part she wasn't quite sure about, except that it made a fine noisy clatter. But there could be no mistaking the authoritative way in which Veda kept lifting her right hand high in the air, or the style with which she crossed her left hand over it. The piece kept mounting to a rousing noisy climax, and then inexplicably it faltered. Veda struck a petulant chord. "I always want to play it *that* way."

"I'll tell Mr. Rachmaninoff when I see him."

Mr. Hannen was slightly ironical about it, but his brows knit, and he began eyeing Veda sharply. Veda, a little chastened, finished. He made no comment, but got up, found a piece of music, and put it in front of her. "Let's try the sight-reading."

Veda rattled through this piece like a human pianola, while Mr. Hannen alternately screwed up his face as though he were in great pain, and stared hard at her. When silence mercifully stole into the room, he walked over to the shelves again, got out a violin case, set it beside Mildred, opened it, and began to resin the bow. "Let's try the accompanying. What's your name again?"

"Miss Pierce."

"Ah—?"

"Veda."

"Have you ever accompanied, Veda?"

"Just a little."

"Just a little, what?"

"—I beg your pardon?"

"I might warn you, Veda, that with young pupils I mix quite a little general instruction, in with the musical. Now if you don't want a clip on the ear, you'll call me *sir*."

"Yes sir."

Mildred wanted to kick up her heels and laugh at a Veda who was suddenly meek and humble. However, she affected not to be listening, and fingered the silk of Mr. Hannen's violin cover as though it was the most interesting piece of sewing she had ever seen. He picked up the violin now, and turned to Veda. "This isn't my instrument, but there must be *something* for you to accompany, so it'll have to do. Sound your A."

Veda tapped a note, he tuned the violin, and set a piece of music on the piano. "All right—a little briskly. Don't drag it."

Veda looked blankly at the music. "Why—you've given me the violin part."

"—?"

"Sir."

"Ah, so I have."

He looked on the shelves for a moment, then shook his head. "Well, the piano part's around somewhere, but I don't seem to see it at the moment. All right, keep the violin part in front of you and give me a little accompaniment of your own. Let's see—you have four measures before I come in. Count the last one aloud."

"Sir, I wouldn't even know how to—"

"Begin."

After a desperate look at the music, Veda played a long, faltering figure that ended somewhere up in the tinkle notes. Then, thumping a heavy bass, she counted: "One, two, three, four *and*—"

Even Mildred could detect that the violin was certainly not Mr. Hannen's instrument. But Veda kept up her bass, and when he stopped, she repeated the long figure, thumped her bass, counted, and he came in again. This went on for a short time, but little by little, Mildred thought, it was getting smoother. Once, when Mr. Hannen stopped, Veda omitted the long figure. In its place, she repeated the last part of the air he had been playing, so that when he came in again it joined up quite neatly. When they finished, Mr. Hannen put the violin away and resumed staring at Veda. Then: "Where did you study harmony?"

"I never studied harmony, sir."

"H'm."

He walked around a few moments, said "Well" in a reflective way, and began to talk. "The technique is simply God-awful. You have a tone like a xylophone that fell in love with a hand organ, but that may respond to—whatever we do about it. And the conceit is almost beyond belief. That certainly will respond. It's responded a little already, hasn't it?"

"Yes sir."

"But—play that bit in the Rachmaninoff again, the way you said you always wanted to play it."

Rather weakly, Veda obeyed. He was beside her on the bench now, and dropped his big paw on the keys as he played after her. A tingle went through Mildred at the way it seemed to reach down into the vitals of the piano, and find sounds that were rich, dark, and exciting. She noted that it no longer seemed hairy and thick, but became a thing of infinite grace. He studied the keys a moment, then said: "And suppose you did play it that way. You'd be in a little trouble, don't you think?" He played another chord or two. "Where would you go from *there*?"

Veda played a few more chords, and he carefully played them after her. Then he nodded. "Yes, it could have been written that way. I really think Mr. Rachmaninoff's way is better—I find a slight touch of banality in yours, don't you?"

"What's banality, sir?"

"I mean it sounds corny. Cheap. It's got that old Poet and Peasant smell to it. Play it an octave higher and put a couple of trills in it, it would be 'Listen to the Mocking Bird' almost before you knew it."

Veda played it an octave higher, twiddled a trill, did a bar of "Listen to the Mocking Bird," and got very red. "Yes sir, I guess you're right."

"But—it makes musical *sense*."

This seemed so incredible to him that he sat in silence for some little time before he went on: "I got plenty of pupils with talent in their fingers, very few with anything in their heads. Your fingers, Veda, I'm not so sure about. There's something about the way you do it that isn't exactly—but never mind about that. We'll see what can be done. But your head—that's different. Your sight-reading is remarkable, the sure sign of a musician. And that trick I played on you, making you improvise an accompaniment to the little gavotte— of course, you didn't really do it well, but the amazing thing was that you could do it at all. I don't know what made me think you could, unless it was that idiotic monkeyshine you pulled in the Rachmaninoff. So—"

He turned now to Mildred. "I want her over here twice a week.

I'm giving her one lesson in piano—my rate is ten dollars an hour, the lesson is a half hour, so it'll cost you five dollars. I'm giving her another lesson in the theory of music, and that lesson will be free. I can't be sure what will come of it, and it isn't fair to make you pay for my experiments. But, she'll learn *something*, and at the very least get some of the conceit knocked out of her."

So saying, he took a good healthy wallop at Veda's ribs. Then he added: "I suppose nothing will come of it, if we're really honest about it. Many are called, in this business, but few are chosen, and hardly any find out how good you have to be before you're any good at all. But—we'll see . . . God, Veda, but your playing stinks. I ought to charge a hundred dollars an hour, just to listen to you."

Veda started to cry, as Mildred stared in astonishment. Not three times in her life had she seen this cold child cry, and yet there she was, with two streams squirting out of her eyes and cascading down on the maroon sweater, where they made glistening silver drops. Mr. Hannen airily waved his hand. "Let her bawl. It's nothing to what she'll be doing before I get through with her."

So Veda bawled, and she was still bawling when they got in the car and started home. Mildred kept patting her hand, and gave up all thought of a little light twitting on the subject of "Sir." Then, in explosive jerks, Veda started to talk. "Oh Mother—I was so afraid— he wouldn't take me. And then—he *wanted* me. He said I had something—in my head. Mother—in my *head!*"

Then Mildred knew that an awakening had taken place in Veda, that it wasn't in the least phony, and that what had awakened was precisely what she herself had mutely believed in all these years. It was as though the Star of Bethlehem had suddenly appeared in front of her.

So Monty was vindicated, but when Mildred snuggled up to him one night in the den, and wanted to talk about it, the result left a great deal to be desired. He lit a cigarette and rehearsed his reasons for thinking Veda "had it"; they were excellent reasons, all in praise of Veda, but somehow they didn't hit the spot. When she tried to break through his habit of treating everything with offhand impersonality, saying wasn't it wonderful, and how did *he* ever think up something like that, he seemed uncomfortable at her kittenishness, and rather curtly brushed her off. To hell with it, he said. He had done nothing that anybody couldn't have done that knew the child, so why give him any credit? Then, as though bored with the whole subject, he began stripping off her stockings.

But there was a great hunger in Mildred's heart: she had to *share* this miracle with somebody, and when she had stood it as long as she could she sent for Bert. He came the next afternoon, to the restaurant, when the place was deserted and she had him to herself. She had Arline serve lunch and told him about it. He had already heard a little, from Mom, who had got a brief version from Veda, but now he got it all, in complete detail. Mildred told about the studio, the Rachmaninoff prelude, the sight-reading, the accompaniment to the violin selection. He listened gravely, except for the laugh he let out over the "Sir" episode. When Mildred had finished he thought a long time. Then, solemnly, he announced: "She's some kid. She's some kid."

Mildred sighed happily. This was the kind of talk she wanted, at last. He went on, then, flatteringly reminding her that she had always said Veda was "artistic," gallantly conceding that he himself had had his doubts. Not that he didn't appreciate Veda, he added hastily, hell no. It was only that he didn't know of any music on Mildred's side or his, and he always understood this kind of thing ran in families. Well, it just went to show how any of us can be wrong, and goddam it, he was glad it had turned out this way. *Goddam* it he was. Then, having polished off the past, he looked at the future. The fingers, he assured Mildred, were nothing to worry about. Because suppose she didn't become a great pianist? From all he had heard, that market was shot anyhow. But if it was like this guy said, and she had talent in her head, and began to *write* music, that was where the real dough was, and it didn't make a bit of difference whether you could play the piano or not. Because, he said dramatically, look at Irving Berlin. He had it straight that the guy couldn't play a note, but with a million bucks in the bank and more coming in every day, *he* should worry whether he could tickle the keys or not. Oh no, Mildred needn't worry about Veda now. The way it looked to *him*, the kid was all set, and before very long she'd be pulling off something big.

Having Veda turn into Irving Berlin, with or without a million bucks in the bank, wasn't exactly what Mildred had in mind for her. In her imagination she could see Veda already, wearing a pale green dress to set off her coppery hair, seated at a big piano before a thousand people, grandly crossing her right hand over her left, haughtily bowing to thunderous applause—but no matter. The spirit was what counted. Bert spun her dreams for her, while she closed her eyes and breathed deeply, and Arline poured him more coffee, from a percolator, the way he liked it. It was the middle of the afternoon before Mildred returned to earth, and said suddenly: "Bert, can I ask a favor?"

"Anything, Mildred."

"It's not why I asked you here. I just wanted to tell you about it. I knew you'd want to hear."

"I know why you asked me. Now what is it?"

"I want that piano, at Mom's."

"Nothing to it. They'll be only too glad—"

"No, wait a minute. I don't want it as a gift, nothing like that at all. I just want to borrow it until I can get Veda a piano that—"

"It's all right. They'll—"

"No, but wait a minute. I'm going to get her a piano. But the kind of piano that she ought to have, I mean a real grand, costs eleven hundred dollars. And they'll give me terms, but I just don't dare take on any more debt. What I'm going to do, I'm going to open a special account, down at the bank, and keep putting in, and I know by next Christmas, I mean a year from now, I can manage it. But just now —"

"I only wish I could contribute a little."

"Nobody's asking you to."

Quickly she put her hand over his and patted it. "You've done plenty. Maybe you've forgotten how you gave me the house outright, and everything that went before, but I haven't. You've done your share. Now it's my turn. I don't mind about that, but I do want them to know, Mom and Mr. Pierce I mean, that I'm not trying to *get* anything from them. I just want to borrow the piano, so Veda can practice at home, and—"

"Mildred."

"Yes?"

"Will you just kindly shut up?"

"All right."

"Everything's under control. Just leave it to me."

So presently the piano was carted down, and on January 2, Mildred went to the bank and deposited $21, after multiplying carefully, and making sure that $21 a week, at the end of a year, would almost exactly equal $1,100.

•   •   •

Mildred was in such a panic over the bank holiday, as well as the other alarums that attended Mr. Roosevelt's inauguration, that she paid scant attention to anything except her immediate concerns. But when her apprehension slacked off, she began to notice that Monty seemed moody and abstracted, with little of the flippancy that was normally part of him. Then, in a speakeasy one night, the sharp way he glanced at the check told her he didn't have much money with him. Then another night, when he revoked an order for a drink he obviously wanted, she knew he was hard up. But it was Veda who let the cat out of the bag. Walking home from the restaurant one night, she suddenly asked Mildred: "Heard the news?"

"What news, darling?"

"The House of Beragon is ge-finished. It is ffft, fa-down-go-boom, oop-a-doop-whango. Alas it is no more. Pop goes the weasel."

"I've been suspecting something like that."

Mildred said this quickly, to cover the fact that she actually had been told nothing at all, and for the rest of the walk home was depressed by the realization that Monty had suffered some sort of fantastic reverses without saying a word to her. But soon curiosity got the better of her. She lit a fire in the den, had Veda sit down, and asked for more details. "Well Mother, I really don't know a great deal about it, except that it's all over Pasadena, and you hardly hear anything else. They had some stock, the Duenna, that's his mother, and the Infanta, that's his sister. Stock in a bank, some-where in the East. And it was assessable, whatever that means. So when the bank didn't open it was most unfortunate. What *is* assessable?"

"I heard some talk about it, when the banks were closed. I think it means that if there's not enough money to pay the depositors, then the stockholders have to make it good."

"*That's* it. That explains about their assets being impounded, and why they've gone to Philadelphia, the Duenna and the Infanta, so papers can't be served on them. And of course when Beragon Brothers, dear old Beragon Brothers, founded in 1893—when they went bust, that didn't help any, either."

"When did that happen?"

"Three or four months ago. Their growers, the farmers that raised the fruit, all signed up with the Exchange, and *that* was what cooked Monty's goose. He didn't have any bank stock. His money was in the fruit company, but when that folded his mother kicked in. Then when the bank went under she had nothing to kick. Anyway there's a big sign on the lawn, 'For Sale, Owner Must Sacrifice,' and Monty's showing the prospective buyers around."

"You mean their *house?*"

"I mean their palatial residence on Orange Grove Avenue, with the iron dogs out front and the peacock out behind—but a buyer had better show up pretty soon, or Monty'll be eating the peacock. It certainly looks as though the old buzzard will have to go to work."

Mildred didn't know whether she was more shocked at the tale she heard or Veda's complete callousness about it. But one thing was clear: Monty wanted no sympathy from her, so for a time she ate with him, drank with him, and slept with him under the pretense that she knew nothing whatever. But presently the thing became so public, what with pieces in the paper about the sale of his polo ponies, the disappearance of the Cord in favor of a battered little Chevrolet, and one thing and another, that he did begin to talk about it. But he always acted as though this were some casual thing that would be settled shortly, a nuisance while it lasted, but of no real importance. Never once did he let Mildred come close to him in connection with it, pat him on the head, tell him it didn't really matter, do any of the things that in her scheme of life a woman was expected to do under these circumstances. She felt sorry for him, terribly upset about him. And yet she also felt snubbed and rebuffed. And she could never shake off the feeling that if he accepted her as his social equal he would act differently about it.

And then one night she came home to find him with Veda, waiting for her. They were in the den, having a furious argument about polo, which continued after she sat down. It seemed that a new team had been organized, called the Ramblers; that its first game would be at San Diego, and that Monty had been invited to make the trip. Veda, an expert on such matters, was urging him to go. "There'd better be *one* eight-goal man with that outfit, or they can stop calling it The Ramblers and call it Mussolini Reviewing the Cavalry, because that's what it's going to be all right. Just a one-way parade of horses, and they won't wake up until the score is about forty to nothing."

"I've got too much to do."

"Such as what?"

"This and that."

"Nothing whatever, if I'm any good at guessing. Monty, you've got to go with them. If you don't, they're sunk. It'll be embarrassing. And they'll simply ruin your horses. After all, *they've* got some rights."

Polo was a complete mystery to Mildred. How Monty could sell his ponies and still be riding them she couldn't understand, and chiefly she couldn't understand *why* he was riding them, or anybody was. And yet it tore her heart that he should want to go, and not be able to, and it kept bothering her long after Veda had gone to bed. When he got up to go she pulled him down beside her, and asked: "Do you need money?"

"Oh Lord no!"

His voice, look, and gesture were those of a man pained beyond expression at an insinuation utterly grotesque. But Mildred, nearly two years in the restaurant business, was not fooled. She said: "I think you do."

"Mildred—you leave me without any idea—what to say to you. I've—run into a little bad luck—that's true. My mother has—we all have. But—it's nothing that involves—small amounts. I can still—hold up my end of it—if that's what you're talking about."

"I want you to play in that game."

"I'm not interested."

"Wait a minute."

She found her handbag, took out a crisp $20 bill. Going over to him she slipped it in the breast pocket of his coat. He took it out, with an annoyed grimace, and pitched it back at her. It fell on the floor. She picked it up and dropped it in his lap. With the same annoyed grimace, very much annoyed this time, he picked it up, started to pitch it back at her again, then hesitated, and sat there snapping it between his fingers, so it made little pistol shots. Then, without looking at her: "Well—I'll pay it back."

"That's all right."

"I don't know when—two or three things have to be straightened out first—but it won't be very long. So—if it's understood to be distinctly a loan—"

"Any way you want."

That week, with the warm June weather, her business took a sharp drop. For the first time, she had to skip an installment on Veda's piano.

. . .

The next week, when he changed his mind about going to a speakeasy that he liked, she slipped $10 into his pocket, and they went. Before she knew it, she was slipping him $10's and $20's regularly, either when she remembered about it, or he stammeringly asked her if he could tap her for another small loan. Her business continued light, and when the summer had gone, she had managed to make only three deposits on the piano, despite hard scrimping. She was appalled at the amount of money he cost, and fought off a rising irritation about it. She told herself it wasn't his fault, that he was merely going through what thousands of others had already gone through, were still going through. She told herself it was her duty to be helping somebody, and that it might as well be somebody that meant something to her. She also reminded herself she had practically forced the arrangement on him. It was no use. The piano had become an obsession with her by now, and the possibility that it was slipping away from her caused a baffled, frustrated sensation that almost smothered her.

And she was all too human, and the cuts she had received from him demanded their revenge. She began to order him around: timid requests that he haul Veda to Mr. Hannen's, so she wouldn't have to take the bus, now became commands; she curtly told him when he was to show up, when he was to be back, whether he was to have his dinner at the restaurant or at the house, and when she would join him afterwards. In a hundred small ways she betrayed that she despised him for taking her money, and on his side, he did little to make things better. Monty, alas, was like Bert. A catastrophic change had taken place in his life, and he was wholly unable to adjust himself to it. In some way, indeed, he was worse off than Bert, for Bert lived with his dreams, and at least they kept him mellow. But Monty was an amateur cynic, and cynics are too cynical to dream. He had been born to a way of life that included taste, manners, and a jaunty aloofness from money, as though it were beneath a gentleman's notice. But what he didn't realize was that all these things rested squarely on money: it was the possession of money that enabled him to be aloof from it. For the rest, his days were dedicated to play, play on which the newspapers cast a certain agreeable importance, but play nevertheless. Now, with the money gone, he was unable to give up the old way of life, or find a new one. He became a jumble of sorry fictions, an attitude with nothing behind it but pretense. He retained something that he thought of as his pride, but it had no meaning, and exhibited itself mainly in mounting bitterness toward Mildred. He carped at her constantly, sneered at her loyalty to Mr. Roosevelt, revealed that his mother knew the whole Roosevelt family, and regarded Franklin Delano as a phony and a joke. His gags about the Pie Wagon, once easily patronizing and occasionally funny, took on a touch of malice, and Veda, ever fashionable, topped them with downright insolence. The gay little trio wasn't quite so gay.

And then one night in the den, when Mildred tucked another $20 into his pocket, he omitted his usual mumble about paying it back. Instead, he took out the bill, touched his forelock with it, and said: "Your paid gigolo thanks you."

"I don't think that was very nice."

"It's true, isn't it?"

"Is that the only reason you come here?"

"Not at all. Come what may, swing high, swing low, for better or for worse, you're still the best piece of tail I ever had, or ever could imagine."

He got this off with a nervous, rasping little laugh, and for a few seconds Mildred felt prickly all over, as though the blood were leaving her body. Then her face felt hot, and she became aware of a throbbing silence that had fallen between them. Sheer pride demanded that she say something, and yet for a time she couldn't. Then, in a low, shaking voice, she said: "Monty, suppose you go home."

"What's the matter?"

"I think you know."

"Well, by all that's holy, I *don't* know!"

"I told you to go."

Instead of going, he shook his head, as though she were incredibly obtuse, and launched into a dissertation on the relations between the sexes. The sense of it was that as long as this thing was there, everything was all right; that it was the strongest bond there was, and what he was really doing, if she only had sense enough to know it, was paying her a compliment. What she really objected to was his language, wasn't it? If he had said it flowery, so it sounded poetic, she would have felt differently, wouldn't she?

But every moment or two he gave the same nervous, rasping laugh, and again she was unable to speak. Then, gathering herself with an effort, she rose to one of her rare moments of eloquence. "If you told me that, and intended it as a compliment, it might have been one, I don't know. Almost anything is a compliment, if you mean it. But when you tell me that, and it's the only thing you have to tell me, then it's not a compliment. It's the worst thing I ever had said to me in my life."

"Oh, so you want the I-love-you scene."

"I want you to go."

Hot tears started to her eyes, but she winked them back. He shook his head, got up, then turned to her as though he had to explain something to a child. "We're not talking about things. We're talking about words. I'm not a poet. I don't even want to be a poet. To me, that's just funny. I say something to you my own way, and wham you go moral on me. Well what do I do now? It's a pure question of prudery, and—"

"That's a lie."

Her lungs were filling with breath now, so much that she felt it would suffocate her. Her face screwed up into the squint, and the glittering tears made her eyes look hard, cold, and feline. She sat perfectly still, her legs crossed, and looked at him, where he stood facing her on the other side of the room. After a long pause she went on, in a passionate, trembling voice. "Since you've known me, that's what I've been to you, a piece of tail. You've taken me to mountain shacks and back-street speakeasies, you've never introduced me to your friends—except for a few men you've brought over to dinner sometimes—or your mother, or your sister, or any member of your family. You're ashamed of me, and now that you're in my debt, you had to say what you just said to me, to get even. It's not a surprise to me. I've known it all along. Now you can go."

"None of that is true."

"Every word of it is true."

"So far as my friends go—"

"They mean nothing to me."

"—It hadn't occurred to me you'd care to meet any of them. Most of them are dull, but if meeting them means anything to you. that's easy fixed. So far as my mother goes—"

"She means nothing to me either."

"—So far as my mother goes, I can't do anything about her now, because she's away, and so is my sister. But you may have forgotten that with this restaurant of yours you keep somewhat peculiar hours. To have arranged a meeting would have been idiotically complicated, so I did the best I could. I took your daughter over there, and if you knew anything about social conventions at all, you'd know that I was dealing in my own way with what otherwise would have been a situation. And certainly my mother took all the interest in Veda she could be expected to take—a little more interest than you seemed to be taking, I sometimes thought."

"I—didn't complain on that score."

In her heart, Mildred knew that Monty was being as dishonest about Veda as he was being about the rest of it. Obviously, he liked Veda, and found her an amusing exhibit to drag around, no doubt because she was precisely the kind of snob that he was himself, and that most of his friends were. And also, by doing so much for the child, he could neatly sidestep the necessity of doing anything about the mother. But to argue about it would jeopardize the enchanted life that Veda now led, so Mildred veered off in a new direction. "Monty, why don't you tell the truth? You look down on me because I work."

"Are you crazy?"

"No. You look down on everybody that works, as you practically admitted to me the first night I was with you. All right, I work. It's not at all elegant work, but it's the only work I can do. I cook food and sell it. But one thing you'd better get through your head sooner or later: You'll have to go to work—"

"Of course I'm going to work!"

"Ha-ha. When?"

"As soon as I get the damned house sold, and this mess straightened out that we've got ourselves into. Until that's over, work, for me, is out of the question. But as *soon* as it's over—"

"Monty, you just make me laugh. I used to be married to a real estate company, and there's no use trying to kid me about houses, and how to get rid of them. There's nothing about that place that can't be put in the hands of an agent, and handled like any other. No, it's not that. You'd rather live there, so you can have an address on Orange Grove Avenue, and cook your own eggs in the morning, and drive over to the club in the afternoon, and have your dinner here with Veda, *and take your spending money from me*—than work. That's all, isn't it?"

"Sure."

His face broke into a sunny smile, he came over, roughly pushed her into a little heap, took her in his arms. "I don't know anybody I'd rather take money from than you. Your paid gigolo is damned well satisfied."

She pushed his arms away, trying to repulse him. But she was taken by surprise, and her struggles had no steam in them. Try as she would, she couldn't resist the physical effect he had on her, and when she finally yielded, the next hour was more wanton, more shamefully exciting, than any she remembered. And yet, for the first time, she felt an undertone of disgust. She didn't forget that not once had the $20 bill been mentioned, not once had he offered to give it back. They parted amicably, he apologizing for the offending remark, she telling him to forget what she had said, as she was upset, and didn't mean it. But both of them meant it, and neither of them forgot.

Chapter 11

"B ABY, WHAT ARE you doing about Repeal?"

"You mean Repeal of Prohibition?"

"Yeah, just that."

"Why, I don't see how it affects me."

"It affects you plenty."

Mrs. Gessler, having coffee with Mildred just before closing time, began to talk very rapidly. Repeal, she said, was only a matter of weeks, and it was going to stand the whole restaurant business on its head. "People are just crazy for a drink, a decent drink, a drink with no smoke or ether or formaldehyde in it, a drink they can have out in the open, without having to give the password to some yegg with his face in a slot. And places that can read the handwriting on the wall are going to cash in, and those that can't are going to pass out. You think you've got a nice trade here, don't you? And you think it'll stick by you, because it likes you, and likes your chicken, and wants to help a plucky little woman get along? It will like hell. When they find out you're not going to serve them that drink, they're going to be sore and stay sore. They're going to tag you for a back number and go some place where they get what they want. You're going to be out of luck."

"You mean I should sell *liquor?*"

"It'll be legal, won't it?"

"I wouldn't even consider such a thing."

"Why not?"

"Do you think I'd run a *saloon?*"

Mrs. Gessler lit a cigarette, began snapping the ashes impatiently into Mildred's Mexican ashtrays. Then she took Mildred to task for prejudice, for stupidity, for not being up with the times. Mildred, annoyed at being told how to run her business, argued back, but for each point she made Mrs. Gessler made two points. She kept reminding Mildred that liquor, when it came back, wasn't going to be the same as it had been in the old days. It was going to be respectable, and it was going to put the restaurant business on its feet. "That's what has ailed eating houses ever since the war. That's why you're lucky to get a lousy 85 cents for your dinner, when if you could sell a drink with it, you could get a buck, and maybe a buck and a quarter. Baby, you're not talking sense, and I'm getting damned annoyed at you."

"But I don't know anything about liquor."

"I *do*."

Something about Mrs. Gessler's manner suggested that this was what she had been trying to lead up to all the time, for she lit another cigarette, eyed Mildred sharply, and went on: "Now listen: You know and I know and we all know that Ike's in the long- and short-haul trucking business. Just the same, Repeal's going to hit him hard. We'll have to do something, quick, while he reorganizes. That means *I'll* have to do something. So how's this? You put in the booze, and I'll take charge of it for you, for a straight ten per cent of what I take in, plus tips, if, as, and when there any, and if, as, and when I'm not too proud to pick them up—which ain't likely, baby. It ain't even possible."

"You? A *bartender?*"

"Why not? I'll be a damned good one."

This struck Mildred so funny that she laughed until she heard a girdle seam pop. In spite of work, worry, and everything she could do about it, she was getting the least little bit fat. But Mrs. Gessler didn't laugh. She was in dead earnest, and for the next few days nagged Mildred relentlessly. Mildred still regarded the whole idea as absurd, but on her trips downtown in connection with the pie business, she began to hear things. And then, as state after state fell in line for Repeal, she hardly heard anything else: every proprietor, from Mr. Chris to the owners of the big cafeterias, was in a dither to know what to do, and she began to get frightened. She had to talk to somebody, and on such matters she hadn't much confidence in Bert, and none at all in Monty. On a sudden inspiration she called up

Wally. She saw him quite a lot, in connection with their real estate relations, but their previous relation, by the curious twists of human memory, had by tacit consent been completely erased, so it had never existed. Wally came over one afternoon, listened while Mildred explained her quandary, then shook his head. "Well I don't know what you're backing and filling about. Course you'll sell liquor."

"You mean I'll have to, to hold my trade?"

"I mean there's *dough* in it."

He looked at her with his familiar stare, that was at the same time so vague and so shrewd, and her heart gave a little thump. It was the first time, for some reason, that this aspect of the problem had occurred to her. He went on, a little annoyed at her stupidity: "What the hell? Every drink you sell will be about eighty per cent profit, even at what you have to pay for your liquor. And it'll pull in more people for the dinner trade. If Lucy Gessler wants to take it over, then O.K. If she don't know about booze, I don't know who does. Get going on it, and get going now. It's coming, fast. And be sure you put on your sign, *Cocktails*. That's what they're waiting for. Put a red star in front of it, so they know *you* know it's important."

"Will I need some kind of a license?"

"I'll fix that up for you."

So the next time Mrs. Gessler came in, she found Mildred in a different frame of mind. She nodded approval of what Wally had said about the sign, then became coldly businesslike about other obligatory preparations. "I'll need a bar, but there's no room for one until you make alterations, so I'll have to get along with a portable. It'll be a perambulator thing that I'll wheel from table to table—the same as most other places are going to use, temporarily. It'll have to be specially made and it'll cost you about three hundred bucks. Then I'll need a couple of hundred dollars' worth of liquor. I ought to have more, but it'll be all I can get, in the beginning. Then I want a couple of leather seats, near the door, with a low table between. Between trips to the tables, I'll be running my own little soiree over there, and I'll sell plenty of drinks to people waiting to be seated for dinner. Then I'll want a special bus, assigned to me alone. Your kid Pancho has a pal that'll do, by the name of Josie. He won't be available for general work, because he'll have to wash glasses for me all the time, and wash them the way I want them washed, and bring beer from the icebox when I call for it, and ice whatever wine we sell, and he'll have all he can do, just helping me. Then I'll need a full set of cocktail, highball, and wine glasses—not too many, but we'll have to have the right glasses for the right drinks. Then, let's see. You'll need pads of special bar checks, to run separate from the others. It's the only way we can keep it all straight. That's about all I can think of now."

"How much, all in all?"

"About five hundred to start—for the bar, glasses, furniture, and checks. The liquor will be over and above the five hundred, but you won't pay till the Monday after delivery, and by that time we ought to have a few dollars coming in."

Mildred gulped, told Mrs. Gessler she would let her know next day. That night she lay awake, and her mind darted first to this scheme, then to that, whereby she could furnish five hundred dollars. She kept a little reserve of two or three hundred dollars, but she dared not dip into it, as sad experience had taught her that emergencies arose constantly that demanded instant cash. It was a long time before her mind darted at last to the only way she could get the money: by robbing the special account for Veda's piano. It now amounted to $567, and the moment she thought of it she tried not to think of it, and began once more her frantic questing for schemes. But soon she knew this was what she had to do; knew that Veda couldn't have her piano for Christmas. Then once more rage began to suffocate her—not at Mrs. Gessler, or Repeal, or any of the circumstances that made this new outlay necessary, but at Monty, for the money he had cost her, those endless $10s and $20s which now, if she had them, would see her through. She worked herself into such a state that presently she had to get up, put on a kimono, and make herself a cup of tea, so she could quiet down.

Christmas morning Mildred woke up with one of her rare hangovers. It had indeed been a gay night at the little restaurant, for the bar, opening promptly on December 6, had outdone all that had been expected of it. Not only had it taken in large sums itself, but it had drawn a bigger dinner trade, and a better dinner trade. Mrs. Gessler, in gabardine slacks of the same brick-red as the waitresses' uniforms, white mess jacket with brass buttons, and red ribbon around her hair, seemed to catch the diners' fancy, and certainly she was expert enough to please the most fastidious. Tips went up, and when the kitchen celebration finally got going, it was exceedingly festive. Hans, the baker, was supposed to be off at night, but he showed up anyway, and got the party started with a bang by feeling Sigrid's leg. Sigrid was a Swedish girl Mildred had hired mainly for her looks, and then found out was one of the best waitresses she had ever seen. Then, just to be impartial, Hans felt Arline's leg, and Emma's, and Audrey's. Emma and Audrey had been taken on the day after the opening, just to forestall the possibility of another jam-up. The ensuing squeals were enjoyed by Pancho and Josie, who sat apart, not quite of things, yet not quite out of them; and by Mrs. Kramer, an assistant cook Mildred was training. They were emphatically not enjoyed by Carl, a seventeen-year-old who drove the little second-hand delivery truck Mildred had bought, and painted cream, with *"Mildred Pierce, Pies,"* lettered on it in bold red script. He concentrated on ice cream and cake, and eyed Hans's efforts with stony disapproval, to the great delight of Arline, who kept screaming that he was learning "the facks of life."

Mildred had sat down with them, and put out wine and whiskey, and taken two or three drinks herself. What with the liquor, and the thanks she received for the $10 she had given each of them, she began to feel so friendly that she weakened in her resolve to give Monty nothing whatever for Christmas. First she took his orchids out of the icebox and pinned them on, to a loud chorus of applause. Then she had another drink, went over to the cash box, and smooched four $10 bills. These she put in a little envelope and wrote on it, "Merry Christmas, Monty." Then, hearing from Mrs. Gessler that he had arrived, she went into the dining room, weaving slightly, and elaborately took him outside. Under the trees she slipped the envelope into his pocket and thanked him for the orchids, which she said were the most beautiful she had ever had. Then she invited him to smell them. Laughing a little, obviously delighted at her condition, he reminded her that orchids had no smell. "Smell'm anyway." So he smelled, and reported that the orchids still had no smell, but that she smelled fine. She nodded, satisfied, and kissed him. Then she took him inside, where Bert, Wally, Mrs. Gessler, and Veda were sitting at a table, having a little celebration of their own.

And yet the evening had had an unpleasant finish: Monty and Veda began whispering together, and went into gales of laughter at some joke of their own. Mildred heard the words "varlets' yulaba-loo," and concluded, probably correctly, that they were laughing at the party in the kitchen. She launched into a long, boozy harangue on the rights of labor, and how anybody who worked for a living was as good as anybody else. Wally tried to shush her down and Mrs. Gessler tried to shush her down, but it was no use. She went on to the bitter end. Then, somewhat inconsistently, she lurched to her feet, went to the kitchen, and asked how people could enjoy themselves with all that yelling going on. This had the effect of ringing down the curtain, front and rear.

Now, as she got up and dressed, she had a sour recollection of the harangue, and a still sourer recollection of the four $10's that had followed their predecessors down a bottomless rathole. She had given Letty the day off, so she went to the kitchen, made herself coffee, and drank it black. Then, hearing Veda's water running, she knew she had to hurry. She went to her bedroom, got a pile of packages out of the closet, and took them to the living room. Quickly she arranged a neat display around the base of the tree that had already been set up and decorated. Then she took out her own offering and looked at it. It was a wrist watch. She had put off buying it until the last moment, hoping the profits from the bar would permit her to order the piano anyway. But the unforeseen had again intervened. During the first hectic days of Repeal, Mrs. Gessler had a devil's own time finding liquor, and for much of it had to pay cash. So the hope died, and at the last minute Mildred had dashed downtown and bought this gaud for $75. She listened close and heard its tiny tick, but it didn't sound much like a grand piano. Glumly she wrapped it, wrote a little card, tucked it under the ribbon. Then she set it beside the package from Bert.

She had hardly stood up to survey the general effect when there came a tap on the door, and Veda, in her most syrupy Christmas voice, asked: "May I come in?" Mildred managed a soft smile, and opened the door. Suddenly Veda was smothering her with kisses, wishing a merry Christmas to "you darling, darling Mother!" Then, just as suddenly, the kisses stopped and so did the greetings. Veda was staring at the Pierce upright, and by the look on her face Mildred knew she had been told about the grand, by Bert, by Monty, by the cashier at the bank, by somebody—and had expected to see it there, as a fine surprise, this Christmas morning.

Mildred licked her lips, opened her mouth to make explanations, but at the cold look on Veda's face, she couldn't. Nervously she said something about there being a great many presents, and hadn't Veda better make a list, so she would be sure who sent what? Veda made no reply, but stooped down and began pulling ribbons. When she got to the wrist watch she examined it with casual interest, laid it aside without comment. At this Mildred went back to her bedroom, lay down on the bed, tried to stop trembling. The trembling went on. Presently the bell rang, and she heard Bert's voice. Going to the living room again, she was in time to hear Veda ecstatically thank him for the riding boots he had given her, and call him "you darling, darling father." A little scene ensued, with Bert saying the boots could be exchanged it they weren't the right fit, and Veda trying them on. They were perfect, said Veda, and she wasn't going to take them off all day. She was even going to *sleep* in them.

But Veda never once looked at Mildred, and the trembling kept on. In a few minutes Mildred asked Bert if he was ready, and he said any time she was. They went to the kitchen for the flowers they were going to put on Ray's grave, but Bert quickly closed the door. Jerking his thumb toward the living room he asked: "What's the matter with her? She sick?"

"It's about the piano. What with the bar and one thing and another I couldn't get it. This Christmas, I mean. But somebody kindly tipped her off."

"Not me."

"I didn't say so."

"What *did* you give her?"

"A wrist watch. It was a nice watch, a little one, the kind they're all wearing, and you'd think she'd at least—"

But the trembling had reached Mildred's mouth by now, and she couldn't finish. Bert put his arm around her, patted her. Then he asked: "Is she coming with us?"

"I don't know."

They went out the back door to get the car out of the garage, and Mildred drove. As they were backing down the drive, Bert told her to hold it. Then, lightly, he tapped the horn. After a few seconds, he tapped it again. There was no response from the house. Mildred eased into the street, and they drove to the cemetery. Mildred threaded her way slowly along the drive, so as not to disturb the hundreds of others who were out there too. When they came to the Pierce plot she stopped and they got out. Taking the flowers, they walked over to the little marker that had been placed there by the Pierces a short time before. It was a plain white stone, with the name, and under it the dates of the brief little life. Bert mumbled: "They wanted to put a quotation on it, 'Suffer the little children,' whatever it is, but I remembered you like things plain."

"I like it just like it is."

"And another thing they wanted to put on it was: 'Erected by her loving grandparents Adrian and Sarah,' but I told them 'Hey, keep your shirt on. You'll get your names in this marble orchard soon enough without trying to beat the gun in any way.' "

This struck Mildred as funny, and she started to titter, but somewhere down the drive a child began to laugh. Then a great lump rose in her throat and Bert quickly walked away. As she stood there she could hear him behind her, walking back and forth. She stood a long time. Then she put the flowers on the grave, paused for one last look, turned, and took his arm. He laced his fingers through hers, squeezed hard.

When Mildred got home, she found Veda exactly where she had left her: in the chair near the Christmas tree, the boots still on, staring malevolently at the Pierce upright. Mildred sat down and opened a package Bert had brought with him when he came, a jar of preserved strawberries from Mrs. Biederhof. For a few moments, except for the crackle of paper, there was silence. Then, in her clearest, most affected drawl, Veda said: "Christ, but I hate this dump."

"Is there anything in particular that you object to?"

"Oh no, Mother, not at all, not at all—and I do hope you don't begin changing things around, just to please me. No, there's nothing in particular. I just hate every lousy, stinking part of it, and if it were to burn down tomorrow I wouldn't shed a furtive tear from the Elixir of Love, by Gaetano Donizetti, seventeen ninety-eight–eighteen forty-eight."

"I see."

Veda picked up a package of the cigarettes Mildred kept on hand for Monty, lit one, and threw the match on the floor. Mildred's face tightened. "You'll put out that cigarette and pick up that match."

"I will like hell."

Mildred got up, took careful aim, and slapped Veda hard, on the cheek. The next thing she knew, she was dizzy from her head to her heels, and it seemed seconds before she realized, from the report that was ringing in her ears, that Veda had slapped her back. Blowing smoke into Mildred's face, Veda went on, in her cool, insolent tone: "Glendale, California, Land Where the Orange Tree Blows, from Mignon, by Ambroise Thomas, eighteen eleven–eighteen ninety-six. Forty square miles of nothing whatever. A high-class, positively restricted development for discriminating people that run filling stations, and furniture factories, and markets, and pie wagons. The garden spot of the world—in the pig's eye. A wormhole, for grubs!"

"Where did you hear that?"

Mildred had sat down, but at these last words she looked up. She was wholly familiar with Veda's vocabulary, and she knew that this phrase was not part of it. At her question, Veda came over, leaned down close. "Why you poor goddam sap—do you think he'd marry *you?*"

"If I were willing, yes."

"Oh! Yee gods and little fishes hear my cynical laughter, from Pagliacci, by Ruggiero Leoncavallo, eighteen fifty-eight–nineteen nineteen. If you were willing—! Pardon me while I regain my shattered composure. Stupid, don't you know what he sees in you?"

"About what you see, I think."

"No—it's your legs."

"He—told you—*that?*"

"Why certainly."

Veda's manner showed that she relished Mildred's consternation. "Of course he told me. We're very good friends, and I hope I have a mature point of view on these matters. Really, he speaks very nicely about your legs. He has a theory about them. He says a gingham apron is the greatest provocation ever invented by woman for the torture of man, and that the very best legs are found in kitchens, not in drawing rooms. 'Never take the mistress if you can get the maid,' is the way he puts it. And another thing, he says a pretty varlet is always agreeably grateful, and not too exacting, with foolish notions about matrimony and other tiresome things. I must say I find his social theories quite fascinating."

Veda went on at some length, snapping her cigarette and when it went out lighting another one and throwing the match on the floor. But for some time Mildred found her taunts nothing but a jumble. She was so stunned at the discovery that this man, whom she had put up with because he brought Veda closer to her, had all the time been sneering at her behind her back, making fun of her most intimate relations with him, setting the child against her, that every part of her seemed to have turned to jelly. Presently, however, words began to have meaning again, and she heard Veda saying: "After all, Mother, even in his darkest days, Monty's shoes are custom-made."

"They ought to be. They cost me enough."

Mildred snapped this out bitterly, and for a second wished she hadn't. But the cigarette, suddenly still in midair, told her it was news to Veda, quite horrible news, and without further regret, she rammed home her advantage: "You didn't know that, did you?"

Veda stared incredulously, then decided to play it funny. "You buy his shoes? Yee gods and little—"

"His shoes and his shirts and his drinks and everything else he's had in the last few months, including his polo dues. And you needn't call on your gods and little fishes any more, or mention any more dates from the operas. If you want to see some dates I have them all written down, with an exact amount beside each one. Miss Pierce, you made a slight mistake. It's not my legs that he likes me for, it's my money. And so long as it's that, we'll see who's the varlet and who's the boss. It may interest you to know that *that's* why he's such a very good friend of yours. He doesn't haul you over to your music lesson because he wants to. In fact, he often complains about it. He does it because he has to. And surprising though it be to you, he'll marry me, or not marry me, or do anything I say, so his proud gentlemanly belly can have something to eat."

Mildred got up, something haughty in her manner for a moment suggesting Veda. "So you see, what he sees in me *is* about what you see, isn't it? And unfortunately, you're in exactly the position he's in, too. You have to do what I say. The hand that holds the money cracks the whip. And I say there'll be no more money for you, not one cent, until you take back everything you've said, and apologize for it."

Veda's answer was to abandon the grand manner, and become a yelling, devilish adolescent of fourteen. Coldly, Mildred listened to her curses, watched her kick at the Pierce upright with Bert's riding boots. "And that's the piano you're going to practice on, until I get ready, in my own good time, to buy you another."

Veda screamed at the top of her lungs, then leaped at the piano and began playing the Can-Can from Orpheus. Mildred didn't know what it was, but she knew it was wild, obscene music. Picking up her coat, she stalked out of the house and headed up the street toward the restaurant.

So far as Monty was concerned, Mildred knew this was the end, but she didn't do anything about it at once. She received him as usual when he dropped in at the restaurant that night, and the next two or three nights. She even submitted to his embraces, deriving a curious satisfaction from the knowledge that his access to the very best legs was rapidly drawing to a close. Stoppage of the spending money brought Veda to her milk, as no beating had ever done, and when it did, Mildred forgave her quite honestly, in a teary little scene two or three days after Christmas. It was almost automatic with her by now to acquit Veda of wrong-doing, no matter how flagrant the offense. In her mind, the blame was all Monty's, and presently she knew exactly how she would deal with him, and when. It would be at the New Year's party he had invited her to, a week or so before. "I thought I'd ask Paul and Louise Ewing—polo players, but you might like them. We could meet at my house around ten, have a drink, then go in to the Biltmore, for the noisy part."

This had obviously been an effort to kill two birds with one stone, to give some plausibility to what he had said about her hours, and at the same time introduce her to somebody, quite as though he would have done so all along if only the right kind of evening had presented itself. She had taken it as evidence of a change of heart, and accepted. Indeed, she had more than accepted. She had consulted anxiously with Mrs. Gessler over what she should wear, and gone into Bullock's and picked out an evening gown. Then she had gone into a veritable agony over the question of a coat. She didn't have a fur coat, and the prospect of making her debut in the world of mink with nothing but her battered blue haunted her horribly. But Mrs. Gessler, as usual, stepped into the breach. She knew a lady, it seemed, with a brocade coat. "It's a beautiful thing, baby, ashy rose, all crusted with gold, just what you want with your hair. It's really a Chinese mandarin's coat, but it's been recut, and you couldn't put a price on it. There's nothing like it on sale anywhere. It'll be the snappiest thing in the room, even at the Biltmore, and—she's broke. She needs the money. I'll see what I can do."

So for $25, Mildred got the coat, and when the dress arrived, she caught her breath at the total effect. The dress was light blue, and gave something to the rose of the coat, so she was a-shimmer with the delicate colors that her general colorlessness needed. She bought gold stockings and gold shoes, and her panic changed to smug complacency. All this had been before Christmas, and her choice of the New Year's party, as the occasion for the break with Monty may possibly have been prompted by a matter-of-fact determination not to let such a costume go to waste, as well as a vivid recollection of the $40 she had contributed to the expense. However, no such motive obtruded on her own virtuous consciousness. It was merely, she told herself, that a resolve had to be made, and New Year's morning was a very good time to make it. As she rehearsed the scene mentally, it became clear in its details, and she knew exactly how she would play it. At the Biltmore, she would be gay, and rattle her rattle, and throw her balloon, and tell the story of Harry Engel and the anchors. Back at Monty's house, she would watch the Ewings take their departure, and then, at his invitation to come in, she would decline, and climb into her car. Then, at his surprised look, she would make a little speech. She would say nothing of Veda, or money, or legs. She would merely remark that all things had to come to an end some time, and it looked as though he and she had reached that point. It had been very pleasant, she had enjoyed his company, every minute of it, she wished him the very best in the world, and she certainly hoped he would regard her as his friend. But—and at this point she saw herself putting out a graceful hand, and in case he merely stood there looking at it, as stepping on the starter.

The whole thing, perhaps, was a little stuffy, and certainly it was sing-songy as she kept adding to it. But it was her valedictory, and no doubt her privilege to deliver it any way she chose.

December 31, 1933, dawned dark in California, and before the morning was over, quite a little rain was falling. By mid-afternoon, tall tales interrupted the broadcasts: of washouts in the hills, of whole families evacuated from this village nad that village, of roads blocked, of trains held in Arizona pending dispatcher's orders. But in Glendale, except for the wet, and quite a little rubble that washed down on the streets, nothing ominous met the eye, and Mildred viewed the downpour as an annoyance, a damper on business, but nothing to get excited about. Around five o'clock, when it didn't let up, she stopped Mrs. Kramer from sectioning more chickens, on the ground that nobody would be there to eat them, and they could wait until next day. When Arline, Emma, and Audrey successively called up to say they couldn't get there, she thought little of it, and when Sigrid came, she set her to cleaning silver.

Around six, Monty called up to know if she had cold feet. Laughing, she asked: "What from?"

"Well, it's a little wet."

"Do you mean *you're* getting cold feet?"

"No, not at all. Just being the perfect host and giving you one last chance to back out if you want to."

"Why, this little shower is nothing."

"Then I'll be expecting you."

"Around ten."

By seven thirty not one customer had showed up, and Mrs. Gessler abruptly suggested that they close, and begin getting Mildred dressed, if she was still fool enough to go to the damned party. Mildred agreed, and started her preparations to lock up. Then she, Mrs. Gessler, Mrs. Kramer, Pancho, Josie, and Sigrid all burst out laughing at the discovery that there *were* no preparations—no dishes to wash, no bottles to put out, no cash to count. Mildred simply cut the lights and locked the door, and as the others went scuttling off into the night, she and Mrs. Gessler climbed into her car and drove down Pierce Drive. It was a little windswept, a little rough from the stones that had washed down on it, but otherwise as usual. Mildred parked close by the kitchen door and dived inside, then held out her hand to Mrs. Gessler.

She was surprised to find Letty and Veda there. Letty had been afraid to start home, and timidly asked Mildred if she could spend the night. Veda, due long ago at the Hannens' for dinner, a party, and an overnight visit, said Mrs. Hannen had called to say the party had been postponed. At this, Mrs. Gessler looked sharply at Mildred, and Mildred went calmly to her room and began taking off her uniform.

By nine, Mildred was powdered, puffed, perfumed, and patted to that state of semi-transparency that a woman seems to achieve when she is really dressed to go out. Her hair, waved the day before, was fluffed out softly; her dress adjusted to the last fold and flounce; her face fashioned to the fish-eyed look that marks the last stage of such rites. Letty was entranced, and even Veda admitted that "you really look quite nice, Mother." Mildred stood before the full-length mirror for a final critical inspection, but Mrs. Gessler disappeared for a final look at the night. When she came back she camped on the bed, and looked moodily at Mildred. "Well, I hate to say it after taking all that trouble over you, but I wouldn't go to that party, if I were you."

"Why, for heaven's sake?"

"Because it's bad out there. You call that idiot up and tell him you're not coming."

"Can't."

"Oh he'll understand. He'll be relieved."

"His phone's disconnected."

"It would be. Then send him a wire. It won't be delivered till tomorrow, but it'll prove you got manners."

"I'm going."

"Baby, you *can't*."

"I said I'm going."

Irritated, Mrs. Gessler ordered Veda to get the trench coat she wore to school, and her galoshes. Mildred protested, but when Veda appeared with the things, Mrs. Gessler went to work. She pinned Mildred's dress up, so it was a sort of sash around her hips, with a foot of white slip showing. Then she put on the galoshes, over the gold shoes. Then she put on the evening coat, and pulled the trench coat over it. Then she found a kerchief, and bound it tightly around Mildred's head. Mildred, suddenly transformed into something that looked like Topsy, sweetly said good-bye to them all. Then she went to the kitchen door, reached out into the wet, and pulled open the car door. Then she hopped in. Then she started the motor. Then she started the wiper. Then she tucked the robe around her. Then, waving gaily to the three anxious faces at the door, she started the car, and went backing down to the street.

Turning into Colorado Boulevard, she laughed. Snug in her two coats, with the motor humming smoothly and the wiper chattering cheerfully against the glass, she thought it funny that people should get so excited over a little rain.

Heading down into Eagle Rock, she was halted by two men with lanterns. One of them came over, and in a hoarse voice asked: "Pasadena?"

"Yes."

"You can't get through. Not without you detour."

"Well? Which way do I go?"

He took off his hat, swooshed the water out of it, then quickly put it on again and gave intricate directions as to how she was to drive up to the hills, then turn and follow along the higher ground until she came to Colorado Boulevard again. "That is, if you don't hit washouts. But believe me, lady, unless you got to get there tonight, it'll be a whole lot better to turn back."

Mildred, perfectly familiar with the road, took up her journey again. She came to a washout, where part of the hill had slid down on the road, but one track was still open, and she slipped easily by. She came back to Colorado Boulevard at a point not far from the high bridge, so popular with suicides at the time, and went splashing across. At the traffic circle she turned right into Orange Grove Avenue. Except for a few tree limbs that had blown down on it, and a lot of leaves, it was clear. As she rolled over its shining black expanse, she laughed again at the way people got all worked up over nothing.

On the portico of the Beragon mansion a light was lit. She turned in through the pillars and followed the drive up past the big trees, the iron dogs, and the marble urn. She parked at the steps, and had hardly cut the motor when Monty popped out of the door, in a dinner coat, and stared as though he could hardly believe his eyes. Then he yelled something at her, popped in the house again, and emerged, carrying a big doorman's umbrella with one hand and dragging a gigantic tarpaulin with the other. The tarpaulin he hurriedly threw over her hood to keep the rain out of the motor. The umbrella he opened for her, and as she made a nimble jump for the portico, said: "God, I had no idea you'd show up. It didn't even enter my mind."

"You put the light on, and got all dressed up. If you don't look out I'll begin wondering who you *were* expecting."

"All that was before I turned on the radio and heard what it's really like out there. How in the *hell* did you get here anyway? For the last hour it's been nothing but a story of bridges out, roads blocked, whole towns under water, and yet—here you are."

"Don't believe everything you hear."

Inside, Mildred saw the reason for the tarpaulin he had produced so unexpectedly, quite as though he kept such things around in case they were needed. The whole place was under gray, ghostly cloths that covered rugs, furniture, even paintings. She shivered as she looked into the great dark drawing room, and he laughed. "Pretty gloomy, hey? Not quite so bad upstairs." He led the way up the big staircase, snapping on lights and then snapping them off when she had passed, through several big bedrooms, all under cloths as the drawing room was, to a long narrow hall, at the end of which was the tiny apartment where he lived. "This is my humble abode. How do you like it?"

"Why it's—quite nice."

"Really servants' quarters, but I moved into them because I could have a little fire—and they seemed cozier, somehow."

The furnishings had the small, battered, hand-me-down look of servants' quarters, but the fire was friendly. Mildred sat down in front of it and slipped off the galoshes. Then she took off the kerchief and trench coat, and unpinned her dress. His face lit up as she emerged like a butterfly from her very drab cocoon, and he turned her around, examining every detail of her costume. Then he kissed her. For a moment he had the old sunny look, and she had to concentrate hard to remember her grievances. Then he said such grandeur deserved a drink. She was afraid that with a drink she couldn't remember any grievances at all, and asked if they hadn't better wait until the Ewings got there. "The—who did you say?"

"Isn't that their name?"

"Good God, they can't get here."

"Why not?"

"They live on the other side of Huntington Avenue, and it's three feet deep in water, and—how in the *hell* did you get here? Haven't you heard there's a storm going on? I think you were hiding two blocks up the street, and just pretended to drive over from Glendale."

"*I* didn't see any storm."

Following him into the bedroom, to see if she could be of help with the drink, she got a shock. It was a tiny cubicle, with one window and a hummocksy bed, on which were her trench coat and a cocktail service, consisting of a great silver shaker, a big B on its side, and beautiful crystal glasses. But not seven feet away, in the smallest, meanest bathroom she had ever seen, he was chopping away at a piece of ice he had evidently procured earlier in the day. Near him, on a small table, she could see a little two-burner gas fixture, a box of eggs, a package of bacon, and a can of coffee. Wishing she hadn't come, she went back and resumed her seat by the fire.

He served the drinks presently, and she had two. When he reached for the shaker to pour her a third, she stopped him. "If I'm going to drive, I think I've had enough."

"Drive? Where to?"

"Why—isn't the Biltmore where we're going?"

"Mildred—we're not going anywhere."

"Well we certainly are."

"Listen—"

He stepped over and snapped on a small radio. An excited announcer was telling of bridges down between Glendale and Burbank, of a wrecked automobile on the San Fernando Road, of the fear that a whole family had been lost with the car. She tossed her head petulantly. "Well my goodness, the Biltmore's not in Burbank."

Wherever it is, and however we got to get to it, we have to cross the Los Angeles River, and by last report it's a raging torrent, with half the bridges out and three feet of water boiling over the rest. We're not going. The New Year's party is here."

He filled her glass and she began to sulk. In spite of the liquor, the main idea of the evening was still clear in her mind, and this turn of events was badly interfering with it. When he put his arm around her, she didn't respond. Amiably, he said she was a very problematical drunk. On two drinks she'd argue with Jesus Christ, on three she'd agree with Judas Iscariot. Now would she kindly tilt over No. 3, so she'd be in a frame of mind to welcome the New Year the way it deserved? When she didn't touch the drink, he asked for her key, so he could put her car in the garage. When she made no move to give it to him, he went downstairs.

Somewhere in the house, water began to drip. She shivered, for the first time really becoming aware of the rain that was cascading down the windows, roaring on the roof. She began to blame him for that too. When he came back, and took a sharp look at her face, he seemed a little bored. "Well, if you still feel like that, I suppose there's nothing to do but go to bed. . . . I pulled that cloth clear over your car, so it'll probably be all right. I have green pajamas and red. Which do you prefer?"

"I'm not going to bed."

"You're not very amusing here."

"I'm going home."

"Then goodnight. But in case you change your mind, I'll put out the green pajamas, and—"

"I haven't gone yet."

"Of course you haven't. I'm inviting—"

"*Why did you tell her that?*"

What with the liquor, the rain, and his manner, her grievances had heavy compression behind them now, and she exploded with a snarl that left her without the least recollection of all the stuffy little things she had intended to say. He looked at her in astonishment. "Tell whom what? If you don't mind my asking."

"You know perfectly well what I'm talking about. How could you say such things to that child? And who gave you the right to talk about my legs anyhow?"

"Everybody else does. Why not me?"

"*What?*"

"Oh come, come, come. Your legs are the passion of your life. They all but get a cheer when you appear with them in that Pie Wagon, and if you don't want them talked about, you ought to wear your skirts longer. But you *do* want them talked about, and looked at, and generally envied, so why this howling fit? And after all, they *are* damned good-looking."

"We're talking about my child."

"Oh for God's sake, what do you mean, child? If she's a child, she's forgotten more about such things than you'll ever know. You ought to keep up with the times. I don't know how it was once— maybe the sweet young things were told by their mothers at the age of seventeen and were greatly surprised, you can't prove it by me. But now—they know all there is to know before they've even been told about Santa Claus. Anyway, she knows. What am I supposed to do? Act like a zany when I drive off with you at night and don't bring you back until the next morning? Do you think she doesn't know where you've been? Hell, she even asks me how many times."

"And you tell her?"

"Sure. She greatly admires my capacity—and yours. Yours she simply can't get over. 'Who'd think the poor mope had it in her?'"

As Monty mimicked Veda, Mildred knew this was nothing he had inventer, as a sort of counteroffensive. Her rage mounted still higher. She said "I see," then said it over again, three or four times. Then, getting up and going over to him, she asked: "And how about the best legs being found in kitchens, not in the drawing room?"

"What in the hell are you talking about?"

"You know what I'm talking about."

Monty stared, touched his brow, as though in a great effort of recollection. Then, snapping his fingers briskly, he said: "Oh, I knew there was something familiar about that. Yes, I did give a little dissertation along those lines one afternoon. We passed a girl—she had on a uniform of some sort, and an apron—quite a pretty little thing, especially around the ankles. And I got that off—what you've just quoted. Nothing original, I assure you. I had almost forgotten it . . . How does that concern us?"

He was plausible, circumstantial, casual, but a little flicker around the eyes betrayed him. Mildred didn't answer his question. She came over close, and there was something snakelike about her as she said: "That's a lie. You weren't talking about any girl you saw on the street. You were talking about me."

Monty shrugged and Mildred went back to her chair and sat down. Then she began to talk slowly, but with rising stridency. She said he had deliberately tried to set Veda against her, to hold her up to ridicule, to make the child think of her as an inferior, somebody to be ashamed of. "I see it all now. I always thought it was funny she never invited any of these people over here in Pasadena to see *her* once in a while. Not that I don't give her the opportunity. Not that I don't remind her that you can't accept invitations all the time without giving any in return. Not that I didn't do my part. But no. Because you were filling her up with all this foolishness she's been ashamed to ask these people over. She actually believes Glendale is not good enough for them. She thinks I'm not good enough. She—"

"Oh for God's sake shut up."

Monty's eyes were black now, and had little hard points of light in them. "In the first place, what invitations did she accept? My mother's, right here in this house. Well, we went all over that once, and we're not going over it again. And to the Hannens'. And so far as I know the only invitation Charlie and Roberta ever got out of you was an invitation to go over and buy their dinner in that Pie Wagon, and they did go over, and—"

"No check was ever presented to them."

"O.K., then you're square. For the rest, who the hell would expect a kid of fourteen to be doing something about every cocktail party I dragged her to? She asked about it, and I said it would be silly. Come on. What else?"

"That may be all right for older people. But there have been plenty of others she's met, girls her own age—"

"No, there haven't. And right there's where I suggest you get better acquainted with your own daughter. She's a strange child. Girls her own age don't interest her. She likes older women—"

"If they're rich."

"Anyway, she's damned nice to them. And it's unusual as hell. And you can't blame them for liking it. And liking her. But as for her trying to throw some kind of a shindig for them, what are you trying to do, make me laugh?"

In some elusive, quicksilver way that she couldn't get her finger on, Mildred felt the argument slipping away from her, and like Veda, she abandoned logic and began to scream: "You've set her against me! I don't care a bit for your fine talk—*you've set her against me!*"

Monty lit a cigarette, smoked sullenly a few moments without speaking. Then he looked up. "Ah! So this is why you came. Stupid of me not to have thought of it sooner."

"I came because I was invited."

"On a night like this?"

"It's as good a time as any other."

"What a nice little pal *you* turned out to be . . . Funny—I had something to say, too."

He looked with a little self-pitying smile into the fire, evidently decided to keep his intentions to himself, then changed his mind. ". . . I was going to say you'd make a fine wife for somebody—if you didn't live in Glendale."

She had been feeling outpointed, but at this all her self-righteousness came back. Leaning forward, she stared at him. "Monty, you can still say that? After what I've said to you? Just to have somebody take care of you, you'd ask me to marry you? Haven't you any more self-respect than that?"

"Ah, but that's what I *was* going to say."

"Monty, don't make it any worse than it is. If I got excited about it, you were going to let it stay said. If I didn't, you were going to pretend that was what you *were* going to say. Gee, Monty, but you're some man, aren't you?"

"Now suppose you listen to what I *am* going to say."

"No, I'm going home."

She got up, but he leaped at her, seized her by both arms, and flung her back in her chair. The little glittering points of light in his eyes were dancing now, and his face was drawn and hard. "Do you know why Veda never invites anybody to that house of yours? Do you know why nobody, except that string bean that lives next door, ever goes there?"

"Yes—because you set her against me and—"

"Because you *are* a goddam varlet, and you're afraid to have people come there, because you wouldn't know what to do about them—you just haven't got the nerve."

Looking into his contorted face, she suddenly had the same paralyzed, shrunken feeling she had had the morning Miss Turner told her off, and sent her over to the housekeeper's job, because there was nothing else she could do. And she kept shrinking, as Monty went on, pouring a torrent of bitter, passionate invective at her. "It's not her. It's not me. It's you. Doesn't that strike you as funny? That Veda has a hundred friends, here, there, everywhere she goes, and that you haven't any? No, I'm wrong—you have one. That bartender. And that's all. Nobody ever gets invited to your house, nobody—"

"What are you talking about? How can I give parties, or invite people, with a living to make? Why you—"

"Living, my eye! That's the alibi, not the reason. You damned little kitchen scullion, you'll tell *me* who's setting your child against you? *Me?* Listen, Mildred. Nobody but a varlet would give one second's thought to what you've been talking about tonight. Because that's the difference. A lady doesn't care. A varlet does."

He walked around, panting, then turned on her again. "And I like a fool, like a damned idiot, I once thought maybe I'd been mistaken, that you were a lady, and not a varlet. That was when you handed me the $20 bill that night, and I took it. And then I took more. I even gave you credit for something, God knows what it is, some sense of humor that only an aristocrat ever has, and *asked* you for money. And then what? Could you go through with it? The very thing that you yourself started? A lady would have cut her heart out before she let *me* know the money meant anything. But you, before I had even fifty bucks out of you, you had to make a chauffeur out of me, didn't you? To get your money's worth? A lackey, a poodle dog.

You had to rub it in. Well no more. I've taken my last dime off you, and God willing, before my sun goes down, I'll pay you back. Why you scum, you—waitress. I guess that's one reason I love Veda. She wouldn't pick up a tip. That's one thing she wouldn't do—and neither would I."

"Except from me."

White with rage, she opened her evening bag, took out a crisp $10 bill, threw it at his feet. He took the fire tongs, picked it up, dropped it on the fire. When the flame flared up he took out a handkerchief and mopped his face.

For a time, nothing was said by either of them, and when their panting had died down, Mildred began to feel ashamed, defeated, and miserable. She had said it all, had goaded him to say it all too, those things that she knew he felt, and that left her crumpled and unable to answer. Yet nothing had been settled: there he was and there she was. As she looked at him, she saw for the first time that he was tired, worn, and haggard, with just a touch of middle age dragging at what she had always thought of as a youthful face. Then a gush of terrible affection for him swept over her, compounded of pity, contempt, and something motherly. She wanted to cry, and suddenly reached over and rubbed his bald spot. For a long time, it had been a little joke between them. He made no move, but he didn't repulse her either, and when she leaned back she felt better. Then again she heard the rain, and for the first time was afraid of it. She drew the coat around her. Then she picked up Manhattan No. 3, drank half of it, set it down again. Without looking at her, he filled her glass. They sat a long time, neither of them looking at the other.

Then abruptly, as though he had solved a very difficult problem, he banged his fist on the arm of his chair, and said: "Damn it, what this needs is the crime of rape!"

He came over, put one arm around her, slipped the other under her legs, and carried her into the bedroom. A little moaning laugh escaped her as he dumped her down on the hummocksy bed. She felt weak and drugged. In a moment, the brocaded coat was off, was sliding to the floor. She thought of her dress, and didn't care: she wanted him to rip it off her, to tear it away in shreds, if he had to, so he got her out of it. But he wasn't ripping it off. He was fumbling with the zipper, and for a moment her fingers were over his, trying to help. Then something stirred inside of her, an unhappy recollection of what she had come for, of what had been piling up between them these last few months. She fought it off, tried to make it sink under the overwhelming blend of liquor, man, and rain. It wouldn't sink. If she had lifted a mountain, it couldn't have been harder than it was to put both palms in Monty's face, push him away, squirm off the bed, and lurch to her feet. She grabbed both coats, ran into the other room. He was after her, trying to drag her back, but she fought him off as she snatched up the galoshes and dashed into the dark hall.

Somehow, she got through the ghostly rooms, down the stairs, and to the front door. It was locked. She twisted the big brass key, and at last was on the portico, in the cold wet air. She pulled on both coats, stepped into the galoshes. Then suddenly the light came on, and he was beside her, reaching for her, trying to pull her back. She dashed out into the rain, yanked the cloth off the car, let it fall in the mud, and jumped in. As she snapped on the lights and started the motor, she could see him under the light, gesticulating at her, expostulating with her. There was nothing of passion in his face now. He was angrily telling her not to be a fool, not to go out in that storm.

She started out. On Orange Grove Avenue more tree limbs were down, and it didn't look so sleek and harmless. She pulled in to the curb, found the kerchief in the trench coat pocket, tied it around her head. Then, cautiously, feeling a throb of fright every time the car bucked in the wind, she went on. As she turned at the traffic circle, she caught the lights of another car, behind.

There were no men with lanterns now, nothing but the black, wild, and terrible night. She got over the bridge without trouble, but when she came to the detour, she was afraid, and waited until the other car caught up a little. Then she went on, noting with relief that the other car turned into the detour too. She had no trouble for a mile or so, and then she came to the washout. To her dismay it had spread: the road was completely blocked. All resolution having deserted her, she stopped and waited, to see what the other car was going to do. It stopped and she watched. A door slammed, and she strained her eyes to see. Then Monty's face was at the window, not six inches from her own. Water was pouring off an old felt hat, and off the slicker that was buttoned to his ears. Furiously he pointed at the washout. "Look at that! It never occurred to you there'd be something like that, did it? Damn it, the trouble you're putting me to!"

For a moment or two, as he savagely ordered her to lock the car, get out, and come back with him, she had a happy, contented feeling, as though he were her father, she a bad little girl that would be taken care of, anyway. Then once more her fixed resolve rose in her. She shifted into reverse and backed. She backed past his car, came to a corner, headed into it. When she had followed the new road a few feet, she saw it led down into Eagle Rock. It was full of rubble, and she proceeded by inches, rolling and braking, then rolling on again. Then ahead of her she saw that the rubble had stopped, that a black shining road lay ahead. She stepped on the gas. It was the check of the car that told her the black shining road was black shining water. When she stepped on the brake the car slid right on. The lights went out. The motor stopped. The car stopped. She was alone in a pool that extended as far as she could see. When she took her foot off the brake she felt it splash into a puddle. She screamed.

The rain was driving against her, and she wound up the window. Outside, she could hear the purling of the torrent against the wheels, and in a moment or two the car began to move. She guided it to the right, and when she felt it catch the curb, pulled up the hand brake. Then she sat there. In a few minutes, her breath had misted the glass so she could see nothing. Then the door beside her was jerked open, and once more Monty was standing there. He had evidently gone back to his car to take off his trousers, for as the slicker floated on the pool she could see he was in his shorts. He braced his right arm against the door jamb. "All right, now throw your legs over my arm, and put your arm around my neck. Hold on tight, and I think I can get you to the top of the hill."

She lifted her feet to the seat, took off the gold shoes and stockings, put them in the dashboard compartment. Then she put on the galoshes, over her bare feet. Then she wriggled out of both coats and the dress. The dress and the brocaded coat she stuffed over the shoes, closed the compartment and locked it. Then, shivering, she got into the trench coat. Then she motioned to Monty to move his hand. When he did, she pulled the door shut and snapped the catch. Then she slipped out the opposite door, locking it. A yelp came out of her as she stepped off the running board and felt the water around her thighs, and the current almost swept her off her feet. But she held on to the door handle and steadied herself. Above her was a high bank, evidently with some sort of sidewalk on top of it. Paying no attention to Monty and his barely audible shouts, she scrambled up, and then slipped, slid, and staggered home through the worst storm in the annals of the Los Angeles weather bureau, or of any weather bureau.

She passed many cars stalled as hers was stalled, some deserted, some full of people. One car, caught between vast lakes of water, was standing near a curb, its top lights on, filled with people in evening clothes, helpless to do anything but sit. She slogged on, up the long hill to Glendale, down block after block of rubble, torrents, seas of water. Her galoshes filled repeatedly, and periodically she stopped, holding first one foot high behind her, then the other, to let the water run out. But she couldn't let the sand and pebbles out, and they cut her feet cruelly. She was in a hysteria of weakness, cold, and pain when she finally reached Pierce Drive, and half ran, half limped, the rest of the way to the house.

Veda and Letty, like two frightened kittens, hadn't slept very well that night, and when lights began to snap on in the house, and a sobbing, mud-spattered, staggering apparition appeared at their door, they screamed in terror. When they realized it was Mildred, they dutifully followed her to her room, but it was seconds before, they got readjusted to the point of helping her out of her clothes and getting her into bed. But suddenly Letty recovered from her fright, and was soon running around frantically, getting Mildred what she needed, especially whiskey, coffee, and a hot-water bottle. Veda sat on the bed, chafing Mildred's hands, spooning the scalding coffee into her mouth, pushing the covers close around her. Presently she shook her head. "But Mother, I simply can't understand it. Why didn't you stay with him? After all, it wouldn't have been much of a novelty."

"Never mind. Tomorrow you get your piano."

At Veda's squeal of delight, at the warm arms around her neck, the sticky kisses that started at her eyes and ended away below her throat, Mildred relaxed, found a moment of happiness. As the gray day broke, she fell into a deep sleep.

Chapter 12

FOR SOME TIME after that, Mildred was too busy to pay
much attention to Veda. Relieved of Monty, she began to have
money, above installments on the piano and everything else. In spite
of hard times, her business grew better; the bar shook down into a
profitable sideline; most important of all, she paid off the last of the
$4,000 she had owed for the property, and the last of her equipment
notes. Now the place was hers, and she took a step she had been
considering for some time. The pies put a dreadful strain on her
kitchen, so she built an annex, out back of the parking space, to
house them as a separate unit. There was some little trouble about
it, on account of the zoning regulations. But when she submitted
acceptable exterior plans, which made it look like a rather large private garage, and agreed to display no advertising except the neon
sign she was already using, the difficulty was smoothed out. When it
was finished, she added pastries to her list, clever items suitable for
restaurant perambulators, and had little trouble selling them. Hans
presently needed an assistant, and then another. She bought a new
truck, a really smart one. About the same time she turned in the car,
never quite recovered from the battering it took in the storm, and
bought a new one, a sleek maroon Buick with white tires that Veda
kissed when the dealer delivered it.

But when Ida, who was a regular visitor now, saw the annex, she
grew thoughtful, and then one night started a campaign to get Mildred to open a branch in Beverly, with herself as manager. "Mildred,
I know what I'm talking about. That town is just crying for a place

that will put out a real line of ready desserts. Think of the entertaining they do over there. Them movie people giving parties every night, and the dessert nothing but a headache to them women. And look how easy you can give them what they want—why you're making all that stuff right now. And look at the prices you'll get. And look at the sidelines you got. Look at the fountain trade. Look at the sandwich trade. And I can do it all with four girls, a fountain man, a short-order cook, and a dish-washer."

Mildred, not wanting to assume risk when she had a certainty, was in no hurry about it. But she drove over to Beverly and made inquiries, and began to suspect that Ida was right. Then, snooping around one afternoon, she ran into a vacant property that she knew would be right for location. When she found out she could get a lease for an absurdly small rental, she made up her mind. There followed another hectic month of furniture, fixtures, and alterations. She wanted the place done in maple, but Ida obstinately held out for light green walls and soft, upholstered booths where people would find it comfortable to sit. Mildred gave way, but on the day of the opening she almost fainted. Without consulting her, Ida had ordered a lot of preserves, cakes, health breads, and other things she knew nothing about. Ida however said *she* herself knew all about them, at any rate all that was necessary to know. By the end of the week, Mildred was not only convinced, but completely flabbergasted. Ida's report was ecstatic: "Mildred, we're in. In the first place I got a lunch trade that's almost like the Brown Derby. People that don't *want* planked whitefish and special hamburgers. They want those little sandwiches I got, and the fruit salads, and you just ought to hear the comment. And I don't hardly get them cleared out before I got a college trade, wonderful refined kids on their way home from Westwood that want a chocolate soda or a malt before they start playing tennis. And when they go my tea trade starts, and on top of that I got a little dinner trade, people that want to eat light before they catch a preview or something. And then on top of that I got a late trade, people that just want a cup of chocolate and a place to talk. From twelve noon until twelve midnight I got *business*. And the take-out trade from those people, it's enough to take your breath away." The receipts bore her out. Ida was to get $30 a week, plus 2 per cent of the gross. She had hoped, in time, to make $50 a week. That very first Saturday night Mildred wrote her a check for $53.71.

But it wasn't all smooth sailing. Mrs. Gessler, when she heard what Mildred was up to, flew into a rage, and wanted to know why Ida had been singled out to manage the Beverly branch, instead of herself. Mildred tried to explain that it was all Ida's idea, that some people are suited to one thing, some to another, but got nowhere. Mrs. Gessler continued bitter, and Mildred grew worried. She had come to depend on her tall, thin, profane bartender as she depended on nobody else, not only for shrewd business advice but also for some sort of emotional support that her nature demanded. Losing her would be a calamity, and she began to consider what could be done.

At that time there was considerable talk about the rise of Laguna Beach, a resort along the coast, a few miles below Long Beach. Mildred began to wonder if it would be a good place for still another branch, with Mrs. Gessler in charge. She drove down a number of times and looked it over. Except for one place, she found no restaurants that impressed her, and unquestionably the resort was coming up, not only for summer trippers but for year-round residents as well. Again it was the lease that decided her. She found a large house, with considerable land around it, on a bluff, overlooking the ocean. With an expert eye, she noted what would have to be done to it, noted that the grounds would be expensive to keep up. But when the terms were quoted to her, they were so low that she knew she could make a good profit if she got any business at all. They were so low that for a brief time she was suspicious, but the agent said the explanation was simple enough. It had been a private home, but it couldn't be rented for that, as it was entirely too big for most of the people who came down from the city just to get a coat of tan. Furthermore, the beach in front of it was studded with rocks and was therefore unsuitable to swimming. For all ordinary purposes it was simply a turkey, and if she could use it, it was hers at the rate quoted. Mildred inspected the view, the house, the grounds, and felt a little tingle inside. Abruptly, she paid $25 cash for a ten-day option, and that night held Mrs. Gessler after closing time for a little talk. But she barely got started when Mrs. Gessler broke in: "Oh shut up, will you for God's sake shut up?"

"But—aren't you *interested?*"

"Does a duck like water? Listen, it's halfway between L.A. and San Diego, isn't it? Right on the main line, and Ike still has his trucks. It's the first honest-to-God's chance he's had to get started again, in a legal way, since—well, you know. And it gets him out of this lousy place. Do you want me bawling right on your shoulder?"

"What's the matter with this place?"

"It's not the place, it's him. O.K., I'm working, see, and he has to find something to do with himself, at night. So he finds it. He says it's pool, and he does come home with chalk all over him, I'll say that for him. But he's a liar. It's a frazzle-haired blonde that works in one of those antique furniture factories on Los Feliz. Nothing serious maybe, but he sees her. It's what I've been so jittery about, if you've got to know. And now, if I can just get him out of here, and in business again so he can hold his head up—well, maybe that'll be that. Go on, tell me some more."

So once again Mildred was in a flurry of alterations, purchases of inventory, and arguments about policy. She wanted a duplicate of the Glendale place, which would specialize in chicken, waffles, and pies, and operate a small bar as a sideline. Mrs. Gessler, however, had other ideas. "Do they come all the way to the ocean just to get chicken? Not if I know them. They want a shore dinner—fish, lobster, and crab—and that's what we're giving them. And that's where we make the dough. Don't forget: fish is cheap. But we've got to have a little variety, so we give them steak, right from our own built-in charcoal broiler."

When Mildred protested that she knew nothing about steaks, or fish, or lobster, or crab, and would be helpless to do the marketing, Mrs. Gessler replied she could learn. It wasn't until she sent for Mr. Otis, the federal meat inspector who had been romantic about her in her waitress days, that her alarm eased a little. He came to the Glendale restaurant one night, and confirmed her suspicions that there were about a hundred different ways to lose money on steaks. But when he talked with Mrs. Gessler he was impressed. He told Mildred she was "smart," and probably knew where she was coming out. It depended mainly, he said, on the chef, and to Mildred's surprise he recommended Archie, of Mr. Chris's establishment. Archie, he assured her, had been wasted for years in a second-class place, but "he's still the best steak man in town, bar none. Any bum can cook fish and make money on it, so don't worry about that. But on steaks, you've got to have somebody that knows his stuff. You can't go wrong on Archie."

So Mildred stole Archie off Mr. Chris, and under his dour supervision installed the built-in charcoal broiler. Presently, after signs had been put up along the road, and announcements inserted in the Los Angeles papers, the place opened. It was never the snug little gold mine that Ida's place was, for Mrs. Gessler was careless of expenses, and tended to slight the kitchen in favor of the bar. But her talent at making a sort of club out of whatever she touched drew big business. The ingenuity with which she worked out the arrangements drew Mildred's reluctant admiration. The big living room of the house was converted into a maple-paneled bar, with dim lights. The rooms behind it were joined together in a cluster of small dining rooms, each with a pleasant air of intimacy about it. One of them opened on a veranda that ran around the house, and out here were tables for out-door drinkers, bathing suiters, and the overflow trade. But the most surprising thing to Mildred was the flower garden. She had never suspected Mrs. Gessler of any such weakness, but within a few weeks the whole brow of the bluff was planted with bushes, and here, it appeared, was where Mrs. Gessler spent her mornings, spading, pruning, and puttering with a Japanese gardener. The expense, what with the water and the gardener, was high, but Mrs. Gessler shrugged it off. "We're running a high-class dump, baby, and we've got to have something. For some reason I don't understand, a guy with an old-fashioned on the table likes to listen to the bumblebees." But when the flowers began to bloom, Mildred paid without protest, because she liked them. At twilight, just before the dinner rush, she would stroll among them, smelling them and feeling proud and happy. On one of these strolls Mrs. Gessler joined her, and then led her a block or two down the main road that ran through the town. Then she stopped and pointed, and across the street Mildred saw the sign:

GESSLER
LONG & SHORT DISTANCE
HAULING
DAY & NIGHT
SERVICE

Mrs. Gessler looked at it intently. "He's on call all the time, too. All he needed was a chance. Next week he's getting a new truck, streamlined."

"Is everything all right upstairs?"

Mildred had reference to the terms of Mrs. Gessler's employment.

She didn't get $30 a week and 2 per cent of the gross, as Ida did. She got $30 and 1 per cent, the rest of her pay being made up of free quarters in the upper part of the house, with light, heat, water, food, laundry, and everything furnished. Mrs. Gessler nodded. "Everything's fine. Ike loves those big rooms, and the sea, and the steaks, and—well, believe it or not he even likes the flowers. 'Service with a gardenia'—he's thinking of having it lettered on the new truck. We're living again, that's all."

Mildred never cooked anything herself now, or put on a uniform. At Glendale, Mrs. Kramer had been promoted to cook, with an assistant named Bella; Mrs. Gessler's place was taken by a man bartender, named Jake; on nights when Mildred was at Beverly or Laguna, Sigrid acted as hostess, and wore the white uniform. Mildred worked from sun-up, when her marketing started, until long after dark; she worked so hard she began to feel driven, and relieved herself of every detail she could possibly assign to others. She continued to gain weight. There was still something voluptuous about her figure, but it was distinctly plump. Her face was losing such little color as it had had, and she no longer seemed younger than her years. In fact, she was beginning to look matronly. The car itself, she discovered, took a great deal out of her, and she engaged a driver named Tommy, older brother to Carl, who drove the truck. After some reflection she took him to Bullock's and bought him a uniform, so he could help on the parking lots. When Veda first saw him in this regalia, she didn't kiss him, as she had kissed the car. She gave her mother a long, thoughtful look, full of something almost describable as respect.

And in spite of mounting expenses, the driver, the girl Mildred engaged to keep the books, the money kept rolling in. Mildred paid for the piano, paid off the mortgages Bert had plastered on the house; she renovated, repainted, kept buying new equipment for all her establishments, and still it piled up. In 1936, when Mr. Roosevelt came up for reelection, she was still smarting from the tax she had paid on her 1935 income, and for a few weeks wavered in her loyalty. But then business picked up, and when he said "we planned it that way," she decided she had to take the bitter with the sweet, and voted for him. She began to buy expensive clothes, especially expensive girdles, to make her look thin. She bought Veda a little car, a Packard 120, in dark green, "to go with her hair." On Wally's advice, she incorporated, choosing Ida and Mrs. Gessler as her two directors, in addition to herself. Her big danger, Wally said, was the old woman in Long Beach. "O.K., she's crossing against the lights, Tommy had his brakes on when he hit her, she's not hurt a bit, but when she finds out you've got three restaurants just watch what she does to you. And it works the other way around too. Sooner or later you're going to have those five people that got ptomaine poisoning, from the fish, or say they did. And what those harpies do to you, once they get in court, will be just plain murder. You incorporate, your *personal* property is safe." The old woman in Long Beach, to say nothing of the five harpies on their pots, fretted Mildred terribly, as many things did. She bought fantastic liability insurance, on the car, on the pie factory, on the restaurants. It was horribly expensive, but worth it, to be safe.

Through all the work, however, the endless driving, the worry, the feeling there were not enough hours in the day for all she had to do, one luxury she permitted herself. No matter how the day broke, she was home at three o'clock in the afternoon, for what she called her "rest." It was a rest, to be sure, but that wasn't the main idea. Primarily it was a concert, with herself the sole auditor. When Veda turned sixteen, she persuaded Mildred to let her quit high school, so she could devote her whole time to music. In the morning she did harmony, and what she called "paperwork." In the afternoon she practiced. For two hours she practiced exercises, but at three she began to practice pieces, and it was then that Mildred arrived. Tiptoeing in the back way, she would slip into the hall, and for a moment stand looking into the living room, where Veda was seated at the satiny black grand. It was a picture that never failed to thrill her: the beautiful instrument that she had worked for and paid for, the no less beautiful child she had brought into the world; a picture moreover, that she could really call her own. Then, after a soft, "I'm home, darling," she would tiptoe to her bedroom, lie down, and listen. She didn't know the names of many of the pieces, but she had her favorites, and Veda usually played one. There was one in particular, something by Chopin, that she liked best of all, "because it reminds me of that song about rainbows." Veda, somewhat ironically, said: "Well Mother, there's a reason"; but she played it, nevertheless. Mildred was delighted at the way the child was coming along: warm, shy intimacy continued, and Mildred laughed to think she had once supposed that Monty had something to do with it. This, she told herself, was what made everything worth while.

One afternoon the concert was interrupted by a phone call. Veda answered, and from the tone of her voice, Mildred knew something was wrong. She came in and sat on the bed, but to Mildred's "What is it, darling?" returned no answer at once. Then, after a few moments of gloomy silence, she said: "Hannen's had a hemorrhage."

"Oh my, isn't that awful!"

"He knew it was coming on. He had two or three little ones. This one caught him on the street, while he was walking home from the post office. The ambulance doctor made a mess of it—had him lifted by the shoulders or something—and it's a lot worse than it might have been. Mrs. Hannen's almost in hysterics about it."

"You have to go over there. At once."

"Not today. He's all packed in icebags, and they give him some kind of gas to inhale. It's just hell."

"Is there something I could do? I mean, if there are any special dishes he needs, I can send anything that's wanted, hot, all ready to serve—"

"I can find out."

Veda stared at the Gessler house, now for rent. Then: "God, but I'm going to miss that damned he-bear."

"Well my goodness, he's not *gone* yet."

Mildred said this sharply. She had the true California tradition of optimism in such matters; to her it was almost blasphemous not to hope for the best. But Veda got up heavily and spoke quietly. "Mother, it's bad. I know from the way he's been acting lately that he's known it would be bad, when it came. I can tell from the way she was wailing over that phone that it's bad . . . And what I'm going to do I don't know."

Special dishes, it turned out, were needed desperately, on the chance that the stricken man could be tempted to eat, and in that way build up his strength. So daily, for a week, a big hamper was delivered by Tommy, full of chicken cooked by Mildred herself, tiny sandwiches prepared by Ida, cracked crab nested in ice by Archie, sherries selected by Mrs. Gessler. Mildred Pierce, Inc., spit on its hands to show what it could do. Then one day Mildred and Veda took the hamper over in person, together with a great bunch of red roses. When they arrived at the house, the morning paper was still on the grass, a market circular was stuffed under the door. They rang, and there was no answer. Veda looked at Mildred, and Tommy carried the things back to the car. That afternoon, a long, incoherent telegram arrived for Mildred, dated out of Phoenix, Ariz., and signed by Mrs. Hannen. It told of the wild ride to the sanitarium there, and begged Mildred to have the gas turned off.

Three days later, while Mildred was helping Ida get ready for the Beverly luncheon rush, Veda's car pulled up at the curb. Veda got out, looking half combed and queer. When Mildred unlocked the door for her, she handed over the paper without speaking, went to a booth, and sat down. Mildred stared at the unfamiliar picture of Mr. Hannen, taken before his hair turned white, read the notice of his death with a blank, lost feeling. Then, noting that the funeral was to be held in New York, she went to the phone and ordered flowers. Then she called Western Union, and dictated a long telegram to Mrs. Hannen, full of "heart-felt sympathy from both Veda and myself." Then, still under some dazed compulsion to do something, she stood there, trying to think what. But that seemed to be all. She went over and sat down with Veda. After a while Veda asked one of the girls to bring her coffee. Mildred said: "Would you like to ride to Laguna with me, darling?"

"All right."

For the rest of the day, Veda tagged at Mildred's heels, silent about Mr. Hannen, but afraid, apparently, to be alone. The next day she hung around the house, and when Mildred came home at three, the piano was silent. The day after that, when she still moped, Mildred thought it time to jog her up a bit. Finding her in the den, she said: "Now darling, I know he was a fine man, and that you were very fond of him, but you did all you could do, and after all, these things happen, and—"

"Mother."

Veda spoke quietly, as one would speak to a child. "It isn't that I was fond of him. Not that I didn't love the shaggy brute. To me he'll always be the one and only, and—oh well, never mind. But—he taught me *music*, and—"

"But darling there are other teachers."

"Yes, about seven hundred fakes and advertisers in Los Angeles alone, and I don't know one from another, and besides—"

Veda broke off, having evidently intended to say something, and then changed her mind. Mildred felt something coming, and waited.

But Veda evidently decided she wasn't going to say it, and Mildred asked: "Can't you make inquiries?"

"There's one man here, just one, that Hannen had some respect for. His name is Treviso, Carlo Treviso. He's a conductor. He conducts a lot of those operas and things out at the Hollywood Bowl. I don't know if he takes piano pupils or not, but he might know of somebody."

"Do you want me to call him up?"

Veda took so long answering that Mildred became impatient, and wanted to know what it was that Veda was holding back, anyway. "Has it anything to do with money? You know I don't begrudge anything for your instruction, and—"

"Then—call him up."

Mr. Treviso's studio was located in downtown Los Angeles, in a building with several signs beside the door, and as Mildred and Veda walked up to the second floor, a bedlam of noises assailed their ears; tenors vocalizing, pianists running dizzy scales, violinists sawing briskly in double stops. They didn't get in to Mr. Treviso at once. Their knock was answered by a short, fat woman with an Italian accent, who left them in a windowless anteroom and went into the studio. At once there were sounds from within. A baritone would sing a phrase, then stop. Then there would be muffled talk. Then he would sing the same phrase again, and there would be more talk. This went on and on, until Mildred became annoyed. Veda, however, seemed mildly interested. "It's the end of the Pagliacci Prologue, and he can't hit the G on pitch. Well, there's nothing to do about *him*. Treviso might just as well save his time."

"To say nothing of *my* time."

"Mother, this is a wop. So we sit."

Presidently the baritone, a stocky, red-faced boy, popped through the door and left sheepishly, and the woman came out and motioned them in. Mildred entered a studio that was rather different from Mr. Hannen's. It was almost as large, but nothing like as austere. The great black piano stood near the windows, and the furniture matched it, in size as well as elegance. Almost covering the walls were hundreds of photographs, all of celebrities so big that even Mildred had heard of some of them, and all inscribed personally to Mr. Treviso. That gentleman himself, clad in a gray suit with black piping on the waistcoat, received them as a ducal counselor might have received a pair of lesser ladies in waiting. A tall, thin Italian of perhaps fifty, with bony face and somber eyes, he listened while Mildred explained what they had come for, then bowed coldly and waved them to seats. When Veda cut in with what Mildred had neglected to mention, that she had studied with Mr. Hannen, he became slightly less formal, struck a tragic pose, and said: "Poor Charl'. Ah poor, poor Charl'." Then he paid tribute to the Hannen tone, and said it marked him as a great artist, not merely as a pianist. Then, smiling a little, he permitted himself to reminisce. "I first know Charl', was in 1922. We make tour of Italy together, I play Respighi program wit' orchestr', Charl' play Tschaikowsky concerto. Was just after Mussolini come in, and Charl', 'e was afraid somebody make him drink castor hoil. Was bad afraid. 'E buy gray spat, black 'at, learn Giovanezza, change, name to Annino, do ever' little t'ing to look like wop. So last concert, was in Turino. After concert, all go to little cafe, 'ave last drink, say good-bye. So concertmaster, 'e stand up, whole place is right away quiet. And concertmaster, 'e make little spich, tell how fine Charl' play Tschaikowsky concerto, say whole orchestr' want make Charl' little gift, express happreciation. 'E give Charl' big mahogany box, look like 'ave gold cup in it, somet'ing pretty nice. Charl', 'e make little spich too, say t'anks boys, sure is big surprise. 'E open box—was roll toilet paper!"

Mr. Treviso's smile had broadened into a grin, and his black eyes sparkled so brightly they almost glared. Mildred, whether because of the anecdote itself, or the recent death of its subject, or the realization that she was in the presence of a point of view completely alien to her, wasn't amused, though she smiled a little, to be polite. But Veda affected to think this was the funniest thing she had ever heard in her life, and egged Mr. Treviso on to more stories. He looked at his watch and said he would now listen to her play.

The Veda who sat down at the piano was a quite different Veda from the one who had so airily entertained Mr. Hannen three years ago. She was genuinely nervous, and it occurred to Mildred that her encouragement to Mr. Treviso's story-telling might have been a stall for time. She thought a moment, then with grim face launched into a piece known to Mildred as the Brahms Rhapsody. Mildred didn't like it much. It went entirely too fast for her taste, except for a slow part in the middle, that sounded a little like a hymn. However, she sat back comfortably, waiting for the praise that Mr. Treviso would bestow, and that she would tell Ida about that night.

Mr. Treviso wandered over to the window, and stood looking down at the street. When Veda got to the slow part, he half turned around, as though to say something, then didn't. All during the slow part he stared down at the street. When Veda crashed into the fast part again, he walked over and closed the piano, elaborately giving Veda time to get her hands out of the way. In the bellowing silence that followed, he went to the far corner of the studio and sat down, a ghastly smile on his face, as though he had been prepared for burial by an undertaker who specialized in pleasant expressions.

It was an appreciable interval before it dawned on Mildred what he had done, and why. Then she looked toward the piano to suggest that Veda play one of her slower pieces. But Veda was no longer there. She was at the door, pulling on her gloves, and before Mildred could say anything, she dived out the door. Mildred jumped up, followed, and in the hall called to her. But Veda was running down the stairs and didn't look up. The next Mildred knew, Tommy was driving them home, and Veda was sitting with writhing face and clenched hands, staring horribly at the floor. Even as Mildred looked, a white line appeared on the back of one of the gloves, and it popped.

All the way home Mildred fumed at the way Mr. Treviso had treated them. She said she had never seen anything like that in her life. If he didn't like the way Veda had played the piece, he could have said so like a gentleman, instead of acting like that. And the very idea, having an appointment with two ladies for four o'clock, keeping them waiting until a quarter to five, and then, when they had barely got in the door, telling them a story about *toilet paper*. If that was the only man in Los Angeles that Mr. Hannen had any respect for, she certainly had her opinion of Mr. Hannen's taste. A lot of this expressed Mildred's very real irritation, but some of it was to console Veda, by taking her side after an outrageous episode. Veda said nothing, and when they got home she jumped out of the car and ran in the house. Mildred followed, but when she got to Veda's room, it was locked. She knocked, then knocked again, sharply. Then she commanded Veda to open the door. Nothing happened, and inside there was silence. Letty appeared, and asked in a frightened way what the trouble was. Paying no attention to Letty, Mildred ran out to the kitchen, grabbed a chair, and ran outside. A sudden paralyzing fear had come over her as to what Veda might be doing in there. Putting the chair near the house, she stood on it and raised the screen. Then she stepped into the room. Veda was lying on the bed, staring at the ceiling in the same unseeing way she had stared at the floor of the car. Her hands were still clenching and unclenching, and her features looked thick. Mildred, who had expected at the very least to see an empty iodine bottle lying around somewhere, first felt relieved, then cross. Unlocking the door, she said: "Well, my goodness, you don't have to scare everybody to death."

"Mother, if you say my goodness one more time I shall scream, I shall scream!"

Veda spoke in a terrible rasping whisper, then closed her eyes. Stiffening, and stretching out her arms as though she were a figure on a crucifix, she began to talk to herself, in a bitter voice, between clenched teeth. "You can kill it—you can kill it right now—you can drive a knife through its heart—so it's dead, dead, *dead*—you can forget you ever tried to play the piano—you can forget there ever was such a thing as a piano—you can—"

"Well my g—. Well for heaven's sake, the piano isn't the only thing on earth. You could—you could *write* music." Pausing, Mildred tried to remember what Bert had said that day, about Irving Berlin, but just then Veda opened her eyes. "You damned, silly-looking cluck, are you trying to drive me *insane?* . . . Yes, I could write music. I can write you a motet, or a sonata, or a waltz, or a cornet solo, with variation—anything at all, anything you want. And not one note of it will be worth the match it would take to burn it. You think I'm hot stuff, don't you? You, lying there every day, dreaming about rainbows. Well, I'm not. I'm just a Glendale Wunderkind. I know all there is to know about music, and there's one like me in every Glendale on earth, every one-horse conservatory, every tank-town university, every park band. We can read anything, play anything, arrange anything, and we're just no good. Punks. Like you. God, now I know where I get it from. Isn't that funny? You start out a Wunderkind, then find out you're just a goddam punk."

"Well, if that's the case, it certainly does seem peculiar that he wouldn't have known it. Mr. Hannen, I mean. And told you so. Instead of—"

"Do you think he didn't know it? And didn't tell me? He told me every time he saw me—my tunes stunk, my playing stunk, everything I did stunk—but he liked me. And he knew how I felt about it. Christ, that was something, after living with *you* all my life. So we went on with it, and he thought perhaps Old Man Maturity, as he called him, might help out, later. He will like hell. In this racket you've got it or you haven't, and—*will you wipe that stupid look off your face and stop acting as if it was somebody's fault?*"

"It certainly would seem, after all that work—"

"Can't you understand anything at all? They don't pay off on work, they pay off on talent! *I'm just no good!* I'M NO GODDAM GOOD AND THERE'S NOTHING THAT CAN BE DONE ABOUT IT!"

When a shoe whizzed past her head, Mildred went out, picked up her handbag, and started over to Beverly. She felt no resentment at this tirade. She had got it through her head at last that something catastrophic had happened to Veda, and that it was completely beyond her power to understand. But that wouldn't stop her from trying, in her own way, to think what she could do about it.

Chapter 13

IN A DAY OR SO, feeling that Veda was the victim of some sort of injustice, Mildred decided that the Messrs. Hannen and Treviso weren't the only teachers in Los Angeles; that battles aren't won by quitting, but by fighting hard; that Veda should go on with her music, whether the great masters liked it or not. But when she outlined this idea to Veda, the look from the bed cut her off in the middle of a sentence. Then, unable to give up the idea that Veda was "talented," she decided that aesthetic dancing was the thing. There was a celebrated Russian dancer who often dined at Laguna, and this authority was sure that with Veda's looks and good Russian instruction, things might still be straightened out. But at this Veda merely yawned. Then Mildred decided that Veda should enter one of the local schools, possibly Marlborough, and prepare herself for college. But this seemed a bit silly when Veda said: "But Mother, I can't roll a hoop any more."

Yet Veda continued to mope in her room, until Mildred became thoroughly alarmed, and decided that whatever the future held, for the present something had to be done. So one day she suggested that Veda called up some of her friends and gave them a little party. Conquering her loyalty to the house, the conviction that it was good enough for anything Veda might want to do in it, she said: "If you don't want to ask them here, why not Laguna? You can have a whole room to yourself. I can have Lucy fix up a special table, there's an orchestra we can get, and afterwards you can dance or do anything you want."

"No, Mother. Thanks."

Mildred might have persisted in this, if it hadn't been for Letty, who heard some of it. In the kitchen she said to Mildred: "She ain't going to see none of them people. Not them Pasadena people."

"Why not?"

"Don't you *know*? After she's been Mr. Hannen's candy kid? The one that was going to New York and play the pyanner so they'd all be hollering for her? You think she's going to see them people now, and just be Veda? Not her. She's the queen, or she don't play. She ain't giving no party, and you ain't either."

"I've simply got to do something."

"Can't you leave her *alone*?"

Letty, a devoted worshipper of Veda's by now, spoke sharply, and Mildred left the kitchen, lest she lose her temper. Leaving Veda alone was something that hadn't entered her mind, but after she cooled off she thought about it. However, she was incapable of leaving Veda alone. In the first place, she had an honest concern about her. In the second place, she had become so accustomed to domineering over the many lives that depended on her, that patience, wisdom, and tolerance had almost ceased to be a part of her. And in the third place, there was this feeling she had about Veda, that by now permeated every part of her, and colored everything she did. To have Veda play the piece about rainbows, just for her, was delicious. To have her scream at her was painful, but bearable, for at least it was she that was being screamed at. To have her lying there on the bed, staring at the ceiling, and not even thinking about her, was an agony too great to be borne. Even as she was trying to be detached, to weigh Letty's remark fairly, she was deciding that where Veda really belonged was in pictures, and meditating a way whereby a director, one of Ida's customers, could be induced to take an interest. This brilliant scheme, however, was never put to the test. Veda snapped out of it. Appearing at Laguna one night, she blithely ordered a cocktail, downed a $3.50 steak, and mingled sociably with everybody in the place. Casually, before she left, she asked Mildred if she could order some new clothes, explaining she had been embarrassed to go anywhere "in these rags." Mildred, delighted at any sign of reviving interest, overlooked the cocktail and told her to order anything she wanted.

She was a little stunned when the bills began to come in, and they footed up to more than $1,300. And she was disturbed when she saw the clothes. Up to now, Veda had worn the quiet, well-made, somewhat sexless toggery sanctioned by Pasadena as suitable to girls of her age. Now, in big, expensive hats and smart, striking dresses, with powder, rouge, and lipstick thick on her face, she hardly looked like the same girl. She was, by any standard, extraordinarily good-looking. Her hair, still a soft, coppery red, was cut and waved to flow over her shoulders. Her freckles were all gone, leaving the upper part of her face, which so much resembled Bert's, even handsomer than it had been before: the shadows under her eyes gave her true beauty, and if the light blue of the eyes themselves, as well as the set of the resolute mouth, were a little hard, they were also suggestive of the modern world, of boulevards, theatres, and streamlined cars. She had grown but little these last three years. Though her carriage enhanced her height, she was actually but a shade taller than Mildred. And her figure had filled out, or taken on form, or undergone some elusive change, so the Dairy was no longer the bulging asymmetry it had been in the days when Monty complained about it. It melted pleasantly, even excitingly, into the rest of her. But what shook up Mildred, when this new finery arrived, was the perception that this child was no longer a child. At seventeen she was a woman, and an uncommonly wise one at that. Mildred tried to like the clothes, couldn't. Unable to indict them, she harped on the three-quarter mink coat, the exact model she had picked out for herself, years before, and never yet bought. Querulously, she said such a purchase should never have been made "without consulting her." But when Veda slipped it on, and called her "darling Mother," and kissed her, and begged to be allowed to keep it, she gave in.

Thereafter, she hardly saw Veda. In the morning, when she went out, Veda was still asleep, and at night, when she came in, Veda wasn't home yet, and usually didn't arrive until two or three in the morning. One night, when Veda's car backed and started several times before making the garage, and the footsteps sounded heavy in the hall, Mildred knew that Veda was drunk. But when she went to Veda's door, it was locked, and there was no answer to her knock. Then one afternoon, when she came home for her rest, Veda's car was there, and so was a dreadful girl, named Elaine. Her place of residence, it turned out, was Beverly, her occupation actress, though when Mildred asked what pictures she had acted in, the answer was merely, "character parts." She was tall, pretty, and cheap, and Mildred instinctively disliked her. But as this was the first girl Veda had

ever chosen as a friend, she tried to "be nice to her." Then Mildred
began to hear things. Ida cornered her one night, and began a long,
whispered harangue. "Mildred, it may be none of my business, but
it's time you knew what was going on with Veda. She's been in here
a dozen times, with that awful girl she goes around with, and not
only here but at Eddie's, across the street, and at other places. And
all they're up to is picking up men. And the men they pick up!
They're driving all around in that car of Veda's, and sometimes
they've got one man with them and sometimes it's five. Five, Mildred. One day there was three inside, sitting all over the girls' laps,
and two more outside, one on each running board. And at Eddie's
they *drink* . . ."

Mildred felt she had to talk to Veda about this, and one Sunday
morning screwed up her courage to start. But Veda elected to be
hurt. "After all, Mother, it was you that said I couldn't lie around
here all the time. And just because that prissy Ida—oh well, let's not
get on that subject. There's nothing to be alarmed at, Mother. I may
go into pictures, that's all. And Elaine may be a bum—well there's
no use being silly about it. I grant at once that she's nothing but a
tramp. But she knows directors. Lots of them. All of them. And you
have to know directors to get a test."

Mildred tried conscientiously to accept this version, reminded
herself that the picture career had been her own idea, too. But she
remained profoundly miserable, almost physically sick.

One afternoon, at the Glendale restaurant, Mildred was checking
inventory with Mrs. Kramer when Arline came into the kitchen and
said a Mrs. Lenhardt was there to see her. Then, lowering her voice,
Arline added excitedly: "I think it's the director's wife."

Mildred quickly scrubbed up her hands, dried them, and went
out. Then she felt her face get prickly. Arline had said Mrs. Lenhardt, but the woman near the door was the very Mrs. Forrester to
whom she had applied, years before, for the job as housekeeper. She
had just time to recall that Mrs. Forrester had expected to be married again when the lady turned, then came over beaming, with out-
stretched glove and alarming graciousness. "Mrs. Pierce? I've been
looking forward *so* much to meeting you. I'm Mrs. Lenhardt, Mrs.
John Lenhardt, and I'm *sure* we're going to work out our little problem *splendidly*."

This greeting left Mildred badly crossed up, and as she led Mrs. Lenhardt to a table she speculated wildly as to what it might mean. She had a panicky fear that it had something to do with that visit years before, that Veda would find out she had once actually applied for a servant's job, that the consequences would be horrible. As she faced her visitor, she suddenly made up her mind that whatever this was about, she was going to deny everything; deny that she had ever seen Mrs. Forrester before, or been to her house, or even considered a position as housekeeper. She had no sooner made this decision than she saw Mrs. Forrester eyeing her sharply. "But haven't we met *before*, Mrs. Pierce."

"Possibly in one of my restaurants."

"But I don't *go* to restaurants, Mrs. Pierce."

"I have a branch in Beverly. You may have dropped in for a cup of chocolate some time, many people do. You probably saw me there. Of course, if I'd seen you I'd remember it."

"No doubt that's it."

As Mrs. Lenhardt continued to stare, Arline appeared and began dusting tables. It seemed to Mildred that Arline's ears looked bigger than usual, so she called her over, and asked Mrs. Lenhardt if she could offer her something. When Mrs. Lenhardt declined, she pointedly told Arline she could let the tables go until later. Mrs. Lenhardt settled into her coat like a hen occupying a nest, and gushed: "I've come to talk about our children, Mrs. Pierce—our *babies*, I'm almost tempted to say, because that's the way I really feel about them."

"Our—?"

"Your little one, Veda—she's such a *lovely* girl, Mrs. Pierce. I don't know *when* I've taken a child to my heart as I have Veda. And . . . my boy."

Mildred, nervous and frightened, stared for a moment and said: "Mrs. Lenhardt, I haven't any idea what you're talking about."

"Oh come, come, Mrs. Pierce."

"I don't know what you mean."

Mildred's tone was sharp, and Mrs. Lenhardt looked at her steadily, her lips smiling, her eyes not believing. Then she broke into a high, shrill laugh. "Oh of course you don't! How stupid of me, Mrs. Pierce. I should have explained that my boy, *my* baby, is Sam Forrester."

As Mildred still stared, Mrs. Lenhardt saw at last that this might not be pretence. Her manner changing, she leaned forward and asked eagerly: "You mean Veda hasn't told you anything?"

"Not a word."

"Ah!"

Mrs. Lenhardt was excited now, obviously aware of her advantage in being able to give Mildred her own version of this situation, whatever it was, first. She stripped off her gloves and shot appraising glances at Mildred for some time before proceeding. Then: "Shall I begin at the beginning, Mrs. Pierce?"

"Please."

"They met—well it seems only yesterday, actually it was several weeks ago, at my house. My husband, no doubt you've heard of him—he's a director, and he was considering Veda for a part. And as he so often does with these kids, when we have a little party going on, he asked her over—Veda and her little friend Elaine, another lovely child, Mrs. Pierce. My husband has known her for years, and—"

"Yes, I've met her."

"So it was at my own house, Mrs. Pierce, that Veda and Sam met. And it was *simply* love at first sight. It must have been, because that boy of mine, Mrs. Pierce, is so sincere, so—"

"You mean they're *engaged?*"

"I was coming to that. No, I wouldn't say they were engaged. In fact I *know* that Sammy had no such thing in mind. But Veda has somehow got the idea that—well, I *understand* it, of course. Any girl wants to get married, but Sam had no such thing in mind. I want that made clear."

Mrs. Lenhardt's voice was becoming a little high, a little strident, and she waggled a stiff forefinger at Mildred as she went on. "And I'm *quite* sure you'll agree with me, Mrs. Pierce, that any discussion of marriage between them would be *most* undesirable."

"Why?"

So far as Mildred was concerned, marriage for Veda would have been a major calamity, but at Mrs. Lenhardt's manner she bristled with hot partisanship. Mrs. Lenhardt snapped: "Because they're nothing but children! Veda can't be over nineteen—"

"She's seventeen."

"And my boy is twenty. That's too young. Mrs. Pierce, it's entirely too young. Furthermore, they move in two different worlds—"

"What different worlds?"

Mildred's eyes blazed, and Mrs. Lenhardt hastily backed off. "That isn't quite what I mean, Mrs. Pierce, of course. Let us say different *communities*. They have different backgrounds, different ideals, different friends. And of course, Sam has always been used to a great deal of money—"

"Do you think Veda hasn't?"

"I'm sure she has everything you can give her—"

"You may find she's been used to just as much as your boy has, and more. I'm not exactly on relief, I can tell you."

"But you didn't let me *finish*, Mrs. Pierce. If Veda's accustomed to wealth and position, so much the *more* reason that this thing should not for a second be considered. I want to make this clear: if Sammy gets married, he'll be *completely* on his own, and it will certainly be hard for two young people, both born with silver spoons in their mouths, to live on what *he* can earn."

Having made this clear, Mrs. Lenhardt tried to calm down, and Mildred tried to calm down. She said this was the first she had heard of it, and she would have to talk with Veda before she could say what she thought. But as Mrs. Lenhardt politely agreed that this was an excellent idea, Mildred began to have a suspicion that the whole truth had not been told. Suddenly and sharply she asked: "Why should Veda feel this way about it, and your boy not?"

"Mrs. Pierce, I'm not a mind reader."

Mrs. Lenhardt spoke angrily, the color appearing in her cheeks. Then she added: "But let me tell you one thing. If you, or that girl, or anybody, employ any more *tricks*, trying to blackmail my boy into—"

"Trying to—*what?*"

Mildred's voice cracked like a whip, and for a few moments Mrs. Lenhardt didn't speak. Apparently she knew she had said too much, and was trying to be discreet. Her effort was unsuccessful. When her nostrils had dilated and closed several times, she exploded: "You may as well understand here and now, Mrs. Pierce, that I shall *prevent* this marriage. I shall prevent it in any way that I can, and by legal means, if necessary." The way she said "*necess'ry*" had a very ominous sound to it.

By now the reality behind this visit was beginning to dawn on Mildred, and she became calm, cold, calculating. Looking up, she saw Arline at her dusting again, her ears bigger than ever. Calling her, she told her to straighten the chairs at the next table, and as she approached, turned pleasantly to Mrs. Lenhardt. "I beg your pardon. For the moment I wasn't listening."

Mrs. Lenhardt's voice rose to a scream. "I say if there are any more threats, any more officers at my door, any more of these tricks she's been playing—I shall have her arrested, I shall have her prosecuted for blackmail, I shall not hesitate for one moment, for I've quite reached the limit of my patience!"

Mrs. Lenhardt, after panting a moment, got up and swept out. Mildred looked at Arline. "Did you hear what she said?"

"I wasn't listening, Mrs. Pierce."

"I asked if you heard what she said."

Arline studied Mildred for a cue. Then: "She said Veda was trying to blackmail her boy into marrying her and if she kept it up she'd have the law on her."

"Remember that, in case I need you."

"Yes'm."

That night Mildred didn't go to Laguna or to Beverly. She stayed home, tramping around, tortured by the fear that Arline had probably told everybody in the restaurant by now, by uncertainty as to what dreadful mess Veda had got herself into, by a sick, nauseating, physical jealousy that she couldn't fight down. At eleven, she went to her room and lay down, pulling a blanket over her but not taking off her clothes. Around one, when Veda's car zipped up the drive, she took no chances on a locked door, but jumped up and met Veda in the kitchen. "Mother! . . . My, how you startled me!"

"I'm sorry, darling. But I have to talk to you. Something has happened."

"Well—at least let me take off my hat."

Mildred went to the den, relieved that she had smelled no liquor. In a minute or two Veda came in, sat down, lit a cigarette, yawned. "Personally, I find pictures a bore, don't you? At least Nelson Eddy pictures. Still, I suppose it's not his fault, for it isn't how he sings but what he sings. And I suppose he has nothing to do with how dreadfully long they are."

Miserably, Mildred tried to think how to begin. In a low, timid voice, she said: "A Mrs. Lenhardt was in to see me today. A Mrs. John Lenhardt."

"Oh, really?"

"She says you're engaged to marry her son, or have some idea you want to marry him, or—something."

"She's quite talkative. What else?"

"She opposes it."

In spite of her effort, Mildred had been unable to get started. Now she blurted out: "Darling, what *was* she talking about? What does it all mean?"

Veda smoked reflectively a few moments, then said, in her clear, suave way: "Well, it would be going too far to say it was my idea that Sam and I get married. After the big rush they gave me, with Pa breaking his neck to get me a screen test and Ma having me over morning, noon and night, and Sonny Boy phoning me, and writing me, and wiring me that if I *didn't* marry him he'd end his young life—you might say it was a conspiracy. Certainly I said nothing about it, or even thought about it, until it seemed advisable."

"What do you mean, advisable?"

"Well Mother, he was certainly very sweet, or seemed so at any rate, and they were most encouraging, and I hadn't exactly been happy since—Hannen died. And Elaine did have a nice little apartment. And I was certainly most indiscreet. And then, after the big whoop-de-do, their whole attitude changed, alas. And here I am, holding the bag. One might almost say I was a bit of a sap."

If there was any pain, any tragic overtone, to this recital, it was not audible to the ordinary ear. It betrayed regret over folly, perhaps a little self-pity, but all of a casual kind. Mildred, however, wasn't interested in such subtleties. She had reached a point where she had to know one stark, basic fact. Sitting beside Veda, clutching her hand, she said: "Darling, I have to ask you something. I have to, I have to. Are you—going to have a baby?"

"Yes Mother, I'm afraid I am."

For a second the jealousy was so overwhelming that Mildred actually was afraid she would vomit. But then Veda looked at her in a pretty, contrite way, as one who had sinned but is sure of forgiveness, and dropped her head on Mildred's shoulder. At this the sick feeling left, and a tingle went through Mildred. She gathered Veda to her bosom, held her tight, patted her, cried a little. "Why didn't you tell me?"

"I was afraid."

"Of me? Of Mother?"

"No, no! Of the suffering it would bring you. Darling Mother, don't you know I can't bear to see you unhappy?"

Mildred closed her eyes for a moment, to savor this sweet blandishment. Then, remembering, she asked: "What did she mean about officers?"

"You mean police?"

"I—guess so. At her door."

"My, that *is* funny."

Veda sat up, lit another cigarette, and laughed in a silvery, ironical way. "From what I've learned of the young man *since* this happened, I'd say that any girl from Central Casting, perhaps all eight thousand of them for that matter, could have sent officers to his door. He has a very inclusive taste. Well, that's really funny, when you stop to think about it, isn't it?"

Hoping for more saccharine remarks, Mildred asked Veda if she'd like to sleep with her, "just for tonight," but Veda said it was something she'd have to face alone, and went to her room. All through the night, Mildred kept waking with the jealousy gnawing at her. In the morning, she went to the Glendale restaurant and called Bert. Dispensing with Tommy, she went down to Mrs. Biederhof's corner and picked him up. Then, starting for the hills, she started to talk. She put in everything that seemed relevant, beginning with Mr. Hannen's hemorrhage, and emphasizing Veda's forebodings about it. When she got to Mr. Treviso, Bert's face darkened, and he exclaimed at the "rottenness" of a dirty wop that would treat a young girl that way. Then, finding the going more difficult, Mildred told about Elaine, the drinking, and Ida's harrowing tales. Then, disconnectedly, hardly able to speak any more, or to drive, she told about Mr. Lenhardt. Then, trying to tell about her talk with Veda, she broke down completely, and blurted: "Bert! She's going to have a baby! She's in a family way!"

Bert's grip tightened on her arm. "Hold it! Stop this goddam car. I got to—get some place where I can move around."

She stopped, and pulled to one side, on Foothill Boulevard. He got out, began tramping up and down beside the car. Then he began to curse. He said goddammit, he was going to kill that son of a bitch if it was the last thing he did on earth. He said he was going to kill him if they hung him for it and his soul rotted in hell. With still more frightful oaths, he went into full particulars as to where he was going to buy the gun, the way he would lay for the boy, what he would say when he had him face to face, and how he would let him have it. Mildred watched the preposterous little figure striding up and down, and a fierce, glowing pride in him began to warm her. Even his curses gave her a queer, morbid satisfaction. But after a while she said: "Get in, Bert."

He climbed in beside her, held his face in his hands, and for a moment she thought he was going to weep. When he didn't, she started the car and said: "I know you'd kill him, Bert. I know you would, and I glory in you for it. I love you for it." She took his hand, and gripped it, and tears came to her eyes, for he had reached her own great pain, somehow, and by his ferocity, eased it. "But—that wouldn't do Veda any good. If he's dead, that's not getting her anywhere."

"That's right."

"What are we going to do?"

Gagging over her words, Mildred presently broached the subject of an operation. It was something she knew little about, and hated, not only on account of its physical aspect, but because it went counter to every instinct in her wholly feminine nature. Bert cut her off with a gesture. "Mildred, girls die in that operation. They die. And we're not going to let her die. We lost one, and that's enough. By God, I'll say she's not going to have any operation, not to make it easy for a dirty little rat that took advantage of her and now wants to do a run-out."

Bert now turned toward Mildred, his eyes flashing. "He's going to marry her, that's what he's going to do. After he's given her child a name, then he can do his run-out. He *better* do a run-out, and do it fast, before I catch up with him. He can go to hell, for all I give a damn, but before he does, he'll march up beside her and say 'I do.' I'll see to that."

"It's the only thing, Bert."

Mildred drove along, and presently had a hollow feeling they were right back where they started. It was all very well to say the boy had to marry Veda, but how could they make him do it? Suddenly she burst out: "Bert, I'm going to get a lawyer."

"It's just what I've been thinking."

"You and I, we can't do a thing. Precious time is going by, and something has to be done. And the first thing is to get that lawyer."

"O.K. And get him quick."

When Mildred got home, Veda was just getting up. Closing the door, she addressed the tousled girl in the green kimono. "I told your father. We had a talk. He agrees that we need a lawyer. I'm going to call up Wally Burgan."

"Mother, I think that's an excellent idea . . . As a matter of fact, I've already called him up."

"You—*what?*"

Veda spoke sleepily, and a little impatiently. "Mother, can't you see that I'm trying to arrange things myself, without putting you to all kinds of trouble about it? I've been trying to spare you. I want to make things easy for you."

Mildred blinked, tried to adjust herself to this astounding revelation.

Wally arrived around three. Mildred brought him to the privacy of the den, then went and sent Letty on an errand that would take her all afternoon. When she got back to the den, Veda was there, in a simple little blue frock that had cost Mildred $75, and Wally was looking at the pictures of Bert attending the banquets. He said things certainly did look familiar, and casually got down to business. He said he had done a little inquiring around, and the situation was about what he figured it was. "The kid comes into dough on his twenty-first birthday, that's the main thing. How much I don't exactly know, but it's well up in six figures. He's got to inherit. There's no way the mother, or the stepfather, or any of them can juggle the books to keep him out of it, and once he dies, whoever is married to him at the time cuts in for her share of the community property. That's what this is all about, and it's all it's all about. That's why they're breaking their necks to head it off. It's got nothing to do with their being too young, or loving each other, or not loving each other, or the different ways they've been brought up, or any of the stuff that mother has been dishing out. It's nothing but the do-re-mi—the old army game."

When Wally stopped Mildred drew a deep breath and spoke slowly, raising her voice a little: "Wally, I'm not interested in whether he inherits, or how much he inherits, or anything of that kind. So long as I'm here, I don't think Veda will be in want. But a situation has been created. It's a terrible situation for Veda, and the only thing that boy can do about it is marry her. If he's a decent boy, he'll do the right thing on his own initiative, regardless of what his family says. If he's not, he'll have to be made. Wally, that woman had a great deal to say that I haven't told Veda, but that I have witnesses to substantiate—about law, and what she'll do, and other things. *I'll go just as far as she will.* If it's the only way, I want that boy arrested—and you can tell him he can be very glad it's only the police he has to face, instead of Bert."

"Arresting him may be a little tough."

"Haven't we got laws?"

"He's skipped."

Wally shot a glance at Veda, who considered a few moments, then said: "I think you'd better tell her."

"You see, Mildred, just happens we already thought of that. Two, three days, maybe a week ago, I took Veda over to the sheriff's office and had her swear out a warrant for Sam. No statutory rape, nothing unpleasant like that. Just a little morals charge, and same afternoon, couple of the boys went over to serve it. He wasn't there. And so far—"

"So that's what she meant by officers!"

Veda stirred uneasily under Mildred's accusing eyes. "Well Mother, if you're talking about what I said last night, I didn't know at that time that any officers had actually *been* there."

Mildred turned on Wally. "It does seem to me that on a thing of this kind, a matter as serious as this, I should have been the first one you would have talked to about it. Why the very idea, of legal steps being taken without my knowing anything whatever about it!"

"Now just hold your horses a minute."

Wally's eyes became very cold, and he got up and marched up and down in front of Mildred before he went on. "One thing you might consider: I've got a little thing called legal ethics to consider. Sure, I'd have been willing to talk to you. We've talked plenty before, haven't we? But when my client makes an express stipulation that I not talk to you, why—"

When Mildred turned, Veda was ready. "Mother, it's about time you got it through your head that after all, I, and not you, am the main figure in this little situation, as you call it. I'm not proud of it. I readily admit it's my own fault, and that I've been very foolish. But when I act on that assumption, when I try to relieve you of responsibility, when I try to save you unhappiness, it does seem to me you could give me credit for some kind of decent motives, instead of going off the handle in this idiotic way."

"I *never* in all my *life*—!"

"Now, Mother, nobody was asking any help from you, and as Wally has taken my case as a great favor to me, I think the least you can do is let him tell us what to do, as I imagine he knows much more about such things than you do."

As Mildred subsided, a little frightened at Veda's tone, Wally resumed in the casual way he had begun: "Well, so far as his doing anything goes, I'd say the next move was up to them. Way I look at it, we've taken Round 1. When we got out that warrant, that showed we meant business. On a morals charge, all the jury wants to know is the age of the girl—after that it's dead open and shut. When they got him under cover quick, that shows they know what they're up against. And what they're up against is tough. So long as that warrant is out against him, he dare not come back to the state of California, he can't go back to college, or even use his right name. Course there's a couple of other things we might do, like suing the mother, but then we're in the newspapers, and that's not so good. I'd say leave it like it is. Sooner or later they got to lead to us, and the more we act like we don't care, the prettier we're sitting."

"But Wally!"

Mildred's voice was a despairing wail. "*Wally!* Time is going on! Days are passing, and look at this girl's condition! We can't wait! We—"

"I think we can leave it to Wally."

Veda's cool tone ended the discussion, but all that day and all that night Mildred fretted, and by next morning she had worked herself into a rage. When Tommy reported, at noon, she had him drive her over to Mrs. Lenhardt's, to "have it out with her." But as they whirled up the drive, she saw the house man that had let her in, that morning long ago, talking to the driver of a delivery truck. She knew perfectly well *he* would remember her, and she called shrilly to Tommy to drive on, she had changed her mind. As the car rolled around the loop in front of the house, she leaned far back, so she wouldn't be seen. Then she had Tommy drive her to Ida's, and telephoned Bert. Leaving Tommy in Beverly, she again picked up Bert at Mrs. Biederhof's corner, and headed up to the hills.

Bert listened, and began shaking his head. "Gee Mildred, I wish you'd told me you had Wally Burgan in mind. I'm telling you, I don't like the guy, and I don't like the way he does business. Telling him to step on the gas is like—well, he's been liquidating Pierce Homes for eight years now, hasn't he? And they're not liquidated yet. He's not trying to get Veda married. He's just running up a bill."

They rode along, each trying to think of something, and suddenly Bert had it. "To hell with him! What we want is to find that boy, isn't it? Isn't that right?"

"That's it! Instead of—"

"What this needs is a private detective."

A hot, savage thrill shot through Mildred. At last she knew they were getting somewhere. Excitedly they talked about it, and then Bert told her to get him to a drugstore, or any place where he could get to a phone book. She stopped in San Fernando, and Bert hopped out before the car stopped rolling. He was back in a minute or two, a slip of paper in his hands. "Here's three, with phone numbers and addresses. I'd say let's go first to this Simons agency. I've heard of it, for one thing, and it's right there in Hollywood, not too far away."

The Simons Detective Agency was located in a small, one-story office on Vine Street, and Mr. Simons turned out to be a friendly little man with bushy black hair. He listened attentively as Bert stated the problem, and refrained from asking embarrassing questions. Then he tilted back in his chair and said he saw no particular difficulty. He got jobs of this sort all the time, and on most of them was able to show results. However, since time seemed to be of the essence, there would be certain expenses, and he would have to ask for an advance. "I'd have to have two fifty before I can start at all. First, to get the young man's picture and other information I'll need, I'll have to put an operative to work, and he'll cost me ten dollars a day. Then I'll have to offer a reward, and—"

"Reward?"

Mildred suddenly had visions of a horrible picture tacked up in postoffices. "Oh, don't worry, Mrs. Pierce." Mr. Simons seemed to divine her fear. "This is all strictly confidential, and nobody'll know anything. Just the same, we work through our connections, and they're not in business for their health. I'd say, on this, a $50 reward should be ample. Then there's the printing of our fliers, and the pay of a girl to address a couple thousand envelopes, and . . ."

Bert suggested that half the advance should be paid now, the other half when the boy was found, but Mr. Simons shook his head. "This is all the money I'll have to pay out before I can start at all. Mind, I haven't said anything yet about my services. Of course, other places may do it cheaper, and you're perfectly welcome to go where you please. But, as I always say, the cheaper the slower in this business—and, the riskier."

Mildred wrote the check. On the way home, both of them applauded themselves handsomely for what they had done, and agreed it should be between themselves, with nothing said to Wally or Veda until they had something to "lay on the line," as Bert put it. So for several days Mildred was ducking into phone booths and talking in guarded tones to Mr. Simons. Then one afternoon he told her to come in. She picked up Bert, and together they drove to the little frame office. Mr. Simons was all smiles. "We had a little luck. Of course it wasn't really luck. In this business, you can't be too thorough. We found out that when he left town, the young man was. driving one of his stepfather's cars, and just because I was able to put that information on the flier, now we've got something. Here's the itemized bill, and if you'll just let me have the check while the girl is typing out the address for you . . ."

Mildred wrote a check for $125, mainly for "services." Mr. Simons put a card in her hand, with an address on it. "That's a dude ranch near Winslow, Ariz. The young man is using his right name, and I don't think you'll have any trouble locating him."

Driving back, they stared at one of Mr. Simons's fliers, bearing the weak, handsome face of the boy they had chosen for a son-in-law. Then, nervously, they discussed what was to be done, and came to the conclusion, in Bert's phrase, that they had to "go through with it." When Mildred dropped him off, they agreed that the time had come to get action out of Wally, and rather grimly Mildred drove home. Going to the kitchen, she sent Letty on another protracted errand. Then, when the girl had gone, she hurried into the den and called Wally. Shrilly, she told what she had done, and read him the address furnished by Mr. Simons. He said hey wait a minute, till he got a pencil. Then he made her repeat the address slowly, and then said: "Swell. Say, that's a help. It's a good thing to have, just in case."

"What do you mean, in case?"

"In case they get tough."

"Aren't you calling the sheriff's office?"

"No use going off half-cocked. We've got them right where we want them, and as I said before, our play is to make them come to us. Just let it ride, and—"

"Wally, I want that boy arrested."

"Mildred, why don't you let me—"

Mildred slammed up the receiver and jumped up, her eyes blazing, her hat slightly askew. When she turned to dash out, Veda was at the door. At once she launched into a denunciation of Wally. "That man's not even trying to do anything. I've told him where that boy is. I had a detective find out—and still he does nothing. Well that's the last he'll hear from me! *I'm* going over to the sheriff's office myself!"

Quivering with her high, virtuous resolve, Mildred charged for the door. She collided with Veda, who seemed to have moved to block her path. Then her wrist was caught in a grip like steel, and slowly, mercilessly, she was forced back, until she plunged down on the sofa. "You'll do nothing of the kind."

"Let go of me! What are you pushing me for? What do you mean I'll do nothing of the kind?"

"If you go to the sheriff's office, they'll bring young Mr. Forrester back. And if they bring him back, he'll want to marry me, and that doesn't happen to suit me. It may interest you to know that he's been back. He sneaked into town, twice, and a beautiful time I had of it, getting him to be a nice boy and stay where Mamma put him. He's quite crazy about me. I saw to that. But as for matrimony, I beg to be excused. I'd much rather have the money."

Mildred took off her hat, and stared at the cold, beautiful creature who had sat down opposite her, and who was now yawning, as though the whole subject were a bit of a bore. The events of the last few days began ticking themselves off in her mind, particularly the strange relationship that had sprung up, between Veda and Wally. The squint appeared, and her face grew hard. "Now I know what that woman meant by blackmail. You're just trying to shake her down, shake the whole family down, for money. You're *not* pregnant, at all."

"Mother, at this stage it's a matter of opinion, and in my opinion, I am."

Veda's eyes glinted as she spoke, and Mildred wanted to back down, to avoid one of those scenes from which she always emerged beaten, humiliated, and hurt. But something was swelling within her, something that began in the sick jealousy of a few nights before, something that felt as though it might presently choke her. Her voice shook as she spoke. "How could you do such a thing? If you had loved the boy, I wouldn't have a word to say. So long as I thought you had loved him, I didn't have a word to say, not one word to blame you. To love is a woman's right, and when you do, I *hope* you give everything you have, brimming over. But just to pretend you loved him, to lead him on, to get money out of him—*how* could you do it?"

"Merely following in my mother's footsteps."

"What did you say?"

"Oh, stop being so tiresome. There's the date of your wedding, and there's the date of my birth. Figure it out for yourself. The only difference is that you were a little younger at that time than, I am now—a month or two anyway. I suppose it runs in families."

"Why do you think I married your father?"

"I rather imagine he married you. If you mean why you got yourself knocked up, I suppose you did it for the same reason I did—for the money."

"What money?"

"Mother, in another minute I'll be getting annoyed. Of course he has no money now, but at the time he was quite rich, and I'm sure you knew it. When the money was gone you kicked him out. And when you divorced him, and he was so down and out that the Biederhof had to keep him, you quite generously stripped him of the only thing he had left, meaning this lovely, incomparable, palatial hovel that we live in."

"That was his idea, not mine. He wanted to do his share, to contribute something for you and Ray. And it was all covered with mortgages, that he couldn't even have paid the interest on, let alone—"

"At any rate, you took it."

By now, Mildred had sensed that Veda's boredom was pure affectation. Actually she was enjoying the unhappiness she inflicted, and had probably rehearsed her main points in advance. This, ordinarily, would have been enough to make Mildred back down, seek a reconciliation, but this feeling within kept goading her. After trying to keep quiet, she lashed out: "But why? *Why*—will you tell me that? Don't I give you everything that money can buy? Is there one single thing I ever denied you? If there was something you wanted, couldn't you have come to me for it, instead of resorting to—blackmail. Because that woman was right! That's all it is! Blackmail! Blackmail! *Blackmail!*"

In the silence that followed, Mildred felt first frightened, then coldly brave, as the feeling within drove her on. Veda puffed her cigarette, reflected, and asked: "Are you sure you want to know?"

"I dare you to tell me!"

"Well, since you ask, with enough money, I can get away from you, you poor, half-witted mope. From you, and your Pie Wagon, and your chickens, and your waffles, and your kitchens, and everything that smells of grease. And from this shack, that you blackmailed out of my father with your threats about the Biederhof, and its neat little two-car garage, and its lousy furniture. And from Glendale, and its dollar days, and its furniture factories, and its women that wear uniforms and its men that wear smocks. From every rotten, stinking thing that even reminds me of the place—or you."

"I see."

Mildred got up and put on her hat. "Well it's a good thing I found out what you were up to, when I did. Because I can tell you right now, if you had gone through with this, or even tried to go through with it, you'd have been out of here a little sooner than you expected."

She headed for the door, but Veda was there first. Mildred laughed, and tore up the card Mr. Simons had given her. "Oh you needn't worry that I'll go to the sheriff's office now. It'll be a long time before they find out from me where the boy is hiding, or you do either."

Again she started for the door, but Veda didn't move. Mildred backed off and sat down. If Veda thought she would break, she was mistaken. Mildred sat motionless, her face hard, cold, and implacable. After a long time the silence was shattered by the phone. Veda jumped for it. After four or five brief, cryptic monosyllables, she hung up, turned to Mildred with a malicious smile. "That was Wally. You may be interested to know that they're ready to settle."

"Are you?"

"I'm meeting them at his office."

"Then get out. Now."

"I'll decide that. And I'll decide when."

"You'll get your things out of this house right now or you'll find them in the middle of Pierce Drive when you come back."

Veda screamed curses at Mildred, but presently she got it through her head that this time, for some reason, was different from all other times. She went out, backed her car down to the kitchen door, began carrying out her things, and packing them in the luggage carrier. Mildred sat quite still, and when she heard Veda drive off she was consumed by a fury so cold that it almost seemed as though she felt nothing at all. It didn't occur to her that she was acting less like a mother than like a lover who has unexpectedly discovered an act of faithlessness, and avenged it.

Chapter 14

IT WAS AT least six months after this that Bert called up to invite her to the broadcast. For her, it had been a dismal six months. She had found out soon enough where Veda was staying. It was in one of the small, swank apartment houses on Franklin Avenue, in Hollywood. Every fiber of her being had wanted to pay a visit there, to take back what she had said, to reestablish things as they had been, or try to. But when this thought entered her mind, or rather shot through her heart like a hot arrow, she set her face as if it had been cast in metal, and not once did she even drive past Veda's door. And yet, even in her loneliness, her relation with Veda was developing, twisting her painfully, like some sort of cancer. She discovered rye, and in the boozy dreams of her daily rest, she pictured Veda as going from bad to worse, as hungering and mending threadbare finery, until she had to come back, penitent and tearful, for forgiveness. This view of the future was somewhat obscured by the circumstance that Mildred didn't know exactly how much Veda had obtained from the Lenhardts, and thus couldn't calculate, with any degree of accuracy, when destitution was likely to strike. But Bert contributed a thought that assisted drama, if not truth. Bert, having tried unsuccessfully to stand on his rights as a father to bluff information out of Wally, and having threatened even to "hold up the settlement" unless full data were furnished, had learned only that his consent was not needed for a settlement; all the Lenhardts wanted was a release from Veda, a signed letter denying promises, intimidation, or pregnancy. But the episode had left him with a lower opinion of Wally's honesty than he had had before, if that were possible, and he hatched the theory that "Wally would have every damned cent of it before the year was out, didn't make a bit of difference what they paid, or what he got, or what she got." On this theory Mildred eagerly seized, and pictured the cheated Veda, not only as cold, hungry, and in rags, but as horribly bruised in spirit, creeping to the strong, silent mother who could cope with Wally or anybody else. When the scene materialized almost daily before her eyes, with a hundred little variations and embellishments, she always experienced the same brief ecstasy as she lifted the weeping Veda into her arms, patted her, inhaled the fragrance of the soft, coppery hair, and bestowed love, understanding, and forgiveness. One slight incongruity she overlooked: Veda in real life, rarely wept.

At Bert's mention of a broadcast it took her a moment or two to collect her wits. "What broadcast?"

"Why, Veda."

"You mean she's playing on the air?"

"Singing, the way I get it."

"Veda? *Singing?*"

"Maybe I better come over."

By the time he got there, she was a-tremble with excitement. She found the radio page of the *Times*, and there, sure enough, was Veda's picture, with the news that "the popular singer will be heard tonight at 8:30, on the Hank Somerville (Snack-O-Ham) program." Bert had seen the Examiner, but hadn't seen the *Times*, and together they looked at the picture, and commented on how lovely Veda looked. When Mildred wanted to know how long this had been going on, meaning the singing, Bert said quickly you couldn't prove it by him, as though to disclaim participation in secrets that had been withheld from Mildred. Then he added that the way he got it, Veda had been on the air quite a lot already, on the little afternoon programs that nobody paid any attention to, and that was how she'd got this chance on a big national hook-up. Mildred got the rye she had been sipping, poured two more drinks, and Bert revealed that his invitation had really been Mrs. Biederhof's idea. "She figured it meant a lot more to you than it would to her, so that's how I came to call you up."

"It was certainly nice of her."

"She's a real friend."

"You mean we'll go to the *studio?*"

"That's it. It's going out from the NBC studio right here in Hollywood, and we'll be able to see it and hear it."

"Don't we have to have tickets?"

". . . I got a couple."

"How?"

"It's taken care of."

"From Veda?"

"Never mind. I got 'em."

At the look on Mildred's face, Bert quickly crossed over, took her hand. "Now what's the use of acting like that? Yes, she called me up, and the tickets are there waiting for me. And she'll call you up, of course she will. But why would she be calling you in the morning, like she did me? She knows you're never home then. And then another thing, she's probably been busy. I hear they run those singers ragged, rehearsing them, the day of a broadcast. O.K., they've got her there, where she can't get to a phone or anything, but that's not her fault. She'll call. Of course she will."

"Oh no. She won't call me."

As Bert didn't know the full details of Veda's departure from home, his optimism was understandable. He evidently regarded the point as of small importance, for he began to talk amiably, sipping his rye. He said it certainly went to show that the kid had stuff in her all right, to get a spot like that with a big jazz band, and nobody giving her any help but herself. He said he knew how Mildred felt, but she was certainly going to regret it afterwards if she let a little thing like this stand in the way of being there at the kid's first big chance. Because it was a big chance all right. The torch singers with these big name bands, they're in the money, and no mistake about it. And sometimes, if they had the right hot licks on their first broadcast, they hit the big time overnight.

Mildred let a wan, pitying smile play over her face. If Veda had got there, she said, it was certainly all right with her. Just the same, it certainly seemed funny, the difference between what Veda might have been, and what she was. "Just a year or two ago, it was a pleasure to listen to her. She played all the classical composers, the very best. Her friends were of the best. They weren't my friends, but they were of the best. Her mind was on higher things. And then, after Mr. Hannen died, I don't know what got into her. She began going around with cheap, awful people. She met that boy. She let Wally Burgan poison her mind against me. And now, Hank Somerville.

Well, that's the whole story—from Beethoven to Hank Somerville, in a little over a year. No, I don't want to go to the broadcast. It would make me too sad."

Truth to tell, Mildred had no such critical prejudice against Mr. Somerville, or the torch canon, as her remarks might indicate. If Veda had called her up, she would have been only too glad to regard this as "the first move," and to have gone adoringly to the broadcast. But when Veda called Bert, and didn't call her, she was sick, and her sickness involved a bad case of sour-grapes poisoning: so far as she was concerned, torch was the lowest conceivable form of human endeavor. Also, she hated the idea that Bert might go without her. She insisted that he take Mrs. Biederhof, but he got the point, and miserably mumbled that he guessed he wouldn't go. Then suddenly she asked what advantage there was in going to the studio. He could hear it over the radio. Why not ride with her to Laguna and hear it there? He could have his dinner, a nice big steak if he wanted it, and then later she would have Mrs. Gessler put the radio on the veranda, and he could hear Veda without going to a lot of useless trouble. At the mention of steak, poor Bert perked up, and said he'd often wanted to see her place at Laguna. She said come right along, she'd be starting as soon as Tommy brought the car. He said O.K., and went legging it home to change into clothes suitable to a high-class place.

At Laguna, Mildred was indifferent to the impending event, and had little to say to the girls, the cooks, and the customers who kept telling her about Veda's picture in the paper, and asking her if she wasn't excited that her daughter was on the air. Bert, however, wasn't so reticent. While his steak was on the fire, he held court in the bar, and told all and sundry about Veda, and promised that if hot licks were what it took, the kid had them. When the hour drew near, and Mrs. Gessler plugged in the big radio on the veranda, he had an audience of a dozen around him, and extra chairs had to be brought. Two or three were young girls, there were two married couples, and the rest were men. Mildred had intended to pay no attention to the affair at all, but along toward 8:25, curiosity got the better of her. With Mrs. Gessler she went outside, and there was a lively jumping up to give her a seat. One or two men were left perched on the rail.

The first hint she got that Veda's performance might not be quite the torchy affair that Bert had taken for granted came when Mr. Somerville, early in the program, affected to faint, and had to be revived, somewhat noisily, by members of his band. The broadcast had started in the usual way, with the Krazy Kaydets giving the midshipmen's siren yell and then swinging briskly into "Anchors Aweigh." Then Mr. Somerville greeted his audience, and then he introduced Veda. When he asked if Veda Pierce was her real name, and she said it was, he wanted to know if her voice was unduly piercing. At this the kaydets rang a ship's gong, and Veda said no, but her scream was, as he'd find out if he made any more such remarks. The studio audience laughed, and the group on the veranda laughed, especially Bert, who slapped his thigh. A man in a blue coat, sitting on the rail, nodded approvingly. "She put that one across all right."

Then Mr. Somerville asked Veda what she was going to sing. She said the Polonaise from Mignon, and that was when he fainted. While the kaydets were working over him, and the studio audience was laughing, and the ship's gong was clanging, Bert leaned to the man in the blue coat. "What's it about?"

"Big operatic aria. The idea is, it's a little over the kaydets' heads."

"Oh, now I get it."

"Don't worry. They'll knock it over."

Mildred, who found the comedy quite disgusting, paid no attention. Then the kaydets crashed into the introduction. Then Veda started to sing. Then a chill, wholly unexpected, shot up Mildred's backbone. The music was unfamiliar to her, and Veda was singing in some foreign language that she didn't understand. But the voice itself was so warm, rich, and vibrant that she began to fight off the effect it had on her. While she was trying to get readjusted to her surprise, Veda came to a little spray of rippling notes and stopped. The man in the blue coat set his drink on a table and said: "Hey, hey, *hey!*"

After a bar or two by the orchestra, Veda came in again, and another chill shot up Mildred's back. Then, as cold prickly waves kept sweeping over her, she really began to fight her feelings. Some sense of monstrous injustice oppressed her: it seemed unfair that this girl, instead of being chastened by adversity, was up there, in front of the whole world, singing, and without any help from her. Somehow, all the emotional assumptions of the last few months were stood on their head, and Mildred felt mean and petty for reacting as she did, and yet she couldn't help it.

Soon Veda stopped, the music changed slightly, and the man in the blue coat sipped his drink. "O.K. so far. Now for the flying trapeze." When Veda started again, Mildred gripped her chair in sheer panic. It seemed impossible that anybody could dare such dizzy heights of sound, could even attempt such vocal gymnastics, without making some slip, some dreadful error that would land the whole thing in ruin. But Veda made no slip. She went on and on, while the man in the blue coat jumped down from the rail, squatted by the machine, and forgot his drink, forgot everything except what was pouring out into the night. Bert and the others watched him with some sort of fascinated expectancy. At the end, when the last, incredibly high note floated over the finale of the orchestra, he looked up at Mildred. "Jesus Christ, did you hear it? Did you—"

But Mildred didn't wait for him to finish. She got up abruptly and walked down toward Mrs. Gessler's flowers, waving back Bert and Mrs. Gessler, who called after her, and started to follow. Pushing through the bushes, she reached the bluff overlooking the sea, and stood there, lacing her fingers together, screwing her lips into a thin, relentless line. This, she needed nobody to tell her, was no descent from Beethoven to Hank Somerville, no cheap venture into torch. It was the coming true of all she had dreamed for Veda, all she had believed in, worked for, dedicated her life to. The only difference was that the dream that had come true was a thousand times rosier than the dream she had dreamed. And come what might, by whatever means she would have to take, she knew she would have to get Veda back.

This resolve remained hot in her mouth, but back of it, like a fishbone across her throat, was her determination that Veda, and not herself, would have to make the first move. She tried to put this aside, and drove to Veda's one morning with every intention of stopping, ringing the bell, and going in. But as she approached the little white apartment house, she hurriedly told Tommy to drive on without stopping, and leaned far back in the car to avoid being seen, as she had done that morning at Mrs. Lenhardt's. She felt hot-faced and silly, and the next time she decided to visit Veda she drove the car herself, and went alone. Again she went by without stopping. Then she took to driving past Veda's at night, and peeping, hoping to see her. Once she did see her, and quickly pulled in at the curb. Taking care not to slam the car door, she slipped out of the car and crept to the window. Veda was at a piano, playing. Then suddenly the miracle voice was everywhere, going through glass and masonry as though they were air. Mildred waited, a-tremble, until the song was finished, then ran back to her car and drove off.

But the broadcasts continued, and Mildred's feeling of being left out in the cold increased, until it became intolerable. Veda didn't appear again on the Snack-O-Ham program. To Mildred's astonishment, her regular spot on the air was Wednesdays, at 3:15, as part of the Treviso Hour, offered by star pupils of the same Carlo Treviso who had once closed the piano so summarily over her knuckles. And then, after listening to two of these broadcasts, and drinking in Veda's singing and everything the announcer said about her, Mildred had an idea. By making use of Mr. Treviso, she could compel Veda to call her on the phone, to thank her for favors rendered. After that, pride would be satisfied and almost anything might happen.

So presently she was in the same old anteroom, with the same old vocalizing going on inside, and her temper growing hotter and hotter. But when Mr. Treviso finally received her, she had herself under what she thought was perfect control. As he gave no sign of recognition, she recalled herself to him, and he looked at her sharply, then bowed, but otherwise made no comment. She then made her little speech, which sounded stiff, and no doubt was supposed to sound stiff. "Mr. Treviso, I've come on a matter that I shall have to ask you to keep confidential, and when I tell you the reason, I'm sure you'll be only too glad to do so. My daughter Veda, I believe, is now taking lessons from you. Now for reasons best known to herself, she prefers to have nothing to do with me at the moment, and far be it from me to intrude on her life, or press her for explanations. Just the same, I have a duty toward her, with regard to the expenses of her musical education. It was I, Mr. Treviso, who was responsible for her studying music in a serious way, and even though she elects to live apart from me, I still feel that her music is my responsibility, and in the future, without saying anything to her, without saying one word to her, Mr. Treviso, I'd like you to send your bills to me, and not to her. I hope you don't find my request unreasonable."

Mr. Treviso had seated himself, and listened with his death-mask smile, and for some moments he studied his fingernails attentively. Then he stood up. "Am ver' sorry, Madame, but dees is subject w'ich I cannot discuss wit' you."

"Well I'm very sorry too, Mr. Treviso, but I'm afraid you'll have to discuss it with me. Veda is my daughter, and—"

"Madame, you excuse me, 'ave engagement."

With quick strides, he crossed to the door, and opened it as though Mildred were the queen of Naples. Nothing happened. Mildred sat there, and crossed her still shapely legs in a way that said plainly she had no intention of going until she had finished her business. He frowned, looked at his watch. "Yes, himportant engagement. You excuse me? Please."

He went out, then, and Mildred was left alone. After a few minutes, the little fat woman came in, found a piece of music, sat down at the piano, and began to play it. She played it loud, and then played it again and again, and each time she played it was louder and still louder. That went on perhaps a half hour, and Mildred still sat there. Then Mr. Treviso came back and motioned the little fat woman out of the room. He strode up and down for a few minutes, frowning hard, then went over and closed the door. Then he sat down near Mildred, and touched her knee with a long, bony forefinger, "Why you want dees girl back? Tell me that?"

"Mr. Treviso, you mistake my motives. I—"

"No mistake, no mistake at all. I tell Veda, well you pretty lucky, kid, somebody else pay a bill now. And she, she got no idea at all, hey? Don't know who to call up, say thanks, sure is swell, how you like to see me again, hey?

"Well that wasn't my idea. Mr. Treviso, but I'm sure, if Veda did happen to guess who was paying the bill, and called up about it, I could find it in my heart to—"

"Listen, you. I tell you one t'ing. Is make no difference to me who pay. But I say to you: you want to 'ear dees girl sing, you buy a ticket. You pay a buck. You pay two bucks. If a ticket cost eight eighty, O.K. you pay eight eighty, but don't you try to 'ear dees girl free. Because maybe cost you more than a whole Metropolitan Grand Opera is wort'."

"This is not a question of money."

"No by God, sure is not. You go to a zoo, hey? See little snake? Is come from India, is all red, yellow, black, ver' pretty little snake. You take 'ome, hey? Make little pet, like puppy dog? No—you got more sense. I tell you, is same wit' dees Veda. You buy ticket, you look at a little snake, but you no take home. No."

"Are you insinuating that my daughter is a snake?"

"No—is a coloratura soprano, is much worse. A little snake, love mamma, do what papa tells, maybe, but a coloratura soprano, love nobody but own goddam self. Is son-bitch-bast', worse than all a snake in a world. Madame, you leave dees girl alone."

As Mildred sat blinking, trying to get adjusted to the wholly unexpected turn the interview had taken, Mr. Treviso took another turn around the room, then apparently became more interested in his subject than he had intended. He sat down now, his eyes shining with that Latin glare that had so upset her on her first visit. Tapping her knee again, he said: "Dees girl, she is coloratura, inside, outside, all over."

"What *is* a coloratura soprano?"

"Madame, is special fancy breed, like blue Persian cat. Come once in a lifetime, sing all a trill, a staccato ha-ha-ha, a cadenza, a tough stuff—"

"Oh, now I understand."

"Cost like 'ell. If is *real* coloratura, bring more dough to a grand opera house than big wop tenor. And dees girl, is coloratura, even a bones is coloratura. First, must know all a rich pipple. No rich, no good."

"She always associated with nice people."

"Nice maybe, but must be rich. All coloratura, they got, 'ow you say?—da *gimmies*. Always take, never give. O.K., you spend plenty money on dees girl, what she do for you?"

"She's a mere child. She can't be expected to—"

"So—she do nothing for you. Look."

Mr. Treviso tapped Mildred's knee again, grinned. "She even twiddle la valiere. All a coloratura, sit back like a duchess, twiddle a la valiere." And he gave a startling imitation of Veda, sitting haughtily erect in her chair, twiddling the ornament of her neck chain.

"She's done that since she was a little girl!"

"Yes—is a funny part."

Warming up now, Mr. Treviso went on: "All a coloratura crazy for rich pipple, all take no give, all act like a duchess, all twiddle a la valiere, all a same, every one. All borrow ten t'ousand bucks, go to Italy, study voice, never pay back a money, t'ink was all friendship. Sing in grand opera, marry a banker, get da money. Got da money, kick out a banker, marry a baron, get da title. 'Ave a sweetie on a side, guy she like to sleep wit'. Den all travel together, all over Europe, grand opera to grand opera, 'otel to 'otel—a baron, 'e travel in

Compartment C, take care of dog. A banker, 'e travel in Compartment B, take care of luggage. A sweetie, 'e travel in Drawing Room A, take care of coloratura—all one big 'appy family. Den come a decoration from King of Belgium—first a command performance, Theatre de la Monnaie, den a decoration. All coloratura 'ave decoration from King of Belgium—first a command performance, Theatre de la Monnaie, den a decoration. All coloratura 'ave decoration from King of Belgium, rest of a life twiddle a la valiere, talk about a decoration."

"Well—Los Angeles is some distance from Belgium—"

"No, no distance. Dees girl, make you no mistake, is big stuff. You know what make a singer? Is first voice, second voice, t'ird voice—yes, all know dees gag. Was Rossini's gag, but maybe even Rossini could be wrong. Must 'ave voice, yes. But is not what make a singer. Must 'ave music, *music* inside. Caruso, 'e could no read one note, but 'e have music in a soul, is come out ever' note 'e sing. Must have rhythm, feel a beat of a music before conductor raise a stick. And specially coloratura—wit'out rhythm, wit'out music, all dees ha-ha-ha is vocalize, not'ing more. O.K., dees Veda. I work on dees girl one week. She sing full chest, sound very bad, sound like a man. I change to head tone, sound good, I t'ink, yes, 'ere is a voice. 'Ere is one voice in a million. Den I talk. I talk music, music, music. I tell where she go to learn a sight-read, where learn 'armonia, where learn piano. She laugh, say maybe I 'ave somet'ing she can read by sight. On piano is a *Stabat Mater*, is 'ard, is tricky, is Rossini, is come in on a second beat, sing against accompaniment t'row a singer all off. I say O.K., 'ere is little t'ing you can read by sight. So I begin play Inflammatus, from a Rossini *Stabat Mater*. Madame, dees girl hit a G on a nose, read a whole Inflammatus by sight, step into a C like was not'ing at all—don't miss one note. I jump up, I say Jesus Christus, where you come from? She laugh like 'ell. Ask is little 'armonia I want done maybe. Den tell about Charl', and I remember her now. Madame, I spend two hours wit' dees girl dees afternoon, and I find out she know more music than I know. Den I really look dees girl over. I see dees deep chest, dees big bosom, dees 'igh nose, dees big antrim sinus in front of a face. Den I know what I see. I see what come once in a lifetime only—a great coloratura. I go to work. I give one lesson a day, charge one a week. I bring dees girl along fast, fast. She learn in six mont' what most singer learn in five year, seven year. Fast, fast, fast. I remember Malibran, was artist at fifteen. I remember Melba, was artist at sixteen. Dees girl, was born wit' a music in a soul, can go fast as I take. O.K., you 'ear Snack-O-Ham program?"

"Yes I did."

"A Polonaise from Mignon, is tough. She sing like Tetrazzini. Oh, no, Madame, is not far from Los Angeles to Belgium for dees girl. Is no good singer. Is great singer. O.K., ask a pipple. Ask a pipple tuned in on a Snack-O-Ham."

Mildred, who had listened to this eulogy as one might listen to soul-nourishing organ music, came to herself with a start, and murmured: "She's a wonderful girl."

"No—is a wonderful singer."

As she looked at him, hurt and puzzled, Mr. Treviso stepped nearer, to make his meaning clear. "Da girl is lousy. She is a bitch. Da singer—is not."

This seemed to be all, and Mildred got up. "Well—we're all entitled to our opinion, but I would like it, if you don't mind, if you'd send your bills hereafter to me—"

"No, Madame."

"Have you any *particular* objection?"

"Yes, Madame. I no enjoy a snake bite. You come in 'ere, you try make me play little part, part in intrigue to get your daughter back—"

"Mr. Treviso, that is your surmise."

"Is no surmise. For last two weeks, ever since Snack-O-Ham broadcast, dees little bitch 'ave told me a poor dumb mother will try get 'er back, and a first t'ing she do is come in here, offer pay for singing lesson."

"She—!"

"Yes! Dees girl, she live for two t'ing. One is make a mother feel bad, odder is get back wit' all a rich pipple she know one time in Pasadena. I tell you, is snake, is bitch, is coloratura. You want Veda back, you see Veda self. I 'ave not'ing to do wit' dees intrigue. She ask me, I say you not been 'ere at all—any'ow, I no see."

Mildred was so shaken up by Mr. Treviso's last revelation, that she wasn't capable of plans, schemes, or intrigues for the rest of that day. She felt as if she had been caught in some shameful act, and drove herself with work so as not to think about it. But later that night, things began to sort themselves out into little piles. She found some consolation in the certitude that at least *Veda* wouldn't know what she had done. And then, presently, she sat up in bed, hot excitement pulsing all through her. At last she knew, from that disclosure of Veda's desire to get back with the rich Pasadena people, how she would get her, how she would make even a coloratura come groveling, on her knees.

She would get Veda through Monty.

Chapter 15

WITHOUT MAKING any special effort to do so, Mildred had kept track of Monty these last three years, had even had a glimpse of him once or twice, on her way back and forth to Laguna. He was exactly where she had left him: in the ancestral house, trying to sell it. The place, no more salable, even in its palmiest days, than a white elephant, had a run-down look to it by now. The grass was yellow, from lack of water; across the lawn, in a bleary row were half a dozen agents' signs; the iron dogs looked rusty; and one of the pillars, out front, had evidently been hit by a truck, for there was a big chip out of it, with raw brick showing through. However, though she knew where to find him, Mildred didn't communicate with Monty at once. She went to the bank, opened her safe-deposit box, and made an accurate list of her bonds. She looked at her balances, both checking and savings. She went to Bullock's, bought a new dress, new hat, new shoes. The dress was simple, but it was dark blue, and she felt it slenderized her. The hat was big, dark, and soft. She then called an agent, and without giving her name, got the latest asking price on the Beragon mansion.

All this took two or three days. Just how exact her plan was it would be hard to say. She was wholly feminine, and it seems to be part of the feminine mind that it can tack indefinitely upwind, each tack bearing off at a vague angle, and yet all bearing inexorably on the buoy. Perhaps she herself didn't quite know how many tacks she would have to make to reach the buoy, which was Veda, not Monty. At any rate, she now sent him a telegram, saying she wanted help in picking a house in Pasadena, and would he be good enough to call her around eight that night, "at the Pie Wagon?"

She was a little nervous that evening, but was as casual when Monty called as though there were no buoys in her life whatever. She explained chattily that she simply had to move soon, to live in some place that was more centrally located; that Pasadena would be most convenient, and would he be good enough to ride around with her, and let her get her bearings before she actually got around to picking out a house? He seemed a little puzzled, but said he would do what he could, and how about calling some agents, so they could ride around too, and show what they had? Agents, she said, were exactly what she wanted to avoid. She could see them any time. What she wanted was to get the feel of a town that he knew a great deal better than she did, perhaps peep at a few places, and get some idea where she wanted to live. Monty said he had no car at the moment, and could she pick him up? She said that was exactly what she wanted to do, and how about the next afternoon at three?

She dressed with a great deal of care the next afternoon, and when she surveyed herself in the long mirror, it was with quite a little satisfaction. For the last few months, perhaps as a result of the woe that had weighted her down, she hadn't put on any more weight, and the special girdle certainly held her belly in quite nicely. The new dress had a smart, casual look to it, and was of a becoming length, so that enough of her legs showed, but not too much. The big hat gave her a slightly flirty, Merry Widow look. The shoes flattered her feet, and set off the whole costume with a bit of zip. She tried a silver fox fur, decided it was right, and wore it. In truth, although she didn't look quite as she imagined she did, she looked rather interesting. She looked like a successful woman of business, with the remains of a rather seductive figure, a face of little distinction but considerable authority, a credit to that curious world that had produced her, southern California.

It didn't suit her plans to have Tommy along, so she stepped into the car herself and was pleased at the expert way she handled it. She went zipping over the bridge to Pasadena, from the traffic circle down Orange Grove Avenue. When she got to the Beragon mansion, Monty was sitting on the steps waiting for her. She went roaring up the drive, stopped in front of him, said "Well!" and held out her hand. He took it, then jumped in beside her. Both were smiling, but a little pang shot through her at the change in him. He wore slacks, but they were cheap and unpressed. His bald spot was bigger: it had grown from the size of a quarter to the size of a big silver dollar. He was thin and lined, and had a brooding, hang-dog look that was very different from the jaunty air he had once had. As to how she looked, he made no comment, and indeed indulged in no personal talk of any kind. He said he wanted her to see a place in the Oak Knoll section, quite decent, very reasonable. Would she care to drive over there? She said she'd love to.

By the time they had looked at places in the Oak Knoll section, the Altadena section, and the South Pasadena section, and nothing quite suited her, he seemed a little irritated. From the glib way he quoted prices, she knew he *had* called up the agents, in spite of her telling him not to, and that he would get a little split if she bought. But she paid no attention, and around five headed for Orange Grove Avenue again, to bring him home. Rather curtly, he said good-bye, and got out, and started inside, and then, as a sort of afterthought, stood waiting for her to leave. Pensively, she sat at the wheel, looking at the house, and then she cut the motor, got out, and stood looking at it. Then she let a noisy sigh escape her, and said, "Beautiful, beautiful!"

"It *could* be, with a little money spent on it."

"Yes, that's what I mean . . . What do they want for it, Monty?"

For the first time that afternoon, Monty really looked at her. All the places he had taken her to had been quoted around ten thousand dollars: evidently it hadn't occurred to him she could possibly be interested in this formidable pile. He stared, then said: "Year before last, seventy-five flat—and it's worth every cent of it. Last year, fifty. This year, thirty, subject to a lien of thirty-one hundred for unpaid taxes—all together around thirty-three thousand dollars."

Mildred's information was that it could be had for twenty-eight and a half, plus the tax lien, and she noted ironically that he was a little better salesman than she had given him credit for. However, all she said was: "Beautiful, beautiful!" Then she went to the door, and peeped in.

It had changed somewhat since her last visit, that night in the rain. All the furniture, all the paintings, all the rugs, all the dust cloths, were gone, and in places the paper hung down in long strips. When she tiptoed inside, her shoes gritted on the floor, and she could hear gritty, hesitant echoes of her steps. Keeping up a sort of self-conscious commentary, he led her through the first floor, then up to the second. Presently they were in his own quarters, the same servants' apartment he had occupied before. The servants' furniture was gone, but in its place were a few oak pieces with leather seats, which she identified at once as having come from the shack at Lake Arrowhead. She sat down, sighed, and said it certainly would feel good to rest for a few minutes. He quickly offered tea, and when she accepted he disappeared into the bedroom. Then he came out and asked: "Or would you like something stronger? I have the heel of a bottle here."

"I'd love something stronger."

"I'm out of ice and seltzer, but—"

"I prefer it straight."

"Since when?"

"Oh I've changed a lot."

The bottle turned out to be Scotch, which to her taste was quite different from rye. As she gagged over the first sip he laughed and said: "Oh you haven't changed much. On liquor I'd say you were about the same."

"That's what *you* think."

He checked this lapse into the personal, and resumed his praise of the house. She said: "Well you don't have to sell me. I'm already sold, if *wanting* it is all. And you don't have to sit over there yelling at me, as though I was deaf. There's room over here, isn't there?"

Looking a little foolish, he crossed to the settee she was occupying. She took his little finger, tweaked it. "You haven't even asked me how I am, yet."

"How are you?"

"Fine."

"Then that's that."

"How are you?"

"Fine."

"Then that's that."

She tweaked his little finger again. He drew it away and said: "You know, gentlemen in my circumstances don't have a great deal of romance in their lives. If you keep this up, you might find yourself the victim of some ravening brute, and you wouldn't like that, would you?"

"Oh, being ravened isn't so bad."

He looked away quickly and said: "I think we'll talk about the house."

"One thing bothers me about it."

"What's that?"

"If I should buy it, as I'm half a mind to, where would you be? Would there be a brute ravening around somewhere, or would I have it all to myself?"

"It would be all yours."

"I see."

She reached again for his finger. He pulled it away before she caught it, looking annoyed. Then, rather roughly, he put his arm around her. "Is that what you want?"

"H'm-h'm."

"Then that's that."

But she had barely settled back when he took his arm away. "I made a slight mistake about the price of this house. To you, it's twenty-nine thousand, five hundred, and eighty. That'll square up a little debt I owe you, of five hundred and twenty dollars, that's been bothering me for quite some time."

"You owe me a debt?"

"If you try, I think you can recall it."

He looked quite wolfish, and she said "Booh!" He laughed, took her in his arms, touched the zipper on the front of her dress. Some little time went by, one half of him, no doubt, telling him to let the zipper alone, the other half telling him it would be ever so pleasant to give it a little pull. Then she felt her dress loosen, as the zipper began to slide. Then she felt herself being carried. Then she felt herself, with suitable roughness, being dumped down on the same iron bed, on the same tobacco-laden blankets, from which she had kicked the beach bag, years before, at Lake Arrowhead.

"Damn it, your legs are still immoral."

"You think they're bowed?"

"Stop waving them around."

"I asked you—"

"No."

Around dark, she grew sentimentally weepy. "Monty, I couldn't live here without you. I couldn't, that's all."

Monty lay still, and smoked a long time. Then, in a queer, shaky voice he said: "I always said you'd make some guy a fine wife if you didn't live in Glendale."

"Are you asking me to marry you?"

"If you move to Pasadena, yes."

"You mean if I buy this house."

"No—it's about three times as much house as you need, and I don't insist on it. But I will not live in Glendale."

"Then all *right!*"

She snuggled up to him, tried to be kittenish, but while he put his arm around her he continued somber, and he didn't look at her. Presently it occurred to her that he might be hungry, and she asked if he would like to ride to Laguna with her, and have dinner. He thought a moment, then laughed. "You'd better go to Laguna alone, and I'll open myself another can of beans. My clothes, at the moment, aren't quite suitable to dining out. Unless, of course, you want me to put on a dinner coat. That mockery of elegance happens to be all I have left."

"We never had that New Year's party yet."

"Oh didn't we?"

"And we don't *have* to go to Laguna . . . I love you in a dinner coat, Monty. If you'll put one on, and then drive over with me while I put on *my* mockery of elegance, we can step out. We can celebrate our engagement. That is, if we really are engaged."

"All right, let's do it."

She spanked him on his lean rump, hustled him out of bed, and jumped out after him. She was quite charming in such moments, when she took absurd liberties with him, and for one flash his face lit up, and he kissed her before they started to dress. But he was somber again when they arrived at her house. She put out whiskey, ice, and seltzer, and he made himself a drink. While she was dressing he wandered restlessly about, then put his head in her bedroom and asked if he could put a telegram on her phone. "I'd like Mother to know."

"Would you like to talk to her?"

"It's a Philadelphia call."

"Well my goodness, you act as if it was Europe. Certainly call her up. And you can tell her it's all settled about the house, at thirty thousand, *without* any foolish deductions of five hundred and twenty dollars, or whatever it was. If that's what's been worrying her, tell her not to worry any more."

"I'd certainly love to."

He went to the den, and she went on with her dressing. The blue
evening dress was long since outmoded, but she had another one, a
black one, that she liked very well, and she had just laid it out when
he appeared at the door. "She wants to speak to you."

"Who?"

"Mother."

In spite of success, money, and long experience at dealing with
people, a qualm shot through Mildred as she sat down to the phone,
in a hastily donned kimono, to talk to this woman she had never
met. But when she picked up the receiver and uttered a quavery
hello, the cultured voice that spoke to her was friendship itself.
"Mrs. Pierce?"

"Yes, Mrs. Beragon."

"Or perhaps you'd like me to call you Mildred?"

"I'd love it, Mrs. Beragon."

"I just wanted to say that Monty has told me about your plan to
be married, and I think it splendid. I've never met you, but from all
I've heard, from so many, many people, I always felt you were the
one wife for Monty, and I secretly hoped, as mothers often do, that
one day it might come to pass."

"Well that's terribly nice of you, Mrs. Beragon. Did Monty tell
you about the house?"

"He did, and I do want you to be happy there, and I'm sure you
will. Monty is so attached to it, and he tells me you like it too—and
that's a big step toward happiness isn't it?"

"I would certainly think so. And I do hope that some time you'll
pay us a visit there, and, and—"

"I'll be delighted. And how is darling Veda?"

"She's just fine. She's singing, you know."

"My dear, I heard her, and I was astonished—not really of
course, because I always felt that Veda had big things in her. But
even allowing for all that, she quite bowled me over. You have a very
gifted daughter, Mildred."

"I'm certainly glad you think so, Mrs. Beragon."

"You'll remember me to her?"

"I certainly will, Mrs. Beragon."

She hung up flushed, beaming, sure she had done very well, but
Monty's face had such an odd look that she asked: "What's the
matter?"

"*Where* is Veda?"

"She—took an apartment by herself, a few months ago. It bothered her to have all the neighbors listening while she vocalized."

"That must have been messy."

"It was—terrible."

Within a week, the Beragon mansion looked as though it had been hit by bombs. The main idea of the alterations, which were under the supervision of Monty, was to restore what had been a large but pleasant house to what it had been before it was transformed into a small but hideous mansion. To that end the porticoes were torn off, the iron dogs removed, the palm trees grubbed up, so the original grove of live oaks was left as it had been, without tropical incongruities. What remained, after all this hacking, was so much reduced in size that Mildred suddenly began to feel some sense of identity with it. When the place as it would be began to emerge from the scaffolding, when the yellow paint had been burned off with torches and replaced with a soft white wash, when green shutters were in place, when a small, friendly entrance had taken the place of the former Monticello effect, she began to fall in love with it, and could hardly wait until it was finished. Her delight increased when Monty judged the exterior sufficiently advanced to proceed with the interior, and its furnishings. His mood continued dark, and he made no allusions to the five hundred and twenty dollars, or Glendale, or anything of a personal kind. But he seemed bent on pleasing Mildred, and it constantly surprised her, the way he was able to translate her ideas into paint, wood, and plaster.

About all she was able to tell him was that she "liked maple," but with this single bone as a clue, he reconstructed her whole taste with surprising expertness. He did away with paper, and had the walls done in delicate kalsomine. The rugs he bought in solid colors, rather light, so the house took on a warm, informal look. For the upholstered furniture he chose bright, inexpensive coverings, enunciating a theory to Mildred: "In whatever pertains to comfort, shoot the works. A room won't look comfortable unless it is comfortable, and comfort costs money. But on whatever pertains to show, to decoration alone, be a little modest. People will really like you better if you aren't so *damned* rich." It was a new idea to Mildred, and appealed to her so much that she went around meditating about it, and thinking how she could apply it to her restaurants.

He asked permission to hang some of the paintings of his ancestors, as well as a few other small pictures that had been stored for him by friends. However, he didn't give undue prominence to these things. In what was no longer a drawing room, but a big living room, he found place for a collection of Mildred Pierce, Inc.: Mildred's first menu, her first announcements, a photograph of the Glendale restaurant, a snapshot of Mildred in the white uniform, other things that she didn't even know he had saved—all enlarged several times, all effectively framed, all hung together, so as to form a little exhibit. At first, she had been self-conscious about them, and was afraid he had hung them there just to please her. But when she said something to this effect, he put down his hammer and wire, looked at her a moment or two, then gave her a compassionate little pat. "Sit down a minute, and take a lesson in interior decorating."

"I love lessons in decorating."

"Do you know the best room I was ever in?"

"No, I don't."

"It's that den of yours, or Bert's rather, over in Glendale. Everything in that room meant something to that guy. Those banquets, those foolish-looking blueprints of houses that will never be built, are a part of him. They do things to you. That's why the room is good. And do you know the worst room I was ever in?"

"Go on, I'm learning."

"It's that living room of yours, right in the same house. Not one thing in it—until the piano came in, but that's recent—ever meant a thing to you, or him, or anybody. It's just a room, I suppose the most horrible thing in the world . . . A home is not a museum. It doesn't have to be furnished with Picasso paintings, or Sheraton suites, or Oriental rugs, or Chinese pottery. But it does have to be furnished with things that mean something to *you*. If they're just phonies, bought in a hurry to fill up, it'll look like that living room over there, or the way this lawn looked when my father got through showing how much money he had . . . Let's have this place the way *we* want it. If you don't like the Pie Wagon corner, I do."

"I love it."

"Then it stays."

From then on, Mildred began to feel proud of the house and happy about it, and particularly relished the last hectic week, when hammer, saw, phone bell, and vacuum cleaner mingled their separate songs into one lovely cacophony of preparation. She moved Letty over, with a room of her own, and Tommy, with a room and a private bath. She engaged, at Monty's request, Kurt and Frieda, the couple who had worked for Mrs. Beragon before "es went kaput," as Kurt put it. She drove to Phoenix, with Monty, and got married.

For a week after this quiet courthouse ceremony she was almost frantic. She had addressed Veda's announcement herself, and the papers were full of the nuptials, with pictures of herself and lengthy accounts of her career, and pictures of Monty and just as lengthy accounts of *his* career. But there was no call from Veda, no visit, no telegram, no note. Many people dropped in: friends of Monty's, mostly, who treated her very pleasantly, and didn't seem offended when she had to excuse herself, in the afternoon at any rate, to go to work. Bert called, with all wishes for her happiness, and sincere praise for Monty, whom he described as a "thoroughbred." She was surprised to learn that he was living with Mom and Mr. Pierce. Mrs. Biederhof's husband having struck oil in Texas, and she having joined him there. Mildred had always supposed Mrs. Biederhof a widow, and so apparently had Bert. Yet the call that Mildred hoped for didn't come. Monty, well aware by now that a situation of some sort existed with regard to Veda, rather pointedly didn't notice her mood, or make any inquiries about it.

And then one night at Laguna, Mrs. Gessler appeared around eight in a bright red evening dress, and almost peremptorily told Mildred to close the place, as she herself was invited out. Mildred was annoyed, and her temper didn't improve when Archie took off his regimentals at nine sharp, and left within a minute or two. She was in a gloomy irritable humor going home, and several times called Tommy down for driving too fast. Until she was at the door of her new house, she didn't notice that a great many cars seemed to be parked out front, and even then they made no particular impression on her. Tommy, instead of opening for her, rang the bell twice, then rang it twice again. She was opening her mouth to say something peevish about people who forget their keys, when lights went up all over the first floor, and the door, as though of its own accord, swung slowly open, wide open. Then, from somewhere within, a voice, the only voice in the world to Mildred, began to sing. After a long time Mildred heard a piano, realized Veda was singing the Bridal Chorus from Lohengrin. "Here comes the bride," sang Veda, but "comes" was hardly the word. Mildred floated in, seeing faces, flowers, dinner coats, paper hats, hearing laughter, applause, greetings, as things in a dream. When Veda, still singing, came over, took her in her arms, and kissed her, it was almost more than she could stand, and she stumbled hurriedly out, and let Monty take her upstairs, on the pretext that she must put on a suitable dress for the occasion.

A few years before, Mildred would have been incapable of presiding over such a party: her commonplaceness, her upbringing, her sense of inferiority in the presence of "society people," would have combined to make her acutely miserable, completely incompetent. Tonight, however, she was a completely charming hostess and guest of honor, rolled into one. In the black evening dress, she was everywhere, seeing that people had what they wanted, seeing that Archie, who presided in the kitchen, and Kurt, Frieda, and Letty, assisted by Arline and Sigrid from the Pie Wagon itself, kept things going smoothly. Most of the guests were Pasadena people, friends of Veda's and Monty's but her waitress training, plus her years as Mildred Pierce, Inc., stood her in good stead now. She had acquired a memory like a filing cabinet, and had everybody's name as soon as she heard it, causing even Monty to look at her with sincere admiration. But she was pleased that he had asked such few friends as she had: Mrs. Gessler, and Ida, and particularly Bert, who looked unusually handsome in his dinner coat, and helped with the drinks, and turned music for Mr. Treviso when Veda, importuned by everybody, graciously consented to sing.

Mildred wanted to cry when people began to leave, and then discovered that the evening had hardly begun. The best part came when she, and Veda, and Monty sat around in the small library, across from the big living room, and decided that Veda should spend the night, and talked. Then Monty, not at all reverent in the presence of art, said: "Well goddammit, how did you get to be a singer? When I discovered you, practically pulled you out of the gutter, you were a pianist, or supposed to be. Then I no sooner turn my back then you turn into some kind of a yodeler."

"Well goddammit, it was an accident."

"Then report."

"I was at the Philharmonic."

"Yes, I've been there."

"Listening to a concert. And they played the Schubert Unfinished. And afterwards I was walking across the park, to my car, and I was humming it. And ahead of me I could see him walking along—"

"Who?"

"*Treviso.*"

"Oh yes, the Neapolitan Stokowski."

"So I had plenty of reason for not wanting to meet the honorable signor, because I'd played for him once, and he wasn't at all appreciative. So I slowed down, to let him get ahead. But then he stopped, and turned around, and looked, and then he came over to me and said: 'Was that you singing?' Well, I have to explain that I wasn't so proud of my singing just about that time. I used to sing Hannen's songs for him, whenever he wrote one, but he used to kid me about it, because I sang full chest, and sounded exactly like a man. He called me the Glendale Baritone. Well, that was Charlie, but I didn't know why I had to take any kidding off Treviso. So I told him it didn't concern him whether I was singing or not, but he grabbed me by the arm, and said it concerned him very much, and me. Then he took a card from his pocket, and a pen, and ran under a light, and wrote his address on it, and handed it to me, and told me to be there the next day at four o'clock, that it was important. So that night I had it out with myself. I knew, when he handed me the card, that he had no recollection he had ever seen me before, so there was no question of kidding. *But*—did I want to unlock that door again or not?"

"What door?"

Monty was puzzled, but Mildred knew which door, even before Veda went on: "Of music. I'd driven a knife through its heart, and locked it up, and thrown the key away, and now here was Treviso, telling me to come down and see him tomorrow, at four o'clock. And do you know why I went?"

Veda was dead serious now, and looking at them both as though to make sure they got things straight. "It was because once he had told me the truth. I had hated him for it, the way he had closed the piano in front of me without saying a word, but it was his way of telling me, and it was the truth. So I thought maybe he was telling me the truth now. So I went. And for a week he worked on me, to get me to sing like a woman, and then it began to come the right way, and I could hear what he had heard that night out there in the park. And then he began to tell me how important it was that I become a musician. I had the voice, he said, if I could master music.

And he gave me the names of this one and that one, who could teach me theory, and sight-reading, and piano, and I don't know what-all."

"Oh yeah?"

"Yeah, and did I get my revenge, for that day when he closed the piano on me. I asked him if there was a little sight-reading he wanted done, and he handed me the Inflammatus from Rossini's *Stabat Mater*. Well nuts. I went through that like a hot knife through butter, and he began to get excited. Then I asked him if he had a little job of arranging he wanted done, and then I told him about Charlie, and reminded him I'd been in there before. Well, if he'd hit gold in Death Valley he couldn't have acted more like a goof. He went all over me with instruments, little wooden hammers that he used on my knuckles, and caliper things that went over my nose, and gadgets with lights on them that went down my throat. Why he even—"

Veda made curious, prodding motions just above her midriff, while Monty frowned incredulously. "Yes! Believe it or not, he even dug his fingers into the Dairy. Well! I didn't exactly know what to think, or do."

Veda could make a very funny face when she wanted to, and Monty started to laugh. In spite of herself, so did Mildred. Veda went on: "But it turned out he wasn't interested in love. He was interested in meat. He said it enriched the tone."

"The *what?*"

Monty's voice rose to a whoop as he said this, and the next thing they knew, the three of them were howling with laughter, howling at Veda's Dairy as they had howled at Mrs. Biederhof's bosom, that first night, many years before.

When Mildred went to bed her stomach hurt from laughter, her heart ached from happiness. Then she remembered that while Veda had kissed her, that first moment when she had entered the house, she still hadn't kissed Veda. She tiptoed into the room she had hoped Veda would occupy, knelt beside the bed as she had knelt so many times in Glendale, took the lovely creature in her arms and kissed her, hard, on the mouth. She didn't want to go. She wanted to stay, to blow through the holes in Veda's pajamas. And when she got back to her room she couldn't bear it that Monty should be there. She wanted to be alone, to let these little laughs come bubbling out of her, to think about Veda.

Monty agreed to withdraw to the tackroom as he called the place where he stored his saddles, bridles, and furniture from the shack, with complete good humor—with more good humor, perhaps, than a husband should show, at such a request.

Chapter 16

MILDRED NOW ENTERED the days of her apotheosis. War was crashing in Europe, but she knew little of it, and cared less. She was drunk with the glory of the Valhalla she had entered: the house among the oaks, where dwelt the girl with the coppery hair, the lovely voice, and the retinue of admirers, teachers, coaches, agents, and thieves who made life so exciting. For the first time, Mildred became acquainted with theaters, opera houses, broadcasting studios, and such places, and learned something of the heartbreak they can hold. There was, for example, the time Veda sang in a local performance of *Traviata*, given at the Philharmonic under the direction of Mr. Treviso. She had just had the delightful sensation of beholding Veda alone on stage for at least ten minutes, and at the intermission went out into the lobby, to drink in the awestruck comment of the public. To her furious surprise, a voice behind her, a man's voice, with effeminate intonation, began: "So that's La Pierce, radio's gift to the lyric muse. Well, there's no use telling me, you can't raise singers in Glendale. Why the girl's simply nauseating. She gargles it over her tonsils in that horrible California way, she's off pitch half the time, and as for acting—did you notice her routine, after Alfredo went off? She had no routine. She planted one heel on that dime, locked both hands in front of her, and just stayed there until . . ."

While Mildred's temples throbbed with helpless rage, the voice moved off somewhere, and another one began, off to one side: "Well, I hope you all paid close attention to the critique of operatic acting, by one who knows nothing about it—somebody ought to *tell* that fag that the whole test of operatic acting is how few motions they have to make, to put across what they're trying to deliver. John Charles Thomas, can he make them wait till he's ready to shoot it! And Flagstad, how to be an animated Statue of Liberty! And Scotti, I guess he was nauseating. He was the greatest of them all. Do you know how many gestures he made when he sang the Pagliacci Prologue? One, just one. When he came to the F—poor bastard, he could never quite make the A flat—he raised his hand, and turned it over, palm upward. That was all, and he made you *cry* . . . This kid, if I ever saw one right out of that can, she's it. So she locked her hands in front of her, did she? Listen, when she folded one sweet little paw into the other sweet little paw, and tilted that pan at a forty-five degree angle, and began to warble about the delicious agony of love—I saw Scotti's little girl. My throat came up in my mouth. Take it from me, this one's in the money, or will be soon. Well, hell, it's what you pay for, isn't it?"

Then Mildred wanted to run after the first man, and stick out her tongue at him, and laugh. Some things, to be sure, she tried not to think about, such as her relations with Monty. Since the night Veda came home, Mildred had been unable to have him near her, or anybody near her. She continued to sleep alone, and he, for a few days, to sleep in the tackroom. Then she assigned a bedroom to him, with bath, dressing room, and phone extension. The only time the subject of their relations was ever discussed between them was when she suggested that he pick out his furniture himself; on that occasion, she had tried to be facetious, and said something about their being "middle-aged." To her great relief, he quickly agreed, and looked away, and started talking about something else. From then on, he was host to the numerous guests, master of the house, escort to Mildred when she went to hear Veda sing—but he was not her husband. She felt better about it when she noted that much of his former gaiety had returned. In a way, she had played him a trick. If, as a result, he was enjoying himself, that was the way she wanted it.

And there were certain disturbing aspects of life with Veda, as for example the row with Mr. Levinson, her agent. Mr. Levinson had signed Veda to a radio contract singing for *Pleasant*, a new brand of mentholated cigarettes that was just coming on the market. For her weekly broadcast Veda received $500, and was "sewed," as Mr. Levinson put it, for a year, meaning that during this period she could do no broadcasting for anybody else. Mildred thought $500 a week a fabulous stipend for so little work, and so apparently did Veda, until Monty came home one day with Mr. Hobey, who was president of Consolidated Foods, and had decided to spend part of his year in Pasadena. They were in high spirits, for they had been in college together: it was Mr. Hobey's mountainous, shapeless form that reminded Mildred that Monty was now in his forties. And Mr. Hobey met Veda. And Mr. Hobey heard Veda sing. And Mr. Hobey experienced a slight lapse of the senses, apparently, for he offered her $2,500 a week, a two-year contract, and a guarantee of mention in 25% of Consol's national advertising, if she would only sing for *Sunbake*, a new vitamin bread he was promoting. Veda, now sewed, was unable to accept, and for some days after that her profanity, her studied, cruel insults to Mr. Levinson, her raving at all hours of the day and night, her monomania on this one subject, were a little more than even Mildred could put up with amiably. But while Mildred was trying to think what to do, Mr. Levinson revealed an unexpected ability to deal with such situations himself. He bided his time, waited until a Sunday afternoon, when highballs were being served on the lawn out back, and Veda chose to bring up the subject again, in front of Mildred, Monty, Mr. Hobey, and Mr. Treviso. A pasty, pudgy little man in his late twenties, he lit a cigar, and listened with half-closed eyes. Then he said: "O.K., ya dirdy li'l rat. Now s'pose ya take it back. Now s'pose ya 'pologize. Now s'pose ya say ya sorry."

"I? Apologize? To *you?*"

"I got a offer for ya."

"What offer?"

"Bowl."

"Then, accept . . . If the terms are suitable."

Mr. Levinson evidently noted how hard it was for Veda to say anything at all about terms, for the Hollywood Bowl is singer's heaven. He smiled a little, and said: "Not so fast, baby. It's kind of a double offer. They'll take Pierce or they'll take Opie Lucas—they leave it to me. I handle ya both, and Opie, she don't cuss me out. She's nice."

"A contralto's no draw."

"Contralto gets it if you don't 'pologize."

There was silence in the sunlight, while Veda's mouth became thick and wet, and Mr. Treviso smiled at a dancing mote, looking like a very benign cadaver. After a long time, Veda said: "O.K., Levy. I apologize."

Mr. Levinson got up, walked over to Veda, and slapped her hard, on the cheek. Monty and Mr. Hobey jumped up, but Mr. Levinson paid no attention. His soft, pendulous lower lip hanging down, he spoke softly to Veda: "What ya say now?"

Veda's face turned pink, then crimson, then scarlet, and her light blue eyes stared at Mr. Levinson with a fixity characteristic of certain varieties of shark. There was another dreadful pause, and Veda said: "O.K."

"Then O.K. And lemme tell ya someth'n, Pierce. Don't ya start noth'n with Moe Levinson. Maybe ya don't know where ya comin' out." Before sitting down, Mr. Levinson turned to Mr. Hobey. "Opie Lucas, she's free. She's free and she's hot. You want her? For twenny-five hunnerd?"

". . . No."

"I thought not."

Mr. Levinson resumed his seat. Monty and Mr. Hobey resumed their seats. Mr. Treviso poured himself a spoonful of the red wine he had elected, instead of a highball, and shot a charge of seltzer into it.

For the rest of the summer Mildred did nothing, and Veda did nothing, but get ready for this appearance at the Bowl. There were innumerable trips to buy clothes: apparently a coloratura couldn't merely buy a dress, and let it go at that. All sorts of questions had to be considered, such as whether the material took up light, from the spots, or reflected it, whether it gave, or whether it took. Then the question of a hat had to be decided. Veda was determined she must have one, a little evening affair that she could remove after the inter-mission, "to give some sense of progression, a gain in intimacy." These points were a little beyond Mildred, but she went eagerly to place after place, until a dressmaker in the Sunset Strip, near Beverly Hills, seemed to be indicated, and presently made the dress. It was, Mildred thought, incomparably lovely. It was bottle-green, with a pale pink top, and a bodice that laced in front. With the little green bonnet it gave a sort of French garden-party effect. But Veda tried it on a dozen times, unable to make up her mind whether it was right. The question, it seemed, was whether it "looked like vaudeville." "I can't come out looking like both Gish sisters," said Veda, and when

Mildred replied that neither of the Gish sisters had ever been in vaudeville, so far as she knew, Veda stared in the mirror and said it was all the same thing. In the end, she decided the bodice was "too much," and took it off. In truth, Mildred thought, the dress did look a little fresher, a little simpler, a little more suitable to a girl of twenty, than it had before. Still unsatisfied, Veda decided presently she would carry a parasol. When the parasol arrived, and Veda entered the living room, one night, as she would enter the Bowl, she got a hand. Mildred knew, and they all knew, that this was it.

Then there was the question of the newspapers, and how they should be handled. Here again, it seemed out of the question merely to call up the editors, tell them a local girl was going to appear, and leave the rest to their judgment. Veda did a great deal of telephoning about the "releases," as she called them, and then when the first item about her came out, she went into a rage almost as bad as the one that had been provoked by Mr. Hobey. At the end of an afternoon in which she tried vainly to locate Mr. Levinson, that gentleman arrived in person, and Veda marched around in a perfect lather: "You've got to stop it, Levy, you've got to kill this society girl stuff right now! And the Pasadena stuff! What do they want to do, kill my draw? And get me razzed off the stage when I come on? How many society people are there in this town, anyway? And how many Pasadena people go to concerts? Glendale! And radio! And studied right here in Los Angeles! There's twenty-five thousand seats in that place, Levy, and those boobs have got to feel that I'm their little baby, that I'm one of them, that they've got to come out there and root for me."

Mr. Levinson agreed, and seemed to regard the matter as important. Mildred, despite her worship of Veda, felt indignant that she should now claim Glendale as her own, after all the mean things she had said about it. But the mood passed, and she abandoned herself to the last few days before the concert. She took three boxes, holding four seats each, feeling sure that these would be enough for herself, Monty, and such few people as she would care to invite. But then the Bowl began calling up, saying they had another lovely box available, and she began remembering people she hadn't thought of before. In a day or so, she had asked Mom and Mr. Pierce, her mother and sister, Harry Engel and William, Ida and Mrs. Gessler, and Bert. All accepted except Mrs. Gessler, who rather pointedly declined. Mildred now had six boxes, with more than twenty guests expected, and as many more invited to the supper she was giving, afterwards.

According to Bert, who sat on the edge of her box and unabashedly held her hand, it had been a magnificent job of promotion, and the thing was a sell-out. So it seemed, for people were pouring through all entrances, and Bert pointed to the upper tiers of seats, already filling up, by which, he said, "you could tell." Mildred had come early, so she "wouldn't miss anything," particularly the crowd, and knowing that all these people had come just to hear her child sing. It was almost dark when Monty, who had driven Veda, slipped into the box and shook hands with Bert. Then the orchestra filed into the shell, and for a few minutes there was the sound of tuning. Then the lights went up, and the orchestra came to attention. Mildred looked around, and for the first time felt the vastness of the place, with these thousands of people sitting there waiting, and still other thousands racing up the ramps and along the aisles, to get to their seats. Then there was a crackle of applause, and she looked around in time to see Mr. Treviso, who was to conduct, mounting his little stand, bowing to the audience and to the orchestra. Without turning around, Mr. Treviso raised his hand. The audience stood. Bert and Monty stood, both very erect, both with stern, noble looks on their faces. Bewildered, Mildred stood. The orchestra crashed into the "Star-Spangled Banner," and the crowd began to sing.

The first number, called the *Fire Bird*, meant nothing to Mildred. She couldn't make out, after reading her program, whether there was to be a ballet or not, and she wasn't at all certain, after it finished, whether there had been one or not. She concluded, while Mr. Treviso was still acknowledging his applause, that if there had been one she would have noticed it. He went out, the lights went up, and for a long time there was a murmur like the murmur of the ocean, as the later comers ran, beckoned to each other, and followed hurrying ushers, to find their seats. Then the murmur died off a little. The lights went out. A drawstring pulled tight on Mildred's stomach.

The parasol, wide open and framing the bonnet in a luminous pink circle, caught the crowd by surprise, and Veda was in the center of the stage before they recovered. Then they decided they liked it, and the applause broke sharp. For a moment Veda stood there, smiling at them, smiling at the orchestra, smiling at Mr. Treviso. Then, expertly, she closed the parasol, planted it on the floor in front of her, and folded both hands over its rather high handle. Mildred, having learned to note such things by now, saw that it gave her a piquant, foreign look, and something to do with her hands. The first number, "Caro Nome," from *Rigoletto*, went off well, and Veda was recalled for several bows. The second number, "Una Voce Poco Fa" from the *Barber of Seville*, ended the first half of the concert. The lights went up. People spilled into the aisles, smoking, talking, laughing, visiting. Bert was sitting on the box again, saying it was none of his business, but in his opinion that conductor could very well have allowed Veda to sing an encore after all that applause. By God, that was an ovation if he ever heard one. Monty, not much more of an authority in this field than Bert was, but at least a little more of an authority, said it was his impression that no encores were ever sung in the first half of a program. All that, said Monty, in his understanding at least, was reserved for the end. Mildred said she was sure that was the case. Bert said then it was his mistake and that explained it. Because if he knew anything about it, these people were eating it up, and it did look as though Treviso would want to give the kid a break, if he could. All agreed that the people were eating it up.

The New World Symphony had little effect on Mildred, except that three airplanes went over while it was being played, and she became terrified lest one go over while Veda was singing, and ruin everything. But the sky was clear when she appeared again, looking much smaller than she had in the first half, quite girlish, a little pathetic. The parasol was gone, and the bonnet, instead of being on Veda's head, was carried in her hand. A single orchid was pinned to Veda's shoulder, and Mildred fiercely hoped that it was one of the six *she* had sent. The program said merely "Mad Scene from Lucia di Lammermoor," but there seemed to be a little more tension than usual before Mr. Treviso raised his stick, and presently Mildred knew she was present at a tremendous vocal effort. She had never heard one note of this music before, so far as she knew: it must have been rehearsed at the studio, not at home. After the first few bars, when she sensed that Veda was all right, that she would make no slip, that she would get through to the end, Mildred relaxed a little, permitted herself to dote on the demure, pathetic little figure, pour-

ing all this elaborate vocal fretwork out at the stars. There came a
tap on her shoulder, and Mr. Pierce was handing her a pair of opera
glasses. Eagerly she took them, adjusted them, levelled them at
Veda. But after a few moments she put them down. Up close, she
could see the wan, stagey look that Veda turned on the audience,
and the sharp, cold, look that she constantly shot at Mr. Treviso,
particularly when there was a break, and she was waiting to come in.
It shattered illusion for Mildred. She preferred to remain at a distance, to enjoy this child as she seemed, rather than as she was.

The number was quite long, was in fact the longest number Mildred had ever heard, but when it was done the sound that swept
over the vast amphitheatre was like thunder. Veda came out for bow
after bow, and presently, after her dozenth or so reappearance, she
came out followed by Mr. Treviso, and without hat or any encum-
brance, just a simple, friendly little girl, hoping to be liked. A gentleman with a flute stepped forward, carrying a chair, and camped near
Veda. When she saw him she went over and shook his hand. Then
Mr. Treviso took the orchestra briskly through the introduction of
"Lo, Hear the Gentle Lark," and there was a ripple of applause, for
this was one of the things that Veda had made popular on the radio.
When she got through there were cheers, and she began a whole
series of her radio numbers: "Love's Old Sweet Song," Schubert's
"Ave Maria," an arrangement of the "Blue Danube Waltz" that per-
mitted her to do vocal gingerbread while the orchestra played the
tune, and a Waldteufel waltz Mr. Treviso had dug up for her, called
"Estudiantina."

Many of these had been called for, with insistent shouting, by the
audience, and toward the end, the orchestra sat back and listened
while Mr. Treviso accompanied her on the piano that had been
pushed out during the intermission. Now Veda came out, and said:
"Even if it's not a song that's supposed to be sung on a symphony
program, may I sing a song just because I want to sing it?" As the
audience broke into amiable applause, Monty looked at Mildred,
and she sensed something coming. Then Mr. Treviso played a short
introduction, and Veda began the song about rainbows that had
been Mildred's favorite back in the happy days when she used to
come home for her rest, and Veda would play the numbers she liked
to hear.

It was all for her.

Veda began it, but when she finished it, or whether she finished it, Mildred never quite knew. Little quivers went through her, and they kept going through her the rest of the night, during the supper party, when Veda sat with the white scarf wound around her throat, during the brief half hour, while she undressed Veda, and put the costume away; in the dark, while she lay there alone, trying to sleep, not wanting to sleep.

This was the climax of Mildred's life.

It was also the climax, or would have been if she hadn't got it postponed, of a financial catastrophe that had been piling up on her since the night she so blithely agreed to take the house off Mrs. Beragon's hands for $30,000, and pay the tax lien of $3,100. She had expected, when she made that arrangement, to do the major part of the financing through the Federal Homes Administration, about which she had heard. She received her first jolt when she paid a visit to this authority, and found it made no loans of more than $16,000. She had to have at least $20,000, and wanted $25,000. She received another jolt when she went to her bank. It was willing to lend her whatever she wanted, seemed to regard her as an excellent risk, but refused to lend anything at all until repairs were made to the property, particularly in the way of a new roof.

Up to then, she had known there would be outlays, but thought of them vaguely as "a couple of thousand to put the place in order, and a few thousand to furnish it." After the bank's report, however, she had to consider whether it wouldn't be better to give the place a complete overhaul, so that she would have a property that somebody might conceivably want to buy, instead of a monstrosity. That was when Monty was called into consultation. She didn't tell him about the financial problem, but she was delighted when he hit on the plan of restoring the house to what it had been before Beragon, Sr., put into effect his bizarre ideas for improvement. But while this satisfied the bank, and qualified her for a $25,000 loan, it cost upwards of $5,000, and cleaned out her personal cash. For the furnishings, she had to sell bonds. When she married Monty he had to have a car, or she thought he had. This meant $1,200 more. To get the money, and cover one or two other things that had come up by then, she dipped into the reserves of the corporation. She drew herself a check for $2,500 and marked it "bonus." But she didn't use a check from the big checkbook used by Miss Jaeckel, the lady she employed to keep the books. She used one of the blanks she always carried in her handbag, in case of emergency. She kept saying to herself that she must tell Miss Jaeckel about the check, but she didn't do it. Then, in December of 1939, to take care of Christmas expenses, she gave herself another bonus of $2,500, so that by the first of the year there was a difference of $5,000 between what Miss Jaeckel's books showed and what the bank was actually carrying on deposit.

But these large outlays were only part of her difficulties. The bank, to her surprise, insisted on amortization of her loan as well as regular interest payments, so that to the $125 a month in carrying charges were added $250 in reduction charges, a great deal more than she had anticipated. Then Monty, when he sold her Kurt and Frieda at $150 a month, put her to somewhat heavier expenses in the kitchen than she had expected. Then the endless guests, all of whom seemed to have the thirst of a caravan of camels, ran up the bill for household entertainment to an appalling figure. The result was that she was compelled to increase her salary from the corporation. Until then, she had allowed herself $75 a week from each of the corporation's four component parts: the Pie Wagon, the pie factory, the Beverly restaurant, and the Laguna restaurant, or $300 a week in all. This was so grotesquely in excess of her living expenses that the money piled up on her account, and it was so much less than the corporation's earnings that a nice little corporate reserve piled up too. But when she hiked it to $400, the reserve ceased growing, and in fact Miss Jaeckel, with stern face, several times notified her that it would be necessary to transfer money from *Reserve*, which was carried on a special account, to *Current Cash*, which was carried on another account. These transfers of $500 each Mildred O.K.'d hurriedly, and with averted eyes, feeling miserable, and like a thief.

Reserve, being a sort of sacred cow outside the routine bookkeeping system, didn't often come into Miss Jaeckel's purview, so there was no immediate danger she would learn of Mildred's withdrawals. And yet in March of 1940, when Miss Jaeckel made up the income statements, and took them down to the notary and swore to them, and left them, with the tax checks, for Mildred's signature, Mildred was in a cold sweat. She couldn't now face Miss Jaeckel and tell her what she had done. So she took the statements to an accountant, and swore him to secrecy, and told him what she had done, and asked him to get up another set, which she herself would swear to, and which would conform with the balance at the bank. He seemed upset, and asked her a great many questions, and took a week making up his mind that nothing unlawful had been done, so far. But he kept emphasizing that *"so far,"* and looking at Mildred in an accusing way, and he charged $100 for his services, an absurd sum for what amounted to a little recopying, with slight changes. She paid him, and had him forward the checks, and told Miss Jaeckel she had mailed them herself. Miss Jaeckel looked at her queerly, and went back to her little office in the pie factory without comment.

Then, within a week or two, two things happened, of an elusive, tantalizing sort, and it was hard to say what was cause and what was effect, but the Laguna business took an alarming drop, and didn't recover. The Victor Hugo, one of the oldest and best of the Los Angeles restaurants, opened a place not far from Mrs. Gessler's place, and at once did a thriving trade. And Mrs. Gessler, white-lipped and tense, informed Mildred one night that "that little bitch, that trollop from Los Feliz Boulevard, had moved down here."

"Is Ike seeing her?"

"How do I know who Ike sees? He out on call half the time, and who knows where he goes, or when he comes back."

"Can't you find out?"

"I've found out, or tried to. No, he's not seeing her, that I know of. Ike's all right, if he gets half a break. But she's *here*. She's working in that pottery place, up the road about three miles, in a smock, and—"

After that, it didn't seem to Mildred that Mrs. Gessler quite had her mind on her work. Trade slacked off, and Mildred couldn't think of any way to get it back. She cut prices, and that didn't help. She would have closed the place down, but she was bound by a lease, unless she could get rid of it, and the other three places wouldn't yield enough to pay rent under the lease, and maintain her establishment in Pasadena too. It was almost weekly now that Miss Jaeckel came to her for more cash, and the transfers from *Reserve*, instead of being $500 each, dwindled to $250, to $150, to $100, to $50, and still the spiral was going downwards. Mildred lived a queer, unnatural life. By day she was nervous, worried, hunted, afraid to look Miss Jaeckel in the eye, sure all her employees were whispering about her, suspecting her, accusing her. By night, when she came home to Monty, to Veda, to the inevitable guests, she abandoned herself to quiet, mystical, intense enjoyment. In these hours, she sealed herself off from the crises of the day, permitted herself no anxious thoughts, stared at Veda, drew deep, tremulous breaths.

But there came a day when *Reserve,* on the books, was $5,003.61 and at the bank was $3.61. She had to tell a long story to Miss Jaeckel, to cover her inability to make another transfer. Two days after that she couldn't pay her meat bill. Bills of all kinds, in the restaurant business, are paid on Monday, and failure to pay is a body blow to credit. Mr. Eckstein, of Snyder Bros. & Co., listened to Mildred with expressionless eyes, and agreed to deliver meat until she "straightened this little matter out." But all during the following week, Archie was raging at the inferior quality of the top sirloins, and Mrs. Gessler had to be restrained from calling Mr. Eckstein personally. By Monday, Snyder Bros. were paid, but Mildred was asking time on other bills, particularly her liquor bill, most of which she owed Bodega, Inc. And then one day Wally Burgan strolled into the Pie Wagon, and it developed that he had been retained by several of her creditors. He suggested a little conference. As most of the trouble seemed to be at Laguna, how would she like to meet them down there the following night? They could have dinner, and then talk things over. The following night was the night Veda was to sing at the Bowl. Mildred shrilly said it was impossible, she had to be at the Bowl; nothing could interfere. Then, said Wally, how about one night next week? How about Monday?

The delay made matters worse, for Monday saw more unpaid bills, and in addition to Mr. Eckstein, Mr. Rossi of the Bodega, and representatives of three wholesale grocers, Mildred had to face Mr. Gurney and several small-fry market men who had previously been flattered if she so much as said good morning. Wally, however, kept everything on a courteous plane. He enjoined silence about the matter in hand while dinner was being served, lest waitresses hear things. He insisted that Mildred give him the check for the creditors' banquet, as he somewhat facetiously called it. He encouraged her to talk, to lay her cards on the table, so something could be arranged. He kept reminding her that nobody wanted to make trouble. It was to the interest of all that she get on her feet again, that she become the A1 customer she had been in the past.

Yet, at the end of two or three hours of questions, of answers, of figures, of explanations, the truth at last was out, and not even Mildred's stammering evasions could change it: All four units of the corporation, even the Laguna restaurant, would be showing a profit if it were not for the merciless milking that Mildred was giving them in order to keep up the establishment in Pasadena. Once this was in the open there was a long, grave pause, and then Wally said: "Mildred, you mind if we ask a few questions about your home finances? Kind of get that a little straightened out?"

"That's nobody's business but mine."

"None of it's anybody's business, so far as that goes. If we just went by what was our business, we'd have gone to court already, asked for receivers, and strictly kept our questions to ourselves. We didn't do that. We wanted to give you a break. But looks like we're entitled to little consideration too don't it? Looks like we could go into what *we* think is important. Maybe you don't think so. Maybe that's where the trouble is. It's you that's behind the eight ball, not us."

". . . What do you want to know?"

"How much does Veda pay in?"

"I don't charge my own child board, I hope."

"She's the big expense though, isn't she?"

"I don't keep books on her."

"This is what I'm getting at: Veda, she's making plenty. She had some dough, that I got for her, and she was smart the way she invested it. She's dragging down $500 a week from Pleasant, and even after she pays all them agents, teachers, and chiselers, she must have quite a lot left over. Well, wouldn't you be justified in deducting an amount to pay for her keep? If you did, that would kind of ease the pressure all around."

Mildred opened her mouth to say she couldn't do any deducting, that she had nothing to do with Veda's income. Then, under Wally's bland manner she noted something familiar, something cold. As her heart skipped a beat, she knew she mustn't fall into any traps, mustn't divulge any of her arrangements with Veda. She must stall, say this was something she hadn't thought of before, insist there were legal angles she would have to look into before she would know how she felt. So mumbling, she kept watching and saw Mr. Rossi look at Mr. Eckstein. Then she knew what this was about. Wally was engineering a little deal. The creditors were to get their money, the corporation was to be placed on a sounder basis, and Veda was to foot the bill. It didn't occur to her that there was an element of justice in this arrangement: that the creditors had furnished her with goods, and were entitled to payment; that Veda earned large sums, and had run a lengthy bill. All she knew was that hyenas were leaping at her chick, and her craftiness, her ability to stall, deserted her. She became excited, said that no child of hers was going to be made the victim of any such gyp, if she had anything to do with it. Then, looking Wally in the eye, she went on: "And what's more, I don't believe you or anybody has any right, even any legal right, to take what belongs to me, or what belongs to my child, to pay the bills of this business. Maybe you've forgotten, Mr. Wally Burgan, that it was you that had me incorporate. It was you that had the papers drawn up, and explained the law to me. And your main talking point was that if I incorporated, then my personal property was safe from any and all creditors of the corporation. Maybe you've forgotten that, but I haven't."

"No, I haven't forgotten it."

Wally's chair rasped as he stood to face her, where she was already standing, a few feet back from the big round table. "I haven't forgotten it, and you're quite right, nobody here can take one dime of your money, or your personal property, or Veda's, to satisfy the claims they got, makes no difference how reasonable the claims may be. They can't touch a thing, it's all yours and a yard wide. All they can do is go to court, have you declared a bankrupt, and take over. The court will appoint receivers, and the receivers will run it. You'll be out."

"All right, then I'll be out."

"You'll be out, and Ida'll be in."

". . . Who?"

"You didn't know that, did you?"

"That's a lie. She wouldn't—"

"Oh yes she would. Ida, she cried, and said at first she wouldn't even listen to such a thing, she was such a good friend of yours. But she couldn't get to you, all last week, for a little talk. You were too busy with the concert. Maybe that hurt her a little. Anyway, now she'll listen to reason, and we figure she can run this business as good as anybody can run it. Not as good as you, maybe, when you've got your mind on it. But better than a stagestruck dame that would rather go to concerts than work, and rather spend the money on her child than pay her creditors."

At the revelation about Ida, tears had started to Mildred's eyes, and she turned her back while Wally went on, in a cold, flat voice: "Mildred, you might as well get it through your head you got to do three things. You got to cut down on your overhead, so you can live on what you make. You got to raise some money, from Veda, from the Pierce Drive property, from somewhere, so you can square up these bills and start over. And you got to cut out this running around and get down to work. Now, as I said before, there's no hard feelings. We all wish you well. Just the same, we mean to get our money. Now you show us some action by a week from tonight, and you can forget it, what's been said. You don't, and maybe we'll have to take a little action ourselves."

It was around eleven when she drove up to the house, but she tapped Tommy on the shoulder and stopped him when she saw the first floor brightly lit, with five or six cars standing outside. She was on the verge of hysteria, and she couldn't face Monty, and eight or ten polo players, and their wives. She told Tommy to call Mr. Beragon aside and tell him she had been detained on business and wouldn't be in until quite late. Then she moved forward, took the wheel, and drove out again into Orange Grove Avenue. It was almost automatic with her to turn left at the traffic circle, continue over the bridge, and level off for Glendale and Bert. There was no light at Mom's, but she knew he was home, because the car was in the garage, and he was the only one who drove it now. At her soft tap he opened a window, and told her he would be right out. At the sight of her face, he stood for a moment in his familiar, battered red bathrobe, patted her hand, and said goddammit this was no place to talk. Mom would be hollering, wanting to know what was going on, and Pop would be hollering, trying to tell her, and it just wouldn't work. He asked Mildred to wait until he got his clothes on, and for a few minutes she sat in the car, feeling a little comforted. When he came out, he asked if she'd like him to drive, and she gladly moved over while he pulled away from the curb in the easy, grand style that nobody else quite seemed to have. He said it sure was one swell car, specially the way it held the road. She hooked her arm through his.

"Veda has to kick in."
They had driven to San Fernando, to Van Nuys, to Beverly, to the ocean, and were now in a little all-night cocktail bar in Santa Monica. Mildred, breaking into tears, had told the whole story, or at least the whole story beginning with Veda's return home. The singular connection that Monty had with it, and particularly the unusual circumstances of her marriage, she conveniently left out, or perhaps

she had already forgotten them. But as to recent events she was flagitiously frank, and even told about the two $2,500 checks, as yet undiscovered by Miss Jaeckel. At Bert's whistle there was a half-hour interlude, while he went into all details of this transaction, and she spoke in frightened whispers, yet gained a queer spiritual relief, as though she were speaking through the lattice of a confessional. And there was a long, happy silence after Bert said that so far as he could see, there had been no actual violation of the law. Then solemnly he added: "Not saying it wasn't pretty damn foolish."

"I *know* it was foolish."

"Well then—"

"You don't have to *nag* me."

She lifted his hand and kissed it, and then they were back to the corporation and its general problem. It could only be solved, he had insisted, through Veda. Now, on his second highball, he was even more of that opinion. "She's the one that's costing you money, and she's the one that's making money. She's got to pay her share."

"I never wanted her to know."

"I never wanted her to know, either, but she found out just the same, when I hit the deck. If she'd had a little dough when Pierce Homes began to wobble, and I'd taken it, and Pierce Homes was ours right now, she'd be better off, wouldn't she?"

Mildred pressed Bert's hand, and sipped her rye, then she held his hand tight, and listened to the radio for a minute or two, as it began moaning low. She hadn't realized until then that Bert had been through all this himself, that she wasn't the only one who had suffered. Bert, in a low voice that didn't interfere with the radio, leaned forward and said: "And who the hell put that girl where she is today? Who paid for all that music? *And* that piano? *And* that car? *And* those clothes? And—"

"You did your share."

"Mighty little."

"You did a lot." Intermingling of Pierce Homes, Inc., with Mildred Pierce, Inc., plus a little intermingling of rye and seltzer, had brought Bert nearer to her than he had ever been before, and she was determined that justice must be done him. "You did plenty. Oh we lived very well before the Depression, Bert, as well as any family ever lived in this country, or any other. And a long time. Veda was eleven years when we broke up, and she's only twenty now. I've carried on nine years, but it was eleven for you."

"Eleven years and eight months."

Bert winked, and Mildred quickly clutched his hand to her cheek. "All right, eleven years and eight months, if you've got to bring that up. And I'm *glad* it was only eight months, how do you like that? Any boob can have a child nine months after she gets married. But when it was only eight, that proves I loved you, doesn't it?"

"Me too, Mildred."

Mildred covered his hand with kisses, and for a time they said nothing, and let the radio moan. Then Bert said: "You want me to talk to that girl?"

"I can't ask her for money, Bert."

"Then I'll do it. I'll drop over there this afternoon, and bring it up friendly, and let her know what she's got to do. It's just ridiculous that you should have your back to the wall, and she be living off you, and rolling in dough."

"No, no. I'll mortgage the house. In Glendale."

"And what good will that do you? You raise five grand on it, you square up for a few weeks, and then you're right back where you started. She's got to kick in, and keep on kicking."

They ran up the beach to Sunset Boulevard and rode homeward in silence. Then unexpectedly Bert pulled over, stopped, and looked at her. "Mildred, you've got to do it yourself."

". . . Why?"

"Because you've got to do it tonight."

"I can't, it's late, she'll be asleep—"

"I can't help how late it is, or whether she's asleep, or she's not asleep. You've got to see her. Because you forgot, and I forgot, and we both forgot who we're dealing with. Mildred, you can't trust Wally Burgan, not even till the sun comes up. He's a cheap, chiseling little crook, we know that. He was my pal, and he crossed me, and he was your pal, and he crossed you. But listen, Mildred: He was Veda's pal too. Maybe he's getting ready to cross *her*. Maybe he's getting ready to grab her dough—"

"He can't, not for corporate debts—"

"*How do you know?*"

"Why, he—"

"That's it, he told you. Wally Burgan told you. You believe everything he says? You believe *anything* he says? Maybe that meeting tonight was just a phony. Maybe he's getting ready to compel you to take over Veda's money, as her guardian, so he can attach it. She's still a minor, remember. Maybe you, I, and Veda will all have papers slapped on us today. Mildred, you're seeing her tonight. And you're getting her out of that house, so no process server can find you. You're meeting me at the Brown Derby in Hollywood for breakfast, and by that time *I'll* be busy. There'll be four of us at that table, and the other one will be a lawyer."

Conspiratorial excitement carried Mildred to Veda's room, where necessity might never have driven her there. It was after three when she came up the drive, and the house was dark, except for the hall light downstairs. She put the car away, walked on the grass to keep from making a noise, and let herself in the front door. Putting the light out, she felt her way upstairs, carefully staying on the carpeting, so her shoes would make no clatter. She tiptoed along the hall to Veda's room and tapped on the door. There was no answer. She tapped again, using the tips of her fingers, to make only the softest sound. Still there was no answer. She turned the knob and went in. Not touching any light switch, she tip-toed to the bed, and bent down to touch Veda, and speak to her, so she wouldn't be startled. Veda wasn't there. Quickly she snapped on the bed light, looked around. Nobody was in the room, and it hadn't been slept in. She went to the dressing room, to the bathroom, spoke softly. She opened a closet. Veda's things were there, even the dress she had put on tonight, before Mildred went to Laguna. Now puzzled and a little alarmed, Mildred went to her own room, on the chance Veda had gone there to wait for her, and fallen asleep, or something. There was no sign of Veda. Mildred went to Monty's room, and rapped. Her tempo was quickening now, and it was no finger rap this time. It was a sharp knuckle rap. There was no answer. She rapped again, insistently. Monty, when he spoke, sounded sleepy, and quite disagreeable. Mildred said it was she, to let her in, she had to see him. He said what about, and why didn't she go to bed and let him sleep? She rapped again, imperiously this time, and commanded him to let her in. It was about Veda.

When he finally came to the door, half opened it, and found what Mildred wanted, he was still more annoyed. "For God's sake, is she an infant? Suppose she's not there, what do I do then? I went to bed—I don't know what she did. Maybe she went somewhere. Maybe she had a blowout. Maybe she's looking at the moon. It's a free country."

"She didn't go anywhere."

"How do you know?"

"Her dress is there."

"Couldn't she have changed it?"

"Her car is there."

"Couldn't she have gone with somebody else?"

This simple possibility hadn't even occurred to Mildred, and she was about to apologize and go back to her room when she became aware of Monty's arm. He was leaning on it, but it was across the door, in a curious way, as though to bar her from the room. Her hand, which was resting on the door casing, slipped up, flipped the light switch. Veda was looking at her, from the bed.

Monty, his voice an emasculated, androgynous yell, crammed all the bitterness, the futility of his life into a long, hysterical denunciation of Mildred. He said she had used him for her special purposes ever since she had met him. He said she was incapable of honor, and didn't know what it meant to stand by her commitments. He recalled the first $20 she had given him, and how she had later begrudged it. He worked down to their marriage, and correctly accused her of using him as bait to attract the errant Veda. But, he said, what she had forgotten was that he was live bait, and the quarry and the bait had fallen in love, and how did she like that? And what was she going to do about it? But there was considerable talk about money mixed in with the chase, and what it added up to was that he had shown his independence of one woman who had been keeping him, with a pie wagon, by switching over and letting another woman keep him, with a voice.

Mildred, however, barely heard him. She sat in the little upholstered chair, near the door, her hat on the side of her head, her handbag in her lap, her toes absurdly turned in. But while her eyes were on the floor, her mind was on the lovely thing in the bed, and again she was physically sick at what its presence there meant. When Monty had talked some little time, stalking gauntly about in his pajamas, Veda interrupted him with affectionate petulance: "Darling! Does it make any difference what such nitwits do, or whether they pay, or even know what a commitment is? Look what a pest she is to me. I literally can't open my mouth in a theater, or a radio studio, or anywhere, that she isn't there, bustling down the aisle, embarrassing me before people, all to get *her* share of the glory, if any. But what do I do? I certainly don't go screaming around the way *you're* doing. It would be undignified. And very—" here Veda stifled a sleepy yawn—"*very* bad for my throat . . . Get dressed now, and we'll clear out, and leave her to her pie plates, and by lunchtime it'll merely seem funny."

Monty went to his dressing room, and for a time there was silence, except for Mildred's breathing, which was curiously heavy. Veda found cigarettes on the floor, and lit one, and lay there smoking in the way she had acquired lately, sucking the smoke in and letting it out in thick curls, so it entered her mouth but didn't reach her throat. Mildred's breathing became heavier, as though she were an animal, and had run a distance, and was panting. Monty came out, in tweeds, a blue shirt, and tan shoes, his hat in one hand, a grip in the other. Veda nodded, squashed out her cigarette. Then she got up, went to Monty's mirror, and began combing her hair, while little cadenzas absentmindedly cascaded out of her throat, and cold drops cascaded over Mildred's heart. For Veda was stark naked. From the massive, singer's torso, with the dairy quaking in front, to the slim hips, to the lovely legs, there wasn't so much as a garter to hide a patch of skin.

Veda, still humming, headed for the dressing room, and Monty handed her the kimono, from the foot of the bed. It was then that Mildred leaped. But it wasn't at Monty that she leaped, her husband, the man who had been untrue to her. It was at Veda, her daughter, the girl who had done no more than what Mildred had once said was a woman's right. It was at a ruthless creature seventeen years younger than herself, with fingers like steel from playing the piano, and legs like rubber from riding, swimming, and all the recreations that Mildred had made possible for her. Yet this athlete crumpled like a jelly fish before a panting, dumpy little thing in a black dress, a hat over one ear, and a string of beads that broke and went bouncing all over the room. Somewhere, as if from a distance, Mildred could hear Monty, yelling at her, and feel him, dragging at her to pull her away. She could feel Veda scratching at her eyes, at her face, and taste blood trickling into her mouth. Nothing stopped her. She clutched for the throat of the naked girl beneath her, and squeezed hard. She wrenched the other hand free of Monty, and clutched with that too, and squeezed with both hands. She could see Veda's face getting red, getting purple. She could see Veda's tongue popping out, her slaty blue eyes losing expression. She squeezed harder.

She was on the floor, beside the bed, her head ringing from heavy blows. Across the room, in the kimono now, huddled in a chair, and holding on to her throat, was Veda. She was gasping, and Monty was talking to her, telling her to relax, to lie down, to take it easy. But Veda got to her feet and staggered out of the room. Mildred, sensing some purpose in this exit, and taking its evil nature for granted, scrambled up and lurched after her. Monty, pleading for an end to "this damned nonsense," followed Mildred. Letty and Frieda, in night dresses, evidently aroused by the commotion, stared in fright at the three of them, as Veda led the way down the big staircase. They made in truth a ghastly procession, and the gray light that filtered in seemed the only conceivable illumination for the hatred that twisted their faces.

Veda turned into the living room, reeled over to the piano, and struck a chord. Then her breath came fast, as though she was going to vomit, but Mildred, a horrible intuition suddenly stabbing at her, knew she was trying to sing. No sound came. She struck the chord again, and still there was no sound. On the third try, a dreadful croak, that was like a man's voice and yet not like a man's voice, came out of her mouth. With a scream she fell on the floor, and lay there, writhing in what appeared to be convulsions. Mildred sat down on the bench, sick with the realization of what she had done. Monty began to weep hysterically, and to shout at Mildred: "Came the dawn! . . . Came the dawn—God, what a dawn!"

Chapter 17

IT WAS CHRISTMAS again on Pierce Drive, a balmy golden California Christmas. Mildred, after the most crushing period of her life, was beginning to live again, to hope that the future might hold more than pain, or even worse, shame. It wasn't the mad, spinning collapse of her world that had paralyzed her will, left her with the feeling that she must wear a veil, so she needn't look people in the eye. The loss of Mildred Pierce, Inc., had been hard. It had been doubly hard because she would always know that if Wally Burgan had been a little less brutal, if Mrs. Gessler had been a little more loyal, and not gone off on her four-day drunk, telephoning the news of Ike's blonde at hourly intervals, with reversed charges, from Santa Barbara to San Francisco—she might have weathered the storm. These calls had been one of the features of her stay in Reno, that six-week fever dream in which she constantly listened to Mr. Roosevelt, and couldn't get it through her head that she couldn't vote for him this year, as she would be a resident of Nevada, not of California. And it had been hard, the wilting discovery that she could no longer do business under her own name. That, it turned out, was still owned by the corporation, and she thought bitterly of the many debts she owed to Wally.

But what had left her with a scar on her soul that she thought nothing could ever heal, was a little session, lasting barely an hour, with a stenographer and a pair of attorneys. It seemed that Veda, the day after she left the hospital, reported as usual at the broadcasting studio, for rehearsal with the Pleasant Orchestra. The rough, male voice that came out of the amplifiers wasn't quite what Pleasant had contracted for, and the conductor had called the rehearsal off. Veda, that day and the day after, had insisted that she was willing to go through with her contract. Thereupon Pleasant had gone to court to have the contract annulled, on the ground that Veda was no longer able to fulfill it.

Veda's attorney, brother of Mr. Levinson, her agent, felt it necessary to prove that Veda's vocal condition was due to no fault of her own. Thus it was that Mildred, before she moved out of the Beragon mansion and advertised it for rent, before she went to Reno for the divorce, before she even got the ice bags off her head, had to give a deposition, telling about the quarrel, and how she had throttled Veda, so she had lost her voice. This was painful enough, even though neither attorney pressed her for an exact account of what the quarrel was about, and let her ascribe it to "a question of discipline." But the next day, when the newspapers decided this was a strange, exciting, and human story, and published it under big headlines, with pictures of Mildred and Veda, and insets of Monty, and hints that Monty might have been back of the "question of discipline," then indeed was the albatross publicly hung on Mildred's neck. She had destroyed the beautiful thing that she loved most in the world, and had another breakdown, and couldn't get up for some days.

Yet when Veda came to Reno, and elaborately forgave her, and there were more pictures, and big stories in the papers, Mildred was weepily grateful. It was a strange, unnatural Veda who settled down with her at the hotel, a wan, smiling wraith who talked in whispers, on account of the condition of her throat, and seemed more like the ghost of Veda than Veda herself. But at night, when she thought about it, it all became clear to Mildred. She had done Veda a wrong, and there was but one way to atone for it. Since she had deprived Veda of her "means of livelihood," she must provide the child a home, must see that she would never know want. Here again was a familiar emotional pattern, with new excuses. But Bert felt about it as she did. She sent him $50, asking if he could come up and see her, and explaining that she couldn't go to see him, as she wasn't permitted to leave the state of Nevada until her divorce was granted. He came up the next weekend, and she took him for a long ride, down toward Tonopah, and they threshed it out. Bert was greatly moved by the details of Veda's arrival, and forgiveness. Goddammit, he said, but that made him feel good. It just went to show that when the kid was seeing the right kind of people, she was true blue inside, just what you'd want her to be. He agreed that the least Mildred could do was provide Veda a home. To her stammering inquiry as to whether he wanted to help her provide it, he gravely said he didn't know anything he'd like better. He was up for two more weekends, and after the divorce there was a quiet courthouse wedding. To Mildred's surprise, Veda wasn't the only guest. Mr. Levinson showed up, saying he happened to be in town on business, and was a sucker for rice.

The days after Thanksgiving had been bleak and empty for Mildred: she couldn't get used to it that the Pie Wagon was no longer hers, that she had nothing to do. And she couldn't get used to it that she was cramped for small money. She had mortgaged the house on Pierce Drive, into which she had now moved, obtaining $5,000. But most of this had been spent in Reno, and the rest of it was rapidly melting. Yet she had resolved they were going to have Christmas, and bought Bert a new suit, and Veda one of the big automatic phonographs, and several albums of records. This bit of recklessness restored her to a touch of her old self, and she was a little gay as Letty announced dinner. Bert had made eggnog, and it felt warm and pleasant, and as the three of them went back to the dining room she suddenly remembered she had bumped into Mr. Chris the day before, at the Tip-Top, and he was furious at the pies that were being delivered to him by Mildred Pierce, Inc. "He couldn't believe it when I told him I had nothing more to do with it, but when I asked him how he'd like to have some of *my* pies, he almost kissed me. 'Hokay, hokay, any time, bring 'm in, appliss, limmon, e poomkin!' "

She was so pleased at the way she imitated Mr. Chris's dialect that she started to laugh, and they all started to laugh. Then Bert said if she felt like making pies again, just leave the rest to him. He'd sell them. Veda laughed, pointed at her mouth, whispered that she'd eat them. Mildred wanted to jump up and kiss her, but didn't.

The doorbell rang. Letty went to answer it, returned in a moment with a puzzled look on her face. "The taxi man's there, Mrs. Pierce."

"Taxi? I didn't order any taxi."

"Yes'm, I'll tell him."

Veda stopped Letty with a gesture. "I ordered it."

"*You* ordered it."

"Yes, Mother."

Veda got up from her untouched turkey, and calmly faced Mildred. "I decided some time ago that the place for me is New York, and I'm leaving in a little while from Union Air Terminal, in Burbank. I mcant to tell you."

Bewildered, Mildred blinked at Veda's cold, cruel eyes, noted that Veda was now talking in her natural voice. A suspicion flashed into her mind. "Who are you going with?"

"Monty."

"Ah."

All sorts of things now began to flit through Mildred's mind, and piece themselves together: remarks by Mr. Hobey, the Sunbake promoter, the big forgiveness scene in Reno, featured by the newspapers, the curious appearance of Mr. Levinson at her wedding. Then, while Veda still stood coldly smiling, Mildred began to talk, her tongue licking her lips with quick, dry motions like the motions of a snake's tongue. "I see it now . . . You didn't lose any voice, you just thought faster than anybody else, that night . . . If you could make me say I choked you, then you could break your contract with Pleasant, the company that gave you your first big chance. You used to sing full chest, like a man, and you could do it again, if you had to. So you did, and you made me swear to all that, for a court record, so the newspapers could print it. But then you found out you'd gone a little too far. The newspapers found out about Monty, and that wasn't so good for the radio public. So you came to Reno, and had pictures of yourself taken, with me in your arms. And at my wedding, to your father. And you even invited that Levinson to be there, as though he meant anything to me. Anything to cover up, to hide what had really been going on, the love affair you'd been having with your mother's husband, with your own stepfather."

"Anyway, I'm going."

"And I know perfectly well why you're going. Now the publicity has blown over a little, you're going to sing for Sunbake, for $2,500 a week. All right—but this time, don't come back."

Mildred's voice rose as she said this, and Veda's hand involuntarily went to her throat. Then Veda went to her father, and kissed him. He kissed her, and patted her, but his eyes were averted, and he seemed a little cold. Then she left. When the taxi door slammed, and it had noisily pulled away, Mildred went to the bedroom, lay down, and began to cry. Perhaps she had something to cry about. She was thirty-seven years old, fat, and getting a little shapeless. She had lost everything she had worked for, over long and weary years. The one living thing she had loved had turned on her repeatedly, with tooth and fang, and now had left her without so much as a kiss or a pleasant good-bye. Her only crime, if she had committed one, was that she had loved this girl too well.

Bert came in, with a decisive look in his eye and a bottle of rye in his hand. In masterful fashion he sloshed it once or twice, then sat down on the bed. "Mildred."

"Yes?"

"To hell with her."

This remark only served to step up the tempo of Mildred's sobs, which were approaching a wail already. But Bert took hold of her and shook her. "I said, to hell with her!"

Through the tears, the woe, Mildred seemed to sense what he meant. What it cost her to swallow back her sobs, look at him, squint, and draw the knife across an umbilical cord, God alone knows. But she did it. Her hand tightened on his until her finger nails dug into his skin, and she said: "O.K., Bert. To hell with her!"

"Goddam it, that's what I want to hear! Come on, we got each other, haven't we? Let's get stinko."

"Yes—let's get stinko."

DOUBLE
INDEMNITY

Chapter 1

I DROVE OUT TO Glendale to put three new truck drivers on a brewery company bond, and then I remembered this renewal over in Hollywoodland. I decided to run over there. That was how I came to this House of Death, that you've been reading about in the papers. It didn't look like a House of Death when I saw it. It was just a Spanish house, like all the rest of them in California, with white walls, red tile roof, and a patio out to one side. It was built cock-eyed. The garage was under the house, the first floor was over that, and the rest of it was spilled up the hill any way they could get it in. You climbed some stone steps to the front door, so I parked the car and went up there. A servant poked her head out. "Is Mr. Nirdlinger in?"

"I don't know, sir. Who wants to see him?"

"Mr. Huff."

"And what's the business?"

"Personal."

Getting in is the tough part of my job, and you don't tip what you came for till you get where it counts. "I'm sorry, sir, but they won't let me ask anybody in unless they say what they want."

It was one of those spots you get in. If I said some more about "personal" I would be making a mystery of it, and that's bad. If I said what I really wanted, I would be laying myself open for what every insurance agent dreads, that she would come back and say, "Not in." If I said I'd wait, I would be making myself look small, and that never helped a sale yet. To move this stuff, you've got to get

in. Once you're in, they've got to listen to you, and you can pretty
near rate an agent by how quick he gets to the family sofa, with his
hat on one side of him and his dope sheets on the other.

"I see. I told Mr. Nirdlinger I would drop in, but—never mind.
I'll see if I can make it some other time."

It was true, in a way. On this automobile stuff, you always make it
a point that you'll give a reminder on renewal, but I hadn't seen him
for a year. I made it sound like an old friend, though, and an old
friend that wasn't any too pleased at the welcome he got. It worked.
She got a worried look on her face. "Well—come in, please."

If I had used that juice trying to keep out, that might have got me
somewhere.

I pitched my hat on the sofa. They've made a lot of that living
room, especially those "blood-red drapes." All I saw was a living
room like every other living room in California, maybe a little more
expensive than some, but nothing that any department store
wouldn't deliver on one truck, lay out in the morning, and have the
credit O.K. ready the same afternoon. The furniture was Spanish,
the kind that looks pretty and sits stiff. The rug was one of those 12
x 15's that would have been Mexican except it was made in Oakland, California. The blood-red drapes were there, but they didn't
mean anything. All these Spanish houses have red velvet drapes that
run on iron spears, and generally some red velvet wall tapestries to
go with them. This was right out of the same can, with a coat-of-
arms tapestry over the fireplace and a castle tapestry over the sofa.
The other two sides of the room were windows and the entrance to
the hall.

"Yes?"

A woman was standing there. I had never seen her before. She was
maybe thirty-one or two, with a sweet face, light blue eyes, and dusty
blonde hair. She was small, and had on a suit of blue house pajamas.
She had a washed-out look.

"I wanted to see Mr. Nirdlinger."

"Mr. Nirdlinger isn't in just now, but I am Mrs. Nirdlinger. Is
there something I could do?"

There was nothing to do but spill it. "Why no, I think not, Mrs.
Nirdlinger, thanks just the same. Huff is my name, Walter Huff, of
the General Fidelity of California. Mr. Nirdlinger's automobile coverage runs out in a week or two, and I promised to give him a re-

minder on it, so I thought I'd drop by. But I certainly didn't mean to bother you about it."

"Coverage?"

"Insurance. I just took a chance, coming up here in the daytime, but I happened to be in the neighborhood, so I thought it wouldn't hurt. When do you think would be a good time to see Mr. Nirdlinger? Could he give me a few minutes right after dinner, do you think, so I wouldn't cut into his evening?"

"What kind of insurance has he been carrying? I ought to know, but I don't keep track."

"I guess none of us keep track until something happens. Just the usual line. Collision, fire, and theft, and public liability."

"Oh yes, of course."

"It's only a routine matter, but he ought to attend to it in time, so he'll be protected."

"It really isn't up to me, but I know he's been thinking about the Automobile Club. Their insurance, I mean."

"Is he a member?"

"No, he's not. He's always intended to join, but somehow he's never got around to it. But the club representative was here, and he mentioned insurance."

"You can't do better than the Automobile Club. They're prompt, liberal in their view of claims, and courteous straight down the line. I've not got a word to say against them."

That's one thing you learn. Never knock the other guy's stuff.

"And then it's cheaper."

"For members."

"I thought only members could get it."

"What I mean is this. If a man's going to join the Automobile Club anyway, for service in time of trouble, taking care of tickets, things like that, then if he takes their insurance too, he gets it cheaper. He certainly does. But if he's going to join the club just to get the insurance, by the time he adds that $16 membership fee to the premium rate, he's paying more. Figure that in, I can stil save Mr. Nirdlinger quite a little money."

She talked along, and there was nothing I could do but go along with it. But you sell as many people as I do, you don't go by what they say. You feel it, how the deal is going. And after a while I knew this woman didn't care anything about the Automobile Club. Maybe the husband did, but she didn't. There was something else, and this was nothing but a stall. I figured it would be some kind of a proposition to split the commission, maybe so she could get a ten-spot out of it without the husband knowing. There's plenty of that going on. And I was just wondering what I would say to her. A reputable agent don't get mixed up in stuff like that, but she was walking around the room, and I saw something I hadn't noticed before. Under those blue pajamas was a shape to set a man nuts, and how good I was going to sound when I started explaining the high ethics of the insurance business I didn't exactly know.

But all of a sudden she looked at me, and I felt a chill creep straight up my back and into the roots of my hair. "Do you handle accident insurance?"

Maybe that don't mean to you what it meant to me. Well, in the first place, accident insurance is sold, not bought. You get calls for other kinds, for fire, for burglary, even for life, but never for accident. That stuff moves when agents move it, and it sounds funny to be asked about it. In the second place, when there's dirty work going on, accident is the first thing they think of. Dollar for dollar paid down, there's a bigger face coverage on accident than any other kind. And it's the one kind of insurance that can be taken out without the insured knowing a thing about it. No physical examination for accident. On that, all they want is the money, and there's many a man walking around today that's worth more to his loved ones dead than alive, only he don't know it yet.

"We handle all kinds of insurance."

She switched back to the Automobile Club, and I tried to keep my eyes off her, and couldn't. Then she sat down. "Would you like me to talk to Mr. Nirdlinger about this, Mr. Huff?"

Why would she talk to him about his insurance, instead of letting me do it? "That would be fine, Mrs. Nirdlinger."

"It would save time."

"Time's important. He ought to attend to this at once."

But then she crossed me up. "After he and I have talked it over, then you can see him. Could you make it tomorrow night? Say seven-thirty? We'll be through dinner by then."

"Tomorrow night will be fine."

"I'll expect you."

I got in the car bawling myself out for being a fool just because a woman had given me one sidelong look. When I got back to the office I found Keyes had been looking for me. Keyes is head of the

Claim Department, and the most tiresome man to do business with in the whole world. You can't even say today is Tuesday without he has to look on the calendar, and then check if it's this year's calendar or last year's calendar, and then find out what company printed the calendar, and then find out if their calendar checks with the World Almanac calendar. That amount of useless work you'd think would keep down his weight, but it don't. He gets fatter every year, and more peevish, and he's always in some kind of a feud with other departments of the company, and does nothing but sit with his collar open, and sweat, and quarrel, and argue, until your head begins spinning around just to be in the same room with him. But he's a wolf on a phoney claim.

When I got in there he got up and began to roar. It was a truck policy I had written about six months before, and the fellow had burned his truck up and tried to collect. I cut in on him pretty quick.

"What are you beefing to me for? I remember that case. And I distinctly remember that I clipped a memo to that application when I sent it through that I thought that fellow ought to be thoroughly investigated before we accepted the risk. I didn't like his looks, and I won't—"

"Walter, I'm not beefing to you. I know you said he ought to be investigated. I've got your memo right here on my desk. That's what I wanted to tell you. If other departments in this company would show half the sense that you show—"

"Oh."

That would be like Keyes, that even when he wanted to say something nice to you, he had to make you sore first.

"And get this, Walter. Even after they issued the policy, in plain disregard of the warning on your memo, and even with that warning still looking them in the face, day before yesterday when the truck burned—they'd have paid that claim if I hadn't sent a tow car up there this afternoon, pulled the truck out, and found a pile of shavings under the engine, that proved it up on him that he started the fire himself."

"Have you got him?"

"Oh, he confessed. He's taking a plea tomorrow morning, and that ends it. But my point is, that if you, just by looking at that man, could have your suspicions, why couldn't they—! Oh well, what's the use? I just wanted you to know it. I'm sending a memo to Norton about it. I think the whole thing is something the president of this company might very well look into. Though if you ask me, if the president of this company had more . . ."

He stopped and I didn't jog him. Keyes was one of the holdovers from the time of Old Man Norton, the founder of the company, and he didn't think much of young Norton, that took over the job when his father died. The way he told it, young Norton never did anything right, and the whole place was always worried for fear he'd pull them in on the feud. If young Norton was the man we had to do business with, then he was the man we had to do business with, and there was no sense letting Keyes get us in dutch with him. I gave Keyes's crack a dead pan. I didn't even know what he was talking about.

When I got back to my office, Nettie, my secretary, was just leaving. "Goodnight, Mr. Huff."

"Goodnight, Nettie."

"Oh—I put a memo on your desk, about a Mrs. Nirdlinger. She called, about ten minutes ago, and said it would be inconvenient for you to call tomorrow night about that renewal. She said she'd let you know when to come."

"Oh, thanks."

She went, and I stood there, looking down at the memo. It crossed my mind what kind of warning I was going to clip to *that* application, if, as, and when I got it.

If any.

Chapter 2

T HREE DAYS LATER she called and left word I was to come at three-thirty. She let me in herself. She didn't have on the blue pajamas this time. She had on a white sailor suit, with a blouse that pulled tight over her hips, and white shoes and stockings. I wasn't the only one that knew about that shape. She knew about it herself, plenty. We went in the living room, and a tray was on the table. "Belle is off today, and I'm making myself some tea. Will you join me?"

"Thank you, no, Mrs. Nirdlinger. I'll only be a minute. That is, if Mr. Nirdlinger has decided to renew. I supposed he had, when you sent for me." Because it came over me that I wasn't surprised that Belle was off, and that she was just making herself some tea. And I meant to get out of there, whether I took the renewals with me or not.

"Oh, have some tea. I like tea. It makes a break in the afternoon."

"You must be English."

"No, native Californian."

"You don't see many of them."

"Most Californians were born in Iowa."

"I was myself."

"Think of that."

The white sailor suit did it. I sat down. "Lemon?"

"No thanks."

"Two?"

"No sugar, just straight."

"No sweet tooth?"

She smiled at me and I could see her teeth. They were big and white and maybe a little bit buck.

"I do a lot of business with the Chinese. They've got me out of the American way of drinking tea."

"I love the Chinese. Whenever I make chow mein I buy all the stuff at the same place near the park. Mr. Ling. Do you know him?"

"Known him for years."

"Oh, you *have!*"

Her brow wrinkled up, and I saw there was nothing washed-out about her. What gave her that look was a spray of freckles across her forehead. She saw me looking at them. "I believe you're looking at my freckles."

"Yes, I was. I like them."

"I don't."

"I do."

"I always used to wear a turban around my forehead when I went out in the sun, but so many people began stopping by, asking to have their fortunes told, that I had to stop it."

"You don't tell fortunes?"

"No, it's one California accomplishment I never learned."

"Anyway I like the freckles."

She sat down beside me and we talked about Mr. Ling. Now Mr. Ling wasn't anybody but a Chinese grocery dealer that had a City Hall job on the side, and every year we had to bond him for $2,500, but you'd be surprised what a swell guy he turned out to be when we talked about him. After a while, though, I switched to insurance. "Well, how about those policies?"

"He's still talking about the Automobile Club, but I think he's going to renew with you."

"I'm glad of that."

She sat there a minute, making little pleats with the edge of her blouse and rubbing them out. "I didn't say anything to him about the accident insurance."

"No?"

"I hate to talk to him about it."

"I can understand that."

"It seems an awful thing to tell him you think he ought to have an accident policy. And yet—you see, my husband is the Los Angeles representative of the Western Pipe and Supply Company."

"He's in the Petroleum Building, isn't he?"

"That's where he has his office. But most of the time he's in the oilfields."

"Plenty dangerous, knocking around there."

"It makes me positively ill to think about it."

"Does his company carry anything on him?"

"Not that I know of."

"Man in a business like that, he ought not to take chances."

And then I made up my mind that even if I did like her freckles, I was going to find out where I was at. "I tell you, how would you like it if I talked with Mr. Nirdlinger about this? You know, not say anything about where I got the idea, but just bring it up when I see him."

"I just *hate* to talk to him about it."

"I'm telling you. *I'll* talk."

"But then he'll ask me what I think, and—I won't know what to say. It's got me worried sick."

She made another bunch of pleats. Then, after a long time, here it came. "Mr. Huff, would it be possible for me to take out a policy *for* him, without bothering him about it at all? I have a little allowance of my own. I could pay you for it, and he wouldn't know, but just the same all this worry would be over."

I couldn't be mistaken about what she meant, not after fifteen years in the insurance business. I mashed out my cigarette, so I could get up and go. I was going to get out of there, and drop those renewals and everything else about her like a red-hot poker. But I didn't do it. She looked at me, a little surprised, and her face was about six inches away. What I did do was put my arm around her, pull her face up against mine, and kiss her on the mouth, hard. I was trembling like a leaf. She gave it a cold stare, and then she closed her eyes, pulled me to her, and kissed back.

"I liked you all the time."

"I don't believe it."

"Didn't I ask you to tea? Didn't I have you come here when Belle was off? I liked you the very first minute. I loved it, the solemn way you kept talking about your company, and all this and that. That was why I kept teasing you about the Automobile Club."

"Oh, it was."

"Now you know."

I rumpled her hair, and then we both made some pleats in the blouse. "You don't make them even, Mr. Huff."

"Isn't that even?"

"The bottom ones are bigger than the top. You've got to take just so much material every time, then turn it, then crease it, and then they make nice pleats. See?"

"I'll try to get the hang of it."

"Not now. You've got to go."

"I'm seeing you soon?"

"Maybe."

"Well listen, I *am*."

"Belle isn't off every day. I'll let you know."

"Well—*will* you?"

"But don't *you* call *me* up. I'll let you know. I promise."

"All right then. Kiss me good-bye."

"Good-bye."

I live in a bungalow in the Los Feliz hills. Daytime, I keep a Filipino house boy, but he don't sleep there. It was raining that night, so I didn't go out. I lit a fire and sat there, trying to figure out where I was at. I knew where I was at, of course. I was standing right on the deep end, looking over the edge, and I kept telling myself to get out of there, and get quick, and never come back. But that was what I kept telling myself. What I was doing was peeping over that edge, and all the time I was trying to pull away from it, there was something in me that kept edging a little closer, trying to get a better look.

A little before nine the bell rang. I knew who it was as soon as I heard it. She was standing there in a raincoat and a little rubber swimming cap, with the raindrops shining over her freckles. When I got her peeled off she was in sweater and slacks, just a dumb Hollywood outfit, but it looked different on her. I brought her to the fire and she sat down. I sat down beside her.

"How did you get my address?" It jumped out at me, even then, that I didn't want her calling my office asking questions about me.

"Phone book."

"Oh."

"Surprised?"

"No."

"Well I like that. I never heard such conceit."

"Your husband out?"

"Long Beach. They're putting down a new well. Three shifts. He had to go down. So I hopped on a bus. I think you might say you're glad to see me."

"Great place, Long Beach."

"I told Lola I was going to a picture show."

"Who's Lola?"

"My stepdaughter."

"Young?"

"Nineteen. Well, *are* you glad to see me?"

"Yeah, sure. Why—wasn't I expecting you?"

We talked about how wet it was out, and how we hoped it didn't turn into a flood, like it did the night before New Year's, 1934, and how I would run her back in the car. Then she looked in the fire a while. "I lost my head this afternoon."

"Not much."

"A little."

"You sorry?"

"—A little. I've never done that before. Since I've been married. That's why I came down."

"You act like something really happened."

"Something did. I lost my head. Isn't that something?"

"Well—so what?"

"I just wanted to say—"

"You didn't mean it."

"No. I did mean it. If I hadn't meant it I wouldn't have had to come down. But I do want to say that I won't ever mean it again."

"You sure?"

"Quite sure."

"We ought to try and see."

"No—please . . . You see, I love my husband. More, here lately, than ever."

I looked into the fire a while then. I ought to quit, while the quitting was good, I knew that. But that thing was in me, pushing me still closer to the edge. And then I could feel it again, that she wasn't saying what she meant. It was the same as it was that first afternoon I met her, that there was something else, besides what she was telling me. And I couldn't shake it off, that I had to call it on her.

"Why 'here lately'?"

"Oh—worry."

"You mean that down in the oilfields, some rainy night, a crown block is going to fall on him?"

"Please don't talk like that."

"But that's the idea."

"Yes."

"I can understand that. Especially with this set-up."

". . . I don't quite know what you mean. What set-up?"

"Why—a crown block will."

"Will what?"

"Fall on him."

"Please, Mr. Huff, I asked you not to talk like that. It's not a laughing matter. It's got me worried sick . . . What makes you say that?"

"*You're* going to drop a crown block *on* him."

"I—*what!*"

"Well, you know, maybe not a crown block. But something. Something that's accidentally-on-purpose going to fall on him, and then he'll be dead."

It nailed her between the eyes and they flickered. It was a minute before she said anything. She had to put on an act, and she was caught by surprise, and she didn't know how to do it.

"Are you—joking?"

"No."

"You must be. Or you must be crazy. Why—I never heard of such a thing in my life."

"I'm not crazy, and I'm not joking, and you've heard of such a thing in your life, because it's all you've thought of since you met me, and it's what you came down here for tonight."

"I'll not stay here and listen to such things."

"O.K."

"I'm going."

"O.K."

"I'm going this minute."

"O.K."

So I ran away from the edge, didn't I, and socked it into her so she knew what I meant, and left it so we could never go back to it again? I did not. That was what I tried to do. I never even got up when she left, I didn't help her on with her things, I didn't drive her back, I treated her like I would treat an alley cat. But all the time I knew it would be still raining the next night, that they would still be drilling at Long Beach, that I would light the fire and sit by it, that a little before nine the doorbell would ring. She didn't even speak to me when she came in. We sat by the fire at least five minutes before either one of us said anything. Then she started it. "How could you say such things as you said to me last night?"

"Because they're true. That's what you're going to do."

"*Now?* After what you've said?"

"Yes, after what I've said."

"But—Walter, that's what I've come for, again, tonight. I've thought it over. I realize that there have been one or two things I've said that could give you a completely wrong impression. In a way, I'm glad you warned me about them, because I might have said them to somebody else without knowing the—construction that could be put upon them. But now that I do know, you must surely see that—anything of that sort must be out of my mind. Forever."

That meant she had spent the whole day sweating blood for fear I would warn the husband, or start something, somehow. I kept on with it. "You called me Walter. What's your name?"

"Phyllis."

"Phyllis, you seem to think that because I can call it on you, you're not going to do it. You *are* going to do it, and I'm going to help you."

"*You!*"

"I."

I caught her by surprise again, but she didn't even try to put on an act this time. "Why—I couldn't have anybody help me! It would be—impossible."

"You couldn't have anybody help you? Well let me tell you something. You had better have somebody help you. It would be nice to pull it off yourself, all alone, so nobody knew anything about it, it sure would. The only trouble with that is, you can't. Not if you're going up against an insurance company, you can't. You've got to have help. And it had better be help that knows its stuff."

"What would you do this for?"

"You, for one thing."

"What else?"

"Money."

"You mean you would—betray your company, and help me do this, for me, and the money we could get out of it?"

"I mean just that. And you better say what you mean, because when I start, I'm going to put it through, straight down the line, and there won't be any slips. But I've got to know. Where I stand. You can't fool—with this."

She closed her eyes, and after a while she began to cry. I put my arm around her and patted her. It seemed funny, after what we had been talking about, that I was treating her like some child that had lost a penny.

"Please, Walter, don't let me do this. We can't. It's simply—insane."

"Yes, it's insane."

"We're going to do it. I can feel it."

"I too."

"I haven't any reason. He treats me as well as a man can treat a woman. I don't love him, but he's never done anything to me."

"But you're going to do it."

"Yes, God help me, I'm going to do it."

She stopped crying, and lay in my arms for a while without saying anything. Then she began to talk almost in a whisper.

"He's not happy. He'll be better off—dead."

"Yeah?"

"That's not true, is it?"

"Not from where he sits, I don't think."

"I know it's not true. I tell myself it's not true. But there's something in me, I don't know what. Maybe I'm crazy. But there's something in me that loves Death. I think of myself as Death, sometimes. In a scarlet shroud, floating through the night. I'm *so* beautiful, then. And sad. And hungry to make the whole world happy, by taking them out where I am, into the night, away from all trouble, all unhappiness . . . Walter, this is the awful part. I know this is terrible. I tell myself it's terrible. But to me, it doesn't *seem* terrible. It seems as though I'm doing something—that's really best for him, if he only knew it. Do you understand me, Walter?"

"No."

"Nobody could."

"But we're going to do it."
"Yes, we're going to do it."
"Straight down the line."
"Straight down the line."

A night or two later, we talked about it just as casually as if it was a little trip to the mountains. I had to find out what she had been figuring on, and whether she had gummed it up with some bad move of her own. "Have you said anything to him about this, Phyllis? About this policy?"
"No."
"Absolutely nothing?"
"Not a thing."
"All right, how are you going to do it?"
"I was going to take out the policy first—"
"Without him knowing?"
"Yes."
"Holy smoke, they'd have crucified you. It's the first thing they look for. Well—anyway that's out. What else?"
"He's going to build a swimming pool. In the spring. Out in the patio."
"And?"
"I thought it could be made to look as though he hit his head diving or something."
"That's out. That's still worse."
"Why? People do, don't they?"
"It's no good. In the first place, some fool in the insurance business, five or six years ago, put out a newspaper story that most accidents happen in people's own bathtubs, and since then bathtubs, swimming pools, and fishponds are the first thing they think of. When they're trying to pull something, I mean. There's two cases like that out here in California right now. Neither one of them are on the up-and-up, and if there'd been an insurance angle those people would wind up on the gallows. Then it's a daytime job, and you never can tell who's peeping at you from the next hill. Then a swimming pool is like a tennis court, you no sooner have one than it's a community affair, and you don't know who might come popping in on you at any minute. And then it's one of those things where you've got to watch for your chance, and you can't plan it in

advance, and know where you're going to come out to the last decimal point. Get this, Phyllis. There's three essential elements to a successful murder."

That word was out before I knew it. I looked at her quick. I thought she'd wince under it. She didn't. She leaned forward. The firelight was reflected in her eyes like she was some kind of leopard. "Go on. I'm listening."

"The first is, help. One person can't get away with it, that is unless they're going to admit it and plead the unwritten law or something. It takes more than one. The second is, the time, the place, the way, all known in advance—to us, but not to him. The third is, audacity. That's the one that all amateur murderers forget. They know the first two, sometimes. But that third, only a professional knows. There comes a time in any murder when the only thing that can see you through is audacity, and I can't tell you why. You know the perfect murder? You think it's this swimming pool job, and you're going to do it so slick nobody would ever guess it. They'd guess it in two seconds, flat. In three seconds, flat, they'd prove it, and in four seconds, flat, you'd confess it. No, that's not it. The perfect murder is the gangster that goes on the spot. You know what they do? First they get a finger on him. They get that girl that he lives with. Along about six o'clock they get a phone call from her. She goes out to a drugstore to buy some lipstick, and she calls. They're going to see a picture tonight, he and she, and it's at such and such a theater. They'll get there around nine o'clock. All right, there's the first two elements. They got help, and they fixed the time and the place in advance. All right, now watch the third. They go there in a car. They park across the street. They keep the motor running. They put a sentry out. He loafs up an alley, and pretty soon he drops a handkerchief and picks it up. That means he's coming. They get out of the car. They drift up to the theater. They close in on him. And right there, in the glare of the lights, with a couple hundred people looking on, they let him have it. He hasn't got a chance. Twenty bullets hit him, from four or five automatics. He falls, they scram for the car, they drive off—and then you try to convict them. You just try to convict them. They've got their alibis ready in advance, all airtight, they were only seen for a second, by people who were so scared they didn't know what they were looking at—and there isn't a chance to convict them. The police know who they are, of course. They round them up, give them the water cure—

and then they're habeas-corpused into court and turned loose. Those guys don't get convicted. They get put on the spot by other gangsters. Oh yeah, they know their stuff, all right. And if we want to get away with it, we've got to do it the way they do it, and not the way some punk up near San Francisco does it, that's had two trials already, and still he's not free."

"Be bold?"

"Be bold. It's the only way."

"If we shoot him it wouldn't be accident."

"That's right. We don't shoot him, but I want you to get the principle through your head. Be bold. It's the only chance to get away with it."

"Then how—?"

"I'm coming to that. Another trouble with your swimming pool idea is that there's no money in it."

"They'd have to pay—"

"They'd have to pay, but this is a question of how much they'd have to pay. All the big money on an accident policy comes from railroad accidents. They found out pretty quick, when they began to write accident insurance, that the apparent danger spots, the spots that people think are danger spots, aren't danger spots at all. I mean, people always think a railroad train is a pretty dangerous place to be, or they did, anyway, before the novelty wore off, but the figures show not many people get killed, or even hurt, on railroad trains. So on accident policies, they put in a feature that sounds pretty good to the man that buys it, because *he's* a little worried about train trips, but it doesn't cost the company much, because it knows he's pretty sure to get there safely. They pay double indemnity for railroad accidents. That's just where we cash in. You've been thinking about some piker job, maybe, and a fat chance I'd be taking a chance like this for that. When we get done, we cash a $50,000 bet, and if we do it right, we're going to cash it, don't make any mistake about that."

"Fifty thousand dollars?"

"Nice?"

"My!"

"Say, this is a beauty, if I do say it myself. I didn't spend all this time in this business for nothing, did I? Listen, he knows all about this policy, and yet he don't know a thing about it. He applies for it, in writing, and yet he don't apply for it. He pays me for it with his own check, and yet he don't pay me. He has an accident happen to him and yet he don't have an accident happen to him. He gets on the train, and yet he don't get on it."

"What *are* you talking about?"

"You'll find out. The first thing is, we've got to fix him up with that policy. I sell it to him, do you get that?—except that I don't sell him. Not quite. I give him the works, the same as I give any other prospect. And I've got to have witnesses. Get that. There's got to be somebody that heard me go right after him. I show him that he's covered on everything that might hurt the automobile, but hasn't got a thing that covers personal injury to himself. I put it up to him whether a man isn't worth more than his car. I—"

"Suppose he buys?"

"Well—suppose he does? He won't. I can bring him within one inch of the line and hold him there, don't you think I can't. I'm a salesman, if I'm nothing else. But—I've got to have witnesses. Anyway, one witness."

"I'll have somebody."

"Maybe you better oppose it."

"All right."

"You're all for the automobile stuff, when I start in on that, but this accident thing gives you the shivers."

"I'll remember."

"You better make a date pretty quick. Give me a ring."

"Tomorrow?"

"Confirm by phone. Remember, you need a witness."

"I'll have one."

"Tomorrow, then. Subject to call."

"Walter—I'm so excited. It does terrible things to me."

"I too."

"Kiss me."

You think I'm nuts? All right, maybe I am. But you spend fifteen years in the business I'm in, maybe you'll go nuts yourself. You think it's a business, don't you, just like your business, and maybe a little better than that, because it's the friend of the widow, the orphan, and the needy in time of trouble? It's not. It's the biggest gambling wheel in the world. It don't look like it, but it is, from the way they figure the percentage on the OO to the look on their face when they cash your chips. You bet that your house will burn down, they bet it won't, that's all. What fools you is that you didn't *want* your house to burn down when you made the bet, and so you forget it's a bet. That don't fool them. To them a bet is a bet, and a hedge bet don't look any different than any other bet. But there comes a time, maybe, when you *do* want your house to burn down, when the money is worth more than the house. And right there is where the trouble starts. They know there's just so many people out there that are out to crook that wheel, and that's when they get tough. They've got their spotters out there, they know every crooked trick there is, and if you want to beat them you had better be good. So long as you're honest, they'll pay you with a smile, and you may even go home thinking it was all in a spirit of good clean fun. But you start something, and then you'll find out.

All right, I'm an agent. I'm a croupier in that game. I know all their tricks, I lie awake nights thinking up tricks, so I'll be ready for them when they come at me. And then one night I think up a trick, and get to thinking I could crook the wheel myself if I could only put a plant out there to put down my bet. That's all. When I met Phyllis I met my plant. If that seems funny to you, that I would kill a man just to pick up a stack of chips, it might not seem so funny if you were back of that wheel, instead of out front. I had seen so many houses burned down, so many cars wrecked, so many corpses with blue holes in their temples, so many awful things that people had pulled to crook the wheel, that that stuff didn't seem real to me any more. If you don't understand that, go to Monte Carlo or some other place where there's a big casino, sit at a table, and watch the face of the man that spins the little ivory ball. After you've watched it a while, ask yourself how much he would care if you went out and plugged yourself in the head. His eyes might drop when he heard the shot, but it wouldn't be from worry whether you lived or died. It would be to make sure you didn't leave a bet on the table, that he would have to cash for your estate. No, he wouldn't care. Not that baby.

Chapter 3

Then another thing I call your attention to, Mr. Nirdlinger, a feature we've added in the last year, at no extra cost, is our guarantee of bail bond. We furnish you a card, and all you have to do, in case of accident where you're held responsible, or in any traffic case where the police put you under arrest, is to produce that card and if it's a bailable offense, it automatically procures your release. The police take up the card, that puts us on your bond, and you're free until your case comes up for trial. Since that's one of the things the Automobile Club does for members, and you're thinking about the Automobile Club—"

"I've pretty well given that idea up."

"Well then, why don't we fix this thing up right now? I've pretty well outlined what we do for you—"

"I guess we might as well."

"Then if you'll sign these applications, you'll be protected until the new policies are issued, which will be in about a week, but there's no use your paying for a whole week's extra insurance. There's for the collision, fire, and theft, there's for the public liability—and if you don't mind sticking your name on these two, they're the agent's copies, and I keep them for my files."

"Here?"

"Right on the dotted line."

He was a big, blocky man, about my size, with glasses, and I played him exactly the way I figured to. As soon as I had the applications, I switched to accident insurance. He didn't seem much interested, so I made it pretty stiff. Phyllis cut in that the very idea of accident insurance made her shiver, and I kept on going. I didn't quit till I had hammered in every reason for taking out accident insurance that any agent ever thought of, and maybe a couple of reasons that no agent ever had thought of. He sat there drumming with his fingers on the arms of his chair, wishing I would go.

But what bothered me wasn't that. It was the witness that Phyllis brought out. I thought she would have some friend of the family in to dinner, maybe a woman, and just let her stay with us, there in the sitting room, after I showed up around seven-thirty. She didn't. She brought the stepdaughter in, a pretty girl, named Lola. Lola wanted to go, but Phyllis said she had to get the wool wound for a sweater she was knitting, and kept her there, winding it. I had to tie her in, with a gag now and then, to make sure she would remember what we were talking about, but the more I looked at her the less I liked it. Having to sit with her there, knowing all the time what we were going to do to her father, was one of the things I hadn't bargained for.

And next thing I knew, when I got up to go, I had let myself in for hauling her down to the boulevard, so she could go to a picture show. Her father had to go out again that night, and he was using the car, and that meant that unless I hauled her she would have to go down by bus. I didn't want to haul her. I didn't want to have anything to do with her. But when he kind of turned to me there was nothing I could do but offer, and she ran and got her hat and coat, and in a minute or two there we were, rolling down the hill.

"Mr. Huff?"

"Yes?"

"I'm not going to a picture show."

"No?"

"I'm meeting somebody. At the drugstore."

"Oh."

"Would you haul us both down?"

"Oh—sure."

"You won't mind?"

"No, not a bit."

"And you won't tell on me? There are reasons why I don't want them to know. At home."

"No, of course not."

We stopped at the drugstore, and she jumped out and in a minute came back with a young guy, with an Italian-looking face, pretty good-looking, that had been standing around outside. "Mr. Huff, this is Mr. Sachetti."

"How are you, Mr. Sachetti. Get in."

They got in, and kind of grinned at each other, and we rolled down Beachwood to the boulevard. "Where do you want me to set you down?"

"Oh, anywhere."

"Hollywood and Vine all right?"

"Swell."

I set them down there, and after she got out, she reached out her hand, and took mine, and thanked me, her eyes shining like stars. "It was darling of you to take us. Lean close I'll tell you a secret."

"Yes?"

"If you hadn't taken us we'd have had to walk."

"How are you going to get back?"

"Walk."

"You want some money?"

"No, my father would kill me. I spent all my week's money. No, but thanks. And remember—don't tell on me."

"I won't."

"Hurry, you'll miss your light.

I drove home. Phyllis got there in about a half hour. She was humming a song out of a Nelson Eddy picture. "Did you like my sweater?"

"Yeah, sure."

"Isn't it a lovely color? I never wore old rose before. I think it's going to be really becoming to me."

"It's going to look all right."

"Where did you leave Lola?"

"On the boulevard."

"Where did she go?"

"I didn't notice."

"Was there somebody waiting for her?"

"Not that I saw. Why?"

"I was just wondering. She's been going around with a boy named Sachetti. A perfectly terrible person. She's been forbidden to see him."

"He wasn't on deck tonight. Anyway, I didn't see him. Why didn't you tell me about her?"

"Well? You said have a witness."

"Yeah, but I didn't mean her."

"Isn't she as good a witness as any other?"

"Yeah, but holy smoke there's a limit. A man's own daughter, and we're even using her—for what we're using her for."

An awful look came over her face, and her voice got hard as glass. "What's the matter? Are you getting ready to back out?"

"No, but you coud have got somebody else. Me, driving her down to the boulevard, and all the time I had this in my pocket." I took out the applications, and showed them to her. One of those "agent's copies" was an undated application for a $25,000 personal accident policy, with double indemnity straight down the line for any disability or death incurred on a railroad train.

It was part of the play that I had to make two or three calls on Nirdlinger in his office. The first time, I gave him the bail-bond guarantee, stuck around about five minutes, told him to put it in his car, and left. The next time I gave him a little leather memo book, with his name stamped on it in gilt, just a little promotion feature we have for policy holders. The third time I delivered the automobile policies, and took his check, $79.52. When I got back to the office that day, Nettie told me there was somebody waiting for me in my private office. "Who?"

"A Miss Lola Nirdlinger and a Mr. Sachetti, I think she said. I didn't get his first name."

I went in there and she laughed. She liked me, I could see that. "You surprised to see us again?"

"Oh, not much. What can I do for you?"

"We've come in to ask a favor. But it's your own fault."

"Yeah? How's that?"

"What you said the other night to Father about being able to get money on his car, if he needed it. We've come in to take you up on it. Or anyway, Nino has."

That was something I had to do something about, the competition I was getting from the Automobile Club on an automobile loan. They lend money on a member's car, and I got to the point where I had to, too, if I was going to get any business. So I organized a little finance company of my own, had myself made a director, and spent about one day a week there. It didn't have anything to do with the insurance company, but it was one way I could meet that question that I ran into all the time: "Do you lend money on a car?" I had mentioned it to Nirdlinger, just as part of the sales talk, but I didn't know she was paying attention. I looked at Sachetti. "You want to borrow money on your car?"

"Yes sir."

"What kind of car is it?"

He told me. It was a cheap make.

"Sedan?"

"Coupe."

"It's in your name? And paid for?"

"Yes sir."

They must have seen a look cross my face, because she giggled. "He couldn't use it the other night. He didn't have any gas."

"Oh."

I didn't want to lend him money on his car, or anything else. I didn't want to have anything to do with him, or her, in any way, shape, or form. I lit a cigarette, and sat there a minute. "You sure you want to borrow money on this car? Because if you're not working now, what I mean if you don't absolutely see your way clear to pay it back, it's a sure way to lose it. The whole second-hand car business depends on people that thought they could pay a small loan back, and couldn't."

She looked at me very solemnly. "It's different with Nino. He isn't working, but he doesn't want this loan just to have money to spend. You see, he's done all his work for his Sc.D., and—"

"Where?"

"U.S.C."

"What in?"

"Chemistry. If he can only get his degree, he's sure of work, he's been promised that, and it seems such a pity to miss a chance for a really good position just because he hasn't taken his degree. But to take it, he has to have his dissertation published, and pay this and that, for his diploma for instance, and that's what he wants this money for. He won't spend it on his living. He has friends that will take care of that."

I had to come through. I knew that. I wouldn't have, if it didn't make me so nervous to be around her, but all I could think of now was to say yes and get them out of there. "How much do you want?"

"He thought if he could get $250, that would be enough."

"I see. I see."

I figured it up. With charges, it would amount to around $285, and it was an awfully big loan on the car he was going to put up. "Well—give me a day or two on it. I think we can manage it."

They went out, and then she ducked back. "You're awfully nice to me. I don't know why I keep bothering you about things."

"That's all right, Miss Nirdlinger, I'm glad—"

"You can call me Lola, if you want to."

"Thanks, I'll be glad to help any time I can."

"This is secret, too."

"Yes, I know."

"I'm terribly grateful, Mr. Huff."

"Thanks—Lola."

The accident policy came through a couple of days later. That meant I had to get his check for it, and get it right away, so the dates would correspond. You understand, I wasn't going to deliver the accident policy, to him. That would go to Phyllis, and she would find it later, in his safe deposit box. And I wasn't going to tell him anything about it. Just the same, I had to get his check, in the exact amount of the policy, so later on, when they checked up his stubs and his cancelled checks, they would find he had paid for it himself. That would check with the application in our files, and it would also check with those trips I had made to his office, if they put me on the spot.

I went in on him pretty worried, and shut the door on his secretary, and got down to brass tacks right away. "Mr. Nirdlinger, I'm in a hole, and I'm wondering if you'll help me out."

"Well I don't know. I don't know. What is it?"

He was expecting a touch, and I wanted him to be expecting a touch. "It's pretty bad."

"Suppose you tell me."

"I've charged you too much for your insurance. For that automobile stuff."

He burst out laughing. "Is that all? I thought you wanted to borrow money."

"Oh. No. Nothing like that. It's worse—from my point of view."

"Do I get a refund?"

"Why sure."

"Then it's better—from my point of view."

"It isn't as simple as that. This is the trouble, Mr. Nirdlinger. There's a board, in our business, that was formed to stop cut-throating on rates, and see to it that every company charges a rate sufficient to protect the policy holder, and that's the board I'm in dutch with. Because here recently, they've made it a rule that *every* case, every case, mind you, where there's an alleged mischarge by an agent, is to be investigated by them, and you can see where that puts me. And you too, in a way. Because they'll have me up for fifteen different hearings, and come around pestering you till you don't know what your name is—and all because I looked up the wrong rate in the book when I was out to your house that night, and never found it out till this morning when I checked over my month's accounts."

"And what do you want me to do?"

"There's one way I can fix it. Your check, of course, was deposited, and there's nothing to do about that. But if you'll let me give you cash for the check you gave me—$79.52—I've got it right here with me—and give me a new check for the correct amount—$58.60 then that'll balance it, and they'll have nothing to investigate."

"How do you mean, balance it?"

"Well, you see, in multiple-card bookkeeping—oh well, it's so complicated I don't even know if I understand it myself. Anyway, that's what our cashier tells me. It's the way they make their entries."

"I see."

He looked out the window and I saw a funny look come in his eye. "Well—all right. I don't know why not."

I gave him the cash and took his check. It was all hooey. We've got a board, but it doesn't bother with agents' mistakes. It governs rates. I don't even know if there's such a thing as multiple-card bookkeeping, and I never talked with our cashier. I just figured that when you offer a man about twenty bucks more than he thought he had when you came in, he wouldn't ask too many questions about why you offer it to him. I went to the bank. I deposited the check. I even knew what he wrote on his stub. It just said "Insurance." I had what I wanted.

. . .

It was the day after that that Lola and Sachetti came in for their loan. When I handed them the check she did a little dance in the middle of the floor. "You want a copy of Nino's dissertation?"

"Why—I'd love it."

"It's called 'The Problem of Colloids in the Reduction of Low-Grade Gold Ores.'"

"I'll look forward to it."

"Liar—you won't even read it."

"I'll read as much as I can understand."

"Anyway, you'll get a signed copy."

"Thanks."

"Good-bye. Maybe you're rid of us for a while."

"Maybe."

Chapter 4

ALL THIS, what I've been telling you, happened in late winter, along the middle of February. Of course, in California February looks like any other month, but anyway it would have been winter anywhere else. From then on, all through the spring, believe me I didn't get much sleep. You start on something like this, and if you don't wake up plenty of times in the middle of the night, dreaming they got you for something you forgot, you've got better nerves than I've got. Then there were things we couldn't figure out, like how to get him on a train. That was tough, and if we didn't have a piece of luck, maybe we never would have put it over. There's plenty of people out here that have never been inside a train, let alone taken a ride on one. They go everywhere by car. That was how he traveled, when he traveled, and how to make him use a train just once, that was something that gave us a headache for quite some time. We got a break on one thing though that I had sweated over plenty. That was the funny look that came over his face when I got that check. There was something back of it, I knew that, and if it was something his secretary was in on, and especially if he went out after I left and made some crack to the secretary about getting $20 he didn't expect, it would look plenty bad later, no matter what kind of story I made up. But that wasn't it. Phyllis got the low-down on it, and it startled me, how pretty it broke for us. He charged his car insurance to his company, under expenses, and his secretary had already entered it when I came along with my proposition. She had not only entered it, but if he went through with what I wanted, he still had his cancelled check to show for it, the first one, I mean. All he had to do was keep his mouth shut to the secretary and he could put his $20 profit in his pocket, and nobody would be the wiser. He kept his mouth shut. He didn't even tell Lola. But he had to brag to somebody how smart he was, so he told Phyllis.

Another thing that worried me was myself. I was afraid my work would fall off, and they'd begin talking about me in the office, wondering why I'd begun to slip. That wouldn't do me any good, later I mean, when they began to think about it. I had to sell insurance while this thing was cooking, if I never sold it before. I worked like a wild man. I saw every prospect there was the least chance of selling, and how I high-pressured them was a shame. Believe it or not, my business showed a 12% increase in March, it jumped 2% over that in April, and in May, when there's a lot of activity in cars, it went to 7% over that. I even made a hook-up with a big syndicate of second-hand dealers for my finance company, and that helped. The books didn't know anything to tell on me. I was the candy kid in both offices that spring. They were all taking off their hats to me.

"He's going to his class reunion. At Palo Alto."

"When?"

"June. In about six weeks."

"That's it. That's what we've been waiting for."

"But he wants to drive. He wants to take the car, and he wants me to go with him. He'll raise an awful fuss if I don't go."

"Yeah? Listen, don't give yourself airs. I don't care if it's a class reunion or just down to the drugstore, a man would rather go alone than with a wife. He's just being polite. You talk like you're not interested in his class reunion, and he'll be persuaded. He'll be persuaded so easy you'll be surprised."

"Well I like that."

"You're not supposed to like it. But you'll find out."

That was how it turned out, but she worked on him a whole week and she couldn't change him on the car. "He says he'll have to have it, and there'll be a lot of things he'll want to go to, picnics and things like that, and if he doesn't have it he'll have to hire one. Besides, he hates trains. He gets trainsick."

"Can't you put on an act?"

"I did. I put on all the act I dare put, and still he won't budge. I put on such an act that Lola is hardly speaking to me any more. She thinks it's selfish of me. I can try again, but—"

"Holy smoke no."

"I could do this. The day before he's to start, I could bang the car up. Mess up the ignition or something. So it had to go in the shop. Then he'd *have* to go by train."

"Nothing like it. Nothing even a little bit like it. In the first place, if you've already put on an act, they'll smell something, and believe me Lola will be hard to talk down, later. In the second place, we need the car."

"*We* need it?"

"It's essential."

"I still don't know—what we're going to do."

"You'll know. You'll know in plenty of time. But we've got to have the car. We've got to have two cars, yours and mine. Whatever you do, don't pull any monkey business with the car. That car's got to run. It's got to be in perfect shape."

"Hadn't we better give up the train idea?"

"Listen, it's the train or we don't do it."

"Well my goodness, you don't have to snap at me."

"Just pulling off some piker job, that don't interest me. But this, hitting it for the limit, that's what I go for. It's all I go for."

"I was just wondering."

"Quit wondering."

Two or three days later was when we had our piece of luck. She called me at the office around four in the afternoon. "Walter?"

"Yes."

"Are you alone?"

"Is it important?"

"Yes, terribly. Something has happened."

"I'll go home. Call me there in a half hour."

I was alone, but I don't take chances on a phone that runs through a switchboard. I went home, and the phone rang a couple of minutes after I got there. "The Palo Alto trip is off. He's broken his leg."

"What!"

"I don't even know how he did it, yet. He was holding a dog or something, a neighbor's dog that was chasing a rabbit, and slipped and fell down. He's in the hospital now. Lola's with him. They'll be bringing him home in a few minutes."

"I guess that knocks it in the head."

"I'm afraid so."

I was at dinner before it came to me that instead of knocking it in the head, maybe this fixed it up perfect. I walked three miles, around the living room, wondering if she'd come that night, before I heard the bell ring.

"I've only got a few minutes. I'm supposed to be on the boulevard, buying him something to read. I could cry. Whoever heard of such a thing?"

"Listen, Phyllis, never mind that. What kind of break has he got? I mean, is it bad?"

"It's down near the ankle. No, it's not bad."

"Is it in pulleys?"

"No. There's a weight on it, that comes off in about a week. But he won't be able to walk. He'll have to wear a cast. A long time."

"He'll be able to walk."

"You think so?"

"If you get him up."

"What do you mean, Walter?"

"On crutches, he can get up, if you get him up. Because with his foot in a cast, *he won't be able to drive*. He'll have to go by train. Phyllis, this is what we've been hoping for."

"You think so?"

"And then another thing. I told you, he gets on that train but he don't get on it. All right, then. We've got a question of identification there, haven't we? Those crutches, that foot in a cast—there's the most perfect identification a man ever had. Oh yeah, I'm telling you. If you can get him off that bed, and make him think he ought to take the trip anyway, just as a vacation from all he's been through —we're in. I can feel it. We're in."

"It's dangerous, though."

"What's dangerous about it?"

"I mean, getting a broken leg case out of bed too soon. I used to be a nurse, and I know. It's almost certain to affect the length. Make one leg shorter than the other, I mean."

"Is that all that's bothering you?"

It was a minute before she got it. Whether one leg was going to be shorter than the other, that was one thing he didn't have to worry about.

Decoration Day they don't have mail delivery, but the day watchman sends over to the General Fidelity box and gets it. There was a big envelope for me, marked personal. I opened it and found a booklet. It was called "Colloids in Gold Mining. An examination of methods in dealing with the problem." Inside, it was inscribed, "To Mr. Walter Huff, in appreciation of past favors, Bernanino Sachetti.

Chapter 5

HIS TRAIN WAS TO leave at 9:45 at night. Around four o'clock, I drove down to San Pedro Street and talked employers' liability to the manager of a wine company. There wasn't a chance of landing him until August, when the grapes came in and his plant opened up, but I had a reason. He explained why he wasn't ready to do business yet, but I put on an act and went back to the office. I told Nettie I thought I had a real prospect, and to make out a card for him. The card automatically gave the date of the first call, and that was what I wanted. I signed a couple of letters, and around five-thirty I left.

I got home around six, and the Filipino was all ready to serve dinner. I had seen to that. This was June 3, and I should have paid him on the first, but I had pretended I had forgotten to go to the bank, and put him off. Today, though, I had stopped at the house for lunch, and paid him. That meant that when night came he could hardly wait to go out and spend it. I said O.K., he could serve dinner, and he had the soup on the table before I even got washed up. I ate, as well as I could. He gave me steak, mashed potatoes, peas, and carrots, with fruit cup for dessert. I was so nervous I could hardly chew, but I got it all down somehow. I had hardly finished my coffee when he had everything washed up, and had changed to cream-colored pants, white shoes and stockings, a brown coat, and white shirt open at the neck, ready to go out with the girl. It used to be that what a Hollywood actor wore on Monday a Filipino house boy wore on Tuesday, but now, if you ask me, it's the other way around, and the boy from Manila beats Clark Gable to it.

He left around a quarter to seven. When he came up to ask if there was anything else for him to do, I was taking off my clothes getting ready to go to bed. I told him I was going to lie there and do a little work. I got some paper and pencils and made a lot of notes, like I was figuring up the public liability stuff for the man I talked to in the afternoon. It was the kind of stuff you would naturally save and put in the prospect's folder. I took care there was a couple of notes on the date.

Then I went down and called the office. Joe Pete, the night watchman, answered. "Joe Pete, this is Walter Huff. Do me a favor, will you? Go up to my office, and right on top of the desk you'll find my rate book. It's a looseleaf book, with a soft leather back, and my name stamped in gold on the front, and under that the word 'rates.' I forgot to bring it home, and I need it. Will you get it and send it up to me by messenger, right away?"

"O.K., Mr. Huff. Right away."

Fifteen minutes later he rang back and said he couldn't find it. "I looked all over the desk, Mr. Huff, and through the office besides, and there's no such book there."

"Nettie must have locked it up."

"I can call her if you want, and ask where she put it."

"No, I don't need it that bad."

"I'm sorry, Mr. Huff."

"I'll have to get along without it."

I had put that rate book in a place where he'd never find it. But it was one person that had called me at home that night, and I was there, working hard. There'd be others. No need to say anything to him that would make him remember the date. He had to keep a log, and enter everything he did, not only by date, but also by time. I looked at my watch. It was 7:38.

A quarter to eight the phone rang again. It was Phyllis. "The blue."

"Blue it is."

That was a check on what suit he would wear. We were pretty sure it would be the blue, but I had to be sure, so she was to duck down to the drugstore to buy him an extra tooth brush, and call. No danger of its being traced, there's no record on dial calls. Soon as she hung up I dressed. I put on a blue suit too. But before that I wrapped up my foot. I put a thick bandage of gauze on it, and over that adhesive tape. It looked like the tape was wrapped on the ankle, like a cast for a broken leg, but it wasn't. I could cut it off in ten seconds when I was ready to. I put the shoe on. I could barely lace it, but that was how I wanted it. I checked on a pair of horn-rim glasses, like he wore. They were in my pocket. So was 58 inches of light cotton rope, rolled small. So was a handle I had made, like stores hook on packages, but heavier, from an iron rod. My coat bulged, but I didn't care.

Twenty minutes to nine I called Nettie. "Did you see my rate book before I left?"

"Indeed I didn't, Mr. Huff."

"I need it, and I don't know what I did with it."

"You mean you lost it?"

"I don't know. I phoned Joe Pete, and he can't find it, and I can't imagine what I did with it."

"I can run in, if you want, and see if I can—"

"No, it's not that important."

"I didn't see it, Mr. Huff."

Nettie lives in Burbank, and it's a toll call. The record would show I called from the house at 8:40. As soon as I got rid of her I opened the bell box and tilted half a visiting card against the clapper, so if the phone rang it would fall down. Then I did the same for the doorbell clapper, in the kitchen. I would be out of the house an hour and a half, and I had to know if the doorbell rang or the phone rang. If they did, that would be while I was in the bathroom taking a bath, with the door shut and the water running, so I didn't hear. But I had to know.

Soon as I had the cards fixed I got in my car and drove over to Hollywoodland. It's just a few minutes from my house. I parked on the main street, a couple of minutes' walk from the house. I had to be where a car wouldn't attract any attention, but at the same time I couldn't be so far off that I had to do much walking. Not with that foot.

Around the bend from the house is a big tree. There's no house in sight of it. I slipped behind it and waited. I waited exactly two minutes, but it seemed like an hour. Then I saw the flash of headlights.

The car came around the bend. She was at the wheel, and he was beside her with his crutches under his elbow on the door side. When the car got to the tree it stopped. That was exactly according to the play. Next came the ticklish part. It was how to get him out of the car for a minute, with the bags in back and everything all set, so I could get in. If he had been all right on his two feet there would have been nothing to it, but getting a cripple out of a car once he gets set, and especially with a well person sitting right beside him, is like getting a hippopotamus out of a car.

She opened up just like I had coached her. "I haven't got my pocketbook."

"Didn't you take it?"

"I thought so. Look on the back seat."

"No, nothing back there but my stuff."

"I can't think what I've done with it."

"Well come on, we'll be late. Here, here's a dollar. That'll be enough till you get back."

"I must have left it on the sofa. In the living room."

"Well all right, all right, you left it on the sofa in the living room. Now get going."

She was coming to the part I had taken her over forty times. She was all for *asking* him to step out and get it. I finally beat it into her head that if she did that, she was just setting herself up to him to ask her why *she* didn't step out and get it, so he wouldn't have to unlimber the crutches. I showed her that her only chance was to talk dumb, not start the car, and wait him out, until he would get so sore, and so worried over the time, that he would make a martyr out of himself and get it himself. She kept at it, just like she was coached.

"But I want my pocketbook."

"What for? Isn't a buck enough?"

"But it's got my lipstick in it."

"Listen, can't you get it through your head we're trying to catch a train? This isn't an automobile trip, where we start when we get ready. It's a railroad train, and it goes at nine-forty-five, and when it goes it goes. Come on. Start up."

"Well if you're going to talk that way."

"What way?"

"All I said was that I wanted my—"

He ripped out a flock of cusswords, and at last I heard the crutches rattling against the side of the car. As soon as he was around the bend, hobbling back to the house, I dove in. I had to dive in the front door and climb over the seat into the back, so he wouldn't hear the back door close. That's a sound that always catches your ear, a car door closing. I crouched down there in the dark. He had his bag and his briefcase on the seat.

"Did I do it all right, Walter?"

"O.K. so far. How did you get rid of Lola?"

"I didn't have to. She was invited to something over at U.C.L.A. and I took her to the bus at seven."

"O.K. Back up, now, so he won't have so far to walk. Try and smooth him down."

"All right."

She backed up to the door and he got in again. She started off. Believe me it's an awful thing to kibbitz on a man and his wife, and hear what they really talk about. Soon as she got him a little smoothed down, he began to beef about Belle, the way she passed things at dinner. She panned Belle for the way she broke so many dishes. Then they got switched off to somebody named Hobey, and a woman named Ethel, that seemed to be Hobey's wife. He said he was through with Hobey and Hobey might as well know it. She said she used to like Ethel but the high-hat way she's been acting lately was too much. They figured it out whether they owed Hobey and Ethel a dinner or the other way around, so they found out they were one down, and decided that after they knocked that one off that was going to be the end of it. When they got that all settled, they decided he was to take a taxi wherever he went, up in Palo Alto, even if it did cost a little money. Because if he had to slog along on crutches everywhere he went, he wouldn't have a good time, and besides he might strain his leg. Phyllis talked just like he was going to Palo Alto, and she didn't have a thing on her mind. A woman is a funny animal.

Back where I was, I couldn't see where we were. I was even afraid to breathe, for fear he'd hear me. She was to drive so she didn't make any sudden stops, or get herself tangled in traffic, or do anything that would make him turn his head around to see what was back of us. He didn't. He had a cigar in his mouth, and lay back in the seat, smoking it. After a while she gave two sharp raps on the horn. That was our signal that we had come to a dark street we had picked out, about a half mile from the station.

I raised up, put my hand over his mouth, and pulled his head back. He grabbed my hand in both of his. The cigar was still in his fingers. I took it with my free hand and handed it to her. She took it. I took one of the crutches and hooked it under his chin. I won't tell you what I did then. But in two seconds he was curled down on the seat with a broken neck, and not a mark on him except a crease right over his nose, from the crosspiece of the crutch.

Chapter 6

WE WERE RIGHT UP WITH IT, the moment of audacity that has to be the the part of any successful murder. For the next twenty minutes we were in the jaws of death, not for what would happen now, but for how it would go together later. She started to throw the cigar out, but I stopped her. He had lit that cigar in the house, and I had to have it. She held it for me, and wiped the end of it as well as she could, while I went to work with the rope. I ran it across his shoulders, just below the neck, under his arms, and across his back. I tied it hard, and hooked the handle on, so it caught both sections of the rope, and drew them tight. A dead man is about the hardest thing to handle there is, but I figured with this harness we could do it, and do it quick.

"We're there, Walter. Shall I park now or drive around the block?"

"Park now. We're ready."

She stopped. It was on a side street, about a block from the station. That stumped us for a while, where to park. If we went on the regular station parking lot, it was a 10 to 1 shot that a redcap would jerk the door open to get the bags, and we'd be sunk. But parking here, we would be all right. If we got a chance, we were to have an argument about it in front of somebody, with me complaining about how far she made me walk, to cover up on something that might look a little funny, later.

She got out and took the bag and briefcase. He was one of the kind who puts his toilet articles in a briefcase, for use on the train, and that was a break for me, later. I wound up all windows, took the crutches, and got out. She locked the car. We left him right where he was, curled down on the seat, with the harness on him.

She went ahead with the bag and briefcase, and I came along behind, with the bandaged leg half lifted up, walking on the crutches. That looked like a woman making it easy for a cripple. Really, it was a way to keep the redcap from getting a good look at me when he took the bags. Soon as we got around the corner, in sight of the station, here came one, running. He did just what we figured on. He took the bags from her, and never waited for me at all.

"The nine forty-five for San Francisco, Section 8, Car C."

"Eight in Car C, yas'm. Meet you on the train."

We went in the station. I made her drop back on me, so if anything came up I could mumble to her. I had the glasses on, and my hat pulled down, but not too much. I kept my eyes down, like I was watching where I put the crutches. I kept the cigar in my mouth, partly so it covered some of my face, partly so I could screw my face out of shape a little, like I was trying to keep the smoke out of my eyes.

The train was on a siding, out back of the station. I made a quick count of the cars. "Holy smoke, it's the third one." It was the one that both conductors were standing in front of, and not only them, but the porter, and the redcap, waiting for his tip. Unless we did something quick, it would be four people that had a good look at me before I went in the car, and it might hang us. She ran on ahead. I saw her tip the redcap, and he went off, all bows. He didn't pass near me. He headed for the far end of the station, where the parking lot was. Then the porter saw me, and started for me. She took him by the arm. "He doesn't like to be helped."

The porter didn't get it. The Pullman conductor did.

"Hey!"

The porter stopped. Then he got it. They all turned their backs and started to talk. I stumped up the car steps. I got to the top. That was her cue. She was still down on the ground, with the conductors. "Dear."

I stopped and half turned. "Come back to the observation platform. I'll say good-bye to you there, and then I won't have to worry about getting off the train. You still have a few minutes. Maybe we can talk."

"Fine."

I started back, through the car. She started back, on the ground, outside.

All three cars were full of people getting ready to go to bed, with most of the berths made up and bags all out in the aisle. The porters weren't there. They were at their boxes, outside. I kept my eyes down, clinched the cigar in my teeth, and kept my face screwed up. Nobody really saw me, and yet everybody saw me, because the minute they saw those crutches they began snatching bags out of the way and making room. I just nodded and mumbled "thanks."

When I saw her face I knew something was wrong. Outside on the observation platform, I saw what it was. A man was there, tucked back in a corner in the dark, having a smoke. I sat down on the opposite side. She reached her hand over. I took it. She kept looking at me for a cue. I kept making my lips say, "Parking . . . parking . . . parking." After a second or two she got it.

"Dear."

"Yes?"

"You're not mad at me any more? For where I parked?"

"Forget it."

"I thought I was headed for the station parking lot, honestly. But I get all mixed up in this part of town. I hadn't any idea I was going to make you walk so far."

"I told you, forget it."

"I'm terribly sorry."

"Kiss me."

I looked at my watch, held it up to her. It was still seven minutes before the train would leave. She needed a six-minute start for what she had to do. "Listen, Phyllis, there's no use of you waiting around here. Why don't you blow?"

"Well—you don't mind?"

"Not a bit. No sense dragging it out."

"Good-bye, then."

"Good-bye."

"Have a good time. Three cheers for Leland Stanford.'"

"I'll do my best."

"Kiss me again."

"Good-bye."

For what I had to do, I had to get rid of this guy, and get rid of
him quick. I hadn't expected anybody out there. There seldom is
when a train pulls out. I sat there, trying to think of something. I
thought he might leave when he finished his cigarette, but he didn't.
He threw it over the side and began to talk.

"Women are funny."

"Funny and then some."

"I couldn't help hearing that little conversation you had with your
wife just now. About where she parked, I mean. Reminds me of an
experience I had with my wife, coming home from San Diego."

He told the experience he had with his wife. I looked him over. I
couldn't see his face. I figured he couldn't see mine. He stopped
talking. I had to say something.

"Yeah, women are funny all right. Specially when you get them
behind the wheel of a car."

"They're all of that."

The train began to roll. It crawled through the outskirts of Los
Angeles, and he kept on talking. Then an idea came to me. I remembered I was supposed to be a cripple, and began feeling through
my pockets.

"You lose something?"

"My ticket. I can't find it."

"Say, I wonder if I've got my ticket. Yeah, here it is."

"You know what I bet she did? Put that ticket in my briefcase,
right where I told her not to. She was to put it here in the pocket of
this suit, and now—"

"Oh, it'll turn up."

"Don't that beat all? Here I've got to go and hobble all through
those cars, just because—"

"Don't be silly. Stay where you are."

"No, I couldn't let you—"

"Be a pleasure old man. Stay right where you are and I'll get it for
you. What's your space?"

"Would you? Section 8, Car C."

"I'll be right back with it."

                    •   •   •

We were picking up speed a little now. My mark was a dairy sign, about a quarter of a mile from the track. We came in sight of it and I lit the cigar. I put the crutches under one arm, threw my leg over the rail, and let myself down. One of the crutches hit the ties and spun me so I almost fell. I hung on. When we came square abreast of the sign I dropped off.

Chapter 7

THERE'S NOTHING SO DARK as a railroad track in the middle of the night. The train shot ahead, and I crouched there, waiting for the tingle to leave my feet. I had dropped off the left side of the train, into the footpath between the tracks, so there wouldn't be any chance I could be seen from the highway. It was about two hundred feet away. I stayed there, on my hands and knees, straining to see something on the other side of the tracks. There was a dirt road there, that gave entry to a couple of small factories, further on back. All around it were vacant lots, and it wasn't lit. She ought to be there by now. She had a seven-minute start, the train took six minutes to that point, and it was an eleven-minute drive from the station to this dirt road. I had checked it twenty times. I held still and stared, trying to spot the car. I couldn't see it.

I don't know how long I crouched there. It came to me that maybe she had bumped somebody's fender, or been stopped by a cop, or something. I seemed to turn to water. Then I heard something. I heard a panting. Then with it I heard footsteps. They would go fast for a second or two, and then stop. It was like being in a nightmare, with something queer coming after me, and I didn't know what it was, but it was horrible. Then I saw it. It was her. That man must have weighed 200 pounds, but she had him on her back, holding him by the handle, and staggering along with him, over the tracks. His head was hanging down beside her head. They looked like something in a horror picture.

I ran over and grabbed his legs, to take some of the weight off her. We ran him a few steps. She started to throw him down. "Not that track! The other one!"

We got him over to the track the train went out on, and dropped him. I cut the harness off and slipped it in my pocket. I put the lighted cigar within a foot or two of him. I threw one crutch over him and the other beside the track.

"Where's the car?"

"There. Couldn't you see it?"

I looked, and there it was, right where it was supposed to be, on the dirt road.

"We're done. Let's go."

We ran over and climbed in and she started the motor, threw in the gear. "Oh my—his hat!"

I took the hat and sailed it out the window, on the tracks. "It's O.K., a hat can roll,—*get going!*"

She started up. We passed the factories. We came to a street.

On Sunset she went through a light. "Watch that stuff, can't you, Phyllis? If you're stopped now, with me in the car, we're sunk."

"Can I drive with that thing going on?"

She meant the car radio. I had it turned on. It was to be part of my alibi, for the time I was out of the house, that I knocked off work for a while and listened to the radio. I had to know what was coming in that night. I had to know more than I could find out by reading the programs in the papers. "I've got to have it, you know that—"

"Let me alone, let me drive!"

She hit a zone, and must have been doing seventy. I clenched my teeth, and kept quiet. When we came to a vacant lot I threw out the rope. About a mile further on I threw out the handle. Going by a curb drain I shot the glasses into it. Then I happened to look down and saw her shoes. They were scarred from the track ballast.

"What did you carry him for? Why didn't you let me—"

"Where were you? *Where were you?*"

"I was there. I was waiting—"

"Did I know that? Could I just sit there, with *that* in the car?"

"I was trying to see where you were. I couldn't see—"

"Let me alone, *let me drive!*"

"Your shoes—"

I choked it back. In a second or two, she started up again. She raved like a lunatic. She raved and she kept on raving, about him, about me, about anything that came in her head. Every now and then I'd snap. There we were, after what we had done, snarling at each other like a couple of animals, and neither one of us could stop. It was like somebody had shot us full of some kind of dope. "Phyllis, cut this out. We've got to talk, and it may be our last chance."

"Talk then! Who's stopping you?"

"First then: You don't know anything about this insurance policy. You—"

"How many times do you have to say that?"

"I'm only telling you—"

"You've already told me till I'm sick of hearing you."

"Next, the inquest. You bring—"

"I bring a minister, I know that, I bring a minister to take charge of the body, how many times have I got to listen to that—*are you going to let me drive?*"

"O.K., then. Drive."

"Is Belle home?"

"How do I know? No!"

"And Lola's out?"

"Didn't I tell you?"

"Then you'll have to stop at the drugstore. To get a pint of ice cream or something. To have witnesses you drove straight home from the station. You got to say something to fix the time and the date. You—"

"Get out! Get out! I'll go insane!"

"I can't get out. I've got to get to my car! Do you know what that means, if I take time to walk? I can't complete my alibi! I—"

"I said get out!"

"Drive on, or I'll sock you."

When she got to my car she stopped and I got out. We didn't kiss. We didn't even say good-bye. I got out of her car, got in mine, started, and drove home.

When I got home I looked at the clock. It was 10:25. I opened the bell box of the telephone. The card was still there. I closed the box and dropped the card in my pocket. I went in the kitchen and looked at the doorbell. That card was still there. I dropped it in my pocket. I went upstairs, ripped off my clothes, and got into pajamas and slippers. I cut the bandage off my foot. I went down, shoved the bandage and cards into the fireplace, with a newspaper, and lit it. I watched it burn. Then I went to the telephone and started to dial. I still had one call-back to get, to round out the late part of my alibi. I felt something like a drawstring pull in my throat, and a sob popped out of me. I clapped the phone down. It was getting me. I knew I had to get myself under some kind of control. I swallowed a couple of times. I wanted to make sure of my voice, that it would sound O.K. A dumb idea came to me that maybe if I would sing something, that would make me snap out of it. I started to sing the "Isle of Capri." I sang about two notes, and it swallowed into a kind of a wail.

I went in the dining room and took a drink. I took another drink. I started mumbling to myself, trying to get so I could talk. I had to have something to mumble. I thought of the Lord's Prayer. I mumbled that, a couple of times. I tried to mumble it another time, and couldn't remember how it went.

When I thought I could talk, I dialed again. It was 10:48. I dialed Ike Schwartz, that's another salesman with General.

"Ike, do me a favor, will you? I'm trying to figure out a proposition on a public liability bond for a wine company to have it ready for them tomorrow morning, and I'm going nuts. I came off without my rate book. Joe Pete can't find it, and I'm wondering if you'll look up what I want in yours. You got it with you?"

"Sure, I'll be glad to."

I gave him the dope. He said give him fifteen minutes and he'd call back.

I walked around, digging my fingernails into my hands, trying to hold on to myself. The drawstring began to jerk on my throat again. I began mumbling again, saying over and over what I had just said to Ike. The phone rang. I answered. He had it figured for me, he said, and began to give it to me. He gave it to me three different ways, so I'd have it all. It took him twenty minutes. I took it down, what he said. I could feel the sweat squeezing out on my forehead and running down off my nose. After a while he was done.

"O.K., Ike, that's just what I wanted to know. That's just how I wanted it. Thanks a thousand times."

Soon as he hung up everything cracked. I dived for the bathroom. I was sicker than I had ever been in my life. After that passed I fell into bed. It was a long time before I could turn out the light. Then I lay there staring into the dark. Every now and then I would have a chill or something and start to tremble. Then that passed and I lay there, like a dope. Then I started to think. I tried not to, but it would creep up on me. I knew then what I had done. I had killed a man. I had killed a man to get a woman. I had put myself in her power, so there was one person in the world that could point a finger at me, and I would have to die. I had done all that for her, and I never wanted to see her again as long as I lived.

That's all it takes, one drop of fear, to curdle love into hate.

Chapter 8

I GULPED DOWN SOME orange juice and coffee, and then went up in the bedroom with the paper. I was afraid to open it in front of the Filipino. Sure enough, there it was, on Page 1:

OIL MAN, ON WAY TO JUNE RALLY, DIES IN TRAIN FALL

H. S. Nirdlinger, Petroleum Pioneer, Killed In Plunge from Express En Route to Reunion At Leland Stanford.

With injuries about the head and neck, the body of H. S. Nirdlinger, Los Angeles representative of the Western Pipe & Supply Company and for a number of years prominently identified with the oil industry here, was found on the railroad tracks about two miles north of this city shortly before midnight last night. Mr. Nirdlinger had departed on a northbound train earlier in the evening to attend his class reunion at Leland Stanford University, and it is believed he fell from the train. Police point out he had fractured his leg some weeks ago, and believe his unfamiliarity with crutches may have caused him to lose his balance on the observation platform, where he was last seen alive.

Mr. Nirdlinger was 44 years old. Born in Fresno, he attended Leland Stanford, and on graduation, entered the oil business, becoming one of the pioneers in the opening of the field at Long Beach. Later he was active at Signal Hill. For the last three years he had been in charge of the local office of the Western Pipe & Supply Company.

Surviving are a widow, formerly Miss Phyllis Belden of Mannerheim, and a daughter, Miss Lola Nirdlinger. Mrs. Nirdlinger, before her marriage, was head nurse of the Verdugo Health Institute here.

Twenty minutes to nine, Nettie called. She said Mr. Norton wanted to see me, as soon as I could possibly get down. That meant they already had it, and I wouldn't have to put on any act, going in there with my paper and saying this is the guy I sold an accident policy to last winter. I said I knew what it was, and I was right on my way.

I got through the day somehow. I think I told you about Norton and Keyes. Norton is president of the company. He's a short, stocky man about 35, that got the job when his father died and he's so busy trying to act like his father he doesn't seem to have time for much else. Keyes is head of the Claim Department, a holdover from the old regime, and the way he tells it young Norton never does anything right. He's big and fat and peevish, and on top of that he's a theorist, and it makes your head ache to be around him, but he's the best claim man on the Coast, and he was the one I was afraid of.

First I had to face Norton, and tell him what I knew, or anyway what I was supposed to know. I told him how I propositioned Nirdlinger about the accident policy, and how his wife and daughter opposed it, and how I dropped it that night but went over to his office a couple of days later to give him another whirl. That would check with what the secretary saw. I told him how I sold him, then, but only after I promised not to say anything to the wife and daughter about it. I told how I took his application, then when the policy came through, delivered it, and got his check. Then we went down in Keyes's office and we went all over it again. It took all morning, you understand. All while we were talking phone calls and telegrams kept coming in, from San Francisco, where Keyes had our investigators interviewing people that were on the train, from the police, from the secretary, from Lola, after they got her on the phone to find out what she knew. They tried to get Phyllis, but she had strict instruction from me not to come to the phone, so she didn't. They got hold of the coroner, and arranged for an autopsy. There's generally a hook-up between insurance companies and coroners, so they can get an autopsy if they want it. They could demand it, under a clause in their policy, but that would mean going to court for an order, and would tip it that the deceased was insured, and that's bad all the way round. They get it on the quiet, and in this case they had to have it. Because if Nirdlinger died of apoplexy, or heart failure, and fell off the train, then it wouldn't any longer be accident, but death from natural causes, and they wouldn't be liable. About the middle of the afternoon they got the medical report. Death was from a broken neck. When they heard that they got the inquest postponed two days.

By four o'clock, the memos and telegrams were piled on Keyes's desk so he had to put a weight on top of them to keep them from falling over, and he was mopping his brow and so peevish nobody could talk to him. But Norton was getting more cheerful by the minute. He took a San Francisco call from somebody named Jackson, and I could tell from what he said that it was this guy I had got rid of on the observation platform before I dropped off. When he hung up he put one more memo on top of the others and turned to Keyes. "Clear case of suicide."

If it was suicide, you see, the company wouldn't be liable either. This policy only covered accident.

"Yeah?"

"All right, watch me while I check it over. First, he took out this policy. He took it out in secret. He didn't tell his wife, he didn't tell his daughter, he didn't tell his secretary, he didn't tell anybody. If Huff here, had been on the job, he might have known—"

"Known what?"

"No need to get sore, Huff. But you've got to admit it looked funny."

"It didn't look funny at all. It happens every day. Now if *they* had tried to insure *him*, without *him* knowing, *that* would have looked funny."

"That's right. Leave Huff out of it."

"All I'm saying, Keyes, is that—"

"Huff's record shows that if there had been anything funny, he'd have noted it and we'd have known it. You better find out something about your own agents."

"All right, skip it. He takes out this policy in absolute secrecy. Why? Because he knew that if his family knew what he had done,

they would know what he was up to. They knew what was on his
mind, we can depend on that, and when we go into his books and
his history, we'll find out what the trouble was. All right, next point,
he fractured his leg, but he didn't put a claim in. Why? That looks
funny, don't it, that a man had an accident policy, and didn't put a
claim in for a broken leg? *Because he knew he was going to do this,
and he was afraid if he put a claim in the family would find out
about this policy and block him off*."

"How?"

"If they called us up, we'd cancel on him, wouldn't we? You bet
we would. We'd return his unused premium so fast you couldn't see
our dust, and he knew it. Oh no, he wasn't taking a chance on our
doctor going out there to look at his leg and tipping things off.
That's a big point."

"Go on."

"All right, he figures an excuse to take a train. He takes his wife
with him to the station, he gets on the train, he gets rid of her. She
goes. He's ready to do it. But he runs into trouble. There's a guy out
there, on the observation platform, and for this he don't want any
company. You bet he doesn't. So what does he do? He gets rid of
him, by putting up some kind of a story about not having his ticket,
and leaving it in his briefcase, and as soon as this guy goes, he takes
his dive. That was the guy I just talked to, a man by the name of
Jackson that went up to Frisco on a business trip and is coming back
tomorrow. He says there's no question about it, he had the feeling
even when he offered to get Nirdlinger's briefcase for him that he
was trying to get rid of him, but he didn't quite have the heart to say
no to a cripple. In my mind, that clinches it. It's a clear case of
suicide. You can't take any other view of it."

"So what?"

"Our next step is the inquest. We can't appear there, of course,
because if a jury finds out a dead man is insured they'll murder us.
We can send an investigator or two, perhaps, to sit in there, but
nothing more than that. But Jackson says he'll be glad to appear and
tell what he knows, and there's a chance, just a chance, but still a
chance, that we may get a suicide verdict anyway. If we do, we're in.
If we don't, then we've got to consider what we do. However, one
thing at a time. The inquest first, and you can't tell what the police
may find out; we may win right in the first round."

Keyes mopped his head some more. He was so fat he really suffered in the heat. He lit a cigarette. He drooped down and looked away from Norton like it was some schoolboy and he didn't want to show his disgust. Then he spoke. "It was not suicide."

"What are you talking about? It's a clear case."

"It was not suicide."

He opened his bookcase and began throwing thick books on the table. "Mr. Norton, here's what the actuaries have to say about suicide. You study them, you might find out something about the insurance business."

"I was raised in the insurance business, Keyes."

"You were raised in private schools, Groton, and Harvard. While you were learning how to pull bow oars there, I was studying these tables. Take a look at them. Here's suicide by race, by color, by occupation, by sex, by locality, by seasons of the year, by time of day when committed. Here's suicide by method of accomplishment. Here's method of accomplishment subdivided by poisons, by fire-arms, by gas, by drowning, by leaps. Here's suicide by poisons subdivided by sex, by race, by age, by time of day. Here's suicide by poisons subdivided by cyanide, by mercury, by strychnine, by thirty-eight other poisons, sixteen of them no longer procurable at prescription pharmacies. And here—here, Mr. Norton—are leaps subdivided by leaps from high places, under wheels of moving trains, under wheels of trucks, under the feet of horses, from steamboats. *But there's not one case here out of all these millions of cases of a leap from the rear end of a moving train.* That's just one way they don't do it."

"They could."

"Could they? That train, at the point where the body was found, moves at a maximum of fifteen miles an hour. Could any man jump off it there with any real expectation of killing himself?"

"He might dive off. This man had a broken neck."

"Don't trifle with me. He wasn't an acrobat."

"Then what are you trying to tell me? That it was on the up-and-up?"

"Listen, Mr. Norton. When a man takes out an insurance policy, an insurance policy that's worth $50,000 if he's killed in a railroad accident, and then three months later he *is* killed in a railroad accident, it's not on the up-and-up. It can't be. If the train got wrecked

it might be, but even then it would be a mighty suspicious coincidence. A *mighty* suspicious concidence. No, it's not on the up-and-
up. But it's not suicide."

"Then what do you mean?"

"You know what I mean."

". . . Murder?"

"I mean murder."

"Well wait a minute, Keyes, wait a minute. Wait till I catch up
with you. What have you got to go on?"

"Nothing."

"You must have *something*."

"I said nothing. Whoever did this did a perfect job. There's nothing to go on. Just the same, it's murder."

"Do you suspect anybody?"

"The beneficiary of such a policy, so far as I am concerned, is
automatically under suspicion."

"You mean the wife?"

"I mean the wife."

"She wasn't even on the train."

"Then somebody else was."

"Have you any idea who?"

"None at all."

"And this is all you have to go on?"

"I told you, I have nothing to go on. Nothing but those tables and
my own hunch, instinct, and experience. It's a slick job, but it's no
accident, and it's no suicide."

"Then what are we going to do?"

"I don't know. Give me a minute to think."

He took a half hour to think. Norton and I, we sat there and
smoked. After a while, Keyes began to bump the desk with the palm
of his hand. He knew what he meant, you could see that.

"Mr. Norton."

"Yes, Keyes."

"There's only one thing for you to do. It's against practice, and in
some other case I'd oppose it. But not in this. There's a couple of
things about this that make me think that practice is one of the
things they're going to count on, and take advantage of. Practice in a
case like this is to wait, and make them come to you, isn't it? I advise
against that. I advise jumping in there at once, tonight if possible,
and if not tonight, then certainly on the day of that inquest, and

filing a complaint against that woman. I advise filing an information of suspected murder against her, and smashing at her as hard and as quick as we can. I advise that we demand her arrest, and her detention too, for the full forty-eight hours incommunicado that the law allows in a case of this kind. I advise sweating her with everything the police have got. I particularly advise separating her from this accomplice, whoever he is, or she is, so we get the full value of surprise, and prevent their conferring on future plans. Do that, and mark my words you're going to find out things that'll amaze you."

"But—*on what?*"

"On nothing."

"But Keyes, we can't do a thing like that. Suppose we don't find out anything. Suppose we sweat her and get nothing. Suppose it *is* on the up-and-up. Look where that puts us. Holy smoke, she could murder us in a civil suit, and a jury would give her every nickel she asks for. I'm not sure they couldn't get us for *criminal* libel. And then look at the other side of it. We've got an advertising budget of $100,000 a year. We describe ourselves as the friend of the widow and orphan. We spend all that for goodwill, and then what? We lay ourselves open to the charge that we'd accuse a woman of *murder* even, rather than pay a just claim."

"It's not a just claim."

"It will be, unless we prove different."

"All right. What you say is true. I told you it's against practice. But let me tell you this, Mr. Norton, and tell you right now: Whoever pulled this was no punk. He, or she, or maybe the both of them, or the three of them or however many it took—knew what they were doing. They're not going to be caught just by your sitting around hoping for clues. They thought of clues. There aren't any. The only way you're going to catch them is to move against *them*. I don't care if it's a battle or a murder case, or whatever it is, surprise is a weapon that *can* work. I don't say it will work. But I say it can work. And I say nothing else is going to work."

"But Keyes, we can't do things like that."

"Why not?"

"Keyes, we've been over that a million times, every insurance company has been over it a million times. We have our practice, and you can't beat it. These things are a matter for the police. We can help the police, if we've got something to help with. If we discover information, we can turn it over to them. If we have our suspicions,

we can communicate them to them. We can take any lawful, legiti-
mate step—but as for this—"

He stopped. Keyes waited, and he didn't finish.

"What's unlawful about this, Mr. Norton?"

"Nothing. It's lawful enough—but it's wrong. It puts us out in
the open. It leaves us with *no* defenses—in case we miss on it. I
never heard of a thing like that. It's—tactically wrong, that's what
I'm trying to say."

"But strategically right."

"We've got our strategy. We've got our ancient strategy, and you
can't beat it. Listen, it *can* be suicide. We can affirm our belief that
it's suicide, at the proper time, and we're safe. The burden of proof
is on her. That's what I'm trying to say. Believe me, on a keg of
dynamite like this, I don't want to get myself in the position where
the burden of proof is on us."

"You're not going to move against her?"

"Not yet, Keyes, not yet. Maybe later, I don't know. But so long
as we can do the conservative, safe thing, I don't get mixed up with
the other kind."

"Your father"

"Would have done the same thing. I'm thinking of him."

"He would not. Old Man Norton could take a chance."

"Well I'm not my father!"

"It's your responsibility."

I didn't go to the inquest, Norton didn't, and Keyes didn't. No
insurance company can afford to let a jury know, whether it's a coroner's jury or any other kind of jury, that a dead man is insured. It
just gets murdered if that comes out. Two investigators were sent
over, guys that look like everybody else and sit with the newspaper
men. We got what happened from them. They all identified the
body and told their story, Phyllis, the two conductors, the red-cap,
the porter, a couple of passengers, the police, and especially this guy
Jackson, that pounded it in that I tried to get rid of him. The jury
brought in a verdict "that the said Herbert S. Nirdlinger came to his
death by a broken neck received in a fall from a railroad train at or
about ten o'clock on the night of June 3 in a manner unknown to
this jury." It took Norton by surprise. He really hoped for a suicide
verdict. It didn't me. The most important person at that inquest
never said a word, and I had beat it into Phyllis's head long before

that he had to be there, because I had figured on this suicide stuff, and we had to be ready for it. That was the minister that she asked to come with her, to confer with the undertaker on arrangements for the funeral. Once a coroner's jury sees that it's a question of burial in consecrated ground, the guy could take poison, cut his throat, and jump off the end of a dock, and they would still give a verdict, "in a manner unknown to this jury."

After the investigators told their story, we sat around again, Norton, Keyes, and myself, in Norton's office this time. It was about five o'clock in the afternoon. Keyes was sore. Norton was disappointed, but still trying to make it look like he had done the right thing. "Well, Keyes, we're no worse off."

"You're no better off."

"Anyway, we haven't done anything foolish."

"What now?"

"Now? I follow practice. I wait her out. I deny liability, on the ground that accident is not proved, and I make her sue. When she sues, then we'll see what we see."

"You're sunk."

"I know I'm sunk, but that's what I'm going to do."

"What do you mean you know you're sunk?"

"Well, I've been talking to the police about this. I told them we suspect murder. They said they did too, at first, but they've given up that idea. They've gone into it. They've got their books too, Keyes. They know how people commit murder, and how they don't. They say they never heard of a case where murder was committed, or even attempted, by pushing a man off the rear end of a slow-moving train. They say the same thing about it you say. How could a murderer, assuming there was one, be sure the man would die? Suppose he only got hurt? Then where would they be? No, they assure me it's on the up-and-up. It's just one of those freak things, that's all."

"Did they cover everybody that was on that train? Did they find out whether there was a single one of them that was acquainted with this wife? Holy smoke, Mr. Norton, don't tell me they gave up without going into that part. *I tell you, there was somebody else on that train!*"

"They did better than that. They covered the observation car steward. He took a seat right by the door, to mark up his slips for the beginning of the trip, and he's certain nobody was out there with

Nirdlinger, because if anybody had passed him he would have had to move. He remembers Jackson going out there, about ten minutes before the train pulled out. He remembers the cripple going by. He remembers Jackson coming back. He remembers Jackson going out there again with the briefcase, and Jackson coming back, the second time. Jackson didn't report the disappearance right away. He just figured Nirdlinger went in a washroom or something, and as a matter of fact, it wasn't till midnight, when he wanted to go to bed and he still had the briefcase that he supposed had Nirdlinger's ticket in it, that he said anything to the conductor about it. Five minutes after that, at Santa Barbara, was where the Los Angeles yardmaster caught the conductor with a wire and he impounded Nirdlinger's baggage and began taking names. There was nobody out there. This guy fell off, that's all. We're sunk. It's on the up-and-up."

"If it's on the up-and-up, why don't you pay her?"

"Well wait a minute. That's what I think. That's what the police think. But there's still considerable evidence of suicide—"

"Not a scrap."

"Enough, Keyes, that I owe it to my stockholders to throw the thing into court, and let a jury decide. I may be wrong. The police may be wrong. Before that suit comes to trial, we may be able to turn up plenty. That's all I'm going to do. Let a jury decide, and if it decides we're liable, then I pay her, and do it cheerfully. But I can't just make her a present of the money."

"That's what you'll be doing, if you allege suicide."

"We'll see."

"Yeah, we'll see."

I walked back with Keyes to his office. He snapped on the lights. "He'll see. I've handled too many cases, Huff. When you've handled a million of them, you know, and you don't even know how you know. This is murder . . . So they covered the porter, did they. Nobody went out there. How do they know somebody didn't swing aboard from the outside? How do they know—"

He stopped, looked at me, and then he began to curse and rave like a maniac. "Didn't I tell him? Didn't I tell him to drive at her right from the start? Didn't I tell him to have her put under arrest, without waiting for this inquest? Didn't I tell him—"

"What do you mean, Keyes?" My heart was pounding, plenty.

"He was never on the train!"

He was yelling now, and pounding the desk. "He was never on the train at all! Somebody took his crutches and went on the train for him! Of course that guy had to get rid of Jackson! He couldn't be seen alive beyond the point where that body was to be put! And now we've got all those sworn identifications against us—"

"Those what?" I knew what he meant. Those identifications at the inquest were something I had figured on from the start, and that was why I took such care that nobody on that train got a good look at me. I figured the crutches, the foot, the glasses, the cigar, and imagination would be enough.

"At the inquest! How well did any of those witnesses see this man? Just a few seconds, in the dark, three or four days ago. Then the coroner lifts a sheet on a dead man, the widow says yes, that's him, and of course they all say the same thing. And now look at us! If Norton had thrown the gaff into her, all those identifications and everything else about it could have been challenged, the police would have waked up, and we might be somewhere. But now—! So he's going to let her sue! And just let him try, now, to break down those identifications. It'll be impossible. Any lawyer can crucify those witnesses if they change their story now. So that's being conservative! That's playing it safe! That's doing what the old man would have done! Why, Huff, Old Man Norton would have had a confession out of that woman by now. He'd have had a plea of guilty out of her, and already on her way to do a life stretch in Folsom. And now look at us. Just look at us. The very crux of the thing is over already, and we've lost it. We've lost it . . . Let me tell you something. If that guy keeps on trying to run this company, the company's sunk. You can't take many body blows like this and last. Holy smoke. Fifty thousand bucks, and all from dumbness. Just sheer, willful stupidity!"

The lights began to look funny in front of my eyes. He started up again, checking over how Nirdlinger got knocked off. He said this guy, whoever he was, had left his car at Burbank, and dropped off the train there. He said she met him there, and they drove down in separate cars, with the corpse in one of them, to the place where they put the body on the track. He figured it up that she would have time to get to Burbank, and then get back in time to buy a pint of ice cream at the drugstore at 10:20, when she showed up there. He even had that. He was all wrong on how it was done, but he was so near right it made my lips turn numb just to listen to him.

"Well, Keyes, what are you going to do?"

". . . All right, he wants to wait her out, make her sue—that suits me. He's going to cover the dead man, find out what he can about why he maybe committed suicide. That suits me. I'm going to cover *her*. Every move she makes, everything she does, I'm going to know about it. Sooner or later, Huff, that guy's got to show. They'll have to see each other. And as soon as I know who he is, then watch me. Sure, let her sue. And when she goes on the witness stand, believe me, Huff, Norton's going to eat it. He's going to eat every word he's said, and the police may do some eating too. Oh no. I'm not through yet."

He had me, and I knew it. If she sued, and lost her head on the witness stand, God knows what might happen. If she didn't sue, that would be still worse. Her not trying to collect on that policy, that would look so bad it might even pull the police in. I didn't dare call her up, because for all I knew even now her wires might be tapped. I did that night what I had done the other two nights, while I was waiting on the inquest. I got stinko, or tried to. I knocked off a quart of cognac, but it didn't have any effect. My legs felt funny, and my ears rang, but my eyes kept staring at the dark, and my mind kept pounding on it, what I was going to do. I didn't know. I couldn't sleep, I couldn't eat, I couldn't even get drunk.

It was the next night before Phyllis called. It was a little while after dinner, and the Filipino had just gone. I was even afraid to answer, but I knew I had to. "Walter?"

"Yes. First, where are you? Home?"

"I'm in a drugstore."

"Oh. O.K., then, go on."

"Lola's acting so funny I don't even want to use my own phone any more. I drove down to the boulevard."

"What's the matter with Lola?"

"Oh, just hysteria, I guess. It's been too much for her."

"Nothing else?"

"I don't think so."

"All right, shoot, and shoot quick. What's happened?"

"An awful lot. I've been afraid to call. I had to stay home until the funeral, and—"

"The funeral was today?"

"Yes. After the inquest."

"Go on."

"The next thing, tomorrow they open my husband's safe deposit box. The state has something to do with that. On account of the inheritance tax."

"That's right. The policy's in there?"

"Yes. I put it in there about a week ago."

"All right then, this is what you do. It'll be at your lawyer's office, is that it?"

"Yes."

"Then you go there. The state tax man will be there, under the law he has to be present. They'll find the policy, and you hand it to your lawyer. Instruct him to put your claim in. Everything waits until you do that."

"Put the claim in."

"That's right. Now wait a minute, Phyllis. Here's something you mustn't tell that lawyer—yet. They're not going to pay that claim."

"What!"

"They're not going to pay it."

"Don't they have to pay it?"

"They think it's—suicide—and they're going to make you sue, and put it in the hands of a jury, before they pay. Don't tell your lawyer that now, he'll find it out for himself later. He'll want to sue, and you let him. We'll have to pay him, but it's our only chance. Now Phyllis, one other thing."

"Yes."

"I can't see you."

"But I want to see you."

"We don't dare see each other. Suicide is what they hope for, but they're mighty suspicious all the way around. If you and I began seeing each other, they might tumble to the truth so fast it would make your blood run cold. They'll be on your trail, for what they can find out, and you simply must not communicate with me at all, unless it's imperative, and even then you must call me at home, and from a drugstore, never the same drugstore twice in succession. Do you get me?"

"My you sound scared."

"I am scared. Plenty. They know more than you'd think."

"Then it's really serious?"

"Maybe not, but we've got to be careful."

"Then maybe I'd better not sue."

"You've *got* to sue. If you don't sue, then we *are* sunk."

"Oh. Oh. Yes, I can see that."

"You sue. But be careful what you tell that lawyer."

"All right. Do you still love me?"

"You know I do."

"Do you think of me? All the time?"

"All the time."

"Is there anything else?"

"Not that I know of. Is that all with you?"

"I think so."

"You better hang up. Somebody might come in on me."

"You sound as though you want to get rid of me."

"Just common sense."

"All right. How long is this all going to take?"

"I don't know. Maybe quite some time."

"I'm dying to see you."

"Me too. But we've got to be careful."

"Well then—good-bye."

"Good-bye."

I hung up. I loved her like a rabbit loves a rattlesnake. That night I did something I hadn't done in years. I prayed.

Chapter 9

It was about a week after that that Nettie came into my private office quick and shut the door. "That Miss Nirdlinger to see you again Mr. Huff."

"Hold her a minute. I've got to make a call."

She went out. I made a call. I had to do something to get myself in hand. I called home, and asked the Filipino if there had been any calls. He said no. Then I buzzed Nettie to send her in.

She looked different from the last time I had seen her. Then, she looked like a kid. Now, she looked like a woman. Part of that may have been that she was in black, but anybody could see she had been through plenty. I felt like a heel, and yet it did something to me that this girl liked me. I shook hands with her, and sat her down, and asked her how her stepmother was, and she said she was all right, considering everything, and I said it was a terrible thing, and that it shocked me to hear of it. "And Mr. Sachetti?"

"I'd rather not talk about Mr. Sachetti."

"I thought you were friends."

"I'd rather not talk about him."

"I'm sorry."

She got up, looked out the window, then sat down again. "Mr. Huff, you did something for me once, or anyhow I felt it was for me—"

"It was."

"And since then I've always thought of you as a friend. That's why I've come to you. I want to talk to you—as a friend."

"Certainly."

"But only as a friend, Mr. Huff. Not as somebody—in the insurance business. Until I feel I know my own mind, it has to be in the strictest confidence. Is that understood, Mr. Huff?"

"It is."

"I'm forgetting something. I was to call you Walter."

"And I was to call you Lola."

"It's funny how easy I feel with you."

"Go ahead."

"It's about my father."

"Yes?"

"My father's death. I can't help feeling there was something back of it."

"I don't quite understand you, Lola. How do you mean, back of it?"

"I don't know what I mean."

"You were at the inquest?"

"Yes."

"One or two witnesses there, and several people later, to us, intimated that your father might have—killed himself. Is that what you mean?"

"No, Walter, it isn't."

"Then what?"

"I can't say. I can't make myself say it. And it's so awful. Because this isn't the first time I've had such thoughts. This isn't the first time I've been through this agony of suspicion that there might be something more than—what everybody else thinks."

"I still don't follow you."

"My mother."

"Yes."

"When she died. That's how I felt."

I waited. She swallowed two or three times, looked like she had decided not to say anything at all, then changed her mind again and started to talk.

"Walter, my mother had lung trouble. It was on account of that that we kept a little shack up at Lake Arrowhead. One weekend, in the middle of winter, my mother went up to that shack with her dearest friend. It was right in the middle of the winter sports, when everything was lively up there, and then she wired my father that she and this other woman had decided to stay on for a week. He didn't think anything of it, wired her a little money, and told her to stay as long as she wanted; he thought it would do her good. Wednesday of that week my mother caught pneumonia. Friday her condition became critical. Her friend walked twelve miles through snowdrifts, through the woods, to get a doctor—the shack isn't near the hotels. It's on the other side of the lake, a long way around. She got into the main hotel there so exhausted she had to be sent to a hospital. The doctor started out, and when he got there my mother was dying. She lived a half hour."

"Yes?"

"Do you know who that best friend was?"

I knew. I knew by the same old prickle that was going up my back and into my hair. "No."

"Phyllis."

". . . Well?"

"What were those two women doing in that shack, all that time, in the dead of the winter? Why didn't they go to the hotel, like everybody else? Why didn't my mother telephone, instead of wiring?"

"You mean it wasn't she that wired?"

"I don't know what I mean, except that it looked mighty funny. Why did Phyllis tramp all that distance to get a doctor? Why didn't she stop some place, and telephone? Or why didn't she put on her skates, and go across the lake, which she could have done in a half hour? She's a fine skater. Why did she take that three-hour trip? *Why didn't she go for a doctor sooner?*"

"But wait a minute. What did your mother say to the doctor when he—"

"Nothing. She was in high delirium, and besides he had her in oxygen five minutes after he got there."

"But wait a minute, Lola. After all, a doctor is a doctor, and if she *had* pneumonia—"

"A doctor is a doctor, but you don't know Phyllis. There's some things I could tell. In the first place, she's a nurse. She's one of the best nurses in the city of Los Angeles—that's how she met my mother, when my mother was having such a terrible fight to live. She's a nurse, and she specialized in pulmonary diseases. She would know the time of crisis, almost to a minute, as well as any doctor would. And she would know how to bring on pneumonia, too."

"What do you mean by that?"

"You think Phyllis wouldn't be capable of putting my mother out in the night, in that cold, and keeping her locked out until she was half frozen to death—you think Phyllis wouldn't do that? You think she's just the dear, sweet, gentle thing that she looks like? That's what my father thought. He thought it was wonderful, the way she trudged all that distance to save a life, and less than a year after that he married her. But I don't think so. You see—I know her. That's what I thought, the minute I heard it. And now—this."

"What do you want me to do?"

"Nothing—yet. Except listen to me."

"It's pretty serious, what you're saying. Or at any rate intimating. I suppose I know what you mean."

"That's what I mean. That's exactly what I mean."

"However, as I understand it, your mother wasn't *with* your father at the time."

"She wasn't with my mother either. At the time. But she had been."

"Will you let me think this over?"

"Please do."

"You're a little wrought up today."

"And I haven't told you all."

"What else?"

". . . I can't tell you. That, I can't make myself believe. And yet —never mind. Forgive me, Walter, for coming in here like this. But I'm so unhappy."

"Have you said anything to anybody about this?"

"No, nothing."

"I mean—about your mother? Before this last?"

"Not a word, ever, to anybody."

"I wouldn't if I were you. And especially not to—your step-mother."

"I'm not even living home now."

"No?"

"I've taken a little apartment. Down in Hollywood. I have a little income. From my mother's estate. Just a little. I moved out. I couldn't live with Phyllis any more."

"Oh."

"Can I come in again?"

"I'll let you know when to come. Give me your number."

·   ·   ·

I spent half the afternoon trying to make up my mind whether to tell Keyes. I knew I ought to tell him, for my own protection. It was nothing that would be worth a nickel as evidence in court, and for that matter it was nothing that any court would admit as evidence, because that's one break they give people, that they have to be tried for one thing at a time, and not for something somebody thinks they did two or three years before this happened. But it was something that would look mighty bad, if Keyes found out I knew it, and hadn't told him. I couldn't make myself do it. And I didn't have any better reason than that this girl had asked me not to tell anybody, and I had promised.

About four o'clock Keyes came in my office and shut the door.

"Well, Huff, he's showed."

"Who?"

"The guy in the Nirdlinger case."

"*What?*"

"He's a steady caller now. Five nights in one week."

". . . Who is he?"

"Never mind. But he's the one. Now watch me."

That night I came back in the office to work. As soon as Joe Pete made his eight o'clock round on my floor I went to Keyes's office. I tried his desk. It was locked. I tried his steel filing cabinets. They were locked. I tried all my keys. They didn't work. I was about to give it up when I noticed the dictation machine. He uses one of them. I took the cover off it. A record was still on. It was about three quarters filled. I made sure Joe Pete was downstairs, then came back, slipped the ear pieces on and started the record. First a lot of dumb stuff came out, letters to claimants, instructions to investigators on an arson case, notification of a clerk that he was fired. Then, all of a sudden, came this:

Memo. to Mr. Norton
Re. Agent Walter Huff
Confidential—file Nirdlinger

With regard to your proposal to put Agent Huff under surveillance for his connection with the Nirdlinger case, I disagree absolutely. Naturally, in this case as in all cases of its kind, the agent is automatically under suspicion, and I have not neglected to take necessary steps with regard to Huff. All his statements check closely with the facts and with our records, as well as with the dead man's records. I have even checked, without his knowledge, his whereabouts the night of the crime, and find he was at home all night. This in my opinion lets him out. A man of his experience can hardly fail to know if we attempt to watch his movements, and we should thus lose the chance of his cheerful cooperation on this case, which so far has been valuable, and may become imperative. I point out to you further, his record which has been exceptional in cases of fraud. I strongly recommend that this whole idea be dropped.

Respectfully

I lifted the needle and ran it over again. It did things to me. I don't only mean it was a relief. It made my heart feel funny.

But then, after some more routine stuff, came this:

Confidential—file Nirdlinger

SUMMARY—investigators' verbal reports for week ending June 17th:

Daughter Lola Nirdlinger moved out of home June 8, took up residence in two-room apartment, the Lycee Arms, Yucca Street. No surveillance deemed necessary.

Widow remained at home until June 8, when she took automobile ride, stopped at drugstore, made phone call, took ride two succeeding days, stopped markets and store selling women's gowns.

Night of June 11, man caller arrived at house 8:35, left 11:48. Description:—Tall, dark—age twenty-six or -seven. Calls repeated June 12, 13, 14, 16. Man followed night of first visit, identity ascertained as Beniamino Sachetti, Lilac Court Apartments, North La Brea Avenue.

I was afraid to have Lola come down to the office any more. But finding out they had no men assigned to her meant that I could take her out somewhere. I called her up and asked her if she would go with me to dinner. She said she would like it more than anything she could think of. I took her down to the Miramar at Santa Monica. I said it would be nice to eat where we could see the ocean, but the real reason was I didn't want to take her to any place downtown, where I might run into somebody I knew.

We talked along during dinner about where she went to school, and why she didn't go to college, and a whole lot of stuff. It was kind of feverish, because we were both under a strain, but we got along all right. It was like she said. We both felt easy around each other somehow. I didn't say anything about what she had told me, last time, until we got in the car after dinner and started up the ocean for a ride. Then I brought it up myself.

"I thought over what you told me."

"Can I say something?"

"Go ahead."

"I've had it out with myself about that. I've thought it all over, and come to the conclusion I was wrong. It's very easy when you love somebody terribly, and then suddenly they're gone from you, to think it's somebody's fault. Especially when it's somebody you don't like. I don't like Phyllis. I guess it's partly jealousy. I was devoted to my mother. I was almost as devoted to my father. And then when he married Phyllis—I don't know, it seemed as though something had happened that couldn't happen. And then—these thoughts. What I felt instinctively when my mother died became a dead certainty when my father married Phyllis. I thought that showed why she did it. And it became a double certainty when this happened. But I haven't a thing to go on, have I? It's been terribly hard to make myself realize that, but I have. I've given up the whole idea, and I wish you'd forget that I ever told you."

"I'm glad, in a way."

"I guess you think I'm terrible."

"I thought it over. I thought it over carefully, and all the more carefully because it would be most important for my company if they knew it. But there's nothing to go on. It's only a suspicion. That's all you have to tell."

"I told you. I haven't even got that any more."

"What you would tell the police, if you told them anything, is already a matter of public record. Your mother's death, your father's death—you haven't anything to add to what they already know. Why tell them?"

"Yes, I know."

"If I were you, I would do nothing."

"You agree with me then? That I haven't anything to go on?"

"I do."

That ended that. But I had to find out about this Sachetti, and find out without her knowing I was trying to find out.

"Tell me something. What happened between you and Sachetti?"

"I told you. I don't want to talk about him."

"How did you come to meet him?"

"Through Phyllis."

"Through—?"

"His father was a doctor. I think I told you she used to be a nurse. He called on her, about joining some association that was being formed. But then when he got interested in me, he wouldn't come to the house. And then, when Phyllis found out I was meeting him, she told my father the most awful stories about him. I was supposed not to meet him, but I did. There was something back of it, I knew that. But I never found out what it was, until—"

"Go on. Until what?"

"I don't want to go on. I told you I gave up any idea that there might be something—"

"Until what?"

"Until my father died. And then, quite suddenly, he didn't seem interested in me any more. He—"

"Yes?"

"He's going with Phyllis."

"And—?"

"Can't you see what I thought? Do you have to make me say it? . . . I thought maybe they did it. I thought his going with me was just a blind for—something, I didn't know what. Seeing her, maybe. In case they got caught."

"I thought he was with you—that night."

"He was supposed to be. There was a dance over at the university, and I went over. I was to meet him there. But he got sick, and sent word he couldn't come. I got on a bus and went to a picture show. I never told anybody that."

"What do you mean, sick?"

"He did have a cold, I know that. A dreadful cold. But—please don't make me talk any more about it. I've tried to put it out of my mind. I'm getting so I can believe it isn't true. If he wants to see Phyllis, it's none of my business. I mind. I wouldn't be telling the truth if I said I didn't mind. But—it's his privilege. Just because he does that is no reason for me to—think this of him. That wouldn't be right."

"We won't talk about it any more."

I stared into the darkness some more that night. I had killed a man, for money and a woman. I didn't have the money and I didn't have the woman. The woman was a killer, out-and-out, and she had made a fool of me. She had used me for a cat's paw so she could have another man, and she had enough on me to hang me higher than a kite. If the man was in on it, there were two of them that could hang me. I got to laughing, a hysterical cackle, there in the dark. I thought about Lola, how sweet she was, and the awful thing I had done to her. I began subtracting her age from my age. She was nineteen, I'm thirty-four. That made a difference of fifteen years. Then I got to thinking that if she was nearly twenty, that would make a difference of only fourteen years. All of a sudden I sat up and turned on the light. I knew what that meant.

I was in love with her.

Chapter 10

RIGHT ON TOP OF THAT, Phyllis filed her claim. Keyes denied liability, on the ground that accident hadn't been proved. Then she filed suit, through the regular lawyer that had always handled her husband's business. She called me about half a dozen times, always from a drugstore, and I told her what to do. I had got so I felt sick the minute I heard her voice, but I couldn't take any chances. I told her to be ready, that they would try to prove something besides suicide. I didn't give her all of it, what they were thinking and what they were doing, but I let her know that murder was one of the things they would cover anyway, so she had better be ready for it when she went on the stand. It didn't feaze her any. She seemed to have almost forgotten that there was a murder, and acted like the company was playing her some kind of a dirty trick in not paying her right away. That suited me fine. It was a funny sidelight on human nature, and especially on a woman's nature, but it was just exactly the frame of mind I would want her in to face a lot of corporation lawyers. If she stuck to her story, even with all Keyes might have been able to dig up on her, I still didn't see how she could miss.

That all took about a month, and the suit was to come up for trial in the early fall. All during that month, three or four nights a week, I was seeing Lola. I would call for her, at the little apartment house where she was living, and we would go to dinner, and then for a drive. She had got a little car, but we generally went in mine. I had gone completely nuts about her. Having it hanging over me all the time, what I had done to her, and how awful it would be if she ever found out, that had something to do with it, but it wasn't all. There was something so sweet about her, and we got along so nice, I mean we felt so happy when we were together. Anyway I did. She did too, I knew that. But then one night something happened. We were parked on the ocean road, about three miles above Santa Monica. They have places where you can park and sit and look. We were sitting there, watching the moon come up over the ocean. That sounds funny, don't it, that you can watch the moon come up over the Pacific Ocean? You can, just the same. The coast here runs almost due east and west, and when the moon comes up, off to your left, it's pretty as a picture. As soon as it lifted out of the sea, she slipped her hand into mine. I took it, but she took it away, quick.

"I mustn't do that."

"Why not?"

"Lots of reasons. It's not fair to you, for one."

"Did you hear me squawk?"

"You do like me, don't you?"

"I'm crazy about you."

"I'm pretty crazy about you too, Walter. I don't know what I'd have done without you these last few weeks. Only—"

"Only what?"

"Are you sure you want to hear? It may hurt you."

"Better hear it than guess at it."

"It's about Nino."

"Yes?"

"I guess he still means a lot to me."

"Have you seen him?"

"No."

"You'll get over it. Let me be your doctor. I'll guarantee a cure. Just give me a little time, and I'll promise to have you all right."

"You're a nice doctor. Only—"

"Another 'only'?"

"I *did* see him."

"Oh."

"No, I was telling the truth just now. I haven't talked with him. He doesn't know I've seen him. Only—"

"You sure have a lot of 'only's.'"

"Walter—"

She was getting more and more excited, and trying not to let me see it.

"—He didn't do it!"

"No?"

"This is going to hurt you terribly, Walter. I can't help it. You may as well know the truth. I followed them last night. Oh, I've followed them a lot of times, I've been insane. Last night, though, was the first time I ever got a chance to hear what they were saying. They went up to the Lookout and parked, and I parked down below, and crept up behind them. Oh, it was horrible enough. He told her he had been in love with her from the first, but felt it was hopeless—until this happened. But that wasn't all. They talked about money. He's spent all of that you let him have, and still he hasn't got his degree. He paid for his dissertation, but the rest he spent on her. And he was talking about where he'd get more. Listen, Walter—"

"Yes?"

"If they had done this together, she'd have to let him have money, wouldn't she?"

"Looks like it."

"They never even mentioned anything about her letting him have money. My heart began to beat when I realized what that meant. And then they talked some more. They were there about an hour. They talked about lots of things, and I could tell, from what they said, that he wasn't in on it, and didn't know anything about it. I could tell! Walter, do you realize what that means? *He didn't do it!*"

She was so excited her fingers felt like steel, where they were clutched around my arm. I couldn't follow her. I could see that she meant something, something a whole lot more important than that Sachetti was innocent.

"I don't quite get it, Lola. I thought you had given up the idea that *anybody* was in on it."

"I'll never give it up! . . . Yes, I did give it up, or try to. But that was only because I thought if there was something like that, *he* must have been in on it, and that would have been too terrible. If he had anything to do with it, I knew it couldn't be that. I *had* to know it, to believe it. But now—oh no, Walter, I haven't given it up. She did it, somehow. I know it. And now, I'll get her. I'll get her for it, if it's the last thing I do."

"How?"

"She's suing your company, isn't she? She even has the nerve to do that. All right. You tell your company not to worry. I'll come and sit right alongside of you, Walter. I'll tell them what to ask her. I'll tell them—"

"Wait a minute, Lola, wait a minute—"

"I'll tell them everything they need to know. I told you there was plenty more, besides what I told you. I'll tell them to ask her about the time I came in on her, in her bedroom, with some kind of foolish red silk thing on her, that looked like a shroud or something, with her face all smeared up with white powder and red lipstick, with a dagger in her hand, making faces at herself in front of a mirror—oh yes, I'll tell them to ask her about that. I'll tell them to ask her why she was down in a boulevard store, a week before my father died, pricing black dresses. That's something she doesn't know I know. I went in there about five minutes after she left. The saleslady was just putting the frocks away. She was telling me what lovely numbers they were, only she couldn't understand why Mrs. Nirdlinger would be considering them, because they were really mourning. That was one reason I wanted my father to take that trip, so I could get him out of the house and find out what she was up to. I'll tell them—"

"But wait a minute, Lola. You can't do that. Why—they can't ask her such things as that—"

"If they can't, I can! I'll stand right up in court and yell them at her. I'll be heard! No judge, no policeman, or *anybody*—can stop me. I'll force it out of her if I have to go up there and choke it out of her. *I'll make her tell! I'll not be stopped!*"

Chapter 11

I DON'T KNOW WHEN I decided to kill Phyllis. It seemed to me that ever since that night, somewhere in the back of my head I had known I would have to kill her, for what she knew about me, and because the world isn't big enough for two people once they've got something like that on each other. But I know when I decided *when* to kill her, and *where* to kill her and *how* to kill her. It was right after that night when I was watching the moon come up over the ocean with Lola. Because the idea that Lola would put on an act like that in the courtroom, and that then Phyllis would lash out and tell her the truth, that was too horrible for me to think about. Maybe I haven't explained it right, yet, how I felt about this girl Lola. It wasn't anything like what I had felt for Phyllis. That was some kind of unhealthy excitement that came over me just at the sight of her. This wasn't anything like that. It was just a sweet peace that came over me as soon as I was with her, like when we would drive along for an hour without saying a word, and then she would look up at me and we still didn't have to say anything. I hated what I had done, and it kept sweeping over me that if there was any way I could make sure she would never find out, why then maybe I could marry her, and forget the whole thing, and be happy with her the rest of my life. There was only one way I could be sure, and that was to get rid of anybody that knew. What she told me about Sachetti showed there was only one I had to get rid of, and that was Phyllis. And the rest of what she told me, about what she was going to do, meant I had to move quick, before that suit came to trial.

I wasn't going to leave it so Sachetti could come back and take her away from me, though. I was going to do it so he would be put in a spot. Police are hard to fool, but Lola would never be quite sure he hadn't done it. And of course if he did one, so far as she was concerned he probably did the other.

My next day at the finance company, I put through a lot of routine stuff, sent the file clerk out on an errand, and took out the folder on Sachetti. I slipped it in my desk. In that folder was a key to his car. In our finance company, just to avoid trouble in case of a repossess, we make every borrower deposit the key to his car along with the other papers on his loan, and of course Sachetti had had to do the same. That was back in the winter when he took out the loan on his car. I slipped the key out of its envelope, and when I went out to lunch I had a duplicate made. When I got back I sent the file clerk on another errand, put the original key back in its envelope, and returned the folder to the file. That was what I wanted. I had the key to his car, and nobody there even knew I had the folder out of the file.

Next I had to get hold of Phyllis, but I didn't dare ring her. I had to wait till she called. I sat around the house three nights, and the fourth night the phone rang.

"Phyllis, I've got to see you."

"It's about time."

"You know the reason I haven't. Now get this. We've got to meet, to go over things in connection with this suit—and after that, I don't think we have anything to fear."

"Can we meet? I thought you said—"

"That's right. They've been watching you. But I found out something today. They've cut down the detail assigned to you to one shift, and he goes off at eleven."

"What's that?"

"They did have three men assigned to you, in shifts, but they weren't finding out very much, so they thought they'd cut down the expense, and now they've only got one. He goes on in the afternoon, and goes off at eleven o'clock, unless there's something to hold him. We'll have to meet after that."

"All right. Then come up to the house—"

"Oh no, we can't take a chance like that. But we can meet. Tomorrow night, around midnight, you sneak out. Take the car and sneak out. If anybody drops in the evening, get rid of them well before eleven o'clock. Get rid of them, turn out all lights, have the place looking like you had gone to bed well before this man goes off. So he'll have no suspicions whatever."

The reason for that was that if Sachetti was going to be with her the next night, I wanted him to be well out of there and home in bed, long before I was to meet her. I had to have his car, and I didn't want the connections to be so close I had to wait. The rest of it was all hooey, about the one shift I mean. I wanted her to think she could meet me safely. As to whether they had one shift on her, or three, or six, I didn't know and I didn't care. If somebody followed her, so much the better, for what I had to do. They'd have to move fast to catch me, and if they saw her deliberately knocked off, why that would be just that much more Mr. Sachetti would have to explain when they caught up with him.

"Lights out by eleven."

"Lights out, the cat out, and the place locked up."

"All right, where do I meet you?"

"Meet me in Griffith Park, a couple of hundred yards up Riverside from Los Feliz. I'll be parked there, and we'll take a ride, and talk it over. Don't park on Los Feliz. Park in among the trees, in the little glade near the bridge. Park where I can see you, and walk over."

"In between the two streets?"

"That's it. Make it twelve-thirty sharp. I'll be a minute or two ahead of time, so you can hop right in and you won't have to wait."

"Twelve-thirty, two hundred yards up Riverside."

"That's right. Close your garage door when you come out, so anybody passing won't notice the car's out."

"I'll be there, Walter."

"Oh, and one other thing. I traded my car in since I saw you. I've got another one." I told her the make. "It's a small dark-blue coupe. You can't miss it."

"A blue coupe?"

"Yes."

"That's funny."

I knew why it was funny. She'd been riding around in a blue coupe for the last month, the same one if she only knew it, but I didn't tumble. "Yeah, I guess it's funny at that, me driving around in that oil can, but the big car was costing too much. I had a chance for a deal on this one, so I took it."

"It's the funniest thing I ever heard."

"Why?"

"Oh—nothing. Tomorrow night at twelve-thirty."

"Twelve-thirty."

"I'm just dying to see you."

"Same here."

"Well—I had something to talk to you about, but I'll let it wait till tomorrow. Good-bye."

"Good-bye."

When she hung up I got the paper and checked the shows in town. There was a downtown theater that had a midnight show, and the bill was to hold over the whole week. That was what I wanted. I drove down there. It was about ten-thirty when I got in, and I sat in the balcony, so I wouldn't be seen by the downstairs ushers. I watched the show close, and paid attention to the gags, because it was to be part of my alibi next night that I had been there. In the last sequence of the feature I saw an actor I knew. He played the part of a waiter, and I had once sold him a hunk of life insurance, $7,000 for an endowment policy, all paid up when he bought it. His name was Jack Christolf. That helped me. I stayed till the show was out, and looked at my watch. It was 12:48.

Next day around lunch time I called up Jack Christolf. They said he was at the studio and I caught him there. "I hear you knocked them for a loop in this new one, 'Gun Play.' "

"I didn't do bad. Did you see it?"

"No, I want to catch it. Where's it playing?"

He named five theaters. He knew them all. "I'm going to drop in on it the very first chance I get. Well say old man, how about another little piece of life insurance? Something to do with all this dough you're making."

"I don't know. I don't know. To tell you the truth, I might be interested. Yes, I might."

"When can I see you?"

"Well, I'm busy this week. I don't finish up here till Friday, and I thought I would go away for a rest over the weekend. But next week, any time."

"How about at night?"

"Well, we might do that."

"How about tomorrow night?"

"I tell you. Ring me home tomorrow night, around dinner time, some time around seven o'clock. I'll let you know then. If I can make it, I'll be glad to see you."

That would be why I went to that particular picture tonight, that I had to talk to this actor tomorrow night, and I wanted to see his picture, so I could talk about it and make him feel good.

About four o'clock I drove up through Griffith Park, and checked it over close, what I was going to do. I picked a spot for my car, and a spot for Sachetti's car. They weren't far apart, but the spot for my car was close to one end of the bridle path, where they ride horses in the daytime. It winds all over the hills there, but right above this place it comes out on the automobile road up above. I mean, up high in the hills. This park, they call it a park, but it's really a scenic drive, up high above Hollywood and the San Fernando Valley, for people in cars, and a hilly ride for people on horses. People on foot don't go there much. What I was going to do was let her get in and then start up the hill. When I came to one of those platforms where the road is graded to a little flat place so people can park and look over the valley, I was going to pull in, and say something about parking there, so we could talk. Only I wasn't going to park. The car was accidentally on purpose, going to roll over the edge, and I was going to jump. As soon as I jumped I was going to dive into the bridle path, race on down to my car, and drive home. From where I was going to park Sachetti's car to where I was going to run her over the edge was about two miles, by road. But by bridle path it was only a hundred yards, on account of the road winding all through the hills for an easy grade, and the bridle path being almost straight up and down. Less than a minute after the crash, before even a crowd could get there, I would be away and gone.

I drove up the hill and picked the place. It was one of the little lookouts, with room for just one or two cars, not one of the big ones. The big ones have stone parapets around them. This one didn't have any. I got out and looked down. There was a drop of at least two hundred feet, straight, and probably another hundred feet after that where the car would roll after it struck. I practiced what I was going to do. I ran up to the edge, threw the gear in neutral, and pushed open the door. I made a note I would only half close my door when she got in, so I could open it quick. There was a chance she would grab the emergency as the car went over and save herself, and then have the drop on me. There was a chance I wouldn't jump clear, and that I would go over the edge with her. That was O.K. On this, you have to take a chance. I ate dinner alone, at a big downtown seafood house. The waiter knew me. I made a gag with him, to fix it on his mind it was Friday. When I finished I went back to the office and told Joe Pete I had to work. I stayed till ten o'clock. He was down at his desk, reading a detective story magazine when I went out.

"You're working late, Mr. Huff."

"Yeah, and I'm not done yet."

"Working home?"

"No, I got to see a picture. There's a ham by the name of Jack Christolf I've got to talk to tomorrow night, and I've got to see his picture. He might not like it if I didn't. No time for it tomorrow. I've got to catch it tonight."

"They sure do love theirself, them actors."

I parked near the theater, loafed around, and around eleven o'clock I went in. I bought a downstairs seat this time. I took a program and put it in my pocket. I checked, it had the date on it. I still had to talk with an usher, fix it on her mind what day it was, and pull something so she would remember me. I picked the one on the door, not the one in the aisle inside. I wanted enough light so that she could see me well.

"Is the feature on?"

"No sir, it's just finished. It goes on again at 11:20."

I knew that. That was why I had gone in at 11 o'clock instead of sooner. "Holy smoke, that's a long time to wait . . . Is Christolf in all of it?"

"I think only in the last part, sir."

"You mean I've got to wait till one o'clock in the morning to see that ham?"

"It'll be on tomorrow night too, sir, if you don't care to wait so long tonight. They'll refund your money at the box office for you."

"Tomorrow night? Let's see, tomorrow's Saturday, isn't it?"

"Yes sir."

"Nope, can't make it. Got to see it tonight."

I had that much of it. Next I had to pull something so she would remember me. It was a hot night, and she had the top button of her uniform unbuttoned. I reached up there, and buttoned it, quick. I took her by surprise.

"You ought to be more careful."

"Listen, big boy, do I have to drip sweat off the end of my nose, just to please you?"

She unbuttoned it again. I figured she would remember it. I went in.

As soon as the aisle usher showed me a seat, I moved once, to the other side of the house. I sat there a minute, and then I slipped out, through a side exit. Later, I would say I stayed for the end of the show. I had my talk with Christolf, for a reason for being there late. I had my talk with Joe Pete, and his log would prove what day it was. I had the usher. I couldn't prove I was there clear to the end, but no alibi ought to be perfect. This was as good a one as most juries hear, and a whole lot better than most. As far as I could go with it, it certainly didn't sound like a man that was up to murder.·

I got in the car and drove straight to Griffith Park. That time of night I could make time. When I got there I looked at my watch. It was 11:24. I parked, cut the motor, took the key and turned off the lights. I walked over to Los Feliz, and from there down to Hollywood Boulevard. It's about half a mile. I legged it right along, and got to the boulevard at 11:35. I boarded a street car and took a seat up front. When we got to La Brea it was five minutes to twelve. So far, my timing was perfect.

I got off the car and walked down to the Lilac Court Apartments, where Sachetti lived. It's one of those court places where they have a double row of bungalows off a center lane, one-room shacks mostly that rent for about $3 a week. I went in the front. I didn't want to come up to the park from outside where I would look like a snooper if anybody saw me. I walked right in the front, and down past his bungalow. I knew the number. It was No. 11. There was a light inside. That was O.K. That was just like I wanted it.

I marched straight through, back to the auto court in the rear, where the people that live there keep their cars. Anyway, those of them that have cars. There was a collection of second-, third-, fourth-, and ninth-hand wrecks out there, and sure enough right in the middle was his. I got in, shoved the key in the ignition and started it. I cut on the lights and started to back. A car pulled in from the outside. I turned my head so I couldn't be seen in the headlights, and backed on out. I drove up to Hollywood Boulevard. It was exactly twelve o'clock. I checked his gas. He had plenty.

I took it easy, but still it was only 12:18 when I got back to Griffith Park. I drove up into Glendale, because I didn't want to be more than two or three minutes ahead of time. I thought about Sachetti and how he was going to make out with his alibi. He didn't have one, because that's the worst alibi in the world to be home in bed, unless you've got some way to prove it, with phone calls or something. He didn't have any way to prove it. He didn't even have a phone.

Just past the railroad tracks I turned, came on back, went up Riverside a little way, turned facing Los Feliz, and parked. I cut the motor and the lights. It was exactly 12:27. I turned around and looked, and saw my own car, about a hundred yards back of me. I looked into the little glade. No car was parked there. She hadn't come.

I held my watch in my hand. The hand crept around to 12:30. Still she hadn't come. I put my watch back in my pocket. A twig cracked—off in the bushes. I jumped. Then I wound down the window on the right hand side of the car, and sat there looking off in the bushes to see what it was. I must have stared out there at least a minute. Another twig cracked, closer this time. Then there was a flash, and something hit me in the chest like Jack Dempsey had hauled off and given me all he had. There was a shot. I knew then what had happened to me. I wasn't the only one that figured the world wasn't big enough for two people, when they knew that about each other. I had come there to kill her, but she had beaten me to it.

I fell back on the seat, and I heard footsteps running away. There I was, with a bullet through my chest, in a stolen car, and the owner of the car the very man that Keyes had been tailing for the last month and a half. I pulled myself up by the wheel. I reached up for the key, then remembered I had to leave it in there. I opened the door. I could feel the sweat start out on my head from what it took out of me to turn the handle. I got out, somehow. I began staggering up the road to my car. I couldn't walk straight. I wanted to sit down, to ease that awful weight on my chest, but I knew if I did that I'd never get there. I remembered I had to get the car key ready, and took it out of my pocket. I got there and climbed in. I shoved the key in and pulled the starter. That was the last I knew *that* night.

Chapter 12

I DON'T KNOW IF YOU'VE ever been under ether. You come
out of it a little bit at a time. First a kind of a gray light shines
on one part of your mind, just a dim gray light, and then it gets
bigger, but slow. All the time it's getting bigger you're trying to gag
the stuff out of your lungs. It sounds like an awful groan, like you
were in pain or something, but that's not it. You try to gag it out of
your lungs, and you make those sounds to try and force it out. But
away inside somewhere your head is working all the time. You know
where you're at, and even if all kind of cock-eyed ideas do swim
through that gray light, the main part of you is there, and you can
think, maybe not so good, but a little bit.

It seemed to me I had been thinking, even before I began to come
to. I knew there must be somebody with me there, but I didn't
know who it was. I could hear them talking, but it wouldn't quite
reach me what they were saying. Then I could hear it. It was a
woman, telling me to open my mouth for a little ice, that would
make me feel better. I opened my mouth. I got the ice. I figured the
woman must be a nurse. Still I didn't know who else was there. I
thought a long time, then figured it out I would open my eyes just a
little bit and close them quick, and see who was in the room. I did
that. At first I couldn't see anything. It was a hospital room, and
there was a table pushed up near the bed, with a lot of stuff on it. It
was broad daylight. Over my chest the covers were piled high, so
that meant a lot of bandages. I opened my eyes a little bit further
and peeped around. The nurse was sitting beside the table watching

me. But over back of her was somebody. I had to wait till she moved to see who it was, but I knew anyway even without seeing.

It was Keyes.

It must have been an hour that I lay there after that, and never opened my eyes at all. I was all there in the head by that time. I tried to think. I couldn't. Every time I tried to gag more ether out, there would come this stab of pain in my chest. That was from the bullet. I quit trying to gag out the ether then and the nurse began talking to me. She knew. Pretty soon I had to answer her. Keyes walked over.

"Well, that theater program saved you."

"Yeah?"

"That double wad of paper wasn't much, but it was enough. You'll bleed a little bit for a while where that bullet grazed your lung, but you're lucky it wasn't your heart. Another eighth of an inch, and it would have been curtains for you."

"They get the bullet?"

"Yeah."

"They get the woman?"

"Yeah."

I didn't say anything. I thought it was curtains for me anyway, but I just lay there. "They got her, and I got plenty to tell you boy. This thing is a honey. But give me a half hour. I got to go out and get some breakfast. Maybe you'll be feeling better then yourself."

He went. He didn't act like I was in any trouble, or he was sore at me, or anything like that. I couldn't figure it out. In a couple of minutes an orderly came in. "You got any papers in this hospital?"

"Yes sir, I think I can get you one."

He came back with a paper and found it for me. He knew what I wanted. It wasn't on Page 1. It was in the second section where they print the local news that's not quite hot enough to go on the front page. This was it:

MYSTERY SHROUDS
GRIFFITH PARK
SHOOTING
Two Held After Walter Huff, Insurance Man, Is Found
Wounded at Wheel of Car on Riverside
Drive After Midnight

Police are investigating the circumstances surrounding the shooting of Walter Huff, an insurance man living in the Los Feliz Hills, who was found unconscious at the wheel of his car in Griffith Park shortly after midnight last night, a bullet wound in his chest. Two persons were held pending a report on Huff's condition today. They are:

Lola Nirdlinger, 19.

Beniamino Sachetti, 26.

Miss Nirdlinger gave her address as the Lycee Arms Apartments, Yucca Street, and Sachetti as the Lilac Court Apartments, La Brea Avenue.

Huff apparently was shot as he was driving along Riverside Drive from the direction of Burbank. Police arriving at the scene shortly afterward found Miss Nirdlinger and Sachetti at the car trying to get him out. A short distance away was a pistol with one chamber discharged. Both denied responsibility for the shooting, but refused to make any further statement.

They brought me orange juice and I lay there trying to figure that out. You think I fell for it, do you? That I thought Lola had shot me, or Sachetti maybe, out of jealousy, something like that? I did not. I knew who shot me. I knew who I had a date with, who knew I was going to be there, who wanted me out of the way. Nothing could change me on that. But what were these two doing there? I pounded on it awhile, and I couldn't make any sense out of it, except a little piece of it. Of course Lola was following Sachetti again that night, or thought she was. That explained what she was doing there. But what was he doing there? None of it made sense. And all the while I kept having this numb feeling that I was sunk, and not only sunk for what I had done, but for what Lola was going to find out. That was the worst.

It was almost noon before Keyes came back. He saw the paper. He pulled up a chair near the bed. "I've been down to the office."

"Yeah?"

"It's been a wild morning. A wild morning on top of a wild night."

"What's going on?"

"Now I'll tell you something you don't know. This Sachetti, Huff, this same Sachetti that plugged you last night, is the same man we've been tailing for what he might know about that other thing. That Nirdlinger case."

"You don't mean it."

"I do mean it. I started to tell you, you remember, but Norton got these ideas about keeping all that stuff confidential from agents, so I didn't. That's it. The same man, Huff. Did I tell you? Did I tell Norton? Did I say there was something funny about that case?"

"What else?"

"Plenty. Your finance company called up."

"Yeah?"

"They popped out with what we'd have known in the first place, I mean me and Norton, if we had taken you into our confidence completely from the beginning. If you had known about this Sachetti, you could have told us what we just found out today, and it's the key to the whole case."

"He got a loan."

"That's right. He got a loan. But that's not it. That's not the important thing. *He was in your office the day you delivered that policy to Nirdlinger.*"

"I couldn't be certain."

"We are. We checked it all up, with Nettie, with the finance company records, with the records in the policy department. He was in there, and the girl was in there, and that's what we've been waiting for. That gives it to us, the hook-up we never had before."

"What do you mean, hook-up?"

"Listen, we know Nirdlinger never told his family about this policy. We know that from a check we've made with the secretary. He never told anybody. Just the same the family *knew* about it, didn't they?"

"Well—I don't know."

"They knew. They didn't put him on the spot for nothing. They knew, and now we know *how* they knew. This ties it up."

"Any court would assume they knew."

"I'm not a court. I'm talking about for my own satisfaction, for my own knowledge that I'm right. Because look, Huff, I might demand an investigation on the basis of what my instinct tells me. But I don't go into a courtroom and go to bat with it without knowing. And now I know. What's more, this ties the girl in."

"The—who?"

"The girl. The daughter. She was there, too. In your office, I mean. Oh yeah, you may think it funny, that a girl would pull something like that on her own father. But it's happened. It's happened plenty of times. For fifty thousand bucks it's going to happen plenty of times again."

"I—don't believe that."

"You will, before I get done. Now listen Huff. I'm still shy something. I'm shy one link. They put you on the spot for something you could testify to when this suit comes up, I can see that. But what?"

"What do you mean, what?"

"What is it you know about them they would knock you off for? Their being in your office, that's not enough. There must be something else. Now what is it?"

"I—don't know. I can't think of anything."

"There's something. Maybe it's something you've forgotten about, something that doesn't mean anything to you but is important to them. Now what is it?"

"There's nothing. There *can't* be."

"There's something. There must be."

He was walking around now. I could feel the bed shake from his weight. "Keep it on your mind, Huff. We've got a few days. Try to think what it is."

He lit a cigarette, and pounded around some more. "That's the beauty of this, we've got a few days. You can't appear at a hearing until next week at the earliest, and that gives us what we need. A little help from the cops, a few treatments with the rubber hose, something like that, and sooner or later this pair is going to spill it. Especially that girl. She'll crack before long . . . Believe me this is what we've been waiting for. It's tough on you, but now we've got them where we can really throw the works into them. Oh yeah, this is a real break. We'll clean this case up now. Before night, with luck."

I closed my eyes. I couldn't think of anything but Lola, a lot of cops around her, maybe beating her up, trying to make her spill something that she knew no more about than the man in the moon. Her face jumped in front of me and all of a sudden something hit it in the mouth, and it started to bleed.

"Keyes."

"Yeah?"

"There was something. Now you speak of it."

"I'm listening boy."

"I killed Nirdlinger."

Chapter 13

H E SAT THERE STARING at me. I had told him everything he needed to know, even about Lola. It seemed funny it had only taken about ten minutes. Then he got up. I grabbed him.

"Keyes."

"I've got to go, Huff."

"See that they don't beat her."

"I've got to go now. I'll be back after a while."

"Keyes, if you let them beat her, I'll—kill you. You've got it all now. I've told you, and I've told you for one reason and one reason only. It's so they won't beat her. You've got to promise me that. You owe me that much. Keyes—"

He shook my hand off and left.

While I was telling him I hoped for some kind of peace when I got done. It had been bottled up in me a long time. I had been sleeping with it, dreaming about it, breathing with it. I didn't get any peace. The only thing I could think of was Lola, and how she was going to find out about it at last, and know me for what I was.

About three o'clock the orderly came in with the afternoon papers. They didn't have any of what I had told Keyes. But they had been digging into their files, after the morning story, and they had it about the first Mrs. Nirdlinger's death, and Nirdlinger's death, and now me being shot. A woman feature writer had got in out there and talked with Phyllis. It was she that called it the House of Death, and put in about those blood-red drapes. Once I saw that stuff I knew it wouldn't be long. That meant even a dumb cluck of a woman reporter could see there was something funny out there.

It was half past eight that night before Keyes came back. He shooed out the nurse as soon as he came in the room, and then went out a minute. When he came back he had Norton with him, and a man named Keswick that was a corporation lawyer they called in on big cases, and Shapiro, the regular head of the legal department. They all stood around, and it was Norton that started to speak. "Huff."

"Yes sir."

"Have you told anybody about this?"

"Nobody but Keyes."

"Nobody else?"

"Not a soul . . . God, no."

"There have been no policemen here?"

"They've been here. I saw them out in the hall. I guess it was me they were whispering about. The nurse wouldn't let them in."

They all looked at each other. "Then I guess we can begin. Keyes, perhaps you had better explain it to him."

Keyes opened his mouth to say something, but Keswick shut him up, and got Norton into a corner. Then they called Keyes over. Then they called Shapiro. I could catch a word, now and then. It was some kind of a proposition they were going to make to me, and it was a question of whether they were all going to be witnesses. Keswick was for the proposition, but he didn't want anybody to be able to say he had been in on it. They finally settled it that Keyes would make it on his own personal responsibility, and the rest of them wouldn't be there. Then they all tiptoed out. They didn't even say good-bye. It was funny. They didn't act like I had played them or the company any particularly dirty trick. They acted like I was some kind of an animal that had an awful sore on his face, and they didn't even want to look at it.

After they left Keyes sat down. "This is an awful thing you've done, Huff."

"I know it."

"I guess there's no need my saying more about that part."

"No, no need."

"I'm sorry. I've—kind of liked you, Huff."

"I know. Same here."

"I don't often like somebody. At my trade, you can't afford to.
The whole human race looks—a little bit crooked."

"I know. You trusted me, and I let you down."

"Well—we won't talk about it."

"There's nothing to say . . . Did you see her?"

"Yes. I saw them all. Him, her, and the wife."

"What did she say?"

"Nothing . . . I didn't tell her, you see. I let her do the talking.
She thinks Sachetti shot you."

"For what?"

"Jealousy."

"Oh."

"She's upset about you. But when she found out you weren't
badly hurt she—. Well, she—"

"—Was glad of it."

"In a way. She tried not to be. But she felt that it proved Sachetti
loved her. She couldn't help it."

"I see."

"She was worried about you, though. She likes you."

"Yeah, I know. She . . . likes me."

"She was following you. She thought you were him. That was all
there was to that."

"I figured that out."

"I talked to *him*."

"Oh yeah, you told me. What was he doing there?"

He did some more of his pounding around then. The night light
over my head was the only light in the room. I could only half see
him, but I could feel the bed shake when he marched.

"Huff, there's a story."

"Yeah? How do you mean?"

"You just got yourself tangled up with an Irrawaddy cobra, that's
all. That woman—it makes my blood run cold just to think of her.
She's a pathological case, that's all. The worst I ever heard of."

"A what?"

"They've got a name for it. You ought to read more of this modern psychology, Huff. I do. I wouldn't tell Norton. He'd think I was
going highbrow or something. I find it helpful though. There's
plenty of stuff in my field where it's the only thing that explains what
they do. It's depressing, but it clears up things."

"I still don't get it."

"You will . . . Sachetti wasn't in love with her."

"No?"

"He's known her. Five or six years. His father was a doctor. He had a sanatorium up in the Verdugo Hills about a quarter mile from this place where she was head nurse."

"Oh yeah. I remember about that."

"Sachetti met her up there. Then one time the old man had some tough luck. Three children died on him."

The old creepy feeling began to go up my back. He went on. "They died of—"

"—Pneumonia."

"You heard about it?"

"No. Go on."

"Oh. You heard about the Arrowhead business."

"Yes."

"They died on him, and there was an awful time and the old man took the rap for it. Not with the police. They didn't find anything to concern them. But with the Department of Health and his clientele. It ruined him. He had to sell his place. Not long after that he died."

"Pneumonia?"

"No. He was quite old. But Sachetti thought there was something funny about it, and he couldn't shake it out of his mind about this woman. She was over there too much, and she seemed to take too much interest in the children up there. He had nothing to go on, except some kind of a hunch. You follow me?"

"Go on."

"He never did anything about it till the first Mrs. Nirdlinger died. It happened that *one* of those children was related to that Mrs. Nirdlinger, in such fashion that when that child died, Mrs. Nirdlinger became executrix for quite a lot of property the child was due to inherit. In fact, as soon as the legal end was cleared up, Mrs. Nirdlinger came into the property herself. Get that, Huff. That's the awful part. Just *one* of those children was mixed up with property."

"How about the other two?"

"Nothing. Those two children died just to cover the trail up a little. Think of that, Huff. This woman would even kill two extra children, just to get the one child that she wanted, and mix things up so it would look like one of those cases of negligence they sometimes have in those hospitals. I tell you, she's a pathological case."

"Go on."

"When the first Mrs. Nirdlinger died, Sachetti elected himself a one-man detective agency to find out what it was all about. He wanted to clear his father for one thing, and the woman had become an obsession with him for another thing. I don't mean he fell for her. I mean he just had to know the truth about her."

"Yeah, I can see that."

"He kept up his work at the university, as well as he could, and then he made a chance to get in there, and talk with her. He already knew her, so when he went up there with some kind of a proposition to join a physicians'-and-nurses' association that was being formed, he figured she wouldn't think anything of it. But then something happened. He met this girl, and it was a case of love at first sight, and then his fine scheme to get at the truth about the wife went on the rocks. He didn't want to make the girl unhappy, and he really had nothing to go on, so he called it off. He didn't want to go to the house after what he suspected about the wife, so he began meeting the girl outside. Just one little thing happened, though, to make him think that maybe he had been right. The wife, as soon as she found out what was going on, began telling Lola cock-eyed stories about him, and got the father to forbid Lola to see him. There was no reason for that, except that maybe this woman didn't want anything named Sachetti within a mile of her, after what happened. Do you follow this?"

"I follow it."

"Then Nirdlinger got it. And suddenly Sachetti knew he had to go after this woman to mean it. He quit seeing Lola. He didn't even tell her why. He went up to this woman and began making love to her, as hard as he knew. That is, almost as hard as he knew. He figured, if it was her he was coming to see, she'd not forbid him to come, not at all. You see, she was Lola's guardian. But if Lola got married, the husband would be the guardian, and that would mix it all up on the property. You see—"

"Lola was next."

"That's it. After she got you out of the way for what you knew about her, Lola was next. Of course at this time Sachetti didn't know anything about you, but he did know about Lola, or was pretty sure he knew."

"Go on."

"That brings us down to last night. Lola followed him. That is, she followed his car when you took it. She was turning into the parking lot when you pulled out."

"I saw the car."

"Sachetti went home early. The wife chased him out. He went to his room and started to go to bed, but he couldn't shake it out of his mind that something was going on that night. For one thing, being chased out looked funny. For another thing, the wife had asked him earlier in the day a couple of things about Griffith Park, when they closed the roads down there for the night, and which roads they closed—things that could only mean she had something cooking in that park late at night sometime, he didn't know when. So instead of going to bed, he decided to go up to her house and keep an eye on her. He went out to get his car. When he found it gone, he almost fainted, because Lola had a key to it. Don't forget, he knew Lola was next."

"Go on."

"He grabbed a cab and went down to Griffith Park. He began walking around blind—he didn't have any idea what was up, or even when to look. He started at the wrong place—at the far end of the little glade. Then he heard the shot. He ran over, and he and Lola got to you about the same time. He thought Lola was shot. She thought he was shot. When Lola saw who it was, she thought Sachetti shot him, and she was putting on an act about it when the police got there."

"I get it now."

"That woman, that wife, is an out-and-out lunatic. Sachetti told me he found five cases, all before the three little children, where patients died under her while she was a nurse, two of them where she got property out of it."

"All of pneumonia?"

"Three. The other two were operative cases."

"How did she do it?"

"Sachetti never found out. He thinks she found out some way to do it with the serum, combining with another drug. He wishes he could get it out of her. He thinks it would be important."

"Well?"

"You're sunk, Huff."

"I know it."

"We had it out this afternoon. Down at the company. I had the whip hand. There was no two ways about it. I called it long ago, even when Norton was still talking suicide."

"You did that all right."

"I persuaded them the case ought never to come to trial."

"You can't hush it up."

"We can't hush it up, we know that. But having it come out that an agent of this company committed murder is one thing. Having it plastered all over every paper in the country for the two weeks of a murder trial is something else."

"I see."

"You're to give me a statement. You're to give me a statement setting forth every detail of what you did, and have a notary attest it. You're to mail it to me, registered. You're to do that Thursday of next week, so I get it Friday."

"Next Thursday."

"That's right. In the meantime, we hold everything, about this last shooting, I mean, because you're in no condition to testify at a hearing. Now get this. There'll be a reservation for you, under a name I'll give you, on a steamer leaving San Pedro Thursday night for Balboa and points south. You take that steamer. Friday I get your statement and at once turn it over to the police. That's the first I knew about it. That's why Norton and his friends left just now. There's no witnesses to this. It's a deal between you and me, and if you ever try to call it on me I'll deny it, and I'll prove there was no such deal. I've taken care of that."

"I won't try."

"As soon as we notify the police, we post a reward for your capture. And listen Huff, if you're ever caught, that reward will be paid, and you'll be tried, and if there's any way we can help it along, you're going to be hung. We don't want it brought to trial, but if it is brought to trial, we're going through with it to the hilt. Have you got that?"

"I've got it."

"Before you get on that boat, you'll have to hand to me the registry receipt for that statement. I've got to know I've got it."

"What about her?"

"Who?"

"Phyllis?"

"I've taken care of her."

"There's just one thing, Keyes."

"What is it?"

"I still don't know about that girl, Lola. You say you hold everything. I guess that means you hold her and Sachetti, pending the hearing. The hearing that's not going to be held. Well, listen. I've got to know no harm comes to her. I've got to have your solemn word on that, or you'll get no statement, and the case will come to trial, and all the rest of it. I'll blow the whole ship out of water. Do you get that, Keyes? What about her?"

"We hold Sachetti. He's consented to it."

"Did you hear me? What about her?"

"She's out."

"She's—what?"

"We bailed her out. It's a bailable offense. You didn't die, you see."

"Does she know about me?"

"No. I told you I told her nothing."

He got up, looked at his watch, and tiptoed out in the hall. I closed my eyes. Then I felt somebody near me. I opened my eyes again. It was Lola.

"Walter."

"Yes. Hello, Lola."

"I'm terribly sorry."

"I'm all right."

"I didn't know Nino knew about us. He must have found out. He didn't mean anything. But he's—hot-tempered."

"You love him?"

". . . Yes."

"I just wanted to know."

"I'm sorry that you feel as you do."

"It's all right."

"Can I ask something? That I haven't any right to ask?"

"What is it?"

"That you do not prosecute. That you not appear against him. You don't have to, do you?"

"I won't."

". . . Sometimes I almost love you, Walter."

She sat looking at me, and all of a sudden she leaned over close. I turned my head away, quick. She looked hurt and sat there a long time. I didn't look at her. Some kind of peace came to me then at last. I knew I couldn't have her and never could have had her. I couldn't kiss the girl whose father I killed.

When she was at the door I said good-bye and wished her good luck, and then Keyes came back.

"O.K. on the statement, Keyes."

"It's the best way."

"O.K. on everything. Thanks."

"Don't thank me."

"I feel that way."

"You've got no reason to thank me." A funny look came in his eyes. "I don't think they're going to catch up with you, Huff. I think —well maybe I'm doing you a favor at that. Maybe you'd rather have it that way."

Chapter 14

WHAT YOU'VE JUST READ, if you've read it, is the statement. It took me five days to write it, but at last, on Thursday afternoon, I got it done. That was yesterday. I sent it out by the orderly to be registered, and around five o'clock Keyes dropped by for the receipt. It'll be more than he bargained for, but I wanted to put it all down. Maybe she'll see it sometime, and not think so bad of me after she understands how it all was. Around seven o'clock I put on my clothes. I was weak, but I could walk. After a bite to eat I sent for a taxi and went down to the pier. I went to bed right away, and stayed there till early this afternoon. Then I couldn't stand it any longer, alone there in the stateroom, and went up on deck. I found my chair and sat there looking at the coast of Mexico, where we were going past it. But I had a funny feeling I wasn't going anywhere. I kept thinking about Keyes, and the look he had in his eye that day, and what he meant by what he said. Then, all of a sudden, I found out. I heard a little gasp beside me. Before I even looked I knew who it was. I turned to the next chair. It was Phyllis.

"You."

"Hello, Phyllis."

"Your man Keyes—he's quite a matchmaker."

"Oh yeah. He's romantic."

I looked her over. Her face was drawn from the last time I had seen her, and there were little puckers around her eyes. She handed me something.

"Did you see it?"

"What is it?"

"The ship's paper."

"No, I didn't. I guess I'm not interested."

"It's in there."

"What's in there?"

"About the wedding. Lola and Nino. It came in by radio a little after noon."

"Oh, they're married?"

"Yes. It was pretty exciting. Mr. Keyes gave her away. They went to San Francisco on their honeymoon. Your company paid Nino a bonus."

"Oh. It must be out then. About us."

"Yes. It all came out. It's a good thing we're under different names here. I saw all the passengers reading about it at lunch. It's a sensation."

"You don't seem worried."

"I've been thinking about something else."

She smiled then, the sweetest, saddest smile you ever saw. I thought of the five patients, the three little children, Mrs. Nirdlinger, Nirdlinger, and myself. It didn't seem possible that anybody that could be as nice as she was when she wanted to be, could have done those things.

"What were you thinking about?"

"We could be married, Walter."

"We could be. And then what?"

I don't know how long we sat looking out to sea after that. She started it again. "There's nothing ahead of us, is there Walter?"

"No. Nothing."

"I don't even know where we're going. Do you?"

"No."

". . . Walter, the time has come."

"What do you mean, Phyllis?"

"For me to meet my bridegroom. The only one I ever loved. One night I'll drop off the stern of the ship. Then, little by little I'll feel his icy fingers creeping into my heart."

". . . I'll give you away."

"What?"

"I mean: I'll go with you."

"It's all that's left, isn't it?"

Keyes was right. I had nothing to thank him for. He just saved the state the expense of getting me.

We walked around the ship. A sailor was swabbing out the gutter outside the rail. He was nervous, and caught me looking at him. "Theres a shark. Following the ship."

I tried not to look, but couldn't help it. I saw a flash of dirty white down in the green. We walked back to the deck chairs.

"Walter, we'll have to wait. Till the moon comes up."

"I guess we better have a moon."

"I want to see that fin. That black fin. Cutting the water in the moonlight."

The captain knows us. I could tell by his face when he came out of the radio room a little while ago. It will have to be tonight. He's sure to put a guard on us before he puts into Mazatlan.

The bleeding has started again. The internal bleeding, I mean, from the lung where the bullet grazed it. It's not much but I spit blood. I keep thinking about that shark.

I'm writing this in the stateroom. It's about half past nine. She's in her stateroom getting ready. She's made her face chalk white, with black circles under her eyes and red on her lips and cheeks. She's got that red thing on. It's awful-looking. It's just one big square of red silk that she wraps around her, but it's got no armholes, and her hands look like stumps underneath it when she moves them around. She looks like what came aboard the ship to shoot dice for souls in the *Rime of the Ancient Mariner*.

I didn't hear the stateroom door open, but she's beside me now while I'm writing. I can feel her.

The moon.

SERENADE

Chapter 1

I WAS IN THE TUPINAMBA, having a bizcocho and coffee, when this girl came in. Everything about her said Indian, from the maroon rebozo to the black dress with purple flowers on it, to the swaying way she walked, that no woman ever got without carrying pots, bundles, and baskets on her head from the time she could crawl. But she wasn't any of the colors that Indians come in. She was almost white, with just the least dip of café con leche. Her shape was Indian, but not ugly. Most Indian women have a rope of muscle over their hips that give them a high-waisted, mis-shapen look, thin, bunchy legs, and too much breast-works. She had plenty in that line, but her hips were round, and her legs had a soft line to them. She was slim, but there was something voluptuous about her, like in three or four years she would get fat. All that, though, I only half saw. What I noticed was her face. It was flat, like an Indian's but the nose broke high, so it kind of went with the way she held her head, and the eyes weren't dumb, with that shiny, shoe-button look. They were pretty big, and black, but they leveled out straight, and had kind of a sleepy, impudent look to them. Her lips were thick, but pretty, and of course had plenty of lipstick on them.

It was about nine o'clock at night, and the place was pretty full, with bullfight managers, agents, newspaper men, pimps, cops and almost everybody you can think of,

except somebody you would trust with your watch. She
went to the bar and ordered a drink, then went to a table
and sat down, and I had a stifled feeling I had had before, from the thin air up there, but that wasn't it this
time. There hadn't been any woman in my life for quite
some while, and I knew what this meant. Her drink
came, and it was coca-cola and Scotch, and I thought that
over. It might mean that she was just starting the evening,
and it might mean she was just working up an appetite,
and if it meant that I was sunk. The Tupinamba is more
of a café than a restaurant, but plenty of people eat there,
and if that was what she expected to do, my last three
pesos wouldn't go very far.

I had about decided to take a chance and go over there
when she moved. She slipped over to a place about two
tables away, and then she moved again, and I saw what
she was up to. She was closing in on a bullfighter named
Triesca, a kid I had seen a couple of times in the ring,
once when he was on the card with Solorzano, that
seemed to be their main ace at the time, and once after
the main season was over, when he killed two bulls in a
novillada they had one Sunday in the rain. He was a wow
with the cape, and just moving up into the money. He
had on the striped suit a Mexican thinks is pretty nifty,
and a cream-colored hat. He was alone, but the managers,
agents, and writers kept dropping by his table. She didn't
have much of a chance, but every time three or four or
five of them would shove off she would slip nearer. Pretty
soon she dropped down beside him. He didn't take off
his hat. That ought to have told me something, but it
didn't. All I saw was a cluck too stuck on himself to
know how to act. She spoke, and he nodded, and they
talked a little bit, and it didn't look like she had ever
seen him before. She drank out, and he let it ride for a
minute, then he ordered another.

When I got it, what she was in there for, I tried to lose
interest in her, but my eyes kept coming back to her.
After a few minutes, I knew she felt me there, and I
knew some of the other tables had tumbled to what was
going on. She kept pulling her rebozo around her, like it
was cold, and hunching one shoulder up, so she half had

her back to me. All that did was throw her head up still higher, and I couldn't take my eyes off her at all. So of course a bullfighter is like any other ham, he's watching every table but his own, and he had no more sense than to see these looks that were going round. You understand, it's a dead-pan place, a big café with a lot of mugs sitting around with their hats on the back of their heads, eating, drinking, smoking, reading, and jabbering Spanish, and there wasn't any nudging, pointing, or hey-get-a-load-of-this. They strictly minded their business. Just the same, there would be a pair of eyes behind a newspaper that weren't on the newspaper, or maybe a waitress would stop by somebody, and say something, and there'd be a laugh just a little louder than a waitress's gag is generally worth. He sat there, with a kind of a foolish look on his face, snapping his fingernail against his glass, and then I felt a prickle go up my spine. He was getting up, he was coming over.

A guy with three pesos in his pocket doesn't want any trouble, and when the room froze like a stop-camera shot, I tried to tell myself to play it friendly, to get out of it without starting something I couldn't stop. But when he stood there in front of me he still had on that hat.

"My table, he interest you, ha?"

"Your—what?"

"My table. You look, you seem interest, Señor."

"Oh, now I understand."

I wasn't playing it friendly, I was playing it mean. I got up, with the best smile I could paste on my face, and waved at a chair. "Of course. I shall explain. I shall gladly explain." Down there you make it simple, because spig reception isn't any too good. "Please sit down."

He looked at me and he looked at the chair, but it looked like he had me on the run, so he sat down. I sat down. Then I did something I wanted to do for fifteen minutes. I lifted that cream hat off his head, like it was the nicest thing I knew to do for him, slipped a menu card under it, and put it on a chair. If he had moved I was going to let him have it, if they shot me for it. He didn't. It caught him by surprise. A buzz went over the room. The first round was mine.

"May I order you something, Señor?"

He blinked, and I don't think he even heard me. Then
he began looking around for help. He was used to having
a gallery yell *Olé* every time he wiped his nose, but it had
walked out on him this time. It was all deadpan, what he
saw, and so far as they were concerned, we weren't even
there. There wasn't anything he could do but face me,
and try to remember what he had come for.

"The explain. Begin, please."

I had caught him with one he wasn't looking for, and I
decided to let him have another, right between the eyes.
"Certainly. I did look, that is true. But not at you. Believe me, Señor, not at you. And not at the table. At the
lady."

". . . You—tell me this? You tell me this thing?"

"Sure. Why not?"

Well, what was he going to do? He could challenge me
to a duel, but they never heard of a duel in Mexico. He
could take a poke at me, but I outweighed him by about
fifty pounds. He could shoot me, but he didn't have any
gun. I had broken all the rules. You're not supposed to
talk like that in Mexico, and once you hand a Mexican
something he never heard of, it takes him about a year to
figure out the answer. He sat there blinking at me, and
the red kept creeping over his ears and cheeks, and I gave
him plenty of time to think of something, if he could, before I went on. "I tell you what, Señor. I have examined
this lady with care, and I find her very lovely. I admire
your taste. I envy your fortune. So let us put her in a lottery, and the lucky man wins. We'll each buy her a
ticket, and the one holding the highest number buys her
next drink. Yes?"

Another buzz went around, a long one this time. Not
over half of them in there could speak any English, and it
had to be translated around before they could get it. He
took about four beats to think it through, and then he
began to feel better. "Why I do this, please? The lady,
she is with me, no? I put lady in *lotería*, what you put in,
Señor? You tell me that?"

"I hope you're not afraid, Señor?"

He didn't like that so well. The red began to creep up

again, but then I felt something behind me, and I didn't
like that so well either. In the U.S., you feel something
behind you, it's probably a waiter with a plate of soup,
but in Mexico it could be anything, and the last thing
you want is exactly the best bet. About half the population of the country go around with pearl-handled automatics on their hips, and the bad part about those guns is
that they shoot, and after they shoot nothing is ever done
about it. This guy had a lot of friends. He was a popular
idol, but I didn't know of anybody that would miss me. I
sat looking straight at him, afraid even to turn around.

He felt it too, and a funny look came over his face. I
leaned over to brush cigarette ashes off my coat, and out
of the tail of my eye I peeped. There had been a couple
of lottery peddlers in there, and when he came over they
must have stopped in their tracks like everybody else.
They were back there now, wig-wagging him to say yes,
that it was in the bag. I didn't let on. I acted impatient,
and sharpened up a bit when I jogged him. "Well,
Señor? Yes?"

"Sí, sí. We make lotería!"

They broke pan then, and crowded around us, forty or
fifty of them. So long as we meant business, it had to be
hands off, but now that it was a kind of a game, anybody
could get in it, and most of them did. But even before
the crowd, the two lottery peddlers were in, one shoving
pink tickets at me, the other green tickets at him. You
understand; there's hundreds of lotteries in Mexico, some
pink, some green, some yellow, and some blue, and not
many of them pay anything. Both of them went through
a hocus-pocus of holding napkins over the sheets of tickets, so we couldn't see the numbers, but my man kept
whispering to me, and winking, meaning that his numbers were awful high. He was an Indian, with gray hair
and a face like a chocolate saint, and you would have
thought he couldn't possibly tell a lie. I thought of
Cortés, and how easy he had seen through their tricks,
and how lousy the tricks probably were.

But I was different from Cortés, because I wanted to
be taken. Through the crowd I could see the girl, sitting
there as though she had no idea what was going on, and

it was still her I was after, not getting the best of a dumb bullfighter. And something told me the last thing I ought to do was to win her in a lottery. So I made up my mind I was going to lose, and see what happened then.

I waved at him, meaning pick whatever one he wanted, and there wasn't much he could do but wave back. I picked the pink, and it was a peso, and I laid it down. When they tore off the ticket, they went through some more hocus-pocus of laying it down on the table, and covering it with my hat. He took the green, and it was half a peso. That was a big laugh, for some reason. They put his hat over it, and then we lifted the hats. I had No. 7. He had No. 100,000 and something. That was an Olé. I still don't get the chemistry of a Mexican. Out in the ring, when the bull comes in, they know that in exactly fifteen minutes that bull is going to be dead. Yet when the sword goes in, they yell like hell. And mind you, there's nothing as much like one dead bull as another dead bull. In that café that night there wasn't one man there that didn't know I was framed, and yet when the hats were lifted they gave him a hand, and clapped him on the shoulder, and laughed, just like Lady Luck had handed him a big victory.

"So. And now. You still look, ha?"

"Absolutely not. You've won, and I congratulate you, de todo corazón. Please give the lady her ticket, with my compliments, and tell her I hope she wins the Bank of Mexico."

"Sí, sí, sí. And so, Señor, adiós."

He went back with the tickets, and I put a little more hot leche into my coffee, and waited. I didn't look. But there was a mirror back of the bar, so I could see if I wanted to, and just once, after he had handed her the tickets, and they had a long jibber-jabber, she looked.

It was quite a while before they started out. I was between them and the door, but I never turned my head. Then I felt them stop, and she whispered to him, and he whispered back, and laughed. What the hell? He had licked me, hadn't he? He could afford to be generous. A whiff of her smell hit me in the face, and I knew she was standing right beside me, but I didn't move till she spoke.

"Señor."

I got up and bowed. I was looking down at her, almost touching her. She was smaller than I had thought. The voluptuous lines, or maybe it was the way she held her head, fooled you.

"Señorita."

"*Gracias*, thanks, for the *billete*."

"It was nothing, Señorita. I hope it wins for you as much as it lost for me. You'll be rich—*muy rico*."

She liked that one. She laughed a little, and looked down, and looked up. "So. *Muchas gracias*."

"*De nada*."

But she laughed again before she turned away, and when I sat down my head was pounding, because that laugh, it sounded as though she had started to say something and then didn't, and I had this feeling there would be more. When I could trust myself to look around, he was still standing there near the door, looking a little sore. From the way he kept looking at the *damas*, I knew she must have gone in there, and he wasn't any too pleased about it.

In a minute, my waitress came and laid down my check. It was for sixty centavos. She had waited on me before, and she was a pretty little *mestiza*, about forty, with a wedding ring she kept flashing every time she got the chance. A wedding ring is big news in Mexico, but it still doesn't mean there's been a wedding. She pressed her belly against the table, and then I heard her voice, though her lips didn't move and she was looking off to one side: "The lady, you like her *dirección*, yes? Where she live?"

"You sure you know this *dirección*?"

"A *paraquito* have told me—just now."

"In that case, yes."

I laid a peso on the check. Her little black eyes crinkled up into a nice friendly smile, but she didn't move. I put the other peso on top of it. She took out her pencil, pulled the menu over, and started to write. She hadn't got three letters on paper before the pencil was jerked out

of her hand, and he was standing there, purple with fury.
He had tumbled, and all the things he had wanted to say
to me, and never got the chance, he spit at her, and she
spit back. I couldn't get all of it, but you couldn't miss
the main points. He said she was delivering a message to
me, she said she was only writing the address of a hotel I
had asked for, a hotel for Americanos. They must like to
see a guy framed in Mexico. About six of them chimed in
and swore they had heard me ask her the address of a
hotel, and that that was all she was giving me. They
didn't fool him for a second. He was up his own alley
now, and speaking his own language. He told them all
where to get off, and in the middle of it, here she came,
out of the damas. He let her have the last of it, and then
he crumpled the menu card up and threw it in her face,
and walked out. She hardly bothered to watch him go.
She smiled at me, as though it was a pretty good joke,
and I got up. "Señorita. Permit me to see you home."

That got a buzz, a laugh, and an Olé.

I don't think there's ever been a man so moony that a
little bit of chill didn't come over him as soon as a
woman said yes, and plenty of things were going through
my head when she took my arm and we headed for the
door of that café. One thing that was going through was
that my last peso was gone at last, that I was flat broke in
Mexico City with no idea what I was going to do or how
I was going to do it. Another thing was that I didn't
thank them for their Olé, that I hated Mexicans and
their tricks, and hated them all the more because the
tricks were all so bad you could always see through them.
A Frenchman's tricks cost you three francs, but a Mexican is just dumb. But the main thing was a queer echo in
that Olé, like they were laughing at me all the time, and
I wondered, all of a sudden, which way we were going to
turn when we got out that door. A girl on the make for a
bullfighter, you don't exactly expect that she came out of
a convent. Just the same, it hadn't occurred to me up to
that second that she could be a downright piece of trade
goods. I was hoping, when we reached the main street,
that we would turn right. To the right lay the main part

of town, and if we headed that way, she could be taking me almost anywhere. But to our left lay the Guauhtemolzin, and that's nothing but trade.

We turned left.

We turned left, but she walked so nice and talked so sweet I started hoping again. Nothing about an Indian makes any sense. He can live in a hut made of sticks and mud, and sticks and mud are sticks and mud, aren't they? You can't make anything else out of them. But he'll take you in there with the nicest manners in the world, more dignity than you'd ever get from a dozen dentists in the U.S., with stucco bungalows that cost ten thousand dollars apiece, kids in a private school, and stock in the building and loan. She went along, her hand on my arm, and if she had been a duchess she couldn't have stepped cleaner. She made a little gag out of falling in step, looked up once or twice and smiled, and then asked me if I had been long in Mexico.

"Only three or four months."

"Oh. You like?"

"Very much." I didn't, but I wanted anyway to be as polite as she was. "It's very pretty."

"Yes." She had a funny way of saying yes, like the rest of them have. She drew it out, so it was "yayse." "Many flowers."

"And birds."

"And señoritas."

"I wouldn't know about them."

"No? Just a little bit?"

"No."

An American girl would have mauled it to death, but when she saw I didn't want to go on with it, she smiled and began talking about Xochimilco, where the best flowers grew. She asked me if I had been there. I said no, but maybe some day she would take me. She looked away at that, and I wondered why. I figured I had been a little previous. Tonight was tonight, and after that it would be time to talk about Xochimilco. We got to the Guauhtemolzin. I was hoping she would cross. She turned, and we hadn't gone twenty yards before she stopped at a crib.

I don't know if you know how it works in Mexico.

There's no houses, with a madame, a parlor, and an electric piano, anyway not in that part of town. There's a row of adobe huts, one story high, and washed blue, or pink, or green, or whatever it happens to be. Each hut is one room deep, and jammed up against each other in the way they are, they look like a barracks. In each hut is a door, with a half window in it, like a hat-check booth. Under the law they've got to keep that door shut, and drum up trade by leaning out the window, but if they know the cop they can get away with an open door. This door was wide open, with three girls in there, two of them around fourteen, and looking like children, the other big and fat, maybe twenty-five. She brought me right in, but then I was alone, because she and the other three went out in the street to have a palaver, and I could partly catch what it was. They all four rented the room together, so three of them had to wait outside when one of them had a customer, but I seemed to be a special case, and if I was going to spend the night, her friends had to flop somewhere else. Most of the street got in it before long, the cop, the café woman on the corner, and a flock of girls from the other cribs. Nobody sounded sore, or surprised, or made dirty cracks. A street like that is supposed to be tough, but from the way they talked, you would have thought it was the junior section of the Ladies' Aid figuring out where to bunk the minister's brother-in-law that had blown in town kind of sudden. They acted like it was the most natural thing in the world.

After a while they got it straightened out to suit them, who was to go where, and she came back and closed the door and closed the window. There was a bed in there, and a chest of drawers in the early Grand Rapids style, and a washstand with a mirror over it, and some grass mats rolled up in a corner, for sleeping purposes. Then there were a couple of chairs. I was tilted back on one, and as soon as she had given me a cigarette, she took the other. There we were. There was no use kidding myself any longer why Triesca hadn't taken off his hat. My lady love was a three-peso whore.

She lit my cigarette for me, and then her own, and inhaled, and let the smoke blow out the match. We smoked, and it was about as electric as a stalled car. Across the street in front of the café, a mariachi was playing, and she nodded her head once or twice, in time with the music. "Flowers, and birds—and mariachis."

"Yes, plenty of them."

"You like mariachi? We have them. We have them here."

"Señorita."

"Yes?"

". . . I haven't got the fifty centavos. To pay the mariachi. I'm—"

I pulled my pockets inside out, to show her. I thought I might as well get it over with. No use having her think she'd hooked a nice American sugar papa, and then letting her be disappointed. "Oh. How sweet."

"I'm trying to tell you I'm broke. Todo flat. I haven't got a centavo. I think I'd better be going."

"No money, but buy me *billete*."

"And that was the last of it."

"I have money. Little bit. Fifty centavos for mariachi. Now—you look so."

She turned around, lifted the black skirt, and fished in her stocking. Listen, I didn't want any mariachi outside the window, serenading us. Of all things I hated in Mexico, I think I hated the mariachis the worst, and they had come to make a kind of picture for me of the whole country and what was wrong with it. They're a bunch of bums, generally five of them, that would be a lot better off if they went to work, but instead of that they don't do a thing their whole life, from the time they're kids to the time they're old men, but go around plunking out music for anybody that'll pay them. The rate is fifty centavos a selection, which breaks down to ten centavos, or about three cents a man. Three play the violin, one the guitar, and one a kind of bass guitar they've got down there. As if that wasn't bad enough, they sing. Well, never mind how they sing. They gargle a bass falsetto that's enough to set your teeth on edge, but all music gets sung the way it deserves, and it was what they sang that got me down. You hear Mexico is musical. It's not. They do nothing

but screech from morning till night, but their music is
the dullest, feeblest stuff that ever went down on paper,
and not one decent bar was ever written there. Yeah, I
know all about Chavez. Their music is Spanish music
that went through the head of an Indian and came out
again, and if you think it sounds the same after that, you
made a mistake. An Indian, he's about eight thousand
years behind the rest of us in the race towards whatever
we're headed for, and it turns out that primitive man is
not any fine, noble brute at all. He's just a poor fish.
Modern man, in spite of all this talk about his being
effete, can run faster, shoot straighter, eat more, live
longer, and have a better time than all the primitive men
that ever lived. And that difference, how it comes out in
music. An Indian, even when he plays a regular tune,
sounds like a seal playing My-Country-'Tis-of-Thee at a
circus, but when he makes up a tune of his own, it just
makes you sick.

Well, maybe you think I'm getting all steamed up over
something that didn't amount to anything, but Mexico
had done plenty to me, and all I'm trying to say is that if
I had to listen to those five simple-looking mopes outside
the window, there was going to be trouble. But I wanted
to please her. I don't know if it was the way she took the
news of my being broke, or the way her eyes lit up at the
idea of hearing some music, or the flash I got of that
pretty leg, when I was supposed to be looking the other
way, or what. Whatever it was, her trade didn't seem to
make much difference any more. I felt about her the way
I had in the café, and wanted her to smile at me some
more, and lean toward me when I spoke.

"Señorita."

"Yes?"

"I don't like the mariachi. They play very bad."

"Oh, yes. But they only poor boy. No estoddy, no take
lessons. But play—very pretty."

"Well—never mind about that. You want some music
that's the main thing. Let me be your mariachi."

"Oh—you sing?"

"Just a little bit."

"Yes, yes. I like—very much."

I went out, slipped across the street, and took the guitar from No. 4. He put up a squawk, but she was right after me, and he didn't squawk long. Then we went back. There's not many instruments I can't play, some kind of way, but I can really knock hell out of a guitar. He had it tuned cockeyed, but I brought it to E, A, D, G, B, and E without snapping any of his strings, and then I began to go to town on it. The first thing I played her was the prelude to the last act of Carmen. For my money, it's one of the greatest pieces of music ever written, and I had once made an arrangement of it. You may think that's impossible, but if you play that woodwind stuff up near the bridge, and the rest over the hole, the guitar will give you almost as much of what the music is trying to say as the whole orchestra will.

She was like a child while I was tuning, leaning over and watching everything I did, but when I started to play, she sat up and began to study me. She knew she had never heard anything like that, and I thought I saw the least bit of suspicion of me, as to who I was and what the hell I was doing there. So when I went down on the low E string, on the phrase the bassoon has in the orchestra, I looked at her and smiled. "The voice of the bull."

"Yes, yes!"

"Am I a good *mariachi?*"

"Oh, fine *mariachi.* What is the *música?*"

"Carmen."

"Oh. Oh yes, of course. The voice of the bull."

She laughed, and clapped her hands, and that seemed to do it. I went into the bullring music of the last act and kept stepping the key up, so I could make kind of a number out of it without slowing down for the vocal stuff. There came a knock on the door. She opened, and the *mariachi* was out there, and most of the ladies of the street. "They ask door open. So they hear too."

"All right, so they don't sing."

So we left the door open, and I got a hand after the bullring selection, and played the intermezzo, then the prelude to the opera. My fingers were a little sore, as I had no calluses, but I went into the introduction to the Habanera, and started to sing. I don't know how far I got.

What stopped me was the look on her face. Everything I had seen there was gone, it was the face at the window of every whorehouse in the world, and it was looking right through me.

" . . . What's the matter?"

I tried to make it sound comical, but she didn't laugh. She kept looking at me, and she came over, took the guitar from me, went out and handed it to the *mariachi* player. The crowd began to jabber and drift off. She came back, and the other three girls were with her. "Well, Señorita—you don't seem to like my singing."

"*Muchas gracias, Señor.* Thanks."

"Well—I'm sorry. Good evening, Señorita."

"*Buenos noches, Señor.*"

Next thing I knew I was stumbling down the Bolivar, trying to wash her out of my mind, trying to wash everything out of my mind. A block away, somebody was coming toward me. I saw it was Triesca. She must have gone out and phoned him when I left. I ducked around a corner, so I wouldn't have to pass him. I kept on, crossed a plaza, and found myself looking at the Palacio de Bellas Artes, their opera house. I hadn't been near it since I flopped there three months before. I stood staring at it, and thought how far I had slid. Flopping in Rigoletto, in probably the lousiest opera company in the world, before an audience that didn't know Rigoletto from Yankee Doodle, with a chorus of Indians behind me trying to look like lords and ladies, a Mexican tenor on one side of me that couldn't even get a hand on *Questa o Quella,* and a coffee cake on the other side that scratched fleas while she was singing the *Cara Nome*—that seemed about as low as I could get. But I had wiped those footprints out, with my can. I had tried to serenade a lady that was easy serenaded, and I couldn't even get away with that.

I walked back to my one-peso hotel, where I was paid up to the end of the week, went to my room, and undressed without turning on the light, so I wouldn't see the concrete floor, the wash basin with rings in it, and the lizard that would come out from behind the bureau. I got in bed, pulled the lousy cotton blanket up over me, and lay there watching the fog creep in. When I closed my eyes I'd see her looking at me, seeing something in me, I didn't know what, and then I'd open them again and look at the fog. After a while it came to me that I was afraid of what she saw in me. There would be something horrible mixed up in it, and I didn't want to know what it was.

Chapter 2

As WELL AS. I CAN REMEMBER, that was in June, and I didn't see her for a couple of months. Never mind what I did in that time, to eat. Sometimes I didn't eat. For a while I had a job in a jazzband, playing a guitar. It was in a nightclub out on the Reforma, and they needed me bad. I mean, the place was for Americans, and the music they handed out was supposed to be the McCoy, but it wasn't. I went to work, and got them so they could play the hot stuff hot and the blue stuff blue, anyway a little bit, and polished up a couple of them so they could take a solo strain now and then, just for variety. Understand, you couldn't do much. A Mexican's got a defective sense of rhythm. He sounds rhythmic on the cucaracha stuff, but when you slow him down to foxtrot time, he can't feel it. He just plays it mechanically, so when people get out on the floor they can't dance to it. Still, I did what I could, and figured a few combos that made them sound better than they really were, and business picked up. But then a guy with a pistol on his hip showed up one night and wanted to see my papers, and I got thrown out. They got Socialism down there now, and one of the rules is that Mexico belongs to the Mexicans. They're out of luck, no matter how they play it. Under Diaz, they turned the country over to the foreigners, and they had prosperity, but the local boys didn't get much of it. Then they had the Revolution, and fixed it up so that whatever was going on, the local boys had to run it. The only trouble is, the local boys don't seem to be very good at it. They threw me out, and then they had Socialism, but they didn't have any jazzband. Business fell off, and later I heard the place closed.

After that, I even had to beg to stay on at the hotel until I got the money from New York, which wasn't ever coming, as they knew as well as I did. They let me use the room, but wouldn't give me any bedclothes or service. I had to sleep on the mattress, under my clothes, and haul my own water. Up to then, I had managed to keep some kind of press in my pants, so I could anyway bum a meal off some American in Butch's café, but I couldn't even do that any more, and I began to look like what I was; a beachcomber in a spig town. I wouldn't even have eaten if it hadn't been for shagging my own water. I started going after it in the morning, and because the tin pitcher wouldn't fit under the tap in the washroom at the end of the hall. I had to go down to the kitchen. Nobody paid any attention to me, and then an idea hit me, and next time I went down at night.. There was nobody there, and I ducked over to the icebox. They've got electric iceboxes all over Mexico, and some of them have combinations on them, like safes, but this one hadn't. I opened it up, and a light went on, and sure enough, there was a lot of cold stuff in there. I scooped some frijoles into a glass ashtray I had brought down, and held them under the pitcher when I went up. When I got back to my room I dug into them with my knife. After that, for two weeks, that was what I lived on. I found ten centavos in the street one day, and bought a tin spoon, a clay soapdish, and a cake of soap. The soapdish and the soap I put on the washstand, like they were some improvements of my own I was putting in, since they wouldn't give me any. The spoon I kept in my pocket. Every night when I'd go down, I'd scoop beans, rice, or whatever they had, and sometimes a little meat into the soapdish, but only when there was enough that it wouldn't be missed. I never touched anything that might have counted, and only took off the top of dishes where there was quite a lot of it, and then smoothed them up to look right. Once there was half a Mexican ham in there. I cut myself off a little piece, under the butt.

And then one morning I got this letter, all neatly type-written, even down to the signature, on a sheet of white business paper.

> Calle Guauhtemolzin 44b,
> Mexico, D. F.
> A 14 de agosto.

Sr. John Howard Sharp,
Hotel Dominguez,
Calle Violeta,
Ciudad.
Mi Querido Jonny:

En vista de que no fue posible verte ayer en el mercado al ir a las compras que ordinaria-mente hago para la casa en donde trabajo, me veo pre-cidada para dirigirte la presente y manifestarte que dormí inquieta con motivo de tus palabras me son vida y no pudiendo permanecer sin contacto contigo te digo que hoy por la noche te espero a las ocho de la noche para que platiquemos, por lo que así espero estaras presente y formal.

Se despide quien te ama de todo corazón y no te olivida,
JUANA MONTES

How she got my name and address didn't bother me. The waitress at the Tupinamba would have been good for that. But the rest of it, the date I was supposed to have with her yesterday, and how she couldn't sleep for thinking about me, didn't make any sense at all. Still, she wanted to see me, that seemed to be the main point, and it was a long time before sundown. I was down past the point where I cared how she had looked at me, or what it meant, or anything like that. She could look at me like I was a rattlesnake, for all I cared, so she had a couple of buns under the bed. I went back upstairs, shaved, and started up there, hoping something about it might lead to a meal.

When I rapped on the door the window opened, and

the fat one poked her head out. The four of them were just getting up. The window closed, and Juana called something out to me. I waited, and pretty soon she came out. She had on a white dress this time, that must have cost all of two pesos, and white socklets, and shoes. She looked like some high school girl in a border town. I said hello and how had she been, she said very well, *gracias*, and how had I been? I said I couldn't complain, and edged toward the door to see if I could smell coffee. There didn't seem to be any. Then I took out the letter and asked her what it meant.

"Yes. I ask you to come. Yes."

"I caught that. But what's all this other stuff about? I didn't have any date with you—that I know of."

She kept studying me, and studying the letter, and hungry as I was, and bad as she had walloped me that night, and dumb as it had been up to now, I couldn't help having this same feeling about her I had had before, that was mainly what any man feels toward a woman, but partly what he feels toward a child. There was something about the way she talked, the way she held her head, the way she did everything, that got me in the throat, so I couldn't breathe right. It wasn't child, of course. It was Indian. But it did things to me just the same, maybe worse on account of it being Indian, because that meant she was always going to be like that. The trouble was, you see, that she didn't know what the letter said. She couldn't read.

She called the fat one out, and had her read it, and then there was the most indignant jabbering you ever heard. The other two came out and got in it, and then she grabbed me by the arm. "The auto. You make go, yes?"

"Well, I could once."

"Come, then. Come quick."

We went down the street, and she turned in at a shack that seemed to be a kind of a garage. It was full of wrecks with stickers pasted on the windshield, that seemed to be held for the sheriff or something, but halfway down the line was the newest, reddest Ford in the world. It shone like a boil on a sailor's neck. She went up to it, and began

waving the letter in one hand and the key in the other.
"So. Now we go. Calle Venezuela."

I got in, and she got in, and it was a little stiff, but it
started, and I rolled it through the murk to the street. I
didn't know where the Calle Venezuela was, and she
tried to show me, but she didn't have the hang of the
one-way streets, so we got tangled up so bad it took us a
half hour to get there. As soon as I backed up to park she
jumped out and ran over to a colonnade, where about
fifty guys were camped out on the sidewalk, back of tables
with typewriters on them. They all wore black suits. In
Mexico, the black suit means you got plenty of education, and the black fingernails mean you got plenty of
work. When I got there, she was having an argument
with one guy, and after a while he sat down to his machine, stuck a piece of paper in it, wrote something, and
handed it to her. She came over to me waving it, and I
took it. It was just two lines, that started off "Querido Sr.
Sharp" instead of "Querido Jonny," and said she wanted
to see me on a matter of business.

"This letter, big mistake."

She tore it up.

Well, never mind the fine points. The result of the big
Socialist educational program is that half the population
of the city have to come to these mugs to get their letters
written, and that was what she had done. But the guy
had been a little busy, and didn't get it quite straight
what she had said, and fixed her up with a love letter. So
of course, she had to go down there and get what she had
paid for. I didn't blame her, but I still didn't know what
she wanted, and I was still hungry.

"The auto—you like, yes?"

"It's a knockout." We were coming up the Bolivar
again, and I had to keep tooting the horn, according to
law. The main thing they put on cars for Mexican export
is the biggest, loudest horn they can find in Detroit, and
this one had a double note to it that sounded like a couple of ferryboats passing in an East River fog. "Your business must be good."

I didn't mean to make any crack, but it slipped out on me. If it meant anything to her at all, she passed it up.

"Oh no. I win."

"How?"

"The *billete*. You remember?"

"Oh. My *billete*?"

"Yes. I win, in *lotería*. The auto, and five honnerd pesos. The auto, is very pretty. I can no make go."

"Well, I can make it go, if that's all that's bothering you. About those five hundred pesos. You got some of them with you?"

"Oh yes. Of course."

"That's great. What you're going to do is buy me a breakfast. For my belly—muy empty. You get it?"

"Oh, why you no say? Yes, of course, now we eat."

I pulled in at the Tupinamba. The restaurants don't open until one o'clock, but the cafés will take care of you. We took a table up near the corner, where it was dark and cool. Hardly anybody was in there. My same old waitress came around grinning, and I didn't waste any time. "Orange juice, the biggest you got. Fried eggs, three of them, and fried ham. Tortillas. Glass of milk, *frío*, and café con crema."

"*Bueno*."

She took iced coffee, a nifty down there, and gave me a cigarette. It was the first I had had in three days, and I inhaled and leaned back, and smiled at her. "So."

"So."

But she didn't smile back, and looked away as soon as she said it. It was the first time we had really looked at each other all morning, and it brought us back to that night. She smoked, and looked up once or twice to say something, and didn't, and I saw there was something on her mind besides the *billete*. "So—you still have no pesos?"

"That's more or less correct."

"You work, no?"

"I did work, but I got kicked out. Just at present, I'm not doing anything at all."

"You like to work, yes? For me?"

". . . Doing what?"

"Play a guitar, little bit, maybe. Write a letter, count money, speak *Inglés*, help me, no work very hard. In Mexico, nobody work very hard. Yes? You like?"

"Wait a minute. I don't get this."

"Now I have money, I open house."

"Here?"

"No, no, no. In Acapulco. In Acapulco, I have very nice friend, big *político*. Open nice house, with nice music, nice food, nice drink, nice girls—for American."

"Oh, for Americans."

"Yes. Many Americans come now to Acapulco. Big steam-boat stop there. Nice man, much money."

"And me, I'm to be a kind of a combination professor, bartender, bouncer, glad-hander, secretary, and general bookkeeper for the joint, it that it?"

"Yes, yes."

"Well."

The food came along, and I stayed with it a while, but the more I thought about her proposition the funnier it got to me. "This place, it's supposed to have class, is that the idea?"

"Oh yes, very much. My *político* friend, he say American pay as much as five pesos, gladly."

"Pay five—what?"

"Pesos."

"Listen, tell your *político* friend to shut his trap and let an expert talk. If an American paid less than five dollars, he'd think there was something wrong with it."

"I think you little bit crazy."

"I said five bucks—eighteen pesos."

"No, no. You kid me."

"All right, go broke your own way. Hire your *político* for manager."

"You really mean?"

"I raise my right hand and swear by the holy mother of God. But—you got to get some system in it. You got to give him something for his money."

"Yes, yes. Of course."

"Listen, I'm not talking about this world's goods. I'm talking about things of the spirit, romance, adventure, beauty. Say, I'm beginning to see possibilities in this. All right, you want that American dough, and I'll tell you what you've got to do to get it. In the first place, the dump has got to be in a nice location, in among the hotels, not back of the coconut palms, up on the hill. That's up to your *político*. In the second place, you don't do anything but run a little dance hall, and rent rooms. The girls came in, just for a drink. Not mescal, not tequila. Chocolate ice-cream soda, because they're nice girls. that just dropped in to take a load off their feet. They wear hats. They come in two at a time, because they're so well brought up they wouldn't dream of going in any place alone. They work in the steamboat office, up the street, or maybe they go to school and just came home for vacation. And they've never met any Americans, see, and they're gigling about it, in their simple girlish way, and of course, we fix it up, you and I, so there's a little introducing around. And they dance. And one thing leads to another. And next thing you know, the American has a room from you, to take the girl up. You don't really run that kind of place, but just because it's him, you'll make an exception—for five dollars. The girl doesn't take anything. She does it for love, see?"

"For what?"

"Do I know the *Americano*, or don't I?"

"I think you just talk, so sound fonny."

"It sounds fonny, but it's not just talk. The *Americano*, he doesn't mind paying for a room, but when it comes to a girl, he likes to feel it's a tribute to his personality. He likes to think it's a big night for her, too, and all the more because she's just a poor little thing in a steamboat office, and never had such a night in her life until he came along and showed her what life could be like with a real guy. He wants an adventure—with him the hero. He wants to have something to tell his friends. But don't have any bums sliding up to take their *foto*. He doesn't like that."

"Why not? The *fotógrafo*, he pay me little bit."

"Well, I tell you. Maybe the *fotógrafo* has a heart of gold, and so has the *muchacha*, but the *Americano* figures the *foto* might get back to his wife, or threaten to, specially if she's staying up at the hotel. He wants an adventure, but he doesn't want any headache. Besides, the *fotos* have got a Coney Island look to them, and might give him the idea it was a cheap joint. Remember, this place has class. And that reminds me, the *mariachi* is going to be hand-picked by me, and hand-trained as well, so maybe somebody could dance to the stuff when they play it. Of course, I don't render any selections on the guitar. That's out. Or the piano, or the violin, or any other instrument in my practically unlimited repertoire. And that *mariachi*, they wear suits that we give them, with gold braid down the pants, and turn those suits in every night when they quit. It's our own private *mariachi*, and as fast as we get money to buy more suits we put on more men, so it's a feature. The main thing is that we have class, first, last, and all the time. No Americano, from the time he goes in to the time he goes out, is going to get the idea that he can get out of spending money. Once they get that through their heads, we'll be all right."

"The Americanos, are they all crazy?"

"All crazy as loons."

It seemed to be settled, but after the gags wore off I had this sick feeling, like life had turned the gray-white color of their sunlight. I tried to tell myself it was the air, that'll do it to you at least three times a day. Then I tried to tell myself it was what I had done, that I had no more pride left than to take a job as pimp in a coast-town whorehouse, but what the hell? That was just making myself look noble. It was, anyway, some kind of work, and if I really made a go of it, it wouldn't make me squirm. It would make me laugh. And then I knew it was this thing that was drilling in the back of my head, about her. There hadn't been a word about that night, and when she looked at me her eyes were just as blank as though I'd been some guy she was talking to about the rent. But I knew what those eyes could say. Whatever it was she had seen in me that night, she still saw it, and it was between us like some glass door that we could see through but couldn't talk.

She was sitting there, looking at her coffee glass and

not saying anything. She had a way of dozing off like that, between the talk, like some kitten that falls asleep as soon as you stop playing with it. I told you she looked like some high school girl in that little white dress. I kept looking at her, trying to figure out how old she was, when all of a sudden I forgot about that and my heart began to pound. If she was to be the madame of the joint, she couldn't very well take care of any customers herself, could she? Then who was going to take care of her? By her looks, she needed plenty of care. Maybe that was supposed to be my job. My voice didn't quite sound like it generally does when I spoke to her.

". . . Señorita, what do I get out of this?"

"Oh—you live, háve nice cloth, maybe big hat with silver, yes? Some pesos. Is enough, yes?"

"—And entertain the señoritas?"

I don't know why I said that. It was the second mean slice I had taken since we started out. Maybe I was hoping she'd flash jealous, and that would give me the cue I wanted. She didn't. She smiled, and studied me for a minute, and I felt myself getting cold when I saw there was the least bit of pity in it. "If you like to entertain señoritas, yes. Maybe not. Maybe that's why I ask you. No have any trouble."

Chapter 3

EARLY NEXT MORNING I shaved, washed, and packed. My earthly possessions seemed to be a razor, brush, and cake of soap, two extra shirts, a pair of extra drawers I had washed out the night before, a pile of old magazines, and the black-snake whip I had used when I sang Alfio. They give you a whip, but it never cracks, and I got this mule-skinner's number with about two pounds of lead in the butt. One night on the double bill a stagehand laid it out for Pagliacci, and the Nedda hit me in the face with it. I still carry the scar. I had sold off all the costumes and scores, but couldn't get rid of the whip. I dropped it in the suitcase. The magazines and my new soap-dish I put on top of it, and stood the suitcase in the corner. Some day, maybe, I would come back for it. The two extra shirts I put on, and tied the necktie over the top one. The extra drawers I folded and put in one pocket, the shaving stuff in another. I didn't mention I was leaving, to the clerk, on my way out. I just waved at him, like I was on my way up to the postoffice to see if the money had come, but I had to slap my hand against my leg, quick. She had dropped a handful of pesos in my pocket, and I was afraid he'd hear them clink.

The Ford was an open roadster, and I lost a half hour getting the boot off and the top up. It was an all-day run to Acapulco, and I didn't mean to have that sun beating down on me. Then I rolled it out and pulled down to 44h. She was on the doorstep, waiting for me, her stuff piled up around her. The other girls weren't up yet. She was all dressed up in the black dress with purple flowers that she had had on when I first saw her, though I thought the white would have been better. The main baggage seemed to be a round hatbox, of the kind women traveled with fifteen years ago, only made of straw and stuffed full of clothes. I peeled off the extra shirts and put them and the hatbox in the rumble seat. Then there was the grass mat that she slept on, rolled up and tied. I stuck that in, but it meant I couldn't close the rumble. Those mats, they sell for sixty centavos, or maybe twenty cents, and it didn't hardly look like it was worth the space, but it was a personal matter, and I didn't want to argue. Then there was a pile of *rebozos*, about every color there was, but mainly black. I put them in, but she ran out and took one, a dark purple, and threw it over her head. Then there was the cape, the *espada*, and the ear. It was the first time I ever saw a bullfighter's cape, the dress cape, I mean, not the fighting cape, up close so I could really look at it. I hated it because I knew where she had got it, but you couldn't laugh off the beauty of

it. I think it's the only decently made thing you'll ever
see in Mexico, and maybe it's not even made there. It's
heavy silk, each side a different color, and embroidered so
thick it feels crusty in your hands. This one was yellow
outside, crimson in, and against that yellow the needle-
work just glittered. It was all flowers and leaves, but not
in the dumb patterns you see on most of their stuff. They
were oil-painting flowers, not postcard flowers, and the
colors had a real tone to them. I folded it, put a rebozo
around it, to protect it from dust, and laid it beside the
hatbox. The espada, to me, was just one more grand-op-
era prop. It's what they use to stick the bull with, and I
didn't even take it out of the scabbard to look at it. I
threw it down in the bottom.

While I was loading the stuff in, she was standing
there stroking the ear. I wouldn't have handled it with
tongs. Sometimes, when a bullfighter puts on a good
show, they give him an ear. The crowd begins to yell
about it, and then one of the assistants goes over and cuts
an ear off the bull, where he's lying in the dirt with the
mules hooking on to his horns. The bullfighter takes it,
holds it up so you can see all the blood and slime, and
goes around with it, bowing every ten steps. Then he
saves it, like a coloratura saves her decoration from the
King of Belgium. After about three months it's good and
rank. This one she had, there were pieces of gristle hanging out of it, and it stunk so you could smell it five feet
away. I told her if it went on the front seat with us the
deal was off, and she could throw it back there with the
espada. She did, but she was plenty puzzled.

The window popped open then, and the fat one
showed, with some kind of a nightgown on, and her hair
all frazzled and ropy, and then the others ones were beside her, and there was a lot of whispering and kissing,
and then we got in and got started. We lost about ten
minutes, out on the edge of town, when we stopped to
gas up, and another five when we came to a church and
she had to go in and bless herself, but finally, around
eight o'clock we leveled off. We passed some wooden
crosses, another little feature they've got. Under Socialism, it seems that there's only one guy that really knows

how it works, and if some other guy thinks he does, it's a counter-revolutionary act, or, in unsocialist lingo, treason. So back in 1927, a guy named Serrano thought he did, and they arrested him and his friends down in Cuernavaca, and started up to Mexico with them in a truck. But then up in Mexico somebody decided it would be a good idea if they never got there at all, and some of the boys started out in a fast car to meet them. They fastened their hands with baling wire, lined them up beside the road, and mowed them down with a machine gun. Then they said the revolution was over, and the American papers handed it to them that they had a stable government at last, and that a strong man could turn the trick, just give him the chance. So wooden crosses mark the spot, an inspiring sight to see.

We had some coffee in Cuernavaca, then pushed on to Taxco for lunch. That was the end of the good road. From there on it was just dust, curves, and hills. She began to get sleepy. A Mexican is going to sleep at one o'clock, no matter where he is, and she was no exception. She leaned her head against the side, and her eyes drooped. She wriggled, trying to get set. She slipped off her shoes. She wiggled some more. She took off a string of beads around her neck, and unfastened two buttons. She was open to her brassiere. Her dress slipped up, above her knees. I tried not to look. It was getting hotter by the minute. I didn't look, but I could smell her.

I gassed in Chilpancingo, around four o'clock, and bathed the tires with water. That was what I was afraid of, mostly, that in that heat and sliding all over that rough road, we would have a blow-out. I peeled down to my undershirt, knotted a handkerchief around my head to catch sweat, and we went on. She was awake now. She didn't have much to say. She slipped off her stockings, held her bare legs in the air stream from the hood vent, and unbuttoned another button.

We were down in what they call the *tierra caliente*, now, and it turned cloudy and so muggy the sweat stood out on my arms in drops. After Chilpancingo I had been looking for some relief, but this was the worst yet. We had been running maybe an hour when she began to lean forward and look out, and then she told me to stop. "Yes. This way."

I rubbed the sweat out of my eyes and looked, and saw something that maybe was intended to be a road. It was three inches deep in dust, and cactuses were growing in the middle of it, but if you concentrated we could see two tracks. "That way, hell. Acapulco is the way we're going. I looked it up."

"We go for Mamma."

". . . What was that you said?"

"Yes. Mama will cook. She cook for us. For the house in Acapulco."

"Oh, I see."

"Mamma cook very nice."

"Listen. I haven't had the honor of meeting Mamma, but I've just got a hunch she's not the type. Not for the high-class joint we're going to run. I tell you what. Let's get down there. If worse comes to worst, *I'll* cook. I cook very nice, too. I studied in Paris, where all the good cooks go when they die."

"But Mamma, she have the *viveres*."

"The what?"

"The food, what we need. I send Mamma the money, I sent last week. She buy much things, we take. We take Mamma, Papa. All the *viveres*."

"Oh, Papa too."

"Yes, Papa help Mamma cook."

"Well, will you tell me where you, me, Mamma, Papa, and the *viveres* are going to ride? By the way, do we take the goat?"

"Yes, this way, please."

It was her car, and I turned into the road. I had gone about a hundred yards when the wheel jerked out of my hands and I had to stamp on the brake to keep from going down a gully that must have been two hundred feet deep. I mean, it was that rough, and it didn't get any better. It was uphill and down, around rocks the size of a truck, through gullies that would have bent the axles of anything but a Ford, over cactuses so high I was afraid they would foul the transmission when we went over them. I don't know how far we went. We drove about an hour, and the rate we were moving, it might have been five miles or twenty, but it seemed more like fifty. We passed a church and then a long while after that, we began to pass Mexicans with burros, hurrying along with them. That's a little point about driving in Mexico they don't tell you about. You meet these herds of burros, going along loaded up with wood, fodder, Mexicans, or whatever it is. The burro alone doesn't give you much trouble. He knows the rules of the road as well as you do, and gets out of the way in time, even if he's a little grouchy about it. But if he's got a Mexican herding him along, you can bet on it that that Mexican will shove him right in line with your fender and you do nothing but stand on your brake and curse and sweat and cake up with their dust.

It was the way they were hurrying along, though, that woke me up to what it looked like outside. The heat and dust were enough to strangle you, but the clouds were hanging lower all the time, and over the tops of the ridges smoky scuds were slipping past, and it didn't look good. After a long time we passed some huts, by twos and threes, huddled together. We kept on, and then we came to a couple more huts, but only one of them seemed to have anybody in it. She reached over and banged on the horn and jumped out, and ran up to the door, and all of a sudden there was Mamma, and right behind her, Papa. Mamma was about the color of a copper pot, all dressed up in a pink cotton dress and no shoes, to go to Acapulco. Papa was a little darker. He was a nice, rice mahogany after it's had about fifteen coats of dark polish. He came out in his white pajama suit, with the pants rolled up to his bare knees, and took off his big straw hat and shook hands. I shook hands. I wondered if there had been a white iceman in the family. Then I pulled up the brake and got out.

Well, I said she ran up to the door, but that wasn't quite right. There wasn't any door. Maybe you never saw an Indian hut, so I better tell you what it looks like. You can start with the colored shanties down near the railroad track in New Orleans, and then, when you've got them clearly in mind, you can imagine they're the Waldorf-Astoria Hotel, and that the Mexican hut is a shanty standing beside it. There's no walls, or roofs, or anything like you're used to seeing. There's four sides made of sticks, stuck down in the ground and wattled together with twigs, about as high as a man's head. In the middle of the front side is a break, and that's the door. The chinks between the twigs are filled up a little bit with mud. Just plain mud, smeared on there and most of it falling off. And on top is a thatch of grass, or palmetto, or whatever grows up on the hill, and that's all. There's no windows, no floor, no furniture, no pictures of the Grand Canyon hanging on the walls, no hay-grain-and-feed calendars back of the clock, with a portrait of a cowgirl on top of a horse. They've got no need for calendars, because in the first place they couldn't figure out what the writing was for, and in the second place they don't care what day it is. And they've got no need for a clock, because they don't care what time it is. All I'm trying to say is, there's nothing in there but a dirt floor, and the mats they sleep on, and down near the door, the fire where they do their cooking.

So that was where she came from, and she ran in there, barefooted like they were, and began to laugh and talk, and pat a dog that showed up in a minute, and act like any other girl that's come home after a trip to the city. It went on quite a while, but the clouds weren't hanging any higher, and I began to get nervous. "Listen, this is all very well, but how about the viveres?"

"Yes, yes. Mamma have buy very good estoff."

"Fine, but let's get it aboard."

It seemed to be stored in the other hut, the one that nobody was living in. Papa ducked in there and began to carry out iron plates for cooking tortillas, machetes, pots, and jars and such stuff. One or two of them were copper, but most of them were pottery, and Mexican pottery means the worst pottery in the world. Then Mamma showed up with baskets of black beans, rice, ground corn, and eggs. I stowed the stuff in the rumble seat, shoving the pots in first. But pretty soon it was chock up to the top, and, when I came to the baskets I had to lash them to the side with some twine that they had so they rode the running board. Some of the stuff, like the charcoal, wasn't even in baskets. It was done up in bundles. I lashed that too. The eggs I finally found a place for in back, on top of her hatbox. Each egg was wrapped in cornhusk, and I figured they would ride all right there and not break.

Then Papa came grinning out with a bundle, bigger than he was, of brand-new mats, all rolled up and tied. I couldn't figure out why they were so nuts about mats, but later I found out. He mussed up my whole rumble seat by dragging out the mat she had brought, unrolling his pile, rolling out her mat with the others and tying them up again. Then he lashed them to the side on top of the charcoal. I stood on the fender, grabbed the top and rocked the car. The twine broke and the mats fell out in the dirt. He laughed over that. They got a funny sense of humor. Then he got a wise look on his face, like he knew how to fix it, and went out back of the hut. When he showed again he was leading a burro, all saddled up with a rack. He opened the mats again, split them into two piles and rolled them separate. Then he lashed them to the burro, one pile on each side. Then he led the burro to the car and tied him to the rear bumper.

I untied the burro, took the mats off him, and rolled them into one pile again. I lifted them. They weren't so heavy. I hoisted them on to the top so one end was on the top, the other on the rumble seat, where it was open, and lashed them on to the top brace. I went in the hut. Juan was tying up one more basket, the old lady squatting on the stove bricks, smoking a cigar. She jumped up, ran out the door and around back, and came back with a bone. Juana had to untie the basket again, and in it was the dog. The old lady dropped the bone in, Juana put the top on and tied it up.

I went out, took the key out of my pocket, got in, and started the car. I had to back up to turn around, and all three of them started to scream and yell. It wasn't Spanish. I think it was pure Aztec. But you could get the drift. I was stealing the car, the *viveres*, everything they had.

Up to then I was nothing but a guy going nuts, and trying to get started in time to get there if we ever were going to get there. But the way they acted gave me an idea. I put her in first, hauled out of there, and kept on going.

Juana was right after me, screaming at the top of her voice, and jumped on the running board. "You estop! You steal auto! You steal *viveres*. You estop! You estop now!"

I did like hell stop. I stayed in first, so she wouldn't get shaken off, but I kept on over the hill, sounding like a load of tin cans with all that stuff back there, until Mamma and Papa were *todo* out of sight. Then I threw out and pulled up the brake.

"Listen, Juana. I'm not stealing your car. I'm not stealing anything—though why the hell you couldn't have bought all this stuff in Acapulco where you could get it cheap, instead of loading up here with it, that's something I don't quite understand. But get this: Mamma, and Papa and the burro, and that dog—they're not coming."

"Mamma, she cook, she—"

"Not tonight she doesn't. Tomorrow maybe we'll come back and get her, though I doubt it. Tonight I'm off, right now. I'm on my way. Now if you want to come—"

"So, you steal my car, yes."

"Let's say borrow it. Now make up your mind."

I opened the door. She got in. I switched on the lights and we started.

By that time I would say it was about seven o'clock. It was dark from the clouds, but it still wasn't night. There was a place down the line called Tierra Colorado that we might make before the storm broke, if I could ever get back to the main road. I had never been there, but it looked like there would be some kind of a hotel, or anyway cover for the car, with all that stuff in it. I began to force. I had to go up the hills in first, but coming down I'd let her go, with just the motor holding her. It was rough, but the clock said 20, which was pretty good. Well, you take a chance on a road like that, you're headed for a fall. All of a sudden there was a crash and a jerk, and we stopped. I pedaled the throttle. The motor was dead. I pulled the starter, and she went. We had just hit a rock, and stalled. But after that I had to go slower.

Up to then I was still sweating from the air and the work. So was she. Then we topped a rise and it was like we had driven into an icebox. She shivered and buttoned her dress. I had just about decided I would have to stop and put on my coat when we drove into it. No sheet of water, nothing like that. It just started to rain, but it was driving in on her side, and I pulled up. I put on my coat, then made her get out and lifted up the seat to get the side curtains. I felt around in there with my hand. There wasn't a wrench, a jack, or tool of any kind, and not a piece of a side curtain.

"Nice garage you picked."

In Mexico you even have to have a lock on your gasoline tank. It was a wonder they hadn't even stripped her of the lights.

We got in and started off. By now it was raining hard, and most of it coming in on her. While I was hunting for curtains she had dug out a couple of rebozos and wrapped them around her, but even that woven stuff stuck to her like she had just come out of a swimming pool. "Here. You better take my coat."

"No, gracias."

It seemed funny, in the middle of all that, to hear that soft voice, those Indian manners.

The dust had turned to grease, and off to the right, down near the sea, you could hear the rumble of thunder, how far off you couldn't tell, with the car making all that noise. I wrestled her along. Every tilt down was a skid, every tilt up was a battle, and every level piece was a wrench, where you were lifting her out of holes she went in, up to her axles. We were sliding around a knob with the hill hanging over us on one side, and dropping under us on the other, so deep you couldn't see the bottom. The drop was on my side, and I had my eyes glued to the road, crawling three feet at a time, because if we took a

skid there it was the end. There was a chock overhead, all
the top braces strained, and something went bouncing
down the gully the size of a five-gallon jug. I was on the
brake before it hit the ground, and after a long time I
heard her breathe. The engine was still running and I
went on. It must have been a minute before I figured out
what that was. The rain had loosened a rock above us, and
it came down. But instead of coming through and killing
us, it had hit the end of the mat roll and glanced off.

It cut the fabric, though, and as soon as we rounded
the knob that was the end of the top. The wind got
under it, and it ripped and the rain poured down on me.
It was coming from my side now. Then the mats began
to roll, and there came another rip, and it poured down
on her.

"Very bad."

"Not so good."

We passed the church, and started down the hill. I had
to use brake and motor to hold her, but down at the bottom it looked a little better ahead, so I lifted my foot to
give her the gun. Then I stamped on the brake so hard
we stalled cold. What lay ahead, in the rain, looked like a
wet sand flat where I could make pretty good time. What
it was was yellow water, boiling down the arroyo so fast
that it hardly made a ripple. Two more feet and we
would have been in, up to the radiator. I got out, went
around the car and found I had a few feet clear behind. I
got in, started, and backed. When I could turn around I
did, and went sliding up the hill again, the way we had
come. Where we were going I didn't know. We couldn't
get to Tierra Colorado, or Acapulco, or any place we
wanted to go, that was a cinch. We were cut off. And
whether we could make Mamma's hut, or any hut, was
plenty doubtful. With the top flapping in ribbons, and
all that water beating in, that motor was due to short any
minute, and where that would leave us I hated to think.

We got to the top of the hill and started down the
other side, past the church. Then I woke up. "All right,
get in the church there, out of the wet. I'll be right after
you."

"Yes, yes."

She jumped out and ran down there. I pulled off to one side, set the brake, and fished out my knife. I was going to cut those mats loose and use some of them to blanket the motor, and some of them to protect the seat and stuff in back until I could carry it in there. But the main thing I thought about was the car. If that didn't go, we were sunk. While I was still trying to get the knife open with my wet fingernail she was back. "Is close."

"What was that?"

"The church, is close. Is lock. Now we go on, yes. We go back to Mamma."

"We will like hell."

I ran over to the doors, shook them and kicked them. They were big double doors and they were locked all right. I tried to think of some way I could get them open. If I had a jack handle I could have shoved it in the crack and pried, but there wasn't any jack handle. I beat on the doors and cursed them, and then I went back to the car. The engine was still running and she was sitting in it. I jumped in, turned, and pointed it straight at the church. The steps didn't bother me. The church was below the road and they went down, instead of up, and anyway they were just low tile risers, about three inches high, and pretty wide. When she saw what I was going to do, she began to whimper, and beg me not to, and grabbed the wheel to make me stop. "No, no! Not the *Casa de Dios*, please, no! We go back! We go back to Mamma."

I pushed her away and eased the front wheels down the first step. I bumped them down the next two steps, and then the back wheels came down with a slam. But I was still rolling. I kept on until the front bumper was against the doors. I stayed in first, spun the motor, and little by little let in the clutch. For three or four seconds nothing happened, but I knew something had to crack. It did. There came a snap, and I was on the brake. If those doors opened outward I didn't want to tear out their hinges.

I backed up the width of the last step, pegged her there with the brake and got out. The bolt socket had torn out. I pulled the doors open, shoved Juana in, went

back and started to work on the mats again. Then I
thought, what's the matter with you? Don't be a fool. I
ran back and pulled the doors as wide open as they would
go. Then I ran in and began to drag pews around, working by the car lights, until there was an open space right
up the center aisle. Then I went back and drove the car
right in there. I went back and pulled the doors shut.
The headlights were blazing right at the Blessed Sacrament, and she was on her knees at the altar rail, begging
forgiveness for the sacrilegio.

I sat down in one of the pews where it was turned side-
wise, just to sit. I began to worry about the car lights. At
the time it seemed I was thinking about the battery, but
it may have been the Blessed Sacrament, boring into the
side of my head, I don't know. I got up and cut them.
Right away the roar of the rain was five times as loud. In
with it you could hear the rumble of thunder, but you
couldn't see any lightning. It was pitch dark in there, except for one red spot. The sacristy light was burning.
From up near it came a moan. I had to have light. I cut
the switch on again.

Off to one side of the altar was what looked like a vestry
room. I went back there. The water squirted out of my
shoes when I walked. I took them off. Then I took off
my pants. I looked around. There was a cassock hanging
there, and some surplices. I took off everything, wet undershirt, wet drawers, wet socks, and put on the cassock.
Then I took a lighter that was standing in a corner and
started out to the sacristy lamp. I knew my matches
wouldn't work. Walking on a tile floor barefoot you don't
make much noise, and when she saw me with the
lighter, in the cassock, I don't know what she thought, or
if she thought. She fell on her face in front of me and
began to gibber, calling me padre and begging for
absolutión. "I'm not the padre, Juana. Look at me. It's
me."
"Ah, Díos!"
"I'm lighting the candles so we can see."
But I mumbled it low. I pulled down the lamp, lit the

lighter and slipped it up again. Then I went around through the vestry room and up on the altar and lit three candles on one side, crossed over and lit three on the other. I cut the lighter. went back to the vestry room, put it in its place again. Then I went back and cut the car lights.

One funny thing about that that I didn't realize until I snapped that switch. Each time I crossed that altar I went down on one knee. I stood there, looking at the six candles I had lit, and thought that over. It had been twenty years, ever since I had been a boy soprano around Chicago. since I had thought of myself as a Catholic. But they knock it into you. Some of it's there to stay.

I lifted eggs and about fifteen other things from the rumble, until I could get out her hatbox. It was pretty wet but not as wet as the rest of the stuff. I took it back to the vestry room, set it down, then went out and touched her on the shoulder. "Your things are back there. You better get out of that wet dress."

She didn't move.

By that time it must have been about half past eight, and it dawned on me that why I felt so lousy was that I was hungry. I got a candle off the altar, lit it, went back and stuck it to the rear fender of the car, and took stock. I lifted out most of that stuff from the rumble seat, and unlashed what was riding the running board, and all I could see that was doing us any good was the eggs. I unwrapped one and took out my knife to puncture the end so I could suck it, and then I noticed the charcoal. That gave me an idea. There were some loose tiles in the floor and I clawed up a couple of them and carried them to the vestry room and stood them on their sides. Then I got one of the iron plates for cooking tortillas, and laid it across them and carried in the charcoal.

Next thing was how I was going to cook the eggs. There were no skillets or anything like that. And I went through every basket there was and there wasn't any butter, grease or anything you could use for grease. But there was a copper pot, bigger than I wanted but anyway a pot, so that meant that anyway I could boil the eggs. While I was rooting through those beans and rice and stuff that would take all night to cook, I smelled coffee and started looking for it. Finally I hit it, buried in with the rice in a paper bag, and then I found a little coffee pot. The coffee wasn't ground, but there was a metate there for grinding corn, and I mashed up a couple of handfuls with that, and put it in a bowl.

I went in the vestry room with what I had and the next thing was what I was going to use for water. It was dripping through every seam in the room and running down the windows in streams, but it looked kind of tough to get enough of it to cook. Still, I had to get some. Out back I could hear a stream pouring off the roof, so I took the biggest of the bowls and pulled the bolt on the rear door, right back of the altar. But when I opened it I could see a well, just a few steps down the hill. I took off the cassock. It was the only dry thing there was, and I wasn't letting it get wet. I went down to the well stark naked. The rain came down on me like a needle shower and at first it was terrible, but then it felt good. I threw out my chest against it and let it beat me. Then I pulled up the bucket and poured the water in the bowl. When I got back in the church with it I was running water even from my eyeballs. I felt around back of the altar for a closet. Oh, it was coming back to me, fast. I knew where they kept everything. Sure enough, I found a door and opened it, and there they were, the altar cloths, all in a neat pile. I took one, rubbed myself dry with it and put on the cassock. It was warm. I began to feel better.

The choir loft was off to one side and I started there to get a hymn book, so I could tear it up to start the fire. Then I changed my mind. Except for the window, there was no vent in the vestry room, and I didn't want to be smoked out, right at the start. I took four or five pieces of charcoal, laid them in a little pile between my tiles, went back to the altar and got another candle. I held the flame under the charcoal, turning all the time to keep the melting even, and pretty soon I got a little glow. I fed a couple more pieces on, and it glowed still redder. In a min-

ute it was off, and I blew out the candle. There was
hardly any smoke. Charcoal doesn't make much.

I laid the plate over the tiles, put the pot on it, and
dipped some water in the pot. Then I dropped in some
eggs. I started with six, but then I kept thinking how
hungry I was, and I wound up with a dozen. I filled the
coffee pot, scooped in some coffee, and put that on. Then
I sat there, feeding the fire and waiting for the eggs to
boil. They never did. The pot was too big or the fire too
small, or something. The most I got was smoke coming
off the top, but they were cooking all the time, so I
didn't worry much. Anyway, they'd be hot. But the coffee
boiled. The old smell hit me in the nose, and when I
lifted the lid the grounds were simmering around. I took
an egg, went to the back door, broke it, and let the egg
spill out on the ground. The shell I took back and
dropped in the coffee. That was what it needed. It began
to clear.

I watched the eggs some more, and then I thought
about my cigarettes and matches. They were in my coat,
and I went to the car to get it. Then I thought about her
things. I put the cigarettes and matches on the end of the
tortilla plate to dry. Her stuff I took out of the hatbox
and draped them near the fire on a bench that was back
there. What she had I could only half see. It was all
damp, but it smelled like her. One dress was wool, and I
put that nearest the heat, and a pair of shoes, on the floor
near it. Then I got to wondering how we were going to
eat the eggs, even if they ever got cooked. There were no
spoons or anything like that, and I always hated eggs out
of the shell. I went out to the car again and half filled a
little bowl with corn meal. I came back, dipped a little
water into it. I worked it with my fingers, and when it
got pasty I patted some of it into a tortilla, or anyway
into some kind of a flapjack that was big enough to hold
an egg. I put it on the plate to cook, and when it began
to turn color I turned it over. When it was done on both
sides I tasted it. It didn't taste right. I went out and got
some salt I had found and forgotten to take. I mixed a
little salt in, tried another one, and anyway you could eat

it. Pretty soon I had twelve. That was one for each egg,
and I thought that was enough.

All that took a long time, and there wasn't one peep out
of her the whole time I was at work. She had moved
from the altar rail to a pew, but she was still out there, a
rebozo over her head and her bare feet sticking out behind, where she was kneeling with her face in her hands.
I slid in the pew, took her by the arm and led her into
the vestry room. "I told you once to take off that wet
dress. Here's one that's fairly dry, and you go back there
and change it. If your underwear's wet, you better take it
off."

I picked up the woolen dress and shoved her behind
the altar with it. When she came back she had it on. "Sit
on the bench so your feet will be on the warm tiles near
the fire. When those shoes are dry you can put them on."

She didn't. She sat on the bench, but with her back to
the fire, so her feet were on cold tiles. That was so she
could face the altar. She dropped her head in her hands
and began to mutter. I got out my knife, broke an egg
tortilla, and shoved it at her. The egg was half hard and
half soft, but it rode the tortilla all right.

She shook her head. I put the tortilla down, went to the
altar, got three or four candles, lit them, came back and
stuck them around. Then I closed the door, the one that
led to the altar and that I had kept open, to have more
light. That kind of blocked her off on the muttering and
she half turned around. When she saw the tortillas she
laughed. That seemed to help. "Look very fonny."

"Well, maybe they look fonny but I didn't notice you
doing much about them. Anyway, you can eat them."

She picked up the tortilla, half wrapped it around the
egg and bit into it. "Taste very fonny."

"The hell it does."

I had bit into my first one by then, and it hit the spot.
We wolfed them down. She ate five and I ate seven. We
were talking in a natural tone of voice for the first time
since we got in out of the storm, and it came to me it
was because that door that led to the altar was shut. I got
up and closed the other door, the one leading into the

church, and that made it still better. We got to the coffee and there was nothing we could drink it out of but one little bowl, so we took turns. She would take a guzzle and then I would. In a minute I reached for the cigarettes. They were dry, and so were the matches. We lit up and inhaled. They tasted good.

"You feel better now?"

"Yes, gracias. Was very cold, very hongry."

"You still worried about the *sacrilegio*?"

"No, not now."

"There wasn't any *sacrilegio*, you know."

"Yes, very bad."

"No, not a bit. It's the *Casa de Díos*, you know. Everybody's welcome in here. You've seen the burros in here, haven't you? And the goats? On the way to market? The car is just the same. If we had to break the door in, that was only because we didn't have any key. I showed plenty of respect, didn't I? You saw me genuflect every time I crossed, didn't you?"

"Genu—"

"Bow—in front of the Host?"

"Yes, of course."

"No *sacrilegio* there, was there? You're all upset about nothing. Don't worry, I know. I know as much about it as you do. More probably."

"Very bad *sacrilegio*. But I pray. Soon, I confess. I confess to the *padre*. Then, *absolución*. No bad any more."

By that time it must have been somewhere around eleven o'clock at night. The rain hadn't let up, but sometimes it would be heavy, sometimes not so bad. The thunder and lightning would come up and go. There must have been three or four storms rolling up those canyons from the sea, and we'd get it, and it would die away and then we'd get it again. One was coming up now. She began to do what I'd noticed her doing once in the car, hold her breath and then speak, after a second or two when you could almost hear her heart beat. I tumbled that the *sacrilegio* was only part of what was eating on her. Most of it was the storm. "The lightning bother you?"

"No. The *trueno*, very bad."

It didn't look like it would pay to try to explain to her that the lightning was the works, the thunder nothing but noise, so I didn't try. "Try to sing a little. That generally helps. You know *La Sandunga?*"

"Yes, very pretty."

"You sing and I'll be *mariachi.*"

I began to drum on the bench and do a double shuffle with my feet. She opened her mouth to sing, but there came a big clap of thunder just then, and she didn't quite make it. "Outside, I no feel afraid. I like. Is very pretty."

"A lot of people are like that."

"Home, with Mamma, I no feel afraid."

"Well—that's practically outside, at that."

"Here, afraid, very much. I think about the *sacrilegio,* think about many things. I feel very bad."

You couldn't blame her much because it wasn't exactly what you'd call a gay place. I understood how she felt. I felt a little that way myself.

"Anyhow, it's dry. In spots."

The lightning came and I put my arm around her. The thunder broke and the candles guttered. She put her head on my shoulder and hid her face in my neck.

It died off after a while and she sat up. I opened the window a crack to get a little oxygen in the air, and put a couple more sticks of charcoal on the fire. "You had a good dinner?"

"Yes, gracias."

"You feel like a little work?"

". . . Work?"

"Suppose you be fixing us up a place to sleep while I wash up."

"Oh yes—gladly."

I went and brought the mats and and then got out a pile of altar cloths. Then I took the pots, bowls, and water out back and washed them up. I couldn't see very well, but I did the best I could. I had to duck out to the well once or twice, stripped down like I was before, and rub off with the same old cloth, so it took me about a half hour. When I got done I piled the things up inside the door and went in there. She was already in bed. She had taken three or four of the mats and some altar cloths, for herself, and bedded me down across the room.

I blew out the candles we had eaten by, and stepped out on the altar to blow out the ones I had lit there, and then I noticed the other one, the one I had stuck to the car fender, was still burning. I stepped over the rail, went back there and blew it out. Then I started up to the altar again. My legs felt queer and shaky. I slipped in a pew and sat down.

I knew what it was all right, and it came to me then why I had put her to fixing the mats and taken all that time to wash up. I had hoped she would just fix one bed, and then when she didn't, it was like a wallop in the pit of the stomach to me. I had even quit wondering why I was the only man on the face of the earth she wouldn't sleep with. What I hated was that it made any difference to me.

I don't know how long I sat there. I wanted to smoke, and I had the cigarettes and matches with me, but I just held them in my hand. I was over by the choir loft, out of line with the Blessed Sacrament, but I was right in line with the crucifix, and I couldn't make myself light up. Another storm began to come up. I enjoyed it that she was across there in the vestry room, all alone, and scared to death. It kept rolling up, the worst we had had yet. There came two flashes of lightning, and then one terrific shot of thunder right after them. The candles were just guttering up again when there came a blaze of lightning, and the thunder right with it, and every candle up there went out. For a second you couldn't see a thing but the red spot of the sacristy lamp.

Then she began to scream. From where she was, with the door to the altar open like I had left it, maybe she caught it sooner than I did. Or maybe for a split second I had my eyes closed. I don't know. Anyway, the church filled with green light, and then it seemed to settle over the crucifix, so the face looked alive, like it was going to cry out. Then you couldn't see anything but the red spot.

She was screaming her head off now, and I had to have light. I dived for the choir loft, scratched a match, and lit

the organ candles. I don't know how many there were. I
lit them all, so it was a blaze of candles. Then I turned to
go and light the altar candles again, but I would have to
cross in front of the crucifix and I couldn't do it. All of a
sudden I sat down to the organ. It was a small pedal
organ, and I pumped with my bare feet and started to
play. I kept jerking out stops, to make it louder. The
thunder rolled, and the louder it rolled the louder I
played. I didn't know what I was playing, but after a
while I knew it was an *Agnus Dei*. I cut it off and started
a *Gloria*. It was louder. The thunder died off and the rain
came down like all Niagara was over us. I played the *Gloria* over again.

"Sing."

I couldn't see her. She was outside the circle of light,
where I was sitting in the middle. But I could feel her,
up at the altar rail again, and if singing was what she
wanted, that suited me too. I skipped the *Qui Tollis* the
Quoniam, and the rest of it down to the *Credo*, and went
on from there. Don't ask me what it was. Some of it was
Mozart, some of it was Bach, some of it was anybody you
can think of. I must have sung a hundred masses in my
time, and I didn't care which one it was, so I could go on
without a break. I went straight through to the *Dona
Nobis*, and played off soft after I finished it, and then I
stopped. The lightning and thunder had stopped again,
and the rain was back to its regular drumming.

"Yes."

She just whispered it, but she drew it out like she always did, so the end of it was a long hiss. ". . . Just like
the priest."

My head began to pound like it would split. That was
the crown of skunk cabbage, all right, after all the years
at harmony, of sight-reading, of piano, of light opera, of
grand opera in Italy, Germany and France—to be told by
this Indian that couldn't even read that I sounded like a
priest. And it didn't help any that that was just what I
sounded like. The echo of my voice was still in my ears
and there was no getting around it. It had the same
wooden, dull quality that a priest's voice has, without one

particle of life in it, one echo that would make you like it.

My head kept pounding. I tried to think of something to say that would rip back at her, and couldn't.

I got up, blew out all the candles but one, and took that one with me. I started up past the crucifix to cross over to the vestry room. She wasn't at the crucifix. She was out in front of the altar. At the foot of the crucifix I saw something funny and held the candle to see what it was. It was three eggs, in a bowl. Beside them was a bowl of coffee and a bowl of ground corn. They hadn't been there before. Did you ever hear of a Catholic putting eggs, coffee, and corn at the foot of the cross? No, and you never will. That's how an Aztec treats a god.

I crossed over, and stood behind her, where she was crouched down, on her knees, her face touching the floor, and her hands pressing down beside it. She was stark naked, except for a *rebozo* over her head and shoulders. There she was at last, stripped to what God put there. She had been sliding back to the jungle ever since she took off that first shoe, coming out of Taxco, and now she was right in it.

A white spot from the sacristy lamp kept moving back and forth, on her hip. A creepy feeling began to go up my back, and then my head began to pound again, like sledge hammers were inside of it. I blew out the candle, knelt down, and turned her over.

Chapter 4

WHEN IT WAS OVER we lay there, panting. Whatever it was that she had done to me, that the rest of it had done to me, I was even. She got up and went back to the car. There was some rattling back there, and then I felt her

coming back, and got up to meet her. I was getting used
to the dark by then, and I saw the flash of a machete.
She came in on a run, and when she was a couple of
yards away she took a two-handed chop with it. I
stepped back and it pulled her off balance. I stepped in,
pinned her arms, and pressed my thumb against the back
of her hand, right at the wrist. The knife fell on the floor.
She tried to wriggle free. Mind you, neither one of us had
a stitch on. I tightened with one arm, lifted her, carried
her in the vestry room and closed both doors. Then I
dumped her in the bed she had been in, piled in with
her, and pulled up the covers. The fire still made a little
glow, and I lit a cigarette and I smoked it, holding her
with the other arm, then squashed it against the floor.

When she tired, I loosened up a little, to let her blow.
Yes, it was rape, but only technical, brother, only technical. Above the waist, maybe she was worried about the
sacrilegio, but from the waist down she wanted me, bad.
There couldn't be any doubt about that.

There couldn't be any doubt about it, and it kind of
put an end to the talk. We lay there, then, and I had another cigarette. I squashed it out, and from away off
there came a rumble of thunder, just one. She wriggled
into my arms, and next thing I knew it was daylight, and
she was still there. She opened her eyes, closed them
again, and came closer. Of course there wasn't but one
thing to do about that, so I did it. Next time I woke up I
knew it must be late, because I was hungry as hell.

It rained all that day, and the next. We split up on the
cooking after the first breakfast. I did the eggs and she
did the tortillas, and that seemed to work better. I got
the pot to boil at last by setting it right on the tiles without any plate, and it not only made it boil, but saved
time. In between, though, there wasn't much to do, so
we did whatever appealed to us.

The afternoon of the second day it let up for about a half
hour, and we slid down in the mud to have a look at the
arroyo. It was a torrent. No chance of making Acapulco
that night. We went up the hill and the sun came out

plenty hot. When we got to the church the rocks back of it were alive with lizards. There was every size lizard you could think of, from little ones that were transparent like shrimps, to big ones three feet long. They were a kind of a blue gray, and moved so fast you could hardly follow them with your eyes. They leveled out with their tail, somehow, so they went over the rocks in a straight line, and almost seemed to fly. Looking at them you could believe it all right, that they turned into birds just by letting their scales grow into feathers. You could almost believe it that they were half bird already.

We climbed down and stood looking at them, when all of a sudden she began to scream. "Iguana! Iguana! Look, look, big iguana!"

I looked, and couldn't see anything. Then, still as the rock it was lying on, and just about the color of it, I saw the evilest-looking thing I ever laid eyes on. It looked like some prehistoric monster you see in the encyclopedia, between two and three feet long, with a scruff of spines that started at its head and went clear down its back, and a look in its eye like something in a nightmare. She had grabbed up a little tree that had washed out by the roots, and was closing in on him. "What are you doing? Let that goddam thing alone!"

When I spoke he shot out for the next rock like something on springs, but she made a swipe and caught him in mid-air. He landed about ten feet away, with his yellow belly showing and all four legs churning him around in circles. She scrambled over, hit him again, and then she grabbed him. "Machete! Quick, bring machete!"

"Machete, hell, let him go I tell you!"

"Is iguana! We cook! We eat!"

"Eat!—that thing?"

"The machete, the machete!"

He was scratching her by that time, and if she wouldn't let him go I wasn't letting him make hash out of her. I dove in the church for the machete. But then some memory of this animal caught me. I don't know whether it was something I had read in Cortés, or Diaz, or Martyr, or somebody, about how they cooked it when the Aztecs still ran Mexico, or some instinct I had

brought away from Paris, or what. All I knew was that if
we ever cut his head off he was going to be dead, and
maybe that wouldn't be right. I didn't grab a machete. I
grabbed a basket, with a top on it, and dug out there
with it. "The machete! The machete, give me machete!"

He had come to by now, and was fighting all he knew,
but I grabbed him. The only place to grab him was in
the belly on account of those spines on his back, and
that put his claws right up your arm. She was bleeding up
to her elbows and now it was my turn. Never mind how
he felt and how he stunk. It was enough to turn your
stomach. But I gave him the squeeze, shoved him head-
down in the basket, and clapped the top on. Then I held
it tight with both hands.

"Get some twine."

"But the machete! Why no bring—"

"Never mind. I'm doing this. Twine—string—that the
things were tied with."

I carried him in, and she got some twine, and I tied
the top on, tight. Then I set him down and tried to
think. She didn't make any sense out of it, but she let me
alone. In a minute I fed up the fire, took the pot out and
filled it with water. It had started to rain again. I came in
and put the pot on to heat. It took a long while. Inside
the basket those claws were ripping at the wicker, and I
wondered if it would hold.

At last I got a simmer, and then I took the pot off and
got another basket-top ready. I picked him up, held him
way above my head, and dropped him to the floor. I remembered what shock did to him the first time, and I
hoped it would work again. It didn't. When I cut the
string and grabbed, I got teeth, but I held on and socked
him in the pot. I whipped the basket-top on and held it
with my knee. For three seconds it was like I had
dropped an electric fan in there, but then it stopped. I
took the top off and fished him out. He was dead, or as
dead as a reptile ever gets. Then I found out why it was
that something had told me to put him in the pot alive,
and not cook him dead, with his head cut off, like she
wanted to do. When he hit that scalding water he let go.

He purged, and that meant he was clean inside as a whistle.

I went out, emptied the pot, heated a little more water, and scrubbed it clean with cornhusks, from the eggs. Then I scrubbed him off. Then I filled the pot, or about two thirds filled it, with clean water, and put it on the fire. When it began to smoke I dropped him in. "But is very fonny. Mamma no cook that way."

"Is fonny, but inspiration has hit me. Never mind how Mamma does it. This is how I do it, and I think it's going to be good."

I fed up the fire, and pretty soon it boiled. I cut it down to a simmer, and this smell began to come off it. It was a stink, and yet it smelled right, like I knew it was going to smell. I let it cook along, and every now and then I'd fish him up and pull one of his claws. When a claw pulled out I figured he was done. I took him out and put him in a bowl. She reached for the pot to go out and empty it. I almost fainted. "Let that water alone. Leave it there, right where it is."

I cut off his head, opened his belly, and cleaned him. I saved his liver, and was plenty careful how I dissected off the gall bladder. Then I skinned him and took off the meat. The best of it was along the back and down the tail, but I carved the legs too, so as not to miss anything. The meat and liver I stowed in a little bowl. The guts I threw out. The bones I put back in the pot and fed up the fire again, so it began to simmer. "You better make yourself comfortable. It's a long time before dinner."

I aimed to boil about half that water away. It began to get dark and we lit the candles and watched and smelled. I washed off three eggs and dropped them in. When they were hard I fished them out, peeled them, and laid them in a bowl with the meat. She pounded up some coffee. After a long time that soup was almost done. Then something popped into my mind. "Listen, we got any paprika?"

"No, no paprika."

"Gee, we ought to have paprika."

"Pepper, salt, yes. No paprika."

"Go out there to the car and have a look. This stuff needs paprika, and it would be a shame not to have it just because we didn't look."

"I go, but is no paprika."

She took a candle and went back to the car. I didn't need any paprika. But I wanted to get rid of her so I could pull off something without any more talk about the sacrilegio. I took a candle and a machete and went back of the altar. There were four or five closets back there, and a couple of them were locked. I slipped the machete blade into one and snapped the lock. It was full of fire-crackers for high mass and stuff for the Christmas chèche. I broke into another one. There it was, what I was look-ing for, six or eight bottles of sacramental wine. I grabbed a bottle, closed the closets, and came back. I dug the cork out with my knife and tasted it. It was A-1 sherry. I socked about a pint in the pot and hid the bottle. As soon as it heated up a little I lifted the pot off, dropped the meat in, sliced up the eggs, and put them in. I sprin-kled in some salt and a little pepper.

She came back. "Is no paprika."

"It's all right. We don't need it. Dinner's ready."

We dug in.

Well, brother, you can have your Terrapin Maryland. It's a noble dish, but it's not Iguana John Howard Sharp. The meat is a little like chicken, a little like frog-legs, and a little like muskrat, but it's tenderer than any of them. The soup is one of the great soups of the world, and I've eaten Marseilles bouillabaisse, New Orleans crayfish bisque, clear green turtle, thick green turtle, and all kinds of other turtle there are. I think it was still better that we had to drink it out of bowls, and fish the meat out with a knife. It's gelatinous, and flooding up over your lips, it makes them sticky, so you can feel it as well as taste it. She drank hers stretched out on her belly, and after a while it occurred to me that if I got down and stuck my mouth up against hers, we would be stuck, so we experiemented on that for a while. Then we drank some more soup, ate some more meat, and made the coffee. While we were drinking that she started to laugh. "Yeh? And what's so funny?"

"I feel—how you say? Dronk?"

"Probably born that way."

"I think you find wine. I think you steal wine, put in iguana."

"Well?"

"I like, very much."

"Why didn't you say so sooner?"

So I got out the bottle, and we began to swig it out of the neck. Pretty soon we were smearing her nipples with soup, to see if they would stick. Then after a while we just lay there, and laughed.

"You like the dinner?"

"It was lovely dinner, gracias."

"You like the cook?"

"Yes. . . . Yes. . . . Yes. Very fonny cook."

God knows what time it was when we got up from there and went out front to wash up. She helped me this time, and when we opened the door it had stopped raining and the moon was shining. That set us off again. After we got the stuff clean we started to laugh and dance out there in the mud, barefooted. I started to hum some music for it, and then I stopped. She was standing out there in the glare of the moon with that same look on her face she had the first night I met her. But she didn't turn away from me this time. She came closer and looked at me hard. "Sing."

"Oh, the hell with it."

"No, please, sing."

I started over again, what I had been humming, but this time I sang it instead of humming it, and then I stopped again. It didn't sound like a priest any more. I walked over to the edge of the rocks and threw one down the arroyo, with a wide-open throttle. I don't know what it was. It came full and round, the way it once had, and felt free and good. I cut, and had just taken breath for another one when the echo of the first one came back to me. I caught my breath. That echo had something in it my voice had never had before, some touch of sweetness, or excitement, or whatever it was, that I had always lacked. I cut the second one loose, and she came over and stood looking at me. I kept throwing them, each one tone higher than the last. I must have got up to F above the staff. Then I did a turn in the middle of my voice and shot one as high as I dared. When the echo came it had a ring to it almost like a tenor. I turned and ran into the church and up to the organ, to check pitch. It was A flat, and church organs are always high. At orchestra pitch, it was at least an A natural.

I was trembling so bad my fingers shook on the keys. Listen, I was never a great baritone. I guess you begin to place me by now, and after the Don Giovanni revival, and especially after the Hudson-to-Horn hookup, you heard I was the greatest since Bispham, and some more stuff like that. That was all hooey. I was no Battistini, no Amato, no John Charles Thomas. On voice, I was somewhere between Bonelli and Tibbett. On acting, I was pretty good. On music, I was still better. On singing, I was as good as they come. I ought to be, seeing it was all I ever did, my whole life. But never mind all that. I had a hell of a good voice, that's all I'm trying to say, and I had worked on it, lived for it, and let it be a part of me until it was a lot more than just something to make a living with. And I want you to get it straight why it was when this thing happened in Europe, and it cracked up on me for no reason that I could see, and then when I got sold down to Mexico as a broken-down hack that couldn't be sent any place better, and then when I wasn't even good enough for that,—it wasn't only that I was a bum, and down and out. Something in me had died. And now that it had come back, just as sudden as it went, I was a lot more excited than you would be if you found a hundred-dollar bill somewhere. I was more like a man that had gone blind, and then woke up one morning to find out that he could see.

I played an introduction, and started to sing. It was *Eri Tu*, from Ballo in Maschera. But I couldn't be bothered with pedaling that old wreck. I walked out in the aisle, and walked around with it, singing without accompaniment. I finished it, sang it again, and checked pitch. It had pulled a little sharp. That was right, after that long lay-off, it ought to do that. I played a chord for pitch, and started another. I sang for an hour, and hated to quit, but at that high pitch an hour was the limit.

She sat in a pew, staring at me as I walked around. The *sacreligio* didn't seem to bother her much any more. When I stopped, she came in the vestry room with me, and we dropped off what we had on, and lay down. There were six or seven cigarettes left. I kept smoking them. She lay beside me, up on one elbow, still staring at me. When the cigarettes were gone I closed my eyes and tried to go to sleep. She opened one eye, with her finger, and then the the other eye. "That was very beautiful, *gracias.*"

"I used to be a singer."

"Yes. Maybe I made a mistake."

"I think you did."

". . . Maybe not."

She kissed me then, and went to sleep. But the fire was dead, the moon had gone down, and the window was gray before I went to sleep.

Chapter 5

WE PULLED INTO ACAPULCO the next afternoon around five thirty. We couldn't start before four, on account of that busted top, that I had to stow away in the boot. I didn't mean to get sunstroke, so I let her sleep and tried to clean up a little, so I would leave the church about the way I found it, except for a few busted locks and this and that. Getting the car out was a little harder than getting it in. I had to make little dirt run-ways up the steps, soak them with water, and let them bake in the sun, so I could get a little traction for the wheels in reverse. Then I had to tote all the stuff out and load it again. but I had more time, and made a better job of it. When she came out of her siesta, we started off. The arroyo was still a stream, but it was clear water now, and not running deep, so we got across all right.

When we got to Acapulco she steered me around to the hotel where we were going to stop. I don't know if you ever saw a hotel for Mexicans. It was a honey. It was just off the road that skirts the harbor, on the edge of the town, and it was just an adobe barracks, one story high, built around a dirt patio, or court, or whatever you'd call it, and that was all. In each room was a square oil can, what they use to carry water in all over Mexico, and that was the furnishings. You used that to carry your water in, from the well outside, and there wasn't anything else in there at all. Your mat, that you slept on, you were supposed to have with you, and unroll it on the dirt floor yourself. That was why she had been packing all those mats around. Your bedclothes you were supposed to have with you too, except that a Mexican doesn't need bedclothes. He flops as is. The plumbing was al fresco exterior, just over from the well. In the patio was a flock of burros, tied, that the guests had come on, and we parked our car there, and she took her hatbox, the cape, the *espada*, and the ear, and the *hostelero* showed us our room. It was No. 16, and had a fine view of a Mexican with his pants down, relieving his bowels.

"Well, how do you feel?"

"Very nice, *gracias*."

"The heat hasn't got you?"

"No, no. Nicer than Mexico."

"Well, I tell you what. It's too early to eat yet. I think I'll have my suit pressed, then take a walk around and kind of get the lay of the land. Then after sundown, when it's cooler, we'll find a nice place and eat. Yes?"

"Very nice. I look at house."

"All right, but I got ideas on the location."

"Oh, the *político* already have house."

"I see. I didn't know that. All right, then, you see the *político*, have a look at the house, and then we'll eat."

"Yes."

I found a *sastrería*, and sat there while they pressed my suit, but I didn't waste any time on the lay of the land

after that. You think I was going to bookkeep for a
whorehouse now? A fat chance. Those high notes down
the arroyo made everything different. There was a freight-
er laying out there in the harbor, and I meant to dig out
of there, if there was any way in God's world I could
promote passage on her.

It was nearly dark before I found the captain. He was
having dinner at the Hotel de Mexico, out under the canopy. He was a black Irishman, named Conners, about
fifty, with brows that met over his nose, a face the color
of a meerschaum pipe, and blistered sunburned hands
that were thin and long like a blackjack dealer's. He gave
me a fine welcome when I sat down at his table. "My
friend, I don't know your uncle in New York, your
brother in Sydney, or your sister-in-law back in Dublin,
God bless her, nevertheless. I'm not a member of the Ancient, Free, and Accepted Order of Masons, and I don't
care if you ever get the twenty pesos to take you to Mexico City. I'll not buy you a drink. Here's a peso to be off,
and if you don't mind I'll be having my dinner."

I let the peso lay and didn't move. When he had to
look at me again I recited it back to him just like he had
handed it to me. "I have no uncle in New York, no
brother in Sydney, no sister-in-law in Dublin, thanks for
the benediction, nevertheless. I'm not a member of the
Ancient, Free, and Accepted Order of Masons, and I'm
not on my way to Mexico City. I don't want your drink,
and I don't want your peso."

"By your looks, you want something. What is it?"

"I want passage north, if that's where you're headed."

"I'm headed for San Pedro, and the passage will be two
hundred and fifteen pesos, cash of the Republic, payable
in advance, and entitling you to a fine deck stateroom,
three meals a day, and the courtesies of the ship."

"I offer five."

"Declined."

I picked up his peso. "Six."

"Declined."

"I offer sweat. I'll do any reasonable thing to work this

passage out, from swabbing decks to cleaning brass. I'm a pretty fair cook."

"Declined."

"I offer a recipe for Iguana John Howard Sharp that I have just perfected, a dish that would be an experience for you, and probably improve your disposition."

" 'Tis the first sensible thing you have said, but there would be a difficulty getting the iguana. At this season they move up to the hills. Declined."

"I offer six pesos and a promissory note for two hundred and nine. The note I guarantee to redeem."

"Declined."

I watched him eating his fish, and by that time I was beginning to be annoyed. "Listen, maybe you don't get this straight. I intend to haul out of here, and I intend to haul out on your boat. Write up your contracts any way you want. The thing to get through your head is: I'm going."

"You're not. You've taken my peso, so be off."

I lit a cigarette and still sat there. "All right, I'll level it out, and quit the feinting and jabbing. I was a singer, and my voice cracked up. Now it's coming back, see? That means if I ever get out of this hellhole of a country, and get back where the money is, I can cash in. I'm all right. I'm as good as I ever was, maybe better. To hell with the promissory note. I guess that was a little tiresome. I ask you as a favor to haul me up to San Pedro, so I can get on my feet again."

When he looked up, his eyes were smoky with hate. "So you're a singer, then. An American singer. My answer is: It wouldn't be safe for me to take you aboard. Before I was out of the harbor with you I'd drop you into the water to rid the world of you. No! And don't take up any more of my time with it."

"What's the matter with an American singer?"

"I even hate the Pacific Ocean. On the Atlantic side, I can get London, Berlin, and Rome on my wireless. But here what is it? Los Angeles, San Francisco, the blue network, the red network, a castrated eunuch urging me to buy soap—and Victor Herbert!"

"He was an Irishman."

"He was a German."

"You're wrong. He was an Irishman."

"I met him in London when I was a young man, and I talked German with him myself."

"He talked German, through choice, especially when he was with other Irishmen. You see, he wasn't proud of it. He didn't want them to know it. All right, look him up."

"Then he was an Irishman, though I hate to say it.— And George Gershwin! There was an Irishman for you."

"He wrote some music."

"He didn't write one bar of music. Victor Herbert, and George Gershwin, and Jerome Kern, and buy the soap for me schoolboy complexion, and Lawrence Tibbett, singing mush. At Tampico, I got Mozart's Jupiter Symphony, that I suppose you never heard of, coming from Rome. Off Panama, I picked up the Beethoven Seventh, with Beecham conducting it, in London—"

"Listen, never mind Beethoven—"

"Oh, it's never mind Beethoven, is it? You would say that, you soap agent. He was the greatest composer that ever lived!"

"The hell he was."

"And who was? Walter Donaldson, I suppose."

"Well, we'll see."

There were two or three mariachis around, but the place wasn't full yet, so there was a lull in the screeching. I called a man over, and took his guitar. It was tuned right, for a change. My fingers still had calluses on them, from the job in Mexico City, so I could slide up to the high positions without cutting them. I went into the introduction to the serenade from Don Giovanni, and then I sang it. I didn't do any number, didn't try to get any hand, and the rest of them in there hardly noticed me. I just sang it, half-voice, rattled off the finish on the guitar, and put my hand over the strings.

He was to his tamales by now, and he kept putting them down. Then he called the guitar player over, had a long pow-wow in Spanish, and laid down some paper money. The guitar player touched his hat and went off. The waiter took his plate and he stared hard at the table.

". . . It's a delicate point. I've been a Beethoven enthusiast ever since I was a young man, but I've often wondered to myself if Mozart wasn't the greatest musical genius that ever lived. You might be right, you might be right. I bought his guitar, and I'll take it aboard with me. I'm in with a cargo of blasting powder, and I can't clear till I've signed a million of their damned papers. Be at the dock at midnight sharp. I'll lift my hook shortly after."

I left him, my heels lifting like they had grown wings. Everything said lay low until midnight, and never go back to the hotel. But I hadn't eaten yet, and I couldn't make myself go in a café and sit down alone. Along about nine o'clock I walked on up there.

I no sooner turned in the patio before I could see there was something going on. Two or three oil lamps were stuck around, on stools, and some candles. Our car was still where I had left it, but a big limousine was parked across from it, and the place was full of people. By the limousine was a stocky guy, dark taffy-colored, in an officer's uniform with a star on his shoulder and an automatic on his hip, smoking a cigarette. She was sitting on the running board of our car. In between, maybe a couple of dozen Mexicans were lined up. Some of them seemed to be guests of the hotel, some of them the hired help, and the last one was the *hostelero*. Two soldiers with rifles were searching them. When they got through with the *hostelero* they saw me, came over, they grabbed me, stood me up beside him, and searched me too. I never did like a bum's rush, especially by a couple of gorillas that didn't even have shoes.

When the searching was over, the guy with the star started up the line, jabbering at each one in Spanish. That took quite a while. When he got to me he gave me the same mouthful, but she said something and he stopped. He looked at me sharp, and jerked his thumb for me to stand aside. I don't like a thumb any better than I like a bum's rush.

He fired an order at the soldiers then, and they began going in and out of the rooms. In a minute one of them gave a yell and came running out. The guy with the star went in with them, and they came out with our beans, our eggs, our ground corn, our pots, bowls, charcoal, machetes, everything that had been packed on the car. A woman began to wail and the *hostelero* began to beg. Nothing doing. The guy with the star and the soldiers grabbed them and hustled them out of the court and up the street. Then he barked something else and waved his hand. The whole mob slunk to their rooms, and you could hear them in there mumbling and some of them moaning. He walked over to her, put his arm around her, and she laughed and they talked in Spanish. Quick work, getting the stolen stuff back, and he wanted appreciation.

She went into No. 16 and came out with the hatbox and the other stuff. He opened the door of the limousine.

"Where you going with that guy?"

I didn't know I was going to say it. My play was to stand there and let her go, but this growl came out of my mouth without my even intending it. She turned around, and her eyes opened wide like she couldn't believe what she heard. "But please, he is *político*."

"I asked you where you're going with him."

"But yes. You stay here. I come mañana, very early. Then we look at house, yes."

She was talking in a phoney kind of way, but not to fool me. It was to fool him, so I wouldn't get in trouble. She kept staring at me, trying to get me to shut up. I was standing by our car, and he came over and snapped something. She came over and spoke to him in Spanish, and he seemed satisfied. The idea seemed to be that I was an American, and was all mixed up on what it was about. I licked my lips, tried to make myself take it easy, play it safe till I got on that boat. I tried to tell myself she was nothing but an Indian girl, that she didn't mean a thing with me, that if she was going off to spend the night with this cluck it was no more than she had done plenty of times before, that she didn't know any different and it was none of my business anyway. No dice. Maybe if she hadn't looked so pretty out there in the moonlight I might have shut up, but I don't think so. Something had happened back in that church that made me feel she belonged to me. I heard my mouth growl again. "You're not going."

"But he is *político*—"

"And because he's *político*, and he's fixed you up with a lousy sailor's whorehouse, he thinks he's going to take part of his graft in trade. He made a mistake. You're not going."

"But—"

He stepped up, then, and shot a rattle at me in Spanish, so close I could feel the spit on my face. We hadn't been talking loud. I was too sore to yell, and Mexicans say it soft. He finished, straightened up, and jerked his thumb at me again, toward the hotel. I let him have it. He went down. I stamped my foot on his hand, grabbed the pistol out of the holster. "Get up."

He didn't move. He was out cold. I looked at the hotel. All you could hear was this mumbling and moaning. They hadn't heard anything at all. I jerked open the car door and shoved her in, hatboxes and all. Then I ran around, threw the pistol on the seat, jumped in and started. I went out of the court in second, and by the time I hit the road I was in high.

I snapped on the lights and gave her the gun. In a few seconds I was in the town, and then I knew what a mistake I had made when I came out of that court, and cut right instead of left. I had to get out of there, and get out of there quick before that guy came to, and I couldn't turn around. I mean literally I couldn't turn around. The street was so narrow, and so choked with burros, pigs, goats, *mariachis*, and people, that even when you met a car you had to saw by, and a turn was impossible. It was no through street. It went through the town, and then, at the hill, it led up to the big tourist hotel, and that was the end of it. I crawled along now, the sweat coming out on my brow, and got to the bottom of the hill. There was no traffic there, but it was still narrow. I turned right on a side road. I thought I might hit a way, after a block or two, that would lead back where I had come from. I didn't. The street just tapered off into two tracks on an open field, that as far as I could see just wandered up in the hills. I pulled into the field, to turn around. I thought I still might have time to slip back through the town, though it didn't look like even Jess Willard could stay out that long. Then back of me I heard shots, yells, and the screech of a motorcycle siren. It was too late. I was cut off. I doused the lights and bumped over to a grove of coconut palms, where anyway I would be shaded from the moonlight.

I lined up toward the town, so I could see, and tried to think. It all depended on whether I had been noticed, turning off the main street. If I hadn't, I might be able to lay low till the moon went down and they were asleep, then go through the town fast, and be on my way to Mexico City before they even knew I had got away. I tried not to think about the ship.

In a minute or so, the sirens began to screech louder, and three single lights streaked out of town around the harbor. That meant they had no idea I was still around. They thought I was on my way to Mexico, and were out after me. That meant we would be safe here for a little while, maybe the whole night. But where it put me, when I did start up to Mexico, and met those patrols coming back, I hated to think. And Mexico was the only place you could go. There wasn't any other road.

We sat there a long time, and then I knew she was crying. "Why you do this? Why you do this to me?"

"Don't you know? Why I—" I tried to make myself say "I love you," but it stuck in my throat. "I wanted you. I didn't want him to have you."

"That is not true. You go away."

"What makes you say that?"

"You sing now, yes? You sing better anybody in Mexico. You stay in Acapulco, in a house? Why you lie? You go away."

"I never even thought of it."

"Now for me, very bad. No house, no. Maybe he shoot me, yes. I can no work more in Mexico. He is very big político. I—why you do this? Why you do this?"

We sat there some more, and I wondered why I didn't

feel like a heel. She had called it on me all right, and I
had certainly busted up her run of luck with plenty to
spare. But I didn't feel like a heel. I was in a spot, but my
face wasn't red. Then it hit me between the eyes: *I
wasn't going to run out on her.*

"Juana."

"Yes?"

"Listen to me now. I've got some things to say."

"Please, say nothing."

"In the first place, you were right when you said I was
going away, and I did lie to you. While I was out, pretending to look the town over, I arranged passage to the
Estados Unidos del Norte, on a boat. I was to leave at
twelve o'clock."

"I know you lie, when you go out. Yes."

"All right, I lied. You want to hear the rest?"

She didn't answer for a long time. But you could always tell when something was going on inside of her, because her breath would stop for a two beat, and then go
on. She turned her head to me once, and then looked
away. "Yes."

"When I went up to the hotel, I intended to take you
out to dinner, sit around a while, then drift out to the *caballeros,* and not come back. Then you started off with
him, and I knew I wasn't going to let you go, and it
wasn't only that I didn't like him. I wanted you myself,
and I wasn't going to let him have you, or anybody have
you."

"But why?"

"I'll get to that. I'm not done yet. Now I'm going
away. I told you I used to be a singer. I used to be a very
good singer, one of the best in the world, and I made a
lot of money, and I will again. But I can't do anything in
Mexico. I'm going back to my own country, the *Estados
Unidos del Norte.* Now, here's what I'm getting at. Do
you want to come with me?"

"Is that very big country?"

"Much bigger than Mexico."

"How you go?"

"We have the car, and you still have a little money. In
a little while, after things quiet down, we'll slip through

the town and go as far as we can before daylight. Then
tomorrow night, we'll start out again, and with luck we'll
make Mexico City. We'll lay low another day, and the
next night we'll be in Monterey. One more night and
we're at Laredo, and I'll figure a way to get you across.
Once we're in my country, we're all right."

"That is impossible."

"Why?"

"They know the auto. They catch us, sure."

I knew that was right, even before she said it. In the
United States, once you're across a state line, you could
go quite a while without being caught. But down there,
the state line doesn't mean much. Those guys with rifles,
they're federal troops, and with just a car now and then
up that road, there wasn't a chance they would miss us,
night time, day time, or any other time. ". . . In bus, perhaps."

"What was that, Juana?"

"Ride little way, hide auto. Then in morning, take bus.
Maybe they no catch."

"All right, we'll do that."

"But why? Why you no go alone?"

"All right, now we come to the big why. You like me?"

"Yes, much."

"I like you."

I sat looking at her, wondering why I couldn't go the
whole hog, tell her I loved her and be done with it. Then
I remembered how many times I had sung those words,
in three or four different languages, how phoney they
sounded, and how much trouble I had in putting them
across. Then it came to me that I hated them, not for
what they said, but for what they didn't say. They told it
all except what you felt in your bones, your belly, and all
those other places. They said you might die for a woman,
but missed how hungry you could get for her, just to be
near her, just to know she was around. ". . . I could
make it stronger than that, Juana. Maybe I don't have
to."

"They catch us, sure. They kill us."

"You willing to take a chance?"

It was a long time before she said anything, and before

she did she took my hand and pressed it. Then she
looked up, and I knew that whatever it was going to be,
there was no fooling around about it. It was the
works. . . . "Yes."

A little tingle went over me, but what I said was
dumb enough. "Yes, what?"

"What do you mean?"

"Don't you think it's about time for us to pick out
something for you to call me? I can't very well keep on
being *Señor*."

"I call you Hoaney."

I half wished she had picked out something different
than what she had called every Weehawken slob that had
showed up at her crib, but I didn't say anything. Then
something caught my throat. It came to me that she
wasn't calling me "Honey." She was calling me Johnny—
her way. "Kiss me, Juana. That's exactly what I want you
to call me."

The town was dark now, and quiet. I started, pulled out
of the grove, and got over the road. As soon as I could I
went into high, not for speed, but for quiet. With all
that stuff out of the car we didn't make much noise, but
I cut her back to the slowest roll that was in her, and we
crept along until we got to the main street. I stopped,
and listened. I didn't hear anything, so I started up again,
and turned the corner, to the left. I hadn't put the lights
on, and the moon was hanging low over the ocean, so the
right side of the main street was in shadow. I had gone
half a block when she touched my arm. I rolled in to the
curb and stopped. She pointed. About three blocks down
the street, on the left, where the moonlight lit him up,
was a cop. He was walking away from us. He was the only
one in sight. She leaned to me and whispered: "He go,
so."

She motioned with her hand, meaning around the corner. That's how I went. I gave him about five seconds,
then reached for the starter. The car tilted. Somebody
was beside me, on the running board. I still had the gun
beside me. I snatched it and turned. A brown face was

there, not six inches from mine. Then I saw it was Conners.

"Is that you, lad?"

"Yes. God, you gave me a start."

"Where've you been? I've been looking all over for you! I've broken out my hook, I'm ready to go, I'm out of humor with you."

"I got in some trouble."

". . . Don't tell me it was you that hit the general?"

"I did."

His eyes popped open and he began to talk in a whisper. "The penalty is death, lad, the penalty is death."

"Irregardless of that—"

"Not so loud. It's all over town. One of them could be sleeping, and if they hear the English, they'll yell and it'll be the end of you. . . . Did you mind what I said? The penalty is death. He'll take you to the jail and they'll spend an hour booking you, filling out every paper they've got. Then he'll take you out and have them shoot you—for trying to escape."

"If they catch me."

"They'll catch you. For God's sake, come on."

"I'm not coming."

"Did you hear me? The penalty—"

"Since I saw you, there are two of us. Miss Montes, Capitán Conners."

"I'm happy to know you, Miss Montes."

"Gracias, Capitán Conners."

He treated her like a princess, and she acted like one. But then he leaned close and put it in my ear. "You can't do it, man. You can't take up with some girl you met tonight, and you'll be putting her in terrible danger, too. She's a pretty little thing, but hark what I'm telling you. You must come on."

"I didn't just meet her tonight, and she's with me."

He looked up and down the street, and then at his watch. Then looked at me hard. "Lad—do you know the Leporello song?"

"I do."

"Then come on, the pair of you."

He slipped around the car and helped her out. She had the hatbox in her lap. He took it. She carried the other stuff. I grabbed the door, for fear he would slam it mechanically. He didn't. I slipped out on the right side, after her. He pulled us back of the car. "We'll keep the automobile between us and that policeman, down the street."

We tiptoed back to the corner I had just turned, and instead of going the way I had, he pulled us the other way, toward the beach. We came to a crooked alley, and turned into that.

Two minutes after that we trotted out on a dock, and dropped into a launch. Two minutes after that, we were on the deck of the *Port of Cobh*, with beer and sandwiches coming up. Two minutes after that we were slipping past the headland, and I was cocked back with a guitar on my knee, rolling the Leporello song out for him, and she was pouring beer.

Chapter 6

IT WAS A HAPPY WEEK, all right. I didn't sing much, except a little at night, if he wanted it. Most of the time we sat around and fanned about music. She would be with us, and then she wouldn't be. He gave us the royal suite, and the main feature was a shower bath, with sea water coming out of it. It was the first time she had been under one. Maybe it was the first time she ever had a bath, I don't know. Mexicans are the cleanest people on earth. Their face is clean, their feet are clean, their clothes are clean, and they don't stink. But when they bathe, or whether they bathe, I can't tell you. To her it was a new toy, and every time I'd go looking for her I'd find her in there, stripped clean, under the water. I guess I generally hung around. She was something for a sculptor to hire, and she had just enough of the copper in her to make her look like something poured from metal, especially with the water shining on her shoulders. I didn't let her see me look, at first, but then I found out she liked it. She'd stand on her toes, and stretch her arms, and let her muscles ripple, and then laugh. So of course that led to this and that.

The second night out, he got off on a harangue against Verdi, Puccini, Mascagni, Bellini, Donizetti, and "that most unspeakable wop of all, Rossini." That was where I stopped him. "Hold on, hold on, hold on. On those others, I haven't got much to say. I sing them, but I don't talk about them, though Donizetti is a lot better than most people think. But on Rossini, you're crazy."

"The William Tell Overture is the worst piece of music ever written."

"There's music in it, but it's not his best."

"There's no music in it of any kind."

"Well, how's this?"

I picked up the guitar and gave him a little of Semiramide. You can't play a Rossini crescendo on a guitar, but I did what I could. He listened, his face set like flint. I finished and was going to start something else, when he touched my arm. "Play a little of that again."

I played it again, then gave him some Italians in Algiers, and then some Barber. It took quite a while. I know a lot of Rossini. I didn't sing, just played. On the woodwind strain in the Barber overture, I just brushed the strings with my fingers, then for the climax came in big over the hole, and it really sounded like something. I stopped, and he smoked his pipe a long time. " 'Tis fine, musicianly music, isn't it?"

"It's all of that. And it's no worse for being gay, and not taking itself too seriously."

"Aye, it has a twinkle in its eye, and a sparkle in its beat."

"Your friend Beethoven patronized him, the son-of-a-bitch. Told him to keep on writing tunes, that was what he was good for. All Rossini was doing at the time was trying to give him a lift, so he wouldn't have to live like a hog in the dump he found him in."

"If he patronized him it was his right."

"The hell it was. When a Beethoven overture is as good as a Rossini overture, then it'll be his right. Until then, let him keep his goddam mouth shut."

"Lad, lad, you're profaning a temple."

"No, I'm not. You say he's the greatest composer that ever lived, and so do I. He wrote the nine greatest symphonies ever put on paper, and that makes him the greatest composer. But listen, symphonies are not all of music. When you get to the overtures, Beethoven's name is not at the top, and Rossini's is. The idea of a man that could write a thing like the Leonora No. 3 high-hatting Rossini. Why, when those horns sound off, off-stage, it's a cheap vaudeville effect that makes the William Tell Overture sound like a Meistersinger's Prelude, by comparison."

"I confess I don't like it."

"Oh yeah, he would show the boys how to write an overture, wouldn't he? He didn't have overtures in him. You know why? To write an overture, you've got to love the theatre, and he didn't. Did you ever hear Fidelio?"

"I have, and it shames me—"

"But Rossini loved the theatre, and that's why he could write an overture. He takes you into the theatre,— hell, you can even feel them getting into their seats, and smell the theatre smell, and see the lights go up on the curtain. Who the hell told Beethoven he could treat that guy as somebody with an amusing talent that he ought to cultivate?"

"Just the same he was a great man."

I played the minuet from the Eighth Symphony. You can get most of that on the guitar. ". . . That was something to hear. By the way you play him, lad, you think he's a great man yourself, I take it?"

"Yes."

"The other too. From now on I shall listen to him." We were several days out before he got around to Mc-Cormack, and he kind of brought it up offhand, as we were sitting on deck at sundown, like it was just something he happened to think of. But when he found out I

thought McCormack was one of the greatest singers that
ever lived, he began to talk. "So you say the singers admire the fellow?"

"Admire him? Does a ballplayer admire Ty Cobb?"

"Between ourselves, I'm no enthusiast for the art. As
you've observed, I'm a symphony man myself, and I believe the great music of the world has been written for
fiddlers, not singers. But with McCormack I make an exception. Not because he's an Irishman, I give you my
word on that. You were right about Herbert. If there's
one thing an Irishman hates more than a landlord it's another Irishman. 'Tis because he makes me feel music I
had previously been indifferent to. I don't speak of the
ballads he sings, mush a man wouldn't spit into. But I
have heard him sing Händel. I heard him sing a whole
program of Händel at a private engagement in Boston."

"He can sing it, all right."

"Until then, I had not cared for Händel, but he revealed it to me. 'Tis something to be grateful for, the
awakening to Händel. What is the reason for that? I've
heard a million of your Wops, Frogs and Yankees sing
Händel, aye and plenty of Englishmen, but not one of
them can sing it the way that fellow can."

"Well, in the first place, he's good. That's something
you can't quite cut up into pieces and measure off. And
when a man's good, he's generally good all the way down
the line. McCormack has music in him, so he no sooner
opens his trap than there's a tingle to it, no matter what
he sings. He has an instinct for style that never lets him
down. He never drags an andante too slow, or hustles an
allegro too fast. He never turns a dumb phrase, or forces,
or misgauges a climax. When he does it, it's always right,
with a big R. What he did for Händel was to bring it to
life for you. Up to then, you probably thought it was
pale, thin, tinkle-tankle stuff—"

"To my shame I did."

"And then he stepped into it, like a bugler at dawn—"

"That's it, that's it, like a bugler at dawn. You can't
imagine what it was like, lad. He stood there, the most
arrogant figure of a man I ever saw, with his chest thrown
out and his head thrown back, and his thumbs in his lit-

tle black book of words, like a cardinal starting the mass. And without a word, he began to sing. And the sun came up, and the sun came up."

"And in the second place—"

"Yes, lad, in the second place?"

"He had a great voice."

"He could have the Magic Flute in his throat and I'd never know it."

"Well, he goddam near *had* the Magic Flute in his throat, if somebody happened to ask you. And your ears knew it, even if your head didn't. He had a *great* voice, not just a good voice. I don't mean big. It was never big, though it was big enough. But what makes a great voice is beauty, not size, and beauty will get you, I don't care if it's in a man's throat or a woman's leg."

"You may be right. I hadn't thought of it."

"And in the third place—"

"Go on, 'tis instructive to me."

"—There's the language he was born to. John McCormack comes from Dublin."

"He does not. He comes from Athlone."

"Didn't he live in Dublin?"

"No matter. They speak a fine brogue in Athlone, almost as fine as in Belfast."

"It's a fine brogue, but it's not a brogue. It's the English language as it was spoken before all the other countries of the world forgot how to speak it. There's two things a singer can't buy, beg or steal, and that no teacher, coach or conductor can give him. One is his voice, the other is the language that was born in his mouth. When McCormack was singing Händel he was singing English, and he sings it as no American and no Englishman will ever sing English. But not like an Irishman. Not with all that warmth, color, and richness that McCormack puts into it."

" 'Tis pleasant to hear you say that."

"You speak a fine brogue yourself."

"I try to say what I mean."

We were creeping past Ensenada, four or five miles out,

and we smoked a while without saying anything. The sea was like glass, but you could see the hotel in the setting sun, and the white line of surf around the harbor. We smoked a while, but I'm a bit of a bug on that subject of language, and what a man brings on stage with him besides what he was taught. I started up again, and told him how all the great Italian singers have come from the city of Naples, and gave him a few examples of singers with fine voices that never made the grade because they were bums, and people won't listen to bums. About that, I knew plenty. Then I got off on Mexico, and about that, I guess you can realize I was pretty bitter. I began getting it off my chest. He listened, but pretty soon he stopped me. "Not so fast, lad, not so fast. 'Tis instructive that Caruso came from Naples, as McCormack came from Athlone, and that it was part of his gift, but when you speak so of Mexico, I take exception."

"I say they can't sing because they can't talk." -

"They talk soft."

"They talk soft, but they talk on top of their throats—*and they've got nothing to say!* Listen, you can't spend a third of your life on the dirt floor of an adobe hut, and then expect people to listen to you when you stand up and try to sing Mozart. Why, sit down, you goddam Indian, and—"

"I'm losing patience with you."

"Did you ever hear them sing?"

"I don't know if they can sing, and I don't care. But they're a great people."

"At what? Is there one thing they do well?"

"Life is not all doing. It's part being. They're a great people. The little one in there—"

"She's an exception."

"She's not. She's a typical Mexican, and I should know one when I see her by now. I've been sailing these coasts for fifty years. She speaks soft, and holds herself like the little queen that she is. There's beauty in her."

"I told you, she's an exception."

"There's beauty in them."

"Sure, the whole goddam country is a musical comedy

set, if that's what you mean. But when you get past the
scenery and the costumes, what then? Under the surface
what do you find? Nothing!"

"I don't know what I find. I'm no great hand at words,
and it would be hard for me to say what I find. But I
find *something*. And I know this much: if it's beauty I
feel, then it must be under the surface, because beauty is
always under the surface."

"Under the bedrock, in that hellhole."

"I think much about beauty, sitting alone at night, listening to my wireless, and trying to get the reason of it,
and understand how a man like Strauss can put the
worst sounds on the surface that ever profaned the night,
and yet give me something I can sink my teeth into. This
much I know: True beauty has *terror* in it. Now I shall
reply to your contemptuous words about Beethoven. He
has *terror* in him, and your overture writers have not.
Fine music they wrote, and after your remarks I shall listen to them with respect. But you can drop a stone into
Beethoven, and you will never hear it strike bottom. The
eternities and the infinities are in it, and they strike at the
soul, like death. You mind what I'm telling you, there is
terror in the little one too, and I hope you never forget it
in your relations with her."

There wasn't much I could say to that. I had felt the
terror in her, God knows. We lit up again, and watched
Ensenada turn gray, blue and violet. My cigarettes were
all gone by then, and I was smoking his tobacco, and one
of his pipes, that he had cleaned out for me on a steam
jet in the boiler. Not a hundred feet from the ship a
black fin lifted out of the water. It was an ugly thing to
see. It was at least thirty inches high, and it didn't zigzag,
or cut a V in the water, or any of the things it does in
books. It just came up and stayed a few seconds. Then
there was the swash of a big tail and it went down.

"Did you see it, lad?"

"God, it was an awful-looking thing, wasn't it?"

"It cleared up for me what I've been trying to say to
you. Sit here, now, and look. The water, the surf, the colors on the shore. You think they make the beauty of the
tropical sea, aye, lad? They do not. 'Tis the knowledge of

what lurks below the surface of it, that awful-looking
thing, as you call it, that carries death with every move
that it makes. So it is, so it is with all beauty. So it is
with Mexico. I hope you never forget it."

We docked at San Pedro around three in the afternoon,
and all I had to do was walk ashore. He gave me dollars
for our pesos, so I wouldn't have any trouble over that
part, and came down the plank with me. It took about
three seconds. I was an American citizen, I had my passport, they looked at it, and that was all. I had no baggage.
But she was different, and how she was going to get
ashore was making me pretty nervous. He had her below
decks, under cover, and so far so good, but that didn't
mean she was in, by a long way. He didn't seem much
upset, though. He walked through the pier with me, waving at his friends, stopping to introduce me to his broker,
taking it easy. When he got to the loading platform outside, he stood there and lit a cigar his broker had given
him. "Across there is a little cove they call Fish Harbor.
It is reached by a ferry, and you should find out how to
get there this afternoon, but don't arrive before dark, as
you should not be seen hanging around. By the wharves
runs a street, and on the main thoroughfare leading down
to it is a little Japanese restaurant, about a stone's throw
from the water. Be there at nine o'clock, sharp. Order
beer, and drink it slowly till I come."
  He clapped me on the shoulder, and went back to the
ship. I walked down and found how the ferry ran. Then I
went in a lunchroom and had something to eat. Then I
went in a moving picture, so I could sit down. I don't
even know what the show was. Every fifteen or twenty
minutes I would go out in the lobby to look at the clock.
Whatever it was, I saw it twice. Around seven I left the
theatre and walked down to the ferry. It was quite a
while coming, but just about dark it showed up and I
went across. It took about ten minutes. I walked down to
Fish Harbor, found it without having to ask anybody
about it, and then spotted the restaurant. I walked past it,
then found a clock and checked on the time. It was half
past eight. I walked on to where the street turned into a

road, and kept on going until I figured I had covered
three quarters of a mile. Then I turned around and came
back. When I passed the clock it said five minutes to
nine.

I went in and ordered beer. There were five or six guys in
there, fishermen by their looks, and I raised my glass at
them, and they raised back. I didn't want to act like some
mysterious stranger, looking neither right nor left. After
that they paid no attention to me. At ten after he came
in. He shook hands all around in a big way, then sat
down with me, and ordered beer. They seemed to know
him. When his beer came, he sent the Jap out for a cab,
and then began telling me, and telling them, about this
trouble he had on his ship. He had his things packed, and
was already to come ashore, when a launch showed up
out of the night, and began yelling up at the pier for
somebody named Charlie. "They kept it up, until I got
so sick of Charlie I could have thrown a pin at them."

He was pretty funny, but I wasn't in the humor for it.
They were, though. "Who was Charlie?"

"I never did find out. But wait a minute. Of course my
second officer had his face out the hatch, ogling the girls,
and do you know what the young upstart did? He called
out: 'Forget about Charlie! Come aboard, girls. I'll give
you a hand through the hatch—and let a real man take
care of you!' And before I knew it he had a line down,
they had made the launch fast, and they were aboard my
ship!"

"What did you do?"

"I was down there in a flash and I ordered them off! Off
and begone!' I said to them. 'Out of the hatch where you
came in, and let me see no more of you!' "

"Did they go?"

"They did not! They stood laughing at me, and invited
me to go with them! Then the man that was with them
seconded the invitation, and my second officer had the
effrontery to second him. I was so furious I could not
trust myself to speak. But then with an effort, I got myself under control, and I said to him: ' 'Tis an official
matter,' I reminded him, 'to be entered on your papers

and reported to your owners. Get these girls out of here, and at once.' Do you know what those girls said to me?"

"What they say?"

" 'Nuts.' "

That got a laugh. "I argued with them. I pleaded with them, as I didn't want any trouble. At last I had to appeal to the guard on the pier, who was standing there, looking down into the hatch, listening to it. 'Is that right, my man?' I said to him, 'that such entry into a ship is in violation of law? That they must enter by the plank, and pass the guard, otherwise be subject to arrest?"

" 'It is, captain,' he said, 'and they'll not pass the guard if I have anything to do with it.' "

"That seemed to frighten them, and out they went, the girls, the man and my second officer. Him I will deal with in the morning. But what I cannot understand about these American girls is the boldness of them. Not one of them could have been more than nineteen, and where were their mothers all that time? What were they doing in that launch at all? Will you tell me that?"

They all chimed in with what a tough bunch the young girls are nowadays, and then the Jap came in and said the cab was ready. He paid, and we took the valise he had brought with him, and went out and put it in the cab, and he told the driver to wait. Then he started to walk down toward the wharves. "Well, what about her?"

He didn't seem to hear me. " 'Twas a noisy ten minutes. Of course, if the guard on the pier had been observant, he would have noticed that the man in the launch was my first officer. He would also have noticed that whereas three young girls came into the hatch, four of them went out of it."

"Oh."

We got to the wharves, strolled out on one, then strolled back, and stood on the corner, smoking. Out in the basin somewhere a launch started up. In a minute or two it slipped in to the wharf, stopped a second, and she hopped ashore and came running to us. Then it shoved off and disappeared. I had wanted to go down and thank those guys for all they had done for us, but he wouldn't

let me. "I'll tell them all you say. The three girls they
found have no idea what they've been a party to, and the
less they know, the less they have to tell. They will see a
nice picture show, now, and that's enough."

It was always catching me by surprise, how glad I was to
be with her, and I got this catch in my throat when she
came running up to us, laughing like it had all been a big
joke. We walked back to the cab, got in, and told the
driver to take the ferry and go to the nearest Los Angeles
bus stop. She sat in the middle and I took her hand. He
looked out the window. She turned to him, but he kept
staring at the buildings going by. Then she reached out
and took his hand. He came out of it on that. He took
her hand in both of his, and patted it, but it was a minute or two before he said anything. ". . . There's something I'd like to say to both of you. I've enjoyed every
minute of your stay on my ship. I wish you all happiness,
and as you're in love, you may have it. 'Tis a big world,
and I bob around it like a cork in a tub. But should you
ever need me, and should I be there, you have only to
say the word. Only to say the word."

". . . Gracias, Señor Capitán.—. . . This big world, I go
around, too . . . But, you need me—you say word, say
word only."

"Me too."

". . .'Tis a pretty night."

On the ferry the driver went forward to have a smoke,
and we were alone. He sat up and began to talk. "Her
things are all in the valise. It holds them better than her
own little box, especially that sword that she carries with
her. She's wearing no hat, and it would be a good idea if
you were to stow your own hat with her stuff. You're
both well burned by the sun, and without hats you could
well be a couple that has spent a day at the beach, and
arouse no suspicion that you're just off a boat."

I opened the valise, put my hat in it, and he went on.
"Inquire of the busman, and get off as near what they
call the Plaza as you can. In that neighborhood are many
small hotels catering to Mexicans of the town, and you

will attract no attention. Register as Mr. and Mrs. Perhaps you will not believe it, but under American laws you must write it so, and so long as you do, they will not care. In the morning, get up very early, and as soon as you can, get a hat on her. I have packed all her shawls, and forbidden her to carry one, as they will betray her sooner than anything else. I doubt if she has ever had a hat on in her life, so be careful that you pick one yourself, a little hat exactly like all the other hats in the place. When you have bought the hat, buy her a little dress. I know nothing of girls' clothes myself, but her little things make me think of Mexico, and sharper eyes than mine might become suspicious. Buy her a dress like every other dress in the place. When you have bought her a hat and bought her a dress, you can breathe easier about illegal entry. Her accent will attract no attention. In America are as many accents as the countries of the world, and she could have lived here all her life and still speak as she does. But the clothes will mark her. She should meet few Mexicans. There is a belief among them that the United States government pays informers against immigrants of her kind. It does not, but one of them might turn her in for the sake of the legendary reward. As soon as you can, get work. A working man is his own answer to all questions, an idle man is a riddle they all try to guess. It would be a good idea if she learned to read and write."

We got out at the bus stop, and shook hands, and then she put her arms around him and kissed him. He was shaken up as I stepped over to help him into the cab. "And you'll mind what I've been telling you, lad?—about her, and Mexico, and all the rest of it?"

"I'll mind. For the rest of my life."

"See that you do. For the rest of your life."

Chapter 7

WE FOUND A LITTLE HOTEL, a two-dollar joint on Spring Street, and didn't have any trouble. It was about what you would expect, but after Mexico it was like a palace, and they gave us a room with a shower, so she was happy. After she had splashed enough water to suit her, she came and lay in my arms, and I lay there thinking about how we were starting our life together in my own country, and wanted to say something about it, but next thing I knew she was asleep. We got up early the next morning, and as soon as the stores were open, went out to get that hat. Then we got a dress and a light coat. The hat was $1.95, the dress $3.79, and the coat $6. That left us $38 out of her 500 pesos. We stopped by a little restaurant, had a little breakfast, and then I took her back to the hotel and went out to find work.

First thing I did was wire my agent in New York, the one that had sent me down to Mexico. I told her I was all right again, and to see what she could do, as I wanted to get going. Then I bought a Variety, the Hollywood edition, and looked in there to see if any agents carried ads. Quite a few of them did, and the one that seemed to be what I wanted was named Stoessel, and had offices in Hollywood, so I got on a bus and went out there. It took me an hour to get in to see him, and he never even bothered to look at me. "Brother, out here singers are a drug on the market, and they've quit fooling with them. They've had them all, and how many come through? Eddy, MacDonald, Pons, Martini, and Moore—and even Pons and Martini ain't so hot. The rest of them, flops, nothing but flops. And it ain't only that they flop, they have a hell of a time getting stories for them. They're

through with singers. When they want a singer, little
production number maybe, they know where to get him.
Outside of that—out. I'm sorry, but you're in the wrong
place."

"I didn't mean pictures. How about theatres?"

"I could book you twelve weeks straight, right up the
coast, book you in a minute, if you was a name. Without
a name for the marquee, you ain't worth a dime."

"I'm fairly well known."

"I never heard of no John Howard Sharp."

"I sang mainly in Europe."

"This ain't Europe."

"How about night clubs?"

"I don't fool with that small stuff. You want to go on
in a night club, there's plenty of them around. If that interests you, you might pick up quite a little time here and
there, this and that. Try Fanchon and Marco. Maybe
they got a spot for you."

I walked down on Sunset, to Fanchon and Marco.
They were putting up a dance act, and a singer didn't
seem to fit. I went in a radio station. They gave me an
audition, and said they'd let me have some sustaining
time in the afternoon, but they wouldn't pay for it, and
I'd have to bring my own accompanist. I said I'd be back.

Around four o'clock I went in a night club on La Brea,
and they let me sing for them, and then said they'd put
me on, $7.50 a night, tips and meals, report in evening
clothes at nine o'clock. I said I'd let them know. I found
a costume place to go in and rent an evening outfit. The
price was $3 a night, $10 by the week, and that would
leave a little profit, but they had nothing in there that
would fit. I'm six feet, and weighed nearly two hundred,
and that's an out size for a costume place. I went back to
Spring Street. There was a little place still open, and I
went in and bought a second-hand guitar for $5. I wasn't
going to pay an accompanist to get me on the air. With
that guitar, I could do my own accompanying.

I kept that up three or four days. I parked the guitar in
the radio station, and went in there every day at two
thirty. I was to get fifteen minutes, and be announced

under my name, but when I cut myself up into two
pieces, John Howard Sharp, baritone, and Signor Giu-
seppe Bondo, the eminent Italian guitar player, they gave
me a half hour. I'd sing a couple of numbers, and then
I'd introduce the Signor, and the Signor would announce
his selections in a high voice, in Italian. Then I'd try to
translate, and get it all wrong, so if I said it was to be
Hearts and Flowers, the Signor would play Liebestraum,
or something like that. The station manager thought that
was a pretty good gag, and made us a regular feature, and
put our names in the paper. After the second day he got
twenty or thirty letters about me, and two or three hundred about the Signor, and he got all excited and said he
was going to find a sponsor for us. A sponsor, it turned
out, was an advertiser that would pay us.

One of those days, after the broadcast, I took the guitar out with me and went to Griffith Park, where the
Iowa Society was having a picnic, forty or fifty thousand
of them. I thought if I went singing around, there might
be some tips. I had never taken a tip, and I wondered
how I was going to feel about it. I needn't have worried.
The Iowa Society liked me fine, but none of them dug
into their pocket. But next day I went in the Biltmore,
where the Rotary Club was having lunch. I marched
right in with the guitar, just like I was supposed to be
there, and when I got into the dining-room I went to the
center of the U table that they were all sitting around,
hit a chord and started to sing. I picked the Trumpeter,
because you can rip into it right from the start without
any waiting around for a chorus to get started on. A captain and three waiters hustled over to throw me out, but
two or three of them yelled, "Let him alone! Let him
alone!"

I got a hand, and piled a couple of numbers on top of
it. I remember one of them was the Speaks Mandalay.
Then some egg up in the corner began to yell "Pollyochy! Pollyochy!" I didn't think it was a Pagliacci crowd,
so I didn't pay any attention to him, but he kept it up,
and then some of the others yelled "Pollyochy!" too,
mostly to shut him up. So I whammed into the introduction, and began singing the Prologue. It's not my favorite

piece of music, but I do it all right, and at the end of the andante I gave them plenty of A flat. By rights, you sing A flats for dough, and for nothing else, but it had been a long time since anybody wanted to hear mine. I swelled it and cut, and then on the E flat that follows it I shook the windows. When I finished I got a big hand, and gave them some Trovatore and Traviata.

When it was time for the speeches the president, or chairman, or whatever he was, called me up, and told me to wait, and they began making up a pot for me. They borrowed a tray from a waiter and passed it around and when it came back it was full of silver. He handed it to me, and I thanked him, and dumped it in my pocket. I had taken a tip, but I didn't feel anything. I went out in the washroom to count it.

It was $6.75, but we were getting low, getting low. Even with that, we were down to $22, and nobody showing the least interest in John Howard Sharp. Still, there was an outdoor performance of Carmen that night at the Hollywood Bowl, at a dollar and a half top but with some seats at seventy-five cents, so of course we had to go. If you want to know where to find an opera singer the night some opera is being given you'll find him right there, and no other place. A baseball player, for some reason, prefers a ball game.

So I told her to get dressed, so we could eat early, and try to get out there in time to get some kind of decent seat. By that time she had quit playing with the shower bath to play with the hat. She'd put it on, and take it off, and put it on again, and look at herself in the mirror, and ask if she had it on right, then take it off and start all over again. I generally said it looked swell, but it was funny how dumb she was, catching on to how it worked. Up to then, I had always thought of a woman's hat as something that she put on, and forgot about, and that was that. But the way she did it, it was the funniest-looking thing you ever saw in your life. Half the time she would get it on backwards, and even when she didn't, she would pull it down on her head some way that made it look like it didn't even belong to her. I tried the best I could and it was better than her way, but it always looked like a man's necktie would if somebody else tied it for him.

It was a warm night, so she wasn't wearing the coat. She decided to wear the bullfighter's cape. It looked pretty swell, so it was all right with me. When she had laid it out, she came over for me to put the finishing touches on the hat. I fixed it so it looked almost right, and then she went over to the mirror to have a look. She gave it one last pull that made it all wrong, put on the cape, and turned around to be admired. "Am I very pretty?"

"You're the prettiest thing in the world."

"Yes."

The curtain was advertised at eight thirty, and we got there at seven thirty, but I found out I didn't even know what early meant on a night when they're giving opera in the Hollywood Bowl. Most of those people, I think, had been there since breakfast. The best we could get was up on the rim, at least a quarter of a mile from the show. It was the first time I had ever seen the Hollywood Bowl, and maybe you've never been in it. It's so big you can't believe it. It was just about dark when we got there, and they were pouring into it through every ramp, and everywhere you looked there were people. I counted the house as well as I could, and by my figuring when they all got in there would be twenty thousand of them. As it turned out, that was about right. I sat there wondering whether they used amplifiers or what the hell they did. It frightened you to think of singing in such a place.

I looked on the program to see who was singing. I had heard of a couple of them. The José and the Micaela were second-line Metropolitan people. There was a program note on the Carmen. She was a local girl. I knew the Escamillo. He was a wop named Sabini that sang Silvio in Palermo one night when I was singing Tonio. I hadn't heard of him in five years. The rest of them I didn't know.

They played the introduction and the lights went up and
we began to have a good time. I'm telling you, that was
opera that you dream about. They didn't have any curtain. They put the lights up, and there it was, and when
they finished they blacked out and came up with a baby
spot for the bows. The orchestra was down front. Beyond
was a low flight of wide steps, and quite a way beyond
that was the stage, without the shell they use for concerts. On that they built a whole town, the guardhouse
on one side, cafés on the other, the cigarette factory in
back. You had to rub your eyes to believe you weren't in
Spain. The way they lit it was great. They've got a light
box in that Bowl that tops anything. I ever saw. And that
stage town was just filled with people. The performance
seemed to be given with some kind of hook-up between a
ballet school and some local chorus, and they must have
had at least three hundred out there. When the bell rang
and the girls began pouring out of the factory, they
poured out. It was really lunch time. Between acts, they
rolled that stuff off, and rolled on the café for the second
act, and the rocks for the third act, and the bullring entrance for the fourth act. The place is so big that with the
lights down nobody paid any attention to what they were
doing out there. They didn't use any amplifiers. Big as it
was, the acoustics were so perfect you could hear every
whisper. That was the thing I couldn't get over.

The principals were just fair, maybe not as good as
that, except for the two from the Met, but I didn't mind.
They were giving a performance, and that's enough. So
when this little thing happened, I didn't pay any attention to it. A singer can spot trouble a mile away, but I
was there for a good time, so what the hell? But then I
woke up.

What happened was that in the middle of the scene in
the first act, where the soldiers bring Carmen out from
the factory after she's cuffed another girl around, a choris-
ter in a uniform stepped up to the Zuniga, jerked his
thumb backstage, and began to sing the part. The Zuniga
walked off. That was all. They did it so casually that it
almost seemed like part of the opera, and I don't think
twenty people out there thought anything of it. You

would have had to know the opera to have spotted it. I
wondered about it, because the Zuniga had a pretty good
bass voice, and he had been doing all right. But I was listening to the Carmen, and she started the Seguidilla before I tumbled to what was up.

I jumped up, grabbed the bullfighter cape off her,
whipped off my own coat and put it on her, and pointed
down the hill. "Meet me after it's over! You understand?"

"Where you go?"

"Never mind. Meet me there. You got it?"

"Yes."

I skipped around the rim, took the ramp on the run,
ducked back of the stage, and asked a stagehand for the
manager. He pointed to some cars that were parked out
back. I went back there, and sure enough, there was the
Zuniga, still in his captain's uniform, and a fat guy, standing by a car and arguing with somebody inside. I tapped
the fat guy on the shoulder. He batted at me with his
hand and didn't even look. "I'm busy. See me later."

"Goddamn it, I'm singing your Escamillo for you!"

"Get the hell away!"

"What's the matter with you—are you snowed in? You
called this guy off to get dressed—and he can't sing it!"

The Zuniga turned around. "You heard him, Morris. I
can't sing F"s. I can't do it."

"I've heard you do it."

"Transposed, yes."

"They'll set it down for you!"

"How? They can't rescore a whole number between
acts! They got no parts to set it down with!"

"For Christ sake! They can read it down—"

"They can like hell. It's out!"

About that time, the man in the car put his head out,
and it was Sabini. When he saw me he grabbed me and
began kissing me with one side of his mouth and selling
me to the manager with the other. Then he began giving
me an earful of Italian, a mile a minute, explaining to me
he didn't dare get out of his car, didn't even dare be
seen, or his wife's process servers would get him, and that
was why he couldn't sing. Then he did get out, on the far

side, lifted a trunk out of the rumble, and called me around. He began stripping me, and as fast as he got one piece off me, he'd have a piece of the Toreador costume out of the trunk for me to put on. The manager lit a cigarette and stood there watching us. Then he went off. "It's up to the conductor."

There was a big roar from the Bowl that meant the first act was over. Sabini jumped in the car and snapped on the lights. I sat down in front of them and the Zuniga took the make-up kit and began making me up. He stuck on the *coleta* and I tried the hat. It fit. When the manager came back he had a young guy with him in evening clothes, the conductor. I got up and spoke. He looked me over. "You've sung Escamilla?"

"At least a hundred times."

"Where?"

"Paris, among other places. And not at the Opera. At the Comique, if that means anything to you."

"What name did you sing under?"

"In Italy, Giovanni Sciaparelli. In France and Germany my own, John Howard Sharp."

He gave me a look that would have curdled milk, turned his back, and beckoned to the Zuniga.

"Hey, what's the matter?"

"Yes, I've heard of you. And you're washed up."

I cut one loose they must have heard in Glendale.

"Does that sound like I'm washed up? Does it?"

"You lost your voice."

"Yeah, and I got it back."

He kept looking at me, opened his mouth once or twice to say something, then shook his head and turned to the manager. "It's no use, Morris. He can't do it. I just happened to think of that last act. . . . Mr. Sharp, I wish I could use you. It would pull us out of a spot. But for the sake of the ballet school, we've interpolated Arlésienne music into Act IV, and I've scored the baritone into it, and—"

"Oh, Arlésienne, hey? Listen: Cue me in. That's all I ask. Just cue me in!"

You think that's impossible, that a man can go on and sing stuff he never even saw? All right, once there was an old Áborn baritone that's dead now, by the name of Harry Luckstone, brother of Isidore Luckstone, the singing teacher. He had a cousin named Henry Myers, that writes a little music now and then. Myers had written a song, and he was telling Luckstone about it, and Luckstone said fine, he'd sing it.

"I haven't put it on paper yet—"

"All right, I'll sing it."

"Well, it goes like this—"

"God Almighty, does a man have to know a song to sing it? Get going on your goddam piano, and I'll sing it!"

And he sang it. Nobody but another singer knows how good a singer really is. Sure, I sang his Arlésienne for him. I got a look at his score after Act III, and what he had done was put some words to the slow part, let the baritone sing them, then have baritone and chorus sing them under the fast part, in straight counterpoint. I didn't even bother to look what the words were. I bellowed "Auprès de ma blonde, qu'il fait bon, fait bon," and let it go at that. One place I shot past a repeat. The dancers were all frozen on one foot, ready to do the routine again, and there was I, camped on an E that didn't even belong there. He looked up, and I caught his eye, and hung on to it, and marched all around with it, while he spoke to his men and wigwagged to his ballerina. Then he looked up again, and I cut, and yelled, "Ha, ha, ha." He brought his stick down, the show was together again, and I began flapping the cape at the dancers. In the Toreador Song, on the long "Ah" that leads into the chorus, I broke out the cape and made a couple of passes at the bull. Not too much, you understand. A prop can kill a number. But enough that I got that swirl of crimson and yellow into it. It stopped the show, and he let me repeat the second verse.

Some time during the night I had been given a dressing room, and after the last bow I went there. My clothes were there, piled on the table, and Sabini's trunk. Instead of taking off the make-up first, I started with the costume, so he could get away, if he was still around. I had just stripped down to my underwear when the manager came in, to pay me off. He counted out fifty bucks, in fives. While he was doing it the process server came in. He had a summons to appear in court and a writ to attach costumes. It took all the manager and I could do to convince him I wasn't Alessandro Sabini, but after a few minutes he went. I was scared to death he would see the "A. S." on that trunk, and serve the writ anyhow, but he didn't think of that. The conductor came in and thanked me. 'You gave a fine performance, and I'd like you to know it was a pleasure to have somebody up there that could troupe a little."

"Thanks. I'm sorry about that bobble."

"That's what I'm talking about. When you gave me the chance to pull it out of the soup, that was what I call trouping. Anybody can make a mistake, especially when they're shoved out there the way you were, without even a rehearsal. But when you use your head—well, my hat's off to you, that's all."

"They be pleasant words. Thanks again."

"I don't think they even noticed it. Did they, Morris?"

"Notice it? Christ, they give it a hand."

I sat on the trunk, and we lit up, and they began telling me what the production cost, what the hook-up was, and some more things I wanted to know. Up to then I didn't even know their names. The conductor was Albert Hudson, who you've probably heard of by now, and if you haven't you soon will. The manager was Morris Lahr, who you've never heard of, and never will. He runs a concert series in the winter, and manages a couple of singers, and now and then he puts on an opera. There's one like him in every city, and if you ask me they do more for music than the guys that get their name in the papers.

We were fanning along, me in my underwear with my make-up still on, when the door opens and in pops Stoessel, the agent I had been talking to not a week before. He had a little guy with him, around fifty, and they stood looking at me like I was some ape in a cage, and then Stoessel nodded. "Mr. Ziskin, I believe you're right. He's the type. He's the type you been looking for. And he sings good as Eddy."

"I need a big man, Herman. A real Beery type."

"He's better looking than Beery. And younger. A hell of a sight younger."

"But he's rugged. You know what I mean? Tough. But in the picture, he's got a heart like all outdoors, and that's where the singing comes in. A accent I don't mind, because why? He's got a heart like all outdoors, and a accent helps it."

"I know exactly what you mean, Mr. Ziskin."

"O.K., then, Herman. You handle it. Three fifty while he's learning English, and then after the script is ready and we start to shoot, five. Six weeks' guarantee, at five hundred."

Stoessel turned to Hudson and Lahr. "I guess Mr. Ziskin don't need any introduction around here. He's interested in this man for a picture. Tell him that much, will you? Then we give him the rest of it."

Lahr didn't act like he was any too fond of Mr. Ziskin, or Stoessel either, for that matter. "Why don't you tell him yourself?"

"He speak English?"

"He did a minute ago."

"Sure, I speak English. Shoot."

"Well, say, that makes it easy. O.K., then, you heard what Mr. Ziskin said. Get your make-up off put on your clothes, and we'll go out and talk."

"We can talk right now."

I was afraid to take my make-up off, for fear he would know me. They still thought I was Sabini, I could see that, because there hadn't been any announcement about me, and I was afraid if he placed me there wouldn't be any three fifty or even one fifty. I was down, that day, and he knew it. "All right, then, we'll talk right now. You heard Mr. Ziskin's proposition. What do you say?"

"I say go climb a tree."

"Say, that's no way to talk to Mr. Ziskin."

"What the hell do you think a singer works for? Fun?"

"I know what they work for. I handle singers."

"I don't know whether you handle singers. Maybe you

handle bums. If Mr.-Ziskin has got something to say, let
him say it. But don't waste my time talking about three
hunded and fifty dollars a week. If it was a day, that
would be more like it."

"Don't be silly."

"I'm not being silly. I'm booked straight through to
the first of the year, and if I'm going to get out of those
contracts it's going to cost me dough. If you want to pay
dough, talk. If not, just let's stop where we are."

"What's your idea of dough?"

"I've told you. But I've been wanting to break into pictures, and to get the chance, I'll split the difference with
you. I'll do a little better than that. A thousand a week,
and it's a deal. But that's rock bottom. I can't cut it, and
I can't shade it."

We had it hot for a half hour, but I stuck and they
came around. I wanted it in writing, so Stoessel took out
a notebook and pen and wrote a memo of agreement,
about five lines. I got a buck out of my pants and made
him a receipt for that, first of all. That bound them. But
when we got that far I had to tell my name. I hated to
say John Howard Sharp, but I had to. He didn't say anything. He tore out the leaf, waved it in the air, handed it
to Ziskin to sign. "John Howard Sharp—sure, I've heard
of him. Somebody was telling about him just the other
day."

They went, and a boy came in for Sabini's trunk, and
Lahr went out and came back with a bottle and glasses.
"Guy has broke into pictures, we got to have a drink on
that. . . . Where did you say you were booked?"

"With the Santa Fe, mashing down ballast."

"Happy days."

"Happy days."

"Happy days."

The crowd was gone and she was all alone when I ran
down the hill, waving the cape at her. She turned her
back on me, started to walk to the bus stop. I pulled out the
wad of fives Lahr had given me. "Look, look, look!" She
wouldn't even turn her head. I took my coat off her, put

it on, and dropped the cape over her shoulders. ". . . I wait very long time."

"*Business! I been talking business.*"

"Yes. Smell very nice."

"Sure we had a drink. But listen: get what I'm telling you. I been talking business."

"I wait very long."

I let her get to the bus stop, but I didn't mean to ride on a bus. I began yelling for a taxi. There weren't any, but a car pulled up, a car from a limousine service. "Take you any place you want to go, sir. Rates exactly the same as the taxis—"

Did I care what his rates were? I shoved her in, and that did it. She tried to stay sore, but she felt the cushions, and when I took her in my arms she didn't pull away. There weren't any kisses yet, but the worst was over. I halfway liked it. It was our first row over a little thing. It made me feel she belonged to me.

We went to the Derby and had a real feed. It was the first time I had been in a decent place for a year. But I didn't break the big news until we were back at the hotel, undressing. Then I kind of just slid into it. "Oh, by the way, I got a little surprise for you."

"Surprise?"

"I got a job in pictures."

"Cinema?"

"That's right. A thousand a week."

"Oh."

"Hell, don't you get it? We're rich! A thousand a week —not pesos, dollars! Three thousand, six hundred pesos every week! Why don't you say something?"

"Yes, very nice."

I didn't mean a thing to her! But when I took the cape, and stood up there in my drawers, and sang the Toreador song at her, like I had at the Bowl, that talked. She clapped her hands, and sat on the bed, and I gave her the whole show. The phone rang. The desk calling, to ask me to shut up. I said O.K., but send up a boy. When he came I gave him a five and told him to get us some wine. He was back in a few minutes and we got a little tight, the way we had that night in the church. After a while we went to bed, and a long while after that she lay in my arms, running her fingers through my hair. "You like me?"

"Yes, much."

"Did I sing all right?"

"Very pretty."

"Were you proud of me?"

". . . You very fonny fallow, you, Hoaney. Why I be proud? I no sing."

"But I sang."

"Yes. I like. Very much."

Chapter 8

I DIDN'T LIKE HOLLYWOOD. I didn't like it partly because of the way they treated a singer, and partly because of the way they treated her. To them, singing is just something you buy, for whatever you have to pay, and so is acting, and so is writing, and so is music, and anything else they use. That it might be good for its own sake is something that hasn't occurred to them yet. The only thing they think is good for its own sake is a producer that couldn't tell Brahms from Irving Berlin on a bet, that wouldn't know a singer from a crooner until he heard twenty thousand people yelling for him one night, that can't read a book until the scenario department has had a synopsis made, that can't even speak English, but that is a self-elected expert on music, singing, literature, dialogue, and photography, and generally has a hit because somebody lent him Clark Gable to play in it. I did all right, you understand. After the first tangle with Ziskin I kind of got the hang of how you handle things out there to get along. But I never liked it, not even for a second.

It turned out he wasn't the main guy on his lot, or even a piece of the main guy. He was just one producer there, and when I showed up the next morning he seemed even to have forgot my name. I had his piece of paper, so they had to pay me, but I wandered around for a week not knowing what I was supposed to do or where I was supposed to do it. You see, he didn't have his script ready. But my piece of paper said six weeks, and I meant to collect on it. After four or five days they shoved me in what they call a B picture, a Western about a cowboy that hates sheep and the sheep man's daughter, but then he finds some sheep caught in a blizzard and brings them home safe, and that fixes it all up. I couldn't see where it fixed anything, but it wasn't my grief. They had bought some news-reel stuff on sheep caught in the snow, and that seemed to be the main reason for the picture. The director didn't know I could sing, but I got him to let me spot a couple of campfire songs, and on the blizzard stuff, Git Along, Little Dogies, Git Along.

They finished it toward the end of September, and gave it a sneak preview in Glendale. I thought it was so lousy I went just out of curiosity to see how bad they would razz it. They ate it up. On the snow stuff, every time I came around the bend with a lamb in my arms, breaking trail for the sheep, they'd clap and stamp and whistle. Out in the lobby, after it was over, I caught just a few words between the producer, the director, and one of the writers. "B picture hell—it's a feature!"

"Christ, would that help the schedule! We're three behind now, and if we can make an extra feature out of this, would that be a break! Would that be a break!"

"We got to do retakes."

"We got to do it bigger, but it'll get by."

"It'll cost dough, but it's worth it."

She hadn't come with me. We were living in an apartment on Sunset by that time, and she was going to night school, trying to learn how to read. I went home and she had just gone to bed with her reader, Wisdom of the Ages, a book of quotations from poetry, all in big type, that she practiced on. I got out the guitar and some blank music paper that I had, and I went to work. I split up that song, Git Along, Little Dogies, Git Along, into five-part harmony, one part the straight melody, the other four a quartet obligato in long four-beat and eight-beat notes, and maybe you think it wasn't work. That song is nothing extra to start with, and when you try to plaster polyphonic harmony on top of it, it's a job. But after a while I had it done, and went to bed with her to get a little sleep.

Next morning, before they could get together and really think up something dumb, I got the producer, the director, the writer and the sound man together in the producer's office, and I laid it down to them.

"All right, boys, I heard a little of what you said last night. You thought you had a B picture here, and now you find out if it's fixed up a little bit, you can get away with it for a feature. You want to do retakes, put some more money in it, do it bigger. Now listen to me. You don't have to put one extra dime in this if you do what I tell you, and you can make it a wow. The big hit is the snow stuff. You've got at least ten thousand feet of that that you didn't use. I know because I saw it run off one day in the projection room. The problem is, how to get more of that stuff in, and tie it up so it makes sense so they don't get tired of it before you've really made full use of it. All right, this is what we do. We rip out that sound track where I'm singing, and make another one. I do that song, but after the first verse I come in, singing over top of myself, see? My own voice, singing an obbligato to myself on the verse. Then when that's done, I come in and sing another one on top of that. Then I come in on top of that, so before the end of it, there's five voices there—all me—light falsetto for the tenor part, heavier for the middle point, and plenty of beef in the bass. Then we repeat it. At the repeat, we start a tympanum, a kettle drum, just light at first, but keeping time to the slug of his feet, and when he gets in sight of the ranch-house we bang hell out of it, and let the five-part harmony swell out so the thing really gets there. All during that, you keep cutting in the snowy stuff, but not straight cuts. Slow dissolves, so you get a kind of dream effect, to go with the cock-eyed harmony on that song.

And it doesn't cost you a dime. Nothing but my pay, and you've got me anyhow, for another two weeks. How does it hit you?"

The producer shook his head. His name was Beal, and he and the director and the writer had been listening like it was merely painful, my whole idea. "It's impossible."

"Why is it impossible? You can put all those parts on your loops, I know you can. After you've checked your synchronization, you run them off and make your sound track. It's absolutely possible."

"Listen, we got to do it big, see? That means we got to do retakes, we got to put more production in, and if I got to spend money, I'd a hell of a sight rather spend it on that than on this. This way you say, I got to pay an arranger, I got to hire an orchestra—"

"Arranger, hell. It's already arranged. I've got the parts right here. And what orchestra?"

"For the kettle drum, and—"

"I play the kettle drum myself. On every repeat of the song, I tune it up. Just a little higher, to get a sense of climax, a little louder, a little faster. Don't you get it? They're getting near home. It'll build. It'll give you what you're looking for, it—"

"Nah, it's too tricky. Besides, how can a goddamn cowboy be singing quartets with himself out there in the snow? They wouldn't never believe it. Besides, we got to pump up the rest of the picture, the beginning—"

"O.K., we'll do that, and then they'll believe everything. Look."

It had suddenly popped in my mind about my voice coming back at me, that night in the arroyo, and I knew I had something. "In that campfire song, the second one, Home On The Range, we do a little retake and show him singing it at the mountains. His voice comes back, in an echo. It surprises him. He likes it. He begins to fool around with it, and first thing you know, he's singing a duet with himself, and then maybe a trio. We don't do much with it. Just enough that they like it, and we establish it. Then in the snow scene it's not tricky at all. It's his own voice coming back at him from all over that range—out there all alone, bringing home those sheep.

They can believe it then, can't they? What's tricky now?"

"It's not enough. We got to do retakes."

Up to then the sound man had sat like he was asleep. He sat up now and began to make marks on a piece of paper. "It can be done."

"Even if it can be done, it's no good."

"It can be done, and it's good."

"Oh, you're telling me what's good?"

"Yeah, I'm telling you."

The technical guys on a lot, they're not like the rest of them. They know their stuff, and they don't take much off a producer or anybody. "You went and bought ten thousand feet of the prettiest snow stuff I ever saw, and then what did you do? You threw out all but four hundred feet of it. It's a crime to waste that stuff, and the lousy way you fixed up the story, there's no way to get it in but the way this guy says. All right then, do like he says, and get it in. It'll build, just like he says it will. You'll get all those angle shots in, all those far shots of miles of sheep going down that mountain, all but the little bits that you never even tried to get in before, and then toward the end of it, the ranchhouse where they're getting near home. I'll give him a light mix on the first of it, and on all the far shots, and when we get near the end —we cut her loose. That kettle drum, that's O.K. It'll get that tramp-tramp feel to it, and go with the music. The echoes on Home On The Range I can work with no trouble at all. It's O.K. And it's O.K. all down the line. It's the only chance you got. Because listen: either this is a little epic all by itself, or it's a goddam cheapie not worth hell room. Take your pick."

"Epic! That's what I've been trying to get."

"Well then, this is how you get it."

"All right, then, fix it up like he says. Let me know when you've got something for me to look at."

So he, I, and the cutter went to work. When I say work I mean work. It was sing, rewrite the parts, test the mix, run it off, and do it all over again from morning to night, and from night to almost morning, but after a couple of weeks we had it done and they gave it another preview, downtown this time, with the newspapers notified.

They clapped, cheered, and gave it a rising vote. The Times next morning said "Woolies" was "one of the most vital, honest, and moving things that had come out of Hollywood in a long time," and that "John Howard Sharp, a newcomer with only featured billing, easily stole the picture, and is star material, unless we miss our guess. He can act, he can sing, and he has that certain indefinable, je-ne-sais-quoi something. He's distinctly somebody to watch."

So the next day eight guys showed up to sell me a car, two to sell me annuities, one to get me to sing at a benefit, and one to interview me for a fan magazine. I was a Hollywood celebrity overnight. When I went on the lot in the afternoon I got a call to report to the office of Mr. Gold, president of the company. Ziskin was there, and another producer named London. You'd have thought I was the Duke of Windsor. It seemed I wasn't to wait till Ziskin got his script ready. I was to go into another one that was waiting to shoot. They had been dickering with John Charles Thomas for it, but he was tied up. They thought I would do just as well, because I was younger and bigger and looked the part better. It was about a singing lumberjack that winds up in grand opera.

I said I was glad they liked my work, and everything was fine if we could come to terms on money. They looked kind of funny, and wanted to know what I was talking about. We had our agreement, and I was pretty well paid for a man that started in pictures just a little while ago.

"We did have an agreement, Mr. Gold."

"And we still got it."

"It ran out today."

"Get his contract, Ziskin."

"He's sewed for five years, Mr. Gold, absolutely for five years from the date on the contract, with options every six months, same as all our talent, with a liberal increase, two fifty I think it was, every time we take up our option. A fine, generous contract, and frankly, Mr. Sharp, I am much amazed by the attitude you're taking. That won't get you nowheres in pictures."

"Get his contract."

So they sent down for my contract, and a secretary
came up with it, and Gold took a look at it, put his
thumb on the amounts and handed it over. "You see?"

"Yeah, I see everything but a signiature."

"This is a file copy."

"Don't try to kid me. I haven't signed any contract.
That may be the contract you were going to offer me, but
the only thing that's been signed is this thing here, that
ran out today."

I fished out the memo I had got off Ziskin that night
in the dressing-room. Gold began to roar at Ziskin. Ziskin
began to roar at the secretary. "Yes, Mr. Ziskin, the contract came through at least a month ago, but you gave me
strict orders not to have any contracts signed until you
gave your personal approval, and it's been on your desk
all that time. I've called it to your attention."

"I been busy. I been cutting Love Is Love."

The secretary went. Ziskin went. London looked sore.
Gold began drumming on his desk with his fingers.
"O.K., then. If you want a little more dough, something
like that, I guess we can boost you a little. Tell you what
we do. We won't bother with any new contract. You can
sign this one here, and we'll take up the first option right
away, and that'll give you twelve fifty. No use quarreling
about a few hundred bucks. Report on the set tomorrow
morning to Mr. London here, and you better be going
down and getting measured for your costumes so you can
start."

"I'm afraid twelve fifty won't do, Mr. Gold."

"Why not?"

"I prefer to work by the picture."

"O.K., then. Let's see, this is on a six-week shooting
schedule, that'll make seven and a half for the picture. I'll
have new contracts drawn up this afternoon with corre-
sponding options."

"I'm afraid that won't do either."

"What the hell are you getting at?"

"I want fifty thousand for the picture, with no options.
I want to work, but I want every picture a separate deal.
For this one, fifty thousand. When we see how that goes,
we'll talk again."

"Talk like you had good sense."

"Listen, I've been out here a little while now, I know what you pay, and fifty thousand is the price. Very low it is, too, but as you say, I'm new here, and I've got to be reasonable."

London left, talking over his shoulder as he went. "Stop work on the sets. I'll wait for Thomas. If I can't get him I'll take Tibbett, and if I can't get him I'll put an actor in and dub the sound. But I'll be goddamned if I'm paying fifty grand to this punk."

"Well, you heard him, Mr. Sharp. He's the producer. Fifty thousand is out of the question. We might up that seven and and a half to ten, but that would be top. The picture can't stand it, Mr. Sharp. After all, we know what our productions cost."

"I heard him, and now in case you didn't hear me, I'll say it over again. The price is fifty thousand. Now beginning tomorrow I'm taking a little rest. I've been working hard, and I'm tired. But one week from today, if I don't hear from you, I'm taking the plane for New York. I've got plenty of work waiting for me there, and get this: I'm not just talking. I'm going."

"I hate to see you be so foolish."

"Fifty, or I go."

"Why—pictures could make you rich. And you can't get away with this. You're trying to put one over on us. You'll be blackballed all over Hollywood. No studio will have you."

"To hell with that. Fifty or I don't work."

"Oh, to hell with it, hey? I'll goddam well see that you don't work in Hollywood. We'll see if a lousy ham actor can put one like that over on Rex Gold."

"Sit down."

He sat, and he sat pretty quick. "Once more. Fifty or I'm going to New York. You got a week."

"Get out of my office."

"On my way."

I had bought a little car by then, and every day we would start out early for the beach or some place, and every day when we got back, around one o'clock, so she could take her siesta, there would be a memo to call Mr.

Ziskin, or Mr. London, or somebody. I never called. Around five o'clock they would call again, and it would turn out that if I would go over and apologize to Mr. Gold, there might be an adjustment on the price, say up to fifteen thousand, or something like that. I did like hell go over and apologize. I said I had done nothing to apologize for, and the price was still fifty thousand. Somewhere around the fifth day they got up to twenty-five. We were at the Burbank airport, going out to the plane, before they came around. A guy ran up, waving signed contracts. I looked them over. They said fifty thousand, but called for three pictures, one each at that price. I thought fast, and said if they'd pay for my tickets it was all right. He snatched them out of my hand before I even finished. Next day I went into Gold's office and said I heard he wanted to apologize. He took that for a gag and we shook hands.

All that time I was making "Woollies," I hardly saw her at all. By the time I got in from the lot, around seven or eight o'clock, she would be gone to night school. I'd eat dinner alone, then go and get her, and we'd have a little snack at the Derby or somewhere. Then it would be time to go home and go to sleep. Believe me, you work on a picture lot, and don't let anybody tell you different. She'd be still asleep when I left in the morning, and the next night it would be the same thing over again. But that week I took off, we did go out and buy her some clothes. We got four or five dresses, and a fur coat, and some more hats. She loved the fur coat. It was mink, and she would stroke it the way she stroked the bull's ears. And she looked swell in it. But the hats she couldn't get the hang of at all. Between me and the saleswoman, we managed to fix her up with a few that seemed to be all right, a kind of soft brown felt hat that would do for regular dresses and that went nice with the coat, and a big filmy one for night, and a little one for knocking around in the morning, or at night school, and two or three that went with what the saleswoman called sports dresses, the kind of thing they wear at the beach. But she never could get it through her head which hat went with which dress.

'We'd start out for the·beach, and she'd come out of the bedroom with white dress, white shoes, white handbag, and the big floppy evening hat. Or she'd start out in the afternoon with a street dress on, and the fur coat, and one of the sports hats. And I'd have a hard time arguing her out of it, make her put on what she ought to have. "But the hat is very pretty. I like."

"It's pretty, but you can't wear evening hats to the beach. It looks funny. It's all wrong."

"But why?"

"I don't know why. You just can't do it."

"But I like."

"Well, can't you just take my word for it?"

"I no understand."

And then this thing happened that finished me with Hollywood, and everything about Hollywood, for good. Maybe you don't know what it's like to be a big Hollywood actor. Well, it's about like being the winning jockey in the Irish Sweepstakes, only worse. You can't turn around that somebody isn't asking you to some little party he's giving, or begging your autograph for some kid that is home sick in bed, or to take space in some trade paper, or to sing at some banquet for a studio executive. Some of that stuff I had to do, like the banquet, but the parties, I ducked by saying I had to work. But when "Paul Bunyan" was finished, and I was waiting around for re-takes, I got this call from Elsa Chadwick, that played opposite me in it, asking me to a little party at her house the next night, just a few friends, and would I sing? She caught me with my mouth hanging open, and I couldn't think of anything to say. I mumbled something about having an engagement to take a lady to dinner, and she began to gurgle that I should bring her. Of course I should bring her. She would expect us both around nine.

I didn't know what Juana was going to say, but instead of balking, she wanted to go. "Oh yes. I like, very much. This Miss Chadwick, I have seen her, in the cinema. She is very nice."

Next day, early, I was called over to re-shoot a scene, and I forgot about the party till I got home. Juana was under the shower, getting ready to go. By that time I had a Hollywood suit of evening clothes, and I put them on, and went out in the living-room and waited. In about a half hour she came out, and I got this feeling in the pit of my stomach. She had gone out, all by herself, and bought a special dress for the party. Do you know what a Mexican girl's idea of a party dress is? It's white silk, with red flowers all over it, a red rose in her hair, and white shoes with rhinestone buckles. God knows where she found that outfit. It looked like Ramona on Sunday afternoon. I opened my mouth to tell her it was all wrong but took her in my arms and held her to me. You see, it was all for me. She wanted to wear a red *rebozo*, instead of a hat. It was evening, and didn't call for a hat, so I said all right. But when she put it on, that made it still worse. Those *rebozos* are hand-woven, but they're cotton, like everything else in Mexico. I'd hate to tell you what she looked like with that dress, and those shoes, and that cotton shawl over her head.

Chadwick went into a gag clinch with me when we came in, but when she saw Juana the grin froze on her face and her eyes looked like a snake's. There were twenty or thirty people there, and she took us in and introduced us, but she didn't take us around. She stood with us, near the door, rattled off the names in a hard voice. Then she sat Juana down, got her a drink, put some cigarettes beside her, and that was all. She didn't go near her again, and neither did any of the other women. I sat down on the other side of the room, and in a minute they were all around me, particularly the women, with a line of Hollywood chatter, all of it loud and most of it off color. They haven't got the Hollywood touch till they cuss like mule-skinners and peddle the latest dirty crack that was made on some lot. I fed it back like they gave it, but I was watching Juana. I thought of the soft way she talked, and how she never had said a dirty word in her life, and the dignified way she had stood there while she was being introduced, and the screechy way they had acted. And I felt something getting thick in my throat. Who were they to leave her there all alone with a drink and a pack of Camels?

George Schultz, that had done the orchestrations for

"Bunyan," went over to the piano and started to play. "Feel like singing, boy?"

"Just crazy to sing."

"Little Traviata?"

"Sure."

"O.K., give."

He went into the introduction of *Di Provenza il Mar*. But this thing in my throat was choking me. I went over to Juana. "Come on. We're going home."

"You no sing?"

"No. Come on."

"Hey, where are you? That's your cue."

"Yeah?"

"You're supposed to come in."

"I'm not coming in."

"What the hell is this?"

We went out and put on our things and Chadwick followed us to the door. "Well, you don't seem to enjoy my little party?"

"Not much."

"It's mutual. And the next time you come don't show up with a cheap Mexican tart that—"

That's the only time a woman ever took a cuff in the puss from John Howard Sharp. She screamed and three or four guys came out there, screen he-men, all hot to defend the little woman and show how tough they were. I stepped back to let them out. I wanted them out. I was praying they'd come out. They didn't. I took Juana by the arm and started for the car. "There won't be any next time, baby."

"They no like me, Hoaney?"

"They didn't act like it."

"But why?"

"I don't know why."

"I do something wrong?"

"Not a thing. You were the sweetest one there."

"I no understand."

"You needn't even bother to try to understand. But if they ever pull something like that on you, just let me know. That's all I've got to say. Just let me know."

We went to the Golondrina. It's a Mexican restaurant on Olvera Street, a kind of Little Mexico they've got in Los Angeles, with mariachis, pottery, jumping beans, bum silverware, and all the rest of it. If she had dressed for me, I was bound she was going to have a good time if I had to stand the whole city on its ear to give it to her. She had it. She had never been there before, but as soon as they spotted her they all came around, and talked, and laughed, and she was back home. The couple in the floor show made up a special verse of their song for her, and she took the flower out of her hair and threw it out there, and they did a dance with it, and gave her some comedy. Their comedy is a lot of bum cucaracha gags, with a lot of belly-scratching and eye-rolling and finger-snapping, but it was funny to her, so it was funny to me. It was the first time I had ever had a friendly feeling toward Mexico.

Then I sang. A big movie shot is an event in that place, but a Mexican would never pull anything, or let you know he was looking at you. I had to call for the guitar myself, but then I got a big hand. I sang to her, and to the girl in the floor show, and whanged out a number they danced to, and then we all sang the *Golondrina*. It was two o'clock before we left there. When we went to bed I held her in my arms, and long after she was asleep this fury would come over me, about how they had treated her. I knew then I hated Hollywood, and only waited for the day I could clear out of there for good.

Under their contract, they had three months to call me for the next picture, and the way the time was counted, that meant any date up to April 1. It was just before Christmas that I got the wire from the New York agent that she had a tip the Met was interested in me, and would I please, please, let her go ahead on the deal? I began to rave like a crazy man. "Hoaney, why you talk so?"

"Read it! You've been going to school, there's something for you to practice on. Read it, and see what you've been missing all this time."

"What is 'Met'?"

"Just the best opera company in the world, that's all. The big one in New York, and they want me. They want me!—she'd never be sending that unless she knew something. A chance to get back to my trade at last, and here I am sewed up on a lousy contract to make two more pictures that I hate, that aren't worth making, that—"

"Why you make these pictures?"

"I'm under contract, I tell you. I've got to."

"But why?"

I tried to explain contract to her. It couldn't be done. An Indian has never heard of a contract. They didn't have them under Montezuma, and never bothered with them since. "The picture company, you make money for her, yes?"

"Plenty. I don't owe her a dime."

"Then it is right, you go?"

"Right? Did they ever give me anything I didn't take off them with a blackjack? Would they even give me a cup of coffee if I didn't pack them in at the box office? Would they even respect my trade? This isn't about right. It's about some ink on a dotted line."

"Then why you stay? Why you no sing at these Met?"

That was all. If it wasn't right, then to hell with it. A contract was just something that you probably couldn't read anyway. I looked at her, where she was lying on the bed with nothing on but a *rebozo* around her middle, and knew I was looking across ten thousand years, but it popped in my mind that maybe they weren't as dumb ten thousand years ago as I had always thought. Well, why not? I thought of Malinche, and how she put Cortés on top of the world, and how his star went out like a light when he thought he didn't need her any more. ". . . That's an idea."

"I think you sing at these Met."

"Not so loud."

"Yes."

"I think you're a pretty bright girl."

Next day I hopped over to the Taft Building and saw a lawyer. He begged me not to do anything foolish. "In the first place, if you run out on this contract, they can make your life so miserable that you hardly dare go out of doors without some rat shoving a summons at you with a dollar bill in it, and you'll have to appear in court. Do you know what that means? Do you know what those blue summonses did to Jack Dempsey? They cost him a title, that's all. They can sue you. They can sew you up with injunctions. They can just make you wish you never even heard of the law, or anything like it."

"That's what we got lawyers for, isn't it?"

"That's right. You can get a lawyer there in New York, and he can handle some of it. And he'll charge you plenty. But you can't hire as many lawyers as they've got."

"Listen, can they win, that's all I want to know. Can they bring me back? Can they keep me from working?"

"Maybe they can't. Who knows? But—"

"That's all I want to know. If I've got any kind of a fighting chance, I'm off."

"Not so fast. Maybe they don't even try. Maybe they think it's bad policy. But this is the main point: You run out on this contract, and your name is mud in Hollywood from now on—"

"I don't care about that."

"Oh yes you do. How do you know how well you do in grand opera?"

"I've been in it before."

"And out of it before, from all I hear."

"My voice cracked up."

"It may again. This is my point. The way Gold is building you up, Hollywood is sure for you, as sure as anything can be, for quite some time to come. It makes no difference to him if your voice cracks up. He'll buy a voice. He'll dub your sound for you—"

"Not for me he won't."

"Will you for Christ sake stop talking about art? I'm talking about money. I'm telling you that if your pictures really go, he'll do anything. He'll play you straight. He'll fix it up anyway that makes you look good. And most of all, he'll pay you! More than any opera company will ever pay you! It's a backlog for you to fall back on, *but—*"

"Yeah, but?"

"Only as long as you play ball. Once you start some funny business, not only he, but every other picture man in Hollywood turns thumbs down, and that's the end of you, in pictures. There's no black-list. Nobody calls anybody up. They just hear about it, and that's all. I can give you names, if you want them, of bright boys like you that thought they could jump a Hollywood contract, and tell you what happened to them. These picture guys hate each other, they cut each other's throats all the time, but when something like this happens, they act with a unanimity that's touching. Now, have you seen Gold?"

"I thought I'd see you first."

"That's all right. Then there's no harm done. Now before you do anything rash, I want you to see him. There may be no trouble at all. He may want you to sing at the Met, just for build-up. He may be back of it, for all you know. Get over and see him, see if you can fix it up. After lunch, come back and see me."

So I went over and saw Gold. He wanted to talk about the four goals he made in the polo game the day before. When we did get around to it he shook his head. "Jack, I know what's good for you, even if you don't. I read the signs all the time, it's my business to know, and they'll all tell you Rex Gold don't make many mistakes. Jack, grand opera's through."

"What?"

"It's through, finished. Sure, I dropped in at the Metropolitan when I was east last week, saw Tosca, the same opera that we do a piece of in Bunyan, and I'd hate to tell you what they soaked me for the rights on it, too. And what do I see? Well, boy, I'm telling you, we just made a bum out of them. That sequence in our picture is so much better than their job, note for note, production for production, that comparison is just ridiculous. Grand opera is through. Because why? Pictures have stepped in and done it so much better than they can do it that they can't get by any more, that's all. Opera is going the same way the theatre is going. Pictures have just rubbed them out."

"Well—before it dies, I'd like to have a final season in

it. And I don't think the Metropolitan stamp would hurt me any, even in pictures."

"It would ruin you."

"How?"

"I've been telling you. Grand opera is through. Grand opera pictures are through. The public is sick of them. Because why? Because they got no more material. They've done Puccini over and over again, they've done La Bohème and Madame Butterfly so much we even had to fall back on La Tosca for you in Bunyan, and after you've done your Puccini, what you got left? Nothing. It's through, washed up. We just can't get the material."

"Well—there are a couple of other composers."

"Yeah, but who wants to listen to them?"

"Almost anybody, except a bunch of Kansas City yaps that think Puccini is classical, as they call it."

"Oh, so you don't like Puccini?"

"Not much."

"Listen, you want to find out who's the best painter in the world, what do you do? You try to buy one of his pictures. Then you find out what you got to pay. O.K., you want to find out who's the best composer in the world, you try to buy some of his music. Do you know what they charged me, just for license rights, on that scene you did from Tosca? You want to know? Wait, I'll get the canceled vouchers. I'll show you. You wouldn't believe it."

"Listen, Puccini has been the main asset of that publishing house for years, and everybody in grand opera knows it, and that's got nothing to do with how good he is. It's because he came in after we began to get copyright laws, and because he was handled from the beginning for every dime that could be got out of him from guys like you. If you're just finding that out, it may prove you don't know anything about opera, but it doesn't prove anything about Puccini."

"Why do you suppose guys like me pay for him?"

"Probably because you knew so little about opera you couldn't think of anything else. If you had let me help on that script, I'd have fixed you up with numbers that wouldn't have cost you a dime."

"A swell time to be saying that."

"To hell with it. You got Tosca, and it's all right. I'm talking about a release for the rest of the season to go on at the Met."

"And I'm talking about what's good for one of our stars. There's no use our arguing about composers, Jack. Maybe you know what's pretty but I know what sells. And I tell you grand opera is through. And I tell you that from now on you lay off it. The way I'm building you up, we're going to take that voice of yours, and what are we going to do with it? Use it on popular stuff. The stuff you sing better than anybody else in the business. The stuff that people want to hear. Lumberjack songs, cowboy songs, mountain music, jazz—you can't beat it! It's what they want! Not any of this tra-la-la-la-la-la! Christ, that's an ear-ache! It's a back number. Look, Jack: From now on, you forget you ever were in grand opera. You give it to them down-to-earth! Right down there where they want it! You get me, Jack? You get me?"

"I get you."

"What did Gold say?"

"He said no."

"I had an idea that was how he felt. I had him on the phone just now, about something else, and I led around to you in a way that didn't tip it you had been in, but he was telling the world where he stood. Well, I'd play along with him. It's tough, but you can't buck him."

"If I do, what did you say my name would be?"

"Mud. M-U-D, mud."

"In Hollywood?"

"Yes, in Hollywood."

"That's all I wanted to know. What do I owe you?"

When I got home there were four more telegrams, saying the thing was hot, if I wanted it, and a memo New York had been calling. I looked at my watch. It was three o'clock. I called the airport. They had two seats on the four-thirty plane. She came in. "Well, Juana, there they are, read them. The abogado says no, a hundred times no. What do I do?"

"You sing Carmen at these Met?"
"I don't know. Probably."
"Yes, I like."
"O.K., then. Get packed."

Chapter 9

I MADE MY DEBUT in Lucia right after New Year's, sang standard repertoire for a month, began to work in. It felt good to be back with the wops. Then I got my real chance when they popped me on three days' notice into Don Giovanni. I had a hell of a time getting them to let me do the serenade my way, with a real guitar, and play it myself, without the orchestra. The score calls for a prop mandolin, and that's the way the music is written, but I hate all prop instruments on the stage, and hate to play any scene where I have to use one. There's no way you can do it that it doesn't look phoney. I made a gain when I told them that the guitar was tradition, that Garcia used to do it that way, but I lost all that ground when somebody in the Taste Department decided that a real guitar would look too much like the Roxy, and for a day it was all off again. Then I got Wurlitzer's to help me out. They sent down an instrument that was a beauty. It was dark, dull spruce, without any pearl, nickel, or highlights on it of any kind, and it had a tone you could eat with a spoon. When I sounded off on that, that settled it.

I wanted to put it up a half tone, so I could get it in the key of three flats, but I didn't. It's in the key of two sharps, the worst key there is for a singer, especially the high F sharp at the end, that catches a baritone all wrong, and makes him sound coarse and ropy. The F sharp is not in the score, but it's tradition and you have to sing it. God knows why Mozart ever put it in that key, unless it's because two sharps is the best key there is for a mandolin, and he let his singer take the rap so he could bring the accompaniment to life.

But I tuned with the orchestra before the act started, and did it strictly in the original key. I made two moves while I was singing it. Between verses I took one step nearer the balcony. At the end, I turned my back on the audience, stepped under the balcony and played the finish, not to them, but to her. On the F sharp, instead of covering up and getting it over quick, I did a *messa di voce*, probably the toughest order a singer ever tries to deliver. You start it p, swell to ff, pull back to p again, and come off it. My tone wasn't round, but it was pure, and I got away with it all right. They broke into a roar, the *bravos* yipped out all over the house, and that was the beginning of this stuff that you read, that I was the greatest since Bispham, the peer of Scotti, and all the rest of it. Well, I was the peer of Scotti, or hope I was. They've forgotten by now how bad Scotti really was. He could sing, and he was the greatest actor I ever saw, but his voice was just merely painful. What they paid no attention to at all, mentioned like it was nothing but a little added feature, was the guitar. You can talk about your fiddle, your piano, and your orchestra, and I've got nothing to say against them. But a guitar has moonlight in it.

Don Giovanni, the Marriage of Figaro, Thaïs, Rigoletto, Carmen, and Traviata, going bigger all the time, getting toward the middle of February, and still nothing from Gold. No notification to report, no phone calls, nothing. It was Ziskin's picture I was supposed to do next. I saw by the papers he was in town and that night saw him in Lindy's, but I saw him first and we ducked out and went somewhere else. He looked just as foolish as ever, and I began to tell myself he still didn't have his script ready, and I might win by default.

The Hudson-to-Horn hook-up was something the radio people had been working on for a year, and God knows how many ministers, ambassadors, and contact men had to give them a hand, because most of those stations south of the Rio Grande are government-owned, and so are the Canadian. Then after they put it over, they had a hard job selling the time, because they were asking plenty for it, and every country had to get its cut. Finally they peddled it to Panamier. The car was being put out mainly for export, and the hook-up gave it what it needed. The next thing was: Who were they going to feature on the hour, now they had sold it? They had eight names on their list, the biggest in the business, starting with Grace Moore and ending with me. I moved up a couple of notches when I told them I could do spig songs in Spanish. I couldn't, but I figured I was in bed with the right person to learn. Then Paul Bunyan opened, and I went up to the top. I can't tell you what the picture had. Understand, for my money no picture is any good, really any good, but this one was gay and made you feel you wanted to see it over again. The story didn't make any sense at all, but maybe it was because it was so cock-eyed you got to laughing. One place in there they cut in the Macy parade, the one they hold about a month before Christmas, with a lot of balloons coming down Broadway in the shape of animals. One of the balloons was a cow, and when they cut them loose, with prizes offered to whoever finds them, this one floats clear out over Saskatchewan and comes down on the trees near the lumber camp. Then the lumberjack that I was supposed to be, the one that has told them all he's really Paul Bunyan, says it's Babe, the Big Blue Ox that's come down from heaven to pay him a Christmas visit. Then he climbs up in a tree and sings to it, and the lumberjacks sing to it, and believe it or not, it did things to you. Then when the sun comes up and they see what gender Babe really is, they go up the tree after the guy to lynch him, but somebody accidentally touches a cigar to the cow and she blows up with such a roar that all the trees they were supposed to cut down are lying flat on the ground, and they decide it was Mrs. Babe.

That clinched me for the broadcast, and they ate it up when I told them how to put the show together so it would sell cars. "We open up with the biggest, loudest,

five-tone, multiple-action horn you can find, and if you
think that's not important, I tell you I've been down
there, and I know what you've got to give them to sell
cars. You've got to have a horn; first, last, and all the
time you've got to have a horn. I take pitch from that
and go into the *Golondrina*, for the spig trade, blended in
with My Pal Babe, for the Canadian trade. I'll write that
little medley myself, and that's our signature. Then we repeat it, you put your announcer in, and after he stops we
go right on. We do light Mexican numbers, then we'll
turn right around and do some little French-Canadian
numbers, then one light American number, when it's
time for the announcer again. Then we do a grand opera
number and so on for as much time as we've got, and any
comedy you want to put in, that's O.K., too, but watch
they can understand it. On your car, plug the horn, the
lock on the gas tank, the paint job, the speed and the low
gas consumption. That's all. Leave out about the brakes,
the knee-action, and all that. They never heard of it, and
you're just wasting your time. Better let me write those
plugs, and you let your announcers translate them. And
first, last, and again: Sound that horn."

They stuck together a program the way I said, and we
made a record of it one morning with the studio orchestra, then went in an audition room and ran it off. It
sounded like something. The advertising man liked it, and
the Panamier man was tickled to death with it. "It's got
speed to it, you know what I mean? 'Gangway for the
Panamier Eight, she's coming down the road!'—that's
what it says. And the theme song is a honey. Catches
them north, south, and in the middle. Boys, we got something now. That's set. No more if, as, and but about it." I
began to feel good. Why did I want that broadcast? Because it would pay me four thousand a week. Because
they treated me good. Because I had had that flop, and I
could get back at Mexico. Because it made me laugh. Because I could say hello to Captain Conners, wherever he
was out there, listening to it. In other words, for no reason. I just wanted it.

That was around the first of March, and they would go

on the air in three weeks, as soon as they could place ads in the newspapers all up and down the line, and get more cars freighted out, to make deliveries. By that time I had kidded myself that Ziskin would never have his script ready, and that I could forget about Hollywood the rest of my life. I woke up after I left them that day, and walked down to the opera house for the matinee Lucia. A messenger was there, with a registered letter from Gold, telling me to report March 10. I was a little off that day, and missed a cue.

What I did about it was nothing at all, except get the address of a lawyer in Radio City that made a specialty of big theatrical cases. Three days later I got a wire from the Screen Actors' Guild, telling me that as I had made no acknowledgment of Gold's notification to report, the case had been referred to them, that I was bound by a valid contract, and that unless I took steps to comply with it at once, they would be compelled to act under their by-laws, and their agreement with the producers. I paid no attention to that either.

Next morning while I was having a piano run-through of the Traviata duet with a new soprano they were bringing out, a secretary came up to the rehearsal room and told me to please go at once to a suite in the Empire State Building, that it was important. I asked the soprano if she minded doing the rest of it after lunch. When I got up to the Empire State Building, I was brought into a big office paneled in redwood, and marked "Mr. Luther, private." Mr. Luther was an old man with a gray cutaway suit, a cheek as pink as a young girl's, and an eye like blue agate. He got up, shook hands, told me how much he had enjoyed my singing, said my Marcello reminded him of Sammarco, and then got down to business. "Mr. Sharp, we have a communication here from a certain Mr. Gold, Rex Gold, informing us that he has a contract with you, and that any further employment of you on our part, after March 10, will be followed by legal action on his part. I don't know what legal action he has in mind, but

I thought it would be well if you came in and, if you can, inform me what he means, if you know."

"You're the attorney for the opera house?"

"Not regularly, of course. But sometimes when somebody is in Europe, they refer things to me."

"Well—I have a contract with Gold."

"For motion pictures, I judge?"

"Yes."

I told him about it, and made it pretty plain I was through with pictures, contract or no contract. He listened and smiled, and seemed to get it all, why I wanted to sing in opera and all the rest of it. "Yes, I can understand that. I understand it very well. And of course, considering the success we're having with you here, I should certainly hesitate to take any step, or give any advice, that would lose you to us at the height of the season. Of course, a telegram unsupported by any other documents is hardly ground for us to make a decision, and in fact we are not bound to take cognizance of contracts made by our singers until a court passes on them, or in some way compels us to. Just the same—"

"Yes?"

"Have you had any communication from Mr. Gold, aside from his letter of notification?"

"Nothing at all. I did have a wire from the Screen Actors' Guild. But that's all."

"The—what was that again?"

I had the wire in my pocket, and showed it to him. He got up and began to walk around the office. "Ah— you're a member of this Guild?"

"Well—everybody is that works in pictures."

"It's an affiliate of Equity, isn't it?"

"I'm not sure. I think so."

". . . I don't know what their procedure is. It's recently organized, and I haven't heard much about it. But I confess, Mr. Sharp, this makes things very awkward. Contracts, court cases—these things I don't mind. After all, that's what I'm here for, isn't it? But I should be very loath to give any advice that would get the company into any mess with the Federation of Musicians. You realize what's involved here, don't you?"

"No, I don't."

"As I say, I don't know the procedure of your Screen
Actors' Guild, but if they took the matter up with the
musicians, and we had some kind of mess on our hands,
over your singing here until you had adjudicated your
troubles with your own union—Mr. Sharp, I simply have
a horror of it. The musicians are one of the most intelli-
gent, co-operative, and sensible unions we have, and yet,
any dispute, coming at the height of the season—!"

"Meaning what?"

"I don't know. I want to think about it."

I went out, had a sandwich and some coffee, and went
back to the rehearsal hall. We just about got started
when the same secretary came up and said the radio people wanted me to come up right away, that it was terribly
important, and would I please make it as soon as I could.
The soprano went into an act that blistered the varnish
off the piano. At plain and fancy cussing, the coloraturas,
I think, are the best in the business. I got out on the
street, tried to figure out which was uptown and which
down. I thought about Jack Dempsey.

They were all up there, the advertising man, the Panamier man, the broadcasting men, all of them, and there
was hell to pay. They had had a wire from Gold, forbidding them to use My Pal Babe, or any part of it, else be
sued up to the hilt, and warning them not to use me.
The Panamier man raved like an animal. I listened and
began to get sore. "What the hell is he talking about?
You can use that song. I don't know much about law,
but I know that much—"

"We can't use it! We can't use a note of it! It's his!
And those ads have gone out to two hundred key newspapers. We got to kill them by wire, we got to get up a
whole new program—Christ, why didn't you tell us about
this thing? Why did you let us start all this knowing you
had that contact?"

"Will you just hold your horses till tonight?"

"For what? Will you tell me that, for what?"

"Till I can see a lawyer?"

"Don't you suppose I've seen a lawyer? Don't you suppose I've had Gold on the phone three times today while I was trying to find where the hell you were? And I've advertised it! I've advertised the goddam theme song! Golondrina, My Babe—don't that sound sick? And I've advertised you—John Howard Sharp, El Panamier Trovador —don't that sound sicker! Get out, for Christ sake—"

"Well you wait? Just till tonight?"

"Yeah, I'll wait. Why not?"

The lawyer was five floors down in the same building. He didn't have redwood paneling in his office. It was just an office, and he was a brisk little guy named Sholto. I laid it out for him. He leaned back, took a couple of calls, and started to talk. 'Sharp, you haven't got a leg to stand on. You made a contract, a contract that any jury would regard as perfectly fair, and the only thing you can do is go through with it. It may reflect credit on your aesthetic conscience that you prefer opera to pictures, but it doesn't reflect any credit on your moral conscience that you jump a contract just because you want to. As well as I can make out this picture company took you when you were a bum, put you on your feet, and now you want to hand them a cross. I don't say you couldn't lick them in court. Nobody can say what a jury is going to do. But you'll be a bum before you ever get to court. Show business is all one gigantic hook-up, Gold knows it frontwards, backwards, crosswise, and on the bias, and you haven't got a chance. You're sewed. You've got to go back and make that picture."

"Just give up everything, now it's breaking for me, go back and make a picture just because that cluck has an idea that opera is through?"

"What the hell are you trying to tell me? One more picture like this Bunyan and you can walk into any opera house in the world, and the place is yours. You're being built into a gallery draw that not one singer in a million can bring into the theatre with him. Haven't you got any brains? These musicals are quota pictures. They go all over the world. They make you famous from Peru to China and from Norway to Capetown, and from Panama to Suez and back again. Don't you suppose opera houses know that? Don't you think the Metropolitan knows it? Do you suppose all this commotion you've caused is just a tribute to your A flat in Pagliacci? It is like hell."

"I haven't sung Pagliacci."

"All right then, Trovatore."

"And that's all you've got to tell me?"

"Isn't it enough?"

I felt so sick I didn't even bother to go up to the broadcasting offices again. I went down, caught a cab, and went home. It was starting to snow. We had sublet a furnished apartment in a big apartment house on East Twenty-second Street, near Gramercy Park. She had liked it because there were Indian rugs around that looked a little like Mexico, and we had been happier there, for six weeks, than I had ever been in my life. She was in bed with a cold. She never could get it through her head what New York weather was like. I sat down and broke the news. "Well, it's all off. We go back to Hollywood."

"No, please. I like New York."

"Money, Juana. And everything. Back we go."

"But why? We have much money."

"And no place to sing. By tomorrow not even a night club will hire me. Unions. Injunctions. Contracts."

"No, we stay in New York. You take guitar, be a *maria-chi*, just you, Hoaney. You sing for me."

"We got to go back."

I sat beside her, and she kept running her fingers through my hair. We didn't say anything for a long time. The phone rang. She motioned to let it alone. If I hadn't picked it up, our whole life would have been different.

Chapter 10

WINSTON HAWES, the papers said, was one of the outstanding musicians of his time, the conductor that could really read a score, the man that had done more for modern music than anybody since Muck. He was all of that, but don't get the idea he was ever one of the boys. There was something wrong about the way he thought about music, something unhealthy, like the crowds you always saw at his concerts, and what it was I can only half tell you. In the first place I don't know enough about the kind of people he came from, and in the second place I don't know enough about music. He was rich, and there's something about rich people that's different from the rest of us. They come into the world with an inflated idea of their relation to it, and everything they find in it. I got a little flash into that side of him once, in Paris, when I strolled into an art store to look at some pictures that caught my eye. A guy came in, an American, and began a palaver about prices. And the way that guy talked gave me a whole new slant at his kind. He didn't care about art, the way you do or I do, as something to look at and feel. He wanted to own it. Winston was that way about music. He made a whore out of it. You went to his concerts, but you didn't sit out there at his rehearsals, and see him hold men for an hour overtime, at full pay, just because there was some French horn passage that he liked, and wanted it played over and over again—not to rehearse it, but because of what it did to him. And you didn't walk out with him afterwards, and see him all atremble, and hear him tell how he felt after playing it. He was like some woman that goes to concerts because they give her the right vibrations, or make her feel better, or have some other effect on her nitwit insides. All right, you may think it's cock-eyed to compare him with somebody like that, but I'm telling you that in spite of all his technical skill, he was a hell of a sight nearer to that fat poop than he ever was to Muck. That woman was in him, poodle dog, diamonds, limousine, conceit, cruelty and all, and don't let his public reputation fool you. She has a public reputation too, if she hands out enough money. The day the story broke, they compared him with Stanford White, but I'm telling you that to put Winston Hawes in the same class with Stanford White was a desecration.

You can't own music, the way you can own a picture, but you can own a big hunk of it. You can own a composer, that you put on a subsidy while he's writing a piece for you. You can own an audience that has to come to you to hear that piece if it's going to hear it at all. You can own the orchestra that plays it, and you can own the singer that sings it. I first met him in Paris. I hadn't known him in Chicago. He came from a packing family so rich I never even got within a mile of where they lived. And I didn't look him up, even in Paris. He showed up at my apartment one day, sat down at the piano, played off a couple of songs that were there, and said they were lousy, which they were. Then he got up and asked me how I'd like to sing with his band. I was pretty excited. He had started his Petite Orchestra about a year before, and I had gone to plenty of the concerts, and don't you think they weren't good. He started with thirty men, but by now he was up to forty. He raided everywhere, from the opera orchestras, from the chamber music outfits, and he took anybody he wanted, because he paid about twice what any other band paid. He footed the deficit himself, and he didn't have a man that couldn't have played quartets with Heifetz. What they could do to music, especially modern music, was just make it sound about twice as good as even the composer thought it was. He had some stuff with him he wanted me to do, all of it in manuscript. Part of it was old Italian songs he had dug up, where I would have to do baritone coloratura that had been out of date for a hundred years, and how he knew I could do it I don't know. Part of it was a suite by his first viola, that had never been performed yet. It was tough stuff, music that wouldn't come to life at all without the most exact tone shading. But he gave me six rehearsals—count them, six, something you couldn't believe. Cost didn't mean anything to him. When we went on with it I was with those woodwinds like I was one of the bassoons, and the response was terrific. I took out Picquot, the viola, before I took a call myself, and the whole thing was like something you read about.

That part of it, I wouldn't be telling the truth if I didn't admit it was an adventure in music I'll never forget. I sang for him four times, and each time it was something new, something fresh, and a performance better than you even knew you could give. He had a live stick all right. From some of them you get a beat as dead as an undertaker's handshake, but not from him. He threw it on you like a hypnotist, and you began to roll it out, and yet it was all under perfect control. That's the word to remember, perfect. Perfection is something no singer ever got yet, but under him you came as near to it as you're ever going to get.

That was the beginning of it, and it was quite a while before it dawned on me what he really wanted. As to what he wanted, and what he got, you'll find out soon enough, and I'm not going to tell any more than I have to. But I'd like to make this much clear now: that wasn't what I wanted. What I meant to him and what he meant to me were two different things, but once again, I wouldn't be telling the truth if I didn't admit that what he meant to me was plenty. He took to dropping into my dressing room at the Comique while I was washing up, and he'd tell me some little thing I had done, something he had liked, or sometimes, something he hadn't liked. If he had been giving a concert, maybe he had heard only part of the last act, but there would always be something. You think that didn't mean anything to me? Singing is a funny job. You go out there and take those calls, and it's so exciting that when you get back to your dressing room you want to sing, to cut it loose till the windows rattle, just to let off the steam that excitement makes. You go back there and you'll hear them, especially the tenors, so you'd think they had gone crazy. But that excitement is all from out front, from a mob you only half see and never know, and you get so you'd give anything for somebody, for just one guy, that knew what you were trying to do, that spotted your idea without your telling him, that could appreciate you with his head and not with the palms of his hands. And mind you, it couldn't be just anybody. It has to be somebody you respect, somebody that knows.

I began to wait for that visit. Then pretty soon I was singing to him and to nobody else. We'd walk out, go to a café while I ate, then drop over to his apartment off the Place Vendóme, and have a post-mortem on my performance. Then, little by little, he began making suggestions. Then I began dropping in on him in the morning, and he'd take me through some things I had been doing wrong. He was the best coach in the world, bar none. Then he began to take my acting apart, and put it together again. It was he that cured me of all those operatic gestures I got in Italy. He showed me that good operatic acting consists in as few motions as possible, every one of them calculated for an effect, and every one made to count. He told me about Scotti and how he used to sing the Pagliacci Prologue before he got so bad they couldn't use him in Pagliacci. He made one gesture. At the end of the andante, he held out his hand, and then turned it over, palm up. That was all. It said it. He made me learn a whole new set of gestures, done naturally, and he made me practice for hours singing *sotto voce* without using any gestures at all. That's a tough order, just to stand up there, on a cold stage, and shoot it. But I got so I could do it. And I got so I could take my time, give it to them when I was ready, not before. I began to do better in comedy roles, like Sharpless and Marcello. Taking out all that gingerbread, I could watch timing, and get laughs I never got before. I got so I was with him morning, noon and night, and depended on him like a hophead depends on dope.

Then came my crack-up, and when my money was all
gone I had to leave Paris. He stormed about that, wanted
to support me, showed me his books to prove that an allowance for me wouldn't even make a dent in his income.
But it was that storming that showed me where things
had got between him and me, and that I had to break
away from him. I went to New York. I tried to find something to do, but there was nothing I could do except sing,
and I couldn't sing. That was when this agent kidded me
that no matter what shape I was in I was good enough
for Mexico, and I went down there.

I had read in some paper that he had disbanded his orchestra in Paris, but I didn't know he was starting his Little Orchestra in New York until I got there. It made me
nervous. I dropped in, alone, at his first concert, just so I
could say I had, in case I ran into him somewhere. It was
the same mob he had had in Paris, clothes more expensive than you would see even at a Hollywood opening,
gray-haired women with straight haircuts and men's dinner jackets, young girls looking each other straight in the
eye and not caring what you thought, boys following men
around, loud, feverish talk out in the foyer, everybody
coming out in the open with something they wouldn't
dare show anywhere else. His first number was something
for strings by Lalo I had heard him play before, and I left
right after it. Next day, when I saw the review in the
paper I turned the page quick. I didn't want to read it. I
had a note from him after Don Giovanni, and shot it
right back, and one word written on it, "Thanks," with
my initials. I didn't want to write on my own stationery,
or he'd know where I was living. I felt funny about asking for opera house stationery. I was afraid not to answer,
for fear he'd be around to know why.

So that's how things stood when I was sitting beside
Juana and the phone rang. She motioned to let it ring,
and I did for a while, but I still hadn't called Panamier,
and I knew I had them to talk to, even if I had nothing
to say. I answered. But it wasn't Panamier. It was Win-

ston. "Jack! You old scalawag! Where have you been hiding?"

"Why—I've been busy."

"So have I, so busy I'm ashamed of it. I hate to be busy. I like time for my friends. But the moment I'm free as a bird, I've got a fine fire burning, and you can hop in a cab, wherever you are—all I've got is your phone number, and I had a frightful time even getting that—and come up here. I just can't wait to see you."

"Well—that sounds swell, but I've got to go back to Hollywood, right away, probably tomorrow, and that means I'll be tied up every minute, trying to get out of town. I don't see how I could fit it in."

"What did you say? *Hollywood!*"

"Yeah, Hollywood."

"Jack, you're kidding."

"No, I'm a picture star now."

"I know you are. I saw your pictures, both of them. But you can't go back to Hollywood now. Why, you're singing for me, one month from today. I've arranged your whole program. It's out of the question."

"No, I'll have to go."

"Jack, you don't sound like yourself. Don't tell me you've got so big you can't spare one night for a poor dilettante and his band—"

"For Christ sake, don't be silly."

"That sounds more like you. Now what is it?"

"Nothing but what I've told you. I've got to go back there. I don't want to. I hate to. I've tried to get out of it every way I knew, but I'm sewed and I've got no choice."

"That sounds still more like you. In other words, you're in trouble."

"That's it."

"Into the cab and up here. Tell it to Papa."

"No, I'm sorry. I can't. . . . Wait a minute."

She was grabbing for the receiver. I put my hand over it. "Yes, you go."

"I don't want to go."

"You go."

"He's just a guy—I don't want to see."

"You go, you feel better, Juana's nose, very snoddy."

"I'll wipe it, then it won't be snoddy."

"Hoaney, you go. Many people call today, all day long. You no here, you no have to talk, no feel bad. Now, you go. I say you gone out. I don't know where. You go, then tonight we talk, you and I. We figure out."

". . . All right, where are you? I'll be up."

He was at a hotel off Central Park, on the twenty-second floor of the tower. The desk told me to go up. I did, found his suite, rang the bell and got no answer. The door was open and I walked in. There was a big living room, with windows on two sides, so you could see all the way downtown and out over the East River, a grand piano at one end, a big phonograph across from that, scores stacked everywhere, and a big fire burning under a mantlepiece. I opened the door that led into the rest of the suite and called, but there wasn't any answer. And then in a second there he was, bouncing in from the hall, in the rough coat, flannel shirt, and battered trousers that he always wore. If you had met him in Central Park you would have given him a dime. "Jack! How are you! I went down to meet you, and they told me you had just gone up! Give me that coat! Give me a smile, for God's sake! That Mexican sunburn makes you look like Othello!"

"Oh, you knew I was in Mexico?"

"Know it! I went down there to bring you back, but you had gone. What's the idea, hiding out on me?"

"Oh, I've been working."

One minute later I was in a big chair in front of the fire, with a bottle of the white port I had always liked beside me, a little pile of buttered English biscuits beside that, he was across from me with those long legs of his hooked over the chandelier or some place, and we were off. Or anyhow, he was. He always began in the middle, and he raced along about Don Giovanni, about an appoggiatura I was leaving out in Lucia, about the reason the old scores aren't sung the way they're written, about a new flutist he had pulled in from Detroit, about my cape routine in Carmen, all jumbled up together. But not for long. He got to the point pretty quick. "What's this about Hollywood?"

"Just what I told you. I'm sewed on a goddam contract and I've got to go."

I told him about it. I had told so many people about it by then I knew it by heart, and could get it over quick. "Then this man—Gold, did you say his name was?—is the key to the whole thing?"

"He's the one."

"All right then. You just sit here a while."

"No, if you're doing something I'll go!"

"I said sit there. Papa's going to get busy."

"At what?"

"There's your port, there's your biscuits, there's the fire, there's the most beautiful snow I've seen this year, and I've got the six big Rossini overtures on the machine —Semiramide, Tancred, the Barber, Tell, the Ladra, and the Italians, just in from London, beautifully played—and by the time they're finished I'll be back."

"I asked you, where are you going?"

"Goddam it, do you have to bust up my act? I'm being Papa. I'm going into action. And when Papa goes into action, it's the British Fleet. Sip your port. Listen to Rossini. Think of the boys that were gelded to sing the old bastard's masses. Be the Pope. I'm going to be Admiral Dewey."

"Beatty."

"No, I'm Bridley. I'm ready to fire."

He switched on the Rossini, poured the wine, and went. I tried to listen, and couldn't. I got up and switched it off. I was the first time I ever walked out on Rossini. I went over to the windows and watched the snow. Something told me to get out of there, to go back to Hollywood, to do anything except get mixed up with him again. It wasn't over twenty minutes before he was back. I heard him coming, and ducked back to the chair. I didn't want him to see me worrying. ". . . I was astonished that you missed that grace note in Lucia. Didn't you *feel* it there? Didn't you know it *had* to be there?"

"To hell with Lucia. What news?"

"Oh. I had forgotten all about it. Why, you stay, of

course. You go on with the opera, you do this foolish broadcast you've let yourself in for, you sing for me, you make your picture in the summer. That's all. It's all fixed up. Once more, Jack, on all those old recitatives—"

"Listen, this is business. I want to know—"

"Jack, you are so crass. Can't I wave my wand? Can't I do my bit of magic? If you have to know, I happen to control a bank, or my somewhat boorish family happen to control it. They embarrass me greatly, but sometimes they have a kind of low, swinish usefulness. And the bank controls, through certain stocks impounded to secure moneys, credit, and so on—oh the hell with it."

"Go on. The bank controls what?"

"The picture company, dolt."

"And?"

"Listen, I'm talking about Donizetti."

"And I'm talking about a son-of-a-bitch by the name of Rex Gold. What did you do?"

"I talked with him."

"And what did he say?"

"Why—I don't know. Nothing. I didn't wait to hear what he had to say. I told him what he was to do, that's all."

"Where's your phone?"

"Phone? What are you phoning about?"

"I've got to call the broadcasting company."

"Will you sit down and listen to what I'm trying to tell you about appoggiaturas, so you won't embarrass me every time you sing something written before 1905? Varlets in the bank are calling the broadcasting company. That's what we have them for. They're working overtime, calling other varlets in Radio City and making them work overtime, which I greatly enjoy, while you and I take our sinful ease here and watch the snow at twilight, and discuss the grace notes of Donizetti, which will be sung long after the picture company, the bank, and the varlets are dead in their graves and forgotten. Are you following me?"

His harangue on the appoggiaturas lasted fifteen minutes. It was something I was always forgetting about him, his connection with money. His family consisted of an old maid sister, a brother that was a colonel in the Illinois

National Guard, another brother that lived in Italy, and some nephews and nieces, and they had about as much to do with that fortune as so many stuffed dummies. He ran it, he controlled the bank, he did plenty of other things that he pretended he was too artistic even to bother with. All of a sudden something shot through my mind. "Winston, I've been framed."

"Framed? What are you talking about? By whom?"

"By you."

"Jack, I give you my word, the way you sang that—"

"Cut out this goddam foolish act about Lucia, will you? Sure I sang it wrong. I learned that role before I knew anything about style, and I hadn't sung it for five years until I went on with it last month, and I neglected to re-learn it, and that's all that amounts to, and to hell with it. I'm talking about this other. You knew all about it when you called me."

". . . Why, of course I did."

"And I think you put me in that spot."

"I—? Don't be a fool."

"It always struck me pretty funny, that guy Gold's ideas about grand opera, and me, and all the rest of it. Anybody else would want me in grand opera, to build me up. What do you know about that?"

"Jack, that's Mexican melodrama."

"What about this trip of yours? To Mexico?"

"I went there. A frightful place."

"For me?"

"Of course."

"Why?"

"To take you by the scuff of your thick neck and drag you out of there. I—ran into a 'cellist that had seen you. I heard you were looking seedy. I don't like you seedy. Shaggy, but not with spots on your coat."

"What about Gold?"

" . . . I put Gold in charge of that picture company because he was the worst ass I had ever met, and I thought he was the perfect man to make pictures. I was right. He's turned the whole investment into a gold mine. Soon I can have seventy-five men, and 'Little Orchestra' will be one of those affectations I so greatly enjoy. Jack, do you have to expose all my little shams? You know them all. Can't we just not look at them? After all they're nice shams."

"I want to know more about Gold."

He came over and sat on the arm of my chair. "Jack, why should I frame you?"

I couldn't answer him, and I couldn't look at him.

"Yes, I knew all about it. I didn't tell Gold to be an ass, if that's what you mean. I didn't have to. I knew about it, and I acted out one of my little shams. Can't I want my Jack to be happy? Wipe that sulky look off your face. Wasn't it good magic? Didn't Gridley level the fort?"

". . . Yes."

I got home around eight o'clock. I rushed in with a grin on my face, said it was all right, that Gold had changed his mind, that we were going to stay, and let's go out and celebrate. She got up, wiped her snoddy nose, dressed, and we went out, to a hot-spot uptown. It was murder to drag her out, on a night like that, the way she felt, but I was afraid if I didn't get to some place where there was music, and I could get some liquor in me, she'd see I was putting on an act, that I was as jittery inside as a man with a hangover.

I didn't see him for a week or ten days, and the first broadcast made me feel good. I said hello to Captain Conners, and there was a federal kick-back the next morning. Messages to private persons are strictly forbidden. I just laughed, and thought of Thomas. There was a federal kick-back on that "Good night, Mother," too, and they told him he couldn't do it. He just went ahead and did it. That afternoon there came a radiogram from the SS. *Port of Cobh:* TWAS A SOAP AGENTS PROGRAM BUT I ENJOYED IT HELLO YOURSELF AND HELLO TO THE LITTLE ONE CONNERS. So of course I had to come running home with that.

I made some records, went on three times a week at the opera, did another broadcast, and woke up to find I was a household institution, name, face, voice and all, from

Hudson Bay to Cape Horn and back again. The spig papers, the Canadian papers, the Alaskan papers, and all the other papers began coming in by that time, and I was plastered all over them, with reviews of the broadcast, pictures of the car, and pictures of me. The plugs I wrote for the car worked, the horn worked, and all of it worked, so they had to put more ships under charter to make deliveries. Then I had to get Winston's program ready, and began seeing him every day.

I didn't have to see him every day to get the program up. But he dropped into my dressing room one night, the way he had done before, and it was just luck that it was raining, and she still had a hangover from the cold, and had decided to stay home. She was generally out there when I sang, and always came backstage to pick me up. There was a big mob of autograph hunters back there, and instead of locking them out while I dressed, the way I generally did, I let them in, and signed everything they shoved at me, and listened to women tell me how they had come all the way from Aurora to hear me, and let him wait. When we walked out I apologized for it and said there was nothing I could do. "Don't ever come around again. This isn't Paris. Let me drop up to your hotel the morning after, and we'll have the post-mortem then."

"I'd love it! It's a standing date."

From the quick way he said it, and the fact that he had never once asked me where I was living, or made any move to come and see me, it came to me that he knew all about Juana, just like he had known all about Gold. Then I began to have this nervous feeling, that never left me, wondering what he was going to pull next.

What I was going to do with her the night of his concert I didn't know. She had got so she could read the papers now, and had spotted the announcement, and asked me about it. I acted like it was just another job of singing, and she didn't pay much attention to it. Her cold was all right now, and there wasn't a chance she would stay home on that account. I thought of telling her it was a private concert, and that I couldn't get her in, but I knew

that wouldn't work. Going up in the cab, I told her that
as I wouldn't have to dress afterwards, it would be better
if she didn't come backstage. We'd meet in the Russian
place next door. Then I could duck out quick and we'd
miss the mob of handshakers. I showed it to her and she
said all right, then she went in the front way and I
ducked up the alley.

When I got backstage I almost fainted when I found out
what he was up to. I was singing two numbers, one the
aria from the Siege of Corinth for the first part of the
program, the other Walter Damrosch's Mandalay, for the
second part. I had squawked on that Mandalay, because I
thought it was all wrong for a symphony concert. But
when he made me read it over I had to admit it was in a
different class from the Speaks Mandalay, or the Prince
Mandalay, or any of the other barroom Mandalays. It's a
little tone poem all by itself, a piece of real music, with
all the verses in it except the bad one, about the house-
maids, and each verse a little different from the others.
One reason it's never done is that it takes a whole male
chorus, but of course cost never bothered him any. He
got a chorus together, and rehearsed them until they spit
blood, getting a Volga-Boat-Song-dying-away effect he
wanted at the end, and by the time I had gone over it
with them two or three times, we had a real number out
of it.
    But what he was getting ready to do was have them
march on in a body, before I came on, and I had to
throw a fit of temperament to stop it. I raved and cursed,
said it would kill my entrance, and refused to go on if he
did it that way. I said they had to drift in with the orchestra after the intermission, and take their places
without any march-on. But I wasn't thinking about my
entrance. What I was afraid of was that those twenty-four
chorus men, marching on at a Winston Hawes concert,
would be such a murderous laugh that it would tip her off
to what the whole thing was about.

I peeped out before we started, and spotted her. She was

sitting between an old couple, on one side, and one of the critics, alone, on the other, so it didn't look like she would hear anything. In the intermission I peeped out again. She was still sitting there, and so was the old couple. She had sneaked a piece of chewing gum into her mouth, and was munching on that, so everything seemed to be all right, so far.

The chorus were in white ties, and they went on the way I said, and nothing happened. The orchestra played a number and Winston came off. He kidded me about my fit of temperament, and I kidded back. So long as everything was under control, I didn't care. Then I went on. Whether it was what Damrosch wrote, or the way Winston conducted, or the tone of those horns, I don't know, but before the opening chords had even finished, you were in India. I started, and did a good job of it. I clowned the second verse a little, but not too much. The other verses I did straight, and the temple-bell atmosphere kept getting better. When we got to the end, with the chorus dying away behind me, and me hanging above them on the high F, it was something to hear, believe me it was. They broke out into a roar. It had been a program of modern music, most of it pretty scrappy and this was the first thing they had heard that really stuck to their ribs. I took two calls, had the chorus stand, came off, and they called me out again. Then Winston did something that's not done, and that he wouldn't have done for anybody on earth but me. He decided to repeat it.

A repeat is something you do mechanically, God knows why. You've done it once, you've scored with it, and the second time out you do it with your mouth, but your head has already gone home. I went through with it, got every laugh I had got before, coasted along without a hitch. I hit the E flat, the chorus was right with me. I hit the F, and my heart stopped. Hanging up there, over that chorus, was the priest of Acapulco, the guy in the church, singing down the storm, croaking high mass to make the face on the cross stop looking at him.

"Who is these man?"

We were in the cab going down, and it was like the whisper you hear from a coiled rattlesnake.

"What man?"

"I think you know, yes."

"I don't even know what you're talking about."

"You have been with a man."

"I've been with plenty of men. I see men all day long. Do I have to stay with you all the time? What the hell are you talking about?"

"I no speak of man you see all day long. I speak of man you love. Who is these man?"

"Oh, I'm a fairy, is that it?"

"Yes."

"Well, thanks. I didn't know that."

It was a warm night, but on account of the white tie I had to wear a coat. I had been hot as hell going up, but I wasn't hot now. I felt cold and shriveled inside. I watched the El posts going by on Third Avenue, and I could feel her there looking at me, looking at me with those hard black eyes that seemed to bore through me. We got out of the cab, and went on up to the apartment. I put the silk hat in a closet, put the coat in with it, lit a cigarette, tried to shake it off, how I felt. She just sat there on the edge of the table. She had on an evening dress we had got from one of the best shops in town, and the bullfighter's cape. Except for the look on her face, she was something out of a book.

"Why you lie to me?"

"I'm not lying."

"You lie. I look at you, I know you lie."

"Did I ever lie to you?"

"Yes. Once at Acapulco. You know you run away, you tell me no. When you want, you lie."

"We went over that. I meant to run away, and you knew what I meant. Lying, that was just how we got over it easy. Then when I found out what you meant to me, I didn't lie. That's all . . . what the hell squwk have you got? You were all ready to sleep with that son-of-a-bitch—"

"I no lie."

"What has this got to do with Acapulco?"

"Yes, it is the same. Now you love man, you lie."

"I don't—Christ, do I *look* like that?"

"No. You no look like that. We meet in Tupinamba, yes? And you no look like that. I like, much, how you look. Then you make *lotería* for me, and lose *lotería*. And I think, how sweet. He have lose, but he like me so much he make *lotería*. Then I send *muchacha* with address, and we go home, go where I live. But then I know. You know how I know?"

"Don't know, don't care. It's not true."

"I know when you sing. Hoaney, I was street girl, love man, three pesos. Little dumb *muchacha*, no can read, no can write, understand nothing like that. But of man—*all*. . . . Hoaney, these man who love other man, they can do much, very clever. But no can sing. Have no *toro* in high voice, no *grrr* that frighten little *muchacha*, make heart beat fast. Sound like old woman, like cow, like priest."

She began to walk around. My hands were clammy and my lips felt numb. ". . . Then the *político*, he say I should open house, and I think of you. I think maybe, with these man, no like *muchacha*, have no trouble. We got to Acapulco. Rain come, we go in church. You take me. I no want, I think of *sacrilegio*, but you take me. Oh, much *toro*. I like. I think maybe Juana make mistake. Then you sing, oh, my heart beat very fast."

"Just a question of *toro*, hey?"

"No. You ask me come with you. I come. I love you much. I no think of *toro*. Just a little bit. Then in New York I feel, I feel something fonny. I think you think about *contrato*, all these thing. But is not the same. To-night I know. I make no mistake. When you love Juana, you sing nice, much *toro*. When you love man—why you lie to me? You think I no *hear*? You think I no *know*?"

If she had taken a whip to me I couldn't have answered her. She began to cry, and fought it back. She went in the other room, and pretty soon she came out. She had changed her dress and put on a hat. She was carrying the valise in one hand and the fur coat in the other. "I no live with man who love other man. I no live with man who lie. I—"

The phone rang. "—Ah!"

She ran in and answered. "Yes, he is here."

She came out, her eyes blazing and her white teeth showing behind something that was between a laugh and a snarl. "Mr. Hawes."

I didn't say anything and I didn't move. "Yes, Mr. Hawes, the director." She gave a rasping laugh and put on the goddamdest imitation of Winston you ever saw, the walk, the stick, and all the rest of it so you almost thought he was in front of you. "Yes, your sweetie, he wait at telephone, talk to him please."

When I still sat there, she jumped at me like a tiger, shook me till I could feel my teeth rattling, and then ran in to the telephone. "What you want with Mr. Sharp, please? . . . Yes, yes, he will come. . . . Yes, thank you much. Goodbye."

She came out again. "Now, please you go. He have party, want you very much. Now, go to your sweetie. Go! Go! Go!"

She shook me again, jerked me out of the chair, tried to push me out the door. She grabbed up the valise and the fur coat again. I ran in the bedroom, flopped on the bed, pulled the pillow over my head. I wanted to shut it out, the whole horrible thing she had showed me, where she had ripped the cover off my whole life, dragged out what was down there all the time. I screwed my eyes shut, kept pulling the pillow around my ears. But one thing kept slicing up at me, no matter what I did. It was the fin of that shark.

I don't know how long I stayed there. I was on my back after a while, staring at nothing. It was dead quiet outside, and dead still, except for the searchlight from the building on Fourteenth Street, that kept going around and around. I kept telling myself she was crazy, that voice is a matter of palate, sinus, and throat, that Winston had no more to do with what happened to me in Paris than the scenery had. But here it was, starting on me again the same way it had before, and I knew she had called it on me the way it was written in the big score, and that no pillow or anything else could shut it out. I closed my eyes, and I was going down under the waves, with something coming up at me from below. Panic caught me then. I hadn't heard her go out, and I called her. I waited, and called again. There wasn't any answer. My head was under the pillow again pretty soon, and I must have slept because I woke up with the same horrible dream, that I was in the water, going down, and this thing was coming at me. I sat up, and there she was, on the edge of her bed, looking at me. It was gray outside. "Christ, you're there." But some kind of a sob jerked out as I said it, and I put out my hand and took hers.

"It's all true."

She came over, sat down beside me, stroked my hair, held my hand. "Tell me. You no lie, I no fight."

"There's nothing to tell. . . . Every man has got five per cent of that in him, if he meets the one person that'll bring it out, and I did, that's all."

"But you love other man. Before."

"No, the same one, here, in Paris, all over, the one son-of-a-bitch that's been the curse of my life."

"Sleep now. Tomorrow, you give me little bit money, I go back to Mexico—"

"No! Don't you know what I'm trying to tell you? That's out! I hate it! I've been ashamed of it, I've tried to shake it off, I hoped you would never find out, and now it's over!"

I was holding her to me. She began stroking my hair again, looking down in my eyes. "You love me, Hoaney?"

"Don't you know it? Yes. If I never said so, it was just because—did we have to say it? If we felt it, wasn't that a hell of a sight more?"

All of a sudden she broke from me, shoved the dress down from her shoulder, slipped the brassiere and shoved a nipple in my mouth. "Eat. Eat much. Make big *toro!*"

"I know now, my whole life comes from there."

"Yes, eat."

Chapter 11

WE DIDN'T GET UP for two days, but it wasn't like the time we had in the church. We didn't get drunk and we didn't laugh. When we were hungry, we'd call up the French restaurant down the street and have them send something in. Then we'd lie there and talk, and I'd tell her more of it, until it was all off my chest and I had nothing more to say. Once I quit lying to her, she didn't seem surprised, or shocked, or anything like that. She would look at me, with her eyes big and black, and nod, and sometimes say something that made me think she understood a lot more about it than I did, or most doctors do. Then I'd take her in my arms, and afterward we'd sleep, and I felt a peace I hadn't felt for years. All those awful jitters of that last few weeks were gone, and sometimes when she was asleep and I wasn't, I'd think about the Church, and confession, and what it must mean to people that have something lying heavy on their soul. I had left the Church before I had anything on my soul, and the confession business, to me then, was just a pain in the neck. But I understood it now, understood a lot of things I had never understood before. And mostly I understood what a woman could mean to a man. Before, she had been a pair of eyes, and a shape, something to get excited about. Now, she seemed something to lean on, and draw something from, that nothing else could give me. I thought of books I had read, about worship of the earth, and how she was always called Mother, and none of it made much sense, but those big round breasts did, when I put my head on them, and they began to tremble, and I began to tremble.

The morning of the second day we heard the church

bells ringing, and I remembered I was due to sing at the
Sunday night concert. I got up, went to the piano, and
tossed a few high ones around. I was just trying them
out, but I didn't have to. They were like velvet. At six
o'clock we dressed, had a little something to eat, and
went down there. I was in a Rigoletto excerpt, from the
second act, with a tenor, a bass, a soprano, and a mezzo
that were all getting spring try-outs. I was all right. When
we got home we changed to pajamas again, and I got out
the guitar. I sang her the Evening Star song, *Träume,*
Schmerzen, things like that. I never liked Wagner, and
she couldn't understand a word of German. But it had
earth, rain, and the night in it, and went with the humor
we were in. She sat there with her eyes closed, and I sang
it half voice. Then I took her hand and we sat there, not
moving.

A week went by, and still I didn't see Winston. He must
have called twenty times, but she took all calls, and when
it was him she would just say I wasn't in, and hang up. I
had nothing to say to him but goodbye, and I wasn't
going to say that, because I didn't want to play the scene.
Then one day, after we had been out for breakfast, we
stepped out of the elevator, and there he was at the end of
the hall, watching porters carrying furniture into an apartment. He looked at us and blinked, then dived at us with
his hand out. "Jack! Is that you? Well, of all the idiotic
coincidences!"
I felt my blood freeze for fear of what she was going to
do, but she didn't do anything. When I happened not to
see his hand, he began waving it around, and kept chattering about the coincidence, about how he had just
signed a lease for an apartment in this very building, and
here we were. She smiled. "Yes, very fonny."
There didn't seem to be anything to do but introduce
him, so I did. She held out her hand. He took it and
bowed. He said he was happy to know her. She said gracias, she had been at his concert, and she was honored to
know him. Two beautiful sets of manners met in the hall
that day, and it seemed queer, the venom that was back
of them.

The door of the freight elevator opened, and more furniture started down the hall. "Oh, I'll have to show them where to put it. Come in, you two, and have a look at my humble abode."

"Some other time, Winston, we—"

"Yes, gracias, I like."

We went in there, and he had one of the apartments on the south tier, the biggest in the building, with a living room the size of a recital hall, four or five bedrooms and baths, servants' rooms, study, everything you could think of. The stuff I remembered from Paris was there, rugs, tapestries, furniture, all of it worth a fortune, and a lot of things I had never seen. Four or five guys in denim suits were standing around, waiting to be told where to put their loads. He paid no attention to them, except to direct them with one hand, like they were a bunch of bull fiddlers. He sat us down on a sofa, pulled up a chair for himself, and went on talking about how he was sick of hotel living, had about given up all hope of finding an apartment he liked, and then had found this place, and then of all the cock-eyed things, here we were.

Or were we? I said yes, we were at the other end of the hall. We all laughed: He started in on Juana, asked if she wasn't Mexican. She said yes, and he started off about his trip there, and what a wonderful country it was, and I had to hand it to him he had found out more about it in a week than I had in six months. You would have thought he might have conveniently left out what he went down there for. He didn't. He said he went down there to bring me back. She laughed, and said she saw me first. He laughed. That was the first time there was the least little glint in their eyes.

"Oh, I must show you my cricket!"

He jumped up, grabbed a hatchet, and began chopping a small crate apart. Then he lifted out a block of pink stone, a little bigger than a football and about the same shape, but carved and polished into the form of a cricket, with its legs drawn up under it and its head huddled between its front feet. She made a little noise and began to finger it.

"Look at that, Jack. Isn't it marvelous? Pure Aztec, at least five hundred years old. I brought it back from Mexico with me, and I'd hate to tell you what I had to do to get it out of the country. Look at that simplification of detail. If Manship had done it, they'd have thought it was a radical sample of his work. The line of that belly is pure Brancusi. It's as modern as a streamlined plane, and yet some Indian did it before he even saw a white man."

"Yes, yes. Make me feel very *nostâlgica.*"

Then came the real Hawes touch. He picked it up, staggered with it over to the fireplace, and put it down. "For my hearth!"

She got up to go, and I did. "Well, children, you know now where I live, and I want to be seeing a lot of you."

"Yes, gracias."

"And oh! As soon as I'm moved in, I'm giving a little housewarming, and you're surely coming to it—"

"Well, I don't know, Winston, I'm pretty busy—"

"Too busy for my housewarming? Jack, Jack, Jack!"

"Gracias, Señor Hawes. Perhaps we come."

"Perhaps? Certainly you'll come!"

I was plenty shaky when we got to our own apartment. "Listen, Juana, we're getting out of this dump, and we're getting out quick. I don't know what the hell his game is, but this is no coincidence. He's moved in on us, and we're going to beat it."

"We beat it, he come too."

"Then we'll beat it again. I don't want to see him."

"Why you run away?"

"I don't know. It—makes me nervous. I want to be somewhere where I don't have to see him, don't have to think of him, don't have to feel that he's around."

"I think we stay."

We saw him twice more that day. Once, around six o'clock, he rang the buzzer and asked us to dinner, but I was singing and said we would have to eat later. Then, some time after midnight, when we had got home, he dropped in with a kid named Pudinsky, a Russian pianist that was to play at his next concert. He said they were

going to run over some stuff, and for us to come on
down. We said we were tired. He didn't argue. He put
his arm around Pudinsky, and they left. While we were
undressing we could hear the piano going. The kid could
play all right.

"I see his game now."

"Yes. Very fonny game."

"That boy. I'm supposed to get jealous."

"Are you jealous?"

"No. Jealous—what the hell are you talking about?
What difference does it make to me what he does, once
I'm out of it? But it makes me nervous. I—I wish he was
somewhere else. I wish we were all somewhere else."

She lay there for a long time, up on one elbow, looking
down at me. Then she kissed me and went over to her
own bed. It was daylight before I got to sleep.

Next day he was in and out half a dozen times, and the
day after that, and that day after that. I began missing
cues, the first sign you get that you're not right. The
voice was in shape, and I was getting across, but the
prompter began throwing the finger at me. It was the first
time in my life that that had ever happened.

In about a week came the invitation to the housewarming. I tried to beg out of it, said I had to sing that night,
but she smiled and said gracias, we would go, and he put
his arm around her and you would have thought they
were pals, but I knew them both like a book, and could
tell there was something back of it, on both sides. After
he left I got peevish and wanted to know why the hell
she was shoving me into it all the time. "Hoaney, with
this man, it do you no good to run away. He see you no
care, then maybe he estop. He know you have afraid, he
never estop. We go. We laugh, have fine time, no care
. . . You care?"

"For God's sake, no."

"I think yes, little bit. I think we have—how you say—
the goat."

"He's got my goat all right, but not for that reason. I
just don't want any more to do with him."

"Then you care. Maybe not so, how he want. But you have afraid. When you no çare at all, he estop. Now—we no run away. We go, you sing, be fine fallow, no give a damn. And you watch, will be all right."

"If I have to, I have to, but Christ, I hate it."

So we went. I was singing Faust, and I was so lousy I almost did get stuck in the duel scene. But I was washed up by ten thirty, and we came home and dressed. It wasn't any white dress with flowers on it this time. She put on a bottle-green evening dress, and over that the bullfighter's cape, and that embroidered crimson and yellow silk, sliding over the green taffeta, made a rustle you could hear coming, I'm here to tell you, and all those colors, over the light copper of her skin, was a picture you could look at. I put on a white tie, but no overcoat or anything, and about a quarter after eleven we stepped out and walked down the hall.

When we got in there, the worst drag was going on you ever saw in your life. A whole mob of them was in there, girls in men's evening clothes tailored for them, with shingle haircuts and blue make-up in their eyes, dancing with other girls dressed the same way, young guys with lipstick on, and mascara eyelashes, dancing with each other too, and at least three girls in full evening dress, that you had to look at twice to make sure they weren't girls at all. Pudinsky was at the piano, but he wasn't playing Brahms. He was playing jazz. The whole thing made me sick to my stomach as soon as I looked at it, but I swallowed hard and tried to act like I was glad to be there.

Winston had on a purple velvet dinner coat with a silk sash knotted around it, and he brought us in like it was all for us. He introduced us, and got us drinks, and Pudinsky slammed into the Pagliacci Prologue, and I stepped up and sang it, and clowned it with as good a grin as I could get on my face. While they were still clapping, Winston turned around and began to throw the show to Juana. She still hadn't taken off the cape, and he lifted it off her shoulders, and began going into a spasm about it. They all crowded up to look, and when he found out it was a real bullfighter's cape, nothing would suit him but that she had to tell them all about the fine points of bull-fighting. I sat down, and got this feeling it wasn't on the up-and-up, that something was coming. I thought of Chadwick, and wondered if this was another play to show her up. But that wasn't it. Except that Winston would put his arm around Pudinsky every time he saw me look-ing at him, he didn't pull anything. He put her in the spot, and made her explain the whole routine of bull-fighting, and she took the cape to show them, and she was pretty funny, and so was he. Nobody could make a woman look good better than Winston, when he wanted to. Pretty soon somebody yelled out: "How the hell does a man study to be a bullfighter, that's what I want to know."

Winston went down on his knees in front of Juana.

"Yes, will you tell us that? Just what are the practice exercises for a bullfighter?"

"Oh, I explain you."

They all sat down, and Winston squatted at her feet.

"First, the little boy, he wants to be a bullfighter, yes? All little boy want to be bullfighter."

"I always did. I do still."

"So, I tell you how you do. You find nice burro, you know what is burro?"

"A little jackass, something like that?"

"Yes. You get little jackass, you cut two big maguey leaf, you know maguey, yes? Have big leaf, much thick, much sharp—?"

"Century plant?"

"Yes. Tie leaf on head of little jackass, make big horn, like bull—"

"Wait a minute."

Some woman dug up a ribbon, and Winston broke off fronds from a fern, and with the ribbon and the fern leaves, he stuck the horns on his head. Then he got down on his hands and knees in front of Juana. "Go on."

"Yes, just so. You look much like little jackass."

That got a shout. Winston looked up, kicked his heels, and let out a jackass bellow. It was a little funnier than it sounds.

"Then you get little stick, for *espada*, and little red rag, for *muleta*, and practice with little jackass." Somebody dug up a silver-headed cane, and she took it, and the cape, and the two of them began doing a bullfight act in the middle of the floor. The rest of them were screeching and yelling by that time, and I was sitting there, wondering what the hell was up. The buzzer sounded. Somebody went to the door, came back, and touched me on the arm. "Telegram for you, Mr. Sharp."

I went out in the hall.

Harry, one of the bellboys, was out there, and shoved a telegram at me. I opened it. It was nothing but a blank form shoved in an envelope. "Is the messenger still there? He's given you nothing but a blank."

Harry closed the door to the apartment. You could still hear them in there, screeching over the bullfight. "Let me talk quick, Mr. Sharp, so you can get back in there before anybody thinks anything. I had to have a telegram in my hand, so it would look right. . . . There's a man down there, waiting for you. I told him you were out. He went up to your apartment, then he came down again, and he's down there now."

"In the lobby?"

"Yes sir."

"What does he want?"

". . . Mr. Sharp, Tony put through three calls today for this new party, Mr. Hawes. They were all to the immigration service. Tony remembered the number from a year ago, when his brother came from Italy. Tony thinks this man is a federal, come to take Miss Montes away."

"Is Tony on?"

"We're both on. Get back in there, Mr. Sharp, before this Hawes gets tipped off. Get her out of there, and have her press the elevator button twice. Either me or Tony will get her out through the basement, and then you can stall this guy till she gets under cover. Tony thinks his people will take her in. They're fans of yours."

I had a wad of money in my pocket. I took it out and peeled off a ten. "Split that with Tony. There'll be more tomorrow. She'll be right down."

"Yes, sir."

"And thanks. More thanks than I know how to say."

I stepped back in. I took care to be stuffing the telegram in my pocket as I came. Winston jumped up from where he was still galumphing around the floor, and came over. "What is it, Jack?"

"Just some greetings from Hollywood."

"Bad?"

"Little bit."

"Well, what is it? By God, I'd love to wake the sons-of-bitches up and tell them where they get off."

"Wouldn't wake them up, that's the trouble. It's only ten o'clock there. To hell with it, I'll tell you later. And to hell with bullfighting. Let's dance."

"Dance we shall. Hey, professor—music!"

Pudinsky began to bat out more jazz, they grabbed each other, and I grabbed Juana. "Now get a grin on your face. I've got something to tell you."

"Yes, here is nice grin."

I laid it out for her fast. "This Pudinsky thing is nothing but a smoke screen. He's turned in an anonymous tip against you, then you're to be taken to Ellis Island, then I'm to run to him for help, then he's to move heaven and earth—and fail. You're to be sent back to Mexico—"

"And then he gets you."

"So he thinks."

"So I think, too."

"Will you for God's sake stop that and—"

"Why you tremble?"

"I'm plenty scared of him, that's why. Now listen—"

"Yes, I listen."

"Get out of here, quick. Get out on some stall so he thinks you're coming back. Change your dress, pack, as fast as you can. If the buzzer rings, keep still and don't answer. Go to the elevator, ring twice, and the boys will take care of you. Don't call me. Tomorrow I'll reach you through Tony. Here's some money."

I had palmed the wad, and slipped it down the back of her dress. "And once more, step on it!"

"Yes, I step."

She went over to Winston. He was sitting with Pudin-sky, the fern leaves still in his hair. "You want to play *real* bullfight, yes?"

"I just thirst for it."

"Wait. I get things. I come back."

He showed her out, then came over to me. "Lovely girl."

"Yeah, she's all of that."

"I've always said there were two nations under every flag, male and female. I wouldn't give a damn for all the Mexican men that ever lived, but the women are marvelous. What saps their painters are, with all that beauty around them, to spend their days on war, socialism, and politics. Mexican art is nothing but a collection of New Masses covers."

"Whatever it is, I don't like it."

"Who would? But if they could paint her face, that would have been different. Goya could have, but those worthy radicals, no. Well—they don't know what they miss."

I went over, sat down and watched them dance. They were getting lit by now, and it was pretty raw. I wished I had fixed up some signal from the boys, so I would know when she was out. I hadn't, so all I could do was sit there. I was going to wait till he missed her, then go down to the apartment to find her, then come back and say she didn't feel well, and had gone to bed. It would all take time, give her a start, but I had to take the play from him.

I had looked at my watch when she went. It was seven after one. After a hell of a time I slipped back to a bath-room and looked again. It was eleven after. She had been gone four minutes: I came back and sat down again. Pu-dinsky stopped and they all yelled for more. He said he was tired. The buzzer rang. Winston opened, and I began thinking of a stall in case it was the detective. Who stepped in was Juana. She hadn't changed her dress. Over her arm was the cape, in one hand was the *espada*, and in the other the ear.

They had got a little sick of bullfighting, but when they

saw the ear they began to yell again. They passed it around, and felt it, and smelled it, and say "Peyooh!" Winston took it, held it up to his head and wobbled it, and they laughed and clapped. He got down on the floor again and bellowed. Juana laughed. "Yes, now you are no more jackass. Big bull."

He bellowed again. I was getting so nervous I was twitching. I went over to her. "Take that stuff back. I'm fed up on bullfighting, and that ear stinks. Take it back where you got it, and—"

I grabbed for the ear. Winston dodged. She laughed and wouldn't look at me. Something hit me in the belly. When I looked around I saw that one of the fags in woman's clothes had poked me with a broomstick. "Out of my way! I'm a picador! I'm a picador on his old white horse!"

Two or three more of them ran back and got broomsticks, or mops handles, or whatever was there, to be picadors, and began galloping around Winston, poking at him. Every time they touched him he'd bellow. Juana drew the *espada*, and spread the cape with it, like it was a *muletta*. Winston began charging it, on one hand and his knees, still holding the ear with his other hand and wobbling it. Pudinsky began to rip off the bullring music from Carmen. There was so much noise you couldn't even hear yourself think. I walked over and leaned on the piano, with my back to it, till she would get the clowning over and I would have another chance to get her out.

All of a sudden Pudinsky stopped, and this "Ooh!" went around the room. I turned around. She was standing there, like a statue, the way they do for the kill, with her left side to Winston, the sword in her right hand, up at the level of her eyes, and pointing right at him. In her left hand, down in front of him, she held the cape. He was down there looking at it, and wobbling the ear at it. Pudinsky began to play blue chords on the piano.

Winston snorted a couple of times, then looked up at her, like he wanted a cue on what to do next. Then he jumped up, and back, but a sofa caught him. A man yelled. I jumped for the sword arm, but I was too late. That *esapada* thrust isn't something in slow motion, like you maybe have thought from reading the books. It goes like lightning, and next thing I knew the point of the steel was sticking out the back of the sofa, and blood was foaming out of Winston's mouth, and she was over him, talking to him, laughing at him, telling him the detective was waiting to take him down to hell.

It flashed over me, that mob at the novelladas, pouring down out of the *sol*, twisting the tail of the dying bull, yelling at him, kicking at him, spitting on him, and I tried to tell myself I had hooked up with a savage, that it was horrible. It was no use. I wanted to laugh, and cheer, and yell *Olé!* I knew I was looking at the most magnificent thing I had ever seen in my life.

Chapter 12

SHE SPIT INTO THE BLOOD, stepped back, and picked up the cape. For a second all you could hear was Pudinsky, over at the piano, gasping and slobbering in an agony of fright. Then they made a rush for the door, to get out before the police came. They fought to get past each other, the women cursing like men, the fags screaming like women, and when they got to the hall they didn't wait for the elevator. They went piling down the stairway, and some of them fell, and you could hear more curses, and screams, and thuds, where they were kicking each other. She came over and knelt beside me, where I had folded into a chair. "Now, he no get. Goodbye, and remember Juana." She kissed me, jumped up, and rustled out. I sat there, still looking at that thing that was pinned to the sofa, with its head hanging over the back, and the blood drying on the shirt. Pudinsky lifted his head, where it was buried in his hands, saw it, let out a moan, and ran over to a corner, where he put his head down and broke out into more sobs. I picked up a rug to throw on it. Then something twisted in my stomach, and I stumbled back to a bathroom. I hadn't eaten since afternoon, but white stuff began coming up, and even after my stomach was empty it kept retching, and horrible sounds came out of me from the air it forced up. I saw my face in the mirror. It was green.

When I came out two cops were there, and four or five of the fags, and one of the girls in a dinner coat, and a guy in a derby hat. Whether he was the dick that had been waiting for Juana, and he grabbed some of them on the way out, I didn't know. When the cops saw me they motioned me to stand aside, and one of them went back to phone. Pretty soon two more cops came up, and a couple of detectives, and next thing, the place was full of cops. There was one guy that seemed to be a doctor, and another that seemed to be a police photographer. Anyway, he set up a tripod, and began setting off bulbs and throwing them in the fern pot. Pretty soon a cop went over, motioned to me, and he, a detective, and I went out. I didn't have any coat there, but I didn't say anything about it. I didn't know whether they had Juana, or even where she had gone, and I was afraid if I asked them to let me go to the apartment, they would come with me and find her. We went down in the elevator. Harry ran us down. When we got to the lobby, more cops were there, talking to Tony.

We got in a police car, drove down Second Avenue, then down Lafayette Street, and on downtown to a place that seemed to be police headquarters. We got out, went in, and the cops took me in a room and told me to sit down. One of them went out. The other stayed, and picked up an afternoon paper that was on the table. We must have sat an hour, he reading the paper and neither of us saying anything. After a while I asked him if he had a cigarette. He passed over a pack without looking up. I smoked and we sat for another hour. Outside it was beginning to get light.

About six o'clock a detective came in, sat down, and stared at me a while. Then he began to talk. "You was there tonight? At this here Hawes's place?"

"Yes, I was."

"You seen him killed?"

"I did."

"What she kill him for?"

"That I don't know."

"Come on, you know. What you trying to do, kid me?"

"I told you I don't know."

"You live with her?"

"Yes."

"Then what do you mean you don't know? What she kill him for."

"I've got no idea at all."

"Was she in this country illegal?"

I knew by that Tony had spilled what he knew. "That I can't tell you. She might have been."

"What the hell can you tell me?"

"Anything I know I'll tell you."

He roared for a minute about how he could make me tell him, but that was a mistake. It gave me time to think. That illegal entry was a way he could tie me in, and hold me if he wanted to, and I knew the only way I could be of any use to her was to get out of there. Whether they had got her or not I didn't know, but I couldn't be any good sitting behind bars. I kept looking at him, thinking over the entries on my passport, and by the time he began asking questions again I had it all in hand, and thought I could get away with a lie. "So you quit that goddam stalling. One more thing you can't tell me and I'll open you up. Come on. She was in illegal, wasn't she?"

"I told you I don't know."

"Did you bring her in?"

"I did not."

"What? Wasn't you in Mexico?"

"Yes, I was."

"Didn't you bring her in with you?"

"I did not. I met her in Los Angeles."

"How you come in?"

"I rode a bus up to Nogales, caught a ride to San Antonio, and from there took another bus to Los Angeles. I met her about a week after that, in the Mexican quarter. Then I began working for pictures, and we hooked up. Then she came with me to New York."

I saw I had led with my chin on that, on account of the white slave charge. He snapped it back at me before I even finished. "Oh, so you brought her to New York."

"I did not. She paid her own fare."

"What the hell are you trying to tell me? Didn't I say cut that stalling out?"

"All right, ask her."

Then came a flicker in his eye. I had a quick hunch they hadn't got her yet. "Ask her, that's all I've got to say. Don't be silly. I'm not paying any woman's fare from Los Angeles to New York. I heard of the Mann Act too."

"Who turned in the tip against her?"

"That I don't know."

"Come on—"

"I told you I don't know. Now if you'll cut out your goddam nonsense, I'll tell you what I do know, and maybe it'll help you out, I don't know. But you can just drop this third-degree stuff right now, or I'll be starting a little third-degree of my own before long that you may not like so well."

"What do you mean by that?"

"You know what I mean. You're not talking to some Hell's Kitchen gunman. I've got a few friends, see? I don't ask any favors. But I'm claiming my rights, and I'll get them."

"All right, Sharp. Shoot it."

"We went to the party, she and I."

"Yeah, that drag was a funny place for a guy like you."

"He was a pixie, but he was also a musician, and I had worked for him, and when he asked us to his house-warming—"

"Are you a pix?"

"Starting up again, are you?"

"Go on, Sharp. Just checking up."

"So we went. And pretty soon one of the boys came up, and—"

"One of them pixes?"

"One of the bellboys. And I found out there was a guy downstairs waiting to see me. And I found out Hawes had put in three calls that day to the Immigration Office—"

"Then he *did* turn her in?"

"I told you I don't know. I wasn't taking any chances. I told her what the boys had told me, and tried to get her out of there. I told her to leave, and she did, but then she came back with this sword, and they started up again this bullfight game they had been playing—"

"Yeah, we know all about that."

"And she let him have it. And goddam well he had it coming to him. What the hell business was it of his whether she—"

"What he turn her in for?"

"That I don't know either. He had tried to tell me once or twice that living with a girl the way we did wasn't doing me any good, that it was hurting my career—"

"Your singing career?"

"That's right."

"What he have to do with that?"

"He had plenty to do with it. I don't only sing here in New York. I'm under contract to a Hollywood picture company, and he controlled the picture company, or said he did, and he was afraid—"

"Hays office stuff?"

"That's it."

"Oh, I get it now. Go on."

"That's all. It wasn't just morals, take it from me it wasn't, or friendship, or anything like that. It was money, and fear that the Mann Act would ruin one of his big stars, and stuff like that. All right, he went up against the wrong person. She let him have it, and now let him count up his Class A preferred stock."

He asked me a few more questions and then went out. As near as I could tell I had done all right. I had fixed her up with a motive that anyway made sense, him trying to bust us up, and it would look a hell of a sight better after we were married, as I knew we would be before the case ever came to trial. I had kept out of it what was really between Winston and me. I would have even told him that if it would have done her any good, but I knew that one whisper of that would crack everything wide open, and ruin her. I had anyhow made some kind of a stall about the Mann Act and the illegal entry, and they couldn't disprove it unless she told them different, and I knew they'd never get anything out of her. Around seven o'clock they gave me something to eat, and I waited for their next move.

Around eight o'clock a cop came in with one of my traveling cases, with clothes in it. That meant they had been in the apartment. I was still in evening clothes, and began to change. "You got a washroom here?"

"O.K., we'll take you to it. You want a barber?"

All I had in my pocket, after giving her the money was silver, but I counted it. There were a couple of dollars of it. "Yeah, send him in."

He went out, and the cop that was guarding took me down to the washroom. There was a shower there, so I stripped, had a bath, and put on the other clothes. The barber came in and shaved me. I put the evening clothes in the traveling case. They had brought me a hat, and I put that on. Then we went back to the room we had left.

A little after nine I was still pounding on it in my mind, what I could do, and it came to me that one thing I could do was get a lawyer. I remembered Sholto. "I'd like to make a phone call. How about that?"

"You're allowed one call."

We went out in the hall, where there was a row of phones against the wall. I looked up Sholto's number, rang it, and got him on the line. "Oh hello, I was wondering if you'd call. I see you're in a little trouble."

"Yeah, and I want you."

"I'll be right down."

In about a half hour he showed up. He listened to me. About all I could tell him, with the cop sitting there, was that I wanted to get out, but that seemed to be all he wanted to know. "It's probably just a matter of bond."

"What am I held for? Do you know that?"

"Material witness."

"Oh, I see."

"As soon as I can see a bondsman—that is, unless you want to put up cash bond yourself."

"How much is it?"

"I don't know. At a guess, I'd say five thousand."

"Which way is quickest?"

"Oh, money talks."

He had a blank check, and I wrote out a check for ten thousand. "All right, that ought to cover it. I think we can get action in about an hour."

Around ten o'clock he was back, and he, and the cop, and I went over to court. It took about five minutes. An assistant district attorney was there, they set bail at twenty-five hundred, and after Sholto put it up, we went out and got in a cab. He passed over the rest of the cash, in hundred-dollar bills. I handed back ten of them. "Retainer."

"Very well, thanks."

The first thing I wanted to know was whether they had got her yet. When he said they hadn't, I grabbed an early afternoon paper a boy shoved in the window, and read it. It was smeared all over the front page, with my picture, and Winston's picture, but no picture of her. That was one break. As well as I could remember, she hadn't had any picture taken since she had been in the country. It was something we hadn't got around to. There was one story giving Winston's career, another telling about me, and a main story that told what had happened. Everything I had said to the detective was in there, and the big eight-column streamer called her the "Sword-Killer," and said she was "Sought." I was still reading when we pulled up at Radio City.

When we got up to his office I began going over what I had told the detective, the illegal entry stuff and all, and why I had said what I had, but pretty soon he stopped me. "Listen, get this straight. Your counsel is not your co-conspirator in deceiving the police. He's your representative at the bar, to see that you get every right that the law entitles you to, and that your case, or her case, or whatever case he takes, is presented as well as it can be. What you told the detective is none of my affair, and it's much better, at this time, that I know nothing of it. When the time comes, I'll ask for information, and you had better tell me the truth. But at the moment, I prefer not to know of any misrepresentation you've made. From now on, by the way, an excellent plan, in dealing with the police, would be to say nothing."

"I get it."

He kept walking around his office, then he picked up the paper and studied that a while, then walked around some more. "There's something I want to warn you about."

"Yeah. What?"

"It seemed to me I got you out very easily."

"I didn't do anything."

"If they had wanted to hold you, there were two or three charges, apparently, they could have brought against you. All bailable offenses, but they could have kept you there quite a while. They could have made trouble. Also, the bond was absurdly low."

"I don't quite follow you."

"They haven't got her. They may have her, tucked away in some station-house in the Bronx, they may be holding her there and saying nothing for fear of habeas corpus proceedings, but I don't think so. They haven't got her, and it's quite possible they've let you out so they can locate her through you."

"Oh, now I see what you mean."

"You going back to your apartment?"

"I don't know. I suppose so."

". . . You'll be watched. There'll probably be a tail on you day and night. Your phone may be tapped."

"Can they do that?"

"They can, and they do. There may be a dictaphone in there by now, and they're pretty good at thinking of places to put it without your finding it, or suspecting it.

It's a big apartment house, and that makes it all the easier
for them. I don't know what her plans are, and apparently you don't. But it's a bad case. If they catch her, I'll
do everything I can for her, but I warn you it's a bad case.
It's much better that she not be located. . . . Be careful."

"I will."

"The big danger is that she phone you. Whatever you
do, the second she rings up, warn her that she's being
overheard."

"I'll remember that."

"You're being used as a decoy."

"I'll watch my step."

When I got up to Twenty-second Street a flock of reporters were there, and I stuck with them for about ten minutes. I thought it was better to answer their questions
some kind of way, and get rid of them, than have them
trying to get to me all day. When I got up to the apartment the phone was ringing, and a newspaper was on the
line, offering me five thousand dollars for a signed story
of what I knew about it, and about her, and I said no,
and hung up. It started to ring again, and I flashed the
board and told them not to put through any more incom-
ing calls, or let anybody up. The door buzzer sounded. I
answered, and it was Harry and Tony, on hand to tell me
what they knew. I peeled off a hundred-dollar bill as they
started to talk, handed it over, and then remembered
about the dictaphone. We went out in the hall, and they
whispered it. She didn't leave right after it happened. She
went to the apartment, packed, and changed her dress,
and about five or ten minutes later buzzed twice, like I
had told her to. Tony had the car up there all that time,
waiting for her, and he opened, pulled her in, and
dropped her down to the basement. They went out by
the alley, and when they came out on Twenty-third
Street he got her a cab, and she left. That was the last he
saw of her, and he didn't tell it to the police. While he
was doing that, Harry was on the board in the lobby, and
didn't pay much attention when he saw the fags going out,
and neither did the guy from the Immigration Service.

How the cops found it out they didn't know, but they thought the fags must have bumped into one outside, or got scared and thought they better tell it anyway, or something. Tony said the cops were already in Winston's apartment before she left.

They went down and I went in the apartment again. With the phone cut off it was quiet enough now, but I began looking for the dictaphone. I couldn't find anything. I looked out the window to see if anybody was watching the building. There wasn't anybody out there. I began to think Sholto was imagining things.

Around two o'clock I got hungry and went out. The reporters were still down there, and almost mobbed me, but I jumped in a cab and told him to drive to Radio City. As soon as he got to Fourth Avenue I had him cut over to Second again, and come down, and got out at a restaurant around Twenty-third Street. I had something to eat and took down the number of the pay phone. When I got back to the apartment house, I whispered to the boy on the board if a Mr. Kugler called, to put him through. I went upstairs and called the restaurant phone. "Is Mr. Kugler there?"

"Hold the line, I'll see."

I held the line, and in a minute he was back. "No Mr. Kugler here now."

"When he comes in ask him to call Mr. Sharp. S-H-A-R-P."

"Yes sir, I'll tell him."

I hung up. In about twenty minutes the phone rang. "Mr. Sharp? This is Kugler."

"Oh, hello, Mr. Kugler. About those opera passes I promised you, I'm afraid I'll have to disappoint you for the time being. You may have read in the paper I'm having a little trouble now. Can you let me put that off till next week."

"Oh, all right, Mr. Sharp. Any time you say."

"Terribly sorry, Mr. Kugler."

I hung up. I knew then that Sholto knew what he was talking about. I didn't know any Mr. Kugler.

Harry kept bringing up new editions as they came out,

and the stuff that was coming in for me. They still hadn't got her. They found the taxi driver that rode her from Twenty-third Street. He said he took her down to Battery Park, she paid him with a five-dollar bill, so he had to go in the subway to get change, and then went off, carrying the valise. He told how Tony had flagged him, and Tony took another trip down to headquarters. It said the cops were considering the possibility she had jumped in the river, and that it might be dragged. The stuff that was coming in was a flock of telegrams, letters, and cards from every kind of nut you ever heard of, and opera fan, and shyster lawyer. But a couple of those wires weren't from nuts. One was from Panamier, saying the broadcast would temporarily be carried on by somebody else. And one was from Luther, saying no doubt I preferred not to have any more opera appearances until I got my affairs straightened out. The last afternoon edition had a story about Pudinsky. I felt my mouth go cold. He was the one person that might know about Winton and me. If he did he didn't say anything. He said what a fine guy Winston was, what a loyal friend, and defended him for calling up the Immigration people. He said Winston only had my best interests at heart.

I went out to eat around seven o'clock, dodged the reporters again, and had a steak in a place off Broadway. My picture was in every paper in town, but nobody seemed to notice me. One reason was, most of those pictures had been taken while I was in Hollywood, and I had put on a lot of weight since then. I wasn't exactly fat when I arrived from Mexico. Then I had a little trouble with my eyes, and had got glasses. I ate what I could, walked around a little, then around nine o'clock came back to the apartment. All the time I was walking I kept looking back, to see if I was followed. I tried not to, but I couldn't help it. In the cab, I kept twisting around, to see what was back of us.

There was another mountain of stuff when I came in, but I didn't bother to open it. I read back all the newspaper stuff again, and then there didn't seem to be anything to

do but to go to bed. I lay there, first trying to think and
then trying to sleep. I couldn't do either one. Then after
a while I did drop off. I woke up in a cold sweat with
moans coming out of my mouth. The whole day had
been like some kind of a fever dream, chasing in and out
of cabs, dodging reporters, trying to shake the police, if
they were around, reading papers. Now for the first time I
seemed to get it through my head the spot we were in.
She was wanted for murder, and if they caught her they
would burn her in the chair.

What waked me up the next morning was the phone.
Harry was on the board. "I know you said not to call, Mr.
Sharp, but there's a guy on the line, he kept calling all
day yesterday, and now he's calling again, he says he's a
friend of yours, and it's important, and he's got to talk to
you, and I thought I better tell you."
"Who is he?"
"He won't say, but he said I should say the word Acapulco, something like that, to you, and you would know
who it was."
"Put him through."
I hoped it might be Conners, and sure enough when I
heard that "Is that you, lad?" I knew it was. He was
pretty short. "I've been trying to reach you. I've called
you, and wired you, and called again, and again—"
"I cut the phone calls off, and I haven't opened the
last bunch of wires. You'd have been through in a second
if they had told me. I want to see you, I've got to see
you—"
"You have indeed. I have news."
"Stop! Don't say a word. I warn you that my phone is
tapped, and everything you say is being heard."
"That occurred to me. That's why I refused to give my
name. How can I get to you?"
"Wait a minute. Wait a minute. . . . Will you call me
in five minutes? I'll have to figure a way—"
"In five minutes it is."
He hung up, and I tried to think of some way we could
meet, and yet not tip off the cops over the phone where
it would be. I couldn't think. He had said he had news,

and my head was just spinning around. Before I even had half an idea the phone rang again. "Well, lad, what's the word?"

"I haven't any. They're following me too, that's the trouble. Wait a minute, wait a minute—"

"I have something that might work."

"What is it?"

"Do you remember the time signature of the serenade you first sang to me?"

". . . Yes, of course."

"Write those figures down, the two of them, one beside the other. Now write them again, the same way. You should have a number of four figures."

I jumped up, got a pen, and wrote the numbers on the memo pad. It was the Don Giovanni serenade, and time signature is 6/8. I wrote 6868. . . . "All right, I've got it."

"Now subtract from it this number." He gave me a number to subtract. I did it. "That is the number of the pay telephone I'm at. The exchange number is Circle 6. Go out to another pay telephone and call me there."

"In twenty minutes. As soon as I get dressed."

I jumped into my clothes, ran up to a drugstore, and called. Whether they were around the booth, listening to me, I didn't care. They couldn't hear what was coming in at the other end. "Is that you, lad?"

"Yes. What news?"

"I have her. She's going down the line with me. I'm at the foot of Seventeenth Street, and I slip my hawsers at midnight tonight. If you wish to see her before we leave, come aboard some time after eleven, but take care you're not detected."

"How did you find her?"

"I didn't. She found me. She's been aboard since yesterday, if you had answered your phone."

"I'll be there. I'll thank you then.".

I went back to the apartment, cut out the fooling around, and began to think. I checked over every last thing I had to do that day, then made a little program in my mind of what I was to do first, and what I was to do after that. I knew I would be tailed, and I planned it all on that basis. The first thing I did was to go up to Grand Central, and look up trains for Rye. I found there was a local leaving around ten that night. I came out of there, went in a store and bought some needles and thread. Then I went down to the bank. I still had over six thousand dollars in hundred-dollar bills, but I needed more than that. I drew out ten thousand, half of it in thousand-dollar bills, twenty-five hundred more in hundreds, and the rest in fives and tens, with about fifty ones I stuffed all that in my pockets, and went home with it. I remembered about the two shirts I had worn out of the hotel in Mexico, and pulled one just like it. I took two pairs of drawers, put one pair inside the other, sewed the bottoms of each leg together, then quilted that money in, all except the ones, and some fives and tens, that I put in my pockets. I put the drawers on. They felt a little heavy, but I could get my trousers over them without anything showing. Tony came up. They had got out of him how he had called the taxi, and he was almost crying because he had squealed. I told him it didn't make any difference.

When dinner time came, instead of going out I had something sent in. Then I packed. I shoved a stack of newspapers and heavy stuff into a traveling case, and locked it. When I dressed I put on a pair of gray flannel pants I had left over from Hollywood, and over my shirt a dark red sweater. I put on a coat, and over that a· light topcoat. I picked out a gray hat, shoved it on the side of my head. I looked at myself in the mirror and I looked like what I wanted to look like, a guy dressed up to take a trip. After drawing the money, I knew they would expect that. That was why I had planned it the way I had.

At nine thirty, I called Tony, had him take my bag down and call a cab, shook hands with him, and called out to the driver, "Grand Central." We turned into Second Avenue. Two cars started up, down near Twenty-first Street, and one left the curb just behind us as we turned west on Twenty-third. When we turned into Fourth, they turned too. When we got to Grand Central they were still with us, and five guys got out, none of them looking at me. I gave my bag to a redcap, went to the ticket office, bought a ticket for Rye, then went out to the news-stand and bought a paper. When I mixed with the crowd at the head of the ramp I started to read it. Three of the five were there too, all of them reading papers.

The redcap put me aboard, but I didn't let him pick the car. I did that myself. It was a local, all day-coaches, but I wanted one without vestibule. It happened to be the smoker, so that looked all right. I took a seat near the door and went on reading my paper. The three took seats further up, but one of them reversed his seat and sat so he could see me. I didn't even look up as we pulled out, didn't look up as we pulled into a Hundred and Twenty-fifth Street, didn't look up as we pulled out. But when the train had slid about twenty feet, I jumped up, left my bag where it was, walked three steps to the car platform, and skipped off. I never stopped. I zipped right out to a taxi, jumped in, told him to drive to Grand Central, and to step on it. He started up. I kept my eyes open. Nobody was behind us, that I could see.

When he turned into upper Park, I tapped on the glass and said I was too late for my train, that he should go to Eighth Avenue and Twenty-third Street. He nodded and kept on. I took off the hat, the topcoat, and the coat and laid them in a little pile on the seat. When we got to Eighth and Twenty-third I got out, took out a five-dollar bill. "I left some stuff in the car, two coats and a hat. Take them up to Grand Central and check them to leave them. Leave the three checks at the information desk, in my name, Mr. Henderson. There's no hurry. Any time tonight will do."

"Yes sir, yes sir."

He grabbed the five, touched his hat, and went off. I started down Eighth Avenue. Instead of a guy all dressed up to go away, I was just a guy without a hat, walking down for a stroll on a spring night. I looked at my watch. It was a quarter to eleven. I back-tracked up to Twenty-third Street and went into a movie.

At twenty after, I came out, started down Eighth Avenue again, and walked to Seventeenth Street. I took my time, looked in windows, keep peeping at my watch. When I cut over to the pier it was a quarter to twelve. I followed the signs to the *Port of Cobh*, strolled aboard. Nobody stopped me. Up at the winch I saw something that looked familiar. I went up and put my arm around him.

"She's back in your old cabin—and you're late."

I went back there, knocked, and stepped in. It was dark in there, but a pair of arms were around me before I even got the door shut, and a pair of lips were against mine, and I tried to say something, and couldn't and she tried to say something and couldn't and we just sat on one of the berths, and held on to each other.

In almost no time there was a knock on the door and he stepped in. "You'll be going ashore now. Why didn't you get here sooner?"

"What are you talking about?"

"I cast my hawsers in two minutes."

"Hawsers, hell. I'm going with her."

"No, Hoaney. Goodbye, goodbye, now you are free, remember, Juana, but come not. No, I have much money now, I be all right. Now, kiss, I love you much."

"I'm going with you."

"No, no!"

"Lad, you don't know what you're saying. Alone, she can vanish like the mist. With you, she's doomed."

"I'm going with her."

He went out. A bell sounded on the tugboat, and we began to move. We looked out. When we straightened out in the river we were looking at the Jersey side. We slipped past it, and pretty soon we stepped out and found him on the bridge. He was at the far end of it, looking out at the Long Island side. I said something, but he paid no attention, and pointed. A cluster of lights was bearing down on us. "It's a police boat, and she's headed right for us."

We stood watching it, hardly daring to breathe. It came on, then cut across our bows toward Staten Island. We picked up speed. The first swell lifted our nose. She put her hand in mine, and gave it a little squeeze.

Chapter 13

We were in Guatemala, though, before we really knew what we were up against, or I did. The trip down was just one nightmare of biting our fingernails and listening to every news broadcast we could pick up, to see if they were on our trail yet. In between, I stuffed myself with food and beer, to put on more weight, and let my moustache grow, and plucked my eyebrows to give my face a different expression, and stood around in the sun, to tan. All I thought about was that radio, and what it was going to tell us. Then at Havana I was running around like a wild man, still trying to beat them to the punch. I found a tailor shop, and put in a rush order for clothes, and then at a little bootleg printshop I got myself a lot of fake papers fixed up, all in the name of Guiseppe Di Nola and where she figured in them, Lola Deminguez Di Nola. I speak Italian like a Neapolitan, and changed myself into an Italian as fast as the tailor, the printer, the barber, and all the rest of them could work on me. As well as I could tell, I got by all right, and none of them had any idea who I was. But one thing kept gnawing at me, and that was the hello I had said to Conners on that first broadcast. Sooner or later, I knew, somebody was going to remember it and check back, and then we would be sunk. I wanted to get a thousand miles away from that ship, and any place she would touch on her way down to Rio.

I had to work fast, because all we had was a three-day layover. As soon as my first suit was ready, I put my fake papers in a briefcase and went over to Pan-American. I found all we would really need was a vaccination certificate for each of us. The rest was a matter of tourist papers that they furnished. I told them to make out the ticket and that I would have the certificates at the airport in the morning. I went over to American Express and bought travelers' checks, then went down to the boat and got her. I had her put on some New York clothes, and we went ashore. Then we went to a little hotel off the Prado. Conners wasn't there when we left, and I had to scribble a note to him, and call that a goodbye. It seemed a terrible thing to beat it without even shaking his hand, but I was afraid even to leave our hotel address with anyone on board, for fear some U.S. detective would show up and they would tip him off. So far, none of them on the ship knew us. He had run into a strike at Seattle in the winter, and cleared with an entirely new crew, even officers. He had carried us as Mr. and Mrs. Di Nola, and Mr. and Mrs. Di Nola just disappeared.

There was no hotel doctor, but they knew of one, and got him around, and he vaccinated us, and gave us our certificates. About six o'clock I went around to the tailor and got the rest of my suits. They were all right, and so were the shoes, shirts, and the rest of the stuff I had bought. The tropicals were double-breasted, with a kind of a Monte Carlo look, the pin-stripe had white piping on the vest and the gray had black velvet, the hats were fedoras, one green, the other black, with a Panama thrown in to go with the tropicals. The shoes were two-toned. On appearance, I was as Italian as Mussolini, and I was surprised to see I looked quite a lot like him. I got out my razor and gave the moustache an up-cut under each corner. That helped. It was two weeks out now, and plenty black, with some gray in it. Those gray hairs startled me. I hadn't known they were there.

In the morning we went to the airport, showed the certificates, and were passed through. The way the trip broke, we could make better time by going through to Vera Cruz, and then turning south, than by making the change at Mérida. There had been some switch on planes, and that would save us a day. I didn't want to spend one more hour in Mexico than I had to, so I said that suited me. Where we were going I had no idea, except that we were going a long way from Havana, but where we were booked for was Guatemala. That seemed to be a kind of a terminus, and to go on from there we would have to have more papers than they could furnish us with at Havana. She got sick as a dog as soon as we took off, and I, and the steward, and the pilots thought it was airsickness. But when it still kept up, after we got to the hotel in Vera Cruz, I knew it was the vaccination. She was all right, though, the next day, and kept looking down at the country we were going over. We had the Gulf of Mexico under us for a little while after we hauled out of Vera Cruz, and then as we were working down toward Tapachula we were over the Pacific. She had to have all that explained to her. She had never got the oceans quite straight, and how we could leave one, and then pick up another almost before we had time to look at the pictures in the magazines, had to be blue-printed for her, with drawings. To her, I think all countries were square, like a bean patch with lines of maguey around it, and it was hard for her to get through her head how any country, and especially Mexico, could be wide at the top and narrow at the bottom.

At Guatemala, we marched from the plane into the pavilion with a loud speaker blaring the Merry Widow waltz, a barefoot Indian girl gave us coffee, and then after a while an American in a flyer's uniform came and explained to me, in some kind of broken Italian, what I would have to do to go on down the line, if that was what I expected to do. I thanked him, we got our luggage, and went to the Palace Hotel. Then I got to thinking:

Why are we going down the line? Why is Chile any better than Guatemala? Our big danger comes every time we fool with papers, and if we're all right so far, why not let well enough alone, and dig in? We couldn't stay on at the hotel, because it was full of Americans, Germans, English and all kinds of people, and sooner or later one of them would know me. But we might rent a place. I sent her down to the desk to ask how we went about it, and when we found out we didn't have to sign any police forms, we went out and got a house. It was a furnished house, just around the block from the hotel, and the gloomiest dump I ever laid eyes on, with walnut chairs, and horse-hair sofas, and sea shells, and coconut shells carved into skulls, and everything else you could think of. But there was a bathroom in it, and it didn't look like we would find one any better. The lady that owned it was Mrs. Gonzalez, and she wanted it understood that she didn't really have to rent the house, that she came of an old coffee family, that she preferred to live out of town, at the lake, on account of her health. We said we understood that perfectly, and closed at a hundred and fifty quetzals a month. A quetzal exchanges even with a dollar.

So in a couple of days we moved in. I found a Japanese couple that didn't speak any English, Italian, or Spanish, and we had to wigwag, but there was no chance of their finding out too much. I was practicing Spanish morning, noon and night, so she and I would be able to talk in front of other people without using English, and I tried to speak it with an Italian accent, but I still wasn't sure I was getting away with it. With the Japs, though, it was safe around the house.

So then we breathed a little easier, and began to shake down into a routine. Daytime we'd lay around, mostly upstairs, in our bedroom. At night we'd walk down to the park and listen to the band. But we'd always sit well away from it, on a lonely bench. Then we'd come back, flit the mosquitoes, and go to bed. There was nothing else to do, even if we had thought it was safe to do it. Guatemala is the Japan of Central America. They've copied everything. They've got Mexican music, American movies, Scotch whisky, German delicatessens, Roman religion, and everything else imported you can think of. But they forgot to put anything of their own in, and what comes out is a place you could hardly tell from Glendale, California, on a bet. It's clean, modern, prosperous, and dull. And the weather gives you plenty of chance to find out how dull it really is. We hit there in June, at the

height of the rainy season. It's not supposed to rain in
Central America, by the books, but that's wrong. It rains
plenty, a cold, gray rain that sometimes keeps up for two
days at a time. Then when the sun comes out it's so
sticky hot you can hardly breathe, and the mosquitos
start up. The air gets you down almost as bad as it does
in Mexico. Guatemala City is nearly a mile up in the air,
and at night that feeling of suffocation comes over you,
so you think you'll die if you don't get something in your
lungs you can breathe.

Little by little, a change came over her. Mind you,
from the time we left New York we hadn't said one word
about Winston, or what she did, or whether it was right
or wrong, or anything about it. That was done, and we
steered around it. We talked about the Japs, the mosquitoes, where Conners was by now, things like that, and
so long as we jumped at every noise, we seemed to be
nearer than we ever had been. But after that eased off,
and we began to kid ourselves we were safe, she began
moping to herself, and now and then I'd catch her looking at me. Then I noticed that another thing we never
talked about was my singing. And then one night, just as
we started downstairs to go out in the park, just mechanically I did a little turn, and in another second would have
cut loose a high one. I saw this look of horror on her
face, and choked it off. She listened, to see if the Japs
had caught it. They seemed to be in the kitchen, so we
went down. Then it came to me, the spot I was in. On
the way down I hadn't even thought about singing. But
here, and any other place south of the Rio Grande, for
that matter, my voice was just as familiar as bananas. My
picture, in the lumberjack suit, was still plastered all over
the Panamier show windows, Pablo Buñan had played
the town not a month before, even the kids were whistling My Pal Babe. Unless I was going to send her to the
chair, I couldn't ever sing again.

I tried not to think about it, and so long as I could read,
or do something to get my mind off it, I wouldn't. But
you can't read all the time, and in the afternoon I'd get
to wishing she'd wake up from her siesta, so we could

talk, or practice Spanish, and I could shake it off. Then I began to get this ache across the bridge of my nose. You see, it wasn't that I was thinking about the fine music I couldn't sing any more, or the muted song that was lost to the world, or anything like that. It was simpler than that, and worse. A voice is a physical thing, and if you've got one, it's like any other physical thing. It's in you, and it's got to come out. The only thing I can compare it with is when you haven't been with a woman for a long time, and and you get so you think if you don't find one soon, you'll go insane. The bridge of the nose is where your voice focuses, where you get that little pull when you cut loose, and that was where I began to feel it. I'd talk, and read, and eat, and try to forget it, and it would go away, but then it would come back.

Then I began to have these dreams. I'd be up there, and they'd be playing my cue, and it would be time for me to come in, and I'd open my mouth, and nothing would come out of it. I'd be dying to sing, and couldn't. A murmur would go over the house, he'd rap the orchestra to attention, look at me, and start the cue again. Then I'd wake up. Then one night, just after she had gone over to her bed, something happened so we did talk about it. In Central America, they've got radios all over the place, and there were three in the block back of us, and one of them had been setting me nuts all day. It was getting London, and they don't have any of that advertising hooey over there. The whole Barber of Seville had come over in the afternoon, with only a couple of small cuts, and at night they had played the Third, Fifth, and Seventh Beethoven symphonies. Then, around ten o'clock, a guy began to sing the serenade from Don Giovanni, the same thing I had sung for Conners at Acapulco, the same thing I had sung the night I came in big at the Metropolitan. He was pretty good. Then, at the end, he did the same *messa di voce* that I had done. I kind of laughed, in the dark. ". . . Well, he's heard me sing it."

She didn't say anything, and then I felt she was crying. I went over there. "What's the matter?"

"Hoaney, Hoaney, you leave me now. You go. We say goodbye."

"Well—what's the big idea?"

"You no know who that was? Who sing? Just now?"

"No. Why?"

"That was you."

She turned away from me then, and began to shake from her sobs, and I knew I had been listening to one of my own phonograph records, put on the air after the main program was over. ". . . Well? What of it?"

But I must have sounded a little sick. She got up, snapped on the light, and began walking around the room. She was stark naked, the way she generally slept on hot nights, but she was no sculptor's model now. She looked like an old woman, with her shoulders slumped down, her feet sliding along in a flat-footed Indian walk, her eyes set dead ahead, like two marbles, and her hair hanging straight over her face. When the sobs died off a little, she pulled out a bureau drawer, got out a gray *rebozo*, and pulled that over her shoulders. Then she started shuffling around again. If she had had a donkey beside her, it would have been any hag, from Mexicali to Tapachula. Then she began to talk. ". . . So. Now you go? Now we say *adiós*."

"What the hell are you talking about? You think I'm going to walk out on you now?"

"I kill these man, yes. For what he do to you, for what he do to me, I have to kill him. I know these thing at once, that night, when I hear of the *inmigración*, that I have to kill him. I ask you? No. Then what I do? Yes? What I do!"

"Listen, for Christ's sake—"

"What I do? You tell me, what I do?"

"Goddam if I know. Laughed at him, for one thing."

"I say goodbye. Yes, I come to you, say remember Juana, kiss you one time, *adiós*. Yes, I kill him, but then is goodbye. I know. I say so. You remember?"

"I don't know. Will you cut it out, and—"

"Then you come to boat. I am weak. I love you much. But what I do then? What I say?"

"Goodbye, I suppose. Is that all you know to say?"

"Yes. Once more I say goodbye. The *capitán*, he know too, he tell you go. You no go. You come. Once more, I

love you much, I am glad. . . . Now, once more. Three
times, I tell you go. It is the end. I tell you, *goodbye*."

She didn't look at me. She was shooting it at me with
her eyes staring straight again, and her feet carrying her
back and forth with that sliding, shuffling walk. I opened
my mouth two or three times to stall some more, but
couldn't, looking at her. "Well, what are you going to
do? Will you tell me that? Do you know?"

"Yes. You go. You give me money, not much, but little bit. Then I work, get little job, maybe kitchen *muchacha*, nobody know me, look like all other *muchacha*, I
get job, easy. Then I go to priest, confess my *pecado*—"

"That's what I've been waiting for. I knew that was
coming. Now let me tell you something. You confess that
pecado, and right there is where you lose."

"I no lose. I give money to church, they no turn me in.
Then I have peace. Then some time I go back to Mexico."

"And what about me?"

"You go. You sing. You sing for radio. I hear. I remember. You remember. Maybe. Remember little dumb *muchacha*—"

"Listen, little dumb *muchacha*, that's all swell, except
for one thing. When we hooked up, we hooked up for
good, and—"

"Why you talk so? It is the end! Can you no see these
thing? It is the end! You no go, what then? They take
me back. Me only, they never find. You, yes. They take
me back, and what they do to me? In Mexico, maybe
nothing, unless he was *político*. In New York, I know,
you know. The *soldados* come, they put the *pañuelo* over
the eyes, they take me to wall, they shoot. Why you do
these things to me? You love me, yes. *But it is the end!*"

I tried to argue, got up and tried to catch her, to make
her quit that walking around. She slipped away from me.
Then she flung herself down on her bed and lay there
staring up at the ceiling. When I came to her she waved
me away. From that time on she slept in her bed and I
slept in mine, and nothing I could do would break her
down.

I didn't leave her, I couldn't leave her. It wasn't only that I was insane about her. What was between us had completely reversed since we started out. In the beginning, I thought of her like she had said, as a little dumb muchacha that I was nuts about, that I loved to touch and sleep with and play with. But now I had found out that in all the main things of my life she was stronger than I was, and I had got so I had to be with her. It wouldn't have done any good to leave her. I'd have been back as fast as a plane could carry me.

For a week after that, we'd lie there in the afternoon, saying nothing, and then she began putting on her clothes and going out. I'd lie there, trying not to think about singing, praying for strength not to suck in a bellyful and cut it loose. Then it popped in my mind about the priests, and I got in a cold sweat that that was where she was going. So one day I followed her. But she went past the Cathedral, and then I got ashamed of myself and turned around and came back.

I had to do something with myself, though, so when she went I began going to the baseball games. From that you can imagine how much there was to do in Guatemala, that I would go to the baseball game. They've got some kind of a league between Managua, Guatemala, San Salvador, and some other Central American towns, and they get as excited about it as they get in Chicago over a World Series, and yell at the ump, and all the rest of it. Busses run out there, but I walked. The fewer people that got a close look at me, the better I liked it. One day I found myself watching the pitcher on the San Salvador team. The papers gave his name as Barrios, but he must have been an American, or anyway have lived in the United States, from his motion. Most of those Indians handle a ball jerky, and fight it so they make more errors than you could believe. But this guy had the old Lefty Gomez motion, loose, easy, so his whole weight went in the pitch, and more smoke than all the rest of them had put together. I sat looking at him, taking in those motions, and then all of a sudden I felt my heart stop. Was it coming out in me again, this thing that had got me when I met Winston? Was that kid out there really doing things to me that had nothing to do with baseball? Was it having its effect, her putting me out of her bed?

I got up and left. I know now it was just nerves, that when Winston died that chapter ended. But I didn't then. I tried to put it out of my mind, and couldn't. I didn't go to the ball games any more, but then, after a couple of weeks, I got to thinking: Am I going to turn into the priest again? Am I going to give up everything else in this Christ-forsaken dump, and then lose my voice too? It began to be an obsession with me that I had to have a woman, that if I didn't have a woman I was sunk.

She didn't go with me to hear the band play any more. She stayed home and went to bed. One night, when I went out, instead of heading for the park, I flagged a taxi. "La Locha."

"Sí, Señor, La Locha."

I had heard guys at the ball game talking about La Locha's, but I didn't know where it was. It turned out to be on Tenth Avenue, but the district was on a different system from in Mexico. There were regular houses, with red lights over the door, all according to Hoyle. I rang, and an Indian let me in. A whorehouse, I guess, is the same all over the world. There was a big room, with a phonograph on one side, a radio on the other, and an electric piano in the middle, with a stained-glass picture of Niagara Falls in the front, that lit up whenever somebody put in a nickel. The wallpaper had red roses all over it, and at one end was a bar. Back of the bar was an oil painting of a nude, and in the cabinet under it were stacks and stacks of long square cans. When a guy in Guatemala really wants to show the girls a good time, he blows them to canned asparagus.

The Indian looked at me pretty funny, and after he went back, so did the woman at the bar. I thought at first it was the Italian way I was speaking Spanish, but then it seemed to be something about my hat. An Army officer was at a little table, reading a newspaper. He had his hat on, and then I remembered and put mine on. I ordered

cerveza, and three girls came in. They stood on the rail
and began loving me up. Two of them were Indian, but
one of them was white, and she looked the cleanest. I put
my arm around her, and after the other two got their
drinks, they went over with the officer. One of them
turned on the radio, and the other one and the officer
began to dance. My girl and I danced. By rights I guess
she was fairly pretty. She couldn't have been more than
twenty-one or two, and even in the sweater and green
dress she had on, you could see she had a pretty good
shape. But she kept playing with my hand, and everything I'd say to her, she'd answer in a little high squeak
of a voice that got on my nerves. I asked her what her
name was. She said María.

We had another dance, but God knows there was no
point in keeping that up. I asked her if she wanted to go
upstairs, and she was leading me out the door even before
the tune was over.

We went up, she took me in a room, and snapped on
the light. It was just the same old whore's bedroom, except for one thing. On the bureau was a signed photograph of Enzo Luchetti, an old bass I had sung with years
before, in Florence. My heart skipped a beat. If he was in
town, that meant I have to get out, and get out fast. I
picked it up and asked her who it was. She said she didn't
know. Another girl had had the room before she came, a
fine girl that had been in Europe, but she had got en-
ferma and had to leave. I put it down and said it looked
like an Italian. She asked if I wasn't Italian. I said yes.

There didn't seem to be much to do, then, but get at
it. She began dropping off her clothes. I began dropping
off mine. She snapped off the light and we lay down on
the bed. I didn't want her, and yet I was excited, in some
kind of a queer, unnatural way, because I knew I had to
have her. It didn't seem possible that anything could be
over so quick and amount to so little. We lay there, and I
tried to talk to her, but there wasn't anything to talk to.
Then we had another, and next thing I knew I was dressing. Ten quetzals. I gave her fifteen. She got awfully
friendly then, but it was like having a poodle bitch trying
to jump in your lap. It was only a little after ten when I

got home, but Juana was asleep. I undressed in the dark, got into bed, and thought I would get some peace. Next thing, the conductor threw the stick on me, and I tried to sing, and the chorus stood around looking at me, and I began yelling, trying to tell them why I couldn't. When I woke up, those yells were still echoing in my ears, and she was standing over me, shaking me.

"Hoaney! What is it?"

"Just a dream."

"So."

She went back to bed. Not only the bridge of my nose, but the whole front of my face was aching so it was two hours before I dropped off again.

From then on I was like somebody threshing around in a fever, and the more I threshed the worse the fever got. I went around there every night, and when I was so sick of María I couldn't even look at her any more, I tried the Indian girls, and when I got sick of them I went in other places, and tried other Indian girls. Then I began picking girls off the street, and in cafés, and taking them in to cheap hotels off the park. They didn't ask me to register and I didn't volunteer. I paid the money, took them in, and around eleven o'clock left them there and went home. Then I went back to La Locha's and started up with María again. The more I had of them the worse I wanted to sing. And all that time there was only one woman in the world that I really wanted, and that was Juana. But Juana had turned to ice. After that one little flash, when I woke her up with my nightmare, she went back to treating me like she just barely knew me. We spoke, talked about whatever had to be talked about, but whenever I tried to push it further than that, she didn't even hear me.

One night the Pagliacci cue began to play, and I was just about to step through the curtain and face that conductor again. But I was almost used to it by now, and woke up. I was about to drop off again, when a horrible realization came to me. I wasn't home. I was in bed with María. I had been lying there listening to her squeak about how the rains would be over soon, and then the good weather would come, and must have gone to sleep. I was the star customer there by now, and she must have turned off the light and just let me alone. I jumped up, snapped on the light, and looked at my watch. It was two o'clock. I jumped into my clothes, left a twenty-quetzal note on the bureau, and ran downstairs. Things were just getting good down in the main room. The army, the judiciary, the coffee kingdom, and the banana empire were all on hand, the girls were stewed, the asparagus was going down in bunches, and the radio, the phonograph, and the electric piano were all going at once. I never stopped. A whole row of taxis were parked up and down the street outside. I jumped in one, went home. A light was on upstairs. I let myself in and started up there.

Halfway up, I felt something coming at me. I fell back a step and braced myself for her to hit me. She didn't. She shot by me on the stairs, and in the half light I saw she was dressed to go out. She had on red hat, red dress, and red shoes, with gold stockings, and rouge smeared all over her face, but I didn't catch all that until later. All I saw was that she was got up like some kind of hussy, and I took about six steps at one jump and caught her at the door. She didn't scream. She never screamed, or talked loud, or anything like that. She sank her teeth into my hand and grabbed for the door again. I caught her once more, and we fought like a couple of animals. Then I threw her against the door, got my arms around her from behind, and carried her upstairs, with her heels cutting dents in my shins. When we got in the bedroom I turned her loose, and we faced each other panting, her eyes like two points of light, my hands slippery with blood. "What's the rush? Where you going?"

"Where you think? To the Locha, where you come from."

That was one between the eyes. I didn't know she had even heard of La Locha's. But I dead-panned as well as I could.

"What's the locha? I don't seem to place it."

"So, once more you lie."

"I don't even know what you're talking about. I went for a walk and got lost, that's all."

"You lie, now another time you lie. You think these girl no tell me about crazy Italian who come every night? You think they no tell me?"

"So that's where you spend your afternoons."

"Yes."

She stood smiling at me, letting it soak in. I kept thinking I ought to kill her, that if I was a man I'd take her by the throat and choke her till her face turned black. But I didn't want to kill her. I just felt shaky in the knees, and weak, and sick. "Yes, that is where I go, I find little muchacha for company, little muchacha like me, for nice little talk and cup of chocolate after siesta. And what these little muchacha talk? Only about crazy Italian, who come every night, give five-quetzal tip." She pitched her voice into Maria's squeak. "Sí. Cinco quetzales."

I was licked. When I had run my tongue around my lips enough that they stopped fluttering, I backed down. "All right. Once more I'll cut out the lying. Yes, I was there. Now will you stop this show, so we can talk?"

She looked away, and I saw her lips begin to twitch. I went in the bathroom, and started to wash the blood off my hand. I wanted her to follow me in, and I knew if she did, she'd break. She didn't. "No! No more talk! You no go, then I go! Adiós!"

She was down, and out the front door, before I even got to the head of the stairs.

Chapter 14

I RAN OUT ON THE STREET just as a taxi pulled away from the corner. I yelled, but it didn't stop. There was no other taxi in sight, and I didn't find one till I went clear around the block to the stand in front of the hotel. I had him take me back to La Locha's. By that time there were at least twenty cabs parked up and down the street, and things were going strong in all the houses. It kept riding me that even if she had gone in the place, they might lie to me about it, and I couldn't be sure unless I searched the joint, and that meant they would call the cops. I went to the first cab that was parked there and asked him if a girl in a red dress had gone in any of the houses. He said no. I gave him a quetzal and said if she showed, he was to come in La Locha's and let me know. I went to the next driver, and the next, and did the same. By the time I had handed out quetzals to half a dozen of them, I knew that ten seconds after she got out of her cab I would know it. I went back to La Locha's. No girl in a red dress had come, said the Indian. I set up drinks for all hands, sat down with one of the girls, and waited.

Around three o'clock the judiciary began to leave, and after them the army, and then all the others that weren't spending the night. At four o'clock they put me out. Two or three of my taxi drivers were still standing there, and they swore that no girl in a red dress, or any other kind of dress, had come to any house in the street all night. I passed out a couple more quetzals, had one of them drive me home. She wasn't there. I routed out the Japs. It was an hour's job of pidgin Spanish and wig-wagging to find out what they knew, but after a while I got it straight. Around nine o'clock she had started to pack. Then she got a cab, put her things in it, and went out. Then she came back, and when she found out I wasn't home, went out. When she came back the second time, around midnight, she had on the red dress, and kept walking around upstairs waiting for me. Then I came home, and there was the commotion, and she went out again, and hadn't been back since.

I shaved, cleaned the dried blood off my hand, changed my clothes. Around eight o'clock I tried to eat some breakfast and couldn't. Around nine o'clock the bell rang. A taxi driver was at the door. He said some of his friends had told him I was looking for a lady in a red dress. He said he had driven her, and could take me to where he left her. I took my hat, got in, and he drove me around to a cheap hotel, one of those I had been to myself. They said yes, a lady of that description had been there. She had come earlier in the evening, changed her clothes once and gone out, then came back late and left an early call. She hadn't registered. About seven thirty this morning she had gone out. I asked how she was dressed. They just shrugged. I asked if she had taken a cab. They said they didn't know. I rode back to the house, and tried to piece it together. One thing began to stick out of it now. My being out late, that wasn't why she had left. She was leaving anyway, and after she had moved out she had come back, probably to say goodbye. Then when she found I wasn't there she had got sore, gone to the hotel again, changed into the red dress, and come back to harpoon me with how she was going back to her old life. Whether she had gone back to it, or what she had done, I had no more idea than the man in the moon.

I waited all that day, and the next. I was afraid to go to the police. I could have checked on the Tenth Avenue end of it in a minute. They keep a card for every girl on the street, with her record and picture, and if she had gone there, she would have had to report. But once I set them on her trail, that might be the beginning of the end. And I didn't even know what name she was using. So far, even with the drivers and at the hotel, I hadn't given her name or mine. I had spoken of her as the girl in the red dress, but even that wouldn't do any more. If they couldn't remember how she was dressed when she left the hotel, it was a cinch she wasn't wearing red. I lay around, and waited, and cursed myself for giving her five thousand quetzals cash, just in case. With that, she could hide out on me for a year. And then it dawned on me for the first time that with that she could go anywhere she pleased. She could have left town.

I went right over to one of the open-front drugstores, went in a booth, and called Pan-American. I spoke English. I said I was an American, that I had met a Mexican lady at the hotel and promised to give her some pictures I had taken of her, but I hadn't seen her for a couple of days and I was wondering if she had left town. They

asked me her name. I said I didn't know her name, but
they might identify her by a fur coat she was probably
carrying. They asked me to hold the line. Then they said
yes, the porter remembered a fur coat he had handled for
a Mexican lady, that if I'd hold the line they'd see if they
could get me her name and address. I held the line again.
Then they said they were sorry, they didn't have her address, but her name was Mrs. Di Nola, and she had left
on the early plane the day before for Mexico City.

Mexico looked exactly the same, the burros, the goats,
the *pulquerías*, the markets, but I didn't have time for
any of that. I went straight from the airport to the Majes-
tic, a new hotel that had opened since I left there, registered as Di Nola, and started to look for her. I didn't go
to the police, I didn't make any inquiries, and I didn't do
any walking, for fear I'd be recognized. I just put a car
under charter, had the driver go around and around, and
took a chance that sooner or later I'd see her. I went up
and down the Guauhtemolzin until the girls would jeer
at us every time we showed up, and the driver had to
wave and say "postales," to shut them up. Buying post-
cards seemed to be the stock alibi if you were just rub-
bering around. I went up and down every avenue, where
the crowds were thickest, and the more the traffic held us
up, the better it suited me. I kept my eyes glued to the
sidewalk. At night, we drove past every café, and around
eleven o'clock, when the picture theatres closed, we drove
past them, on the chance I'd see her coming out. I didn't
tell him what I wanted, I just told him where to drive.

By the end of that day I hadn't even caught a glimpse
of her. I told the driver to be on deck promptly at eleven
the next morning, which was Sunday. We started out,
and I had him drive me into Chapultepec Park, and I
was sure I'd see her there. The whole city turns out there
every Sunday morning to listen to the band, ride horses,
wink at the girls, and just walk. We rode around for
three hours, past the zoo, the bandstand, the boats in the
lake, the chief of the mounted police and his daughter, so
many times we got dizzy, and still no trace of her. In the
afternoon we kept it up, driving all over the city going

every place there might be a crowd. There was no bullfight. The season for them hadn't started, but we combed
the boulevards, the suburbs, and every place else I could
think of. He asked if I'd need him after supper. I said no,
to report at ten in the morning. It wasn't getting me anywhere, and I wanted to think what I was going to do
next. After dinner I took a walk, to try and figure out
something, I passed two or three people I had known,
but they never gave me a tumble. What left Mexico was
a big, hard, and starved-looking American. What came
back was a middle-aged wop, with a pot on him so big it
hid his feet. When I got to the Palacio de Bellas Artes, it
was all lit up. I crossed toward it, and thought I'd sit on a
stone bench and keep an eye on the crowd that was coming in. But when I got near enough to read the signs I
saw it was Rigoletto they were giving and this dizzy,
drunken feeling swept over me, that I should go in there
and sing it, and take the curse off the flop, and show
them how I could do it. I cut back, and turned the corner into the town.

Next to the bullring box office is a café. I went in
there, ordered an apricot brandy, and sat down. I told
myself to forget about the singing, that what I was trying
to do was find her. The place was pretty full, and three
of four guys were standing in front of one of the booth
tables against the wall. Through them I caught a flash of
red, and my mouth went dry. They went back to their
own table and I was looking right at her.

She was with Triesca, the bullfighter, and more guys
kept coming up to him, shaking his hand, and going
away again. She saw me, and looked away quick. Then he
saw me. He kept looking at me, and then he placed me.
He said something to her, and laughed. She nodded, kept
looking off somewhere with a strained face, and then half
laughed. Then he ogled at me. By the way both of them
were acting I knew he didn't connect me with New York,
and maybe he didn't know anything about the New York
stuff at all. All he saw was a guy that had once taken his
girl away from him, and had then turned out to be a fag.
But that was enough for him. He began putting on an
act that the whole room was roaring at in a minute. Her

face got hard and set. I felt the blood begin to pound in my head.

A mariachi came in. He threw them a couple of pesos, and they screeched three or four times. Then he got a real idea. He called the leader, and whispered, and they started *Cielito Lindo*. But instead of them singing it, he got up and sang it. He sang right at me, in a high, simpering falsetto, with gestures. They laughed like hell. If she had dead-panned, I think I would have sat there and taken it. But she didn't. She laughed. I don't know why. Maybe she was just nervous. Maybe she played it the way the rest of them expected her to play it. Maybe she was still sore about Guatemala. Maybe she really thought it was funny, that I should be following her around like some puppy after she had hooked up with another man. I don't know, and I didn't think about any of that at the time. When I saw that laugh, I got a dizzy, wanton feeling in my head, and I knew that all hell couldn't stop me from what I was going to do.

He got to the end of the verse, and they gave him a laugh and a big hand. He struck a pose for the chorus, and then I laughed too, and stood up. That suprised him, and he hesitated. And then I shot it:

> Ay, Ay, Ay, Ay!
> Canta y no llores
> Porque cantando se alegran
> Cielito lindo
> Los corazones!

It was like gold, bigger than it had ever been, and when I finished I was panting from the excitement of it. He stood there, looking thick, and then came this roar of applause. The mariachi leader began jabbering at me, and they started it again. I sang it through, drunk from the way it felt, drunk from the look on her face. On the second chorus, I sang it right at her, soft and slow. But at the end I put in a high one, closed my eyes and swelled it, held it till the glasses rattled, and then came off it.

When I opened my eyes wide she wasn't looking at me.

She was looking past the bar, behind me. The mob was cheering, people were crowding in from the street, and all over the place they were passing it around, "El Panamier Trovador!" But in a booth was an officer, yelling into a telephone. How long that kept up I don't know. They were all around me, jabbering things for me to sing. Next thing I knew, she was running for the door, Triesca after her. But I was ahead of him. I rammed through the crowd, and when I got to the street I could see the red of her dress, half a block away. I started to run. I hadn't gone two steps before some cops grabbed me. I wrestled with them. From up the street came shots, and people began to run and scream. Then from somewhere came a rattle of Spanish, and I heard the word "gringo." They turned me loose, and I ran on. Ahead of me were more cops, and people standing around. I saw something red on the pavement. When I pushed through she was lying there, and beside her, this quivering smile on his face, was a short guy in uniform, with three stars on his shoulder. It seemed a long time before I knew it was the político from Acapulco. I got it, then, that order to lay off the gringo. He couldn't shoot me. I was too important. But he could shoot her, for trying to escape, or resisting arrest, or whatever it was. And he could stand there, and wait, and get his kick when I had to look at her.

I jumped for him, and he stepped back, but then I turned to water, and I sank down beside her, the cops, the lights, and the ambulance going around and around in a horrible spin. If he had done that to her, what had I done?

Once more I was in the vestry room of the little church near Acapulco, and I could even see the burned place on the bricks where we had made the fire. Indians were slipping in barefooted, the women with rebozos over their heads, the men in white suits, extra clean. Her father and mother were in the first pew, and some sisters and brothers I didn't even know she had. The casket was white, and the altar was banked with the flowers I had had sent down, flowers from Xochimilco, that she liked. The choir loft was full of boys and girls, all in white. The priest came in, started to put on his vestments, and I paid him. He caught my arm. "You sing, yes, Señor Sharp? An *Agnus Dei* perhaps?"

"No."

He shrugged, turned away, and pulled the surplice over his head. This horrible sense of guilt swept over me, like it had a hundred times in the last two days. ". . . Never. . . . Never again."

"Ah."

He just breathed it, and stood looking at me, then his hand traced a blessing for me, and he whispered in Latin. I knew, then, I had made a confession, and received an absolution, and some kind of gray peace came over me. I went out, slipped in the pew with her family, and the music started. They carried her out to a grave on the hillside. As they lowered her down, an iguana jumped out of it and went running over the rocks.

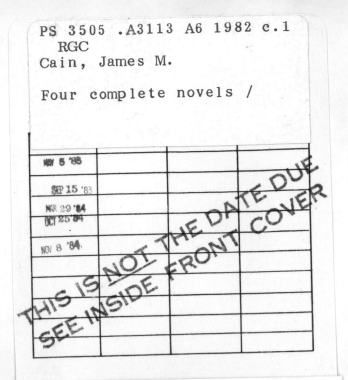